MISTRESS *of the* REVOLUTION

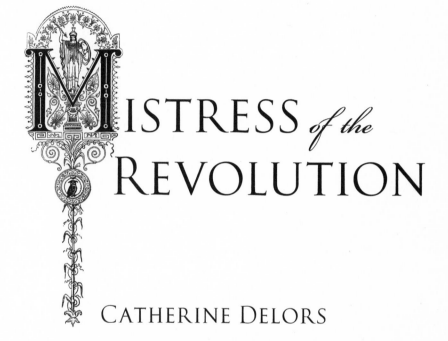

Mistress *of the* Revolution

Catherine Delors

DUTTON

DUTTON
Published by Penguin Group (USA) Inc.
375 Hudson Street, New York, New York 10014, U.S.A.
Penguin Group (Canada), 90 Eglinton Avenue East, Suite 700, Toronto, Ontario M4P 2Y3,
Canada (a division of Pearson Penguin Canada Inc.) · Penguin Books Ltd, 80 Strand, London
WC2R 0RL, England · Penguin Ireland, 25 St Stephen's Green, Dublin 2, Ireland (a division of
Penguin Books Ltd) · Penguin Group (Australia), 250 Camberwell Road, Camberwell, Victoria
3124, Australia (a division of Pearson Australia Group Pty Ltd) · Penguin Books India Pvt Ltd,
11 Community Centre, Panchsheel Park, New Delhi–110 017, India · Penguin Group (NZ), 67
Apollo Drive, Rosedale, North Shore 0632, New Zealand (a division of Pearson New Zealand
Ltd) · Penguin Books (South Africa) (Pty) Ltd, 24 Sturdee Avenue, Rosebank, Johannesburg
2196, South Africa

Penguin Books Ltd, Registered Offices: 80 Strand, London WC2R 0RL, England

Published by Dutton, a member of Penguin Group (USA) Inc.

First printing, March 2008
10 9 8 7 6 5 4 3 2 1

Copyright © 2008 by Laborderie, Inc.

REGISTERED TRADEMARK—MARCA REGISTRADA

LIBRARY OF CONGRESS CATALOGING-IN-PUBLICATION DATA
Delors, Catherine.
    Mistress of the Revolution / Catherine Delors.
        p. cm.
    ISBN 978-0-525-95054-7
    1. Young women—Fiction.   2. Aristocracy (Social class)—France—Fiction.
3. France—Social life and customs—18th century—Fiction.   4. France—History—
Revolution, 1789–1799—Fiction.   5. Forced marriage—Fiction.   6. Widows—Fiction.
7. First loves—Fiction.   8. Exiles—Fiction.   I. Title.
    PS3604.E4473M57 2008
    813'. 6—dc22   2007034494

Printed in the United States of America

For William

It is beautiful to meet someone. It can happen anywhere in the world. Anytime. But the strangest thing is that one does not only meet the living, and that meeting a dead person can change your life.

—ALAIN JOUFFROY

MISTRESS *of the* REVOLUTION

I read this morning in the papers that the corpses of the late King and Queen of France, by order of their brother, the restored Louis the Eighteenth, were exhumed from their graves in the former graveyard of La Madeleine, which has since become a private garden. The remains were removed with royal honours to the Basilica of Saint-Denis, the resting place of the Kings and Queens of France for twelve centuries.

Queen Marie-Antoinette was found soon after the workmen began digging, and the remains of King Louis the Sixteenth were located the next day. A search for the bones of the King's youngest sister, Madame Elisabeth, was also conducted at the cemetery of Les Errancis. The guillotine had filled La Madeleine by the spring of 1794, and the authorities had opened the new graveyard to accommodate its increasing output. That second investigation was unsuccessful. While the King and Queen had each been granted an individual execution and a coffin, Madame Elisabeth had been guillotined towards the end of the Terror as one in a cart of twenty-five prisoners. The remains had been thrown together into a common grave. The bodies, as required by law, had been stripped of all clothing, which, along with their other property, was forfeited to the Nation upon the imposition of the death sentence. Any identification would have become impossible very soon after the burial. Nevertheless, I trust that God will overlook the lack of proper funeral rites, which were denied to many in those days.

Other victims of the guillotine, some of whom I knew and loved, also remain buried at La Madeleine and Les Errancis, royalists and revolutionaries alike, commingled for all eternity in their unmarked graves.

These tidings from Paris have affected my spirits today. I never cry anymore, yet feel tears choking me. I know that I must not allow myself this indulgence, for it is far easier to keep from crying than to quit. Nevertheless, over twenty years have passed since the great Revolution, and it is time for me at last to exhume my own dead and attempt to revive them, however feebly, under my pen.

Some of the events related here are now known only to me, and possibly my daughter. I am not aware of the extent of her recollection because, out of shyness or shame, or a desire not to acknowledge to each other the shared sorrows of the past, we have never talked about those things since our arrival in England in 1794. She was a child then, and may not have understood or remembered much of what she saw or heard. It causes me pain to recall those events, and still more to write about them, but secrecy has been a heavy burden.

1

"Mademoiselle, your cheeks are again smeared with ink," said Sister Suzanne. "What will My Lord the Marquis think when he sees you like this? You are incorrigible. Remember, child, every time you misbehave, you pound the nails of the Good Saviour's cross deeper into His flesh."

I looked up. A drop of ink dripped from my quill and splattered on the shaky capital *H* that had given me so much trouble. I rose and held my hands straight in front of me for Sister Suzanne to hit them with her wooden rule. She ignored them and seized me by the arm to lead me out of the classroom.

"Go clean your face," she said. "Mother Louise needs to see you."

Never before had Sister Suzanne let pass an opportunity to use her rod on my fingers. I was also puzzled by her reference to my brother the Marquis. He visited only during the school holidays, which I spent at the convent. It was late October of the year 1780, and I did not expect any visit from him until Christmas.

I washed my face in the chilly water of the courtyard fountain and, my heart beating fast, went to the Mother Superior's study. There my brother and guardian, Géraud de Montserrat, Marquis de Castel, waited for me. The Marquis, fifteen years my senior, was the embodiment of kindness, elegance and learning. Side curls framed his regular, well-defined features. His hair was powdered and tied by a black silk ribbon. I curtseyed to him. He took me in his arms and kissed me on both cheeks.

"My goodness, Gabrielle," he said, stepping back to look at me, "you have grown much since the summer. You are almost a lady now."

"Yes, My Lord," said Mother Louise, "Mademoiselle de Montserrat is well in advance of her age in many regards. She has made great progress since joining us five years ago. She can now play the harpsichord, read, write and speak French. She knows the rudiments of dancing. She also has a pretty singing voice, the best in our choir, and Sister Béatrice will miss her. I can praise her to her face, for she has no vanity. It is a pity she cannot stay with us a few more years. She has yet much to learn. But of course you are the best judge of that and I understand that Her Ladyship cannot spare her any longer."

So I was going to leave the convent! I was astonished: I was only eleven. The other girls would remain there until their marriage and many would wed in the chapel.

As was customary in all families of any means, I had been taken at birth to a wet nurse, Marie Labro, just outside the town of Vic-en-Carladez, in the province of Auvergne. Mamé Labro had five boys, the youngest of whom, Jacques, was my *frère de lait*, "milk brother," meaning that we had been nursed together. I remained with my nurse until the age of six and shed many tears when my brother announced that I would be taken away from her, not to return to my family, but to become a boarder in the convent of the Benedictine nuns in Vic.

Upon my arrival there, I had the manners of a peasant and faced the contempt of the other schoolgirls, all young ladies of the local nobility and bourgeoisie. I could only speak *la lengo Romano*, the ancient idiom of those parts, and the twenty words of French known to Mamé Labro. The Roman tongue had been the language of poetry in the Middle Ages, but sadly it was no longer taught in schools. Although it was my first language, I never learned to read or write it. It can be harsh and guttural when spoken by men, but in females, in Mamé's mouth in particular, its accents, soft and high-pitched, sounded like a song. I liked them better than the nasal tones of French.

After a month or so at the convent, I had become fluent in the more formal language, but the stigma of my country manners clung to me. Also, as Sister Suzanne liked to say, I shared with Judas, the betrayer of Our Lord Jesus-Christ, at least one characteristic: red hair.

I felt no regrets when my brother handed me into the carriage. I was on my way to the château of Fontfreyde, my birthplace, to meet my mother for the first time in eleven years. I remembered neither her nor my father, who had died when I was still in the care of Mamé Labro.

I asked my brother many questions, but was unable to gather much information beyond assurances that our mother would be delighted to make my acquaintance. We crossed the village of Lavigerie, located in the middle of the Marquis's lands, and passed the gallows. I looked away from the grim wooden structure.

"You see, Gabrielle," said my brother, "I keep my gallows in excellent repair. They serve as a reminder to my vassals that I have the right of high justice over my estates, though I am content to let the royal *Baillage* court in Vic punish the many scoundrels who infest my land. But we must never let others forget who we are, Gabrielle, or forget it ourselves."

This meant that the Marquis could sentence anyone to death, or to any lesser penalty, for crimes committed within his jurisdiction. I recalled the day when Mamé Labro had taken me, along with her sons, to watch a hanging in the main square of Vic. I must have been five. A thief, whose crime had been to pick a merchant's pocket at the Michaelmas cattle fair, had climbed the rungs of a ladder backwards. The noose tight around his neck, he had been pushed to his death. For long minutes he had grimaced and thrashed in agony. Finally the executioner had seized the wretch's legs and pulled sharply to break his neck. Then his accomplice, stripped to his waist, bound to a post of the gallows, had been flogged, then branded on the shoulder with a hot iron. That second thief had been sentenced to two years of hard labour. Mamé had pointed to the mounted constables who were waiting to take him away once the first part of his punishment was over. The sight of the execution, she had assured us, would teach us right from wrong. It would show us what happened to the wicked in this world and give us a hint of what awaited them in the next. She had insisted that I keep my eyes open and not turn away.

Though my milk brother Jacques had held my hand for comfort, that display of cruelty had horrified me. The body of the dead man had been taken down and hung again, this time out of town, from the gallows at the pass of Curebourse, whence it could be seen decaying from miles around. I had been unable to turn my eyes in that direction for weeks, until Jacques had assured me that nothing remained of the corpse and that it was safe to look.

I was relieved to hear that my brother had chosen not to exercise his prerogatives. A man of his kindness could not have anything to do with the gruesome business of justice.

We were soon in sight of the château of Fontfreyde. My brother explained that the current building had replaced the old fortress that had controlled the valley of the Goul River and made our family powerful long before the time of the Crusades. The château, in the traditional style of the high country, had walls of dark stone cemented in white mortar. The steep roofs, designed for the snows of winter, were made of a different kind of stone, resembling the scales of a giant fish. The twin flights of a monumental exterior staircase, decorated with urns and busts, graced the front of the building.

The château was situated in a low spot, in the middle of green meadows, for it rains a great deal in those parts. Oak and birch woods, which had turned gold at the time of my arrival, covered the surrounding mountains. Such was my birthplace and ancestral home, seat of the noble and ancient family of Montserrat. My true name, which I alone remember nowadays, is Marie Gabrielle Aliénor de Montserrat de Castel, or, as most people called me then, Gabrielle de Montserrat.

The trepidation with which I prepared to meet my mother chased all other thoughts from my mind. My brother took me to the main drawing room, where she sat in a tapestry chair. Portraits of ancestors in military or court dress hung on the walls. I curtseyed to Madame de Castel, who gave me her hand to kiss. I was surprised to see that I looked nothing like her. She seemed small and delicate, her hair still black with a few silver threads. She had a thin nose, a strong jaw and piercing dark eyes. Her mouth was a straight line without lips, which did not appear to be often distorted by a smile. She stared at me and turned to my brother:

"I had not expected her to be so bony. Do you think she will grow much taller? And that mass of red hair!"

I had not expected a warm welcome from a parent who had expressed no wish to see me during the first eleven years of my life, but was still mortified by her greeting. The Marquis too seemed embarrassed. He tried to reconcile the truth and my feelings.

"At her age, Madam," he said, "many girls show little promise, but in later years improve considerably. I am sure Gabrielle will become very pretty."

My mother, looking at me, shook her head and sighed. "I had an apartment prepared for you, child. You must be impatient to see it."

I followed a maid to a long, narrow room on the second floor, furnished with a little white bed, an armoire and a large table covered with patterns and pieces of cut fabric not yet sewn together. The sole decoration was the portrait of a gentleman in regimentals, resembling the Marquis except for a rather mischievous smile. He was, the maid informed me, Colonel de Montserrat, a younger brother of my late father. I would sleep alone for the first time in my life in this strange room. I recalled the warmth of Mamé Labro's bed, which I had shared for many years, and even began to regret the sullen companionship of the convent dormitory.

I looked out the window. Once I became tired of the view of the meadows and woods behind the château, I sat on the bed. I took out my book, for I had but one, and read for the hundredth time my favourite stories. That volume, the fairy tales of Perrault, was my most treasured possession, a gift from my brother the Marquis when I was still with Mamé Labro. I could not read then and neither could anyone in the Labro cottage. Yet I had slowly turned the pages, fascinated by the magic of printed words. Their complexity had seemed so daunting that I had been unable to imagine a little person like myself ever mastering such a skill. Also, my brother had told me that the book was written in French, a language barely known to me at the time.

When I was little, the Marquis would sit me on his lap during his Sunday visits to Mamé's cottage and translate the stories into the Roman language while I tenderly and reverently caressed the velvet of his coat. He always departed too quickly, frightening the chickens in the courtyard, and left the Labro household in the middle of their deep bows and curtseys. I watched the dust the hooves of his horse had raised in the dirt lane long after he was gone. I returned to the book to make up my own stories, looking at the pictures for inspiration.

In my strange new bedroom at Fontfreyde, my old friends the princesses, fairies, and cats with enchanted boots brought me their usual comfort. My brother interrupted my reading to take me around the château, a maze of hallways, half-flights of stairs, towers, turrets and parlours, most of which were no longer occupied. In the kitchen, the cook, Joséphine, assisted by a scullery girl, was peeling carrots. They curtseyed to us and Joséphine greeted me in the Roman language, which in itself cheered me. That room had a bright fire burning deep in the vast hearth, within which one could sit on benches located on either side, an arrangement called *cantou* in the Roman language. Hams hung in the upper reaches of the cavernous space. A yellow cat, her eyes closed, her legs stretched, was nursing a kitten almost as large as herself and purring on the brightly coloured pillows on one of the *cantou* benches. Copper kettles on the table were gleaming orange in the light of the fire.

Finally my brother took me to the stables. They were vast enough to accommodate many more than the three horses I found there. My brother's fine bay stallion nickered at us. Two draft horses shifted in their stalls to look at us with curiosity. One of them, by the name of Jewel, black with a white blaze, stood seventeen hands tall, huge even by equine standards.

"He is not yet nine years old and still growing," said my brother, "which is very inconvenient since he will no longer match his companion in harness."

Jewel nibbled with infinite delicacy at my ears and dress. He lowered his giant head against my neck and breathed in noisily. That was the friendliest gesture I had encountered all day. I leaned against his cheek and kissed him. His coat was silky, his mane and tail long and wavy.

I looked up at the Marquis. "Would you teach me to ride, Sir?"

He laughed, a rare occurrence. "Jewel is too large for a lady's horse, but he is gelded and sweet-tempered. I might give it some consideration if you behave like a good girl."

My first supper with my mother and brother was at seven o'clock, in the grand oak-paneled dining parlour. We sat at the fireplace end of a long table lit by two candles. An expanse that could have seated thirty remained in darkness. My brother recited the *Benedicite* before a meal of roast beef with chestnuts was served. He then spoke little while my mother regaled him with tales of the depravities of the servants and tenants. She said nothing to me; indeed she hardly acknowledged my presence.

After dinner, we retired to the main drawing room, where my brother sat down with a worn leather treatise on hunting and my mother a volume of *Christian Thoughts*. I thought it prudent not to fetch my own book and was content to stare at my feet.

"Do you know how to sew, child?" she asked.

"Yes, Madam, I was taught in the convent."

"You might make yourself useful after all. The maids are a sad lot and never seem to finish anything. I wonder why we bother to keep them.

There is a new chemise of mine that was started over a week ago. You will work on it. Do not try to fool me, girl. I want fine, even stitches."

She rang for one of the maids to fetch her workbasket. From that moment, I never lacked occupation at Fontfreyde.

At nine o'clock, all the servants, men and women, entered the room and knelt, along with my brother and mother. She motioned to me to follow suit next to her. The Marquis led the prayers. I made the mistake of sitting on my heels when kneeling, but my mother turned towards me and slapped me on the side of the face. I was reminded of proper manners and corrected my position. At last everyone rose and it was time to retire.

I did not sleep much that first night at Fontfreyde. The wood floor creaked as if someone had been walking in my room. Maybe it was the *drac*, the nasty little fiend that haunted every house, grand or small, in Auvergne and delighted in playing tricks on its inhabitants. The autumn wind shook the old place and filled it with uncanny noises. I thought I heard the racket of the *chaço volanto*, the flying hunt, with its howling hounds, ghost riders and horses at full gallop in midair.

ꙮ 2 ꙮ

My brother gave me the much-awaited riding lessons. Jewel lived up to his name and proved to be the sweetest of animals, although he did keep growing for another year or so. My brother taught me to ride sideways, like a lady. I soon gained confidence and made rapid progress. I also taught myself, when no one was looking, to ride astride. I would fill my pockets with apples and carrots stolen from Joséphine's cellar and lead Jewel away from the château to practice.

I envied the freedom afforded men, who could use both of their legs for balance without having to use the long whip required of a woman on a side saddle. I admired the daring displayed on horseback by my brother, who had been an officer in the Light Cavalry, and knew that I could not hope to match his skill without also riding astride.

My audacity nearly cost me my riding privileges and much more. My mother learned of it and had me summoned to the drawing room. She was seething with anger, her mouth tighter than usual, and slapped me until my face stung.

"Just wait," she said. "Your brother will know of this as soon as he returns from town. Stupid, willful, disobedient girl. All the expense, all the care lavished on your education, all will be for naught. You are no better than your sister Hélène. I will see to it that the Marquis gives you the correction you deserve."

I feared my brother's anger far more than my mother's slaps or any punishment. Even the deprivation of the pleasure of riding would have been nothing compared to the loss of his good opinion. I spent a dreadful afternoon in anticipation of his return.

At last one of the maids told me that I was expected in the Marquis's study. No criminal under examination shook more in front of his judge than I did that day. I stole one look at him. His expression was more severe than I had ever seen it. My sole comfort was that our mother was not there. I knelt before him in silence.

"Mother tells me that you have been riding astride," he said. "Is it true?"

"Yes, Sir. She is very angry with me."

"So am I. I cannot tell you how disappointed I am in you. It must never happen again, Gabrielle, do you hear me?"

"It will not. I would never think of disobeying you, Sir."

"I am not so sure. What I do not like about your conduct is that you hid it from me."

"I did not think it worth mentioning, Sir. If I had thought that it would anger you so, I would never have done it."

"I have an excellent reason, which you are too young to understand, to forbid any riding astride, especially on such a large animal as Jewel. Let me say only that it might later do you a great disservice with the man you will marry. Do you promise that you will never do it again?"

"I do."

"And do you promise never again to conceal anything from me, even if you believe it to be a trivial matter?"

"I do, Sir. It pains me so to have caused you one moment of uneasiness. You have always been so good to me. I terribly feel my own ingratitude. I would welcome any punishment if you would but forgive me."

"Mother has asked me to flog you and deprive you of riding, but I will do neither. I will be content with your promise. Do not cry, dear." He raised me to my feet and took me in his arms. "I love you too much, little sister, not to forgive you. I know that you were only thoughtless and did not mean any harm."

I had gone from utter misery to the most complete happiness I had known in my eleven years. I sobbed on his shoulder while he held me. I never wanted that moment to end.

I liked my new life at Fontfreyde better than my mother's first words of welcome had led me to expect. The Marquise hardly received anyone, except for my brother's few friends and my eldest sister Madeleine, the Countess de Chavagnac, a handsome, dark-haired woman of about thirty. Madeleine's husband, a sallow, unpleasant man, seldom accompanied her. She had two boys, a few years younger than me, both away at school in Clermont. My other sister, Hélène, whom I had yet to meet, was the Abbess of the Convent of Noirvaux, hundreds of miles away.

I often found refuge in the kitchen, where I was assured of Joséphine's welcome. She tried to teach me to cook, but my fingers were cursed.

"Go sit on one of the benches in the *cantou*," she said, "and entertain me with your silly talk. You're the only young, cheerful thing in this old place. You may lick the platters clean after I'm done, but don't touch anything until then. You couldn't boil an egg if you tried. No matter. You'll marry a great lord someday, and you'll be too fine a lady to even know the way to the kitchen in your own house."

I also gained the confidence of the maids, who, when my mother had her back turned, felt free to treat me like their little doll. They were all good souls, elderly and kind. One of them, Antoinette, had been disfigured by smallpox, which had ploughed her face and robbed her of one eye. I had caught the dreaded disease myself when I was in the care of Mamé Labro, but my only memento of it was a tiny round scar on my left temple. At first, I had recoiled from Antoinette, frightened by the dark hollow of her empty orbit, but soon became fonder of her than of the other maids. She sewed for me, hiding from my mother, a doll made of rags, the only one I ever owned.

The maids told me the many tales of the high country, such as the story of the Beast of Gévaudan, which, twenty years earlier, had devoured hundreds of children and shepherdesses. The mayhem lasted until a monstrous brute, the likes of which had never been seen, was shot by a gamekeeper, Chastang, at the end of a nightlong hunt in the forest.

"The Beast recognized Chastang," said Antoinette, looking at me with her only eye. "The man was a *wolf runner*, a witch who had made a pact with those brutes. He could turn into one at will. Then he would lead them to devour Christians."

"And his master, the Count de Morangis, was no better," added Guillemine, another maid, breathless with excitement. "The Bishop accused him from the pulpit of celebrating black masses on the naked body of his youngest sister."

I winced in horror at the idea of a man seeing his sister nude. "Black masses?" I asked.

"A black mass, Mademoiselle," said Guillemine, "is the most wicked blasphemy, a mockery of the Holy Mass. It's a ceremony where an infant is bled to death over a woman lying naked on an altar. And the Count de Morangis forced his sister to take part in such a thing!"

I saw drops of blood falling on the white skin of the young lady; I heard the cries of the child. It was still worse than picturing the mangled remains of the little shepherdesses killed by the Beast. My stomach lurched.

"That's why the Count's vassals feared him like the plague," continued Guillemine. "And they still do, because he's alive and well, the fiend from hell."

Antoinette put her hand on my arm. "Of course, Mademoiselle Gabrielle," she hastened to observe, "that was in Gévaudan, twelve leagues away. The nobility there is far less respectable than here in Carladez. No one would dare compare the Count de Morangis to My Lord the Marquis de Castel, who is so kind."

3

I reached five feet six inches by the age of twelve. "Look at her!" my mother would complain to the Marquis. "No man in his right mind will want a giantess. Heaven help us, I cannot imagine what we are going to do with her."

My breasts and hips soon began to fill out. I stopped growing. Much to my embarrassment, a red down appeared between my thighs. In my bedroom I would stare at my new body, all astonishment at the changes a few months had worked. One night I felt the Colonel's eye following me while I was undressing. I climbed on a chair to cover his portrait with a piece of fabric from the sewing table. I knew that I was being silly but still found it unnerving to disrobe before him. As I reached for the top of the gilded frame, I felt a trickle of warm liquid running down my legs. Horrified, I noticed that it was blood and would not stop. I stuck a remnant of fabric between my thighs. I was, no doubt, dying of some shameful disease. The catastrophe had stricken me because I had done something wrong that would soon be revealed to the entire world. Worse, my brother would learn of it.

The next day Joséphine raised her eyebrow when she saw me. "What have you done now? You look so shamefaced that it must be pretty bad. Tell me, child, I won't say a word to your mother."

I whispered my secret in her ear.

She kissed me. "Poor little dear, I should've known your time had come. Don't fret, it's one of the curses, along with childbirth, set aside as a punishment for us females. It'll come back every moon and won't stop until you're pregnant or become an old woman like me. Yes, from now on, you'll be able to bear children, so you must be careful not to be alone with any man."

I gasped. "What about the Marquis? Should I stop riding with him? How can I tell him of such a thing?"

"No, silly, I wasn't talking about My Lord." She shrugged. "He's your brother, for Heaven's sake. But be mindful of all other men. There'll only be one thing on their minds, pretty as you are. You know what I mean?"

I did not and looked at her blankly.

She sighed. "All right. You've seen what happens when mares are brought here to be covered by My Lord's stallion, haven't you?"

Puzzled, I nodded at her. Indeed, those proceedings took place in a paddock behind the château, under my bedroom window. My brother attended while grooms held the horses' reins. The stallion, upon smelling the mare, threw his head backwards and curled his lips. He raised himself to his full height, his front legs whipping the air, and let out a chilling cry, almost a roar, before beginning his approaches. It was an impressive sight.

"Good," said Joséphine. "Then you must've observed the state of things under the stallion's stomach. The private parts of a man look the same, only less large of course, when he wants to have his way with a girl.

Beware of any scoundrel who'll talk tender to you. When you least expect it, he'll unbutton his breeches, and then he'll raise your skirts and he'll do to you what you've seen done to the mares."

My eyes shut tight, I was trying to banish from my mind the horrific visions evoked by Joséphine's words. I had never considered the fact that men might behave or look like my brother's horse.

"If you let that happen," Joséphine continued, "chances are you'll bear a little bastard nine months later. And even if you weren't with child, you'd still be disgraced. You see, when a girl lets a man meddle with her, it tears something in her nether parts. That's called her maidenhead. It hurts when it rips, and it bleeds quite a bit. But that's not what matters. What matters is that afterwards a girl never looks the same down there."

Joséphine, a dire look on her face, wagged her finger at me. "So even if you managed to hide your shame until your marriage, you wouldn't be able to fool your husband on your wedding night. He'd be awfully angry and he'd lock you in a convent for the rest of your life. Think of it. All because of one lapse." She paused. "Now you've been warned."

"Have no fear, Joséphine," I said with a great deal of conviction. "I will never, ever let any man do those things to me."

"Well, you'll have to let your husband do *those things* to you, of course, and he might teach you some more as well." She patted my cheek. "But that's all you need to know for now."

I winced and put my hand to my stomach.

"Poor dear," she said, "I forgot you're in pain. Let me give you some lime-blossom tea. And don't worry about Her Ladyship. I'll tell her about your curses."

"Oh no, please. She will be so angry with me."

"Of course not. You can't help it, can you? But she needs to know right away since now you're fit to be married."

I shuddered in disgust. "I will never marry."

Joséphine laughed. "Listen to you! As if it was for you to decide."

She provided me with scraps of cloth and instructions for their use. I felt the cruelty with which nature had treated us females. As for the idea of marriage, I hoped that it would never be mentioned again.

A few days later, the Marquis handed me a letter.

"Who is writing you?" he asked.

"It is Félicité de Peylamourgue, Sir. She was my friend at the convent."

Félicité was short, with a round face and dull brown hair. She was also kind and cheerful, though not too clever even by the convent's standards. The prettier, more brilliant girls had despised me in the beginning. Later, once they had found me less stupid than initially believed and worthy of their friendship, I had shunned their company.

"Is she related to Monsieur de Peylamourgue?" asked my brother.

"She is his daughter."

"Good. A minor family, but authentic, ancient nobility. I would not want you to make friends among the vile bourgeoisie. Note that I am giving you this letter sealed."

"Thank you, Sir. I appreciate your trust."

"I know, dearest, but we have to talk about it. Some young ladies become entangled in scandalous romances. On occasion, their friends are complicit in those affairs, in particular by forwarding letters from suitors."

I stared at him. "Sir, I would never do anything so wicked."

"I believe you. Still, I will have to watch you more closely now." He caressed my cheek, smiling. "I remember holding you on my lap when you were a little girl, reading your book aloud. It seems like yesterday. And here you are, already a woman."

I shuddered, shocked that he would broach such a subject. He drew back and looked at me more sternly.

"Now that you are all grown," he continued, "I want you to allow me, to ask me even, to open all of the letters you receive, starting with this one. Likewise you will show me all the letters you write, and I do mean all of them, including to our sister Madeleine. I would be fully within my rights to demand it, but I want to hear you request it. What do you say?"

"You may do what you want."

He frowned. "Of course I may do what I want. That is not what I meant, and you know it. Do not trifle with me, Gabrielle. Will you ask me, your guardian, to read all of your correspondence, as a kindness to you, to protect you from evil?"

"Yes."

"Say it, then."

"I am asking you to read my correspondence."

"As a kindness to you?"

"I am asking you, Sir, as a kindness to me, to please read all of my correspondence. I promise to show you all the letters I write."

"And you will not tell anyone, including of course your correspondents, about this arrangement of ours."

"No, Sir, I will not."

I handed him Félicité's letter. He opened it, perused it and smiled before returning it to me.

"Quite a letter. You are a good girl, Gabrielle."

I received few letters, all from Félicité. I responded to them out of a sense of obligation, but the idea that my correspondence with a school-girl would be read by a grown man chilled my inspiration, if indeed I had any. Although my French spelling and grammar were already good, I was aware of the deficiencies of these childish attempts. It was torture to imagine my brother's contempt as he read them.

During her next visit, Madeleine warned me, as Joséphine had done, never to be alone with a man, though, to my relief, she did not enter into any details. I felt irritated by the interest the news of my curses elicited and the rapidity with which it had spread. It seemed that it would have been more discreet to have Father Marty, the parish priest, read an announcement to that effect from the pulpit after his Sunday sermon.

Life went on very quietly. I would sew and embroider with the maids, who came to work in my bedroom. My mother did not part with her money freely, especially when it came to buying anything for me. She presented me with her old dresses, all made of solid black silk, when their dye began to fade and acquire a brownish tint. The maids and I would turn the fabric inside out and do our best to sew them back into something suitable for me. My mother's gowns were a foot too short for me and we had to add an additional band of fabric at the hem. I knew that I looked strange in my patched clothes, but did not care much about my appearance then. Around the same time, my feet stopped growing, which dispensed with the need to buy me new shoes. I would take mine to the cobbler in Vic to have them mended when the old soles had worn through. This happened often because I was not allowed to wear wooden clogs. They would have made me look, my mother said, like a peasant girl.

I had always liked Vic. It was the *Baillage* seat, with its court of justice, a larger, busier town than Lavigerie. It was built high in the valley of the Cère River, and boasted a cluster of handsome townhouses occupied by the minor nobility and the families of attorneys. From anywhere one had a splendid view of the surrounding mountains. On market days, peasants and traders came from afar to buy and sell horses, sheep and cattle. The fragrance of grilled sausages, wrapped in *bouriols*, thick buckwheat crepes, filled the air.

I would go to the shops in Vic for my mother and take advantage of these errands to visit Mamé Labro. She was as happy as ever to see me, but I lost the friendship of my milk brother Jacques. Since infancy, we had played in the snow in winter and in the freshly cut hay during the long days of June. We had slipped away together to bathe and fish trout by hand in the Cère River.

Now Jacques, whenever he saw me, ran from the cottage without greeting me. I was hurt by his disdain and complained to Mamé.

"It's all for the best, Gabrielle," she said. "Jacques has more sense than you. You are a lady now. It would not be proper for you to be friends with a peasant boy."

It seemed the silliest of explanations.

4

By the age of fourteen, I had acquired the shape of a woman. Yet my mother said nothing about providing me with larger clothes or buying me a new corset, and I was too shy or proud to raise the subject. Such a request would no doubt have been greeted with derision at my vanity, or enquiries about how I thought my family could afford such an expense of finery. I could no longer lace my little girl's corset and now wore on my bosom only my chemise and the bodice of my dress, while covering as much as I could with a kerchief. Even in my innocence, I knew that there was something wrong about my appearance.

One afternoon, my brother entered the room while I was sewing alone, seated on a bench in front of the fireplace in the drawing room. I curtseyed to him and returned to my work.

"Have you seen Mother?" he asked.

"She just went to the kitchen to give Joséphine her instructions for dinner, Sir."

No matter was below our mother's attention when it came to bullying her servants. My back was turned to my brother and my attention was fixed on the petticoat I was hemming for the Marquise. She had indicated in no uncertain terms that she wanted it finished that day. Nothing happened for a minute. Suddenly, the Marquis said in a tone I did not recognize, "Gabrielle, my love, your position is all wrong. Let me show you how to correct it."

Before I understood what he was doing, I felt him standing behind the bench where I was seated, bending over my shoulder. In an instant, he had slipped both of his hands under my kerchief and caught my breasts. He was caressing them while pulling me towards him. In my astonishment and shock, I dared not resist, look up or say a word. Chills were running down my spine. My entire body was tingling in a manner I had never experienced before. The back of my head was now against him and I could feel him trembling. I closed my eyes and heard nothing but his breathing. How long this lasted I cannot say, maybe no more than a few moments. All of a sudden, he pushed me away and was gone without another word.

I wondered whether it had been a dream, so fast had it happened. I tidied my kerchief in a hurry, ran to my room and pressed myself against the closed door, shivering. I still felt the Marquis's hands on my skin. I remembered Joséphine's warnings when I had told her of my first curses. She had said that I had nothing to fear from my brother, and in fact he had not done any of the disgusting things she had mentioned. Yet I knew that what had happened was wrong. The memory of it tortured me.

Antoinette knocked at the door and informed me that I was wanted in the drawing room. There, my mother restored my spirits by slapping me. "What do you mean by leaving your work unfinished on the floor as soon as I turn my back? You are becoming lazier than ever, Gabrielle, and this is saying something. I will have to tell your brother about this."

Fighting tears, I returned to my sewing with an indistinct apology. She expressed at length her disgust at my laziness, carelessness and ingratitude. At supper that night, I dared not meet my brother's eye, nor did he address me. I dreaded that our mother would read our minds like a book and at any moment expose our shame.

"Gabrielle is surlier than usual tonight," she remarked, shaking her head. "No wonder. She must be ashamed of having abandoned her work. You spoil her too much, my son. If you do not take the trouble to give her a serious correction, she will become wild." She turned to me. "Remember, girl, sloth is one of the seven deadly sins. Have you not paid attention to Father Delmas's sermon this morning? Heaven is my witness, I do my best to give you a solid religious education, and what good comes of it?"

After supper, time passed very slowly. I complained of a headache and asked her permission, which was denied, to retire before prayer time. I was haunted by the events of the day and could not sleep that night. Maybe I had done something wrong that had prompted my brother to act in such a manner. What could it be? Was he angry with me? Had I lost his good opinion forever? What if he sent me away?

In such a crisis, I dared not confide in anyone, not even in Joséphine. My brother was after all her lord and master as well as mine. It was also impossible to ask for Madeleine's help. I had promised to show the Marquis all of my letters. In any event, I would have died of shame rather than describe what had happened.

The next morning, the Marquis found me alone again in the drawing room. This time I jumped to my feet as soon as I recognized his step.

"Would you like to go riding with me, Gabrielle?" he asked.

I coloured and made no answer.

"Come, little sister," he said, "I mean you no harm."

I was able to look at him for the first time since the day before, but only for a moment. I could not sustain his eye. He was holding out his hand to me. I took it. Yet when later he helped me into the saddle, as he had always done, it seemed to me, perhaps wrongly, that he was holding me a moment longer than needed. Things could never be the same between us. Suspicion, anticipation and dread crept into my mind at his most innocent move. I knew that he felt it too, and some kind of awkwardness came between us, where there had used to be complete confidence. We rode up the hill and into the woods, and, after some incoherent talk about indifferent things, he asked me to forgive him for what had happened.

"You need not fear its repetition," he said. "However, in order to avoid further temptation, I believe that it would be expedient for both of us to marry."

"I forgive you with all my heart. Indeed, Sir, I have nothing more precious than your friendship. I am so relieved not to have lost it. You should certainly marry if you deem it desirable, but I am very happy at Font-freyde and in no hurry to change my situation. I am only fourteen."

"I agree that it is a bad idea, in general, to make girls marry too young. True, the Church allows them to wed at twelve. Yet in most cases it is too early, if only because they are still unable to comprehend the scope of their new duties and not developed enough to safely bear children. With you, however, I have no such concerns. Your understanding is excellent and you are well formed for your age. I will be sorry to part with you, but you should prepare to the idea of marrying as soon as I receive an eligible offer."

Tears were filling my eyes.

"There is no need for you to fret," continued the Marquis. "Your lack of fortune will probably temper the eagerness of most suitors, though a man may be willing to take you without much."

So my brother was ready to let a stranger take me away from Font-freyde, from my family, from everyone and everything I knew, only to do unspeakable things to me. I was reminded of a wedding song in the Roman language:

> We are leading the poor bride
> As we found her.
> We are taking her away from Poverty
> To deliver her to Starve-to-Death.

The words evoked the harsh fate of a peasant girl, but they now seemed to apply to me too. I began to sob.

"Please, dearest," said my brother, putting his hand on my shoulder, "do not make yourself unhappy. I would never give you to a man whom I would not think worthy of you. I will speak to Mother of what we can afford for your dowry."

I dried my tears and hoped that the Marquis was right about the effect of my fortune on my prospective suitors. Later that day, my mother remarked that I looked like a harlot in my loose clothes. She ordered the carriage and took me to the corset maker in Vic. She did not say anything, however, of marriage or a dowry, nor did I feel any need to broach these subjects.

I soon noticed that young ladies of the neighbouring nobility, accompanied by their mothers, were invited to take tea with us. Dinners entailed too much expense and inconvenience in the Marquise's opinion. After the visitors left, she would criticize the young women's lack or excess of beauty, depending on the case, as well as their immodest attire and unbecoming manners. My brother listened in silence.

5

The year 1784 would bring many changes in my life. I would turn fifteen in July, which filled me with absurd vanity. Mamé Labro, who had always been as proud of me as if I had been her own, admired my tall figure, fair skin, "a true blonde complexion," as she would say, and my hair. When I was little, she had devoted much time to comb, braid and dress it, much to my annoyance.

Mamé's attentions must have attracted the jealousy of her sons. At the age of five, I had awakened one morning to find that one of my braids had been cut while I was asleep. I had been amused and almost wished that the rest of my hair had met with the same fate. Yet Mamé had cried in horror when she had discovered the damage. She had given all five of her sons, for none had come forward to confess to the crime, a flogging with a birch scourge, after which she had made them beg my forgiveness on their knees. My milk brother Jacques had partaken of this punishment. I had been certain of his innocence and pleaded his cause with tears in my eyes, but Mamé had not been moved. My hair had been dressed in a different manner to hide the disaster. The Marquis never suspected that anything was amiss.

Now I was beginning to see things in a different light. I liked my thick locks. Their natural waviness spared me curl papers, hot irons and other instruments used for the torture and beautification of young ladies. I was reaching the age when I found it agreeable to be praised for my looks.

Early during the same year, some legal matters arose involving the estate of Castel, in the neighbouring province of Limousin, from which my brother derived the best part of his income. He was compelled to attend to them himself, and was frequently absent from Fontfreyde for weeks on end. I took to riding by myself to Vic or into the mountains whenever I chose. My mother would scold me upon my return to Font-freyde and I would go back to my sewing without offering any argument in my defense.

On a hot June day, I decided to visit Mamé Labro. Most years, the snows of winter would last into May in the high country, but that spring the weather had been uncommonly mild. The peasants were starting the hay harvest early. I had always loved the smell of cut grass and the circular movement of the men swinging their scythes in perfect cadence. I found the Labro cottage deserted and ran to the fields in search of its inhabitants. They were seated in the shade of a hedge, drinking from a wine bottle during a pause in their work. Sweat stuck their shirts to their chests. Mamé's five sons rose and removed their hats as soon as they saw me. Jacques, sullen as usual, turned away while my nurse greeted me. I always kissed her more than the traditional three times, to feel the softness and firmness of her face under my lips.

"May I help you rake the hay?" I asked.

"Are you out of your senses, dear? What would Her Ladyship say if she heard of it?"

"But I used to do it when I was little."

"Do you think I forgot? The matter with you is that you don't understand the difference between now and then. Go to the river. It'll refresh you. Now run."

I left the Labros and took the direction of the Cère River. I crossed a meadow, then a little wood, before reaching my favourite place, a pebble bank shaped like a half-moon. Upstream, a waterfall emptied into a shallow pool shaded by black cliffs. The darkness of the stone was broken by bursts of ferns and furry mosses growing from the rock faces. There, years earlier, I had caught trout by hand with Jacques.

I undressed to my corset and chemise, which I tied in a knot around my thighs. I gingerly waded into the river, careful not to slip on the green rounded stones of the bottom. The iciness of the water took my breath away. I let the chill penetrate deep into my legs until I could feel the marrow of my bones. Refreshed, I skipped the pebbles I had gathered on the bank and watched the ripples on the glassy surface of the river. I took water into the cup of my hand and let the droplets run down my neck and between my breasts. I shivered with pleasure. It was delicious to feel my skin tingle with cold on that hot day. I was absorbed by the happiness of the moment, lost to any noise but the song of the river.

After a while, I felt a prickling on the back of my neck. I turned around, still knee-deep in the water. A young man of colossal stature was watching me from the bank, smiling, his arms folded. He was dressed with informal elegance, in riding boots, deerskin breeches and a brown velvet waistcoat. His coat and hat were lying on the pebble bank next to my faded gown, moth-eaten stockings and worn-out shoes. His black hair was not powdered and tied like my brother's, but fell straight on his shoulders. What was most noteworthy about the stranger, after his height, was the plainness of his face. The ridges of his jaw and eyebrows were more pronounced than in anyone I had seen before. His nose was long and curved, his skin swarthy, his cheekbones wide and prominent. I wondered how long he had been watching me and I felt colour rise into my cheeks. It was the first time I had seen an intruder in what I considered, now that Jacques shunned my company, my own private domain.

I recovered from my surprise and asked sharply in the Roman language: "Who are you? And what are you doing here?"

"Both pertinent questions, young lady, but I should be the one asking them. My eldest brother owns this land, and you are trespassing. Yet, as a token of my goodwill, I will tell you my name, which is Pierre-André Coffinhal. I came here to bathe in the river, as I like to do every fine day in the summer. However, since you have preceded me, it appears that I will have to forego this pleasure."

He did not look much older than twenty, but his voice was oddly deep for someone so young. He had responded in the Roman language, addressing me in the familiar *thou*. That seemed to indicate that he had taken me for a peasant girl, which suited me very well.

"Are you related to Dr. Coffinhal?" I asked.

"Pierre is one of my brothers, and also my godfather, hence the similarity in our names. In fact, I too am Dr. Coffinhal, for I just completed my medical studies."

I knew the other Dr. Coffinhal well. He lived in Vic, where he was the town physician. My mother fancied herself the prey of various ailments and often had him called to Fontfreyde. He knew how to listen to her. She had the highest opinion of him. He was soft-spoken and handsome, quite different from this brother and godson of his. Another Coffinhal, Jean-Baptiste, the eldest, was an attorney in Vic and handled legal matters for my family. I had seen him before in Fontfreyde and in town, although we could not have met as equals. I knew of still another brother, Joseph Coffinhal, who was a barrister in Paris and whom I had never met.

I now remembered Joséphine mentioning that the youngest son of the family had returned to the high country and was now helping his brother in his medical practice. I did not think it a good idea to tell this new Dr. Coffinhal my real name. My family would not be pleased to learn that a man of lower rank had seen me half-dressed in the river. I vowed to avoid either of the Coffinhals whenever they came to Fontfreyde.

"Please accept my apologies for my intrusion, Doctor," I said. "I will leave the river to your sole enjoyment."

"I was only teasing you. Your presence does not bother me, quite the contrary in fact. You have not told me your name."

The first that came to mind was Gabrielle Labro.

"Are you related to the Labros who live nearby?" he asked.

"I am their daughter. Really, I must go. I was ready to leave when I saw you."

"I know of your family. They are tenants of my brother, and very good people, from what I hear."

He looked down with some curiosity at my clothes, which were lying at his feet. Mortified, I was impatient to leave. I waded towards the beach. The stranger walked to the edge of the water, offered me his hand to help me back to the bank and politely turned away while I dressed.

"Stay for a moment," he said when I was done. "Your mother can spare you for a bit longer."

We sat down a few feet from each other. He asked many questions about the Labros, which I had no trouble answering since I had known them since my infancy, and my life at the cottage. Lying so freely nevertheless made me uneasy. I wanted to put an end to our conversation.

"My mother will become worried if I do not return," I said.

"I am sorry to have delayed you so. Please allow me to walk you back to the cottage. That will give me the opportunity to present my compliments to that excellent woman." He frowned. "However, when I think of it, I suppose that your whole family will be out in the fields, taking advantage of this fine day to finish the hay harvest. How is it that you are not helping? How do you find the time to come here in this season?"

Silently cursing my hasty choice of a false identity and his inquisitiveness, I made no response. The young man grinned.

"Come," he continued, "you must have a poor idea of my intelligence.

Whoever you are, you are no peasant girl. Peasant girls do not wear silk dresses. And your hands, your wrists, and, may I add, your ankles, of which I had the good fortune to catch a glimpse, are far too delicate for farmwork. Your skin is also too fair for you to have spent much time out in the fields. But so far I do not know much about you, except that you are on my brother's land without permission and a shameless liar. Will you please tell me your real name?"

"No."

I was looking down at my feet. He sounded amused by the turn of our conversation, which he pursued, still addressing me familiarly, in French. He spoke it, like me, without any trace of Roman accent.

"Now," he said, "I did observe, over the past few weeks, a young person with your rather peculiar colouring riding through the streets of Vic. I was told that you were Gabrielle de Montserrat, the youngest sister of the Marquis de Castel. By the way, that giant black horse of yours would do very well for me, but it is unsuitable for a lady. Of course *you* did not pay attention to me. Someone like me would have been beneath your notice." He paused. "I hope this teaches you that it is useless to lie, and wrong too."

He caught a loose ringlet on my nape and played with it, his fingertips brushing against the back of my neck, as if it had been the most natural of things.

"A lovely shade of red," he said, "between the colour of dark gold and that of autumn leaves. It suits those grey eyes of yours to perfection."

He had the insolence to address me as *thou* after admitting to knowing who I was. No one, except my brother, Mamé Labro and Joséphine, ever used the familiar form with me. It made me as angry as the liberties he was taking with my hair. I rose to run away from him and his bad manners. Before I had time to turn around, he seized me by the wrist and, without rising, made me sit down again.

"One moment, please," he said. "Would it not be imprudent to turn away so rudely without taking any leave of me? Think that I might tell your brother about this little escapade of yours, of which I do not believe he knows, or would approve if he did. All I am asking in exchange for my silence is that you meet me again here in a few days. If you do, I will be mute as a tomb. You will find me more trustworthy than you yourself have been with me."

There was no harm in agreeing to what he wanted since, in the meantime, I could always change my mind and breach a commitment so extorted. I promised to meet him three days later and, without looking back, ran straight to the cottage, where Jewel was waiting for me. I did not see anyone of the Labro household, nor did I wait for them to come home from the fields. Because of the hot, dry weather, they would be impatient to finish the hay harvest and would not return until after dark.

It is said in French that the night brings counsel. When I undressed at bedtime, I reflected upon the events of that afternoon. I would have been at a loss to describe the impressions the encounter had left on me. The young physician had been rude, but I found this rather reassuring. Joséphine had warned about men who spoke in too friendly a manner. Such was certainly not his case.

Moreover, my brother, if he learned of the meeting, would no doubt forbid any more unchaperoned rides to the river, or anywhere else for that matter. I was not sure that my new acquaintance would have carried out his threat, but I did not wish to take any chance of having my freedom curtailed on account of one incident, however innocent. I concluded that it would be prudent to keep my promise.

The next day, I felt no further hesitation and even began to look forward to that second meeting. The young man was certainly very plain, but his conversation had entertained me and I felt a thrill in meeting someone in secret.

I returned to the Cère River on the appointed day. I chose not to stop by the cottage. Mamé Labro might have become suspicious to see me so soon again. I saw a large, dappled grey horse in the wood and tied Jewel close by. The young physician was waiting for me on the little pebble bank. He greeted me in French with great politeness, this time calling me "Mademoiselle" and addressing me formally.

"Thank you for coming back here," he said. "I dared not hope that you would join me today. I must also admit that I am ashamed of the threat I used. You realized of course that, no matter what, I would never have been so wicked as to tell anyone about our last meeting."

"No indeed. How could I? I do not know you at all."

"I had entertained the hope that perhaps you would come back for the pleasure of my company, but I was apparently too presumptuous."

"I did not find your company very agreeable the other day. You were insolent, but not so much as to preclude the possibility of improvement."

"Thank you, both for your candor and for this chance you are giving me to redeem myself. I will try to make a better impression this time."

We walked along the river and shared our memories of it. He spoke about his own childhood. Like me, he had lost his father at an early age. His eldest brothers, Jean-Baptiste, the lawyer, and Pierre, the physician, of whom he spoke fondly, had replaced his late parent in every respect. Pierre-André had been away at school, first in Clermont, then in Paris, since the age of eleven. His mother had died the year before of a bilious fever.

"Pierre attended her till her last moment," said Pierre-André. "Unfortunately the progress of her illness was very rapid. I was away in Paris and could only return to Vic in time to see her in her coffin. It grieved me not to be able to say good-bye to her, though I know she forgave me. I was her favourite son."

He gazed into the distance. I remained silent.

"Since completing my medical studies," he continued, "I have joined Pierre's practice. He attends to his patients in town while I call upon those in the countryside. It entails riding long distances in all weathers, but I do not mind it. On the contrary, there is nothing I like better than the country around Vic. When I was at school, I always came back here for Christmas and the summer holidays. Indeed I cannot think of a more beautiful place in the world."

"Neither can I. I was born in Lavigerie, but raised here, first by my nurse and then at the convent."

My hand brushed against the tall grass on the side of the lane.

"I am happy to see that we share this opinion of Vic," he said. "Although I prefer this town, I have thought of opening a surgery in Lavigerie, where there is no physician in residence. My late mother, like you, was born there."

"If you were to settle in Lavigerie, you could attend to my own mother. She would be delighted to have a physician at hand."

"My brother Pierre wishes to bring me along during his next visit to Fontfreyde." He frowned. "I know the Marquis by sight only and never had the honour of meeting Her Ladyship. I suspect that I will not answer to her ideas of refinement. She will think that I am just good enough for townspeople and peasants."

"Why do you say this? She is fond of your brother and might like you as well. It is difficult to tell in advance whom she will fancy. What is sure is that she has not a high opinion of me. She finds me stupid."

"A deplorable lack of judgment."

"Unfortunately not. I was taken from the convent at the age of eleven and have not studied anything since. If you knew me better, you would be amazed at my ignorance."

He smiled. "At the very least, your humility should disarm criticism. I find you anything but stupid. If you were, you would not be aware of the deficiencies of your education. You seem very young and—"

"I will turn fifteen in less than three weeks," I interrupted, frowning.

"I am sorry to have offended you. But even if you had already reached the ripe age of fifteen, I would still consider you very young. You will, no doubt, have many opportunities to improve your mind as you grow up. You will read, you will travel, you will mingle in society. I wish more attention were paid to the schooling of young ladies. My late mother, who was the daughter of a mere bourgeois, remained in a convent in Aurillac until she was married at the age of eighteen. It is a pity your family did not value your education more."

"I did not mean any reflection on them," I said. "My brother has always been very kind to me."

"He obviously leaves you free to go wherever you want on your own. If I had a sister so young and delightful as you, I would be less kind and a bit more watchful."

I coloured at that criticism of the Marquis.

"Yet," Pierre-André added, "I should be the last person to complain about it. I might never have had the pleasure of making your acquaintance otherwise."

"Usually my brother rides with me, although we do not come here together. It is only lately that he has been away in Limousin."

"Does he know that, in his absence, you come here to bathe in front of strangers?"

I stopped walking and looked straight at Pierre-André. "It is very rude of you to ask such a question."

"Please forgive me. I seem perversely determined to sink myself in your opinion. You should slap me for my insolence. I deserve it."

"You do, but I would never strike another. My mother often slaps me and I do not like it at all."

"My rudeness will then remain unpunished, which makes me feel my guilt still more. My sole excuse, if I may claim any, is that I do not like the idea of another man finding you here in your chemise."

I resumed walking. "You need not worry. I have come here for years without meeting anyone. That is why you startled me the other day. You reminded me of the poem 'The Wolf and the Lamb,' by La Fontaine. The nuns made me learn it by rote at the convent."

"Rather unflattering for me, and most unfair. If my memory serves me well, the wolf in that story, after finding the lamb drinking in the middle of the river, falsely accuses it of muddying the waters and devours the defenseless animal. I was less fierce and let you escape unscathed. I did not leave a single toothmark on you."

I laughed. "It was only when I first saw you that you reminded me of the wolf. I do not believe now that you would harm me."

"You are right, all the more so because you trust me, but you might have made a less fortunate encounter."

"I am afraid of no one."

"Are you sure?"

I hesitated. "Well, maybe it was a silly thing to say."

"It simply reflects your lack of experience. May life never teach you otherwise."

"Has it taught you otherwise?"

"In some ways. I learned much in medical school."

"How did you like it? Oh, I envy you. You are so fortunate to have lived in great cities. I know next to nothing of them. I am eager to see other places but have never been more than ten leagues from Fontfreyde. Please tell me all about Paris."

He obliged. He spoke well and I could picture unknown places and people as he described them. I had never been so well entertained in anyone's company and did not like to rush home later that afternoon. I told him, truthfully that time, of my early years at the Labro cottage, of my milk brother Jacques, of our childhood friendship and his subsequent disdain for my company.

"One day, five years ago, I told him how pretty I found the wild carnations that grow around here and he twined those flowers into my braids. When we returned to the cottage, very pleased with ourselves, Mamé, instead of complimenting us, as we had expected, reprimanded me for my vanity and gave Jacques a flogging."

"A well-deserved one," said Pierre-André. "I agree with your nurse. No one except me should play with your hair."

I blushed at the thought of what he had done during our first encounter. "Pray what would make you an exception? You are in no position to speak in this manner. I kept my word by coming here again, as I hope you kept yours by being discreet. Now we are done. It is time for me to go home."

"Now I have upset you again. What a poor way of thanking you for your kindness in coming here. I have never spent a more pleasant hour than in your company. Yet I do not want to delay you, no matter how much it pains me to part with you. Now as to the fact that we are done, I disagree." He turned to face me, a grave look on his face. "I, for one, am not done with you. Two days from now I will be waiting for you here. I will make no threats this time. You are free to come back or not, at your pleasure. Either way I will not tell a soul about meeting you. If you care at all for me, as I care for you, you will return. If not, I will remember you for the rest of my life as the prettiest, most unfeeling little liar in the country. I will curse your name, whatever it is. You will never be able to come here again for fear of seeing me, for I will haunt these banks forever, brokenhearted."

I giggled at that depiction, which did not seem to fit him at all.

"Do not laugh," he said seriously. "I mean it."

I knew not what to believe and avoided his eye. We walked in silence through the wood to the spot where we had left our horses. Before reaching it, he took my face between his hands and looked into my eyes. He bent towards me. I opened my mouth to protest, but only let out a moan. At first his lips brushed against mine, then became more insistent. Soon he was kissing me deeply, slowly, deliberately as if we had all the time in the world, or as if the world no longer existed. I had never felt anything of the kind, and enjoyed the novelty of it so much that I found myself kissing him back. I closed my eyes to savor this sensation. He sighed and, much to my regret, let go of me.

"Two days from now," he said, "same hour."

He seized me by the waist to help me into the saddle. He lifted me without any effort but changed his mind and, still holding me in midair, kissed me again.

✒ 6 ✒

I was in a flutter of spirits when I arrived at Fontfreyde. I could not make any sense of what had happened. Why had I let a stranger, a commoner, and a plain one at that, kiss me? In fact, I had kissed him too. And was he so very plain? I was beginning to find him rather handsome, or at least attractive in his own way. Had he been a peasant or a soldier, he would have been considered an uncommonly fine-looking man. Did he really mean what he had said about being brokenhearted if we did not meet again or was he merely mocking me, as his tone had seemed to indicate? Would he be waiting for me in two days? Was it wise to see him again? Truth be told, I knew the answer to this last question. I was playing with fire, but what girl of fifteen is afraid of fire? I was delighted with the game in which I had been drawn. With the innocence and arrogance of youth, I believed that I could control the course of events that would unfold.

Two days later, a heavy summer rain was knocking at the window-panes of Fontfreyde. Without hesitation I threw my winter cloak on my shoulders, grabbed an old hat of my brother's and slipped out. I rode again to the river.

Pierre-André was waiting for me, this time in the wood. One could barely feel any drops there. He helped me dismount and he led me without a word to a shallow cave on the banks of the river. Again, we shared an all too brief hour, sheltered from the rain, enjoying the softness of its noise, mingled with that of running water, and the smell of wet earth. Again we kissed, longer than the last time. I have a beauty mark on the side of my neck, and he kissed me there too, telling me that it was the most enticing thing he had ever seen. He traced the blue lines of my veins on my wrists, which the sleeves of my dress were too short to cover.

"This is the origin of the phrase *blue blood*," he said. "People of noble descent are supposed to have fair skin, but I have never seen any as translucent as yours. Look at my hand: I have no blue blood, either literally, because my complexion is much darker than yours, or figuratively, because I am the grandson of a peasant."

He put his hand against mine. His was twice as large. He kissed the inside of mine and lightly followed the lines there with his fingertips. That simple caress, more than anything else, troubled me. I shuddered, my skin tingling. He never asked my permission before doing anything he pleased, but nothing he did offended me anymore. He now used the familiar form when addressing me. I no longer found it rude, and responded in the same manner. He did not try to touch me on those parts of my body hidden from public view. I rewarded his restraint by giving him my absolute confidence. He was over a foot taller than me, broad-shouldered and muscular, but I did not for a moment entertain the idea that he might take advantage of our isolation. I was not in the least afraid of him.

In that manner we met many times in the course of the following weeks, until there was nothing on my mind but the thought of being with him again. I did not know what the future held for us beyond our next assignation, nor did I wonder about it. The present happiness occupied all of my waking hours, and many of my dreams. My brother was still often away and nothing prevented me from riding to the river.

The heat turned stifling at the beginning of August. I met Pierre-André again on the pebble beach. No breeze was rustling the leaves above us. We were seated next to each other in the dappled shade, my head leaning against his arm. He had taken off his coat and waistcoat, and I my kerchief. My chemise was sticking to my skin under my corset and I felt beads of moisture forming between my breasts. Yet I did not recognize as mine the faint musky scent hovering in the still air. It came from him. To break free from its spell, I turned my attention to the river. Blue and green dragonflies, glittering like jewels, grazed the surface of the water. I looked wistfully at the insects. He read my mind.

"You are dying to go into the water," he remarked.

I bit my lip and made no response. After our first meeting, I had never again bathed in front of him.

"Do it," he said. "Do you not trust me? I already saw you in your chemise, and did not harm you then. What is worrying you now?"

I looked into his eyes. I read a certain amusement there, and no malice.

"Would you do it too?" I thought of the Marquis de Carabas, the hero of one of my favourite fairy tales, who bathed naked in the river. I wondered whether Pierre-André would disrobe. This idea sent ripples of fear down to my stomach.

"No, I will watch you from the bank," Pierre-André said. "Like the first time we met. And I will turn away while you undress. Tell me when I may look."

His smile reassured me. I no longer hesitated. I removed my clothes and, wearing nothing but my chemise and corset, waded into the river. After a few yards, I turned around and looked at him. He was sitting on his haunches, his face averted. I could not resist the impulse to splash him lightly. He moved his head towards me and rose slowly. He was no longer smiling, but gazing at me without a word. I saw his chest heaving under the linen of his shirt. Now he seemed very tall.

I needed to break the silence. "The water feels delightful," I said. "You do not know what you are missing."

"Oh, I do know." His tone was sharp now. "Come back here this moment."

Something within me, stronger than my apprehension, prompted me to walk towards the pebble bank. Before I even reached it, Pierre-André seized my arm to draw me to him. Holding me tight, he kissed me in a new, resentful manner. The trees, the sky, the dark cliffs, the river were swirling around me. Without letting go of my lips, he caught both of my wrists in one of his hands and with the other pushed down on my shoulder.

There was neither brutality nor hesitation in his manner. He did not seem to expect any resistance, nor was I offering any. I knew what he wanted. I realized that I wanted it too. I lay down while he knelt by me. Looking into my eyes, he raised my chemise to my waist. He insinuated one of his thighs, then the other, between mine. His weight now rested upon my hips. He lowered his face to the side of my neck. I felt his breath, his lips, his teeth on my skin as he kissed me relentlessly. I threw my head backwards and moaned.

"My beloved," he whispered. "At last."

I tried to move from under him, not to escape him but to assure myself that there was no turning back now. He pressed down on my hips more firmly. I was his. Waves of desire rose from my loins to my chest. I had experienced the same when he had touched me before, but now they were so strong as to feel like pain. I was afraid, not of him but of what was going to happen. Yet fear only heightened my yearning for him. I spread my thighs wide and, trembling at my own audacity, wrapped my arms around his chest to draw him still closer. I felt his heart beat faster, his muscles tighten under his shirt.

Without warning, everything changed. His face contracted. He rolled over on his back, staring at the sky.

"What is wrong?" I asked. "Are you angry with me?"

He raised himself on one elbow, kissed me lightly on the forehead and pulled my chemise down to my ankles.

"No, I am angry with myself. Meeting you like this, Gabrielle, is the sweetest thing I can imagine, save one. I would not give it up for the world, but it is driving me out of my mind. Many times I have wanted to take you. Nothing could have been easier, but I could not, I still cannot bring myself to act like a thief when you trust me so. I will marry you."

He simply stated a fact that admitted of no discussion. I huddled against him. I wanted his arms to close around me, but he seized my chin to peer into my eyes.

"Look at me," he said. "Will you marry me?"

"Oh yes, I will."

"Do you promise?"

"Yes, I do. If you do not trust me, treat me as your bride already. Do it even if you trust me. I want it. Do whatever you like."

He groaned. "Please stop this, Gabrielle. Do you know what you are doing to me? As if I were not tempted enough. But I cannot take you now, in this manner. I would hurt you, little as I want it."

"It will hurt anyway. I am ready for it."

"What do you know about it, poor innocent? What *I* know is that, my pleasure taken, I would have to send you back to Fontfreyde by yourself, torn, bleeding, maybe regretting your tenderness." He caressed my cheek. "I want you to be my true bride; I want to discover you slowly, gently, tenderly, over an entire night. And afterwards I want to keep you forever."

"But I do not want to deny you anything."

"You are not denying me anything. You gave me your promise. It is all I need for now, my beloved."

He kept me embraced for a long time. I was, to use a trite phrase, the happiest girl in the world.

Yet all too soon it was time to think of returning to Fontfreyde. I tried to imagine my family's reaction to my engagement. True, my brother wanted to see me settled early, but I suspected that my suitor was not the kind of husband the Marquis had in mind for me. Indeed I did not know of any noblewoman who had wed a commoner. I tried to express my misgivings without hurting Pierre-André's pride.

"I am afraid I have not much of a dowry," I said, my head still resting on his shoulder.

He laughed. "I have enough money for both of us, my beloved. I do not want a *sol* from your brother. I am sure that he will be as disagreeable as can be, to make me feel how unworthy I am of marrying into the high and mighty house of Montserrat, but who cares? You are worth it. I will talk to my brothers. They will know how to approach him."

During my ride back home, I tried to imagine my life as Pierre-André's wife. He would take a house for us in town, hire a few maids and a groom. I would be expected to manage it on my own. My mother had no housekeeper in Fontfreyde, nor did she want any, because she liked to direct things herself. Was I too young, too inexperienced to do so? Would Pierre-André be angry with me if the servants were slovenly, the food unappetizing, his shirts not properly washed and ironed? No, he would allow me a few months to become used to my new duties; he would always be kind and patient with me.

And what if I put him to shame by my ignorance? His brothers' wives must be far better educated than I. What had I learned at the convent, beside the alphabet and three tunes on the harpsichord? But he understood that it was not my fault. And he had said that he found me far from stupid. He would take the trouble to instruct me on the many topics of which I knew nothing. He would give me books to read, and I would show my gratitude by the speed of my progress. On winter evenings I would study by the fire, counting the strokes of the clock, waiting to hear the hooves of his horse in the night. He might ride home tired, cold, hungry or sullen after visiting his patients, but I would have a hot meal ready for him. He would tell me of his concerns over supper. Then he would take me in his arms and hold me as he had done that afternoon; he would call me his beloved. He would carry me to bed. It would be *our* bed, where I would give myself to him, where I would fall asleep every night, nestled against him, where I would bear his children, and where someday I would die.

I was still lost in my thoughts as I sat to dinner with my mother and brother. The Marquis had returned that very afternoon. I did not hear half of what my mother said to me and responded to the rest at cross-purposes, to the point where she remarked: "The girl has never been too clever, but she is now turning into a complete simpleton. Mark my words, my son: she will disgrace the family and be the ruin of us."

My brother too seemed absentminded. He turned to our mother and said abruptly: "Gabrielle should have a new dress."

"Well," my mother responded after a pause, "I hope she appreciates your generosity. I am ready to part with one of my gowns if you wish."

"No, Madam, it is not what I meant. I believe that Gabrielle should have a new dress of her own. She looks very pretty in black, with her fair skin, but I was thinking of a more lively colour, more in keeping with her age."

My mother, silenced for once, stared at my brother.

"I am not so destitute, Madam," he continued, "as to be unable to afford a new gown for my sister. You could go to Vic with her tomorrow to buy some fabric."

I had become fully attentive to the conversation. I was, of course, happy to have a new gown. What girl of fifteen would not have been? It was mortifying to be seen by Pierre-André, week after week, in the only two black things I had inherited from my mother. Yet the Marquis's unexpected generosity was unsettling. He could not have heard from Pierre-André's brothers yet. What had he in mind?

My mother ordered the carriage to go to the draper in Vic. For the first time in my life, I indulged in the pleasures of finery. The seemingly limitless choice of textures and colours made my head spin. She picked a greenish satin and raised it to my face.

"With this unfortunate hair of yours," she said, "we are left with very few choices."

"No, Madam," I said, "not the green. It reminds me of the colour of goose droppings. And it makes my skin look sallow. This bright pink silk will do much better."

My mother frowned. "Are you out of your senses, Gabrielle? I will not allow my child to parade around in a colour fit for a loose woman."

At last we settled our differences with the help of the shopkeeper and agreed on a striped material, light pink and white, which happened to be the least expensive.

"It will look lovely on Mademoiselle de Montserrat," said the shopkeeper. "It will highlight the delicacy of her complexion and her beautiful hair. I would recommend this as a pattern for the dress, with the stripes straight in the skirt and cut on the bias in the bodice."

Our purchases that day also included white silk stockings. We even stopped by the cobbler's shop. There were ordered for me, for the first time in years, new shoes, black and elegant with a silver buckle. I thanked my mother, all the more embarrassed that I felt no real gratitude. During the ride back to Fontfreyde, I wanted to ask about the reason for these purchases, but she volunteered no information and I thought it wiser not to press the point.

I met Pierre-André again.

"I spoke with my brothers," he said. "They are astonished at my choice of a bride."

I easily believed it. Although he had too much delicacy to mention it, they must have represented to him that he could do much better in terms of money. I was also sure that they did not relish the prospect of dealing with my brother. Pierre-André could have married any girl of the local bourgeoisie, with a comfortable dowry, whose family would have been delighted by the match.

"Are they unhappy with your choice?" I asked.

"They say that I have set my sights too high. That may be true, but if you have the kindness not to object to it, why should they?" He reached for my hand and kissed it. "They complain that I am always begging for trouble of some kind or other. Both of them, however, find you very pretty, and they understand why I want you so. Pierre, who has seen you many times at Fontfreyde and is always my best ally, convinced Jean-Baptiste to seek your brother's consent. According to them, it will not be enough to take you without a dowry. I should offer some financial inducement to assuage your family's concerns as to the inequality of the match. Jean-Baptiste suggested that I settle 20,000 francs on you by marriage contract and offer an equal sum to your brother as consideration for your *disparagement*. That is what lawyers call the unequal marriage of a noble lady to a commoner, and, like everything else, it has a price."

"I had no idea that such sums could change hands upon the occasion of my wedding."

"You have too modest an opinion of your own claims. I would give anything for the happiness of having you as my wife."

I was saddened by the implicit opinion that my brother's consent to the match could be bought. It did not reflect well on either his financial circumstances, with which, as his lawyer, Jean-Baptiste Coffinhal must have been acquainted, or his avarice.

"What was I thinking?" said Pierre-André. "I have been a brute to tell you about these sordid matters. Your feelings for your brother, after all, are only natural. I should not have hurt them."

"No, I thank you for telling me. I should know of these things since they concern me."

"My beloved, my brothers think that I have a fair chance of success since there is no competing offer from any noble party. They will speak to the Marquis shortly. I wanted to go with them, but they refuse to take me along. They say that I would ruin all of their efforts with what they call my arrogance."

"What if my brother refuses?"

"Do not worry. He will discover that when I want something, I get it sooner or later."

It was the first time that serious concerns had arisen to cloud our happiness. We agreed that our assignations should remain a secret, and that he would pretend to have fallen in love at first sight while casually crossing my path in Vic.

Once at home, I went to work with the help of the maids. The pink and white fabric was sewn into one of the prettiest gowns I ever owned. When I tried it on and looked at my reflection in the mirror, I took a step backwards. I was stunned to see myself for the first time in such finery. I would have liked Pierre-André to see me too, but that was not to be. My mother told me that I had to save the dress for the pilgrimage of Our Lady of Consolation in Thiézac on the 15th of August.

⚜ 7 ⚜

"Our Lady of August," *Nostro Damo d'Agost,* as it is called in the Roman language, is the Festival of the Assumption of the Blessed Virgin. On that day, my mother never missed the pilgrimage of Thiézac. During its celebration, a statue, reputed to have miraculous properties, of Our Lady of Consolation carrying in her arms the Divine Child was removed in the morning from its chapel in the mountains and carried with great ceremony to the village church for the day. This was the only opportunity during the entire year for the faithful to worship it.

I had therefore not been surprised when my mother had asked me to save my new dress for this occasion. For the first time she was paying great attention to my appearance. She harassed the maids while they did my hair. She brought her bottle of rose water and did not spare it. She even lent me, for that occasion only, as she was careful to point out, her best lace kerchief and her gold medal of the Blessed Virgin. The chain was too long for me. The jewel, cold against my skin, rested low on my throat. She arranged the white lace in a manner that uncovered as much of my flesh as decency permitted. She then adjusted a white rose between my breasts as a *babarel*. That is the name given in Auvergne to flowers arranged between a woman's breasts. I had never worn any before and was beginning to feel uneasy but kept my suspicions to myself. We left Fontfreyde early to arrive on time to see the statue of Our Lady carried into town.

Peasants had come down from the most isolated hamlets in the mountains, some in wooden clogs and coats of coarse wool, their hair matted under their broad-brimmed hats. The parish priest, in holiday vestments of gold embroidery, was at the head of the procession, followed by the town aldermen and mounted constables with their sabres drawn. Behind them the statue of Our Lady of Consolation, carved of black wood and dressed in white and gold brocade, was carried on the shoulders of villagers in their Sunday best. All stopped in the square in front of the church. *Cabretaïres*, the high country bagpipers, started to play traditional airs. Dancers, their hands held aloft, formed the wheel patterns of the *bourrées*, the men shouting throaty cries of rejoicing I have never heard in any other country. As a child, I had gladly joined in those dances and learned the accompanying songs, some bawdy, some telling of the heartsickness of lost love. The presence of my family now forced me to stay away. My mother, without paying attention to the music or the dancers, was looking around with a worried expression. Suddenly her face softened. A stranger was walking in our direction. The crowd was parting to make way for him, the men taking off their hats and the women curtseying. He bowed to my mother. He and my brother embraced briefly, calling each other "cousin." The man was introduced to me as the Baron de Peyre.

The Baron was about three inches taller than me, broad-chested and robustly built. He was dressed rather for hunting than for a high holiday, in a plain suit of green cloth and leather boots that came up to his thighs. His hair, straight and thick, without side curls, was longer than was fashionable even at the time, almost down to his waist, and simply tied by a ribbon of black silk behind his neck. I had thought from afar that it was powdered, but, upon closer inspection, I saw that it was naturally of a uniform grey colour that contrasted with the tan of his skin. Apart from of that sign of age, he gave an impression of health and carried himself with a great deal of assurance. His face was wide, his expression good-humoured and his features handsome in a coarse way. I noticed his smell, strong but not unpleasant, reminiscent of horse and smoked ham in winter.

He presented his compliments to my mother, who simpered back, her voice higher-pitched than usual in an attempt at sweetness. She elbowed me sharply to remind me of my manners. I had forgotten to curtsey, lost as I was in my contemplation of the gentleman. He seemed to share my curiosity and looked me over intently, staring in particular at the gold medal and white rose between my breasts. His eyes were still fixed on me when he said to my mother: "Please allow me to offer my congratulations, Madam. Your Ladyship has been blessed with a charming daughter. My little cousin is ripe for marriage."

I felt myself blushing at the crudeness of his compliment. He then seemed to ignore me and turned to my mother to apologize for his clothing.

"I came on horseback," he explained. "There is nothing I find quite as tedious as traveling in a carriage, especially on a fine summer day."

The dances had ended and it was time for Mass. My mother had of course precedence over me, and the Baron should have led her into church, but my brother anticipated him. I was left behind with my cousin and had no choice but to put my hand on his when he offered it. Touching it made me cringe. The Marquis led my mother to the front pew, which was reserved for us, and took his place after her. The Baron and I followed. I had to sit between my brother and him. I arranged the skirts of my pink dress so that they would not touch him.

I had always liked the church of Thiézac, which was decorated inside in pinks, blues and greens, trimmed with gold. Painted statues of saints stood in every niche and corner. The altars were adorned with a multitude of white lilies to honour the Blessed Virgin. However, on that day, my thoughts were very little occupied by my surroundings or the pilgrimage of Our Lady of Consolation. I avoided looking at the Baron but keenly felt his presence next to me. I could not help breathing in his smell, mixed with the scent of the lilies and my own fragrance. At the end of the service, he saw us to our carriage and received from my mother a pressing invitation to call upon us, which was accepted with great cordiality.

I knew little about the Baron, beyond the fact that he was a distant cousin of both my late father and my mother, and a widower. I remembered my mother mentioning his wife's death a few months earlier. At the time, the passing of an unknown relation had been of very little concern to me. I now regretted my lack of attention. As soon as we returned home, I hurried to the kitchen to question Joséphine.

"He's very rich, dear," she said. "He inherited the Cénac estate when his elder brother died. And he married a lady of great wealth. He lost her not too long ago, at the end of May, I think it was. His late wife, poor thing, passed away while giving birth, I think it was for the seventh time. Her infant son followed her the same day and they were buried together. All of the Baron's children died in infancy. So now his heir is Monsieur de Laubrac, his first cousin."

I knew by sight Monsieur de Laubrac, a young man, still single. All of this confirmed my fears. The Baron could afford to take a girl as penniless as I, and would be looking for a young, healthy bride to bear him a son. Joséphine smiled. "Who knows," she said, "maybe you caught his fancy today."

"I do not want him. He is old, for one thing."

"Nonsense. He can't be more than forty-five. That's nothing when a man is in good health. I can't think of a better match for you."

For my part, I found the prospect of any intimacy with him unbearable. Even sitting by his side in church had been agony.

✺ 8 ✺

The next day, fresh from the impressions of Thiézac, I was leading Jewel to a meadow behind the château when I saw two men ride into the courtyard. I recognized Pierre-André's elder brothers, the lawyer, Jean-Baptiste, and Pierre, the physician. My heart stopped for a minute. I hastened to take Jewel back to the stables and returned to the house. I ran to a spare bedroom that afforded a view of the courtyard and waited. After about ten minutes, I saw the brothers mount and leave. I tried in vain to read their expressions.

Then I heard an unexpected noise. A dispute had erupted between my brother and mother. Both of their voices were at their highest pitch, quivering with anger. The bedroom was right above the main drawing room, and I could feel the violence of the words they hurled at each other without understanding them. I was frozen with surprise, because I had never heard my brother raise his voice to our mother. She in turn reserved her barbs for the servants and me. Finally, one of the maids, a terrified look on her face, came to tell me that I was wanted downstairs. As I entered the drawing room, my mother and brother turned to me. Her eyes were red.

"So, Gabrielle," said my brother, his jaw tight, "what have you been doing of late?"

"I do not know of what you are talking, Sir. I saw Messieurs Coffin-hal leave a while ago, that is all."

"And of course, you are unaware of the purpose of their visit?"

"I thought that maybe Maître Coffinhal had come here to discuss some legal matter with you, Sir, and that Mother had summoned the Doctor."

"Are you telling me that you are ignorant of the offer of marriage that has just been made by those men?"

"I am."

"Gabrielle, look at yourself when you lie."

Foolishly, I obeyed and glanced at my reflection in the mirror above the fireplace. My face was flushed.

"Pray tell me," continued the Marquis, "how it is that their younger brother has the insolence to aspire to your hand? He is a country physician, a lawyer's son, which is bad enough. But do you know what his paternal grandfather was? The lowest kind of commoner, a peasant from Pailherols, up in the mountains, a man who would not have dared address any of the Montserrats except on his knees. And now his grandson would marry my sister? How on earth did he conceive the idea?"

"I believe that he knows me by sight, Sir. I met him briefly at the cobbler's shop."

"So you want me to believe that a man in his right mind would seek the hand of a young lady he knows only by sight, without any encouragement from her family, as in one of your fairy tales?" The Marquis paused, his eyes narrowed. "Have *you* given him any encouragement?"

"Certainly not, Sir."

"If you had, you would have done him no favours, for such a match is out of the question. I will never give you to a commoner. Never, do you hear me?" He glared at me. "As for you, Gabrielle, go to your room. There will be no more rides to Vic on your own. From now on, you will not stir from Fontfreyde unless accompanied by Mother or me."

I returned upstairs, upset but not desperate. True, my brother seemed angry, but in time he might relent. I would, in the course of the next days, speak to him outside the presence of our mother. I would throw myself upon his mercy, confess everything and beg his forgiveness for lying to him. He loved me. His heart could not remain closed to me for long. I hoped that he had not been too blunt in his refusal and that the Coffinhal brothers could be convinced to renew their offer. I scrawled a note to Pierre-André to tell him not to lose hope and ask him to communicate with me through Joséphine. I went to the kitchen and begged her to have it sent to Vic.

She frowned when she read the direction. "Young Dr. Coffinhal? My goodness, is he a suitor of yours? Is that why his brothers came here today? No wonder Her Ladyship looked so upset." She looked into the distance. "Remember, when you made me tell your fortune, the first card you drew, that Knight of Swords? You know, that man riding a black horse, his sword drawn."

Indeed a few months earlier I had pestered and coaxed Joséphine until she had fetched her deck of tarot cards.

"Well," she continued, "your young doctor puts me in mind of the Knight of Swords. He's clever and resolute. He speaks well. He commands attention wherever he goes. But he can be arrogant, even cruel. Remember what I told you about the Knight: he spells doom for his enemies, and God knows he has many. And remember how he wields his sword, the sword of justice? He will show his foes no mercy, and receive none."

"But you said yourself that the cards can be tricky, that they deceive us more often than not." I kissed her. "Be good, dear Joséphine. Have my note delivered. Please."

She thought for a minute and sighed. "All right," she said. "But you're a bad girl, and likely to cost me my place."

I had hastened to forget about the Baron, but he painfully reminded me of his existence by calling at Fontfreyde the very next day. After the exchange of usual civilities in the drawing room, there was a pause in the conversation. I dared not raise my eyes and did not know what to do with myself. Even my mother, usually not at a loss for words, was silent for a moment before addressing him.

"Indeed, Sir," she said, "we are flattered to receive a visit from you so soon after having had the honour of meeting you in Thiézac."

"The honour was all mine, dear Madam. I was delighted to make the acquaintance of your youngest daughter. The rumours I had heard of her beauty do not do her justice."

"Ah, Sir, you appeal to the feelings of a mother! I must confess that it is a weakness of mine: I am inordinately fond of our Gabrielle. I should not sing my own child's praises, but I can assure you that you will not find a more dutiful girl in all of Auvergne. She has been given excellent Christian principles. She is a good seamstress too, and she goes to help in the kitchen every day. God knows she has never lacked anything here, but she has not been used to luxury or idleness. She will make a thrifty wife and be content with little, without expecting anything lavish like those young ladies who have been raised with high notions of their own claims."

I blushed with shame at this speech.

"Further, Sir," my mother added, "you will find that Gabrielle has not been infected with those ideas that too fancy an education gives girls nowadays. The Marquis took her from the convent when she was eleven. She can read, write and count. These are all the accomplishments a noblewoman needs to make her husband happy. My eldest daughter thought that Gabrielle could have stayed in the convent a few years longer, but, as I told her—"

The Baron interrupted to remark: "I am not in the least surprised, Madam, to learn of my little cousin's many qualities, but I have yet to hear the sound of her voice."

True, I had never uttered a single word in his presence. He was justified in wondering whether I had been endowed with the power of speech.

"Please forgive her stupidity, Sir," said my mother in a sharper tone. "The child has the most awkward manners. I cannot apologize enough on her behalf." She turned to me. "Say something, girl. Speak to our cousin instead of staring at your feet like a simpleton. You may rest assured that you will receive a serious flogging as soon—"

"Please, dear Madam," the Baron intervened, "do not scold my little cousin. I would be very sorry if she were whipped because of my remark, which was meant not as a reproof but as an expression of curiosity. I find it far more becoming for a female to talk too little than too much."

I raised my eyes to him and said: "Thank you, Sir."

He bowed to me. "I am delighted to hear Mademoiselle de Montserrat speak at last. Her voice is as charming as her person."

His words silenced me. There was another pause in the conversation. He turned to my brother. "Cousin," he asked, "can we have a word between men?"

My mother gestured to me to follow her out of the room. The Baron rose to wish us good-bye.

How I wished I could have stayed behind to listen to that conversation! I had to sit with my mother in her apartment, my forehead resting on the windowpane, watching the courtyard for half an hour. Again and again I pondered each of the Baron's looks and expressions with the same anxiety as if I had been madly in love with him and uncertain of his feelings. At last, I saw him leave the house. My brother accompanied him to the bottom of the front staircase. They embraced each other with great cordiality. I bid my last hopes farewell.

I heard my brother's brisk footstep outside my mother's door. He walked in, smiling, took my hands in his and kissed me on both cheeks.

"Let me offer my congratulations," he said. "Our cousin has proposed and been accepted."

I had expected the blow but remained unable to utter a word, tears running down my cheeks. My mother berated me for my ingratitude. She slapped me. My brother took me by the hand and led me to my own room. There, he sat next to me on the bed, his arm around my shoulders.

"Gabrielle," he said, "tears are useless. My decision is irrevocable. Any other girl would be delighted to have been chosen by the Baron. He speaks like a man truly in love with you. He even had the generosity to decline the modest dowry offered with your hand."

My brother let go of my shoulders and handed me his handkerchief. "The wedding date has been set. Our cousin is impatient to proceed and I see only advantages in keeping the engagement short. The 15th of September has been settled upon, which will allow almost a month for the publication of the banns, the drafting of the marriage contract and other preparations. We also need to obtain the Bishop's dispensation because of your kinship with your fiancé."

My sobs redoubled at the idea that my wedding would take place so soon. I had nothing to lose. I had to tell the truth.

"Please, Sir," I said, "spare me the pain of marrying the Baron. Not him. I beg you. Besides, I am already engaged to another. I have accepted Pierre-André Coffinhal."

My brother blanched. He seized me by the shoulders so hard that I cried aloud in pain and fear. Trembling with rage and shaking me, he made me describe everything that had happened between Pierre-André and me, in what manner, on what parts of my body, how often he had touched me, whether I had enjoyed it, whether I loved him. I had never seen my brother in such a state of fury. Every detail was pried from me. When he saw that I had no more to reveal and that I was choking with tears, he let go of me.

"You had no right," he said, his mouth tight, "to enter into that engagement without my permission. It is void. You seem, along with your lover, to have forgotten that you are under my authority. If what you told me is true, you will be married as soon as can be arranged. If not, beware."

He left, slamming the door. There is a great difference between guessing something we do not like and being assured of it. My brother discovered it that day. He must have surmised that there was more to my meetings with Pierre-André than I had cared to admit before, but had not sought to learn of it. It was not long before I felt the consequences of my disclosure.

I remained on my bed, sobbing, my head buried in the pillows. Later that day, my mother entered the room, followed by the maid Guillemine and Denise Delrieu, the village midwife. The Delrieu woman was also, according to common rumour, a *faiseuse d'anges*, an "angel maker," who would rid distressed females of unborn offspring. She was nicknamed in the Roman language *lou Cabanel*, the Owl, and considered a witch, or a healer, depending on one's opinion of her potions. Like all the children in the village, I had kept away from her cottage.

Startled, I rose. My mother, in her severest voice, ordered me to lie on my bed. I obeyed. Without a word of warning, she raised my skirts up to my waist, caught my knees and spread my legs apart. She ordered the maid to hold my arms above my head. At that time, women did not wear any undergarments under their chemise, and my intimate parts were exposed to the view of the Owl. The crone lit a candle she had taken from the sewing table and approached so close that I felt the heat of the flame between my thighs. I imagined for an instant that she was going to burn me in some witchcraft ritual as a punishment for my misconduct. I cried in horror and tried to rise from the bed, but the maid was holding my arms firmly. The Owl, bending toward me until I felt her head brushing against my skin, examined me and poked at me with the fingers of her free hand. I shuddered at her touch. After a few minutes, she turned to my mother.

"She's intact," said the witch, "fresh as a rose. You needn't worry, My Lady, she'll bleed."

My mother gave an audible sigh. She dismissed the Owl and left without a second look at me. I rose in haste, sick to my stomach, and rearranged my skirts.

Of course I knew the purpose of the examination. I wondered what would have happened had Pierre-André's conduct been less honourable. My engagement to the Baron would certainly have been broken. Yet even that would not have ensured the acceptance of Pierre-André's offer. It was more likely that both of us would have been subjected to my brother's wrath.

That night I did not go down to dinner, nor did anyone ask to see me. Joséphine brought me a tray in my bedroom. She too congratulated me on my good fortune and represented to me all of the advantages of the match. I said nothing, too nauseated to touch the food.

For the next few days Joséphine continued to bring me my meals. There seemed to be an unspoken understanding in Fontfreyde that I was not to leave my bedroom. Yet before the week was over, a maid came to fetch me. She announced that there was company waiting for me in the drawing room. I thought at first that the Baron had come for a courtship visit and fervently hoped that we would be left alone for a moment. I intended to throw myself at his feet and confess my attachment to another. Perhaps he was not cruel. He might take pity on me and release me from our engagement.

I was startled to find a little crowd in the drawing room. In addition to my *fiancé,* I saw my brother, our mother, my sister Madeleine, her husband the Count de Chavagnac, the Chevalier des Huttes, who was a friend of my brother, Monsieur de Laubrac, the Baron's cousin and heir, and still another man, tall and thin, whom I did not know. All faces were solemn. An uneasy silence greeted me. It was broken when Madeleine walked to me to kiss me and offer her congratulations.

The Marquis spoke. "Gabrielle, we are gathered here to sign your marriage contract."

It was customary in France then, and I believe it still is, for future spouses to enter into a written contract formalizing the mutual promises of marriage and settling in advance all financial matters. It was signed by the spouses-to-be and their parents, and also by other family members and friends who attended as witnesses. All persons of substance entered into such contracts before marrying. No Montserrat had ever wed without one. Yet I had not expected mine to be signed so soon.

My brother nodded in the direction of the stranger. "Maître Carrier has just read aloud the articles of the contract. Now it requires your signature."

Carrier was holding several handwritten sheets of paper, bound with string, in his hand. My brother had obviously chosen not to avail himself of the services of Jean-Baptiste Coffinhal, his usual attorney. Carrier put the papers down on a table that stood in the middle of the room and pointed at the back of the last sheet.

"You may sign here, Mademoiselle," he said with a strong Roman accent. He pulled a chair for me and held out a quill.

I was desperately trying to think of a way to delay the proceedings. "What does it say?" I asked Carrier.

"Enough, Gabrielle," said my brother in a stern voice. "A bride-to-be does not ask this kind of question. I, as your guardian, am satisfied with the terms of this contract. So is your future master. It is all that matters. Now I am telling you to sign, and you are going to obey."

I looked at Madeleine in a silent plea for help. She turned away. The Marquis pressed down on my shoulder and made me sit at the table. He took the quill from Carrier's hand to put it in mine.

"Sign," he said.

My brother was bending over me, one of his hands resting on the table and the other still on my shoulder. "Sign," he repeated between his teeth.

I looked around at the rest of the company, but all eyes were now averted, except those of the Baron. *He* was observing me in silence, a few yards away, with a strange smile on his face. I felt a shove on my shoulder. My brother was becoming impatient. I could not muster the courage to defy him in front of my family. I took a deep breath and signed so hastily that I smudged ink on the paper. I rose very fast. Everyone else, Carrier last of all, signed in turn.

Carrier picked up the contract and put it away in a portfolio. I saw the Baron whisper into my mother's ear. She nodded and ordered me to follow her to her little upstairs parlour. Now I did not want to be alone with him. He had watched my attempt at resistance, then my surrender, all without any dismay, any pity. On the contrary, he had been amused. He would never release me from our engagement. And why should he now? Whatever else was in the contract, I knew that it must contain a promise of marriage. And I had signed it, after pledging my faith to Pierre-André! I could not forgive myself for my cowardice.

Once in my mother's parlour, and before we had time to sit, the Baron pulled from his pocket a red leather case emblazoned with a coat of arms. He offered it to me. I took it awkwardly and muttered words of thanks.

"What are you waiting for, girl?" asked my mother. "Do not gape like a half-wit, open it." She simpered at the Baron. "You must forgive her, Sir. She is overcome with your kindness."

I opened the case reluctantly. It contained a pair of earrings, two inches long, gleaming against the white satin lining. Each was made of twelve large oval rubies, the colour of red currants, surrounded by diamonds. The beauty of the stones amazed me, but it gave me no pleasure. I could not think of what to say.

"They were," the Baron explained, "presented by my father to my late mother upon their engagement. My poor departed Dorothée also wore them, but they seem to have been especially designed to shine against the white skin of your lovely neck."

Visions of those unknown dead ladies wearing the earrings came to my mind. "I do not know how to thank you, Sir," I said at last. "I was never given anything so beautiful."

"Indeed, Sir," intervened my mother, "you are spoiling her. This is far more than she deserves. As for you, child, your manners put me to shame. Kiss your fiancé's hand to thank him properly."

I hesitated, repulsed by the idea of touching any part of him. My mother glowered at me. I held my breath and brought his hand as briefly as I could to my lips. He patted my cheek.

"Do not fret, Madam," he said to the Marquise. "After what I saw of your daughter today, I am more satisfied than ever with my choice of a bride. She will learn to show her gratitude suitably once we are married." He smiled at me. "I will see you again, dear little cousin, on our wedding day. I look forward to it more than you can imagine."

With that he bowed and, much to my relief, took his leave. Our courtship was limited to this single occasion. Thus was my marriage decided, with no more regard for my wishes and feelings than if I had been a cow sold at the cattle fair in Vic.

ℳ 10 ℳ

After the signing of my marriage contract, I was allowed to leave my bedroom, and on the next Sunday I attended High Mass with my brother and mother in the church of Lavigerie. We took our places in the seats reserved for the lord and his family in the chancel. Over the years, I had often heard Father Delmas read from the pulpit, after the sermon, the banns of marriage for my brother's vassals. Now the priest cleared his voice to announce, with more solemnity than usual, the forthcoming union between the Noble Lady Marie Gabrielle de Montserrat and the High and Mighty Lord Donatien Aimé François de Laubrac, Baron de Peyre, de Cénaret and de La Clavière, Colonel of the Royal Dragoons and Knight of the Order of Saint-Louis. Father Delmas, after catching his breath, invited anyone aware of any legal impediment to such marriage to step forward. I knew that all eyes were turned towards me. I stared at the stone floor, wishing for it to open and swallow me alive. Excited whispers rippled through the congregation. I would not have been more ashamed if I had stood naked in the middle of the church.

Over the following days, the news of my future marriage became, according to Joséphine, the topic of all conversations from Vic to Auril-lac. I kept wondering what Pierre-André was feeling. The reading of the banns in church had made my engagement public. He must by now have understood that it was all over. Perhaps he had learned that I had signed my marriage contract already, he was now resigned to losing me, he had given up any thought of me. Or maybe he was very angry with me. He thought, with good cause, that I had betrayed him. Those ideas tormented me no less than the prospect of my own fate and were not put to rest until Joséphine told me of an incident that had taken place in Lavigerie.

Pierre-André and my brother happened to ride into town at the same time. Pierre-André, without removing his hat, addressed the Marquis most disrespectfully as "Sir" instead of "My Lord." In a thunderous voice, he told my brother that my family must have lost all common decency to throw a girl of fifteen into the bed of an old swine three times her age. My brother responded that such insolence from a commoner was intolerable, and that he would receive no lessons on what to do with his own sister. Pierre-André replied, among other things, that the nobles' arrogance, which seemed to increase in exact proportion to their poverty, made him sick to his stomach and that all aristocrats, beggarly and wealthy alike, would receive what they deserved sooner than they expected. Both men dismounted. Pierre-André caught my brother by his necktie and threatened to kill him with his bare hands, while the Marquis drew the sword he wore as a sign of his rank. The outcome of the fight would not have been in doubt, for, although Pierre-André was by far the taller and heavier man of the two, he was unarmed. The villagers, alerted by the sound of his voice, had rushed to the scene and managed to separate the combatants, who had gone their separate ways, glowering at each other.

"Of course," said Joséphine, "young Dr. Coffinhal deserves the gallows for assaulting My Lord, and in Lavigerie too, in the middle of the Marquis's jurisdiction."

"Will my brother press charges?"

"I'm sure he'd like to see your suitor hanged, but he has to keep quiet because of the scandal it'd create, with your name mentioned between them in public like that. And he can't fight a commoner in a duel either. So My Lord tried to recruit men among the servants and peasants to have your suitor thrashed for his insolence, but he couldn't find any volunteers. Young Dr. Coffinhal is well known around here. He's strong as a horse and he has quite a temper. People are afraid of him. No one, even with the help of other fellows, wants to risk a broken arm or jaw, or worse, in that kind of expedition."

I was pained by the idea of such an encounter between the two men I loved best. I was also moved at the thought that Pierre-André had not forgotten me and that he pitied the distress of my situation, to the point of putting his life at risk to express his opinion of the match. I wondered whether any of it had reached the Baron's ears, and allowed myself to hope that it might alter his plans.

I visited Joséphine with great punctuality, since she was my best source of information about tidings that concerned me most closely. A few days later, I entered the kitchen as she was running a plucked chicken by the fire to burn the remaining feathers. The acrid smell filled the room. Without a word, she reached into her pocket and slipped into my hand a note, sealed and without any direction, which read as follows:

> *As I write this, my beloved, I do not know whether you are resolved to marry the man your brother has chosen for you. If so, it is all over and you need not read further. But if you do not forsake me, I cannot, I will not, ever abandon you.*
>
> *You may remember Father Marty, who used to be the vicar of Lavigerie and is now the priest of Pailherols. I called on the old renegade yesterday and, after presenting him with a bottle of fine wine, asked about a clandestine wedding between us, without banns, witnesses or your brother's consent. Well, Gabrielle, under canon law, the marriage would be valid. Father Marty, as the officiating priest, would likely be relieved of his duties, but he is tired of Pailherols and does not care. He is ready to celebrate the ceremony. Once married, we will have nothing to fear.*
>
> *I know that it will grieve you to offend your brother. I would not propose this if it were not our only chance. In the eyes of the world, nothing I can offer compares to what your proposed match would afford you. All I have to give you is my appreciation not only of your beauty, but also of your goodness and kindness, and my promise to love you and protect you till death.*
>
> *Listen, Gabrielle, my sweet one, my tender love. I will wait for*

you two days from now, on the 1st of September at midnight at the
crossroads of Escalmels. If you do not join me there, I will know
that I have lost you and you will not hear from me again.
Regardless of your decision, burn this immediately.

I felt as if sunlight had suddenly flooded the kitchen. Pierre-André, against all odds, in spite of my engagement to another man, still wanted me. Joséphine was cutting open the chicken and removing the giblets. She grumbled when I kissed her madly. I threw the note into the fire of the *cantou*, where it burnt with a bright flame, then shriveled to ashes in a moment.

Indeed I remembered Father Marty very well. My family no longer kept a chaplain, and he, as the parish priest of Lavigerie, had come to Fontfreyde to prepare me for my First Communion. Shortly afterwards, he had been arrested in a house of convenience in Aurillac for molesting one of the ladies. My mother had mentioned the scandal at the dinner table. My brother had glanced at me and turned the conversation to a subject more suited to the ears of a maiden. Intrigued, I had sought more information from Joséphine. Gossip had it that, although all secular charges had been dropped against Father Marty, my mother had been so outraged at his conduct that she had obtained from the Bishop of Saint-Flour his removal from his pastoral duties in Lavigerie. Thanks to the good Father's friends at the diocese, he had avoided being stripped of his priesthood. After a few months of severe penance in a monastery, he had been sent to the mountain hamlet of Pailherols, where cattle outnumbered Christians ten to one. According to rumour, he had taken to drinking in the solitude of his new parish.

My marriage to Pierre-André would need to be celebrated and con-summated before I was missed at Fontfreyde in the morning of the 2nd. I was ignorant of the niceties of canon law, but knew that the scandal would then be too great for my family to question the validity of the cer-emony. What would happen next the letter did not say, but I trusted that Pierre-André would have taken steps to secure our escape from the country until things quieted.

At no time did I waiver in my determination to elope. My wedding day was now but two weeks away. If Lord Blue Beard himself, he of the six murdered wives, had sprung alive from the pages of my book of fairy tales, I would have chosen him over the Baron.

The moon was only two days short of full and the weather clear and dry. Escalmels was three miles from Fontfreyde, an easy ride. As a child, nothing would have induced me to venture outside the château at night. Now I had reached an age when I feared brutes of flesh and bone, such as the Baron, far more than werewolves or ghosts.

ᘓ 11 ᘔ

On the night of the 1st of September, I went to my bedroom as usual after prayers. I kissed my rag doll for the last time. I still played with it on occasion, but now I knew that I was bidding my childhood farewell. It was eleven when I wrapped myself in my winter cloak and left the silent château on tiptoe. My heart was beating fast as I unbarred the front door and closed it quietly behind me. I ran down the great stairs and to the stables. Jewel whinnied softly when he caught my scent in the dark. I stroked his face to silence him, put his bridle on and wrapped his hooves in the rags I had prepared. The place was so familiar that I could find my way without the help of a lantern. I led him out of his stall.

As I was ready to cross the threshold of the stables, a dark figure appeared from the shadows and blocked my passage. I felt all warmth leave my body. My brother was standing in front of me. He said calmly: "I know everything. Follow me and keep silent."

I had no intention of doing either. I pushed him away and ran for a few paces, but he caught me. I fought him as long as I could, hoping till the end to escape, but he was stronger, and desperate to stop me. Holding me by the waist with both arms, he dragged me towards the house while I struggled to escape his grip. Since there was no longer any hope in secrecy, I cried at the top of my lungs. Jewel, seeing me attacked, neighed wildly and reared on his back legs. The rags I had tied around his hooves came loose. Sparks flew in the darkness where his shoes hit the cobblestones of the courtyard. Lights appeared at several windows, and faces looked out to discover the cause of the commotion. My brother hissed: "Little bitch! You will not be happy until you have utterly disgraced us."

I heard footsteps. My mother and the servants, in their nightclothes, appeared at the top of the outside stairs. My brother, still struggling to restrain me, shouted at them to all go back to bed, except for my mother and Joséphine. With the help of both, he half-carried, half-dragged me, still screaming, up the front stairs and down to a little cellar. Joséphine kept apples, carrots, and turnips in a sand bin there, and she stored the preserves she made through the course of the year on the shelves that lined the walls. It smelled of mildew and dried fruit. The solid oak door and the lack of any window, except for a tiny opening under the ceiling, precluded any chance of escape. I was dropped on the dirt floor. I heard the door slam behind me and the key turn in the lock. After a time, my brother came back, bringing with him a straw mattress and a blanket, which he threw at me in silence. He locked the door behind him without another look at me. Although I had no light, I knew the cellar well, having come there often with Joséphine. It did not frighten me. I had, in any case, reached depths of despair where fear had no place. It would have been dreadful to marry the Baron knowing that Pierre-André had abandoned me, but the idea that he had still wanted me, and that we now had to forsake each other in spite of our pledge, was unbearable. He would be at that time waiting for me at the crossroads of Escalmels, thinking that I had not the courage, or did not love him enough to join him. My throat was sore from screaming. I reached for the mattress and blanket in the dark. Soon I went to sleep, as much to escape my situation as from exhaustion.

I awoke the next morning when the Marquis brought me a pitcher of water and a piece of dark bread, such as the servants ate. I raised myself on one arm, blinking at his lantern.

"You have no one to blame but yourself for your current position," he said in a stern voice. "If I locked you in your bedroom, you would find a way to escape. You will be safe here until your wedding."

"How did you find out?"

"You are very naive, Gabrielle. Joséphine showed me your suitor's letter before she gave it to you. I could have kept it and you would never have known about it, but I wanted to see whether I could trust you. On this point I no longer have any doubts."

So Joséphine, whom I had believed for years to be my friend, had betrayed me. My anger at her treason added to my other sorrows.

The tiny window barely allowed any daylight to pierce the darkness. I became so accustomed to it that I had to turn away from the dim glow of my brother's lantern. He did not entrust to anyone the task of bringing me my bread and water every morning and night. I counted with anguish the days that still separated me from my marriage.

On the morning of the 14th, my brother appeared as usual. "Father Delmas will hear your confession this afternoon," he said. "You will be married tomorrow and cannot approach the Holy Table without receiving the absolution."

Until then, I had gone to the church of Lavigerie for confession, but my family must have feared that I would take advantage of any outing to run away. I had never liked the idea of imparting my sins to a stranger. During confession, I would always resort to the same short list of sins, such as being lazy and not listening to my mother. The more interesting ones I kept to myself. This time, I would have to repeat the procedure, not in the reassuring darkness of the confessional, but in plain view of the priest in my mother's drawing room. I could imagine her listening at the door.

I felt light-headed after being freed from the confined space of my prison. I put my hand to my eyes as the light inside the house blinded me. My brother seized me roughly by the arm and pushed me into the main drawing room. He left me there. Father Delmas opened his arms in a gesture of welcome.

"Dear, dear child," he said, smiling and shaking his head with indulgence. "What have you done? Yet you need not despair. God will hear you if you show sincere contrition."

He made the sign of the cross, sat down in a chair and pointed at the carpet. I knelt next to him and joined my hands. "Bless me, Father, for I have sinned." I hesitated.

"I am listening, child," he said. "Speak without fear."

"Father, I am on the verge of committing a grievous sin. If I obey my brother, I will marry a man for whom I do not feel the least affection."

He sighed. "My child, your real sin, a mortal one, a sin of pride, is to defy the wishes of your guardian. You have already caused him much sorrow by your disobedience. You must repent to receive the sacrament of penance."

"Father, I do not repent at all. It would be a sin for me to enter the state of matrimony unprepared to love my future husband. I could not make him a good wife without having had time to receive spiritual guidance."

Father Delmas's unctuous smile had been wiped off his face.

"If you listen to me now, child, you will receive all the guidance you need. You are gravely mistaken in your notions. Love, as you understand it, is a fleeting illusion, worse, a lure of the Devil. Matrimony, on the contrary, is a holy sacrament. The kind of affection one finds in that blessed state has nothing in common with the miserable feelings under which you are labouring. The only love God sanctions follows marriage and rewards the fulfillment of its duties; it does not precede it nor determine it. The remission of your sins is fully within your reach, child, if you marry as you are told. My Lord the Marquis, who has the authority of a father under the laws of God and men, has chosen a husband for you. Only by submitting to his wishes can you atone for your outrageous misconduct."

Father Delmas pulled a handkerchief from the pocket of his cassock. "Do you not hear the call of duty? Even if your guardian's choice were misguided, you should still obey him without a whisper of protest."

Still on my knees, I moved back a few feet.

"But he has kept your best interest in mind," Father Delmas continued, mopping sweat from his forehead. "In terms of rank, of fortune, of respectability, you could not do better if you waited ten years for another offer. True, there is a slight disparity of age between My Lord the Baron and you, but even that should be reckoned as an advantage. A younger, less experienced husband might have some trouble asserting his authority given your unfortunate tendency to willfulness. In sum, it is a most eligible match in all respects."

Father Delmas, now standing, was wagging a fat finger in my face. I also rose, glaring at him.

"You shall receive the sacrament of matrimony tomorrow," he continued. "For your penance, recite ten *Paster Nosters* and ten *Aves* and prostrate yourself at your brother's feet. May the Almighty have mercy on you and forgive your sins."

Father Delmas made the sign of the cross and left. My brother, sullen, was waiting for me outside the door. He asked the priest to wait while he took me back to the cellar. After half an hour, the Marquis returned and sat by my side on the straw mattress.

"I have spoken to Father Delmas," he said. "I see that you remain as undutiful as ever."

"So this is how he treats the seal of confession."

"From what I understand, your conversation with him can hardly be deemed a confession, for you expressed only further defiance and no repentance. I cannot tell you how angry I am."

"I beg you to forgive me, Sir. I assure you that my sole wish now is to live quietly at Fontfreyde as in the past. I promise never to see Pierre-André again, if you release me from my engagement to the Baron. I will never again give you the slightest displeasure."

The Marquis glared at me. "How dare you in the same breath beg my forgiveness and refuse to obey me? I am tired, Gabrielle, of all the grief you have already caused and have no intention of serving indefinitely as your jailer. Your failed elopement makes your immediate marriage the only remedy to our plight. Are you, yes or no, going to do as you are told tomorrow?"

I did not hesitate. "No."

For the first time, I heard my brother swear. "You are the most stubborn, ungrateful, undutiful creature I have ever met. I was, however, already prepared for the worst. Read this."

He pulled from his pocket a sheet of paper, which I read by the light of the lantern. It was a request to the King for a *lettre de cachet*. It related how a young lady of the nobility, seduced by a commoner, had attempted to throw herself into the power of her suitor. She was now refusing to obey her guardian and enter into a most advantageous match. The letter concluded by respectfully requesting my imprisonment in the harshest of convents until it pleased the Marquis to take me back.

In France, at that time, anyone, regardless of rank, could be imprisoned upon the order of the King, in any place and for any duration, for any reason or for no reason at all. *Lettres de cachet* were thus requested by families who wished to discreetly rid themselves of spendthrift sons, undutiful wives or rebellious daughters. I knew that my brother's threat was by no means empty. Still, reclusion in a convent seemed more appealing than marrying the Baron.

"One last time," said my brother, "will you obey me?"

"No, Sir."

He took my chin in his hand. "Fine. I will send this to the King. You will only leave this cellar for the convent, where you will spend the rest of your life. You will soon come to regret the treatment I have afforded you here." The Marquis spoke through his clenched teeth. "As for your lover, do you know, Gabrielle, that a man who induces a young woman to flee the protection of her father or guardian is punished by death?"

I felt faint. So Pierre-André had put his life at stake by asking me to elope with him. My brother's letter fell from my hand.

"And there are aggravating circumstances in this case," he continued. "Since you are a noblewoman and your seducer a commoner, he will be sentenced to the wheel. Before taking you to your convent, I will make you watch the execution of that—that—" The Marquis seemed at a loss to find a term vile enough to describe Pierre-André "—that peasant, that scoundrel. You have never seen a criminal broken and exposed on the wheel, have you?"

I shook my head in horror.

"Then I will tell you what to expect, Gabrielle. Your seducer will be led to a scaffold, then stripped of his clothes. The executioner will tie him, flat on his back, to a cross, and hit him with an iron bar on the arms, thighs, legs and loins. Once his limbs and hips are broken, he will be untied. His legs will be folded under his back, and he will be fastened to a small carriage wheel. He will remain exposed in this position, with his head hanging over the rim and his shattered bones piercing his flesh. You will hear him howl in pain and beg for death. At last, at the time set by the court, and not a moment earlier, he will be strangled." My brother paused. "I will make sure that you do not miss any of it."

I was indifferent to my own fate. All that mattered was to save Pierre-André.

"I will marry the Baron tomorrow," I said, "under one condition: you must not press charges. No harm must come to Pierre-André, now or in the future." I looked into my brother's eyes. "You must swear to it on the memory of our late father. Should you breach your promise, Sir, I will run away from my husband's house; I will disgrace the Baron and our family."

The Marquis hesitated for a moment, biting his lip. "You have my word of honour, Gabrielle. I summoned his brothers here on the day after your elopement and told them that he would be arrested if he caused any further scandal. Now I will demand only that he leave and never return to Auvergne. His punishment will be to know that you are in the power of another. Good night, Gabrielle."

The French phrase *la mort dans l'âme* has no English equivalent and can be translated as "with death in one's soul." It comes to mind when I think of my last hours at Fontfreyde. Sometimes we do or endure things that are so wicked, so irretrievably harmful, so contrary to our feelings that part of ourselves is destroyed in the process. I had been taught to believe in the immortality of the soul. That night, I felt that mine died. I slept little and fitfully, startled from time to time by dreams in which some unforeseen and incredible event occurred to prevent my wedding. Alas, I always woke to the same situation and with the same thoughts. Finally, any kind of rest became impossible. I did my best to steady myself and muster my courage.

After what seemed like a few hours, the door was unlocked and my brother appeared. He told me that he would allow me, on my last day at Fontfreyde, to have breakfast in the dining parlour. Before we left the cellar, he reached for my hand. I turned away. My heart felt empty and cold. Nobody, not even my mother, spoke over breakfast. I did not look up from my porridge.

The Marquise took me to my old bedroom. She ordered me to disrobe and step into a round copper tub filled with water. She would not allow me to squat or kneel in it, but insisted that I stand, legs apart, while the maids washed me with sponges. Until then I could not remember having been naked in front of anyone. My mother herself, Joséphine had once told me, always bathed clad in a flannel robe that covered her to her neck.

"How becoming of you," said the Marquise, "to give yourself these little airs of modesty, after what you have done. Your husband will teach you to be less of a prude tonight."

One of the maids pierced my ears with a sewing needle while pressing a cork behind the lobes. I sensed the pain but did not wince. I was trying to no longer feel what was done to me.

"Remember, girl," said my mother, "you must rise to greet your master when you see him approach the bed. I hope that you will not disgrace us by being undutiful."

I stepped into the skirts of my pink gown as I had done on the morning of the Thiézac pilgrimage, but now a tiny bouquet of orange blossoms was nestled between my breasts. I wore the Baron's ruby earrings. They put me in mind, when I looked at my reflection in the mirror, of droplets of blood running down my neck.

I am looking at my eight-year-old granddaughter, whom Aimée insisted on naming Gabriella, much against my wishes. I do not believe it to be an auspicious choice. She is a most endearing child. Her cheeks, round as apples, beg for kisses. She is holding a doll out to me, along with remnants of lilac silk, demanding with the gentle tyranny of children that I make a dress for it matching her own. One thing always gives me a slight shock whenever I look at her: her resemblance to my late husband. Yet it should come as no surprise. The Baron de Peyre was after all her grandfather, but I have never grown accustomed to finding his features in her lovely face. She even has his manners, the same way of holding her head slightly to the side and knitting her brows when she is cross. Like him, she never seems to experience self-doubt. The past has ways of thrusting itself upon us, of reminding us of what we least wish to remember.

I was married in the church of Lavigerie, decorated with white roses for the occasion, on a cold and sunny day, the 15th of September of the year 1784. The ringing of the bells, deafening, shook the air. My brother handed my mother and me out of the carriage. He led me to the altar, holding me firmly by the hand as if afraid that I would run away. My sister Madeleine, her husband, the Count de Chavagnac, Monsieur de Laubrac, the Baron's cousin and heir, among many other family members and friends were in attendance. So were my brother's vassals. The Baron was waiting for me in the chancel in a crimson suit, embroidered with gold, and white silk stockings instead of his usual hunting clothes and leather boots.

I said and did all that was required of me, concentrating on the rituals themselves, trying very hard not to think of what they entailed. Facing the Baron, my eyes downcast, I recited the words that would bind me to him until death: "I, Marie Gabrielle, agree before God of my own free will to take thee, Donatien, for my husband."

He took my right hand in his, around which the priest wrapped his stole while reciting the nuptial benediction. Father Delmas blessed a gold coin and a ring, wide and plain. The Baron placed it first on the thumb of my left hand, then on my index, then on my middle finger while reciting "in the name of the Father, and the Son, and the Holy Ghost." He said "Amen" when he reached the fourth finger, where he left it. He presented me with the coin, which I received with both hands. We both knelt at the foot of the altar. The white nuptial pall was raised over our heads as we received the Church's blessing upon our union.

Through the Mass that followed, I knelt, rose and sat, taking my cues from the congregation without knowing what I was doing. I felt that I had taken leave of my own body and was watching the ceremony from a few paces away. In his sermon, Father Delmas spoke of the meaning of the ring presented to me, which was an *annulus fidei*, a reminder of the faith I had pledged to my husband. The gold coin recalled the price paid in the old days by the groom for the purchase of the bride. It signified the transfer of my custody from my guardian to my husband and was a token of the obedience I now owed the Baron. The wrapping of the stole around our clasped hands meant that we were irrevocably united before God.

After the ceremony, my husband handed me into his carriage. It was the first time we were alone. He lowered the blinds and threw himself upon me. The numbness I had felt in church dissipated in an instant. I resisted. He quieted.

"It is all right, dearest," he said. "You may tease me all you want. I have not much longer to wait now."

Once in Cénac, the Baron led me to the courtyard behind the château, where a dinner had been set for the servants and peasants. The guests rose to cry *Viva la novio*, "Long live the bride." We walked around the long tables to receive their compliments and best wishes. The Baron, grinning, slapped the men on the back and asked them in the Roman language how they liked their new lady. I hung my head, too embarrassed to say anything. At last, he bid everyone to have a good time and took me inside.

I attended an interminable feast in the château, this time for the noble guests. The Baron, in a jolly mood, ate, drank, laughed and talked a great deal. It would have been customary for the wedding dinner to take place at the bride's house, but perhaps my husband did not trust my mother to have a decent meal at Fontfreyde. My imprisonment in the cellar had kept me unaware of the preparations for my own wedding.

I had met my husband only three times before, but had ample opportunity to observe him now. His loud voice was jarring to my ears, and his discourse was punctuated by many words I had never heard before, though I could guess their meaning. I sat, numb and mute, at the opposite end of a table, which had been dressed with great magnificence. All of the local nobility had been invited and the guests were in a joyful mood. My mother, in a new black silk dress trimmed with lace, was seated to the Baron's right hand. She looked happier than I had ever seen her. I could only toy with the food on my plate without bringing it to my lips. My brother was not eating much either, and avoiding my eye. He had risen at the beginning of the dinner and toasted in a perfunctory manner the Baron and Baroness de Peyre. It had been odd to hear for the first time my new name and title. To me, the Baroness de Peyre was my husband's late wife, Dorothée de La Feuillade, a faint ghost, unmourned four months after her death.

After a number of courses, I saw the Baron lean towards my mother and speak to her while looking at me. She smiled at him and gestured to me to follow her. She and Madeleine took me to my new apartment. When I saw the bed there, I threw my arms around my sister's neck.

"Please," I said, "do not leave me here. Take me home with you. I never want to see him again."

My mother pursed her lips. "You see, Madeleine, what I have been suffering. Thank Heaven, we are rid of her at last. I wish the Baron much pleasure with this little bitch. Imagine her being only fifteen and already such a harpy! But then your sister Hélène, when she was thirteen—"

"Please, Madam," interrupted Madeleine, "let us not speak of Hélène at this time. You may leave me with Gabrielle. I am sure she will listen to reason. She is only frightened, poor child."

After the Marquise left, my sister, gently but in a manner that admitted of no opposition, unlaced my dress and corset. She knelt before me to remove my shoes, untie my garters and pull my stockings. When I was stripped to my chemise, she nudged me towards the bed. I clung to her.

"Gabrielle, you must be a good girl," she said. "Are you afraid because you do not know what to expect? I will explain it all if you wish."

"I do know about those things. That is precisely why I did not want to marry him."

She ran her finger on my cheek. "It is wrong to entertain these thoughts now. You undertook before God new duties that you must now fulfill. Why fret over what cannot be avoided?" She smiled. "Besides, dearest, he cannot be so terrible. He seems very much in love with you. I have observed him: he cannot keep his eyes off you."

"I have not noticed anything of the sort."

"I would be surprised if you had," she said, "for you hardly ever look at him. Your modesty is very commendable, but the time has come to be less shy with him." She stroked my hair. "Let him do whatever he wants, and all will be fine."

"But I do not want him to touch me."

"These feelings are normal for a bride, Gabrielle. They will pass once the marriage is consummated and you realize that your fears were groundless. He is a mature man. He will be less rash and more patient than a younger husband."

The Baron, in his dressing gown, his hair untied, appeared. At the same time, I heard drunken clamours in the hallway, followed by hammering at the door. Male voices demanded to see the bride and groom together in bed to toast them one last time. The Baron swore.

"You buggering jackasses," he shouted when he opened the door, "you are frightening my little bride with your racket. Leave us alone."

The guests reluctantly left, some of them trying to peek inside the room before being firmly pushed away by the Baron. Madeleine pressed my hand. I tried to cling to hers, but she kissed me on the forehead and abandoned me to my fate.

The Baron was now free to turn his attention to me. I forgot all about my mother's lecture, Father Delmas's sermon and my sister's words of comfort. Instead of rising to meet my master, I remained in bed, my knees under my chin and my arms around my legs. He ordered me to remove my chemise. I stayed frozen. He seized me by the arm and, without a word, stripped me of it himself. I wrapped one of the sheets around my naked body. That too was torn away from me. I jumped from the bed in terror and without thinking ran for the door. He had no trouble catching me. I bit, I scratched, I fought him with all the energy I could muster. It was futile. He subdued me and carried me to bed, where he kept me pinned on my back, his knee planted in my stomach.

With the belt of his nightgown he bound my hands and tied them to one of the bedposts. I begged for mercy, in vain. He was too busy pawing and kissing me to pay any heed to my pleas. I turned my head away to escape the smell of wine on his breath.

"I have not been mistaken in my choice," he said. "You are still more beautiful than I expected. I cannot wait any longer, little dear."

He slipped his shirt over his head, baring all. I whimpered in horror at the sight of his nakedness. He spread my thighs, knelt between them and lowered himself onto me. I tried to squirm from under him, but his weight, resting on my hips, was crushing me. He proceeded with the main assault, causing me such pain as to convince me that my entire body was tearing apart. My cries, far from giving him pause, seemed to make his lunges more furious. Sweat glued the black hair on his chest and stomach to his skin. I was smothered against his neck, thick as that of a bull. At last, when I thought that I could bear no more, he raised himself on his arms. After a final thrust, deeper and more violent than any before, he arched his back and let out a long roar.

He rolled over by my side, his eyes closed, with a look of exhausted contentment that let me hope that he had fallen asleep. This comfort was short-lived. Apparently refreshed by his rest, he spread my thighs again. I had abandoned any kind of struggle and let him do what he pleased. He examined at length the site of his victory, tender under his fingers like a raw wound.

"There is nothing I like better than this sight," he said. "You just made me very happy, my pretty little bride, although you could have spared yourself some unpleasantness by obeying me from the start. No matter, you will learn fast enough."

He untied me. In my naivete, I thought that the ordeal was over for the night. Before long I saw with horror that his inspection had rekindled his appetite. He had only freed me to shift my position at his pleasure. Once the essential point had been settled to his advantage, he knew that my compliance was assured. He resumed his attentions with undiminished vigour. I lost track of the number of times I had to go through the same agony, which he alternated with bouts of whipping, both, he said, as a punishment and a warning.

"You see, my dear," he said during a lull, "brides are like young horses. Some of them are docile by nature. Others offer a spirited resistance when mounted for the first time. My late Dorothée belonged to the first kind. You obviously fall into the second. It does not bother me, far from it. The effort I put into taming a fine animal is amply rewarded by the satisfaction of finding it afterwards as eager to please as it was troublesome."

I could not imagine how any female could bear that kind of treatment for an entire night. I had visions of myself reduced by the morning to shattered bones and bloody pulp, like a broken body on the wheel. At last, long after I had abandoned any hopes of seeing an end to my misery, he left me in peace and retired to his own apartment. I found my torn chemise on the floor and put it back on.

I was crying in my sleep when a maid drew the drapes and opened the shutters.

"My Lord requests Your Ladyship's company at breakfast without delay," she said.

I would discover that "without delay" was the byword at Cénac, where everyone understood that the Baron was not to be kept waiting. I was still shaken, sore all over, and wanted nothing more than to stay in bed a little longer. Moreover, after my initiation to nuptial bliss, I would have been content never to set eyes again upon my husband. Yet I understood from the maid's alarmed look that it would be unwise not to make haste. I wanted to wash away the filth of the night, but that would have to wait. While the maid was helping me, I saw that I was covered with welts and bruises of various sizes and hoped that she did not notice them.

I joined the lord my master in the dining parlour, where he was eating breakfast with a hearty appetite. I curtseyed to him but could not bring myself to meet his eye. He seemed oblivious to the events of the night and rose to greet me in a good-humoured manner.

He hoped that I had slept well, and told me that, now that we were man and wife, we should settle a few things between ourselves about our future happiness.

"First, Madam," he said, "I am as patient as the next man, but I do not like to be kept waiting at my own table. I will expect the pleasure of your company at seven o'clock without having to send for you. You are no longer at Fontfreyde, where you may have been allowed to spend the whole day in bed. In this house, you will follow my ways, which you cannot expect me to change for the sake of a child of fifteen. Is this understood?"

"Yes, Sir. Please forgive me. I did not know that you were expecting me, or I would have risen earlier. I promise that in the future I will be on time."

"All right, but remember that I might show less indulgence next time. That is not all: we have other important matters to discuss. Some of your habits, frankly, I do not like. You probably know to what I refer. Your brother, for reasons I cannot fathom, has let you run wild all over the country. Although I do not blame you, for you were too young to know any better, I will have to put an end to that nonsense. First, you will be impatient to present me with an heir sooner rather than later, and all that horse riding would not do. Second, I will not have it said that I allow my wife to roam the countryside like a madwoman. There will be no need for you to ride. I do not want to see you within a hundred feet of the stables."

Until then, riding had been the key to all of my moments of freedom. It had not occurred to me that I would be denied that indulgence. Of course, it was possible that a faint echo of my recent adventures had reached the Baron.

"So you wish me to spend all of my time indoors, Sir?"

He sighed. "Of course not, child. You are not listening to me. You may walk in the garden around the château, but do not go beyond that. As for the carriage, you will ask for my permission in advance and tell me where you want to go. I will give the coachman his orders: he receives them from no one but me."

"Could I go hunting with you? I hear that you are fond of it. I am a good horsewoman, Sir. I could keep you company."

He threw his knife and fork onto his plate. I started at the noise of the silver hitting the porcelain. "Have you not heard what I said? I told you that I do not want you to ride. I meant *not at all*, neither on your own, nor with me, nor in anyone else's company. You will pay more attention in the future, Madam."

I was staring at the veal cutlet on my plate.

"Have you listened this time?"

"Yes, Sir."

"Let us hope so. There is also another matter we need to discuss. It has not escaped you, I am sure, that Maryssou manages the entire household. Leave her alone. She is a very good woman, but a bit jealous of her authority, which is understandable because she has been in charge for a long time. You should know that I have the highest regard for her. In any case, you are too young to handle those things yourself and would only make a mess of them."

The previous day, I had noticed that Maryssou woman, the upper servant, dark-haired and handsome. I had tried to smile at her. In response, she had looked at me in an insolent and resentful manner. I had already suspected that she enjoyed some intimacy with the Baron. She was probably no stranger to the fact that the maids had failed to wake me up on time that morning.

"There, my dear," said the Baron. "I thought it better to make things clear from the start. You will find me a liberal and easy master, although I will not be remiss in correcting those wild habits you have been allowed to acquire. If left unchecked, they would do you great harm in my eyes." He pointed his knife at me. "The late Baroness, bless her soul, was surrounded by comfort and attentions till her last breath. But then she never gave any kind of trouble. It would be wise of you to follow in her footsteps. As of now, you are nothing but a spoiled child, but your youth lets me hope that you will be amenable to reason. You do not look like a halfwit, far from it, and you will know your best interest. Now eat. I cannot abide a woman with a poor appetite, nor those who pretend to be indisposed to make themselves interesting."

It was clear that I would not be the mistress of my own house and that I would lead the life of a recluse, expected to produce a child every year until I grew so old, sad and tired that I no longer cared about any of it. Those thoughts of escape that had been so close to my heart only a few weeks earlier now seemed very odd. I felt soiled, defeated and broken, body and soul, after my wedding night. I no longer had anywhere to go, or anyone to go to. It would have been unthinkable to meet Pierre-André now, my disgrace written on my face.

After breakfast, I returned to my apartment, where the maids were changing the bed and, much to my mortification, hanging the bloodstained sheet out of the window.

"What are you doing?" I asked.

"It's always been the custom at Cénac, My Lady, to display it on the day after the master's wedding," one of them said. "My Lord has given orders to follow the old ways."

I said nothing and sought comfort in a hot bath. I did not see the Baron at luncheon, for he had business in Aurillac the whole day.

Early in the afternoon, I took a walk in the garden. There the last roses of the season were withering away, despoiled by the early frosts. I thought of the days when I could ride Jewel on mountain trails and enjoy the freedom of going wherever my fancy took me. I missed the kiss of the rain on my lips, the warmth of the sun and the chill of the wind on my cheeks. Lost in my reverie, I barely paid attention to the noise of the gravel crushing under my feet, when I heard the approach of a rider. Looking up, I recognized my brother. As he dismounted, I silently prayed that he would not notice the soiled bedsheet hanging like a flag of surrender from my window. If he did, he did not remark on it. He looked at me with concern and asked how I was.

"Very well, thank you," I said. "Though I am no longer under lock and key, I have not run away."

"So it appears, Gabrielle, but I was not worried on that account. I came here to see how you are."

"It is thoughtful of you."

He reached for my hand. "Has your husband been kind to you?"

"He is my husband, and it is all that matters now."

"You are still angry with me, Gabrielle."

Tears were welling up in my eyes. "It does not matter. There is no going back. Let us not speak of that, because I find it painful to think of what could have been. Please tell me about Fontfreyde instead. I will probably never return there."

"Why do you say this? I am sure your husband will allow you to visit us."

"He may never permit it. He has forbidden me to ride and I will have to ask for the carriage."

"It must seem harsh to you because of your past habits, but now that you are a married woman, his request does not seem unreasonable."

"He does not make requests; he gives orders."

"Come, Gabrielle, little sister, you sound so bitter and unhappy that you will break my heart. The Baron may be gruff, but he will not ask for anything more than another husband. I knew it would be difficult for you, with your independence of spirit, to be married to any man."

"That is a point on which you and I disagree. But let us talk about more cheerful things."

So he did tell me about Fontfreyde as if I had not seen the old place in years. It lifted my spirits.

After my brother's departure, the day felt empty. The afternoon wore on slowly, evening drew near, until that time just before nightfall, when the sky turns a darker shade of blue and inside candles are lit, shutters closed and curtains drawn. That hour, full of sweet sadness, had been my favourite in Fontfreyde. It became a moment of anguish in my new home. The prospect of the Baron joining me in bed again that night, and every night of our joint lives thereafter, which had been but a distant cloud in the bright light of the morning, began to loom on my mind until it drove away any other thought.

I was careful not to repeat my mistake of the morning by being exactly on time for dinner. I was already shaking when I faced my husband. He took one look at me and hit the table with the palm of his hand. The crystal glasses shook. Both of his hounds rose from their crouching position by his chair and yelped in terror.

"Where, Madam, did you find these rags?" he shouted. "I already saw them at breakfast, but I excused you then because I thought that you had no time to find anything else. Now you have had all day to dress. Do you think that I want my wife to show herself at my table attired like a beggar? Return to your apartment this minute and put on something proper. And throw away these horrors, or give them to the poor if you prefer. Now you will make me wait for my dinner after being late for breakfast. So this is how you thank me for my leniency this morning! Have it your way, my lovely. I will attend to you tonight. I may have to peel all the skin off your back, but I will teach you to mind what I say."

My first movement had been to bolt from the dining parlour, but I knew that I had nothing to gain by it except an immediate beating. I had noticed the night before that, although my husband was far heavier than I, he could outrun me. I fell to my knees.

"Please, Sir," I said, "forgive me. These are my only clothes, except for my wedding gown. I will go put it on immediately if you prefer. I will be only a minute. I am very sorry to have offended you and assure you that it was innocently done."

I omitted to mention that the rest of my wardrobe consisted of another black dress, which I had left at Fontfreyde. I had worn it during my stay in the cellar, where it had acquired a musty smell, not to mention an association with the memories of my captivity.

The Baron swore again and muttered something about marrying into a family of paupers.

"I should have known," he said, "when your old miser of a mother asked whether I wanted to delay our marriage to wait for your *trousseau* to be ready. The damned bitch felt no shame in sending you to me with only the shirt on your back after I had agreed to take you without a *sol*."

It struck me for the first time that I had not been given any *trousseau*, the set of clothes, undergarments and toiletries a bride received from her family as part of her dowry. During the past weeks, such futilities had not entered my mind. Now their omission seemed to entail new troubles for me.

"I became suspicious yesterday," continued the Baron, "when I saw you in the dress you already wore in Thiézac instead of a proper wedding gown. Your mother had it made especially for the pilgrimage, had she not? I have to give her credit for something, though: she knows what catches the eye of a man."

I burst into tears.

"Now, do not be upset, child," he added. "I am not angry with *you*. And you do look lovely in that pink dress."

He raised me to my feet, took me in his arms and patted me on the back in a fatherly manner. "Dry your tears. I will have the carriage ready tomorrow. You will go to Aurillac with Maryssou to order a set of proper clothes. She knows the best shops. You can have 2,000 francs, but tell them, for God's sake, to make haste. Now let us sit to dinner."

I was amazed at the change in his mood and his generosity. I had not had new clothes in years, with the exception of the pink dress.

᠊ᡒ 13 ᠊ᡒ

I saw little of the Baron during the day since he was busy riding, hunting, inspecting his estates, or otherwise occupied in the outdoors pursuits now forbidden to me. After dinner, he would read the papers for a couple of hours without saying more than a few words to me. I took a seat with my sewing on the opposite side of the fireplace, too afraid of him to address him uninvited. He paid less attention to me than to his hounds. Without interrupting his reading, he would once in a while put down his glass of wine to scratch the animals on the back of the head. They closed their eyes with contentment before returning to their position at his feet, their giant muzzles resting between their front paws. Only the noise of the newspaper being folded and the crackling of the logs in the fireplace broke the silence.

When the time came to retire, I never knew whether I would be treated with a sort of rough benevolence or whether he would have thought of some new idea for his enjoyment and my torment. Even in the course of a single night, his mood could become violent, sometimes at the slightest provocation, and often without any apparent reason.

Divorce did not exist then. One could only request an annulment before a religious court for lack of consummation of the marriage, grounds which were not applicable in my case. True, a cottager's wife from Vic had requested a few years earlier from the *Baillage* court a legal separation. Whenever I saw her in town, she always had a black eye or two. Joséphine had told me that her husband had come home one night with half a dozen companions, all drunk. He had dragged her out of bed, lifted her chemise and invited his friends to confirm that she was, as he put it, *a handsome bitch*. That circumstance, deemed offensive to the sanctity of marriage, had prompted the court to allow the poor woman to live separately. Once alone she had sunk into poverty, and had been seen begging for her bread on the streets of Vic. She had soon returned to her husband of her own accord.

In the case of my own marriage, nothing disgraceful ever came to light. Only the servants, who as a rule know every secret in a house, could have known what was happening. The Baron was careful not to leave any clues to his brutality on my face or on those parts of my body exposed to public view, except for bruises on my wrists. I was ashamed of them and, whenever I wore short sleeves, hid them with velvet ribbons, which I tied with a pair of fine diamond clasps he had given me.

Often, without any particular reason, I wept by myself in my bedroom. I was swept by waves of rage. During these episodes, all I could see was a grey blur before my eyes. I felt the urge to howl at the top of my lungs. To calm myself, I would bite my arms so hard that the pain brought me to my senses. During these moments, I felt briefly that I could have spat in my husband's face. Yet I cowered at the very sight of him.

A full month elapsed before I mustered enough courage to ask for the carriage to call on Mamé Labro. Her cottage, which had been my home for many years, now looked as if it belonged to another time and country. I threw myself in her arms.

"Oh, Mamé," I asked, "do you think I have changed?"

She took a step backwards and smiled.

"You look beautiful," she said, "maybe a little paler than before. You're far better dressed, for sure. You've become a fine lady now."

I was indeed wearing an elegant gown of red velvet trimmed with lace, with a white satin underskirt and matching shoes and bonnet. Mamé asked many questions about my new life, which I answered as cheerfully as I could.

As we spoke, my thoughts drifted towards the river. Autumn leaves were twirling in the eddies like flecks of gold. They would be carried down its current, light and buoyant at first, then soggy and brown, until they sank to the bottom and slowly rotted away between the stones of its bed. By the following spring there would be nothing left of them. At last, I asked Mamé Labro without meeting her eye:

"Have you heard any news of the younger Dr. Coffinhal?"

"Yes, he left for Paris to study law. Around the time of your wedding, I believe. He's to be apprenticed to his elder brother, Maître Joseph Coffinhal. From what I've heard, he's given up any idea of practicing medicine." She sighed. "There's no accounting for young people's changes of heart these days."

I was relieved to hear that Pierre-André was free and safe. But we would not meet again. For him too, the short time when our paths had crossed was gone, closed like a book no one ever wanted to read a second time. He would have a new life, new studies, a new profession, maybe soon a new love, in a busy place, far from me and what had briefly brought us together. At the thought of his forgetting me, I was pierced by sorrow. The pain was so sharp that it took my breath away. I closed my eyes to hide my tears.

Indeed I had lost the belief that it was in my power to decide my fate. I now inhabited a place where no joy, no hope, no light, no love could reach. I came to understand that we do not change gradually, peacefully, over time, but that we undergo sudden upheavals that overthrow our best-laid plans, change our character and redesign the shape of our life, all in a matter of moments. I had been robbed of some part of myself, of my youth, my innocence, my cheerfulness, never to recover them.

ᘓ 14 ᘔ

About two months after my wedding, I had reason to suspect that I was with child. I dared not share my thoughts with my husband for fear of angering him by raising futile expectations. He had made no effort to hide his disappointment the month before, once it had become apparent that I had not immediately become pregnant, and for several days I had felt the effects of his displeasure under the guise of a harsher treatment than usual.

"Are you with child?" he asked abruptly one night over dinner.

I twisted my napkin in my hands and kept my eyes fixed on my plate. "I am about two weeks late, Sir. I did not think that you would have noticed anything yet."

"Do you take me for an imbecile? I can recognize a pregnant woman when I see one. Were you waiting to be six months along to tell me about it?"

"I was afraid of disappointing you if I was mistaken."

"You are silly, dear child. Come and give me a kiss."

Amazed, I raised my eyes to him. He was smiling. He made me sit in his lap and pressed me in his arms. "I guess I will have to be a bit more gentle," he said. "We would not want to hurt my son, would we?"

That night, my husband fell asleep in my bed. Until then, he had always left for his own apartment when he was done with me. I looked at him by the light of the candle as he lay on his side, harmless for once, his eyes and lips half-closed. Strands of silky grey hair were spread across his gently heaving chest. Stretching from the breastbone to the left shoulder was a scar, shiny and pale against his olive-coloured skin. One of his arms was resting on my waist. I barely dared breathe lest I wake him. Until then he had only been the man who had the right to seize my body whenever he pleased and do what he liked with it. Now his seed was growing within me. He was my unborn child's father.

My husband seemed to grow fonder of my company and more content with our marriage. He would speak with much confidence and anticipation of his son and make numerous schemes for his education. Those filled me with dread, for it was all too easy to imagine how he would react to the birth of a girl. In the meantime, he stopped beating me and granted me permission to stay in bed past seven whenever I felt tired in the mornings. During the evenings, he spoke to me more and taught me to play *piquet* and backgammon, games that could not even be mentioned in Fontfreyde because my mother considered them the works of the Devil. I would let him win, because it had not escaped me that he could be fierce in his displeasure if he lost.

I had noticed a fine harpsichord in the main drawing room. My fingers caressed the keys with some hesitation at first, then with more assurance as I remembered a piece by Couperin, part of the *Leçons de*

Ténèbres, the "Lessons of Darkness" written for the services of the Holy Week. I had learned it at the convent and was amazed to feel how easily the tunes came back to me. Never before had I found such solace, peace and comfort in music.

I discovered a library on the second floor of the château. The books had been for the most part purchased by the late Baron, who must have been quite different from his younger brother. My husband, if he had read any book in his life, did not consider it worth mentioning, and it was not a subject on which I felt at liberty to question him. Since I had to occupy the ample time I had to myself, I began to read anything that came my way. The library contained a full edition of the Encyclopedia, as well as works by Montesquieu, Rousseau, Diderot, Voltaire and Pascal, one of the greatest minds Auvergne has ever produced. In addition, many works of a more libertine nature, amply illustrated, were included. I began to understand that my husband's tastes were shared by other men.

ℳ 15 ℳ

I cherished the constant companionship of my unborn child, especially after I began to feel it moving and kicking inside me. The Baron seemed to find increased satisfaction in the new shape of my body. He told me that, seen from behind, I was still thin as a reed, that my step was as light and graceful as ever. I carried my child forward, which he interpreted as a promise of male offspring. The servants were not slow in noticing the improvement of my standing. They treated me with more respect and paid greater attention to my requests. For the first time since my marriage, I allowed myself to hope that my life might change for the better.

Those thoughts were very much on my mind, when one winter morning, I opened the door to a drawing room. There I found the Baron embracing Thérèse, the youngest of the chambermaids, a year or two older than me. She was trying to push him away, but he was grasping one of her bare buttocks. With the other arm, he held the back of her skirts aloft above her waist. I knew from personal experience the strength of his grip and guessed that poor Thérèse had not much of a chance to escape. Her back was turned to me, but he was facing me. He noticed my presence and became red in the face without letting go of her. Thérèse could not have seen me. I doubt that she even heard me. I had a sudden inspiration. Putting my index finger to my lips to intimate silence, I smiled and closed the door as quietly as I could. I returned to my apartment, my heart beating wildly, wondering how that chance encounter could change the course of my life at Cénac.

A few minutes later, I heard a knock at my door. The Baron came in and took my hands in his, looking rather sheepish.

"Gabrielle, my dear," he said, "I have a favour to request. I would be very grateful if you could keep quiet about what you just saw. Maryssou, as you know, has rather strict notions. She would dismiss Thérèse if she learned of it."

I looked at him, my voice even, carefully considering my words. "I am surprised to hear it, Sir. You are the master of this house and its inhabitants, including Maryssou."

I pointed at the door to a little dressing room, which could only be accessed through my bedroom and was furnished with a bathtub, a little marble table and a couch.

"Maryssou would never go there unannounced," I continued, "as she does in the servants' quarters or the rest of the château. Feel free, Sir, to use it at your pleasure, right now if you wish."

The Baron seemed delighted. He kissed my hands and cheeks with great affection and could not express his thanks warmly enough. I felt sorry for Thérèse. She seemed like a good girl, pretty and very shy, but she could not, any more than I, or any other eligible female within the house, escape the Baron's attentions. That was part of her fate in being a maid at Cénac, just as it was part of mine by virtue of my marriage.

Thérèse was a simple country girl who did not seem to entertain any loftier ambitions than to keep her place. I felt assured that, when I became incapacitated by my confinement, she could take over my conjugal duties without interfering with the Baron's affections for me as Maryssou would have done. I took pains to know the poor girl better and promoted her, with the Baron's permission, to the place of lady's maid, with double wages.

My husband was happy with our new arrangements and manifested his satisfaction by his increased goodwill towards me. His attentions towards Thérèse did not seem to lessen in the least his interest in me. I even received the honours of the couch during the day whenever my enlarging body captured his fancy on the spur of the moment. I measured the success of my scheme by the increased malevolence of the glares Maryssou cast at me. Soon deep vertical lines began to mark the sides of her mouth.

The Baron would now speak to me in a friendly manner after dinner. He had traveled in Germany and America while in the service and had much to say about people he had met and places he had visited.

"Military life can be damned tedious, my dear," he said, "and its glory is not what one imagines. It was better than taking orders, though. *That* was an idea of my late mother's. She had the most tiresome notions about religion. How she cried, poor woman, when I told her that it was out of the question! Even my father was angry. He said that I was being too fastidious and that one did not need to believe in God to become a bishop." He chuckled. "I simply could not picture myself dressed as a priest. I was shipped to the army. A gentleman has to do his duty, of course, but I found nothing as heartrending as the sight of a field strewn with the dead and the dying after a battle."

"I noticed a scar on your chest. Was it a battle wound?"

"Yes, by a Prussian bayonet at the Battle of Krefeld, during the Seven Years' War. It was the very first time I saw action. I was a second lieutenant then. It is not a fond memory, my dear, and I would rather not talk about it. Even when the Prussians were not trying to hack us to death, and we were not busy returning the favour, it was a miserable life. I will spare you the petty intrigues among the officers, the rivalries between the noblemen and the commoners, for at that time it was still possible for those to be commissioned. That was bad enough, but I have never seen worse specimens of humanity than the rabble under my command. The one way to keep any discipline was to dole out floggings at the slightest infraction. Scoundrels, all of them, thinking only of deserting at the first opportunity, drinking and chasing after whores of the lowest description."

I looked up from the baby cap I was embroidering. "You do not like prostitutes?"

"Hell, no! What could have given you such an idea, child? I wonder how anyone can find pleasure in the company of females who have served hundreds, maybe thousands, of men and are infected with every sort of pox and vermin. One would be a fool not to prefer a fresh little thing like you." He pinched my cheek.

The Baron had been at Court and visited Paris.

I gazed into the fire and sighed wistfully. "I would dearly like to visit those places."

"Do not count on it, my dear. All husbands are cuckolds there. I would not be kindhearted if I found that I had suffered that common misfortune. So, you see, it will save both of us much trouble to stay quietly here, where we lack nothing."

I resumed my sewing with alacrity. "I would never do anything so heinous, Sir."

"Maybe not, but I find that keeping a woman from temptation is the best manner to ensure that she not stray."

"You are of course the sole judge of it, Sir. Still, since I am not to see anything of Court or city life, I would enjoy hearing you speak of it."

"The King is a man of great learning and intelligence," said the Baron, "an excellent horseman and hunter. Unfortunately he is surrounded by a horde of scoundrels, the worst of whom come from his wife's entourage."

"What about the Queen? Is she not beautiful?"

The Baron put down his glass of wine. "She has the long face and thick lips of the Habsburgs, for, as you know, she is the daughter of the late Empress Maria-Theresa of Austria. Yet she fancies herself pretty and encourages the most ridiculous fashions, such as those towers of feathers, flowers, bows and pompons, all held together by pounds of *pommade*, she likes to wear on top of her head. I saw her once with an arrangement of radishes in her hair. I asked around whether she had taken leave of her senses. I was told that she was trying to prove that Frenchwomen would follow any new fashion she promoted, no matter how absurd. Of course no lady in her right mind was ever seen with a headdress of vegetables."

He shook his head in disgust. "But that would be nothing if she did not openly keep lovers, male and female, for she has both tastes. Yes, my dear, she is a *tribade*, she enjoys the intimate company of her own sex. Her favourite used to be the Princess de Lamballe, but now the Duchess de Polignac occupies that place. And there are men too. Nobody knows who sired the Queen's children, including the little Dauphin, heir to the throne. When I was at Court, she could not keep her eyes off the buttons of the Count de Fersen's breeches. He is a Swede. She used to have the decency to reserve her favours for French noblemen, like the Duke de Lauzun, but no, not anymore. She hates France. Do you know what she calls the Parisians? *The frogs of the Seine.*" He shrugged. "They do not like her much either. They too have names for her: *Madame Deficit* and *the Austrian Woman.* With her spendthrift ways and her depravity, she will bring nothing but disgrace upon the sacred person of the King. Now she is with child again, probably by that Fersen scoundrel."

Queen Marie-Antoinette's third pregnancy had just been officially announced. A little prince, Louis-Charles, was born in March of 1785.

Although the Baron expressed little interest in religious matters, we attended High Mass every Sunday.

"We should be seen by the peasants as often as possible," he said. "I despise those noblemen who live in town or at Court. They leave the management of their estates to bailiffs or such rascals, and are content to collect their rents and feudal duties without ever having anything to do with their vassals. Yet God knows that nothing bores me quite as much as that religious tomfoolery."

Indeed he spent the divine service with his eyes closed and his chin resting on his chest. Since we sat in the chancel, the entire congregation saw him sleep. Yet he never failed to awaken with a start at the end of Mass. Before we left the church, I would pause to light a candle and kneel before the altar of the Blessed Virgin in a side chapel, to implore her protection against my husband and the favour of presenting him with a son.

His lack of religious fervor did not make him any less popular with the peasants, who were not fond of the priest themselves and resented the tithes they had to pay him. They credited the Baron for being "without pride." He dressed simply, avoided trampling their crops when hunting and remembered their names and concerns. After Mass, he would stop outside the church to converse with them in the Roman language. Some, bowing and holding their hats with both hands, would then approach him with some plea or other.

Towards the end of my pregnancy, I noticed that Thérèse's eyes were often red and swollen. One morning, I felt a sudden kick from my child and put my hand to my stomach. She burst into tears.

"Thérèse," I said, "I think I know what is ailing you."

Her sobs redoubled.

"How far along are you?"

"About two months, My Lady. I went to a woman in the village, and she gave me some herbs, but nothing's happened yet. My Lord'll throw me out, and then my father'll kill me when he learns of my disgrace."

"Have you seen a midwife?"

"I can't. Everybody'd know of my shame if I did."

I complained of some pain and had the midwife fetched the same afternoon. I asked Thérèse to stay with me during her visit. The girl was indeed with child. When she heard it, she started sobbing again. I took her in my arms and assured her that I would speak to the Baron.

I waited until after he joined me in bed to broach the subject. I had found that it was the time when he was most likely to listen to my requests.

"Thérèse, with child?" he said. "She must be mistaken."

"I had her examined by the midwife, Sir."

"And pray what is it to me? Am I to be taken to task whenever a maid misbehaves under my roof?"

"Certainly not, Sir, but Thérèse is a decent girl. I had the impression that she was a virgin when you took a fancy to her."

He shrugged. "These things are easy to feign, my dear. Some brothels sell the same whore as a maiden fifty times over."

"Thérèse is a simple peasant girl. She could not have secured the means to impose on you. Besides, *you* would not be fooled by such tricks."

"All right, let us admit for the sake of argument that I took her maidenhead. It does not follow that I fathered her child. Any of those rascals I keep as menservants could have impregnated her."

"She could not have strayed without your being informed of it. You know how Maryssou watches the servants. She would have been delighted to shame Thérèse in your eyes and have her dismissed."

The Baron raised himself on one elbow. "Well, now Maryssou will dismiss her as soon as she suspects the truth."

"Please, Sir, do not let it happen. I know your kindness. One of your vassals might, for some monetary consideration, be induced to marry Thérèse. I would consider it the greatest favour to me as well as to her. It would bring me bad luck to throw out a pregnant girl while I am with child."

"What a notion! I will see what can be done." He wagged his finger at me. "But be careful, Gabrielle. Do not imagine that I am completely henpecked yet."

It is, for everyone's sake, better to conclude this kind of arrangement before the bride begins to show. Thérèse, within days, became engaged to marry Pierre Petit, a young peasant who lived in a cottage a half-league from Cénac. He was a tenant of the Baron's and had just purchased a small parcel of his own nearby, which made a little additional money very welcome to him. He was respectably known in the parish and there was no reason to doubt that he would make as good a husband as any other man. Thérèse was overcome with gratitude. Not only did she keep her good name, but she could never have married so well without the Baron's generosity. General opinion pronounced her, just as it had in my case, the most fortunate bride in the world. Of course, some gossip would later attend the premature birth of her child.

In a way I envied her because, unlike me, she had escaped the Baron. I presented her with a sturdy black wedding gown. In those days, peasant women were married in black clothes, since fabric of that colour was more durable than any other, and could be used for a lifetime of funerals, weddings and other formal occasions. I attended the ceremony, congratulated the new spouses and kissed the bride on both cheeks.

Thérèse had to be replaced. My husband entrusted to me, rather than to Maryssou, the choice of my new lady's maid. I invited him to have a look at the applicants. He seemed to be hesitating between two of them, equally comely.

"I will soon need a nursery maid as well," I said. "With your permission, Sir, I will hire both."

A smile lit his face. "Gabrielle, dearest, you are a good girl."

৵ 16 ৶

Monsieur de Laubrac, my husband's cousin, never acknowledged me more than required by common politeness, and sometimes rather less. Since my pregnancy had been announced, he would cast furtive, unfriendly glances at my stomach. Early in the spring of 1785, he braved a fresh coat of snow to introduce his bride, a stout, loud, pockmarked widow of inferior birth, endowed with a fortune of 60,000 francs. That kind of marriage where an impoverished scion of the nobility wedded a woman for her money was called in French *fumer ses terres*, which can be translated by "spreading manure upon one's estate."

Although I experienced little discomfort throughout my pregnancy, the weather became hot and my back began to ache under the weight of my stomach. I often thought of the late Baroness's untimely death in childbirth and wondered whether I would meet the same fate.

Early in the morning of the 15th of August 1785, one year to the day after first meeting the Baron, I felt the first pangs of childbirth. The pain, from dull, became close to unbearable. In spite of the midwife's assurances that all was well, I was convinced that my body was splitting apart and that I would not survive my lying-in. At last I had the relief of hearing, in the late afternoon, the first cry of my child.

"Oh, Madam," announced the midwife, "it's a beautiful little girl. I'd be surprised if she didn't weigh a full nine pounds. Who would have guessed it, with Your Ladyship being so young and slender!"

My heart sank, but my daughter was so pretty that she consoled me as soon as she was handed to me, all bundled up. She had dark blue eyes and the thickest head of black hair I have ever seen in an infant. The maids marveled at her resemblance with me, apart from her colouring. She was perfectly finished, down to the nails of her tiny fingers, which grasped mine with surprising strength.

I dreaded meeting my husband's eye. No one had mustered the courage to break the news to him. I was sitting in bed, holding my child as a shield when he entered my apartment with an eager look. I closed my eyes for a moment and said a silent prayer. My fears were unfounded. His face fell when I made my announcement, but he raised neither his hand nor his voice. With his forefinger, he pulled the white blanket in which our daughter was swaddled away from her face and glanced at her.

"Well," he said, "at least she seems healthy enough, which is a good sign for the others to come. I guess it is not your fault, my dear. Just rest and regain your strength. We will try again soon."

He kissed me on the forehead and left without a second look at our child.

Before giving birth, I had convinced him to allow me to nurse my child. It was less due to the influence of Rousseau's ideas on the question than to the fact that I could not imagine giving it up to a strange woman for years, as my mother had done with me. The Baron had reluctantly agreed on principle but had reserved the right to curtail what he considered a whim to any term he deemed appropriate. Nursing would of course interfere with my ability to become pregnant again. At the time, many ladies of the nobility bore more children than peasant women because they married far younger and did not feed their own offspring. The fact that I had borne a female was likely to shorten the period during which I would be allowed to nurse. Now that I was holding my daughter in my arms, parting with her seemed unthinkable. My aim was to continue feeding her until she could be weaned or was old enough to drink cow's milk.

It remained to name my daughter. I had spent hours thinking of names during my pregnancy, but I had not dared mention to the Baron any that were suitable for a girl.

"What about *Aimée*?" I suggested. "It is the female form of your second Christian name."

"And a ridiculous one for a grown man. But it was my mother's name, and it will do for a girl. Call her whatever you like."

Aimée means "beloved" in French. In happier days, Pierre-André had called me *mon aimée*, "my beloved." It had been a year since I had seen him. During that time, I had married and become a mother. The ideas of love or romance I had once entertained had succumbed on my wedding night. However, in a part of my memory I dared not revisit, a faint echo of past feelings survived. So my little girl was christened Aimée Françoise Marie de Laubrac de Peyre. I called her simply Aimée, to remember that I too had once been beloved. My brother was her godfather and Mademoiselle de Carlat, an elderly maiden aunt of my husband's, her godmother.

"The old sow is rich," the Baron explained, "and we might as well induce her to leave something to the child. I do not believe that daughters should expect to inherit much from their fathers. It is enough of a nuisance to raise them and marry them off. Hopefully this one will be pretty like you. Some fool will fall in love with her and take her without a *sol*."

I agreed readily to the Baron's choice since I did not want my mother, the Marquise de Castel, to be the godmother. It would have seemed bad luck to let her, like a wicked fairy, approach my little girl's cradle.

I had naively imagined that, immediately after giving birth, I would feel and look exactly as I had before my pregnancy. I was surprised to be sore, and horrified, when I rose the next day, to see that my waist had thickened and my stomach looked very strange indeed, as if my skin was now too large for my body. The midwife laughed at me when I asked about it.

"What did Your Ladyship expect?" she asked. "It will be another few days before you feel fine, and you will not get your figure back for weeks or even months, maybe not before your next pregnancy. My Lord must be impatient to father an heir and I would not be surprised if you were again with child before long."

Within three weeks, I was happy to observe that my waist and stomach had returned to their usual proportions.

"You are as slender as ever," my husband remarked, looking down at my kerchief. "Except for your bosom, of course, and I have no complaints about that. Send for that fool of a midwife. You must be fit to resume your duties now."

The midwife concurred. When he grasped me that night, I felt as if a knife were plunged into an open wound. Yet I bore the pain without a whimper or a word of protest, afraid that my little girl would be taken away from me if I angered him by my reluctance. I would have endured much worse to keep her with me. She was thriving and outgrew one set of baby linens after the other. I would hold her for hours, rocking her in my arms and singing to her, while her dark blue eyes remained fixed on my face.

My former maid Thérèse also gave birth to the Baron's offspring. I called on her after she was delivered of a large, healthy boy. Blushing, she asked me whether I would do her the honour of becoming the child's godmother. I agreed. As long as I remained in Auvergne, I followed little Gabriel's progress. I sometimes wondered how many other bastards of the Baron populated the surrounding countryside, unacknowledged and unheeded by their father.

One dark and snowy November afternoon, my husband came to my apartment while I was feeding Aimée. He seldom visited there during the day except to use the dressing room with the maids. I moved to rise and curtsey, my daughter in my arms, but he gestured to me to remain seated. He watched us in silence. Aimée's eyes were slowly closing. The movements of her mouth were becoming lazier. After she dozed off, still clutching my breast with her tiny hands, I gently put her down in the lace-draped cradle where generations of little Peyres had slumbered.

"She is growing like a weed," remarked the Baron. "I am sure that she can be weaned. If not, find her a nurse. What a notion for a noblewoman to feed her own child!" He was staring at my bare breasts. "I have to admit, though, that it does enhance the size of your bosom."

I blushed and began to readjust my bodice. He caught both of my wrists to draw me to him. "Stay as you are, my dear. Let us lie down for a minute."

He led me to the couch. As always, he did, and made me do, what he wanted. Once satisfied, he rose and proceeded to button his breeches and waistcoat. I seized his hand and kissed it.

"Please, Sir," I said, "let me continue to feed our daughter. I beg you. Just for a few weeks longer."

He frowned. "Have you not heard what I said? I have shown much patience with you. We have been married for over a year now, Madam, and you are still giving no sign of presenting me with an heir. You will put an end tomorrow to this nonsense."

I closed my eyes and made no answer.

In anticipation of his decision, which I had been dreading for some weeks, I had begun to introduce into Aimée's diet, much to her annoyance, gruel made from cow's milk. I found a peasant woman nearby who had a boy of the same age and agreed to come to Cénac during the day. I watched, with feelings of bitter jealousy, my daughter root for her breast instead of mine. Aimée was apparently healthy enough to become accustomed to this regimen without any ill effects.

By January of 1786, two months later, I was with child again. I was afraid of bearing another girl. The Baron made no effort to hide his misgivings. We never regained the hopeful feelings of my first pregnancy.

One afternoon in late July, I felt a sharp pain low in my back and was taken to bed. I was only six months along. The midwife kept repeating, a terrified look on her face:

"Don't worry, My Lady, you'll be fine."

"What about my child?" I asked between two pangs. "Is it going to be stillborn?"

"It'll be fine too. Just don't worry."

Her assurances sounded hollow, and I knew that my husband would blame me if anything went wrong. All of a sudden, I heard through the closed door his voice yelling oaths. He had come home earlier than expected and must have been informed that I had gone into labour. He burst into my apartment, booted and still holding his riding whip. My heart stopped for a moment, then started beating so fast that my chest felt ready to burst. I had been until then only moaning, but began crying aloud, not in pain but in terror. The midwife, although she had the good fortune not to be married to him, joined her screams to mine.

"Bitch," he shouted, glaring at me, "what have you done?"

He was advancing fast towards me. Never before, not even during my wedding night, had I been so afraid of him. I gathered my remaining strength to rise and run away, but with one hand he caught me by the shoulder while he raised his whip with the other. Blows were raining on my arms, my breasts, my stomach. I felt something warm gushing between my thighs. I fainted.

I came to my senses too late to see my son alive. The midwife had baptized him in haste so that the poor innocent could attain eternal salvation. It tore my heart to behold the tiny body, so frail, so raw. I mourned that child, whose white coffin had to be pried from my arms for burial. I was not recovered enough to attend his funeral.

The Baron was content afterwards to look at me in a resentful and malevolent manner. I was pronounced fit to resume my duties even sooner than after the birth of Aimée. Yet I failed to become pregnant. I was terrified of having become barren.

After our son's death, the Baron returned to the cruelties he had inflicted at the beginning of our marriage. My heart would still skip a beat at the signs of his anger, but once I was past the first lash, I knew how to detach myself from my own body. As to his other attentions, they no longer repelled me. I did everything he required of me and simply waited for the proceedings to be over. Any resistance, which he would have overcome without difficulty, would only have increased his pleasure and my misery.

Many times did I watch, from the window of my bedroom, the Baron mount his horse in the courtyard and ride away. I bit my lips with envy, remembering his injunction not to approach within a hundred feet of the stables. I knew that it was meant to be taken literally and that any disobedience would be reported by the servants. I sighed as I recalled the happy days of my girlhood, when I was free to ride Jewel into the mountains. That would never be again. I was careful not to indulge in any hopes of a change.

Yet my life was not without its consolations. I had my little girl, who was now past her first birthday. Her eyes were no longer blue, but had turned dark like her father's. Apart from her black hair, she still very much resembled me. She had learned to walk by holding fast to my skirts, and could now say not only "Mama" but also "want" while pointing at the object of her desires. I had presented her with my old rag doll, which she called "Nana" and dragged everywhere. I mended the poor thing, now discoloured and threadbare, over and over again. I even sewed a replacement for it, but Aimée steadfastly refused to even look at the new doll.

Whenever I played the harpsichord, Aimée would listen with rapt attention, propped against the bench. After I was done, I sat her on my lap and guided her tiny forefinger on the keys to produce simple melodies. She giggled in delight while I kissed her dark curls and praised her musical skills.

I found more solace than ever in the little library. Reading about the trials of others made me forget mine. Tales, real or imaginary, of faraway lands made my seclusion in Cénac bearable.

17

The 17th of March 1787 witnessed one of those momentous turns in the course of my life. Around midmorning, while I was reading in my apartment, I heard Maryssou howling, which very much surprised me for she was not given to venting her feelings. My chambermaid, out of breath, burst into the room without knocking.

"Oh, Madam," she said, "a great misfortune had happened. My Lord's been taken ill."

I ran downstairs and saw four peasants carrying a sort of door on which lay my husband. They gently put it down in the vestibule. I cried aloud, took his hand, which was already cold, and looked into his face. His eyes and mouth half-closed, he looked very much as he had done that night when he had fallen asleep in my bed, except for a small cut across the bridge of his nose. In a moment I understood that I was a widow.

I felt no sorrow. Many times during my marriage I had reflected that death only could release me from my servitude, but I had always thought of mine, not his. My first feeling was one of astonishment and shock rather than relief. All of my waking hours had been occupied by the dread of his reactions. Now he was gone, I was free, and I was lost. The only person whose help I could think of enlisting was my brother. I scrawled a note and asked a manservant to deliver it to Fontfreyde. I waited in the parlour, pacing the room.

Shortly after noon, I heard the sound of hooves on the gravel in the courtyard. I ran outside. It was the Marquis. His horse was covered with sweat. I fell into his arms, sobbing. He took me back to the house.

"Gabrielle, what is the matter? I could not make any sense of your note. I rode like hell to find out what is ailing you."

"The Baron is dead. Oh, Sir, I am a widow now."

"Poor child, what a blow this must be."

He called to a servant for a glass of wine, which he made me drink. It steadied me. I was able to sit still.

"Now tell me about it, Gabrielle. How did this happen?"

"He went hunting early this morning, as usual. Baduel, the tenant of the Bousquet farm, found him lying in the snow. He was apparently already dead. This is so sudden. He seemed in excellent health."

"Well, dearest, he indulged in many excesses. The less said about it, the better, I guess."

I grasped his hands. "If you do not help me, Sir, I do not know what will become of my little girl and me. I cannot spend the night here. Please take us back with you to Fontfreyde."

"Be brave, Gabrielle. As his widow, you will wake your husband. His corpse cannot be left unattended. You must spend the first night in prayers by his side."

The idea of spending the night in the Baron's bedroom, where I had never entered, in the company of his dead body, was more than I could bear.

"I have never sat with the dead before. Please, Sir, stay with me tonight."

"If you wish, little sister. Please calm yourself."

The Marquis sent word to Carrier, the Baron's attorney, and had a physician and a priest fetched. He went in search of Maryssou, whom he found sobbing in the kitchen. Under his direction, she had the body of the Baron dressed properly and laid on his bed.

Dr. Roussille, after acknowledging my husband's demise, which he assured me had been due to a sudden rupture of the heart, handed me a vial of medicine.

"Take this in a cup of herb tea, My Lady," he said. "It is laudanum and will quiet you."

I sat to dinner with my brother, and we went to the Baron's bedroom, where he lay, dressed in his finest clothes. A rosary, which I had never seen him use during his life, had been placed in his hands. Two candles were burning on the nightstand, where Father Vidal had left a basin of holy water with instructions to sprinkle the body from time to time. My brother and I each took a chair by the side of the bed. I could not take my eyes off the thing that had been my husband. I imagined that I saw him stirring. If I stopped watching him for a moment, he would rise from the dead to beat me again.

The Marquis, glancing at me, rang for a cup of lime-blossom tea. He poured all the contents of Dr. Roussille's medicine in it and made me drink it. It tasted sweet and strong, like liquor. Within minutes I became dizzy. I was dreaming awake. Wolves with human faces were watching me, and sometimes they came frighteningly close to me. I cried aloud to my brother. He took me in his arms, carried me to a couch in front of the fireplace, lay me down and removed my shoes. He sat next to me and held my feet in his hands. He was talking while caressing my ankles, but I could not understand what he was telling me, as if he had been speaking a foreign language. I needed to hear his voice. It kept the eerie visions from closing upon me. It lulled me to sleep. I fell into a pit of oblivion.

When I woke and raised myself on one elbow, my brother was opening the inside shutters and the grey light of dawn could be glimpsed beyond the woods. Smiling, he walked up to me and ran his fingers on my cheek.

"So, my love," he asked, "are you better this morning?"

I seized his hand. "Please do not leave yet."

"Of course not, little sister."

The Marquis remained another day and night at Cénac.

I was growing accustomed to the idea that I was free at last. Yet my relief was tempered by concerns about the future. I ordered the carriage to go to Aurillac, where I stopped at Maître Carrier's chambers. I had met him during the signing of my marriage contract and on occasion in Cénac when he came to attend to the Baron's business. Although there was nothing objectionable in his manners, he made me uncomfortable and I had always avoided him.

Many say that Carrier was ugly. That is not true. He was tall, thin, a bit stooped and olive-skinned. There was a certain countrified air about him and he spoke French with a thick Roman accent. His father had been a peasant from Yolet, a village close to Vic. Pierre-André, the son of a lawyer and a convent-educated lady of the bourgeoisie, was far more polished in manners and language. Yet that day, the unease I felt in Carrier's presence was not enough to deter me from my purpose. I announced myself to one of his clerks and was shown into his chambers without delay.

"Well, Madam," he said, bowing, "it seems too long since I last had the honour of seeing Your Ladyship. Please allow me to offer my condolences."

"Thank you."

"You had no need to come here. I would have been happy to call on you at Cénac."

"You are very kind, Sir, but what brings me is a delicate matter which I wanted to discuss in your chambers."

He looked straight into my eyes, smiling. "I am honoured by your trust, My Lady. I hope that it will be in my power to assist you."

"You are, of course, familiar with the provisions of my late husband's will."

"I drafted it."

"I need to know its contents."

"Your Ladyship, like the other heirs, will have to wait until I come to Cénac to read the will after the funeral."

"What harm would there be in telling me of its terms now? Please,

Maître Carrier, I am sure that you would not be so unfeeling as to deny a poor widow's request."

"Indeed, Madam, there is nothing I find so moving as a lady in distress." He was not smiling anymore, but watching me, his eyes narrowed, in a manner that made me squirm in my chair. "And I have always felt the most respectful admiration for you."

"Should I be worried?"

"You should be aware of an unfortunate circumstance: you waived, by marriage contract, all of your rights to the assets and estate of the late Baron. Thus he was not bound to leave Your Ladyship a *sol* more than agreed to in the contract."

"And pray what was that?"

"I will not keep you in suspense any longer, Madam. I will go directly to the relevant provisions of the late Baron's will."

He pulled a bundle of papers from a drawer in his desk and read: *"To my beloved wife, the High and Mighty Lady Marie Gabrielle Aliénor de Montserrat de Castel: the sum of 3,000 francs; I also confirm all gifts of jewellery and personal property made by me to said Lady before and during our marriage, without any limitation of value."*

I stared at him in amazement. He paused to look at me, then resumed his reading. *"To my legitimate daughter Aimée Françoise Marie, the sum of 3,000 francs.* Then, Madam, there are various legacies to servants, including a rather generous 1,000 francs to one Marie, or Maryssou Magne, the housekeeper at Cénac. Then we go back to what concerns you: *Should my wife be pregnant at the time of my demise, the sum of 3,000 francs to the child of her body if such child be a female, and to such child the remainder of my estate should it be a male.* And finally: *Should my wife bear a male child, I give her an additional 100,000 francs and for life the income of the Barony of Cénaret.* That, Madam, is 11,000 francs per annum. *Should my wife fail to bear a male child, the remainder of my estate to my cousin, François-Xavier Alexandre de Laubrac."*

Carrier put down the will. "You wanted to know. You do now."

I hid my face in my hands. "Are you telling me, Maître Carrier, that all I can expect is 3,000 francs, with the same sum going to my daughter? Is that what the marriage contract provided?"

"The marriage contract required 3,000 francs for you, Madam, and another 3,000 for each daughter. Of course, the Baron could have left you and your little girl more if he had so chosen."

My cheeks were burning. I interrupted Carrier. "What is the value of my late husband's estate?"

"Probably a little under two million."

"And of that, I am to receive 3,000 francs! What if I were pregnant now?"

"Ah, that would make things interesting. The estate would be held in abeyance until the birth of your child. If it were a female, nothing would change, except that she too would receive 3,000 francs, but the birth of a male would of course be a very fortunate circumstance for you, as well as a severe disappointment to Monsieur de Laubrac, whose hopes are totally contingent upon the absence of a direct heir."

"Thank you, Maître Carrier. You have been most helpful."

He smiled again. "I will always remain, with all due respect, at Your Ladyship's service and that of your honourable family."

✺ 19 ✺

Carrier's words were very much on my mind as I greeted Monsieur de Laubrac and his wife on the day of the Baron's funeral. She was draped in a vast quantity of black crape, which made her frame still more formidable than usual. She smothered me against her bosom.

"Poor, poor child," she said, "so young and such a dreadful misfortune. Fear not, Madam, my husband will not mind your staying another week at Cénac. This will give you ample time to pack your things. As I told the new Baron: *We would not want to rush the dear Dowager Baroness out of her former house, would we?*"

To me, dowagers were ancient ladies with doddering heads and snowy hair. Madame de Laubrac's haste irritated me. The Marquis arrived. Our mother, he explained, had been too grieved by the Baron's death to attend. Madeleine alighted from her carriage and embraced me in silence.

The family repaired to the parish church for the funeral service, which was celebrated with all the pomp required by the Baron's rank. The local nobility attended, along with all of his vassals. The little church could not accommodate such a crowd, and many had to follow the service from outside. The Baron's coffin, covered with a black and silver pall, was then brought back to Cénac, where it was laid to rest in the crypt beneath the chapel, among the dust of his ancestors. It was put down on iron saw-horses, between the bodies of his first wife and elder brother. Dozens of coffins of all sizes, some, like the Baron's, made of lead, and some, older ones, of stone, crowded the confined space. I felt that the ghosts of the Peyre family were rising around me. I had not attended my son's funeral nine months earlier and indeed had never entered the crypt before. I gasped when I saw a tiny box, draped in dusty white silk, resting on a kind of shelf carved in a wall. I was suffocating and sought the support of my brother's arm.

I regained enough composure to return to the house, leaning on him. In the main drawing room, Maître Carrier read the will in front of the assembled family. I kept my eyes down and gave no sign of emotion.

After the attorney was done, I said: "Maître Carrier, I know that all umarried and widowed women must report their pregnancies to a minis-terial officer of the King. You are, I believe, such an officer."

"Indeed."

"Then I must report to you the fact that I am with child."

Carrier grinned. "I will come back tomorrow to take your official declaration, Madam. So after all, this time will be one of congratulations as well as condolences."

Monsieur de Laubrac had recovered enough to hiss to his wife: "The woman is lying."

I raised my eyes. My brother rose, his hand on the hilt of his sword, and faced Monsieur de Laubrac. "You insulted my sister, Sir."

"Surely," intervened Carrier, "Her Ladyship would not make such a claim without good reason."

"You, stay out of this," said Monsieur de Laubrac, red in the face. He turned to my brother. "My deepest apologies to you, My Lord, and to Her Ladyship. I would not dare impugn her veracity."

I put my hand to my stomach. "Your apology is accepted, Sir. Now I will retire to my apartment and take some rest."

I curtseyed to the company. The idea of keeping Monsieur and Ma-dame de Laubrac in suspense for some time gave me great satisfaction. My brother joined me a few minutes later in my apartment. He seized me none too gently by the elbow.

"Gabrielle, what is the meaning of this? Are you really with child?"

"I certainly intend to remain pregnant until further notice."

He released my arm. "How can you make light of such matters? You should know that our sister Hélène wrote Madeleine to offer to receive you among her novices at the Convent of Noirvaux. Your 3,000 francs would not normally be enough of a dowry for Noirvaux, but Hélène will make an exception in your favour. I have also approached the Bishop on your behalf. You will, as a widow, need a dispensation before being allowed to take the veil."

I frowned. "Is this not premature, Sir? I have not expressed the slightest wish to become a nun."

"Do you think we are placed on earth for the sole purpose of following our whims? Your husband is not yet cold in his grave and you are already showing signs of your old willfulness. But you would be wise not to spurn your family's help so hastily. You might find that 3,000 francs is not quite enough to support you in the style to which you have grown accustomed."

I sighed. "I am aware of it. I am not seeking a quarrel with you, Sir. I have entertained the hope that you would take me back. Please let me return to Fontfreyde. You used to be so fond of me when I was little. You were so good to stay with me to wake my husband. How can you forsake me now that your kindness is my only hope?"

The Marquis shook his head. "What are you trying to do, Gabrielle? I love you as much as ever, but I am not weak enough to yield to your entreaties when I know that it would not be proper."

"What could be improper about a brother offering a widowed sister his help? Remember that Aimée is your goddaughter. Noirvaux is not a teaching institution. What would you suggest I do with her if I took the veil?"

"You need not worry on Aimée's account. Mother will raise her at Fontfreyde. I will treat her as my own daughter. As for you, I do not want you back. Do you think I forgot your scandalous affair? You were disgraced by that scoundrel!"

For the first time I raised my voice to my brother. "I was not disgraced, Sir. That scoundrel, as you call him, had respected my innocence. Did he not propose? And was not his offer more advantageous than the one you accepted? He would have settled 20,000 francs on me; he would not have left me destitute as the Baron did. How could you forget it when you arranged my marriage contract?" I glared at the Marquis. "And what about my feelings, Sir? Did you care at all about them?"

"Do you really fail to see what was disgraceful about that business? An alliance with any commoner would have been a stain upon our honour. But to imagine you in that man's power! The thought that he would have been your master is simply unbearable. Under no circumstances would I have let you fall into the paws of that giant brute."

I stared at the Marquis in shock. Until then, I had deceived myself into believing that family pride had been his main motive. Now I recalled how he had touched me that afternoon in the Fontfreyde drawing room. I had been blind. He had been jealous of Pierre-André. My brother had forced me to marry the Baron to keep me away from the man I had loved.

"I understand you now, Sir, better than I ever wished," I said. "Please send my most respectful regards to Mother."

He left without another word. I did not join the guests at the funeral dinner.

🙦 20 🙤

Madeleine declined to interfere. In her eyes, our brother, as the head of the family, was the sole judge of what was to become of me. I had to make plans. I was not with child. I would have to be careful and keep certain things from the maids, who might be bribed by the presumptive heir to spy on me. In a few months I would have to admit my mistake. The new Baron and his wife would then throw me out of Cénac.

My 3,000 francs, added to Aimée's, would give us an income of around 300 francs per annum, just enough to secure modest accommodations in Vic. There I found lodgings consisting of a parlour, two bedrooms and maid's quarters on a second floor on the main street, just a stone's throw from the Coffinhal house. It did not matter, for Pierre-André never visited there anymore. The remainder of my income would barely pay for our food, clothing and the wages of one maid. We would be poor as church mice.

Shortly afterwards, Maryssou announced the visit of the Chevalier des Huttes. The Chevalier, Jean-Baptiste Pagès des Huttes, was about my brother's age and a great friend of his. I had seen him often at Fontfreyde before my marriage. He also was a Captain in the Regiment of the Queen's Bodyguards, the *blue gentlemen*, as they were called because of the colour of their uniforms. The members of that corps, put in charge of Her Majesty's personal security, were recruited among the minor nobility. The Chevalier's duties required him to spend much of his time in the Palace of Versailles. When he was on leave in Auvergne, he resided in his fine house in Vic or his manor in the mountains. He had sometimes been our guest at Cénac and had attended the Baron's funeral.

"I need not ask how you are feeling, My Lady," he said. "You look very well."

"Thank you, Sir, well enough." I could not guess the purpose of his call and waited for him to speak.

"I hear that you are enquiring about lodgings in Vic," he said, "which surprised me in light of your condition."

I looked into his eyes. "Are you, like Monsieur de Laubrac, accusing me of lying?"

"Certainly not, Madam, but the Marquis told me yesterday of your plans to go to Noirvaux if your hopes of giving birth to the Baron's heir were disappointed. Why then would you need lodgings in Vic?"

"These are my brother's plans, not mine. He seems to think, as he did before, that he can dispose of me without any regard for my wishes."

The Chevalier sighed. "I must be the only man in whom he confided before your wedding. He was absolutely right when he forbade your marriage to Pierre-André Coffinhal. In my opinion, that young man's departure is no great loss for Vic. Oh, he is full of intelligence and energy, but he was overly indulged by his late mother. Added to his stature and physical strength, that may explain his insufferable arrogance. And that voice of his! When riding past the inn in Vic, I could hear it through the closed door, booming over the clamours of all the other patrons put together. Even his plainness never seemed to lessen his insolence. By the age of sixteen, he had bedded all of his mother's maids and was turning his sights on mine. I remonstrated with him. Far from expressing contrition, he told me that, though he was ugly, my maids enjoyed his attentions and were eager to continue his acquaintance. According to him, so were most females once they discovered that his size, so to speak, matched his height."

I felt myself blushing to the roots of my hair. "This is, I suppose, the sort of banter to be expected from a man, especially a very young man, when there are no ladies present. It is not fit to be repeated to one."

The Chevalier looked embarrassed. "You are right, Madam. Please forgive me. I am truly sorry to have upset you. I was trying to explain why I thought, and still think, the Marquis justified in forbidding your marriage to the younger Coffinhal. It was characteristic of him to raise his sights to you without thinking twice about it, as if there were no striking disparity between you and him." The Chevalier shook his head. "I am a nobleman, but the Marquis would have balked if I had sought to marry you. Imagine what he, the head of one of the most prominent families in the province, must have felt at the idea of giving his sister to the grandson of a peasant! That would have been a most unsuitable match for you."

I frowned. "True. My brother had a more suitable match in mind."

"Please hear me, My Lady. I do not approve of forced marriages, especially where the bride is so young as to be still a child. It pained me to see you so unhappy during the signing of your marriage contract. I strongly advised the Marquis to find a way to break the engagement, but he disagreed. Now you are no longer under his authority, and I do not like to see you again forced into a path against your inclination."

"You are very kind, Sir. What are you offering beyond your opinion? Are you asking for my hand in marriage to rescue me from the convent?"

He smiled. "Please do not think ill of me, My Lady, if I do not. My purpose, I am afraid, is more prosaic. What I propose is to take you to Paris when I return there in three weeks. One of my closest friends happens to be the Dowager Duchess of Arpajon, your late father's cousin. She is a lady of unimpeachable respectability. She could present you at Court and introduce you to the best society while offering you the benefit of her advice and protection. She likes the company of bright, cheerful young persons. If I told her of your situation, I am sure that she would be delighted to offer you her hospitality."

"Then what would I do? I cannot remain with her forever."

"A lady such as you cannot fail to find a situation at Court or a suitable husband in Paris. I will write the Duchess if you will allow me to do so. Should she accept, I would be happy to convey you to the capital."

"And pray what would you expect in return for this service?"

"The pleasure of Your Ladyship's company during the carriage ride to Paris, which I usually find very tedious on my own."

I must have looked skeptical.

"I may be naive, Madam," added the Chevalier, "but I believe that, on occasion, people, at least decent people, do things because they believe them right, without any expectation of a return. I will consider myself amply repaid if I earn your friendship."

I accepted the Chevalier's offer. The reader, before judging me too harshly, must remember that I was seventeen. When I found myself alone, I did feel some misgivings about the wisdom of my decision. What if the Chevalier took advantage of me? He could argue that I had agreed to elope with him, that I had thrown myself into his power of my own accord. Yet my doubts were swept away by the prospect of discovering the most fascinating city in Europe, which I had often imagined from the descriptions given by Pierre-André and the Baron.

My other choice, since the convent still did not tempt me, was to enjoy the pleasures of genteel poverty in a small town, my life over before I was eighteen. My best prospect in Vic would be, counting on extreme good fortune, to marry some widowed nobleman of a bilious disposition, probably as brutal as my late husband, but less rich and saddled with a family of hostile children. I was not joking when I had suggested to the Chevalier that he wed me. He was relatively young, handsome, good-humoured and sensible, infinitely superior to any other man whom, as a widow with a young daughter, I could expect to marry based on the sole appeal of my charms and 3,000 francs. I would have accepted him on the spot had he proposed.

A week later, the Chevalier came back to show me the Duchess's response. I only remember the sentence: "If your young friend is half as charming as you depict her, I will be fortunate to have such a companion. Bring her to me, by all means, along with her little girl."

I threw my arms around the Chevalier's neck and kissed him on the cheek.

Later on the same day, I entered the stables of Cénac, which had been so stringently forbidden to me. A groom stared at me when I ordered him to saddle one of the horses.

"But, My Lady," he said, "we have no side saddles here."

"No matter. I can use a man's saddle, or still better, I will ride bareback."

He saddled one of the horses in a hurry, muttering under his breath and glancing sideways at me as if I were a madwoman.

"Where will Your Ladyship be going?"

"For a ride."

It was the first time since my marriage that I enjoyed the pleasure of riding. I no longer cared whether I confirmed Monsieur de Laubrac's doubts as to my pregnancy. I called on my former maid Thérèse Petit and my godson, Gabriel, now over one year old and walking around in a very assured way. He was a handsome child, robust for his age and much like his late father in looks and manners. There was the son the Baron had so wished for. Yet neither little Gabriel nor his mother had been remembered in my husband's will. I gave Thérèse one hundred francs as a farewell present. She cried when I took my final leave of her.

I paid another farewell visit. I rode, as I had done so many times in my maiden days, to the Labro cottage. I kissed the whole household good-bye, Jacques included and Mamé last of all. I turned around to look at them one last time. Mamé, surrounded by her sons, waved at me. Tears were rolling freely down my cheeks. I decided to ride to the river, where I had not set foot since my last assignation with Pierre-André, before my marriage. The stones in the middle of its current were still covered with snow, but the merry song of the water held a promise of spring. I stood a long time on the pebble bank, unable to make sense of the past or the future.

∽ 21 ∾

At eight one fine May morning, I waited, my daughter in my arms, for the Chevalier. I left, to the servants' mute astonishment, what had been my home. The Chevalier handed me into his carriage. The first test of his conduct had come. Of course, I sat with Aimée in the back. I waited to see whether he would settle next to me. This would have been inappropriate for a man who was neither my husband nor my brother. To my relief, he sat across from me. I turned around and watched through the rear window of the carriage the square towers of Cénac disappear in the distance. Aimée, a stranger to any feelings of nostalgia, was standing on the seat, cooing and nuzzling up to my cheek and neck.

I was still uneasy and did my best to keep the skirts of my black dress from brushing against the Chevalier's knees. I expected him to pounce on me at the first opportunity, *comme la misère sur le monde*, "like poverty on the world," according to the French saying. The Baron had used the less elegant *comme la vérole sur le bas clergé*, "like the pox on the lower clergy." I was prepared to fight unwanted advances with the utmost energy. His quiet, unaffected demeanour eventually reassured me. It must have had the same effect on Aimée. She sat down, huddled against me, her face hidden in her hands, casting from behind her spread fingers looks of false shyness in his direction. He smiled back. At last she held out her arms to him.

"May I hold her, Madam?" he asked.

"Certainly, if she does not mind. You seem to have made quite an impression, Sir. She is generally very shy around gentlemen, as befits a proper young lady."

Aimée had never been held by her father and had cried, burying her face in my neck, whenever she had heard his voice. She sat on the Chevalier's lap and, looking up, touched his face with her little hand, frowning at the roughness of a man's cheek. She then turned her attention to the silver buttons of his coat, which she tried to put in her mouth. After he dissuaded her from it, she pursed her lips, looked bored and fell asleep in his lap. I had not seen any man before take an interest in a child, especially female, save for my brother. I was reminded of his past tenderness for me and looked out the window to hide my emotion.

We changed horses and stopped for the night at the Inn of the Two Crowns, in Clermont, another novel experience for me. The Chevalier secured the largest apartment for Aimée and me, and the second in size for himself.

"We will dine in your bedroom, Madam," he said. "You should not be exposed to the coarse language and manners of the common room downstairs, especially at night when the patrons tend to be the worse for drink."

My wariness of the Chevalier reappeared. During our meal I desperately tried to keep Aimée awake on my lap though she kept dozing off. The Chevalier remarked that I must be tired and left promptly after dinner for his own apartment after bowing to me and kissing Aimée, now fast asleep in my arms. She smiled when his lips brushed against her round cheek.

I had forgotten, following my marriage, that most men will not force themselves upon a woman. My journey with the Chevalier reminded me of it. I also recalled Pierre-André, whose restraint had been more meritorious because he had wanted me. The Chevalier's perfect manners seem to proceed as much from his indifference towards me as from his delicacy.

The next day, we left the boundaries of Auvergne. I did not know then that I would never again see my native country, the scene of so many memories, happy or not, of my childhood and youth. It is much to our advantage to be denied the gift of foresight for we would not stir otherwise.

⚘ 22 ⚘

After five full days, the Chevalier announced that we were approaching Paris. I opened the window and leaned out the carriage, gaping at the fortified wall being built around the city. We passed across an unfinished gate decorated by columns in the antique style.

"At least Paris will be well defended," I said, choking on the dust of the construction.

The Chevalier shouted to make himself heard above the thunder of hammers and the cries of workmen. "This has nothing to do with the defense of Paris. This wall is being built all around the city for the benefit of the Farmers Generals, to prevent food from entering without being taxed." The Chevalier shook his head bitterly. "I am afraid this will inflame the populace. The Farmers Generals are already hated. They are in charge of tax collection and may raise what they like while paying the Treasury a fixed amount. Now they will be accused of strangling Paris with this new wall."

Parisians are fond of calling provincials *culs-terreux*, which literally translates as "dirty asses," but what struck me in Paris was the filth of the southern districts we first crossed. We followed narrow streets, strewn with garbage and lined with soot-coloured houses, five or six stories high. I saw bands of half-naked children. Raggedy women yelled and shook their fists at each other. A man was relieving himself against a wall. The mere thought of male genitals still was enough to turn my stomach, though I had now been widowed for a few months. I looked away and glanced at the Chevalier, but, either out of delicacy or because he was used to that sight, he seemed to ignore the man.

Soon the streets became wider and took a more prosperous look. I thought I would go deaf from the rattling of the carriages, the swearing of the cart drivers and the cries of the street vendors peddling their wares. We had to stop more than once to give way to other carriages, for wooden stalls, piled high with produce, encroached on the street. I marveled at pyramids of oranges, which, the Chevalier told me, came from Portugal. I remembered my joy when, as a child, I found one of those fruits in my clog in front of Mamé Labro's hearth on Christmas morning. I ate it all too quickly, in spite of Mamé's entreaties to savour it, and refused to wash my hands afterwards in spite of their stickiness. I kept the peel for several days, breathing in its sweet oil until the fragrance was gone. I would not taste another orange until the next Christmas.

A man, perched on planks resting on sawhorses, was playing the violin. A small crowd had formed to listen to him. He paused at the end of each air to point with his bow at scenes painted on a canvas hung behind him. I could not understand what he was saying, though I could hear the shrill accents of his music.

I asked the Chevalier the meaning of the initials *M.A.C.L.*, which I saw painted above the entrances of buildings. He flushed.

"It stands," he said, "for *Maison Assurée Contre L'incendie*, and serves to indicate that the owner of the house has purchased fire insurance. Some, however, give it another, outrageous meaning. Such scoundrels deserve the gallows."

He seemed truly upset and I did not press the point. Before long I would discover the other meaning derisively ascribed to these initials. It was *Marie-Antoinette Cuckholds Louis*. Thus, like any other Parisian, I would be reminded daily of the King's alleged misfortune.

The Chevalier pointed to the monumental gilded gates that marked the entrance to the main courthouse. He said that we would cross the river by way of the *Pont-au-Change*, the Bridge of the Money Changers. I looked out, eager for my first glimpse of the Seine. My face fell when I saw only houses on either side of the street.

"Houses have been built on almost all of the bridges of Paris," said the Chevalier, smiling at my disappointment, "but they are soon to be demolished. They will no longer block the view of river, and the city will be more airy and healthy."

Our route took us through the *Châtelet* district. I have heard that it has since been destroyed on the orders of Napoléon Bonaparte. At the time of my arrival in Paris, this area gave off an odor unlike anything I had smelled before. I remarked to the Chevalier that the gutters were running red.

"The main slaughterhouse is around the corner," he said. "It sends streams of blood flowing down into the river. I once saw an escaped ox, mad with terror, galloping in the middle of this street. Butchers in their soiled aprons, cutlasses in hand, were chasing the poor animal."

The Chevalier pointed to the medieval towers of the criminal court building, called the *Grand Châtelet*.

"It houses some of the most squalid dungeons in the city," he said. "It is also home to the *Morgue*. The bodies found daily in the river or on the streets are kept there until identified or claimed."

I put my hand to my face, dizzy with nausea. It was a relief to leave the *Châtelet* to reach at last the *Marais* district, where the Duchess d'Arpajon lived. *Marais* means "swamp" in French.

"What an odd name for such a beautiful district!" I said, marveling at the elegant mansions on each side of the street.

"True," said the Chevalier. "It used to flood every spring, when the river overflowed after the melting of the snows. It was the aristocratic quarter of choice a century ago, but it has now lost that distinction to the Faubourg Saint-Germain, on the Left Bank."

We passed the jail of La Force. Two hundred years earlier, explained the Chevalier, it had been one of the most magnificent dwellings in Paris, and now it was degraded to the rank of debtors' prison. Little did I guess then the part it would play in my life only a few years later. The Duchess's mansion was on the next street.

After the carriage stopped in the courtyard, I observed that the front of the house was elegantly decorated with columns and sculpted allegories of the four seasons. We alighted and were led up a wide stone staircase to a parlour on the second floor, a vast cheerful room, handsomely furnished. I was reminded of my trepidation upon meeting my mother at the age of eleven. Her Grace the Duchess d'Arpajon, a lady of about sixty, white-haired and blue-eyed, rose to embrace me and kiss me on the cheek. That simple kindness was more than I had ever received from my mother. I felt the prickling of tears in my eyes. She hastened to order the tea things, a welcome sight after a long day of travel. Aimée sat on my lap, where she fell sound asleep.

"Dear Chevalier," said the Duchess, "nothing in your letters quite prepared me for the beauty of my young cousin." She turned to me. "If you will allow it, my dear, I will call you Belle, for you remind me of the youngest sister in the tale of *Beauty and the Beast*. You see, I have a weakness in my old age. I like to be surrounded by young, handsome, cheerful people. I used to be considered quite attractive myself. I can say it because nothing remains of my beauty now. Your presence will remind me of those days. Apart from my friend the Chevalier, who is the last true gentleman left in the kingdom, no young people visit me anymore unless I happen to have under my roof guests like you. Without you, I was reduced to gossiping and playing lotto with ladies as ancient as I."

She put down her cup of tea. "Do not feel sorry for me, dear Belle. I am invited to dinners once in a while because I am still good company. Also I am frightfully fond of the theatre, the opera and gambling, quite a shame at my time of life and given the state of my finances. Before long, dear Belle, you will become familiar with all of my vices. I am afraid I have kept them all in my dotage, save the one I most cherished. Time is most unfair to us females."

I must have looked shocked by such a speech from a lady older than my mother. She patted my hand. "I am sorry, dear, to embarrass you with my loose talk," she continued, her eyes twinkling. "Listen to me, an old sinner. Your blushes make me ashamed of myself, which I have not felt in forty years. I am all the more delighted to have you with me. You may give me some principles before it is too late. And it may be easier to depart for the eternal night with you at my side."

"I should be the one to apologize for my prudishness," I said. "It is one of my flaws, Madam: I colour so easily. I am afraid I will make a fool of myself in Paris with my provincial manners."

"Nonsense, Belle. Your modesty is so rare that it will only add to your allure. You are just what this city needs. Twenty women like you would redeem its morals."

"Your Grace will not find so many here," said the Chevalier.

"I guess not," the Duchess responded. "We shall remain unrepentant then, which will not prevent us from enjoying dear Belle's company."

The Chevalier announced that he had to take his leave to reach his lodgings in the Palace of Versailles, some ten miles to the southwest of Paris, before the night. The Duchess thanked him again for delivering me to her. As he left, he bowed to kiss my hand and wished me the best of luck. Aimée, awakened, wrapped her arms around his knees and cried. I had to pry her away from him.

"If you do not visit us very soon," I said, "you will break my daughter's heart."

"I will call at the first opportunity, Madam."

Aimée could not be persuaded to go to bed without me. The Duchess had ordered a cot prepared in a maid's room, but she kindly agreed to have it moved to mine.

"You are such a funny young person," she said. "In my time, no noble-woman would have thought of keeping her child with her at night."

"I did not do so in my husband's home, Madam, but she has become used to it during our journey from Auvergne. It would be hard for her now to sleep with a stranger in a strange room."

"What do you mean by your *husband's* home, Belle? Was is not yours too?"

"No, as attested by the fact that I had to quit it upon his death."

"That is what the Chevalier wrote me. A very odd business. My late husband did not leave me much, but he at least gave me a small pension and this house for life. What was the Baron thinking? Did he want you to beg for your bread on the streets?"

"I will never know, Madam. He probably thought that my brother would take me back."

"What a pitiful arrangement! But fortunate for me, I suppose. Now, dearest, you can barely keep your eyes open. I do not want to be selfish and keep you late on your first night here. We will take our dispositions for you tomorrow."

My apartment looked out on a garden of trimmed boxwood hedges, in the formal French style, at the back of the house. After putting Aimée to bed, I opened one of the windows. The only noise I could hear in that delightful old-fashioned district was the evening song of the birds. There was nothing to suggest the embrace of the vast city surrounding me. Yet I could sense that I no longer lived in the countryside. The air was milder than in Auvergne, for in May the high country is still in the grip of the last winter frosts. I fell in love with Paris. Indeed I am still under its thrall, in spite of these twenty years of exile. I went to bed happy.

The next day, I joined the Duchess for breakfast at seven o'clock. Like many elderly persons, she liked to rise early. Thanks to my late husband, my habits were the same.

"First, we must take care of your clothes, dear," she said. "Have you anything other than these black dresses?"

"But, Madam, I have been widowed less than three months. It would not be proper for me to quit my mourning so early."

"Then wear white for your mourning. In my opinion that is more than enough for a little widow of seventeen. Have you any Court gowns?"

"No, Madam. Pray what will I need? I know that such attire can be expensive."

"My dear, some of the Queen's gowns cost over 10,000 francs. Mademoiselle Rose Bertin, her dressmaker, has made a fortune."

I smiled in dismay. "I have less than 3,000 francs altogether."

"I would lend you some of my own Court gowns, but they would be too short for you. Do not worry; you can purchase used ones from another lady's chambermaid. I will ask Mélanie to find something suitable for your lovely figure. You must, of course, be presented to the King and Queen in order to be admitted everywhere in Versailles. I will be happy to serve as your *presenting lady* for that occasion. For dinners in town, young women do not dress as they used to do. I am sure that the clothes you brought from Auvergne will be fine for such occasions."

The same day, I wrote my sister, Madame de Montserrat, to thank her for her offer to join her at Noirvaux Abbey. I explained that I did not feel any religious vocation and believed it wrong to take the veil without a more definite calling. I wanted to provide my own explanation for my refusal to enter her convent. I did not know in what light my family had cast my decision to leave for Paris.

Within a week, Mélanie, the Duchess's chambermaid, found a white Court dress suitable for my height, although it needed to be narrowed around the waist. It had a few wine stains on the bodice and smelled of its prior owner's now faded fragrance. I was reminded of the time when I had worn my mother's discards, but this gown was in a very different style, adorned with silver embroidery and grey ribbons. It was designed to be worn over *paniers*, "baskets," giant oval hoopskirts that only allowed the ladies of the Court to go through doors sideways. A long train attached to the waist of the dress. The bodice was cut to leave all of the throat and shoulders bare. It required a special corset, the lacing of which exposed part of the chemise in the back.

My jaw dropped at the sight of this attire. "How can anyone wear anything so immodest in public?" I asked.

"My poor Belle," said the Duchess, laughing, "please remember that I, at my age, have to dress in the same fashion at Court. And the chemise one wears under this corset must be sheer so your back will be almost as visible as your throat and shoulders. Believe me, you will become used to it, like many a modest lady before you."

As the Duchess and I examined the gown, we found a tear in the rows of lace that covered the sleeves to the elbows. Manon, the chambermaid assigned to my service in my new home, looked at the damage.

"Don't worry, My Lady," she said, "that's nothing. My sister Louise is a lace maker and can repair it in a trice. And I'll find some matching grey ribbon to sew over these wine stains."

In the middle of our survey of my new finery, we received a visit from the Marquise de Bastide, the Duchess's daughter. I had never met her before. The Duchess also had a son, who was quartered with his regiment in Lorraine. Being of a taciturn and unsociable nature, he rarely set foot in town or at Court. I would not be introduced to him until the following year.

Madame de Bastide was tall and imposing, with dark hair, regular features and her mother's blue eyes. When we were introduced, she barely took the trouble to nod at me. Instead, she turned her attention to my gown.

"Very pretty," she said, holding the skirt between two fingers and smiling with disdain. "This kind of silver embroidery was very fashionable last year, I believe. Congratulations, Madam. This gown will suit you to perfection."

I was not sorry when she announced that other engagements called her away.

The next day, the gown was ready. Manon laced my new corset, attached the *paniers* to my waist, arranged the skirts and train, and finally tied the bodice. I sat at my dressing table. She covered my shoulders with a vast cloth and proceeded to smear generous quantities of jasmine-scented cream over my hair. I opened my mouth to protest.

"If I don't put *pommade* in Your Ladyship's hair," she said, "the powder won't stick. It'll all fall on your shoulders. Now that wouldn't be too pretty. And your hair wouldn't stay up either."

I sighed and kept silent. This was the first time I had had my hair powdered and dressed in that manner. Half an hour later, it stood in a foot-high array of pinkish grey locks and curls. I thanked Manon in a tone that lacked conviction.

The Duchess nodded with satisfaction. "This is beautiful, Manon. The great Léonard himself, who attends to the Queen, could not do any better."

She sent for her jewellery case and picked diamond necklaces, bracelets, hair ornaments and earrings. She asked me to stand and tried them all on me.

"Your Grace is too good," I said. "I cannot accept—"

She raised her hand to silence me. "I am afraid you have no choice in this matter, Belle. No lady was ever presented without wearing a pound or two of borrowed diamonds."

She arranged a few more ornaments in my hair and added yet another pair of bracelets. I felt like one of those jewel-encrusted casks that display holy relics to the veneration of the faithful. Lips pursed, the Duchess stepped back to judge the effect of the stones.

"There," she said, "this should be enough. Now I will show you the gait expected of a lady at Court. Look at me, Belle, and pay close attention. See how I glide *slowly* as if I were on skates. I *barely* raise my feet off the floor."

I could not repress a smile.

She arched her eyebrow. "Now let us see you do it, dear."

I obeyed, feeling clumsy and utterly silly.

"Not quite good enough," she said. "Try again. Remember, you will be walking on the floors of Versailles, which are waxed often and can be very slippery. Also, you must be careful not to step on the train of the lady in front of you."

I bit my lip and looked at the Duchess with mingled exasperation and desperation, but she was relentless. She would not declare herself satisfied until I glided as easily in my *paniers* as I walked in my regular clothes. Then she made me practice the movements I would perform during my presentation. She played the part of the Queen, then that of the King, and I curtseyed before her until I felt weak in the knees.

"Perfect," she said after a few hours. "Shyness gives most women a sort of awkwardness, but it only makes you more graceful. This dress, which is rather dismal in itself, looks beautiful on you. These grey ribbons recall the colour of your eyes. Of course, all the ladies of the Court will notice that your attire is not new. They would find something wicked to say in any event. You are too exquisitely pretty to escape their criticism."

We had a final rehearsal. The Duchess smiled. Manon clasped her hands, a rapturous look on her round face. Aimée stared in mute amazement at the huge skirts of my gown, at my bare throat, which the Duchess's rows of diamonds did not suffice to cover, at my powdered hair, bedecked with glittering ornaments.

Before I could be presented, the Court genealogist researched my lineage and that of my late husband to verify that our nobility dated back to the year 1400. All was in order. The dreaded day came at last.

❧ 23 ❧

The Duchess and I left early on a fine Sunday morning for Versailles. I was attired in all of my new finery. She wore a black Court gown and the rest of her diamonds. Aimée, much to her chagrin, had to remain in Paris. Children, except those of the royal family, were not seen at Court. I dried her tears and assured her that I would be back very soon.

After the carriage had made its way through an army of street vendors peddling cheap mementos in front of the Palace, we passed two successive sets of gates and alighted in the courtyard reserved for Duchesses. I was awed by the size of the palace. Its wings seemed to extend forever on each side of the central building.

"I never imagined anything so gigantic," I exclaimed.

"What you see is nothing," replied the Duchess. "The main palace occupies only a small fraction of the grounds. And from here, we have not a view of either of the *Trianons*. Each is a separate château within the park of Versailles. A make-believe hamlet, complete with its grotto and farm, was also built for the Queen."

Two sedan chairs, conveyances I had never used before, had been brought for us. We gathered our trains and, with the help of the Duchess's lackeys, pushed our *paniers* into these devices. After much effort, the doors were closed on us. In that manner we were carried into the Palace and up the Marble Staircase, which led to the Queen's Great

Apartments. I felt my chair being lowered to the floor. One of the two lackeys who followed me opened the door. I was in the Hall of the Body-guards, where I saw of the Chevalier des Huttes. He looked very hand-some in his uniform, a blue coat, trimmed in silver braid, and red breeches and waistcoat. He was on duty and only bowed to me with the slightest hint of a smile. The Duchess's sedan chair, covered in red velvet to mark her rank, had been allowed to advance to the next room.

I joined her. We walked to the doors of the Salon of the Nobles, where dozens of ladies were crowded, their bulky *paniers* pressed against each other. The colours of their gowns jarred against the apple-green damask that covered the walls.

"Are you not glad to be wearing white?" whispered the Duchess. "This shade of green is the Queen's favourite colour, and this room was redone according to her directions. Now remember to stay away from the windows whenever you are in her presence. Otherwise she would think that you are flaunting the radiance of your skin. Her complexion is be-ginning to fade and she resents the freshness of younger women."

This remark helped me remember that Marie-Antoinette, though she was the Queen, was not exempt from the petty vanities shared by many women. My heartbeat quieted and my composure returned. I followed the Duchess into the salon. The crowd parted to make way for us. All eyes were on me, and not all were friendly.

At last I saw the Queen standing at the far end of the room. She was dressed in a blue gown embroidered with sapphires and diamonds. I tried to remember what my late husband had said of her. She did have an elon-gated face, a thick lower lip, bulging blue eyes and ruddy cheeks, either naturally or from too much rouge. Yet what her features lacked in fine-ness was compensated by the majesty of her countenance. She was almost as tall as I, but rather stout. Her breasts seemed ready to burst out of her glittering bodice.

The Duchess made a deep curtsey and announced: "Madam, the Bar-oness de Peyre!"

I advanced towards the Queen, pausing three times to curtsey. Then, bowing until my forehead almost touched the floor, I removed my right glove and seized the hem of the Queen's gown to bring it to my lips. The Duchess, during our rehearsals, had warned me that Her Majesty never allowed any lady to complete that part of the ritual. The Queen, with a tap of her fan, did withdraw her skirt before I had time to kiss it. I put on my glove, rose and, careful not to trip on my own train, walked backwards in the direction of the Duchess. My presentation to the Queen was over.

"You did very well, dear," whispered the Duchess.

She then led me out of the Queen's Great Apartments. Followed by our sedan chairs and lackeys, we walked, or rather glided down the *Galerie des Glaces*, named after the giant mirrors reflecting the light from seventeen windows across the long hall. I saw statues of Roman emperors, red marble columns crowned by gilded capitals and painted ceilings celebrating the victories of the reign of Louis the Fourteenth, the Great King. I exclaimed at the number of courtiers, visitors and servants we met.

"Oh, you should have seen Versailles at the time of its glory," remarked the Duchess. "Because of the budget troubles, much of the Households of the King and Queen has been dismissed now."

We reached the King's Bedchamber. A balustrade separated the bed, raised on a dais and draped in red and gold brocade, from a larger area for the reception of the courtiers. There stood a portly man among the lords of his retinue. He wore a huge diamond decoration, the star of the Order of the Holy Ghost, on his silver-embroidered coat. I had seen his sloping forehead, bulbous nose and receding chin on countless coins. His protuberant blue eyes, oddly similar to the Queen's, seemed lost in a fog. I recalled my late husband saying that the King was a man of great learning and intelligence. Appearances can indeed be deceptive.

The First Gentleman of the Bedchamber announced my name. I made another three deep curtseys before the King. Again my forehead brushed against the carpet. At least the étiquette did not require me to kiss any part of His Majesty's clothing. He seized me rather awkwardly by the shoulders, raised me to my feet and embraced me in silence. The Duchess had told me that the late King, famous for his appreciation of female beauty, had always said a few gracious words of welcome on such occasions, but that Louis the Sixteenth often remained mute, especially if the presented lady happened to be pretty.

I was then taken to the apartments of Madame Elisabeth, the King's youngest sister, and likewise presented to her. She was a bit obese like her brother, whom she much resembled. She smiled at me and embraced me in a friendly manner. I would have had to repeat the same ceremony with each of the other members of the royal family, had not they been absent from Versailles that day. At last my presentation was over.

We repaired to the *Salon du Grand Couvert* to attend Their Majesties' dinner. They sat side by side, facing the crowd of courtiers. A row of stools was disposed for Duchesses in a circle ten feet in front of the royal table. My friend sat on one of them while I stood behind her. I was amused to note that the King, his face buried in his plate, noisily devoured dozens of consommés, patés, meats, entremets and desserts, while the Queen did not touch her food at all. She did not even unfold her napkin or remove her gloves. At no time did the royal couple exchange any look or word. Finally the King drained his last glass of wine. He bowed to the Queen and the company to take his leave.

The Duchess remarked that it was time to think of our own dinner. She led me to the apartments of Madame de Polignac, Governess to the Royal Children and the Queens' favourite. I was introduced to her. She was very pretty when one looked straight at her face, but her nose was almost flat and her chin receding. Her profile reminded me of that of a rabbit. Like the other main courtiers, she held open tables in her apartments. Throngs of guests were gathered there for refreshments. Both men and women looked at me in a pointed manner. I heard people ask about me in very audible whispers. Men commented on my personal attributes, and women on my attire. The Duchess d'Arpajon introduced me to many more people. I was by then utterly confused and could not remember anyone's name or title.

Hundreds of dishes were displayed in enormous platters disposed on buffets behind us. Bottles of sweet white wines chilled in silver buckets. We sat at a table while the Duchess's lackeys stood behind our chairs, ready to bring us the drinks and dishes of our choice. We ate patés of foie gras, mushroom crepes, sweetbreads with asparagus, and, for dessert, cream puffs and chocolate mousse, accompanied by Sauternes wine.

After finishing our meal, we returned to the *Galerie des Glaces*, the Hall of Mirrors, where we curtseyed to the Queen again. She seemed more gracious now and honoured the company with a smile. The King waddled by her side, his sword beating awkwardly against his leg at each of his steps. Madame de Polignac followed with the two eldest royal children: Madame Royale, a plump little girl of eight or nine, and the Dauphin, Louis-Joseph, heir to the throne. I was shocked when the Duchess reminded me that he was five, for he was very small for his age. The little prince had a drawn, yellow face and the bent posture of an old man. I felt pity for the Queen and her son. I cannot think of a more cruel fate for a mother than to see her child waste away before her eyes.

That night we attended the Queen's gaming salon. She was seated at a card table, quite different from the woman I had seen before. Here, she was alive, enthralled by the game, the rules of which were unknown to me. All I understood, from the quantity of gold *louis* piled in front of each player and in the middle of the table, was that the stakes were very high. The Duchess de Polignac occupied the chair next to the Queen's. The two friends were whispering to each other and giggling like schoolgirls. A handsome man was seated to the other side of Madame de Polignac.

"He is the Count de Vaudreuil, the Duchess's bosom friend," whispered the Duchess d'Arpajon.

"What about the Duke de Polignac? Does he mind?"

"He stays out of his wife's way and knows better than to care about such trifling matters."

Madame de Polignac looked at me and said something to the Queen's ear. Her Majesty smiled at her friend and addressed me.

"Madam, will you not sit? The Count de Vaudreuil will gladly surrender his place to you."

I obeyed, my heart beating fast. There were but two gold *louis* of twenty-four francs each in my pocket.

"Why, Baroness," said the Queen, "do you not play?" Her manner had become haughty again.

I took a deep breath. "Your Majesty is very kind, but I have neither a taste for games of cards nor the means to indulge in them."

The whole room became silent. After what seemed a very long pause, the Queen said: "How odd! What do you like then, Baroness?"

"I enjoy music and riding, Madam, and more particularly reading."

Madame de Polignac chuckled while the Queen shrugged and turned her attention back to the cards without paying me any further attention. I heard whispers and giggles behind my back. I rose and curtseyed to the Queen as soon as the game was over.

"Would Your Grace mind if we retired?" I asked the Duchess. "I feel exhausted."

"It is still early for a young person like you. The Queen will probably keep gambling all night long."

"I will not. To tell you the truth, Madam, I have never felt so mortified in my life."

The Duchess laughed. "Come, Belle, I hope you will not let that little conversation ruin your evening. In fact, I cannot think of anything more to the point than what you said. But let us retire if you wish."

The Duchess's daughter, the Marquise de Bastide, was a lady-in-waiting to the King's sister-in-law. That function entitled her to lodgings within the Palace itself, a rare and coveted favour. She was, as the other ladies with positions at Court, on duty one week out of three. The Marquise de Bastide happened to be on leave, enjoying the pleasures of Paris, which she relished far more than her functions in Versailles. Her absence allowed us to use her lodgings, which consisted of two tiny rooms under the eaves, with a sort of shelf in a closet where Mélanie, the Duchess's chambermaid, was to sleep. The stench of nearby privies permeated the place.

The Duchess, before going to bed, asked me whether I wanted to spend a few more days at Court.

"My daughter will not resume her service until next week," she said, "so we can follow your inclination and remain here if you wish."

"If Your Grace does not mind, I am ready to return to Paris tomorrow morning. I have never been separated from Aimée for long. Besides, I displayed the most perfect imbecility tonight in front of the Queen and the whole Court. I do not look forward to meeting Her Majesty or Madame de Polignac again."

"I should have warned you, poor dear. The Queen dislikes *pedantic women*. It is what she calls ladies who have read any book from cover to cover. I do not think that she can claim to have done so herself. Neither can her friend Madame de Polignac, which did not prevent her from being appointed Governess to the Royal Children. She, who can barely write her own name!"

The Duchess shook her head. "Furthermore, the Queen has squandered millions at cards. You could not have hit closer to the heart than you did by expressing your disdain for gambling and your love of reading. Do not worry, Belle. What you said will not make the Queen your friend, but by the end of tomorrow you will be the talk of the city."

"I am not sure this is the sort of fame I wish to attain."

"Better this kind than none at all, my dear." She sat on the bed and patted it to invite me to join her. "Apart from the little incident in the gaming salon, what did you think of the Queen?"

"Well, she looked and acted very much like a queen. Her manner was haughty. She barely seemed to see me or anyone else."

"She is shortsighted as a mole, dear Belle, in more ways than one. Her manners are indeed insolent, although they used to be far worse. When she arrived in France as a bride twenty years ago, she stated publicly that she did not understand how anyone over thirty dared show one's face at Court. Look at her now: she is well past that mark herself and does not seem a day younger than her age. And I will never forget the official condolences visit following the death of the late King Louis the Fifteenth, in 1774. The Queen was laughing so hard at me and the other *centuries*, as she called us ancient ladies, that she had to hide her face behind her fan."

I frowned. "That was very unbecoming, Madam, just after the late King's death too."

"And the Queen was twenty then. She should have known better. You are but seventeen, Belle, but I cannot imagine you acting in such a manner."

The door to the apartment next to ours slammed. We heard the voices of a man and a woman, obviously in high spirits. I was reminded of my evenings with my late husband. My body stiffened with the memory. But this lady seemed to be enjoying herself more than I had ever done. Her encouragements and praise were followed by less distinct but still lively exclamations. Her lover, from all appearances a man of few words, soon joined his moans to hers before bellowing with satisfaction. That, however, only interrupted the proceedings without concluding them and the happy couple continued their entertainment late into the night. The Duchess and I could follow in the minutest detail their conversation, which put an end to ours.

≈ 24 ≈

The next morning, I was happy to settle by the Duchess's side in the carriage.

"We will call on my daughter," she said as soon as it was in motion, "and tell her what happened. You know that she is a lady-in-waiting to Madame, the Countess de Provence, who is married to the King's brother. You would have been presented to her yesterday if she had been in Versailles. She will, no doubt, be impatient to make your acquaintance, for she cannot abide the Queen."

"Why not?"

"The Queen thinks of herself as the prettiest woman at Court, and never lets her sister-in-law forget it. Not that Madame, who is indeed no beauty, has any delusions in that regard, but she does not like to be reminded too often of her own plainness."

"It is certainly unkind, and unwise, of the Queen to offend her sister-in-law. What about the other members of the royal family?"

"The Countess d'Artois, who is married to the King's youngest brother, has not much to recommend herself. She causes quite a bit of scandal by her liaisons with the Bodyguards assigned to her service. Some say that her last pregnancy has no other origin."

I gasped in horror. "Is the Chevalier des Huttes—"

The Duchess laughed. "Oh no, dear, I did not mean our friend the Chevalier, of course." She became grave again. "As to the rest of the royal family, they seldom set foot in Versailles, except for state occasions. The Queen herself now hates the Court. She spends as much time as she can in her little château of Trianon, her own private retreat within the grounds of Versailles. She receives only the Duchess de Polignac and her clique there, in addition to the handsome Fersen, of course. Sometimes she also invites Madame Elisabeth, the King's sister, to whom you were presented yesterday. A delightful person, on good terms with everyone. To give you an idea of Madame Elisabeth's generosity, three years ago, she asked the King to forego her New Year's Day present, in order to give her friend, Mademoiselle de Causans, a dowry of 150,000 francs."

"What happened to that Mademoiselle de Causans?"

"She was able to marry the Marquis de Raigecourt, my dear."

"Would he not have married her without her 150,000 francs?"

"Probably not, and such a dowry is not extraordinary. When the Duchess de Polignac's daughter was married, at the age of twelve, to the Duke de Guiche, the Queen requested that the Treasury give the little bride a dowry of 800,000 francs. That is considered high, especially in the current state of the public finances, but there is not a thing the Duchess de Polignac would not obtain from the Queen."

I looked out the window. "So, Madam, what do you think of my chances of remarrying with less than 3,000 francs to my name?"

"To be candid, dear Belle, I think they are slim, unless of course some man loses his head over you, which is always possible."

"The Chevalier des Huttes seemed to think that I could find a husband in Paris."

"If he had any sense at all, he would marry you himself. I have not failed to point this out to him. Where will he find a woman with one tenth of your beauty, your understanding and your sweetness of temper? You would have him if he proposed, would you not?"

"Maybe," I said, blushing.

"You do not fool me, dearest. Of course you would. I cannot forgive him for being such an idiot. The truth is that he is in love with the Queen."

I stared at the Duchess.

"Do not look at me like this, Belle," she added. "She does have that effect on certain men. Do you know why the Chevalier brought you to Paris? He thought you might attract the Queen's benevolent attention. She would indeed gain much by having you as a friend. But the stunted mind of a money-hungry simpleton like Madame de Polignac is what she can grasp. You have nothing to regret, my dear. If the Queen had displayed the slightest hint of a liking for you, the Polignac clique would have thought of some scheme to discredit you in her eyes before the day was over. You have no experience of Court intrigues, and you would not have known what was happening to you."

"My late husband told me that the Duke de Lauzun and the Count de Fersen were the Queen's lovers. Is it true?"

"Only they know," said the Duchess. "What is certain is that the Queen used to be very, very favorably inclined towards Lauzun before he left for the American War. She gave him public marks of her favour and could not bear to spend a day without seeing him. She has become much less friendly towards him. These days, she cares for no one but Fersen. He is admitted several times a week in the Queen's private apartments at Trianon, while enjoying the company of less elegant females on his days of leisure in Paris. The difference between Fersen and Lauzun is that Fersen does not flaunt his successes with other ladies. He always keeps in public that cold manner which so well matches the Queen's." The Duchess shrugged. "Fersen is a hypocrite, like all of those foreigners who presume to criticize the freedom, or the looseness, as they call it, of French morals."

I had already abandoned any hopes of obtaining a place at Court. Versailles did not seem to agree with my temperament. The other option considered by the Chevalier des Huttes, which was to remarry, sounded equally unlikely. I hoped that the Duchess was wrong about my prospects. After all, when I was fifteen, two men had been prepared to take me without a *sol*.

A letter was waiting for me in Paris. Madame de Montserrat, my sister, had responded, which in itself astonished me. I opened the missive, my hands trembling.

> *Thank you, dearest sister, for your letter. I had heard such contradictory accounts of you as to be unable to form any opinion of you. Madeleine had sent word that you had disgraced yourself and the family by eloping with one of Géraud's friends. Then I learned that you were staying in Paris with our cousin the Duchess d'Arpajon, whose reputation is above reproach.*
>
> *I understand your decision not to enter religious life, I even approve of it. I remained a novice myself for three full years before taking my final vows at sixteen, a choice I never regretted. I have found within the walls of Noirvaux a peace that would have eluded me in any other place. Your situation, however, is different. Your letter did not seem to indicate that you are at all prepared to renounce the world. Believe me, the call, when one receives it, is unmistakable. That time may come for you too, perhaps sooner than you expect, but it is clear that you have not been granted that grace yet.*
>
> *What I propose is that you come and visit our community whenever you like. For one thing, as a selfish creature, for one remains selfish or becomes more so in a convent, I will be delighted to meet you at last. You were but an infant when I left Fontfreyde forever, and the last memory I have of you is that of a baby of three weeks in your nurse's arms when she took you away. You already had hair the same colour as mine, much to poor Mother's despair.*
>
> *Moreover, a retreat here, if only of a few weeks, could help you become better acquainted with your real wishes and needs. Prayer works wonders.*

Please continue writing.

May God keep you, dearest sister, under His holy and worthy protection.

✝ *Hélène, Abbess de Noirvaux*

To say that I was delighted with that letter would fall short of describing my feelings. I was impatient to meet Madame de Montserrat and decided to avail myself of her offer as soon as my Paris engagements slowed with the advent of the summer.

✌ 25 ✌

The Chevalier des Huttes called a few days after our return from Versailles. The Duchess had gone out to visit her daughter and Aimée was napping. He was clearly embarrassed.

"You seem to have heard of my debut at Court," I said, smiling. "Please rest easy. My vanity has already recovered."

"It was my fault." The Chevalier bit his lip. "I should have warned you of what to expect. It grieves me to think that, though the Queen is goodness itself, she does not know how to show it. There is not a kinder, more amiable person within her private circle."

"I am sure that you are right. You have known her for many years. I just have the misfortune to be outside her private circle. Please do not worry about me."

"How can I help it? I feel a great deal of responsibility towards you, My Lady. I was the one who brought you here, leading you to expect things that may never happen."

"You are too harsh on yourself, dear Chevalier. You did not promise anything except to deliver me safely to the Duchess's house." I looked out the window. "Did you know that I wrote Madame de Montserrat and that she responded? She invited me to Noirvaux for a retreat."

"I am glad to hear it, My Lady, and will be happy to take you there whenever you wish."

"You are very kind, as usual. In your opinion, Sir, would the Marquis think less ill of me if he knew that I intend to go visit our sister? Do you think he will ever forgive me for moving to Paris?"

"I do not believe that he has forgiven either of us. Yet, My Lady, he may be mollified if he hears that you are going to Noirvaux, even for a short visit."

The Chevalier looked at me gravely. "He has his fair share of worries these days: the situation in Auvergne is less peaceful than it used to be. You have, of course, heard of the new municipal assemblies that will now govern all the parishes. The Marquis presides over that of Lavigerie, as is his right as the titular lord of the town. But then Jean-Baptiste Coffin-hal, his former attorney, who is now the main landowner there, had the insolence to refuse to let the Marquis participate in the deliberations, al-legedly because he can only represent the interests of the nobility and not those of the commoners! What an outrage!" The Chevalier shook his head sadly. "I could have imagined such insult from the younger Cof-finhal, but I expected better from his elder brother."

I could not hear Pierre-André's name without a pang. It seemed that his whole family had now espoused his quarrel with my brother. I knew that my former suitor lived in Paris and often wondered whether he was aware of my presence in town. I never passed the massive towers of the *Grand Châtelet*, half a mile from the Duchess's mansion, without thinking of him. I pictured him in one of the courtrooms at that very moment.

It would have been easy to discover his whereabouts. Many times I was tempted to call on him. I was always stopped by the fear of finding him resentful, hostile, contemptuous or, worse, indifferent. I did not want to hear him say that he no longer cared for me, to face the pain, the humiliation of having him turn me out of his chambers.

Also, since I intend to tell the plain truth in these memoirs, I will not deny that, since we had last met, I had absorbed some of the prejudices of my class. I was a Baroness, albeit a penniless one. I associated only with aristocrats. Not all were wealthy, but all lived in a world of luxury, of idleness, of parties, of pleasure, which was becoming mine. A liaison between a commoner and a noblewoman, a notion that had seemed com-pletely natural to me at fifteen, would have been very odd to them. It had not even entered the Chevalier's mind, when he had brought me to Paris, that I might be tempted to renew with my former suitor.

There may have been still another, maybe more compelling reason: my remembrance of Pierre-André was associated with the season of my life when I had been forced to forsake him and all of my hopes. It would have been unbearable to bring back the anguish of my engagement to a man I had loathed, of those terrible first weeks of my marriage. Time had passed, but the pain of those memories was as fresh as ever.

Whatever the reason, I did not avail myself of the opportunity I now had to meet Pierre-André Coffinhal, when only a few years earlier I would have bartered my soul to run away with him.

26

Not many weeks elapsed before the Viscount de Rivière, one of the Duchess's friends, began to show a lively interest in me.

"Everybody is talking of the opera *Tarare*, which is to open on the 8th," he said. "Salieri has composed it in an entirely novel style. I would be delighted if Your Ladyship allowed me to offer you my box at the Opera for that occasion. I would be honoured to accompany you, and the Duchess, of course."

On the appointed evening, he sent word, with his deepest apologies and regrets, that he was detained in Versailles at the last minute by his duties. The Duchess and I went to the Opera by ourselves in her carriage. I was in a flutter of excitement as we settled in our box, for I had never witnessed such an entertainment before. The air carried the scent of natural flowers and heady perfumes. The din of the conversations from the audience mingled with the sound of the violins being tuned in the orchestra pit. I eagerly looked at the embroidered gowns of the other ladies, hoping that my own attire, a plain white satin dress, was not inadequate for the occasion. I was not wearing any jewellery except for my ruby earrings and wedding band. A few white roses were my sole hair ornament. I noticed two ladies, both glittering with diamonds, taking their seats in a neighbouring box. They were attended by three gentlemen.

All three soon joined us. The Duchess curtseyed to the largest, whose face was covered with red blotches, pustules and pimples. Otherwise he looked very much, in features and corpulence, like the King. I was introduced. He was His Highness the Duke d'Orléans, cousin to His Majesty, recently returned from England. The second man was the famous Duke de Lauzun, about forty years of age, uncommonly handsome and well aware of it. The third one was the Count de Villers. His hair, like that of his companions, was powdered white but his eyebrows were blonde, with a reddish tinge, and pale freckles covered the bridge of his nose and his upper lip. I had never seen such colouring in Auvergne. Another detail surprised me about his person: he was wearing large gold earrings. At the time, noblemen had stopped fancying those ornaments, which tended to be favoured only by the lower classes, in particular sailors and soldiers.

The three visitors sat with us and conversed in a friendly manner with the Duchess, all the time openly eyeing me. I could see the two ladies left behind in the other box also staring at me through their opera glasses. The men did not leave until well after the overture started, which somewhat spoiled my enjoyment of the first act.

"Do you know them well?" I whispered to the Duchess's ear.

"Quite well, dear Belle, but they would never have come here tripping over each other if it were not for your presence. They are not interested in a wizened old woman like me. It is you they have in mind."

"Who are the two ladies in that box? Are they married to these gentlemen?"

The Duchess tapped my wrist with her fan. "You are so funny, dear. Her Highness the Duchess d'Orléans is never seen with her husband, except on state occasions. As to the Duke and Duchess de Lauzun, they have been separated almost as long as they have been married. He squandered his fortune, which was colossal, and part of hers too, on women, gambling and race horses. He is now waiting to inherit a fresh one from his uncle the Duke de Biron. I told you of Lauzun already: in addition to winning the favour of the Queen, he was one of the heroes of the Battle of Yorktown during the American independence war. The English forces led by Colonel Tarleton insisted on surrendering to the *French Duke*, as they called him, and his dashing hussars, rather than to the bedraggled American army. As a reward for his exceptional bravery under fire, Lauzun was chosen to bring the news of the victory to Paris."

The Duchess grinned. "He took advantage of his return here to bed Mrs. Robinson, one of the Prince of Wales's mistresses, thus inflicting a second defeat of sorts on the British. You should know that Lauzun is a regular Don Juan and does not shy away from cuckolding royalty. They say that no woman has ever resisted him. Beware of him, dear Belle, for I am sure that he must be already thinking of adding you to his *tableau de chasse*. He is not discreet either: the entire town knows of his victory the day after he storms the castle. Yet his lack of tact does not seem to impede his further success. Listen to me, a spiteful old woman, for if he showed any interest in me, I would be sure to have him on the spot."

A female singer had reached the end of an aria.

"So, Madam," I asked, "who are the ladies in that box?"

"They are both mistresses to the Duke d'Orléans, dear. The one who is not so young anymore, with the stork's neck, is a Scotswoman, Lady Elliott. He brought her back from England. She has a daughter by the Prince of Wales, but she left the little bastard child behind in that country. She did not wish to encumber herself with that kind of baggage, I suppose. The Duke d'Orléans seems to have grown tired of her. He is now seen quite often with the other lady, the Countess de Buffon, who is much fresher. She cannot be more than a few years older than you. Yet from the way he was looking at you, I am sure he would not mind neglecting either or both of these women if you gave him the slightest encouragement."

I winced. "I do not think, Madam, that I ever beheld anyone so repulsive. These ladies must not be very fastidious in their tastes."

"Well, the Duke d'Orléans is a prince of the royal blood and, after the King, the richest man in the kingdom, with a yearly income of six million. We drove past his palace in town, the *Palais-Royal*. He had several levels of shops built around his gardens. Because the place belongs to a member of the royal family, it is exempt from the surveillance of the police. So his tenants comprise gaming parlours, print shops that specialize in seditious or lewd literature, and of course the most luxurious houses of convenience in Paris."

"I cannot understand why anyone so rich would want to derive part of his income from such trades. What about the third man?"

"Villers? He is not as handsome as Lauzun, nor is he as rich as the Duke d'Orléans, but he owns a good part of Normandy and is very mindful of his money. He can act a bit wild once in a while, but never loses his head. There was talk of him being on friendly terms with my daughter last year, but he seems to have offended her by paying much attention to a visiting English lady. I make it a rule, however, never to espouse my children's quarrels."

"Is he married too?"

"He has been widowed as long as I can remember and seems content with his situation. He is a libertine, like his friends. They are after the same thing, all three of them. Believe me, dear, it is not your hand in marriage."

My attention returned to the opera. I found it fascinating once I became accustomed to the oddity of seeing people walking onto the stage and singing instead of behaving like sensible human beings. The end of the first act brought back the three gentlemen. The ladies, again abandoned, were whispering to each other while looking at me in a rather pointed manner. The Duke d'Orléans placed himself to my right, which made me uneasy. I could not help wondering whether his skin condition was infectious. The Duchess kindly moved away to leave empty the seat to my left. Lauzun and Villers jostled to occupy it.

"Give way to superior rank," said Lauzun.

"Who cares about rank?" replied Villers. "You may be a Brigadier General, but I am not in the service anymore. The Baroness has no use for a beggar like you." He turned to me. "Your Ladyship should tell him to return to my box and to attend to the other ladies."

I smiled. "I would not presume to do so. Why, Sir, do you not settle this dispute by the toss of a coin?"

It was meant in jest, but Villers reached into his waistcoat pocket. He won. Lauzun complained of foul play.

"You are whining, Lauzun," said the prince. "What a pitiful idea the poor Baroness must have of you."

"Quite," said Villers. "Your Highness is right, as usual."

He sat next to me with a satisfied look. "What do you think of tonight's entertainment, My Lady?"

"This is the first time I have the pleasure to watch an opera, Sir. I am delighted with it."

"An *ingénue* and a dowager, all in one. And musical too. Quite unusual, I dare say."

"Yes, I do love music and hope to hear more of it now that I live in Paris."

"Then my box will always be at your service and that of Her Grace. But I will be sure not to invite Lauzun. I am ashamed of his manners."

I smiled. "You need not worry, Sir. I do not know either of you well enough to distinguish between your manners and those of your friend."

Villers turned to Lauzun, who had taken a seat behind me. "Did you hear? Now, in the eyes of the Baroness, I am tainted by association. I would be honoured if Your Ladyship, with the Duchess, of course, could join us for supper later tonight at my house."

"You are very kind, Sir, but Her Grace was telling me not long ago that she feels rather tired."

"I am sorry to hear it. I will call on her tomorrow then, with her permission."

The Duchess could not repress a smile.

꧁ 27 ꧂

The next morning, the Duchess and I rose later than usual and chatted about the opera over a breakfast of tea and croissants. That delicacy had been introduced to France by the Queen upon her arrival from Vienna. We had settled with our reading in the drawing room when the Count de Villers was announced by one of the footmen. After the usual exchange of bows, curtseys and compliments, the conversation turned to one of the Duchess's acquaintances.

"Did you know, Villers," she said, "that the Viscount de Dorval just purchased an estate fifty leagues from Paris, and that he intends to take his wife there? He wants to keep her away from what he calls the corrupt morals of this town! The poor thing visited us yesterday and was inconsolable at the idea of being buried alive in some provincial château."

"Madame de Dorval is a lady of unimpeachable virtue," said Villers, "who never did anything to justify such severity. Did I tell Your Grace about an innocent trick Lauzun and I played on Dorval a few years ago, before he married Mademoiselle de Moret, as she was then called, and her 60,000 francs a year?"

"I remember hearing about it, but you must regale me with the full tale."

"Dorval had been engaged for a few months and his absurd jealousy was already the sport of the entire Court and town. Lauzun and I could not resist the temptation to have some fun at his expense. Since my ears are pierced and I am more slender than my friend, we agreed that I should be the one to play the female character in this prank. We shaved the three hairs on my chest, for, although they were blonde, they would have detracted from my ladylike appearance. The good Madame de Croisy, after being taken into our confidence, had the kindness to lend me a fine pair of diamond earrings and one of her Court dresses, one foot too short for me and quite suitable to make me look like a fool. I was duly coiffed and rouged by one of her chambermaids."

His eyes sparkled. "Thus beautified, I sailed forth into the kitchens of Marly. The Court still went there at the time. I proceeded to kiss every-one, down to the lowest rag washer, on the mouth, act in the most im-modest manner and generally make an ass of myself. Lauzun, meanwhile, ran to Dorval to warn him that Mademoiselle de Moret was committing a thousand follies in the kitchens and was believed to be at the very mo-ment in the passionate embraces of a scullion. You know that Dorval, as Equerry to the King, is in charge of the stables. In his fury, he went there forthwith, ordered all of the grooms to fetch their whips for a punitive expedition and placed himself at their head to storm the kitchens. A regular battle took place between the stable boys and the cooks, the out-come of which was very much to the disadvantage of the kitchen. I watched the engagement from the safety of a cupboard but was unfor-tunately prevented, conspicuous as I was, from leaving the field on the heels of the victors. That almost cost me dearly. The cooks, once aware of my disguise and the part I had played in their defeat, chased me around a table with their knives, threatening to perform a certain operation on me. I was unarmed, outnumbered and impeded in my flight by my *paniers*."

He chuckled. "Lauzun had arrived with Dorval's troops to watch the commotion. He howled with laughter at my plight instead of coming to my rescue. I reached him and was able to draw his sword to keep the rabble at bay. The King's dinner was somewhat in disarray that day, but when His Majesty was told of the reason, he found it an excellent joke, although, as you know, he is exceedingly fond of his food. It would have been a pity to send Lauzun or me to the Bastille for such a trifle. We were young and thoughtless then."

The Duchess was laughing aloud. Torn between amusement and in-dignation, I dared not look at Villers.

"What about Dorval?" asked the Duchess, tears of merriment still in her eyes. "Did he also find it an excellent joke?"

"Your Grace knows him. He can be tiresome about questions of honour. He demanded reparation and I had to meet him the next morning at dawn in the Bois de Boulogne. I gave him a flesh wound in the arm, after which he declared himself satisfied."

I felt Villers turning to me. "You do not seem amused, My Lady," he remarked.

I looked at him. "If I had been Mademoiselle de Moret," I said, "I would not have liked to have my name bandied in such a manner. In my opinion it was you, Sir, and the Duke de Lauzun, not the kitchen boys, who deserved to be whipped."

He grinned. "Indeed you are right. Thanks to you, Madam, I now see my behaviour in an entirely different light. It is not too late for me to receive what I deserve. I would gladly, nay, eagerly, submit to a serious flogging, provided of course that it be inflicted by you."

I felt colour rising into my cheeks. "Then, Sir, your conduct shall remain unpunished. It will not be the first time, I am sure."

"You have a poor opinion of me. I have no one but myself to blame for it, I suppose. I was trying to impress a new acquaintance with my cleverness, and instead I look like a fool and a scoundrel in the eyes of a lady."

"I would be surprised if it were a new occurrence either," I said, smiling.

"Dear Belle," said the Duchess, "I find you very harsh on poor Villers."

"Nothing that I did not deserve," he replied. "I intend from now on to call here, with Your Grace's permission, with great regularity. I wish to receive a daily scolding from the Baroness. Nothing could do me more good. Within months, maybe weeks, Madam, you will be amazed by the improvement of my conduct."

"I am sure, Sir," I said, "that your conduct is well beyond any reform that my censure could ever accomplish. You will make a better use of your time with ladies who appreciate your high spirits."

"I have been calling on such ladies for years, Madam, and look at the result! Besides, I am becoming tired of their society. *You* may succeed where so many have failed, in making me see the error of my ways."

"I cannot believe it. You seem very fond of your ways. Further, I may lack the inclination to take that sort of trouble for you."

He raised his eyebrows. "Do you mean, My Lady, that I am not even worthy of being scolded? Duchess, please intercede for me with your cruel friend."

"Dear Belle, Villers is right. This is not fair. You may not upbraid him while denying him the guidance he so humbly seeks from you."

"Monsieur de Villers is mocking me, Madam, and has no use for my guidance. Yet if you take his side, I will relent."

"It is settled, then," said Villers. "With Your Grace's permission, I will call again tomorrow." He turned to me. "I will convince you, Madam, that not only do I care about your good opinion, but also that I can secure it."

"You will tire of my society long before you reach this goal."

"Time shall tell, Madam."

I heard from another of the gentlemen from the Opera before the day was over. A letter, sealed with green wax, awaited me on my pillow that night. It contained the most ardent professions of love from the Duke de Lauzun, and told of grave illness, if not prompt death, threatening its author if he found me too cruel. I did not let it worry me in that regard.

I told the Duchess about it the next morning, without showing it to her. She laughed.

"Congratulations, Belle, you made at least one conquest already, and not a mean one. Did I not tell you? Dear Lauzun, he never wastes any time and I am sure that he is quite a writer. He always means what he says. That is why he is so persuasive."

"I am anything but persuaded, Madam. What concerns me is that his letter found its way to my bedroom. Do you think the Duke bribed one of your servants?"

"Can you think of any other explanation, dearest?"

"Do you not wish to know who it is?"

"I am afraid it would be futile. Assuming that I were able to discover the culprit, I would have to hire an equally corruptible replacement for him or her."

I resolved to lock my door before going to bed lest the servant who was accommodating enough to bring me Monsieur de Lauzun's correspondence took the further liberty of giving him nightly access to the Duchess's house in general and to my apartment in particular. A steady stream of letters followed. I opened them out of curiosity, to see whether he would send me duplicates in the belief that I would tire of reading them. He never did. I concluded that he must have copied, with minor modifications, letters from a prior affair.

The Duchess was right: he had much to say on the chapter of his feelings and was without any doubt a prolific writer. All of his eloquence, however, failed to touch me. He was a married man. I could not have allowed myself to consider for a second the thought of becoming attached to him.

ᴥ 28 ᴥ

During the summer of 1787, the Duchess and I returned to Versailles on a few Sundays. Neither of us found much pleasure in those outings, and I in particular could not go there without mortifying memories intruding upon my mind. We avoided the Queen's gaming salon and never stayed overnight. The Duchess nevertheless pointed out that, in my situation, I needed to meet as many people as possible and would be unwise to shun the Court altogether.

We would wait among a crowd of other ladies in the Salon of the Nobles, the green room where I had been presented. At noon, the doors to the Queen's Bedchamber flew open. As in the King's apartment, a balustrade divided the room into two areas, one for the giant gilded bed, draped in heavy silks embroidered with flowers, peacock feathers and lilac branches, and the other for the Queen to greet her visitors. We seldom stayed more than a few moments, for many other ladies, their huge *paniers* pressing against our own, awaited their chance to be noticed by the Queen. We soon retreated to the Salon of the Nobles.

The King appeared before one o'clock to lead the Queen to the Royal Chapel. The Duchess and I joined the ladies who glided behind in rows of four. We were ever mindful of the others' trains and hoped that no one would step on ours. The King and Queen would pause on their way to say a few words to the most favoured courtiers. The Duchess always insisted that I walk at the outside of our row of ladies. Thus some of the gentlemen waiting for the royal cortege would step forward and whisper compliments to my ear.

Once in the Salon of Hercules, which led to the entrance to the Royal

Chapel, the Duchess would beckon to her lackey. The man was posted there among a crowd of his fellow servants, all carrying the gold-tasseled red velvet bags that held their mistresses' prayer books. The King and Queen entered the Chapel. It was the cue for the ladies to pick up their trains and rush forward, for any woman who had been presented could hear Mass from the upper galleries on either side of the royal family. There was no more graceful gliding. The ladies jostled, with the help of their lackeys, to secure the seats closest to the King and Queen. Sometimes I pictured my friend and myself trampled under the feet of that elegant mob. The melee subsided at last. We could then sit, arrange our *paniers*, put away our trains and retrieve our prayer books from the depths of the red velvet bag. By that time Mass was already well under way. The Duchess and I found those devotions devoid of spiritual comfort. We preferred to attend Sunday High Mass in Saint Paul-Saint Louis, her parish church in the *Marais* district.

In terms of society too, I liked Paris better than Versailles. In the capital, the new fashion for ladies was to forego hair powder and to wear straw bonnets and simple dresses of white muslin during the day. This suited my finances very well. Instead of the blue sashes favoured by other women, I would choose bright pink ones, while decorating my hats with matching ribbons to highlight the colour of my hair. Most gentlemen, however, still used powder. Only a few wore their hair black, straight and untied, as I remembered Pierre-André had done. These were already called "patriots" and deemed dangerous enemies of the established order of things.

The Duchess took me to parties given by her friends. Some were regular dinners, some informal suppers after the play, the ballet or the opera, and others musical gatherings, where both professional and amateur performers displayed their talents. I was often pressed to sing, which, out of shyness, I avoided as much as I could without appearing affected or ungracious. Impromptu dances often concluded the pleasures of the evening. The Bishop of Autun, Monsieur de Talleyrand, who has since achieved such fame as a diplomat, once said: "Who has not known that time has not known the sweetness of living." It was indeed sweet, although that sweetness was not to last.

The company at those gatherings was carefully chosen, with the most famous painters, singers, composers and writers of the time mingling with people of noble and sometimes royal birth. I made the acquaintance of Mr. Jefferson, Ambassador of the new United States to France. He was a tall man with polished manners and an interesting conversation. I imparted my opinion of him to the Duchess.

"Oh yes, Belle," she said, "he is a fine man, but he is no match for his predecessor, Dr. Benjamin Franklin. A pity you did not meet him. Everyone in Paris, especially the ladies, was enamored of him. He popped up everywhere in his plain clothes, with his bald pate, sometimes crowned by a raccoon's cap. So brilliant, so eccentric, so fascinating a man. Did you know that the Countess Diane de Polignac, sister-in-law to the Queen's favourite, was so infatuated with him that the King became irritated? His Majesty presented her with a porcelain chamber pot, the bottom of which was adorned with Dr. Franklin's picture."

I laughed. "I am indeed sorry not to have met him. He must be quite a man to inspire such jealousy."

"He is, dearest, he is."

Manners in good society were very modest. It would have been the height of insolence for a gentleman to touch, even briefly, any part of a sofa occupied by a lady, let alone to sit next to her, or to offer her his arm for a walk. Only husbands or brothers were allowed those familiarities. Lovers avoided them at all costs. The English custom of shaking hands, especially between persons of different sexes, was considered so vulgar as to be ridiculous. Conversations, however, were freer than anything I had heard before in company.

Upon one occasion, at the end of a supper party, Villers praised the King and his two younger brothers. "The divine providence has been kind to these august princes. Each has been endowed with a particular gift: His Majesty is a skilled locksmith, the Count de Provence a coffee-house wit, and the Count d'Artois a good lover."

That was, of course, a reference to the King's passion for the art of locksmithing, which attracted the derision of the Court, and an allusion to the alleged impotence of both His Majesty and the Count de Provence. The Count d'Artois had apparently been spared that family curse. Everyone laughed except me.

I blushed and could not help asking: "How did you form your opinion of the Count d'Artois, Sir? Do you speak from personal experience?"

Villers smiled at me. "I have not that honour, Madam. Neither His Highness nor I suffer from *the little defect*: both of us prefer the intimate company of the fair sex. But I will not leave your first question unanswered: I heard that assessment of the Count d'Artois from several ladies of my acquaintance, whom of course I may not name."

I looked away to hide my embarrassment.

Once I overcame my initial shyness, I enjoyed society. During my marriage, my pleasure in company had always been marred by the dread of the Baron's jealousy and the anticipation of his wrath. I was now free to feel and express delight at the numerous amusements Paris offered me.

My conversation with the Queen in her gambling salon had ensured my fame. Everyone sought to be introduced to me and I never lacked partners for the dances. Madame d'Arpajon's fond name for me, Belle, was soon in general use in society. My female acquaintances began to address me in that manner.

"Men also use it to refer to you between themselves," said the Duchess.

"Does it not assume too much familiarity?"

"It certainly would if they were to address you in that manner. But as long as they show you all due respect, you have no reason to resent that appellation. I know of many less flattering names they give other ladies behind their backs. Take it as it is meant, as a compliment."

I met Lauzun and Villers, my new acquaintances from the Opera, almost daily. They called at Madame d'Arpajon's together or separately and I would see them in society. The Count de Villers would reiterate the offer of his box at the Opera. In spite of my love of music, I did not avail myself of it, out of a desire to escape the gossip that would ensue as well as to avoid too great a sense of obligation towards him.

I met at a supper the most celebrated painter of that time, Madame Lebrun, a pretty, cheerful woman. We discovered many similarities in our situations. In particular, she told me that she had a little girl, two years older than Aimée, of whom she spoke with true motherly fondness. Madame Lebrun had an unusual quality: she could not bring herself to speak ill of anyone. This may have arisen from her simultaneous employment by numerous people who were, in some manner or other, enemies. In any event, I was delighted to meet someone who would not criticize me behind my back, something I knew other ladies had no scruple about. She concluded our conversation by inviting Aimée and me to visit her.

Aimée was of course too young to attend any formal dinners, but she too discovered the pleasures of Paris. I took her to the boulevards to see the *Fantoccini*, life-size Italian puppets. She cried with terror upon first seeing them, but soon became fascinated and begged to return. She could watch the same show all over again, week after week, each time with fresh enjoyment. I never tired of seeing her delight.

৵ 29 ৵

As predicted by the Duchess, the Countess de Provence, married to the brother of the King, expressed a wish to meet me. The Marquise de Bastide took me to the Luxembourg Palace, Her Highness's residence in Paris, to make the introduction. I had been forewarned not to expect a pretty woman and discovered that, as often, reality outstripped rumour. The bottom half of Her Highness's face was bloated as if her mouth had been full of food, and her eyebrows met above her nose in a single dark bushy line that contrasted with her hair, powdered white. What disconcerted me most in her appearance was a black down on her upper lip and along the side of her cheeks, in the manner of adolescent males. Nevertheless, her eyes were dark, intelligent and expressive. Seated next to Her Highness on a sofa was her reader, Madame de Gourbillon, a tall, large horse of a woman, who looked at me with more curiosity than friendliness.

Her Highness received me far more graciously than the Queen. She rose to embrace me and, much to my surprise, kissed me on the cheek. As she reached me, I was taken aback by her odor, a mix of wine, stale sweat and dirty laundry. After a few seconds, my nostrils recovered and I was able to answer Her Highness's questions with tolerable presence of mind. Before long, Madame de Gourbillon reminded her of a pressing engagement. I took my leave after receiving an invitation to visit Madame at her country house.

"How did you like Her Highness?" asked Madame de Bastide on our way back to the Duchess's.

"At first her appearance surprised me, but she is unaffected and charming. Madame de Gourbillon, however, did not seem so friendly."

"Her Highness is an excellent character, though she suffers from the female version of *the little defect*. Madame de Gourbillon is more than her reader and keeps a close eye on anyone who might poach on her manor. I would not have expected her to behave otherwise towards you. The Count de Provence cannot stand the woman, both personally and because of the scandal her continual presence by his wife's side causes. People of course say the same thing about the Queen and Madame de Polignac, but here it is real. The Countess de Provence is in love with Madame de Gourbillon."

"Could not the Count de Provence detach his wife from her friend?"

"He has tried on many occasions, but the Countess de Provence does not listen to anything he says. She will not hear of being separated from her dear Gourbillon. There is no fondness between husband and wife, if indeed they can be given that name. The Count de Provence is not believed to have consummated the marriage these fifteen years. The poor Countess has many excuses for her peculiar tastes."

A few weeks later I had the honour to be introduced to the Count de Provence, who has since become King Louis the Eighteenth. I felt that, had I had the misfortune to be married to him, I too would have foresworn bathing in an attempt to keep him away.

Before long I availed myself of an opportunity to visit Madame Lebrun, the painter. Her daughter, Julie, was delighted to introduce her dolls to Aimée. While the children played under the supervision of Julie's governess, Madame Lebrun showed me the beautiful paintings owned by her husband, an art dealer. She noticed my interest and recommended that I visit various collections, in particular that of the Duke d'Orléans, famous for its masterpieces of the Italian school. When I told her that I had been at the Luxembourg Palace, she exclaimed that during my next visit there I must see the unique ensemble of monumental paintings by Rubens in the gallery.

She took me to her studio, filled with light and the acrid smell of paint. Urns in the antique style, plaster models of female nudes and draperies in deep reds and greens cluttered the space. I saw, resting on easels, two portraits, one of the Queen and one of the Countess de Provence, in matching white muslin dresses and straw hats decorated with feathers and blue ribbons. Madame Lebrun had captured the likenesses of both princesses while making them appear pretty. In the Queen's portrait, the nose was smaller than in reality, the lips less thick, the eyes less prominent. Yet the features were clearly recognizable. The feat was still more remarkable with regard to the poor Countess de Provence. I complimented Madame Lebrun on the artistry of the paintings.

"Thank you, Madam," she said. "I am putting the finishing touches to both portraits. I intend to exhibit them at the Salon at the end of August."

"I am sure they will meet with great success."

"Alas, Madam, the public's judgment is unpredictable. At the last Salon, my likeness of the Queen with her children was harshly criticized because the frame was too large and costly!"

She walked around me, eyeing me closely. "Your features would be a delight to paint. Do you mind, Madam?"

She led me to a stool. When I was seated, she removed my hat and untied my hair, which she rearranged loosely on my shoulders. With her forefinger, she gently turned my head to the side.

"Such a beautiful profile," she said. "And I would love to capture the colour and abundance of your hair."

"I never had my portrait painted. How much is your fee?"

"From 3,000 francs to 10,000 for wealthy clients."

I smiled. "This makes it an easy decision. The lesser sum represents more than the entire amount of my fortune."

"I would paint your portrait out of sheer pleasure, but my husband would never allow it. He manages all of my business affairs."

"I envy you so much, Madame Lebrun. You are able to support yourself through your art. *I* have neither money nor any means of earning it."

"Indeed I am blessed to spend my time doing something I love. My art has also earned me the patronage of the Queen and other members of the royal family. It allows me to mingle in the best society." She sighed. "As for money, dear Madam, please do not envy me. I am fortunate to have frugal tastes. My husband allows me, on his good days, less than one twentieth of my fee. If he is in dire circumstances, he keeps the whole thing."

There was a little sadness, but no bitterness in her tone. I followed her to the drawing room to take tea with our daughters and the governess.

The Duchess and I were also invited to country estates outside of Paris. The Duke d'Orléans, who did not seemed discouraged by my lack of interest, conveyed us, with his rival mistresses, Lady Elliott and

Madame de Buffon, to his château of Le Raincy for a fishing party. I found Villers and Lauzun there. I had not wanted to appear rude by refusing an invitation from a prince of the royal blood, but fishing could hardly be described as my favourite pastime. A lackey handed me a rod after baiting the line. I held it at arm's length, unable to conceal my distaste. Villers was watching me with more than a little amusement.

"You do not seem fond of fishing, Madam," he remarked.

"I do not like the sight of a squirming worm torn on a hook. I think I will walk by the lake until the fishing part of the entertainment is over."

"I will gladly relinquish fishing for the honour of accompanying you in your walk, My Lady. You must not like hunting either."

"You are mistaken, Sir. I used to love to hunt with my brother, but it was for the pleasure of riding on a fine autumn day, rather than that of killing an animal. As for fishing, I used to do it by hand in rivers when I was a child, but that was quite another sport. I am too restless for this."

"Really? You enjoy riding then?"

"It was one of my greatest pleasures, Sir, but my late husband would not allow it. I have not ridden in almost three years now, save for a few times after I was widowed."

"I have a pretty little mare at my country house. Would you like to ride her, My Lady? You would do me a favour, beside that of your company. She needs the exercise."

I would have been quick to voice the opinion that he could not be at a loss finding ladies to ride his mare, but abstained from comment. I sorely wanted to ride again. Yet I was reluctant to accept the invitation, for the same reason that had made me decline the offer of his box at the Opera on several occasions.

"Poor Baroness," he said, smiling, "your dilemma can be plainly read on your face. You are torn between your love of riding and your dislike of me."

"I do not dislike you. You must know it by now. But I do not trust you at all."

"Is it better than disliking me? But you are wrong not to trust me, My Lady. Ask anybody in town. I have never harmed, molested or violated a single dowager in the course of my entire life. In any case, it was remiss of me not to have invited the Duchess earlier. I know that she is fond of my country house. Will you come there for luncheon the day after to-morrow?"

"I have no riding habit."

"You may come dressed as you like. I will not invite anyone else, except of course the Duchess, so nobody will be there to criticize your attire. And please bring your pretty little daughter."

It was too tempting. I accepted.

₰ 30 ₰

The weather was still fine when the Duchess, Aimée and I set off for Vaucelles, the Count de Villers's country house. It was only one mile from the Charenton Gate, which marked the city's southeastern entrance, but one felt far from Paris. Villers welcomed us to his château, which was a *folie*, a "folly," of recent construction, graceful and small. What was most striking about it was its location. The beautiful gardens, in the formal French style in the front, had in the back of the house been given the look of a natural meadow. The grounds, dotted with cherry trees, sloped gently down towards the banks of the Seine River, just upstream from Paris. Several boats were moored there to a little pier. The Duchess was soon tired and we all walked back to the château, where she settled with Aimée in the oval summer parlour at the back of the house. Its windows opened to the floor onto a marble terrace that overlooked the perspective of the river.

Villers then took me to the stables, where he introduced me to his mare, Margot, a strawberry roan, much smaller than Jewel but just as sweet. She took in my smell with friendly curiosity and accepted the apple I offered her before showing a taste for my straw hat. I ran my hand against her soft gleaming coat, a grayish pink, and rested my head on her shoulder. The memories of happy times with my brother, of my assignations with Pierre-André rushed back to me. I felt a prickling in my eyes and turned away. Villers remained silent for a few minutes.

"I see that you have found clothes suitable for riding after all," he said at last. "I expected to see Your Ladyship arrive dressed as a shepherdess or a milkmaid, which seems to be the fashion these days."

"I grew up in the country and know what peasant women look like. It would feel as if I were mocking them by copying their clothing, which I am sure they would be delighted to exchange for mine."

"You are right, Madam. This affectation of pastoral simplicity strikes me as silly. I am glad that you do not share it. Many ladies of my acquaintance have chided me for not having a dairy, like the Queen's at Versailles, built on the grounds of this house."

"Your house is lovely as it is. You should not change anything under the guise of improving it."

"Thank you. I appreciate your compliment because I know it to be sincere. It is a pity that you did not come here a few months ago, when the cherry trees were blooming. You were not even in Paris then." Villers waved his hand towards the château. "I can take no credit for this place, which was built by my late father. I too find it delightful. I have not deemed it necessary to improve it except to add to the library."

"The library? Would you show it to me?"

"With pleasure, Madam, after luncheon, but please do not expect anything out of the ordinary for a small country house."

He helped me into the saddle and mounted his own horse. We began at a walk and, as the horses warmed and loosened, quickened our pace to a canter. Villers took me around the park and to country lanes beyond its limits. In the happiness of that moment, I lost all sense of time.

"How do you like Margot?" he asked after we had slowed to a walk.

"She is a dear. So pretty and sweet-tempered."

"She was bred on my estate. So were many of the horses you have seen at the races at Longchamp."

"I did not know you were interested in breeding."

"I am. I visit my estates in Normandy regularly. There is no better country to raise horses. The old local stocks are excellent, and one can obtain amazing results by breeding Normand mares with Arabian stallions. Have you ever been to Normandy, My Lady?"

"I never left my native country of Auvergne before coming to Paris this spring."

"Then you have never seen the sea. I hope that you will allow me to take you there someday."

I made no answer and quickened Margot's pace to a gallop.

"You are a fine horsewoman," remarked Villers.

"My brother taught me when I was a child. He is an excellent rider himself. He used to be in the Light Cavalry."

"I cannot recall meeting the Marquis de Castel, though I do remember your late husband very well. When he became Colonel of the Royal

Dragoons, that regiment had the reputation of being the most neglected and insubordinate in the entire army. He restored discipline in a matter of weeks. An iron fist in an iron glove."

"The Baron always made a strong impression on those who met him."

"True. He was unforgettable in his own way. And your brother, the Marquis de Castel, when did he leave the service?"

"Shortly after I was born. Around '73. He was less than twenty, I believe."

"He must be about my age then, or maybe a few years younger. A pity he missed the American War. He would have seen some interesting action against the English. I enjoyed it."

"I had not heard that you had fought for American independence."

"That is how I met Lauzun, Lafayette, Rochambeau, d'Estaing and even Fersen."

"The Count de Fersen?"

"Himself, Madam, the Queen's favourite Swede. I must say, though, that he is the only one of the comrades from America who has not remained my friend. But to return to your brother, how is it that he sent you to Paris to fend for yourself? Does he, unlike you, trust the likes of me?"

I blushed. "That is a question better put directly to him, Sir."

"My apologies. I was not trying to pry. No, to be entirely candid, I was indeed trying to pry, but it was an unsuccessful attempt."

It was just after one in the afternoon, time to rejoin the Duchess and Aimée over a luncheon of cold meats, cake, strawberries and ice cream.

"My dear," said the Duchess, "the exercise makes you still lovelier than usual. Do you not agree, Villers?"

"I would not have dared say so, Madam, because Madame de Peyre already has a dismal opinion of my morals. My paying her such a compliment, however deserved, would only have increased her misgivings. But now that you mention it, yes, I feel free to concur with Your Grace."

"Why do you not strive to improve her opinion of you?"

"That is precisely what I intend to do this very afternoon. I promised to show the Baroness my library. Will Your Grace accompany us?"

"I will keep Aimée company. She is a bit young for books. Go, the two of you."

The library was a room of moderate size, facing north, paneled in various shades of grey. I looked around and noticed that most of the books had been published over the past ten years and were unknown to me. English novels and plays were well represented, both in the original language and in French translation. Villers pulled from the shelves a little volume, bound in pink and gold leather. He handed it to me.

"Please take this one."

"I cannot accept any presents from you."

"I would not have the presumption to offer you any. It is a loan, Madam, and a selfish one. I would like to know your opinion of this work. It was written a few years ago by Laclos, whom you may have met at some of the parties given by the Duke d'Orléans."

It was *Les Liaisons Dangereuses*, "Dangerous Liaisons." I had heard much about it. As I leafed through the pages, some of the illustrations made me blush.

"As you must have noticed already, I am a prude. You should respect my feelings."

"You are no prude. You are shy and modest. I can assure you, My Lady, that, while the illustrations are silly, the text is clever. You must forget that it comes from my library and give me your candid opinion of it. Of course, you should feel free to borrow any other works you like."

I chose a French translation of Shakespeare's tragedies.

When Villers handed us into our carriage later that afternoon, he invited us to come back the following Saturday to join a party of his friends. The Duchess, without taking the trouble to look in my direction, accepted. Aimée fell asleep promptly against my shoulder.

"Do you not think, Madam," I asked during our ride back to Paris, "that it puts us in his debt? And I am afraid of being seen too much with him."

"This does not matter as long as it is clear that you are not his mistress. Besides, if you shun him, people will think that you are resolved to have Lauzun as your lover. It would be far more harmful to your reputation."

"I had not considered this." I looked out the window. "Candidly, Madam, what do you think will happen to me?"

"I wish I could read the future, dear, but it is a gift I have been denied. Or a curse I have been spared."

"Do you think that Monsieur de Villers would marry me?"

"It is unlikely, from what I know of him, but not impossible. He does seem very attracted to you. Would you have him if he proposed?"

"He is pleasant, of suitable rank and younger than my late husband."

"You have not answered my question, dear Belle. Are you in love with him?"

I hesitated. "That would be fairly ridiculous, Madam, would it not? *He* is not in love with me."

"Are you sure? But you are right, my dear, not to commit your feelings until you know more about his. This does not mean that you should discourage his attentions. I will not live forever."

The Duchess, tired by our excursion to Vaucelles, retired early that night. I followed suit after kissing Aimée good night. She now slept in her own bedroom next to mine. I began reading *Dangerous Liaisons* in my bedroom. The web of intrigues woven by the characters fascinated me by its complexity and disgusted me by its malice. I remembered Villers's insistence that I borrow the book. Had he any particular purpose in lending it to me? Was he trying to tell me anything? I put aside the volume and rang for a cup of hot chocolate. As I was sipping it, lying on a sofa by the fireplace, I thought about the Duchess's questions. Would I have Villers if he proposed?

From the standpoint of worldly wisdom, he was an excellent match. His nobility, unlike mine, could not be traced beyond the time of the Crusades, but that disparity was more than compensated by the considerable difference in our respective fortunes. He did not seem brutal like my late husband.

My thoughts took another turn. What would become of me if the Duchess passed away? That question at least was easy to answer: Aimée and I would be without a roof on our heads. My expenses in Paris, modest as they were, had already made a dent in the 3,000 francs the Baron had left me. How long would the remainder last if I had to pay for our own lodgings? Probably no more than a few months. I could picture Aimée and myself retrenching on our expenses until we slowly sank into poverty. I shuddered.

I would be a simpleton to refuse a man such as Villers. Was I in love with him? I had to admit that I enjoyed his company. His conversation entertained me, even when it made me uneasy. If given a choice, I would rather see him than not.

We returned to Vaucelles with Aimée on the appointed day. Lauzun was among the guests, as well as Lafayette, whom I had never met before, and Madame de Bastide, the Duchess's daughter. The conversation turned to politics. The Marquis de Lafayette, a slender man with a long, grave face and a strangely pale complexion, was discussing the recently dismissed *Assemblée des Notables*, to which he had been appointed by the King. During his brief tenure, he had raised the necessity of calling the *Etats-Généraux*, the Estates General, a meeting of representatives of the Clergy, the Nobility and the *Tiers-Etat*, the "Third Estate," meaning the rest of the nation. Those were the three Orders composing all of the French population.

"The Estates General," I said, "have not been called in almost two hundred years. Is not the institution too antiquated to do any good?"

"Have you any better idea, Madam?" he responded in a rather haughty tone. "What matters is not the antiquity or modernity of any institution, but what it may accomplish."

"What could it accomplish that the Assembly of the Notables could not?"

Lafayette sighed. "The Assembly of the Notables, Madam, failed because it lacked the authority to levy new taxes. The Estates General have that power. I can think of no other way out of the current budget crisis. Also, since the Notables had been chosen by the King among the Clergy and the Nobility, they had no incentive to repeal the tax exemptions enjoyed by the privileged classes. What is wrong with the present system, Madam, is that the poorest of citizens are the most heavily taxed, while the wealthiest pay next to nothing in proportion to their fortune."

"You are right, Sir, but would not the problem be the same with the Estates General, where the Third Estate, although it would be represented, would have a minority position?"

"It would certainly be so, My Lady, if the votes were to be counted by Order, as in the past. But the old system could be reformed to give the Third Estate a larger role in the vote, for instance by giving it more members and by allowing each Representative, instead of each Order, a vote."

"Indeed, Sir, but that in itself would be a revolution. The assembly you contemplate would not be the Estates General. What matters is not what one calls an institution, but the manner in which it is designed."

Lafayette's complexion lost its paleness. "Pardon me, Madam. I suppose I should defer to your opinion in these matters."

I smiled with all the grace I could muster. "I would never have the presumption to suggest such a thing, Sir. You know infinitely more than

I about representative assemblies. You have seen them at work in America and were a member of the Assembly of the Notables in this country. It is why I took the liberty of soliciting your opinion."

Lafayette seemed to recover some of his composure.

"What do you think," I added, "are the chances of the King calling the Estates General and accepting the changes you suggest?"

"The King has no choice, Madam. After the failure of the Notables, the financial crisis is worse than ever. No one can resolve it without raising taxes."

I walked away and was soon joined by Villers.

"I followed your conversation with Lafayette," he said. "A lively exchange, more so than he must have expected from one so young as you, Madam. I did not know that you were interested in politics."

Around four o'clock, the entire party walked towards the river. Refreshments were served under a blue-and-white-striped tent, a few dozen yards from the little pier. Lauzun, after asking my permission but without waiting for my response, sat in the chair next to mine. I could not look at him without blushing at the recollection of his letters, the tone of which was becoming more ardent by the day. He kept whispering comments to my ear, as if to establish a footing of intimacy with me before the other guests. He asked me in particular whether I did not think that Lafayette was the most conceited jackass I had ever met. I would have laughed if I had not been embarrassed by such flaunted familiarity. I coloured and looked at Villers across the table. He was watching Lauzun and me with apparent amusement.

I was not sorry to escape as soon as the meal was over.

"Would Your Grace accompany me on a walk into a little wood nearby?" I asked the Duchess as I was helping her rise from her chair.

"Thank you, dear Belle, but I feel a bit tired. I think I will go rest inside for a while with Aimée."

"I would take it as the greatest favour if I were allowed to join you, My Lady," Lauzun hastened to say.

I was ready to decline when Madame de Bastide interjected with a very expressive smile: "I will accompany you, dear Madam, and Monsieur de Lauzun . . . unless of course you do not want any third parties to interfere with your *tête-à-tête.*"

I could no longer refuse. We had gone a few hundred yards into the wilderness when Madame de Bastide put her hand to her forehead and stopped in her tracks like a startled horse. "You will have to excuse me," she said. "A sudden migraine has come upon me."

"I am sorry to hear it," I responded. "Monsieur de Lauzun and I will accompany you back to the château."

"I absolutely refuse to interrupt your walk, dear Madam. Besides, my ailment is of the kind that requires quiet and solitude. I beg you to continue without me."

She almost ran away, leaving me at the mercy of Lauzun.

"I do not feel so well myself," I said. "I will follow in Madame de Bastide's footsteps."

"You should never say that, My Lady, for you do not know where they would lead you. I do. They would not take you far from Villers's bed, and that of many other gentlemen. And pardon me for doubting your truthfulness, but except for your heightened colour, which is extremely becoming, I fail to detect anything amiss with you. Your shyness is delightful, the most refreshing thing in this town. Indeed, you are unique among all the ladies I have known."

Lauzun, having fallen to his knees, seized both of my hands and covered them with kisses. I looked around in alarm.

"Sir, I beg you to rise. Imagine if anyone saw us in this ridiculous position."

He did not move. "I am not ashamed of it, Madam, nor of my feelings for you."

I tried to draw away from him, in vain for he was holding fast to my hands. "But I am, Sir. You forget that you are a married man."

"I confess I do, Madam, except on very rare, mournful occasions. Why do you not?"

"Because I happen to have an excellent memory. Your letters and your conduct today embarrass me more than words can express. Please, Sir, I beg you, as a favour to me, put an end to both. You are used to ladies who welcome your attentions. I cannot be one of those." I hesitated. "I will not even conceal from you that I like you in spite of myself. You amuse me more than anyone else. After this confession, you can hardly doubt my sincerity when I tell you that you are wasting your time."

"You have said more than enough, Madam, to give me hope. Thank you for your encouragement. I shall persevere."

I pulled away from him and ran from the little wood with tears of vexation in my eyes.

These summer days were the longest of the year, sunny and pleasant. Ladies of fashion would ride on the Champs-Elysées in open carriages, called *landaus*, for their own enjoyment and the gawking pleasure of throngs of pedestrians. Although the Duchess had not such a carriage, we were offered seats by her daughter or other ladies and did not miss any outings on that account. We were often accompanied by various gentlemen on horseback, particularly Lauzun and Villers.

During one of these outings, I was alone with Madame de Bastide in her *landau*. Her mother was feeling tired and had remained at home with Aimée. Villers, on horseback, saw us, removed his hat and bowed. He approached the carriage. After a brief exchange of pleasantries and some enquiries into the Duchess's condition, he rode off.

"Monsieur de Villers never fails to astonish me by the insolence of his manners," said Madame de Bastide as soon as his back was turned.

"He seemed genuinely concerned about the Duchess."

"He had to say something to that effect, though I am sure that he could not care less about my mother. Did you happen to notice how abruptly he escaped?"

I had indeed observed that Villers had not tarried, but had not been in the least surprised. His past intimacy with Madame de Bastide and her resentment at his desertion sufficed to explain it.

"Perhaps he had another engagement," I said.

"No doubt. He was impatient to return to the harlots whose company he so relishes. Do you know, my dear, that he has a *petite maison* close to the Saint-Denis Gate?"

She paused. A *petite maison*, a "little house," was a discreet establishment set up by a gentleman for his mistress or mistresses.

"There," added Madame de Bastide, giggling, "he keeps two actresses from the *Théâtre-Français* and a singer from the Opera. Yes, my dear, he maintains a regular little harem. And, because he is as miserly as he is depraved, he shares the expenses of that establishment with the Duke d'Orléans and Monsieur de Lauzun."

"You seem well informed of Monsieur de Villers's private arrangements," I said, forcing a smile.

"I cannot reveal my sources, of course, but you may trust their veracity." She leaned towards me. "But that is not all, my dear," she whispered. "The Duke d'Orléans, Lauzun and Villers meet there to enjoy those three ladies together. Now please picture those nice little orgies."

I could not help wincing. Madame de Bastide put her hand on my arm. "I hope that I am not causing you pain, dear Madam. I have noticed that you seem inclined to welcome Monsieur de Villers's attentions. I wanted, as a friend, to warn you."

"Your concern is duly appreciated."

I did not wish my companion to think that I had been affected by her disclosures and kept the conversation on meaningless nothings until we reached the Duchess's mansion. Madame de Bastide declined to disturb her mother by calling on her so late. I went to my friend's bedroom to make sure that she was comfortable and, after wishing her a good night and seeing Aimée to her bed, retired to my own apartment.

Madame de Bastide's words had upset me. Though I supposed her to be driven by malice, nothing I knew or guessed of Villers was inconsistent with what she had told me. I went to bed in a foul mood, trying to keep my mind away from the Saint-Denis Gate. Villers must by now have reached his *little house* and be engaged in the scenes of debauchery suggested by Madame de Bastide.

Villers renewed his invitations to Vaucelles once the Duchess recovered. At first, I could not look at him without blushing and thinking of my conversation with Madame de Bastide. Yet he was as pleasant as usual and I still looked forward to our rides together. After one of those, we returned to the house and went to the library. I gave him back the books I had borrowed.

"What did you think of them, My Lady?" he asked.

"I finished *Macbeth*, which I found fascinating, and *Hamlet*, which did not make any sense to me. Maybe the translation is to blame. Most likely I am too stupid to understand either. I had not time to read the rest of the tragedies."

He handed me back the volume. "You should keep the book longer then, and read *King Lear*, which is my favourite. And I agree, the translation is uneven. It would be far better for you to learn English."

"How would I do that?"

"I could teach you if you would let me, but there is the small matter of Your Ladyship's distrust of me. Or you could hire an English governess for your daughter and learn the language with her."

"I might give the expense of a governess some consideration if Aimée were older. She is not yet two."

"That leaves me as an instructor." He smiled. "Not only would I charge nothing, My Lady, but I would even pay handsomely for the privilege of giving you any kind of lessons. What about *Dangerous Liaisons*? What did you think of it?"

"I am happy to return it to you. The two main characters, Valmont and Madame de Merteuil, are idle, malicious creatures, occupied only with destroying each other and a few innocents out of pure amusement. I cannot understand why the Duke d'Orléans patronizes the author. What will the other classes of society think of the nobility when they read such horrors?"

"The opinion the lower classes have of us, I am afraid, was already settled long before Laclos wrote his book. As for the Valmont character, I disagree. He lets himself be fooled into abandoning the only woman he ever loved for the sake of the bitch Merteuil and the simpleton Cécile. He is more to be pitied than loathed."

"Do you recognize yourself in him?"

"A pointed question. I would hope to be less of an imbecile if I were placed in his situation. As to Cécile, she receives only what she deserves when she gives Valmont access to her bedroom and her person, not out of love but out of stupidity." He put away the book and shrugged. "She is a maiden but not an innocent. Many people, especially men, tend to confuse those two notions. Not me. Virginity is worthless in my eyes, only innocence is fascinating." Villers looked at me. "You, in your kindness and purity, remind me of Madame de Tourvel, although I suspect that you are made of sturdier material. If your heart were broken, you would bravely live on."

"You do not know me," I said. "And pray what do you know of purity?"

"Some people, good or evil, have transparent souls. You are one of them. Let me warn you, by the way, My Lady: it makes you the most incompetent liar I have ever met. You should never tell an untruth, because you could not fool a child. Your qualities, your feelings, your emotions can be plainly seen on your face like sunshine through a window. This is how I know that you are an innocent. I have made it a sport, I confess, to say in your presence things that I know will shock you, for the selfish pleasure of seeing you blush. And you have not once disappointed me." He smiled. "Your repartees are fast but you never fail to colour. I must strike you as insufferable, and yet I cannot resist that temptation."

"I thought you were naturally crude to everyone. I did not take it as a personal cruelty or compliment."

"Of course not, because you are modest, another unusual quality. Now you are blushing again, and I have said nothing objectionable. Maybe I should stop being so uncouth after all."

Villers's face did not convey his usual amusement.

"Why not show yourself as you really are, Sir, no worse and no better? I would at least appreciate your candor."

"I will try, but Your Ladyship will find that people who have lived at Court or in this city long enough have difficulty remembering who they are."

"It might happen to me too."

"I think not. You should be sent back to your province of Auvergne if there were any risk of it."

I looked out the window. "It pains me to think of returning to my country."

"So I can see. Why?"

"My soul may be transparent, but I do not wish to have my private concerns become the subject of common talk."

"Why do you believe me indiscreet? You do me a grave injustice, My Lady. Unlike Lauzun, I do not publish things that should be kept private."

"Does Monsieur de Lauzun speak disrespectfully of me?"

"Never, Madam. That is not what I meant. Lauzun blabbers all over town about his successes, but he does not boast of what he has not achieved. He is also patient. He can wait for months to obtain what he wants. I have noticed that you do not give him much encouragement, but it will not be enough to dissuade him from persevering. Beware, your reserve may add in his eyes to your other allurements. In the past I have often seen him more interested in the chase than in the kill."

"And you, Sir, are you also interested in the chase?"

"I am not so refined as Lauzun and do not like wasting my time. I can be patient when the object is worth my while, but I do not bother hunting unless I expect to be successful in the end. It is not to say, of course, that I always obtain what I want."

I tried to read *King Lear* that night, but the book kept falling off my hands. I wondered about my last conversation with Villers. He had seemed to imply that he admired me for more than my looks. Had he tried to tell me that he loved me? Was he thinking of marriage? I checked myself. Why would a man like Villers—rich, handsome, fashionable, brilliant, a man who could have any woman he wanted—consider matrimony? For the sake of a penniless, ignorant little widow fresh from her province?

๛ 31 ๛

The summer of 1787 passed in a most agreeable manner. I had turned eighteen in July, a fact I had not revealed to anyone but the Duchess. Lauzun's letters continued unabated, although his professions began to betray some impatience at the slow pace of his progress. The Duchess, Aimée and I still visited Vaucelles more often than we should have, but the attractions of that little estate were difficult to resist. I rode with Villers twice a week and was invited to parties at his house and other nearby châteaux.

In Vaucelles, he showed us a little theatre, all blue and gold, within the house. I found myself on a stage for the first time in my life, an experience that, even without an audience, I found intimidating.

"Would you like me to set up a play, Madam?" asked Villers.

"Certainly, if you wish."

"Which play would you choose?"

"It might be better, Sir, to let the actors pick what they like."

"Do you mean, Madam, that you would not want to act?"

I laughed. "No, Sir, I would not, though I would be happy to watch the performance from the safety of the audience."

He dropped the subject and led us back to the drawing room for tea.

"So, Belle," said the Duchess after we returned to her mansion that night, "you did not seem very interested when Villers mentioned a play."

"I have no objection to private theatricals, Madam, but the mediocrity of the performance does not seem to justify the expense of time and money they entail. Of course to some the pleasure of finding themselves on stage is, like virtue, its own reward."

"True. Last week at my daughter's house, *The Marriage of Figaro*, by Beaumarchais, was poorly acted, as should be expected from a troupe of amateurs. The performers could not remember half of their lines. And Monsieur de Brasson, who was in the audience, ran onto the stage and interrupted the representation with one of his terrible scenes. He thought that his wife smiled too much at Monsieur de Rivière, who was Figaro. She could not help it, poor thing: she played the maid Suzanne, Figaro's fiancée."

"I do not see, Madam, why everyone is so enamored of that play. It has been officially forbidden by the royal censors, but there does not seem to be one château in France where it has not been performed. Why would anyone support such a work? It is witty, but makes noblemen look like scoundrels. It accredits outrageous lies, such as that nonsense about the *lord's right* to the premises of any maiden on his land. All I remember is my brother giving away the bride at many a country wedding. He did so at her father's request. It was an honour for a peasant girl to be led to the altar by her lord. That was the extent of his prerogatives."

"You are right," said the Duchess. "That Beaumarchais fellow is an impertinent liar. Yet he has the support of the Queen, who was the first to defy the King's authority and have the play performed in her own little theatre at Trianon. She even acted the part of the maid Suzanne, all for the benefit of the lackeys she invites to her private representations." The Duchess shook her head in irritation. "She does everything in her power to discredit the monarchy. Look at what happened when her portrait by Madame Lebrun was exhibited at the Salon. I have not seen it yet, but everyone makes a mockery of her by saying that she was painted in her chemise."

"I saw the painting in Madame Lebrun's studio, Madam. The Queen was wearing a simple white muslin gown, not a chemise. I often dress in the same fashion myself."

"It looks lovely on you, my dear, but it is not appropriate for a portrait of the Queen, especially one that is publicly displayed. She should uphold the dignity of the Crown and remember that she is the King's consort, the mother of the Dauphin."

"But the Countess de Provence was painted in the same manner."

"This is different, Belle. The poor Countess could have herself painted in the nude without anyone taking it amiss. Since she is barren, no one questions the parentage of her offspring. Whatever scandal her infatuation with Madame de Gourbillon causes does not matter in terms of succession to the throne. She was even given a part in *The Marriage of*

Figaro when it was played at Trianon by the Queen, but nobody cared." She smiled. "As for Villers, my guess is that, if you do not show more interest in acting, he will abandon the idea of setting up any play at all."

"Indeed, Madam," I said, sighing, "I do not know what to think of Monsieur de Villers or his attentions."

The Duchess became grave again. "Neither do I, my dear. Time shall tell."

Time did tell. During a visit to Vaucelles at the beginning of September, Villers informed me that Margot had injured her hock and could not be ridden. He proposed to have another horse saddled. I declined but expressed a wish to walk to the stables to pay the little mare a visit. The Duchess and Aimée remained in the summer drawing room.

Margot nickered when she caught my smell. I stroked her face and offered her an apple. Villers proposed a walk to the river. I agreed and opened my parasol. He seemed unusually thoughtful.

"How old are you?" he asked abruptly.

Startled, I turned to look at him. "Is it not considered a rude question, Sir?"

"Not when it is asked of one so young as you. Come, Madam, tell me."

"I turned eighteen in July."

"And Your Ladyship did not breathe a word about it! I would have been delighted to invite you here to celebrate the occasion."

"That may be the reason why I chose not to tell you about it."

"Very sly of you, I dare say. You have all the wiles of a schoolgirl and deserve to be punished like one for playing such pitiful tricks. What did the nuns make you do for your penance at the convent? Did you spend dinnertime on your knees in the middle of the refectory?"

"I did, more than once, and they did not spare the rod on my fingers." I smiled. "Yet it does not appear that *you* are in a position to punish me."

"Oh, you may be wrong, Madam. I could embarrass you by giving a party in your honour on the holiday of the Archangel Gabriel. It is, if my memory serves me well, the 29th of this month."

"Please, if you wish to remain my friend, do not. And I am no schoolgirl. I am a widow and a mother."

"You must forgive my impertinence on account of my advanced years. I am old enough to consider ladies of your age as schoolgirls and, indeed, to be their father."

I stared at him.

"Yes, it is true, Madam," he continued, "though it is kind of you to look surprised. You were born the same year as my son."

"I did not know you had grown children."

"My late father made me marry at the age of eighteen. My bride was fourteen and not to my taste, but I was not given much opportunity to voice my complaints. We were introduced on the eve of our wedding. Yet I did not ignore the call of duty. Madame de Villers presented me with an heir ten months later and died in the process."

"Where is your son?"

"I had him raised on my estate of Dampierre, in Normandy. The country is in my opinion a better place than Paris or Versailles for a child to grow up. When he reached the age of twelve, I purchased an ensign's commission for him, as my father had done for me. He has been in the army ever since. He is a First Lieutenant in the Royal Flanders Regiment and, if I may say so, a fine fellow."

"So you have no other children."

"No legitimate ones. As to bastards, I do not know of any, save a pretty little daughter of fifteen. Her mother was a lady of the Court. I am not, of course, at liberty to mention her name, although you might hear it mentioned in connection with mine. I will not bore you with a full account of my adventures, but some gossip may reach you concerning this one and I would rather have you hear the story from me."

Villers bit his upper lip. "The lady's husband, upon learning of our liaison, requested a *lettre de cachet*, which was granted. He personally took her—she was then with child—to the convent in Lorraine where she spent the rest of her short life. I cannot fathom how a man can be so closed to all feelings of pity as to spend several days in a carriage with his young wife, knowing that she is going to be entombed alive at his behest and that he will never see her again. She must have tried all the way to beg his forgiveness, to plead for him to take her back. This is too painful to imagine, even after all these years. She died before reaching one and twenty."

I was astonished at the turn the conversation had taken. He shook his head, lost in his thoughts. "My child is now being raised as another man's daughter. That sad affair taught me a lesson. I have been careful not to father any more bastards. Legitimate children have also been out of the question since I am not one of the warmest advocates for matrimony. I was widowed when I was almost as young as you, Madam, and have never felt any inclination to change my situation. Wedlock is an undertaking suited only to youths who are forced into it or to fortune hunters. I am neither. I have no intention of marrying again."

I looked at the river. The water reflected the glare of the sun. I blinked and turned away.

"Come," he added, "reward my candor with equal sincerity. There is no point in trying to deceive me. You are, as I already told you, a poor liar. From what I saw of your late husband, he must have been a harsh master. Why, Madam, should you be so eager to place yourself under the yoke of a new one? Why give a man such near absolute power? I understand that your finances are a bit awkward, but that in itself is no reason to remarry. Would you not be a thousand times more independent, and in the eyes of reasonable people, just as respectable with a decent, discreet, generous man for your lover?"

I gasped at his insolence. "What have I done to give you the idea that I would stoop so low? Your proposals, Sir, are the grossest insult I have ever received."

"It truly pains me to have upset you, Madam," said Villers, "but I felt that I could not continue my attentions without making my purpose perfectly clear. I never intended to mislead you, nor do I believe that I have done so."

I closed my parasol and stopped walking.

"I too will be candid, Sir. Though I am not surprised by what you are telling me, I am disappointed. I kept hoping for something else, although I knew that those hopes were not very reasonable. I thank you for dispelling my doubts. May we return to the house now?"

We walked back in silence. Once in the house, I barely heard a word of what was said by anyone. I could not bring myself to meet Villers's eye during the rest of the day. I was impatient to leave and hastened our departure. During the carriage ride back to Paris, the Duchess watched me with silent concern. It was only after I put Aimée to bed that my friend asked me what was ailing me. The tears I had been holding back began to roll down my cheeks.

"Oh, Madam," I said, "you were not mistaken. Monsieur de Villers will not marry me."

"My poor child, I have never been so sorry to be right. Did he propose any kind of arrangement?"

"He said something about my taking a lover, and a generous one, but it does not matter. I have no intention of becoming his mistress."

"You are not in love with him, are you?"

I was sobbing. "If I were, Madam, I would never admit it now, either to you or to myself."

She took me in her arms. "My poor dear, do not be so unhappy. If his visits annoy you, my door will be closed to him. You should know that, as long as I live, you will have a home here. I will always be grateful for your company. Take your time, Belle. There are other men."

"Who? The Duke de Lauzun? Worse, the Duke d'Orléans?"

"Poor Orléans! He seems to have made quite an impression on you. But you are not acquainted with everyone in Paris yet, dear, and some whom you have met have not yet had a chance to appreciate you as you deserve."

I took the Duchess's hand in mine. "Dear Madam, would you be angry with me if I visited my sister at Noirvaux? Now seems a perfect time to meet her at last."

"Well, the Chevalier des Huttes could take you there."

"I would rather not wait for his next leave of absence, Madam. Aimée and I can travel to Nantes by the stagecoach, and, if I wrote my sister to announce my visit, her carriage would take us from there to the convent."

The Duchess frowned. "I hope, Belle, that you will not make any rash decisions in the first bitterness of your disappointment. Villers deserves no such honour."

"Do not worry, Madam. The purpose of my journey will be to meet my sister, and also to see for myself whether convent life suits me. I promise not to make any irrevocable decisions in haste."

I purchased two tickets to Nantes for the same night. I waited until after the servants went to bed to prepare my trunk myself lest one of my suitors, through his spies within the house, was informed of my flight. Taking in my arms Aimée, who was barely awake, I kissed the Duchess good-bye.

I had never traveled by public coach before and soon understood the drawbacks of that mode of transportation for a young woman without a male escort. Aimée, rocked by the movement of the carriage, fell fast asleep against me. An ill-favoured fellow with large yellow teeth was seated across from me and tried on several occasions to start a conversation. He was not discouraged by my lack of response. I put an end to such attempts by pretending to doze off while keeping an eye on him. He looked like a thief. I had left all of my jewellery in Paris with the Duchess but did not want to be robbed of the money I had taken for the expenses of my journey. That night at the inn, I avoided the common room and ordered dinner brought to the apartment I shared with Aimée.

The next day, the man renewed his questions. I answered that I was joining my sister in a convent. This silenced him at last. The rest of my fellow travelers seemed harmless enough and, whether because of my youth, the presence of my little girl or the modesty of my dress, no one else harassed me. Madame de Montserrat's carriage was waiting for us in Nantes to take us to Noirvaux, where we arrived late in the afternoon of the fourth day. I was sore and tired, but happy to have left Paris and my worries behind.

Noirvaux Abbey was an imposing stone building situated twenty miles from the boundaries of the city of Nantes. We must have been expected, for the doors swung open before the coachman had time to ring the bell. We alighted in a courtyard and were greeted by a lay sister who invited us to follow her to the Lady Abbess's apartments. I was very affected at the idea of meeting my sister at last and grasped Aimée's hand.

We were shown into a study. A lady, around thirty years of age, rose from behind her desk. I had never seen a face so much like my own. It was a perfect oval, the beauty of which was enhanced by the severity of the white wimple and black veil. She wore the insignia of her rank as an Abbess, a ring adorned with a large amethyst and a gold pectoral cross on a purple ribbon. She smiled and opened her arms in a gesture of welcome.

"Gabrielle, dearest," she said, "at last."

I knelt, seized her hand and brought her ring to my lips. "It is an honour to meet you, Madam."

She raised me to kiss me on the cheek. "I am your sister. I hope that you will call me *Hélène* when we are alone."

Her black habit had caught the attention of Aimée, who was staring at her with some apprehension.

"So this is my niece," she added, smiling. "God has blessed you with a lovely little girl. I cannot look at her without being reminded of Christ's words: *Let the little children come to me.*"

Hélène caressed Aimée's cheek and seemed lost in her thoughts for a moment.

"We will have some time by ourselves later," she added, "but now you should meet our community. Everyone is gathered in the refectory, and impatient to welcome both of you."

Our arrival in the refectory caused a commotion. A group of novices, recognizable by their white veils and youthful appearance, cried aloud with excitement. One look from Hélène silenced them. Nuns in black veils, their hands crossed on their chests, waited more sedately to be introduced to us. Lay sisters in grey habits were disposing refreshments on the tables. The nuns, all noblewomen, were called *Madame* and kept their family name. The lay sisters, who were commoners, were called *Sister*, followed by their religious name. They performed all menial tasks in the convent and several attended Hélène as maids.

Altogether the community comprised thirty nuns, ten novices and over a hundred lay sisters. In addition, Noirvaux housed two dozen ladies who stayed as boarders. A few, who had settled there permanently, had a religious vocation although their married status did not allow them to take holy orders. Most boarders were officers' wives. Under the military regulations of the time, they were not allowed to follow their husbands to their garrisons. The gentlemen temporarily locked their wives in the convent to keep them from any opportunity to stray. From these ladies' conversation, it was easy to discern that they lacked any kind of religious leanings. They missed the amusements of the world and looked forward to the time when it would please their husbands to put an end to their reclusion.

Nuns, novices and boarders alike feted us and admired Aimée's beauty and sweetness. After half an hour of that bustle, Hélène took us to her private rooms, which were vast and as well appointed as any lady's apartment in a château. There we were served hot chocolate by a lay sister. I had been at first intimidated by Hélène's beauty and the dignity of her countenance, but her look of kindness soon reassured me. She spoke of and asked about Mother, the Marquis, Madeleine, Fontfreyde and the servants, in particular poor disfigured Antoinette. All seemed to belong to an ancient past for her. It felt no less distant for me, although I had left Fontfreyde only three years earlier. Tears came to my eyes. Hélène put an end to the conversation and took me to my cell, the name given to the nuns' apartments in convents.

The room she showed me was comfortable and inviting. The bed was hung with immaculate white curtains. A large cross, made of dark wood, was the sole ornament on the whitewashed walls. A cot had been prepared for Aimée, who began to smile shyly at Hélène. In her thoughtfulness, my sister had ordered a harpsichord brought to the room. She let us settle in and returned half an hour later to take us to supper in the refectory. We attended the Office of Complin in the Abbey Church before retiring for the night.

The next day, I joined the rest of the community in its usual activities of worship, prayer, meals and entertainment, of which music composed a great part. I found the monotony of convent life soothing. The choir of female voices during the divine offices was truly beautiful and reminded me of my childhood in the Benedictine Convent in Vic.

Hélène would spend most of her days in her study, attending to both the spiritual direction and the secular business of the Abbey. Its landed property comprised more than fifty parishes, over which it had the right of high justice. It had its own jail, judges and gallows. Hélène told me that its court was then investigating a robbery on the highway to Nantes, during which one of the Abbey's vassals had been severely injured.

The rank of Abbess of Noirvaux also entailed social engagements. Once or twice a week, Hélène gave entertainments, which I attended, in her private dining parlour. The company comprised ladies and gentlemen of the local nobility, as well as those nuns and boarders whom Hélène had invited. Most evenings, however, after we took our meal at her table in the refectory, I followed Hélène to her drawing room. Once we were alone, she would remove her wimple and veil, revealing her short hair. It was indeed very like mine in waviness and colour, only a shade darker.

During those quiet evenings I felt free to tell her of things I had not revealed to anyone. I spoke of my past sorrows, of our brother, of my late husband, even of Pierre-André, without omitting anything, however painful to recall or confess. I also told her of the choices now open to me. She listened and did not speak much herself. I had expected her to give me advice, but she would only ask a few questions about what I felt or thought. She did not try to force her opinion on me, as so many had done before.

"Dearest," she said at last one night, "I have been praying for guidance with regard to you. Taking orders is entering into a mystical union with Christ. It is an atrocious sin to do so without a true vocation, a trespass much worse than marrying without love. It would be to God that you would risk being unfaithful. Last month, I discovered that one of our novices had been sent here solely because she was in love with a penniless cousin. I summoned her father here and explained to him why I would have to dismiss the young lady. He finally agreed to the marriage." Her eyes became stern. "Convents are not convenient repositories for women whom their families wish to discard or punish, but hallowed places where God calls His own. To think or act otherwise is blasphemy."

"What of my other choices?"

"You may have to balance between sins of very different gravity. Contrary to what you believe, incest does not flow only from fully consummated carnal acts, but also from incomplete, tentative touchings. Yes, Gabrielle, what Géraud did when you were fourteen was sufficient to make him guilty of that crime."

I looked at her in amazement.

"Now," she added, "if you were to beg him to take you back, as you are thinking of doing, would you not deliberately expose him, and yourself, to a repetition of the mortal sin he has already committed?"

We remained silent for a long time.

"Gabrielle," Hélène said at last, "what I am going to say I have not revealed to anyone, except under the seal of confession. Apart from Géraud and me, only Mother and Madeleine know of it. This took place when you were still an infant. Géraud was sixteen and I thirteen. I worshiped him. He loved me too." She paused. "You can guess what happened. It lasted an entire summer, while Géraud was on holiday at Fontfreyde. We were seeing each other in secret, in a sort of bedroom in the attic. One night, Father heard a noise and surprised us. You do not remember him, Gabrielle, but he had a fierce temper. He gave Géraud such a thrashing that he left him for dead. I could no longer be married. Think of the scandal if it had been discovered that not only was I disgraced, but that my own brother was the author of my shame! Géraud left immediately. Father purchased for him an ensign's commission in the Light Cavalry. I was crushed by the discovery of our secret and, truth be told, I pined for Géraud. As soon as it was ascertained that I was not with child, I was sent to Noirvaux as a novice."

I stared at Hélène in silence.

"I learned through Madeleine," she continued, "that Géraud did well in the army. By the age of eighteen, he was promoted to the rank of Captain, but he was never allowed to return to Fontfreyde as long as the old Marquis lived. Father died two years later and of course Mother welcomed Géraud back. He has always been her favourite child." She reached for my hand. "Madeleine wrote me that Géraud had taken you from the Benedictine Convent. She said that you resembled me, that Géraud and you were riding all over the country together. I shuddered when I thought of his motives."

"But I always thought he had taken me from the convent because he could no longer afford to keep me there."

"He may not be rich, but his circumstances are more than comfortable. No, Gabrielle, it could not be the true reason. I spent sleepless nights praying for him, and for you. I represented to Madeleine the glaring imprudence of such a situation, which put you, at the age of eleven, daily at his mercy. I even pleaded to be allowed to receive you here, although Noirvaux is not a teaching institution and I do not usually accept children as boarders. Mother would not hear of it. She has always blamed me for seducing Géraud."

I put my hand to my mouth in horror. "Oh, Hélène, what about that night I spent with him, when we were waking the Baron? Do you think he took advantage of me, next to my husband's dead body?"

"Only Géraud can answer these questions. Please do not torment yourself, Gabrielle. The laudanum made you unconscious. God granted you the grace of innocence regardless of what Géraud may have done that night."

"Do you believe that this . . . thing, if indeed it happened, is what prompted the Marquis to want to send me to Noirvaux?"

Hélène shook her head sadly. "The same thought has occurred to me,

Gabrielle. Even if Géraud were innocent of that crime, he may have followed his better instincts by refusing to take you back after your widowhood. He may have tried to protect you and to resist further temptation by sending you away. Géraud is a good man, though a flawed one. A poor sinner, like all of us. Should I tell you this, dearest Gabrielle? I still love him more than anyone else on earth. I want God in His mercy to grant him forgiveness and to receive him among the blessed. I pray daily for Géraud to repent as I have repented myself. Do not fool yourself, Gabrielle. By returning to Fontfreyde, you would throw yourself into the abyss, this time with full knowledge of what you would be doing, and drag him along."

Tears filled my eyes.

"Now, dearest," Hélène continued, "compare that evil to becoming the mistress of a man totally unrelated to you. *That* would be a violation only of the virtue of chastity, especially where neither party is guilty of adultery or an accessory to it. It bears no common measure to the enormity of the crime of incest." She sighed. "Of course, Gabrielle, I have been praying for you to receive God's call. There is nothing I wish more than to receive you here as a novice."

"I have been praying too, but God has not heard me."

"God hears all prayers. In His infinite wisdom, He has not seen fit to answer yours. You must be patient, Gabrielle. It will happen in due time. Tomorrow Mademoiselle de Vaucourt will take the veil. Perhaps you will receive a sign during the ceremony."

The next day the bells rang as for a wedding. Mademoiselle de Vaucourt had relinquished her novice's black habit and white veil. She was dressed in all the finery of a bride. Whether such attire was meant to remind her of the world she was giving up forever, or of her marriage to Christ, I am not learned enough to say. Regardless of the reason, I was struck by the contrast between her ornate wedding gown and the severe clothing of the nuns. The service took place as usual, with a lengthy sermon from Father Marceau, the confessor of the community. At last the time came. I could not help observing that the novice was trembling as she knelt at the foot of the altar. Her mother was sobbing in the front row outside the barred gate separating the chancel from that part of the Abbey Church open to the public. Mademoiselle de Vaucourt declared before the congregation that she was acting of her own free will and pronounced her vows of chastity, poverty and obedience. She left for a few minutes and reappeared to prostrate herself before the altar. She was again wearing her religious habit. But now her veil was black. She had become a nun.

I held Aimée's hand, wondering whether Mademoiselle de Vaucourt had, like me, experienced moments of doubt, of dread, of despair. The ceremony had reminded me of my wedding and my own feelings upon that melancholy occasion. I remained grave and silent during the rest of the day. I asked Hélène for permission to spend the night in prayers in the Abbey Church. After putting Aimée to bed, I prostrated myself before the altar as I had seen Mademoiselle de Vaucourt do, my arms extended on each side of my body to form a cross, my cheek resting on the stone floor until the cold penetrated my flesh and bones. All night I fervently prayed for guidance. I was answered only by my own tears. Hélène joined me at dawn and knelt by my side.

After two weeks in Noirvaux, I was no closer to a decision than when I had entered its walls. The most sensible course of action seemed to remain there until I saw more clearly where my path lay. I wrote the Duchess to inform her of my decision and beg her to forgive me if the delay in my return caused her any sorrow or inconvenience.

The next morning, a lay sister interrupted my music practice to inform me that the Lady Abbess needed to see me. At that hour, after the Office of Lauds, Hélène was occupied with the business of the Abbey. She would not have interrupted her work without an urgent reason. A thousand thoughts crossed my mind, none of them pleasant.

I left Aimée in the care of the lay sister and hurried to Hélène's study. I had the surprise to see a gentleman seated there with his back to me. He rose immediately, turned around and bowed to me. It was Villers. Men were allowed no farther than the apartments of the Lady Abbess, which explained why he had not been taken to my cell.

I stared at him and forgot my manners.

"What are you doing here?" I asked without any form of greeting.

"I wish you a good morning, My Lady, and apologize for disturbing your retreat. I was explaining to Madame de Montserrat that the Duchess d'Arpajon caught a chest cold a few days after your departure. Her condition was not worrisome at first, but she has declined fast. At her age, one can fear the worst. The Marquise de Bastide, who had left Paris to take the waters at La Bourboule in your country of Auvergne, is expected back in Paris shortly. So is her brother. Yet the Duchess's chambermaid tells me that her mistress, feverish as she is, keeps speaking of you and is afraid of dying without seeing you again."

I was torn between concern for the Duchess and anger at Villers's intrusion. I made an effort to regain the appearance of composure.

"Did the Duchess ask you to bring me back to Paris?"

"Before she became too ill to see any visitors, she told me how much she missed you. I proposed to fetch you, Madam, but she refused to let me bother you on account of what she called a trifling illness. Now she is too unwell to receive me, but Mélanie, her chambermaid, told me that the Duchess now wishes for your return more than that of her own children."

I fixed my eyes on his face, breathing fast. "So you took the liberty of coming here of your own accord?"

"Yes, Madam."

"Why did you not inform me of this in writing, as would have been proper?"

"You would have returned my letter unopened. Furthermore, My Lady, I brought my own carriage. It can take you back to Paris, should you decide to return there, much faster than the stagecoach. I know that you do not wish for my company. I would follow the carriage on horseback."

"May I have a moment alone with Madame de Montserrat?"

He bowed again and left.

"Is he the man of whom you spoke?" asked Hélène.

I sat in the chair he had vacated. "He is. I am amazed at his impudence."

Hélène walked to me. "He seems to mean well, dear. I am sure that he would not invent such a lie about our cousin's condition. He knows that any deception of that kind would discredit him forever in your eyes."

I looked away. "You may be right. Still, Hélène, I cannot reconcile myself to the idea that he came here uninvited."

Hélène stroked my cheek. "You will have time to reflect about your feelings later, dearest. The question is what you are going to do now."

I looked up at her. "Do you think I should return to Paris with him?"

"If the Duchess is indeed so ill and wishes to see you, I believe her kindness to you obligates you not to delay your return. Monsieur de Villers is right about his carriage. You will be in Paris faster than on the stage-coach. This does not prevent you from coming back once the Duchess's condition improves."

"I will be so sorry to leave you."

"And I to lose your company. Do not worry, Gabrielle, we will find each other again." She took both of my hands in hers. "Do not waste time now that you have decided to go. God bless you, dearest sister."

In less than an hour, I had packed our baggage and taken a hasty leave of the congregation. Hélène embraced Aimée and me. We knelt to receive her benediction.

Some events have disproportionate consequences upon our fate. Had the Duchess not become ill, had my sister not encouraged me to return to Paris, I would likely have stayed at Noirvaux. I would have shared Hélène's fate. I would not be writing these pages. I cannot chase away these thoughts, but it will not do to anticipate on the rest of my narrative.

ஊ 33 ஒ

Villers handed Aimée and me into the carriage and closed the door behind us without making any move to join us. I was too upset, both by the news about the Duchess and the shock of his arrival at Noirvaux, to pay much attention to the stages of the journey. The next day, it began raining rather heavily. I felt at first that it served Villers right to have to ride in such a downpour. Yet after ten minutes I reflected that it was not kind to let him be drenched on horseback while Aimée and I enjoyed the comforts of his carriage. I pulled on the cord to signal to the coachman to stop. Villers promptly stepped in, settling across from us and taking off his hat and cloak, which were already wringing wet.

"Thank you, My Lady," he said. "I was wondering whether you would let me catch my death. It would, I hope, have weighed heavily upon your conscience."

"You should be grateful for this storm. It drowned my resentment."

"Pray which of us has reason to be resentful? A pretty trick you played on your friends by slipping out of Paris like a thief! Lauzun has stormed every convent in town in search of you. As for me, I guessed that, in an ancient family like yours, there would be at least one close relative at the head of some abbey in the provinces. I made enquiries and discovered the existence of Madame de Montserrat at Noirvaux. I knew where to find you less than a week after your departure. Still I had no intention of intruding upon your retreat. It was only when the Duchess was taken seriously ill that I made use of the knowledge I had gained of your whereabouts. Mélanie, her chambermaid, told me that the poor old lady is literally dying to see you again."

I looked at him in alarm. "So it is true that she is very ill."

"I would never have taken Your Ladyship away from Noirvaux under false pretenses."

"I was not sure of it."

He frowned. "I know, Madam, that I have had the misfortune of offending you by a candid avowal of my intentions, but I do not deserve to be judged so harshly."

"I am no longer offended by your candor, Sir," I said after a pause. "Please accept my apologies."

I spent the rest of the journey worrying whether I would arrive in time to bid my friend farewell. Villers, without my requesting it, resumed following the carriage on horseback after the rain ceased.

We arrived at last in Paris. We were approaching from the Left Bank the *Pont-Neuf*, the New Bridge, where we were to cross the river to reach the *Marais* district. I heard a noise that would become all too familiar in the ensuing years: the many voices of a furious mob. I could smell smoke. Men and women alike shook their fists at the carriage and hurled insults at us.

"Mama, what is this?" cried Aimée. "See these people! They look so angry. Are they going to hurt us?"

I wrapped my arms around her. "Of course not, dear. This has nothing to do with us."

I nevertheless worried about our safety, and that of Villers, who was still riding by the carriage. Yet he seemed unfazed. I saw him speaking to a man on foot, then give the coachman orders I did not hear. He dismounted and stepped into the carriage. I made room for him to sit next to me without thinking about it.

"Welcome to Paris, My Lady," he said. "This happens once a year, if not more often. You will have to tolerate my presence by your side. I make too easy a target on horseback for any scoundrel with a gun. We cannot cross the river here. We will try through the Island of Saint-Louis. The bridges there may be clear."

"What is happening?"

"They are burning Madame de Polignac in effigy. While Your Ladyship was away, the judges of the Parliament of Paris have openly defied the government over the taxation question. New pamphlets, more virulent than usual, have been published against the Queen. It is Her Majesty the mob really wishes to burn, and not in effigy. We must make haste. The French Guards will be here in a moment. I do not want us to be caught between the troops and the rabble."

As we drove away, I saw more people hurrying towards the New Bridge, apparently eager to join in the commotion. I heard shots being fired and cries in the distance. The French Guards must have arrived.

The Island of Saint-Louis was quiet, as was the *Marais*. Now Villers's presence by my side made me uncomfortable. When the carriage stopped in front of the Duchess's mansion, he stepped out and offered me his hand. I ignored it and jumped out on my own. Carrying Aimée in my arms, I ran away without thanking him.

Mélanie exclaimed when she saw us and led me to her mistress. My friend was very pale, racked by a nasty cough and unable to speak. I knelt by her bed and kissed her hand. She pressed mine.

I spent the night sitting in a chair by her side. I must have dozed off in the morning and was awakened by a visit from Dr. Janseau. He found the Duchess slightly improved. Within a week, he pronounced her to be out of danger. Only then did the Duke d'Arpajon visit his mother. He left after ten minutes. The Marquise de Bastide, to whom I had written the day after my arrival to inform her of the Duchess's slight improvement, sent word that it was no longer worth her while to interrupt her stay in La Bourboule. I was sorry for the Duchess, for she deserved better from her children. Their lack of affection made me all the more aware of my many obligations to my friend. Villers did not call during that time but sent a lackey to enquire twice a day after her health.

Following Dr. Janseau's advice, the Duchess, leaning on my arm, was beginning to leave her bed for a few minutes at a time. I would read aloud to her. She once interrupted me in the middle of a comedy by Marivaux I had chosen to lift her spirits.

"Dear Belle," she said, "I am sorry to broach this subject, but we do need to talk about the future."

I opened my mouth to protest. She raised her hand. "I made a new will in your absence, dearest." She looked at me gravely. "As you know, I may not dispose of this house or even of my diamonds. Yet I left you all I can, which, I am sorry to say, does not amount to more than a very few thousand francs. That should, along with the remainder of what you received from your husband's estate, help Aimée and you keep body and soul together for a few months after my death. Yet I cannot bear the thought of leaving you in such a position. I begged my son when he visited the other day to let you stay here for some time after I am no more. He promised, but it may not do you much good. His wife will throw you out of here before I am cold in my grave."

I took her hand in mine, tears in my eyes. "Madam, you have always been so kind to me that I cannot think of what to say. But you are on your way to a complete recovery. Dr. Janseau assured me of it again today."

"Enough of this nonsense. Tell me, have you given the convent any more thought?"

"I still have no religious vocation, Madam. Of course, I could certainly go to Noirvaux as a boarder, and I am sure that Madame de Montserrat would allow me to keep Aimée with me. But if my daughter were raised there, she would not know any other place, she would not meet any other children. Being penniless, she would have no choice later but to take the veil. Oh, Madam, it is so difficult to decide what is right for Aimée and myself. What would you do if you were in my place?"

"This is a question no one likes to answer, but if I were in your place, I would discover what Villers means."

"He has already made clear what he does not mean. Sometimes I regret having been rude to him during our journey back to Paris, but I am still angry with him. Do you think that he fetched me from Noirvaux out of kindness to you and me, or to make me feel that I cannot escape him?"

"Probably both, dearest. If you wish, I will send him a note asking him to call. Please stay away. We will have a more candid talk outside your presence."

Two days later, Villers called on the Duchess. I kept to my apartment and ran downstairs as soon as he was gone.

"Well, dearest," she said, shaking her head sadly, "I represented to him how cruel it would be to force you into a situation that is sure to make you unhappy. I begged him to marry you since he seems to like you so much." She sighed. "He would not hear of it. He said that he would make you happy enough without marrying you."

I looked out the window. "He does not care about me or my feelings."

"He certainly acts as one who likes to follow his own inclination. He told me that he was glad that I was at hand to discuss your situation with him. At least he has retained enough decency not to relish dealing directly with you about such matters." The Duchess forced a smile. "I feel like a regular procuress now. Do not worry, it does not bother me if it can be of any help to you."

"So, Madam, what does Monsieur de Villers propose?"

"My dear, he wishes you to go to Normandy with him for two weeks. Should you accept, you will receive a generous gift from him before your departure."

"And then what would happen? Would I go live with him as his concubine?"

"Of course not, Belle. That would be disgraceful for you both. Upon your return, if you so wished, he would set up a separate establishment for you. In any event, you may keep his gift if you go to Normandy with him and while you are there let him have his way."

I shook my head in anger. "How elegantly put!" I closed my eyes and tried in vain to imagine my life as Villers's mistress. "Please, Madam," I asked, "would you travel with us? It would be the only thing that could make such a journey bearable."

"No, dearest, I still do not feel very strong yet. Besides, it will be better if I stay out of the way. Should you decide to accompany Villers to Normandy, I would rather have you continue with him upon your return to Paris. That would be more likely if you had only one person to please."

"Then who would chaperone us during our stay in Normandy?"

"He says that a widowed aunt of his lives on the estate year round, so appearances would be respected. He would like to receive permission to call on you, which seems a reasonable request." She stroked my cheek, tears in her eyes. "Poor child. The time has come to give him your answer, whatever it is."

Villers returned the next day. I could not meet his eye. He bowed and presented me with a blue leather case emblazoned with a Baron's coronet.

"Please, Madam, be kind enough not to open it until I leave. If you are pleased with its contents, do me the honour of considering them a gift and come with me to Normandy. If not, send them back and tell me to go to hell. I will depart at the end of the week."

He took his leave without giving me time to respond.

I cautiously opened the case and suppressed a cry of surprise. I had expected a gift of jewellery, but not anything on this order. Glittering against a dark blue velvet background was a pair of diamond earrings set in delicate patterns of roses, each ending with three huge teardrop *briolettes*. I had no idea of the value of the jewels, which I could only suppose to be exorbitant if they were not paste. I ran to the Duchess, who exclaimed at their beauty.

The same afternoon, I visited the shop of Monsieur Boehmer, jeweler to the Crown. He adjusted a magnifying lens to his eye and said in a German accent:

"Of course, Madam, I recognize the stones. Your Ladyship will not find another such set of *briolettes* in all of Europe. They are over fifteen carats a piece and of unmatched purity. I put them together myself in the time of the late King, with the idea that he might purchase them as a present for Madame du Barry. They were set in a necklace at the time. Unfortunately, His Majesty died before completing this transaction. They were afterwards purchased on credit by the Prince de Guéméné, who returned them to me at the time of his bankruptcy." He put aside his magnifying glass. "I had commenced negotiations with emissaries of the Sultan in Istanbul when, two weeks ago, My Lord the Count de Villers walked into my modest store and purchased these jewels. He asked me to reset the stones as girandole earrings. These, Madam, are absolutely unique." He smiled. "I cannot imagine them in better hands than those of Your Ladyship."

I cringed at the notion that the man was able to guess the nature of the proposed transaction between Villers and me.

"Very well, Monsieur Boehmer. How much are they worth?"

He handed me back the leather case. "I will not, of course, disclose the amount Monsieur de Villers paid for these stones. Yet I can assure Your Ladyship that one could resell them for no less than 100,000 francs."

I stared at him.

Back home, I opened the case once more and gazed sadly at the glittering stones. They represented the price of my youth, of whatever beauty I possessed and of the last remains of my innocence. God forgive me, I was ready to sell all of these for a pair of earrings.

⚜ 34 ⚜

Two days later, I breakfasted with the Duchess at seven o'clock. My appetite was spoiled by the prospect of my journey. Aimée, on the contrary, had become used to traveling. She knew that she was going to visit a new place and was too excited to remain seated for more than a minute. Manon, the chambermaid assigned to my service since I first arrived in Paris, was to accompany us. She would travel on the box next to the coachman. The bell of the entrance door rang at eight o'clock. Aimée jumped out of her chair and Villers was shown into the dining parlour.

Tears filled my eyes and those of the Duchess as I took my leave. She grasped Villers's arm. "Take good care of Belle, Villers," she said, looking into his eyes, "or I will kill you upon your return."

He kissed her hand, smiling. "Your Grace will not have to resort to such extremities. You have my word of honour that I will be more attentive to Madame de Peyre's comfort than to my own."

Villers handed me into the carriage and sat across from Aimée and me. I remained silent, twisting my gloves in both of my hands. Aimée observed him with great curiosity and tried without much success to attract his attention. He had always treated her with a benevolent indifference that seemed to pique her young pride. I looked out the window to avoid his gaze, which remained fixed on my face. He put me in mind of a fox eyeing a henhouse. The journey was uneventful and the weather fine for the season, for it was already the second half of October. Only when we reached the borders of Normandy did he become more animated. He pointed out new sights and the different style of the houses in the towns and villages we crossed. It was a country of soft rolling hills, as green as the mountains of my native Auvergne, but dotted with apple trees and divided by high earthen hedgerows crowned with hazelnut. The apples were being harvested into heaps in the middle of the fields.

"This is the beginning of the apple harvest," observed Villers. "Have you ever tasted cider, Madam, or watched it being made?"

"Never."

"You will before long. Autumn is in my opinion the most pleasant time of year to visit Normandy. The weather is drier than in any other season, and the days crisp and fine, as if to give us a last taste of sweetness before the bitterness of winter."

"You seem attached to your native country."

"One would have to be heartless not to be. Are you not to yours?"

"Very much so. It seems so long already since I left it, though it has barely been six months."

"Would you travel there with me someday?"

"I would be afraid of meeting anyone of my family, especially my brother."

He smiled. "There seems to be something unusually fearsome about the men of your country. Is the Marquis de Castel anything like the late Baron?"

"Oh no, not at all. The Marquis is soft-spoken and has perfect manners. . . ." I blushed. "I did not mean any disrespect to the memory of my late husband."

"Heaven forbid. Your Ladyship would not want to conjure his ghost. He was terrifying enough when he was alive."

The last hours of the journey passed pleasantly enough. My conversation with Villers made me forget the purpose of our travels. I was only reminded of it when the carriage stopped in the courtyard of the château of Dampierre.

It was a beautiful building of red and white stone, about a century and a half old. Its architect, Villers informed me, was the man who had designed the older part of the château of Versailles. Indeed, it had the same formality, although Dampierre was in my opinion the finer house due to its uniformity of style and elegant proportions. My host took us to a vast drawing room, decorated with mythological paintings depicting gods and goddesses in various states of undress. The room looked out on green meadows such as the ones we had seen during our journey. Villers introduced me to his aunt, Madame de Gouville, who was lying on a sofa, her legs extended under a blanket. She was a frail lady, about fifty years of age or maybe younger because her hair was still entirely black. The ceaseless activity of her dark eyes and her hands, occupied with knitting, contrasted with the paralysis of her lower limbs. Aimée cried aloud at the sight of her and hid in my skirts.

"Please excuse my daughter, Madam," I said. "She is very shy."

Madame de Gouville smiled. "Do not apologize, dear Madam. She is so pretty and the sweetest little thing, I can tell. We shall be great friends, shall we not, my treasure?"

Aimée's only response was a wail of horror. Villers mercifully put an end to that part of the conversation by embracing his aunt. Her eyes fluttered wildly, like flies trapped in a jar.

"Is not my nephew the handsomest man in the kingdom, Madam?" she asked.

I could not think of any response.

"I am afraid Madame de Peyre does not share your fond prejudice, dear Aunt," interjected Villers, "although she is too well bred to express her true opinion. Please tell me how you have been keeping."

"Never better, dear Aurélien. You are too modest. I assure you, Madam," she said, turning to me, "that if I were not his aunt, and so old and decrepit, I would marry him in a second."

"I am not surprised, Madam," said I. "I am sure many ladies share your feelings, but from his own admission Monsieur de Villers is no friend of matrimony."

Madame de Gouville shrugged. "Do not pay any attention to such talk, Madam. It does not mean a thing. All men speak in this manner until they meet the woman who can truly attach them."

"True," I said. "Your nephew must never have set eyes upon any such woman, except of course for the late Madame de Villers."

"Pray tell me," he said, "whether I should walk out of the room to leave both of you at liberty to discuss my marital prospects."

"Nonsense, Aurélien," said Madame de Gouville. "What could we have to say that you cannot hear?" She smiled at me. "He adds to his other qualities the utmost humility."

"Dear Aunt," said Villers, "what are you knitting? Your skill never fails to amaze me."

She was managing her needles, never losing a stitch, while staring at us with her searching eyes. She looked down at her work only once in a while. "You are too kind, Aurélien, as usual. Just stockings for Gauvin's children. Did you know his wife is expecting her ninth lying-in?"

"Who is Gauvin?" I hastened to ask, relieved at the change of subject.

"A cottager," said Villers, "whom I have refrained from turning out solely out of charity. He is always late in his rent and dues. He thanks me by poaching on my land." He turned to Madame de Gouville. "You may tell his wife the next time you see her, dear Aunt, that my gamekeepers have received orders to give him fifty lashes if he is ever caught again."

"I am sure, Sir," I said, "that you are joking. You are too kind to have one of your vassals flogged."

"You are both wrong and right, My Lady. I am perfectly in earnest, and I have indeed been very kind. I yielded to my aunt's entreaties and let the rascal go with a warning the first time, but he is testing the limits of my patience. He is lazy, except when it comes to fathering little Gauvins, and a drunkard. His children have not a shred of clothing on their backs except what has been given to them by my aunt."

"That is indeed generous of you, Madam," I said. "I wish I were as resourceful as you. I cannot knit at all."

Madame de Gouville stared at me. "Can you not, Madam? You must never have been properly taught. Let me show you."

Villers interrupted these offers to observe that I might be looking forward to an early dinner after the fatigues of our journey. We went upstairs to change. Madame de Gouville had to be carried by a footman. Aimée was holding fast to my hand. She could not keep her eyes off the lady's lifeless legs, thin as sticks, dangling from under her skirts like those of her beloved Italian puppets.

I was shown into a lovely apartment upstairs, decorated in rose-coloured silks, that enjoyed the same pleasant view as the drawing room. I noticed a door connecting to another bedroom, which I assumed to be Villers's.

At dinner I became silent again and could barely bring any food to my mouth. I was wondering whether Villers was expecting to "have his way," as he had said to the Duchess, that very night.

"You look tired, Madam," he remarked. "So am I. Shall we retire early?"

I was unsure of what he meant, but when he wished me a good night, he whispered: "You should take plenty of rest. I will not presume to bother you tonight. I have a surprise for you tomorrow."

I was not sure that I would welcome any surprise from him, but went to bed with great relief. I still made sure that all doors were locked.

The next morning, Villers asked me if I was ready for a ride. He had a Normand mare saddled for me. We crossed the town of Dampierre, which extended beyond the gates of the château.

"My grandfather owned the whole town," he said, "and had all the houses rebuilt in the same style. He did not want them to detract from the appearance of the château or ruin the view from its front windows."

"Just as in Versailles."

"On a smaller scale, the difference being that here, my grandfather assumed the construction costs and retained all property rights. I still own every house in town."

I smiled. "And all of the surrounding land, I suppose."

"Yes, Madam, in a twenty-league radius and up to the sea northwards."

"Would you take me there?"

"That was indeed my intention."

We followed country roads and then smaller lanes until we reached a moor. The grass there was shorter and less green than inland. Jackrabbits ran away from us in a flutter of white tails. We dismounted and tied the horses to a stunted tree. The wind was blowing in my face, carrying an unknown scent and the noise of rushing water. We walked until I saw a shimmering surface, woven of an infinity of blue and grey hues, reflecting the light of the clear autumn day. We were at the summit of a cliff. Waves crashed hundreds of feet below in bursts of foam. I was fascinated by their even rhythm and ever-changing shapes. I could not speak. Villers too was silent. I felt a prickling in my eyes, either from the sharpness of the wind or from some new emotion. I do not know how long the spell held. At last I recalled that I was not alone.

"Forgive me," I said, turning to Villers. "I am so taken by the sight of the sea. You must be bored. This is nothing new to you."

"True, but I do not tire of looking at it. And I am never bored in your company. Watching you watch the sea is fascinating."

"Do we have to leave?"

"I am in no hurry. There is no inn nearby, but we could go to a cottage and have some luncheon before returning. Or if you prefer, I can take you to another place farther to the east. The view is not so spectacular as here, but we could ride on the beach."

"I would rather return here. Can one see England from here?"

He smiled. "It is too far away, about thirty leagues. But Portsmouth and the Isle of Wight are due north across the Channel."

Villers took me to a thatched cottage a couple of miles inland. The peasants recognized him and greeted us with loud cries of surprise and alarm. The woman seized a rag and began scouring the table with alacrity, an unusual occurrence judging by the shiny layer of grease covering it. Her husband chased chickens, clucking with indignation, from the bench where I was to sit.

At first I could not understand anything of what the cottagers said. Their dialect and accent were foreign to me, but I gathered from their tone that they were lamenting the lack of notice and apologizing for not receiving us properly. Villers responded in French, mixed with words of their patois, which I did not recognize. They seemed to understand him without any difficulty. The woman served us a meal of buckwheat crepes and salt pork. I ate with a hearty appetite in spite of some misgivings about the cleanliness of the plates. I felt the prickle of cider against the roof of my mouth and winced at its tartness and taste of mold. Yet it quenched my thirst. Before long, I found it delicious.

"You should be careful, Madam," said Villers, smiling. "Cider is not the same as apple juice. It can go to one's head if one is not accustomed to it."

After a while, I was able to understand a few words of the peasants' speech. They called Villers "Our Master," a phrase I had never heard before, as well as "My Lord." At the end of the meal, he drew a silver *écu* from his pocket and left it on the table. They made a show of protesting before accepting it and kissing both of his hands effusively.

We rode back in the direction of the sea.

"I am dizzy," I said. "I may have had too much cider."

"I told you so, although you may not be sober enough to remember it. I can discern two flaws among your many perfections: you are stubborn beyond belief and you never seem to trust anything I say, when all I have in mind is your best interest. I might be able to cure you of the second, but the first one must be constitutional." He paused. "Let us hope that you can at least ride back to Dampierre. If not, I will have to leave you at the cottage and fetch you tomorrow morning. I am sure that Lafosse and his wife will be happy to give up their bed for you tonight."

I remembered with horror seeing in a corner of the only room of the cottage an unmade bed, the curtains of which had been drawn in haste when we had arrived. I sat straight in the saddle.

"You are such a child," Villers continued, grinning, "that one cannot help teasing you. You should know that I would never do anything of the kind. I cannot bring Your Ladyship back to Paris covered with fleas after I promised the Duchess to take good care of you." He looked at me. "Besides, I might avail myself of the pleasure of your company at Dampierre tonight."

That remark and the bite of the wind dispelled any traces of my dizziness. Once we reached the cliffs, I fell again under the thrall of the sea. We walked on the moor until late in the afternoon, when he observed that the sun was already low on the horizon. It was time for us to return if we wished to reach Dampierre before dark. While helping me into the saddle, he asked: "Tonight?"

He looked pleased with my silence.

◞ 35 ◟

I was far more timid as a widow than I had been as a maiden. At fifteen, I had let Pierre-André kiss and caress me. I had enjoyed his attentions and yearned for the closest intimacy with him. Those emotions had been buried and forgotten under the Baron's ministrations.

Villers had never touched me before, save to dance with me, hand me into and out of carriages and help me mount or dismount. He had never made any attempts at further familiarity, either from delicacy or in anticipation of my reaction.

That night, I whimpered when he approached my bed. He looked like a new, strange kind of animal. His hair, without powder and falling in loose curls on his shoulders, was sandy like his eyebrows. Through the opening of his nightgown I could see freckles on his chest, matching those on his face. Silly as it sounds, one of the reasons why I had accepted him as a suitor was his slender build, but I noticed that his muscles were compact and well defined, and that he could have harmed me if he had been so inclined.

Without giving him time to reach me, I bolted from the bed as I had done at the beginning of my wedding night. Since he was standing between the door and me, I sought refuge in the far corner of the room, crouching in my chemise, my fists clenched against my eyes. I heard him walk towards me.

"I changed my mind," I cried. "I cannot do it. Stay away from me. Please forgive me, Sir. Do not hit me."

I felt that he was kneeling next to me.

"Of course not," he said. "Why would I do such a thing? What has happened to you? Please look at me."

I opened my eyes. I read concern and pity in his. I had not had the least intention of disclosing what had been done to me for fear of giving him ideas he might not already have on his own, but my reserve melted away. I gave him a summary of the brutalities of my married life. He put his finger to my lips.

"I have heard enough. What a shame. Poor Belle, so young, so pretty, so delicate. No wonder you are shy. Listen to me: I will never beat you, hurt you, force you. Never. I promise."

I let him take me in his arms like a child and hold me.

"Let me put you back to bed," he said. "You are shivering. Have no fear. I will not do anything without your permission."

He tucked me in bed and lay down on his side next to me without removing his nightgown. I could not keep my eyes off him. He kissed and caressed my cheek. I stiffened, paralyzed with fear, whenever he touched me. He sighed.

"All right, my dear," he said at last. "I am sorry to frighten you so. Please take some rest."

He left. I cried myself to sleep.

The next morning, I dressed and went down to breakfast with much reluctance. I expected Villers to announce, when he set eyes on me, that I was no longer welcome in Dampierre. I would have to return with Aimée to Paris by the next stagecoach. I stopped for a moment at the entrance to the dining parlour, tempted to run back to my apartment. A lackey saw me and hurried to open the door. It was too late to retreat. I took a deep breath and, my eyes downcast, walked as fast as I could to my chair. I felt more than saw Villers rise and bow to me with his usual ease and courtesy. I did not know whether embarrassment or relief was uppermost on my mind. Madame de Gouville, after greeting me in a friendly manner, was watching him and me in turn with some curiosity.

"I hope you are well rested, Madam," said Villers. "I would like to take you this afternoon to Saint-Laurent, a league to the east of the place we visited yesterday."

I dared not look at him and, without accepting or declining, muttered indistinct thanks.

"Very well," he said. "I am glad to hear that Your Ladyship likes the idea. Saint-Laurent it will be then."

He left promptly after breakfast. I spent the rest of the morning in the drawing room with Aimée and Madame de Gouville. My daughter still would not approach within a few steps of the old lady, but could now bring herself to cast furtive glances at her. I directed Aimée's attempts at drawing flowers in pastels and showed these works to Madame de Gouville, who joined me in expressing rapturous admiration. After my little girl tired of the pastels and turned her attention to dressing her doll, the old lady renewed her offer to teach me to knit. I accepted and drew a chair next to her sofa.

"Oh no, dear, not like this," she said. "You pull too hard on the wool. See the result! It is tight as chain mail. No one could ever wear anything like this."

In spite of my perseverance, my progress was slow. I was struggling with the needles, biting my lips, when Villers reappeared, booted and in riding clothes. I had forgotten his existence for a few hours and blushed at his sight.

I ate little and said less during luncheon. Villers did not try to engage me in conversation and was content to listen to Madame de Gouville's account of our morning activities.

"And pray, dear Aunt," he asked, arching his eyebrow, "how proficient do you find Madame de Peyre at knitting? She seemed quite taken by it when I arrived."

Madame de Gouville thought for a minute before answering. "Well, Aurélien, she puts a great deal of effort into it."

"Very commendable," he said. "One should always, dear Aunt, show much indulgence with beginners."

He was repressing a smile. I looked at him with some resentment.

At last it was time to ride. He kept silent. After we left Dampierre, I took advantage of a moment when we were slowing to a walk between two hedgerows. "I am sorry, Sir," I said, "for what happened, or did not happen, last night. You must think that I am a complete simpleton. I am firmly convinced of it myself."

"Please do not apologize. I am the one to blame. I expected too much too soon. From what I knew of your late husband, I should have guessed that you were no stranger to rough treatment."

"It is kind of you to say so, but I breached my pledge to you. I promised more than I could give when I accepted your earrings. I will of course return them to you later today."

"Please keep them at least until the end of our stay in Normandy. I hope that you do not intend to curtail your visit."

"In truth, Sir, I no longer know what to do. I fully expected you to throw me out of your house this morning. Indeed I deserve no better."

He laughed. "What sort of man do you think I am? I would be a fool to deprive myself of the pleasure of your company. I would of course take you back to Paris should you so desire, but it would be much against my own inclination." He turned towards me. "Please say that you will not leave."

I hesitated. He reined in his horse and caught my bridle.

"All right, Madam," he said sternly, "I will no longer try to conceal it. I am indeed terribly angry with you for misleading me in so shameful a manner. I will forgive you only under one condition."

I looked at him, amazed at the change in his tone. "What is it?"

"That you not say another word about last night, those earrings or your return to Paris."

He was smiling. I breathed a sigh of relief.

"This is better," he said. "The very first smile I have seen on your face today. I feared that these dimples in your cheeks were gone forever. Now let us enjoy this moment and forget about anything else."

We climbed down a steep hill covered with pine trees and found ourselves on a beach that extended for miles. The receding tide had uncovered the sand, except for small pools and rivulets. The day was cloudy. Sea, sky and land all seemed to blend into shades of grey. He proposed a race. "I will let you start ahead of me. It would not be fair otherwise because you are riding sidesaddle."

At his signal I left at a full gallop. He followed a minute later. I won and let out a cry of victory. In my joy, I forgot my apprehension and gladly received his congratulations.

Villers helped me dismount. I knelt and touched the sand. It was wet and compact in places, soft and shifting in others. I ran my fingers through it and filled my pockets with seashells, some tiny, ribbed and yellow, and some larger, irregular in shape and lined with pink mother-of-pearl. He was standing a few yards away with a look of amusement on his face.

"Are you mocking me?" I asked. "I am gathering these shells for Aimée. She likes to play with things of this sort."

"So do you, Madam. You are not so much older than your daughter."

"May we return with her someday?"

"Of course. Order and you will be obeyed. We will take the carriage then."

Nothing in his behaviour betrayed any resentment. We were alone on the beach. Yet he was not making any gesture to take advantage of our isolation. At last he pulled his watch and remarked that it was time to leave. We walked back to the spot where we had left the horses.

"Thank you for your kindness, Sir," I said. "When I rose this morning, I certainly did not expect to have such a pleasant day."

"I easily believe it. I never saw anything so pitiable as you at breakfast, with your swollen eyes and uneasy gait. You made me feel like an ogre. I was quite ashamed of myself for causing such misery." He paused, seemingly lost in his thoughts. "Please look at me."

I did.

"If you did me the favour of leaving your door unlocked tonight," he continued, "I still would not touch you against your wishes. Of course, you may also keep it locked if you prefer. There is no need to tell me now what you intend to do. Regardless of what you decide, you should know that it would not enter my mind to be angry with you. You will always retain my good opinion, as I hope that you will not withdraw yours. We should leave now."

Fog was rising from the fields as we rode in silence. By the time we reached Dampierre, servants were lighting the lanterns in the courtyard. I ran to the drawing room to show Aimée the seashells. She was delighted with them, and still more with the prospect of gathering her own in a few days.

I do not recall anything of what was said, eaten or done during dinner that night. I was lost in my thoughts, unsure of what to do. I could not understand myself. I wondered why I had been ready to marry Villers if I did not want to let him approach me. Perhaps I would have been less shy with him had he wed me. I knew that, by accepting to accompany him to Normandy, I had lost my good name. I would be assumed to be his mistress regardless of what happened between us. My hopes of marrying, which had been slim, would become nil. My only choices would be to return to Noirvaux or to become another's mistress. I shuddered at that thought. I remembered how Villers had respected my fears the night before, how he had made me forget my embarrassment during the day. I tried to imagine how another man would have behaved in his place. The comparison was to his advantage.

I left my door unlocked that night. This time, I remained in bed, breathing fast, watching him intently. He lay down on top of the covers in his nightgown as he had done the night before.

"Thank you for trusting me," he said, bringing my hand to his lips.

He whispered words of comfort to my ear. His voice soothed me. I closed my eyes, not to avoid seeing him but to better listen to him. I felt the warmth of his breath on my neck. A strange numbness was spreading into my head and down my spine.

He pulled gently on the ribbon that tied my chemise around my shoulders. I shuddered. He stopped.

"You are not angry with me, my dearest, are you?" he asked.

I shook my head. "No."

He opened my chemise. His lips wandered between my breasts. "I would give anything to see you naked," he said.

I stiffened in fear. "Would you disrobe too?"

"Not if it made you uneasy, my love."

"You promise?"

"Of course."

I knelt on the bed. He followed suit and lifted my chemise.

"Oh, God," he said, "you are beautiful."

I covered my bosom with my hands. He slowly pushed them aside. We were still on our knees, facing each other. Holding me by the waist, he bent to suckle. Only Aimée had feasted on my breasts in this manner. I was troubled to feel the same kind of intimacy with a grown man.

To escape him, I leaned forward onto my stomach and hid my face in the pillows. He played with my hair and stroked my back with his fingertips. The pleasant numbness returned, only stronger. My skin prickled and quivered under his touch. He pulled on one of my hips to gently roll me onto my side. He explored my body with his lips and tongue. My thighs parted of their own accord. I ran my fingers through the locks of his blonde hair. In spite of its colour, it did not look so strange anymore.

The manner in which he was caressing me moved me as nothing had before. No thoughts, no memories clouded my mind. I became tense all over, then felt a sort of pause, as in anticipation of something unknown, before being shaken by successive pulses of pleasure, longer and longer. They emanated from the center of me and rippled through my entire body. The shudder was so powerful that I felt the muscles of my stomach contract as if a hand had kneaded them. It took my breath away; it made me dizzy. At last it subsided.

Villers looked up, smiling. "Are you surprised?"

"I did not expect anything like this."

"What did you expect, dearest?"

"I do not know. Not pleasure." I looked into Villers's eyes as if to question him.

"Do not worry about me," he said. "I cannot think of a more delicious torture than this. You may prolong it all night if you wish."

"I would like to make you happy too."

"Then come here, my love."

He drew me to him. His lips pressed mine open. His embrace tightened until I felt him aroused against my stomach. A wave of fear overcame me. I pushed him away.

"Forgive me," he said. "I startled you." He caressed my face, looking into my eyes. "Have no fear. Even now, I will not force myself on you."

I drew close to him again. He put his hand on my shoulder without holding me tight. I wanted to give him a token of my tenderness, my gratitude, my trust. All I could bring myself to do was to kiss him lightly on the cheek. Inadequate as my gesture was, he seemed to understand it.

"Thank you, my love," he said.

He sat up and blew out the candles. Only then did he remove his nightgown and shirt. I was not so afraid of him in the dim glow of the fire. He lay by my side again and, seizing one of my hands in both of his, slowly kissed every inch of it. I let him guide it by degrees down his chest and stomach until it reached what he wanted me to feel. The skin there was silkier than anything I had touched. He breathed in sharply. I did not recoil.

It was past ten when I woke the next morning. I started when I saw him still in bed with me. He was smiling.

"I have been watching you for a while," he said. "As much as I wanted you, I did not wish to disturb your rest. You looked too pretty asleep."

He was now addressing me as *thou*. This familiarity brought back the memories of the night. I recalled that I was naked. So was he. I blushed. He wrapped his arms around my waist to draw me closer. "So you are again shy. Last night you seemed to have forgotten your timidity. Remember, my dearest, you are mine now, all mine."

He was ready to give me renewed assurances of it. We rose only in time for luncheon.

Aimée ran to me as soon as I entered the drawing room. "Oh, Mama, you slept so long! I wanted to go awaken you with a kiss. Manon would not let me."

"Aimée dearest," said Madame de Gouville, "I already told you that your Mama was tired after her ride yesterday. The sea air has that effect on people who are not accustomed to it."

I stole a look at the old lady. For once her eyes were fixed on her knitting.

"Mama," said Aimée, "Madame Gouville is no witch after all. Look, I can sit next to her on the sofa. I am not afraid of her. But her feet are *really* ugly. She will make a dress for my doll. I can choose the colour."

"I am very sorry, Madam," I said. "I will check Aimée's tongue in the future."

"No, dear Madam, you should not. Your daughter is delightful. Enjoy these precious moments when the truth springs out of the mouths of babes."

The following day, Villers proposed to take Aimée and me to a nearby farm to watch cider making. I accepted and went to my apartment to dress. He knocked at the door five minutes later, while Manon was tying a cherry-coloured sash around the waist of my gown. I blushed at the familiarity of this visit. Manon did not seem equally disturbed by it and, after a curtsey to Villers, hastened to disappear. He looked at my grey dress and said, smiling, "You look lovely, Belle, but your gown is not elegant enough."

"But we are going to a farmhouse. You are wearing riding clothes yourself."

"True, but the peasants expect a *Baroness from Paris*, and they do not see one every day. My poor aunt is the closest they come to a fine lady. You would offend them by arriving dressed too simply."

"Do you think so, Sir?"

He laughed aloud. "Why on earth do you address me as *Sir* now? I will understand, of course, if you keep doing so in public or in front of the servants, but it is ridiculous when we are alone."

I coloured again. "My husband never suggested that I address him otherwise."

"I am not surprised, but *I* will expect something less formal."

"What?"

"Even *Villers* would be better. How about *Aurélien*?" He smiled. "Or would *my love* offend your sense of truthfulness? Shall we settle on *my dear*, then?"

I bit the nail of my little finger. Villers shook his head sadly and took me in his arms. "My poor Belle, I forget how shy you still are. Call me anything you wish then, or nothing at all if you prefer."

I made no response. He kissed me on the forehead. "Now let us find you something suitable to wear."

He walked to the wardrobe and, after a brief inspection, pulled out a dove-coloured silk dress and a hat trimmed with matching ribbons and white ostrich feathers, which he threw on the bed.

Without giving me time to call back Manon, he proceeded to unlace my bodice as deftly as she would have done. The skirts of my grey dress soon lay in a heap at my feet. He now seemed to have forgotten all about the other gown as he caressed my neck and shoulders with his lips.

"Maybe cider making is not so interesting after all," he said. "I can think of a better way of spending an autumn afternoon."

"But I promised Aimée—"

He stopped me with a light kiss. "As you wish, my love. Be assured that you will make amends for this tonight."

He took the dove-coloured gown from the bed and dressed me as skillfully as he had unlaced me, though far more slowly. He paused many times to stroke the exposed parts of my skin. My eyes closed, I shuddered and sought his lips. He pressed them upon mine.

"You too, dearest," he said, "seem to have something other than cider making on your mind. As you will discover, delaying fulfillment only makes it more enjoyable. In the meantime, you are going to call me *my love*."

My head thrown backwards, my eyes still closed, I whispered: "My love . . ."

He rewarded me with a long, deep kiss. "So much better," he said when he drew away from me. "Now let us put the final touches to your attire."

He adjusted my hat and made me wear his diamond earrings. I was still light-headed when he handed Aimée and me into the carriage.

The farm where Villers took us looked more prosperous and inviting than the cottage we had visited a few days earlier. Over two dozen peasants were gathered in a vast barn next to the house. All laughter and conversations came to a sudden halt upon our arrival. The men removed their hats and bowed while the women curtseyed. Everyone, regardless of age and sex, gawked at me.

Villers did not seem disconcerted by the silence. After taking off his hat, he bowed to the farmer's wife, a blonde buxom woman, as he would have done to a duchess, and paid her a compliment in patois. I did not understand what he said, but her cheeks flushed with pleasure as she curtseyed a second time. The din of the voices resumed.

I watched apples burst in a round granite trough under a wooden wheel drawn by a bay horse. The crushed fruit was then shoveled into a tank, where it was pressed between layers of straw. All the peasants, men, women and children, took turns pushing the iron bar moving the press before refreshing their fatigues by generous swigs of the prior year's cider. The clear juice then flowed through into a vat. From there, it was poured into waiting barrels.

A little boy, four or five years old, his eyes fixed on my face, walked to me and touched my skirts. His mother ran after him and raised her arm to slap him. I stopped her in mid-course and, smiling at him, gave him a silver *écu* I carried in my pocket. He accepted it without taking his eyes off me or thanking me, an omission for which his mother more than compensated.

That night in bed, after I made ample amends, Villers asked me what I thought of our outing.

"It was very pleasant," I said, "but everyone was staring at me in a manner I found a little unnerving."

"People around here are not used to new faces. Any stranger elicits a lively curiosity. Moreover, they will probably never see a more beautiful woman than you in their entire lives. Coarse as they are, they know this. I do not begrudge them the pleasure of gawking at you." He stroked my hair. "It does not bother me to see other men lust for you as long as I have you to myself."

On the following days we returned to the beach of Saint-Laurent with Aimée and enjoyed many other outings. Madame de Gouville would stay home and receive upon our return an account of our expeditions from Aimée, who never failed to enquire afterwards into the stage of completion of the new dresses for her doll. I say dresses, for their number had increased to three.

Villers gave us a tour of his stables, which housed no less than fifty stallions. Most of the horses I had seen racing in Paris, except of course those purchased directly from England, came from his farm. He introduced Aimée to a white pony.

"He is in demand as a sire because he is sweet-tempered around children," said Villers. He lowered his voice to a whisper. "Next year she could ride with us. I will teach her if you wish."

Aimée now insisted on visiting the stables at least once a day to visit her new friend and present him with an apple. It did not escape my notice that Villers had implied that, in a year's time, he would still be interested in me. In spite of my tender age, I was already wise enough to know that men tend to drop such hints without meaning anything, thus dispensing with more explicit commitments.

The weather, still dry and sunny, the wind carrying a faint smell of smoke, allowed us to ride every day.

Villers would join me at night, which I found still more enjoyable than seeing him otherwise. Happiness, like my first taste of cider, made me slightly dizzy. I enjoyed that time to the fullest without worrying about the future beyond the end of our allotted fortnight.

"So, Belle," he said one day, "it is almost time for us to leave Normandy."

"Unfortunately. I do not remember ever spending a more pleasant time than these two weeks."

"I am very happy to hear you say so. Does that mean that you would be willing to continue our acquaintance in Paris?"

I looked up at him. "Would you?"

"How can you doubt it? I could not bear the thought of giving you up."

"Could we please stay in Normandy a little longer?"

"Certainly, if you wish, for a few days. Business does not call me to Paris until the month is over."

At the end of an additional week, we had to pack our things.

"It breaks my heart to see you so sad, Belle," said Villers. "Please do not be. We are going to see almost as much of each other in Paris as here. I will secure lodgings for you next to my house. We will still ride together at Vaucelles."

I fixed my eyes on his face. "Maybe, but in Paris you are going to see other women."

"What makes you believe that?" he asked after a pause.

"I know that you have a *little house* near the Saint-Denis Gate and that you keep three ladies there. You share the expenses with the Duke d'Orléans and Monsieur de Lauzun."

"Your information is very detailed," he said. "May I enquire into its source?"

"Madame de Bastide. Is it not true?"

"There is nothing like the malice of a spurned woman. I did not even discard her. *She* demanded that I choose between her and Mrs. Herndon, which did not take me long to decide. Madame de Bastide should have been flattered that I chose as her rival the latter, who is prettier and far more pleasant."

He frowned. "I wonder how she knows of my private arrangements. Probably Lauzun and his loose mouth. I will not insult your intelligence, my dear, by denying her reports. I am not so presumptuous as to expect exclusive access to a certain class of women and, if I have to share them, I would rather do it with my friends."

"Madame de Bastide also said that the Duke d'Orléans, Lauzun and you meet there and enjoy those three ladies together."

His jaw tightened. "Madame de Bastide is an impertinent hussy. I should have induced her, at the time of our intimacy, to join one of those little parties herself. Neither the Duke d'Orléans nor Lauzun would have minded an addition to the usual company, and she might be less inclined now to blabber. But maybe it is better this way. I would not want to lie to you. You should know that I am no different from other men. I cannot be content for long with one woman, no matter how passionately loved."

Tears came to my eyes. "You are disappointed in me. I must be clumsy and inexperienced compared to your other mistresses."

He took me in his arms. "Please do not speak like this, Belle. I would never think of you as *one of my mistresses*. There is nothing in common between you and any of them. I never waited so long for any woman as for you, I never wanted one so much, I never paid such a price for one and, if you must know, you are worth all of it. I never enjoyed myself as much as in your company. No pleasure compares with the possession of the woman one loves. What I feel for you I have never felt before. I am moved to tears, Belle, when I see you so grateful for minor kindnesses that any other woman would not even notice. I love you, and pity you, and admire you, all at the same time."

He brought my hand to his lips. "It does not prevent me from needing a variety of cruder amusements, some of which you might not find to your taste. I would not dare mention them to you, let alone ask you to share in them. Do not worry, you will not notice any decline either in my affections or my attentions. Our return to Paris will not change anything for you."

"It will for you."

"I am afraid that it cannot be helped. I will not love you any less for it, nor will I give you any reasons to be unhappy with our arrangements."

Aimée and I took a fond farewell of Madame de Gouville.

"I am sorry," she said, "that you must leave so soon. I will miss you and your little girl almost as much as my nephew. And what a pity that you leave Dampierre barely more proficient in the art of knitting than when you entered this house! I would still love to teach you."

"True, dear Aunt," said Villers, "but Madame de Peyre has nevertheless used her time wisely."

She made Villers promise to bring us back very soon.

↞ 36 ↠

Upon our return to Paris, Villers left me with the Duchess and promised to call on me the next day. After his departure, my friend took my face in her hands and looked into my eyes.

"Good," she said. "You are happy. Tell me all about Normandy."

"Oh, Madam, it was beautiful. The sea was unlike anything I could have imagined, so vast, changing from moment to moment. The uproar of it is amazing. Normandy is a fine country, green and cheerful. Dampierre, Monsieur de Villers's château, is a handsome building, very elegantly furnished. His aunt took quite a fancy to Aimée." I smiled. "She even tried to teach me to knit."

"And what about Villers, dear?"

I blushed. "He was very kind, Madam."

She laughed. "I guess I will have to be content with this. I knew that he could not be quite as bad as his reputation. I am delighted to hear that you enjoyed yourself so much, dear Belle. We have been very dull here in Paris, except for the news about the Duke d'Orléans. He defied the King in the middle of a session of the Parliament of Paris, which had declined to approve new taxes and borrowing. He publicly said that the King's actions violated the unwritten Constitution of the Kingdom since only the Estates General have the power to create new taxes. For his pains the King exiled him to the château of Villers-Coterets, forty leagues away."

"The Duke d'Orléans may be right about the Constitution of the Kingdom, but I cannot say that I will miss him much."

"I know, dear. Many missed you, though. The Chevalier des Huttes was here in your absence. He had heard of your journey and was angrier than I have ever seen him. He upbraided me for letting you fall prey to *the most depraved libertine in town*, as he calls Villers." She sighed. "I will never understand men, dear Belle. I reminded the Chevalier that none of this would have happened if he had listened to me and married you. I will spare you most of what he said, but he assured me that he would write your brother."

I gasped. "Oh, Madam, does the Chevalier know what mischief will come out of it? I am sure now that the Marquis will come to Paris."

"Nonsense. After declining to provide for you, how could he blame anyone but himself for your situation?"

On the very day of my return, I had the honour of a call from the Duke de Lauzun, no doubt apprized of my arrival by his informant within the Duchess's house.

"So this is how you reward my perseverance, Madam," he said sternly. "I loved you in vain. You spurned my offers and preferred Villers. I will never forgive you."

"I do not feel that I have deserved such severity, Sir. Please remember that I warned you months ago that I would never allow myself to fall in love with you."

"And how, My Lady, was I supposed to know that you were in earnest?"

"Because I always am when I speak of serious matters. Please, Sir, do me the honour of remaining my friend. What I told you about my other feelings was true too. I am sincerely fond of your company."

"I suppose that I will have to become accustomed to your candor. In the meantime, I would be grateful if you could return my letters. This is the sole reason for my visit today."

"I cannot."

"Pray why not if you want to consider me only a friend?"

"Because I burnt them as I received them."

His jaw dropped. "*Burnt* them?"

"I did not mean to upset you, Sir. I would have kept them had I known that you wanted them back. Letters, I believed, were the property of the recipient."

He stared at me. "You cannot be serious. No woman burns love letters."

"I did. Again you will have to believe me. I was embarrassed by them. I did not want to keep them, nor did I wish to return them to you. It would have given you additional opportunities to speak to me of their subject."

"The more I know you, Madam, the more you astonish me. You must be the most extraordinary creature I have ever met." He smiled. "I guess that I will have to grant your request and remain your friend in spite of everything."

"Please do."

He kissed my hand.

The following day, Villers returned to inform me that my lodgings were ready to receive me. It was with great sadness that I took leave of the Duchess. He took Aimée and me in his carriage to Rue Saint-Dominique, on the left bank of the river. We stopped in front of a handsome house, the monotony of its white stone facade interrupted by Corinthian columns. The building, located less than a hundred yards from Villers's mansion, was rented to various tenants, all members of the nobility. My lodgings, small but elegantly appointed, consisted of the entire second floor. The furniture in the main drawing room was of the most delicate marqueterie, inlaid with medallions of Sèvres porcelain. I ran my fingers on the keys of a pianoforte, an instrument that was then rare and very expensive. In the bedroom, which overlooked an enclosed garden, a pattern of flowers and birds graced the draperies, lined in pale blue silk.

Villers ordered a supper brought from his mansion and spent the night with me to prevent me, he said, from feeling lonely. I was indeed not a little intimidated by my new lodgings and new position. I knew only too well that he could expel me from both on a moment's notice. Truth be told, I had missed his company the night before, the first one I had spent alone in weeks. I could not help imagining that he had taken advantage of it to visit his *little house.*

The following morning, as I awakened, he put a ring on the fourth finger of my left hand.

"I would like you to wear it at all times," he said.

I thanked him, staring at the enormous rectangular ruby flanked by two round diamonds.

"What is the matter?" he asked, stroking my cheek. "Are you not pleased by it?"

"The colour of the ruby is extraordinary. The red almost has a pink tinge." I hesitated. "What pains me is that it seems like a mockery of a nuptial ring."

"Dearest," he said, smiling, "all of Paris already knows that you are mine. By wearing this jewel, you will allow me to flaunt it. Why be shy about it?"

Manon, my chambermaid during my months with the Duchess, had agreed to follow me. She was promoted to the rank of head servant. My household was completed by a footman and two other maids, all of whom came from Villers's employ. I suspected that both women, pert and pretty, had passed through his hands at an earlier, possibly not too distant time. They probably would not be adverse to continuing his acquaintance or spying on me on his behalf. As for the footman, Junot, he seemed very ancient for this kind of place, which was usually occupied by robust young men. I could only guess that he had been handed down to me either because he was becoming too old to fulfill his duties with his master, or because his age assuaged any notions of jealousy on Villers's part. It was a shock at first to behold again the red livery of the Baron de Peyre on Junot's back. I had not seen it since leaving Cénac, nor had I missed it. I was not, in any case, in any position to complain about my servants. Villers paid their wages and the rent, in addition to giving me an allowance of five hundred francs on the first of each month.

"You will not need your own carriage," he told me, "since you may borrow any of mine at your pleasure. And I will not hire a cook for you.

Your maids can prepare breakfast and tea. The rest of your meals may be brought from my own house. It is one of the advantages of having you settled so close to me, in addition of course to the convenience of my visits."

Though Villers was always more than generous in his dealings with me, he, unlike most of his friends, did not indulge in extravagant spending. He once told me that such caution was a Normand trait. I must add that, without my asking for it, he confirmed in writing my ownership of the diamond earrings and the ruby ring, thus giving me assurances that I would not be left destitute if he tired of me.

While disdaining the title of husband, Villers seemed to think that being my keeper, or protector, or master, or whatever title of ownership was appropriate for his position, gave him equivalent rights. I obeyed and honoured him no less than if he had married me. The difference was that he could discard me at will.

"If you want to please me, Belle," he said, "and I am sure that such is your wish, you will not allow any men to call on you here. I do not rent these lodgings to allow others the convenience of paying court to you."

At the time, those demands seemed fair to me. I had been removed less than a year from the bonds of matrimony.

↘ 37 ↙

In spite of Villers's injunction, I was to receive a visit from a gentleman within weeks of my settling in Rue Saint-Dominique. As I came home one afternoon from taking tea with the Duchess, Manon ran to me with an agitated look on her usually placid face.

"Oh, Madam," she said, "a gentleman is here. He says he's the Marquis de Castel, your brother. He was told that you weren't at home. But he pushed Junot aside and said that he'd wait for you."

I handed Manon my mantle and braced myself before entering the drawing room.

The Marquis was pacing the room. I did not know whether he would welcome any gestures of affection and made a formal curtsey. He walked to me and took me in his arms.

"Little sister," he said. "At last. We have never been separated so long, have we?"

His fond gesture brought tears to my eyes. "It is kind of you, Sir, to call on me. I feared your anger."

"I know better than to direct it at you. When I reflect upon my own conduct, Gabrielle, there are some circumstances of which I am not proud. In one particular regard I failed you. As your brother, I should have offered you my help and protection after your widowhood; I should have welcomed you back to Fontfreyde."

I looked away, my conversation with Hélène still fresh on my mind.

"I was wrong," the Marquis continued, "when I tried to force religious vows upon you. I see it now. I unwittingly prompted your departure to Paris. Your current life of sin and dissipation, which grieves me so, is my fault. For this, I humbly beg your forgiveness. I offer you now all I should have proposed last spring. Come back to Fontfreyde with me, dearest."

I had expected anything but that offer. It was quite a different thing to discuss the Marquis from afar with Hélène and face him in all of his renewed kindness. I made no answer.

He held out his hand to me. "Gabrielle, do not hesitate. I will make amends for my past unkindness. I promise never to reproach you for your errors, which are no more grievous than mine."

"I do not know how to express my gratitude, Sir."

"Nothing is easier. You need only leave your shameful situation."

I shook my head sadly. "No, Sir. I cannot."

"Why not? What is keeping you here? What is that man to you? If he had the least respect, the least affection for you, he would have married you."

The Marquis had hit close to home. "You may be right, Sir. I am indeed ashamed of my situation. I would leave Monsieur de Villers, I would follow you to Fontfreyde if I were not afraid of what would happen there."

"How can you expect me to believe this?" he said, frowning. "I lost my mind for a moment, years ago. Am I never to be forgiven, never trusted again?" His jaw tightened. "No, there is another reason for your refusal. You are in thrall to that scoundrel. He has debauched you."

I looked at him with tears in my eyes.

"You are now deaf to the call of duty, of virtue, of reason," he continued. "You leave me no choice, Gabrielle, but to call upon your lover."

He stormed out of the room. I could easily guess the outcome of such a visit.

Villers and I were to go together to the *Théâtre-Français* that night. I received from him a note informing me that due to an earlier engagement, unfortunately forgotten, he was unable to accompany me.

I decided to pay Lauzun a visit. I still saw him a great deal, although not outside the presence of Villers. I now called him simply "Lauzun," a familiarity he had requested and to which Villers had not objected. I would under any other circumstances have considered a late unchaperoned visit to his mansion a most imprudent step, but was too worried to care about niceties. I was shown right away into a drawing room, where he was leaning against the mantelpiece. He smiled and bowed.

"How, Madam, should I interpret the unexpected pleasure of your visit at this hour? Have you relented at last, dearest friend?"

"Please do not trifle with me, Lauzun. What happened between my brother and Monsieur de Villers?"

He became grave. "They had an animated and most unpleasant conversation. Their sole point of agreement was to meet at dawn tomorrow in the Bois de Boulogne."

"Are you Monsieur de Villers's second?"

"I have this honour, Madam."

"And who is my brother's second?"

"The Chevalier des Huttes."

"Could you not try to stop this horrible nonsense?"

"I met the Marquis to effect a reconciliation, but he refused to hear me."

"Villers could decline to fight."

"No, Madam, not without being branded a coward. The Marquis expressed himself in such terms as to leave Villers no choice. The insult has been kept private so far, but I have no doubt that your brother would reiterate it in public if he did not receive satisfaction. Villers would be disgraced if he declined. What makes his situation all the more difficult is that he knows that he would lose you if he killed or seriously wounded the Marquis tomorrow."

"True. Do you think that they will stop fighting at the first blood?"

"I cannot say, Madam."

"When is the duel to take place?"

"At eight o'clock in the Bois de Boulogne." He frowned. "I hope that you are not thinking of attending. Ladies never do, nor should they, especially when they are the cause of the dispute."

"I thank you from my heart. Please, Lauzun, as a favour to me, even if you think it is useless, please try again to prevent this."

"I will do my best, my dearest."

I could not sleep that night. It was still dark when I hailed a hackney to go to the Bois de Boulogne. By the time I had reached the appointed place, the sun, a fierce orange, was just above the horizon, piercing the veil of the December fog. Lauzun and the Chevalier were examining the swords. Both expressed astonishment at my arrival and demanded that I leave. I declined. My brother and Villers, in spite of the cold, had already removed their coats, waistcoats and neckties. They looked somber and ignored me. They unbuttoned their shirts to show each other their bare chests as proof that they were not wearing any concealed protection. Lauzun and the Chevalier, having found the swords of equal length, returned them to the combatants. The fight began. I ran towards the duelists, crying to them to stop.

They were about matched, as far as I could judge, in skill as well as in build, although Villers was slightly taller and slimmer. I am no expert in fencing matters, but I observed that my brother's lunges were aimed at his adversary's chest. Villers seemed content to parry the Marquis's attacks and try to disarm him. Within minutes Villers received a cut on his right forearm. Blood dripped from his torn shirtsleeve. Without flinching, he switched his sword to his left hand. My brother pursued his advantage with increased energy.

Blood had been shed and the Marquis had not paused for a moment. He would not rest until he had killed Villers. I could not allow it. I ran to place myself between the combatants. Lauzun and the Chevalier tried to stop me, but I was too fast and eluded them. I found myself in the middle of the fight. Only then did I become aware of my danger. It was too late. My back turned to Villers, I faced my brother as he lunged towards the other man. The Marquis, carried by his momentum, was unable to stop and pierced me in the chest below the left breast.

The sharpness of the pain took my breath away. I saw a grey shadow standing in front of me, taking my hand in hers—for in France death is female—to lead me to a better world. I saw blood flooding the bodice of my dress. I saw Aimée orphaned. I saw my brother standing trial for my murder.

When I came to my senses, Villers and the Marquis, both very pale, were leaning over me. Their seconds were standing behind them, looking barely more composed. The Chevalier caught me by the shoulders and Lauzun by the knees. I was carried to one of the waiting hackneys, the pain in my chest throbbing with each step they took. The driver, upon observing my condition, hastened to climb down from his seat to open the door.

"What happened to her?" he asked. "How is it she's all covered with blood? Wasn't it supposed to be a duel? What if I am in trouble with the police now? And about the upholstery in my hackney? Who's going to pay for that?"

Villers, without a word, handed the driver a purse, which was promptly accepted and put an end to the man's enquiries. Everything faded as darkness closed around me.

I awoke in my bed. Villers was seated by my side, stroking my cheek.

"Do not move, dearest," he said. "You suffered broken ribs and a deep cut, but the surgeon who probed the wound assured me that the blade missed the heart and lung. You were saved, it seems, by the boning of your corset."

"Where is my brother?"

"He quit Paris as soon as you were pronounced out of danger. I believe that he has been shaken enough to leave both of us alone."

"What about your own wound?"

He shrugged. "Nothing worse than the loss of a good shirt."

The surgeon called. A slit had been made in my chemise to allow him to dress the wound without uncovering my breast, for which I was thankful. Villers did not leave my bedside or take his eyes off me during the entire time of the visit.

The Duchess would come and spend a few hours with me every day. I recovered quickly, though my chest remained sore for a while. My only lasting memento of the duel was a thin line of a scar, red at first, which soon turned white and shiny. No one in Parisian society or at Court knew the truth, except for the eyewitnesses and the Duchess. Even Lauzun kept the secret. For this I was grateful.

Villers, although my equal in rank, was much my superior in other regards. Not only his fortune, but his experience of the world and especially his education far exceeded mine.

"If you wish, Belle," he said one day towards the end of my recovery,
"I can help you follow a regular course of study. You have read a great
deal, but in a haphazard manner and without any guidance. I find it
amazing that you know as much as you do after having been given so
little attention. Do not take it amiss if I say that there are huge gaps in
your education, if indeed the kind of schooling you received can be given
that name. You have not learned a word of Latin, Greek or any of the
modern languages."

I had long been aware of my deficiencies. I knew some ladies in Paris
society who had received the most complete of educations and truly envied them. They were not fooled by my shyness, which was genuine, but
which I also used to conceal my ignorance. I accepted Villers's offer
without false pride and applied myself to my studies with a zeal that
amused him. He hired tutors for the classics, English, Italian and German. Within months I was able to hold my own in the more serious
conversations I would have been embarrassed to join earlier for fear of
displaying my ignorance.

Villers also hired Mademoiselle Lenoir, a pianoforte teacher, and
Signor Rosetti, an elderly singing master, to give me lessons twice a
week, the first I had received since leaving the convent at the age of
eleven. I knew that Villers wished to enhance my value as one of his
possessions. It was nonetheless the first time someone took any trouble
over my education and I was more grateful for this than for any other of
his kindnesses. Indeed it was the most valuable gift I ever received
from him.

His concern for my education also comforted me since it seemed to
indicate that he did not intend to discard me soon. It would have made
no sense for him to invest time and money in the accomplishments of a
mistress he did not wish to retain. I had feared at first that he would tire

of me once his fancy for me was satisfied, but, if anything, time only seemed to increase his tenderness.

During the spring of 1788, when Aimée was close to her third birthday, he brought to my lodgings a young woman, whom he introduced as a candidate for the place of governess. Miss Howard was English, shy, plain, with a pleasant smile in spite of teeth rather larger than average. I could not help wondering whether Villers had any designs upon her, or had already enjoyed some intimacy with her, although she did not seem to answer to his standards of female beauty. She came with an excellent recommendation from Mrs. Herndon, who was returning to England with her two girls and whose name I remembered mentioned in connection with that of Villers. The governess did not speak ten words of French, having remained at the service of an English family during her entire stay in Paris.

"All the better," said Villers. "Aimée and you will have to speak English with her. There is no faster way to learn a language."

I found Miss Howard to my liking and she commenced her new duties the following week.

I was soon advanced enough to read English books from the Vaucelles library. Shakespeare and the classics were still too difficult for me, but I discovered Fielding, Smollett, Richardson and other modern authors. Villers also presented me with more libertine works, such as the poetry of the Earl of Rochester, which he made me read aloud in bed under the pretext of checking my English accent. The subject matter often took our attention away from the scholastic aspect of these studies.

Villers would visit me every day, and often spent the night at my lodgings, generally after we went to the play or to dinner. I presided in an unofficial capacity over the entertainments he gave at his mansion. We would also go to Vaucelles and spend a few days at a time there. Whenever we stayed there overnight, the Duchess would accompany us for the sake of appearances. Villers treated her with affectionate respect, like a sort of mother-in-law.

He was no less kind to Aimée. He presented her, as a New Year's gift, with a doll. It had nothing in common with poor worn-out Nana. This new doll, almost as large as Aimée, came with its bed draped in pink silk and its armoire filled with a very elegant *trousseau*. Margaret, for such was the name Aimée would give it, wore a gold watch and a genuine pearl necklace, with matching earrings.

Aimée, when she received this present on the morning of the 1st of January 1788, flushed with pleasure and remained speechless for a few minutes. She looked shyly at Villers, as if afraid that he would change his mind, and dared not touch the doll. He smiled at her. For the first time, she ran to him and kissed his hand. He raised her onto his lap and kissed her back on the cheek. She huddled against him. Tears came to my eyes. I, like my daughter, had been denied the tenderness of a father. I had not the heart to raise any objections to the extravagance of the gift. From then on, Villers and Aimée became close friends.

With regard to society, I was still received in most salons, thanks, I am sure, to the continued patronage of the Duchess. I befriended Emilie de Crécey, blonde, blue-eyed, pretty and unaccountably cheerful. She was married to the Marquis de Brasson, a brutal fellow nicknamed the *Marquis du Bâton*, which could be translated as "My Lord Cudgel." Truth be told, soon after we became friends, she found comfort in the arms of the Count de Maury, notorious even by the lax standards of the times for his many successes with the ladies. This liaison was kept a great secret because of Lord Cudgel's dire temper. I admired Emilie's daring, and she in turn showed no severity in her judgment of me.

At the time, mistresses fell into two categories. The first were the ladies gentlemen "had." Those were married or widowed, equal in rank and often in fortune to their lovers, with whom their liaisons, although generally known, were not flaunted in any scandalous manner. Then there were the women one "kept." Those received a financial compensation for their services. They were indeed barely above prostitutes, except for the fact that they were expected to reserve their favours for their protectors.

My own situation was ambiguous. Because of my rank, I belonged to the class of the women one *had*, but my financial circumstances were no secret, and neither was the source of my new affluence. Thus in the eyes of some, I was no different from a kept woman. I brought the uncertainties of my status to Villers's attention.

"Well, my love," he said, smiling, "I find this sort of distinction silly. I am very happy to *keep* you, and greatly enjoy *having* you too."

Some ladies would remind me of my dubious position. I overheard the Duchess's daughter, Madame de Bastide, tell one of her friends in a rather loud whisper: "The Baroness de Peyre has the finest hair I have ever seen. So abundant, so glossy, and such a remarkable colour. Some call it red, but it is indeed a true *Venetian blonde*, named after the tint the harlots of Venice use to dye their tresses."

Had Villers married me, I would have been spared that sort of re-mark, as well as a host of unpleasant reflections. No one, not even Ma-dame de Bastide, judged me as harshly as I judged myself in my moments of solitude. I have no doubt that I would have fallen in thrall to Villers if he had made me his wife, but I could not help seeing in him a man who did not honour me enough to take that step. As much as I loved him, a part of me never entirely forgave him.

ஜௐ 39 ௐஜ

Villers taught me to appreciate fine paintings and took me to see the gal-leries, which were already open to the public, of the Louvre and the Luxembourg, as well as the private collections of his friends. He was particularly fond of the Italian masters of the Renaissance. He showed me, in his private study, a full-size copy of *The Birth of Venus*, by Botti-celli. I gazed in admiration at the goddess, standing naked on a shell borne by the sea amid a shower of roses.

"I have to be content with this copy," said Villers, "though I would dearly love to own the original. Look at Venus, dearest. Does she remind you of anyone?"

I hesitated, afraid of sounding presumptuous. "Do you think I look like her?"

"Oh, you do. I was struck by the resemblance when I first saw you at the Opera. You have the same colour and abundance of hair, the same exquisite features. Of course this poor Venus has the body of a peasant girl compared to you. *You* are so delicate in the wrists and ankles, so thin in the waist. Also, Boticelli should have given her grey eyes. Yours re-mind me of the colour of the sea, which is as much of a character in the painting as Venus, the Nymph and the Winds."

"Venus is supposed to have been born from the foam of the sea, is she not?"

Villers laughed. "Yes, my love, but not from just any kind of foam. According to the Greek creation myth, the Titan Cronos castrated his

father, Ouranos, god of the sky. The severed genitals fell into the sea and
gave birth to Venus when their contents mixed with the salt water. So,
instead of coming from a womb without semen, as Our Lord Jesus did,
the goddess was born from semen without a womb. In neither case was
conception tainted by copulation, which is almost as fine a notion as
copulation untainted by conception."

"I am trying," I said, smiling, "to picture my mother's reaction to your
parallels between pagan myths and Christian dogma."

He grinned. "If I were granted the privilege of making Her Ladyship's
acquaintance, I would strive to impress her with the depth of my religious erudition. I would for instance point out to her that the seashell
which carries Venus in this painting is both a reminder of the intimate
anatomy of the female sex and the Christian symbol of the purity of the
Blessed Virgin."

"You may be sure of one thing, my dear. I will never introduce you to
my mother. She would accuse you of blasphemy and, maybe worse in her
eyes, of immodesty."

"What a pity! Small minds imagine God to their image. They underestimate Him. Why would He have granted us the ability to think if He
did not intend for us to notice these similarities?" He looked serious
again. "Apart from these doctrinal matters, Belle, I would take it as a
great favour if you no longer cut your hair. In less than a year, it should
be about the same length as that of Venus. As soon as I set eyes on you at
the Opera, I resolved to become the master of your person and hopefully
of your heart. To prove that I have succeeded in both parts of that endea-
vour, you must promise to let your hair grow. Would you be cruel enough
to deny me this innocent satisfaction?"

I noticed that Villers delighted in combing my hair, playing with it
and kissing it. He did not consider it beneath him to order my clothes or
to supervise my toilette. At night he would dismiss Manon to undress me
himself. I was reminded of Aimée playing with her doll. I will not deny
that I enjoyed his attentions.

Villers told me that he wanted to have a portrait of me and had made
arrangements with Madame Lebrun. I went to her studio, full of the pleasure of meeting her again. Yet I noticed an unusual constraint in her
manner. She avoided my eye.

"How do you suggest that I should be painted?" I asked.

She hesitated. "Well, Madam, did Monsieur de Villers not tell you?"

"Tell me of what?"

She blushed. "Well, he wants you painted in the same manner as Boticelli's Venus. I objected at first, because, though I sometimes paint nudes in allegorical compositions, I am not accustomed to have society ladies sit in this manner for me."

I was so astonished at Villers's impudence that I left Madame Lebrun without giving her any sitting.

Villers, when confronted, laughed. "Maybe you are a prude after all, my love."

"Call me whatever you wish, but a picture such as the one you had in mind would be seen by your servants and some of your guests. Moreover, I have no intention of disrobing in front of Madame Lebrun."

He kissed my hand. "Please do not upset yourself, Belle. We will think of something else."

After much discussion, it was agreed that I would be painted as an undine, a water nymph, with my body in profile and my head turned towards the viewer, my hair falling in loose locks, like those of Venus, to my waist. The surroundings, the banks of a river in the middle of a wood, reminded me of the Cère in Auvergne. I persisted in my refusal to be painted entirely nude. Instead I was dressed in a floating drapery in the antique manner, held by two gold clasps on my shoulders and tied under my breasts by a red sash. My arms, one of my legs and most of my throat were uncovered, and whatever was not bare could easily be guessed under the sheerness of my tunic. I could not look at the painting without the utmost embarrassment.

Villers declared himself delighted. I had the honour of joining Boticelli's Venus in his private study. He also asked Monsieur Curtius, the celebrated wax artist, to make a bust of me. Curtius had been drawing master to Madame Elisabeth, the King's youngest sister. He had recently quit his place at Versailles to open a very successful *Salon de Cire,* "Wax Salon," in Paris, where he took the likenesses of all the nobility. I therefore went to his establishment, where his niece and assistant, Mademoiselle Grosholtz, now famous in this country under her married name of Madame Tussaud, placed quills in my nostrils to allow me to breathe and asked me to lie still while she poured warm plaster over my face and neck. I have never been inclined to remain immobile very long and found the experience unnerving.

Three weeks later, I accompanied Villers to Monsieur Curtius's *Salon de Cire* to gaze at my likeness in wax on one of the shelves, next to the "royal family at dinner," an ensemble representing the King and Queen seated at a round table with the Counts de Provence and d'Artois and their respective wives. Mademoiselle Grosholtz pointed out that the Queen's effigy was wearing a real Rose Bertin dress that had been donated by Her Majesty herself.

My own bust was eerily true to life, for real hair had been added, although I did not like the fixed expression of the glass eyes. Villers had requested a duplicate for himself in addition to the bust that remained in Monsieur Curtius's establishment for public display. I do not know what became of these fragile creations in the ensuing storm. My portrait by Madame Lebrun, however, was not lost.

✧ 40 ✧

My life in Paris continued in the same circle, among which I counted a handful of true friends. I entertained no illusions as to the feelings of the rest. The only change in society was the return of the Duke d'Orléans. His exile had increased his popularity, although it had done little to improve either his figure or his complexion. All of those who wished to disoblige the Queen, and they were many, feted him.

I had not received any news from my brother in the months following his duel with Villers, nor had I expected any. It was with trembling hands that I opened his letter.

> *Dearest Gabrielle,*
>
> *I have terrible news. Mother passed away last night. I know that you had your share of disagreements with her, but will nonetheless feel our loss keenly.*
>
> *She seemed fine until shortly before dinnertime, when she was taken violently ill. She had complained of dull pains in her stomach for a few months, but I had not paid as much attention to it as I should have. She was carried to bed, refused to see any physician, and had Father Delmas fetched. She received the last rites around ten and passed away an hour and a half later. It may*

*comfort you to know that she was in no great pain until the very
last.*

*I feel utterly bereft. My grief is all the more acute that you are
not here to share it. I am offering again all I should have proposed
upon your widowhood. The memory of my actions at the time torments me more than you can imagine. Had I been more generous,
you would not have gone to Paris, you would not have fallen into
the hands of a man who is utterly unworthy of you. I would not
have wounded you because of him. I cannot bear the thought that
I have harmed you in so many ways. Please leave your empty
luxuries, your thoughtless pleasures, your false friends. You deserve
better.*

*I cannot think of a greater happiness than to have you with me
here in Fontfreyde. Please, Gabrielle, beloved little sister, listen to
your heart. Come back to me.*

*I remain, dearest Gabrielle, your most devoted brother and
friend,*

The Marquis de Castel

P.S. Your old nurse, Marie Labro, died in her sleep last week.

I agonized over the substance and wording of my response. I braced
myself against a return of my old tenderness. I wrote back to thank my
brother and deplore that it was not in my power to accept his offers.

Aimée and I went into mourning. My grief over the death of my remaining parent was scant. The Marquise de Castel had never shown me
any affection. I could not recall her ever having a fond word or gesture
for me. Mamé's passing, however, filled me with sadness. I remembered
my last image of her, white-haired and frail, leaning on Jacques's arm on
the threshold of her cottage. The banks of my childhood were receding
as I drifted away, lost on unknown waters.

Villers took Aimée and me to Normandy during the summer of 1788. We attended the parties given by the local nobility, and the rustic festivities in celebration of the harvest. Villers and I opened many a country dance in front of the peasantry, outdoors when the weather was fine or in a barn otherwise. I was reminded of the *bourrées* of my childhood in Auvergne, except that the music of the fiddles replaced that of the bagpipes.

Villers taught Aimée to ride, as he had promised the previous year. He was a kind and patient instructor. She listened to him with rapt attention and would gravely sit in her sidesaddle, her eyes closed to become used to the gait of the white pony. She was now able to follow us on horseback in the park of Dampierre.

The sole shadows to dim the joys of the season were the concerns about the harvest. It was less abundant than usual. The weather, usually very wet in Normandy, was drier that year. Hailstorms, which seemed to gather out of nowhere on beautiful sunny days, hacked away at the crops.

In spite of my fondness for Paris, it was with regret that I returned to the capital in early September. On one of the last days of summer, Villers invited Lauzun and Emilie to a *guinguette*, a riverside restaurant near Rue Saint-Dominique. I liked the informal atmosphere of those establishments, although I could not bring myself to taste their specialty, a *matelote* of eels. I had never been able to eat those fish since the day in Joséphine's kitchen at Fontfreyde when I had seen some, tangled in a knot like snakes, devouring one another in a bucket. I was content with small fry, fresh from the river.

We took our seats while Villers ordered a bottle of champagne. I enjoyed the view of the Seine, glittering green in the sun. My eye was wandering over the crowd in the café when my heart skipped a beat. A black-haired man, one head taller than the tallest of the other patrons, was seated there, his back turned to me. I could not see his features, but I felt sure that this was Pierre-André Coffinhal. At his table was a woman wearing a bright yellow dress adorned with scarlet ribbons, her hair a shade of red not found in nature. She had brought her chair next to his and thrown her arms around his neck. She was hanging upon him in such a way that I expected her to sit in his lap. I assumed that she was a dancer or actress, and not one of an exalted station among her peers. I could tell from her profile that she was young and pretty. The man kept looking ahead, accepting her attentions without returning them.

My cheeks were burning. Lauzun joined us and kissed my hand somewhat longer than conventions allowed. He gazed at me, smiling, without letting go of it. His look followed the lines of my neck and caressed my throat before stopping at the bouquet of fragrant violets I had arranged between my breasts as a *babarel*. It was not fashionable in Paris to wear flowers in that manner, but I never heard any gentleman criticize that custom from Auvergne, although some ladies derided it as provincial. I must say that my dress was quite pretty, a simple white muslin with the same flowers embroidered around the bodice and sleeves. It had been ordered by Villers, who had presented me at the same time with girandole amethyst earrings to match the colour of the violets.

"One of my friends is the most fortunate man in Paris, Madam," said Lauzun. "I hope that he is aware of it."

"Certainly," replied Villers. "He is indeed fortunate and you are wasting your time."

A few tables away, the dark-haired man rose and offered his arm to the girl in the yellow dress. It was indeed Pierre-André. He had not changed much, though he seemed to have grown still broader in the chest and shoulders. He saw me while Lauzun was still holding my hand. I read disbelief and fury on Pierre-André's face. He pulled on his girl's arm and left.

I felt a knot in my throat. I thought of our assignations by the river and was reminded of Lord Rochester's poem:

> *I'd give him liberty to toy*
> *And play with me, and count it joy.*
> *Our freedom should be full complete,*
> *And nothing wanting but the feat.*
> *Let's practice, then, and we shall prove*
> *These are the only sweets of love.*

What remained now of the happiness and innocence of those days?

Emilie had informed us earlier that her husband had been detained in

Versailles until the next day. I was nevertheless astonished when I saw the Count de Maury, feigning surprise at the sight of our little gathering, join us. Emilie kept her eyes down but could not repress a smile. I felt sure that they were meeting by design and marveled at their imprudence. To complete the vexations of the day, Maury, barely acknowledging Emilie, paid me the most pointed attentions. He gave such an imitation of infatuation that Emilie blanched and put her hand to her chest. I silently cursed Maury, Lauzun, Pierre-André and all men. Villers, at whom I glanced from time to time, followed the scene with curiosity but without apparent uneasiness. I wondered whether he had noticed that anything was amiss, and tried to hide the turmoil of my feelings.

"So, Belle," he said after we returned to my lodgings, "you were much admired today."

"None of it means anything. Lauzun paid me compliments out of habit and Maury as a cover for his affair with Emilie."

"You are too modest, dearest. You looked, if possible, lovelier than usual, and both of those gentlemen noticed it. But they were not alone. There was a man in particular who looked at you in a rather odd manner. Your beauty seemed to infuriate him. You cannot have missed him: a fellow of gigantic stature, who wore his hair black. And a little hussy, quite pretty but hopelessly vulgar, was on his arm. Each of them, in a different way, was rather conspicuous. From the way he was glaring at you, I would have sworn that he knew you."

"Maybe he was glaring at *you*, for you seem to have been ogling his mistress." I tried to speak in a light-hearted tone, and looked away to hide my tears.

I could not chase from my mind the memory of the red-haired girl with her arms around Pierre-André's neck. How could he let her act in that manner? Who was she? I needed to know her name. Did he love her? The scene at the *guinguette* conjured other, still more unbearable images. I pictured them in bed together. He was holding her, kissing her slowly, deeply, calling her his beloved, as he had done with me long ago. Then he was undressing her, doing to her things he had never done to me.

That tore at me. How dare he love such a woman after he had loved me? Could he not see that her manners, her garish dress, her dyed hair proclaimed that she was nothing more than a courtesan? And yet he was not ashamed of taking her to a public place, of being seen in her company by people he knew, by *me*.

I was amazed to feel such strong emotions. That day was the fourth anniversary of my wedding. Did Pierre-André remember that he had wanted to prevent it, to elope with me, to marry me? My temples were throbbing. I told Villers that I was unwell. He kissed my hand, wished me a prompt recovery and left me to my thoughts.

I felt calmer the next day. I tried to reason away the pangs of jealousy. In all fairness I could hardly expect Pierre-André to shun female company for the rest of his life. Had I not, after promising to be his wife, married another man and then become the mistress of yet another? Had I not been in Villers's company myself at the *guinguette*? I was no longer angry with Pierre-André. Only sadness remained. Then I remembered the looks of utter misery Emilie had cast at Maury and me. She had been jealous too. I felt guilty to have thought only of my own unhappiness and decided to call on her.

She rose to greet me, but turned away when I tried to embrace her. Her eyes were swollen.

"My poor dear," I said, seizing her hands, "I am sorry."

"Oh Belle, I am so miserable! But how do you know that I am with child? Does it show already?"

I stared at her in amazement. I had called on her to assuage her jealousy, and had not imagined any other cause to her uneasiness.

"No, indeed, Emilie, I had no idea." I forced a smile. "My congratulations to you and your husband."

She began to sob. "He will never believe it. He has deserted my bed these six months."

I bit my lip. Her husband was not the sort of fellow to stop at half-measures. I worried for her. "Then you must win back his attentions at all costs. Knowing the risk, Emilie, how could you not take any precautions?"

Emilie looked at me through her tears. "What precautions, Belle?"

I described, with some embarrassment, the sponges soaked in vinegar that Villers had taught me to use. I even told Emilie what I knew of seal-skin condoms. Villers had mentioned those, though he had said that he did not like them.

Emilie's eyes were wide open. "Nobody ever told me of those things, Belle."

"I had been ignorant of them myself before meeting Villers. To his credit, he has always been very careful."

Emilie began to cry again. I patted her on the back.

"What does Maury propose to do?" I asked.

"I have not told him."

"Why not? Is it not his fault too? At least he should have withdrawn to spare you the risk of a pregnancy."

"I dared not ask him. Men do not like to interrupt their pleasure."

"He should have done it without your asking. How selfish, how inconsiderate of him!"

"Do not blame him, Belle. He thought it was safe. He does not know that my husband no longer shares my bed."

I sighed. "You must tell Maury the whole truth now, dear."

Emilie glared at me. "If I do, he will use it as a pretext to leave me. He is in love with *you*. I saw how he looked at you yesterday. He spoke only to you."

"You are mistaken, dear Emilie. Can you not see that he was only trying not to compromise you? It was very, very imprudent of you to ask him to meet you in a public place. He had no choice but to pretend to pay court to me."

Emilie's face brightened. "Do you really think so?"

"Absolutely. He knows, everyone knows, that he would be wasting his time with me. How could I betray both Villers and you?"

She pressed me in her arms. "Belle, dear, you make me so happy! Now I am sure that I will not lose Maury. The situation is not so bad after all. Léonard, my hairdresser, knows a woman who can help me."

I stared at her. "Léonard? You told your hairdresser about this? You cannot be in earnest, Emilie. And who is that woman?"

I pointed out to Emilie the horror and dangers of the procedure she was considering. In vain. She was elated at the thought that Maury would not leave her, and cared nothing about my warnings.

"Of course," she said, "it was silly of me to entertain those ugly suspicions. I see it now. It all arose from something Maury told me last week. It is a great secret. I should probably not breathe a word of it."

"You have said too much already."

Emilie lowered her voice. "Villers asked his procuress to find him a virgin, no more than fifteen. The girl is to arrive this week, fresh from the country. Villers is not taking her to his *little house*. He will set up a separate establishment for her. Neither Orléans nor Lauzun are to know anything about it, because Villers wants to keep her to himself. I imagined that maybe you too had learned of it and wanted to revenge yourself by taking Maury as a lover."

I had to catch my breath. "Rest easy, Emilie. I would never cause a friend such pain."

I abstained from asking Emilie how Maury knew Villers's procuress, and whether he too availed himself of her services. Apparently that part of the story had not piqued my friend's curiosity.

During the carriage ride back to my lodgings, I had the opportunity to indulge in the most unpleasant reflections. Until then I had made an effort not to be unhappy over Villers's infidelities. Now I remembered the haste in which he had left the night before. Of course his new girl had arrived, and he had been impatient to join her. He had spent the night with her. He had been as gentle with her as he had been with me at the beginning of our intimacy. He had taken her maidenhead, something I had not been able to give him. I remembered what he had said, when we had discussed *Dangerous Liaisons*, about virginity being worthless in his eyes. I felt betrayed.

Then I thought again of Pierre-André's girl. My anger subsided. Who was I to despise her? Oh, I was dressed with becoming elegance, my manners were modest, but was there any difference in what she and I were doing to keep body and soul together? I, just like her, was a courtesan. I had become Villers's kept woman, and accepted his other mistresses. No wonder he felt nothing but contempt for me, and acted accordingly.

Villers visited me that night. He seemed absentminded. He remembered an engagement that would unfortunately deprive him of the pleasure of my company. I closed my eyes because the sight of him caused me pain. As he was bending to kiss me good night, I turned away.

"No," I said.

"Why not?"

"You know very well why not. You should leave; you are going to be late."

"I do not care if I am late. I have never seen you look so angry."

"So let me be angry. Go."

"I do not want to part with you in this manner, Belle. I will stay if you wish."

"I do not wish it. Are you forgetting about that engagement of yours?"

"It can wait. Indeed I do not mind giving it up altogether if it upsets you. I will stay with you tonight."

"Please go. I do not want you here. How many times must I ask you to leave?"

He frowned. "Do not speak to me in this manner, Belle. I pay for these lodgings and may stay here as long as I want."

"True. Stay then."

Villers's last remark had opened my eyes. I ran to my bedroom, threw a mantle on my shoulders and put my diamond earrings in my pocket. I proceeded to the nursery, where Aimée was finishing her dinner in the company of Miss Howard. I told the governess that we had to go out and took Aimée's hand in mine, putting my finger to my lips to intimate silence. She insisted on taking her doll Margaret and dressing her warmly on account of the hour. We quietly went down the service staircase. Once on the street, I hailed a hackney.

Half an hour later, we arrived at the Duchess's mansion.

"Dear Belle," she asked, "what is the matter? You look so upset."

"I just left Villers." I threw myself into her arms. "Will Your Grace allow us to spend the night here?"

"Of course, but what do you mean? Did you leave him for good? What happened?"

We sat on the sofa.

"I am tired of being nothing but one of his many whores."

"What are you saying? He loves you. He is only acting like a fool."

"If he loved me, he would have married me or at least kept his other liaisons discreet. He has pushed me, Madam, to the point where I no longer care for him."

"What am I going to tell him if he comes here?"

"The truth. That I do not wish to ever see him again."

She patted my hand. "Belle, please listen to me. Do not do anything that you would regret later. You are angry, and with good cause. Please have a glass of Madeira with me."

The wine calmed me. While I was sipping it, the footman entered the room to announce the Count de Villers. I escaped to my old bedroom. The Duchess joined me half an hour later.

"You took a long time, Madam," I said, "to tell him to go to hell."

"I did not tell him that, Belle. I told him that you wanted him to go to hell. He said that he would have been here earlier, maybe even before your hackney arrived, but he had not realized at first that you had left. When he did, he ran directly to his stables, saddled his horse himself and rode here as fast as he could. He says that you may spend the night here, but he refuses to leave without seeing you to beg your forgiveness."

I raised my eyebrows. "I *may* spend the night here! Indeed I am glad to have his permission. I do not wish to see him. If he will not leave of his own accord, Madam, have him thrown out by your lackeys."

"I have never heard you speak in this manner. Nor have I ever seen him so shaken. Please relent, Belle, and go speak to him."

"I could not bear to see him, Madam, but I will write him if it will help rid you of him without any scandal."

I sat down to my desk and wrote the following note, which I handed to the Duchess:

> *Your conduct, Sir, puzzles me. Tonight at my, or rather your lodgings, you were impatient to leave me for the bed of another mistress. Now that you are at liberty to spend the night there, or the rest of your natural life if you prefer, you choose to come here to disturb my friend's peace and mine.*
>
> *I would take it as a kindness if you would have my things and Aimée's sent here tonight. I took with me only your earrings and your ring, which I have earned through my past services and which I intend to sell to support my daughter and myself without further resorting to your generosity. I relinquish any rights to the other presents you were kind enough to bestow on me.*
>
> *The Duchess told me that you wish to ask for my forgiveness. There is no occasion for it. I have not a thing to reproach you with. You did nothing you had not led me to expect when I first accepted your offers. You have not changed. I have. What I used to tolerate now disgusts me. Do me the honour of believing me when I tell you that I do not wish to see you again, tonight or at any other time.*
>
> *Please leave.*

The Duchess came back a few minutes later.

"He is gone," she said. "He said that he did not want to upset you further and that he would send Manon here with your things. He asked for permission to come back tomorrow morning."

"I will not see him, Madam. Of course, you should feel free to receive him. I know that you have always been fond of him."

"I must admit it. I am very sad for him. How could he make you so angry?"

"He took a new mistress, a fresh one, fifteen years old. She is going to be to him what I was less than a year ago. He has tired of me. He never cared for me."

"I have trouble believing it. I cannot imagine him desperately running after that new girl. He was wrong, very wrong to cause you pain in this manner, but I hope that he will earn your forgiveness."

"You are too tender-hearted, dear Madam. Monsieur de Villers must be enjoying the company of his new conquest as we speak. Thinking of him is a waste of our time."

Villers did call. The Duchess alone received him. This was repeated daily during the following weeks.

Before long I received a visit from Lauzun.

"Please do not tell me that you came here to plead Monsieur de Villers's cause," I said with some exasperation.

"Fear not, dearest friend," he responded, smiling. "He has been extremely fortunate so far. Any other lady in your position would have repaid him in kind and given him a rival long ago. Instead you ran back to the Duchess and are leading the life of a saint. You have spared him, until now at least, the exquisite torture of jealousy, which he has done everything to deserve. If anything, Madam, you have been far too lenient."

I could not help smiling back. "It never entered my mind to seek a new lover. Now that you mention it, Lauzun, that prospect does not appeal to me. I have no intention of going through the same trials twice."

"I hope that Villers has not embittered you against all men. He has received from you nothing but tenderness, obedience and respect. You saved his life at the peril of your own. I have never heard an angry word pass your lips against him. Husbands in this town do not expect from their wives one hundredth of the affection you bestowed on that ingrate. If Madame de Lauzun had treated me in the same manner, I would not have been so inclined to seek my enjoyment elsewhere. And how has he thanked you? By making you unhappy, by giving you a new rival, and what a rival! A country girl with no wits, no allurements beyond youth and a tolerable freshness."

I raised my eyebrow. "You seem acquainted with the young person in question."

"I met her. Villers offered to send her back to her parents, a little late in my opinion, because she had already served him. She refused and has chosen to remain in Paris under the protection of the Duke d'Orléans."

"And yours too maybe?"

"No. I do not like her, especially after the pain she unwittingly caused you." He paused. "If you would only return my affections, Belle, I would not treat you in so shabby a manner. Need I tell you that time has not altered my feelings nor my hopes?"

"You are very kind, dear Lauzun. I thank you for your offers, but I would rather keep you as my friend."

"Friendship does not preclude love. On the contrary, I have retained a great tenderness for most ladies who have honoured me with their favours in the past."

"I would not presume to doubt it. Does Villers know of your visit here?"

"Oh yes, I told him of it. Why hide it from him? He raved like a lunatic. He even wanted to fight me. I had to remind him that it is his fault, not mine, if you no longer want to see him while you still honour me with your friendship. I also pointed out that a duel was the last thing to improve your opinion of him."

Lauzun reached for my hand. "Dearest Belle," he continued, "while you were his, I refrained, albeit with great regret, from pursuing my own designs. Now he has lost you. He had his chance, he squandered it. I would not have been such an idiot."

"No one can tell what you would have done in his place. And in spite of my esteem for you, the reasons why I refused to entertain your suit last year are no less compelling to me now."

"I understand. You are still upset over that wretch. It may be too early to address you. Please forgive me and let me hope."

I laughed. "Lauzun, I must tell you that you are, with your unaccountable persistence, the only person who could amuse me under these circumstances."

"Indeed, dearest friend, I am flattered to have been able to do so. You know the proverb, which is too crude to be repeated in full in front of a lady: *Woman who laughs . . .* "

The proverb was: *Femme qui rit est à demi au lit,* "Woman who laughs is halfway to bed."

I would send Manon on walks with Aimée, whom I did not want to deprive of fresh air, to the nearby Place Royale. Even those outings had to be interrupted during the second half of September, for riots burst out in several districts. Even after order was restored, I did not stir from the Duchess's house for fear of meeting Villers. My friends visited me. Emilie was radiant. She had been mistaken. Despite my remonstrances, she continued her liaison with Maury with the same imprudence as ever. How she could live in such danger was beyond my comprehension.

I also saw the Marquise de Bastide whenever she called on her mother. One day, while Manon stopped me outside the parlour door to discuss the details of a new dress for Aimée, I overheard a conversation that caught my attention.

"So, Madam, you are still saddled with the dear Baroness," said the Marquise. "Speaking of her, whom do you think I saw last night at the Opera? Villers! He had the impudence to come to my box, uninvited of course, to ask whether you would be joining me. As if I could believe for a moment that he cared about you! I told him that I had not the honour of expecting you and asked whether he had heard that Madame de Peyre lived with you once again. He blanched and left without another word. He did not even return to his own box." She laughed. "I never saw him so crestfallen. None of his usual arrogance, now that he has lost the pearl of his harem. His Belle, his prize, his favourite with the porcelain face, has run away!"

"He was here this morning. Poor man. He calls every day to talk about Belle. He cannot bear the loss of her."

"I have to admit that she is delightful. Indeed I have nothing against her, except on your account. She is such a terrible imposition on you."

"Dear," said the Duchess, "please do not speak of Belle in this manner. You know that it pains me."

"Oh, Madam, I too am very fond of her. I even find her naivete charming." Madame de Bastide giggled. "She thought she would attach Villers, I daresay. I would bet you the millions the Queen lost at *pharaon* that the little red-haired simpleton believed he would marry her. . . ."

I had no desire to hear more and, shaking Manon loose, pushed the door open. Madame de Bastide lost her countenance for only an instant before rising to kiss me on the cheek with the utmost friendliness. I bit my tongue not to remind her that my hair was not red, but *Venetian blonde*. Her malice almost made me pity Villers.

✺ 42 ✺

I knew that I could not remain forever with the Duchess, and missed the country air of Vaucelles. Emilie told me of a cottage for rent in the middle of Meudon Forest, a few miles from Paris. The place sounded inexpensive and delightful. Ever wary of the Duchess's servants and their mercenary souls, I took a hackney to Meudon, accompanied by Aimée and Manon. We drove through the forest, where the leaves were turning to shades of russet and gold under the sun of the mild autumn day. I pointed out to my daughter a doe, only yards from the road. At last we arrived at a clearing. There stood the cottage, with a tiny garden in front and, to the side, a wooden table and two benches under an arbor covered with grapevines. We visited the house, which comprised four rooms, a kitchen and an attic. I could picture us very happy in that retreat.

I left Manon and Aimée to their survey of the attic, where a prior tenant had abandoned broken furniture and old trunks. I stepped through the back door to look at the kitchen garden, divided into neat vegetable squares. I froze when I saw Villers standing there, his hat in his hand.

After the first shock of recognition, I observed that he was altered. His cheeks were more hollow than before and his eyes ringed by dark circles. My anger gave way to pity. I suppressed this feeling by reflecting that these were signs not of sorrow but of the fatigues of his increased debauchery in my absence. I blushed, much to my vexation, but he did not seem much more at ease himself. I turned towards the house.

"Please, Belle," he said, "do not run away." Even his voice had changed. It had lost its former assurance.

I faced him. "Leave. You know that I do not want to see you. Your presence here only shows your lack of respect for me."

"I need to speak to you, Belle. I could think of no other way."

"Now you have spoiled this cottage for me. I will not take it if you are to pester me here."

"I will not pester you again. I give you my word of honour that I will never return here if you hear me today."

I walked to the arbor and sat on one of the benches, looking at my watch. "You have five minutes." I pointed at the other bench across the table. He sat there. For a while he seemed to have trouble catching his breath and remained silent.

"Bear with me," he said at last in an unsteady tone. "I am overwhelmed. Every day I have hoped to see you. And now that I am in your presence, I cannot find my words. May I kneel at your feet?"

"No. I will leave if you try to approach."

"Please stay, Belle. I will not move. May I at least tell you of my dreams? In my dreams I kneel before you in silence, I rest my head on your lap. Then you reach for me, you hold me against your breast, you say that you forgive me. Could it happen someday?"

"No. As I wrote you, there is nothing to forgive."

"You know that it is not true, Belle. I made light of the happiness you brought me. I hurt you over a girl who meant nothing to me."

"Why did you do it then?"

"Oh, Belle, I love you so."

I felt myself flush with anger. "You love me? You took a new mistress because you love me? Do you expect me to believe such an absurdity?"

"It is absurd, I know. It took me time to understand why I acted in this manner. The truth is that I fell too much under your thrall for my own comfort. I tried to fight my feelings by keeping my old amusements, but that did not help. I did not stray while we were in Normandy last summer, Belle. Not once. I was angry with myself, and with you too. I dreaded to have my whole happiness depend on you. So I decided to take a new mistress upon our return to Paris."

"And how did you think I would respond to the news?"

"For one thing, I never imagined that it would reach you so soon. I still do not know how it did. Perhaps I thought that you would accept her as you have had the patience to accept the others. It never occurred to me that you would leave me. I was so arrogant, so blind." He sighed. "And I remained blind even after you left me. I was thunderstruck when I discovered your disappearance, but over the following days I convinced myself that you would accept to see me under the Duchess's roof and listen to reason, meaning to me."

He ran his hand over his eyes. "In time I realized that you did not show any signs of relenting. I came to understand that I had indeed lost you. Oh, Belle, it was as if the ground had opened beneath my feet. I know that Lauzun has been calling on you. Even the idea that he can see you, speak to you, touch your hand while I cannot is unbearable. I would like to kill him for that alone." Villers paused. "I have even pictured you yielding to him to take your revenge."

"I would never demean myself by becoming someone's mistress only to spite you."

Villers looked into my eyes. "Are you telling me that nothing ever happened between you and Lauzun?"

"Nothing. It is none of your concern anymore, but I know the pain of jealousy. I do not wish to inflict it needlessly on anyone, not even you."

"Do you love him?"

"You have no right to ask."

"I know, but please put an end to this part of my torment. Do you love him?"

I looked away. "No, I do not."

He closed his eyes and breathed deeply. "Thank you, Belle. You are the soul of kindness. You could have punished me by letting me believe the worst." He paused. "Oh, Belle, you give me hope. More hope than I had allowed myself in weeks. Even if there is nothing left of the feelings you had for me, all may not be lost. I can become worthy of you. My conduct will change; it has changed already. I have not touched a woman since that horrible night when you left me. I already relinquished all rights to my *little house*, without any regret. I no longer have any other mistresses, nor will there be any in the future."

"I do not trust you."

"Whatever my faults, have I ever breached a promise to you? And I know what I want now. If I were so fortunate as to secure your forgiveness, I would not risk losing you again. Losing you is as close to hell as I can imagine. The only thing that still matters to me is to call on the Duchess every day. I talk of you with her, and I can feel your presence. I know that you are there, only a few rooms away, so close and yet unreachable. I kept one of your chemises, Belle. I could not bring myself to send it to you with the rest of your things. It still smells of you, of your fragrance. I sleep with it every night, or rather I go to bed with it because I can no longer sleep. It drives me insane because it reminds me so vividly of you. Yet it is better than not having any memento of you with me. Oh, Belle, I miss you so."

"You have brought all of this misery upon yourself."

His eyes were red. He was biting his upper lip, his chin quivering. "True. I deserve every part of this punishment, harsh as it is. I am not appealing to your sense of justice, I am begging for mercy. Come back to me, Belle, if only out of pity. I should be able to inspire at least that feeling."

Now tears were rolling down his cheeks. I had never seen a man weep and was too embarrassed to say a word.

"I will do everything to regain your affections," he continued in a halting voice. "You may put any conditions upon your return. I will agree to anything. I disgust you, I know. I will stay away from your bed. I will sleep on a couch, on the floor, in another room. Please come back."

I opened my mouth, more in dismay than to speak.

"Oh, Belle, you are going to say no. Wait. Do not say anything."

I kept silent.

"At least allow me to see you," he continued. "Come and ride with me in Vaucelles, as you used to do. Or if you do not want to be alone with me, let me speak to you under the Duchess's roof, in her presence. Please, Belle. Anything."

He hid his face in his hands. His shoulders were shaken by muffled sobs. I found this sight unbearable. I had to put an end to the conversation.

"You may call on the Duchess tomorrow morning," I said. "I will see you then. You must leave now."

Suddenly, with a look of violent emotion on his face, he rose. I recoiled at the idea of the scene that would follow if I let him move closer. I raised my hand.

"No," I said. "Leave now."

He seemed to make an effort to regain his composure. Then, after one long look at me, he bowed and turned away. I watched him walk slowly towards the gate.

I hurried back to the cottage. Fortunately Villers's visit had gone unnoticed by Aimée, who was still exploring the treasures of the attic. She had often asked in a worried tone whether he had died like her papa. I hastened our return to Paris. The cottage did not seem so appealing to me now.

I went to bed that night painfully uncertain of my feelings. The Duchess had told me that Villers was distraught over our separation, but the intensity of his sorrow had shocked me. Perhaps I still cared for him. Yet I regretted my promise. I did not wish to see him the next day.

I received him in the presence of the Duchess. A more awkward visit cannot be imagined. Neither he nor I had anything to say. After a few obligatory sentences, he was content to look at me. I could feel his gaze fixed upon me. I avoided his eye by staring out the window at the creeping vines, which had now turned bright red on the back wall of the garden. The poor Duchess had to bear unaided the burden of the conversation. After ten minutes of that torture, she seemed to have run out of topics, I could not think of any and Villers still gave no signs of leaving. I lost patience and put an end to everyone's misery by rising.

"Your Grace will remember that we promised to call on Madame de Bastide," I said.

"Oh yes, dear. My memory is not what it used to be. You must excuse us, Villers."

He had to rise but still was not taking his leave.

"Would Your Grace . . . ," he said at last. His voice failed him. He cleared his throat. "Would Your Grace, with Madame de Peyre and her daughter, do me the honour of sharing my luncheon on Tuesday at Vaucelles?"

"Well, this is kind of you. Belle, do you remember whether we have any engagement on that day?"

I turned away and made no response. So was his invitation accepted.

Lauzun, either because he was not to be discouraged or because he valued my friendship as much as he said, would still visit me. He was no longer called by that name, though I continued to use it. His uncle the Marshal Duke de Biron had died and left him his title and fortune.

"In addition," I told the Duchess, "he will be appointed Colonel of the French Guards in replacement of the late Marshal."

"Unfortunately not. Everything seemed to make Lauzun, or the Duke de Biron, as we should call him now, the obvious choice: his kinship with the Marshal, his distinguished career during the American war, his popularity with the troops. This is not to be, however. I heard this morning that the Duke du Châtelet has already been appointed Colonel of the French Guards. I need not tell you, Belle, from what quarter that blow came. The Queen herself opposed Lauzun's appointment. She must still be incensed over what she perceived as his desertion of her years ago. It is an affront of the first gravity to our friend, and a mistake too. What an idea to pick a brute like the Duke du Châtelet!"

Villers repeated the previous year's courtship, only sadder and laden with memories of happy and unhappy times. During a visit to Vaucelles on a foggy December afternoon, he helped me into the saddle and adjusted my foot in the stirrup. He gently uncovered my ankle. He caressed it through the silk stocking and pressed his lips to it. Still holding it, he contemplated it for a long time. At last he raised his eyes to my face.

"Have mercy, Belle," he said. "Please come back to me."

My anger had long subsided. It had been replaced by pity and some return of the affection I had felt for him. I relented.

When I arrived at my lodgings after an absence of three months, I was startled to find the place full of fresh flowers in spite of the late season. The hot houses of Vaucelles must have been looted to achieve such a display. The paneling in the drawing room had been painted blue and white, in the manner of the English porcelains I liked. The dining parlour was freshly wallpapered in a *trompe l'œil* motif of windows overlooking Roman ruins and the Mediterranean Sea. I was reminded of the plans Villers and I had once made to travel to Italy to visit such sights. In my bedroom the drapes, upholstery and bed curtains were now of white silk embroidered with butterflies and flowers in various shades of bright pink. Villers had remembered that it was my favourite colour. A red leather case waited for me on the dressing table. I removed my glove and let my fingertips brush against it before I opened it. It contained seven strands of the most beautiful pearls.

Only whispered expressions of surprise passed my lips. I turned towards Villers. He was silent, gazing at me in a shy manner, as if unsure of my approval. That moved me more than any gift, more than all of his preparations for my return. I held out my hand to him. He dropped to his knees to kiss it.

Within a week of my return to Rue Saint-Dominique, Villers was restored to all of his former privileges, which he resumed with a frightening ardor. Perhaps he had not lied when he had said that he had shunned female company during my absence.

❦ 43 ❧

It was decided by the end of 1788 that the Estates General would be called in May of the following year. The price of bread, due to the meager harvest, had risen beyond the means of the poorest. The Parliament of Paris opened an investigation into the causes of the increase, without any result other than fueling the wildest rumours about the Queen's schemes to starve the people.

Nonetheless the news of the upcoming election was greeted with a tide of enthusiasm and the three Orders, the Clergy, the Nobility and the Third Estate, talked of little else. All began drafting the famous *cahiers de doléances*, "booklets of complaints," in which they set forth the unfairness of the current regime and the remedies they wished their representatives to implement.

All the talk was of the drafting of a Constitution for the Kingdom. The founding fathers of the young United States had written one the year before, but it was generally acknowledged that such a form of government was only suitable for smaller, less populated countries and could never be adapted to France, with her twenty-six million inhabitants.

Most reform-minded thinkers argued that the British model ought to be followed, with a King enjoying limited powers, and a dual Parliament. The higher chamber, similar to the House of Lords, could be assembled from a reunion of the Nobility and Clergy, and a House of Commons would be derived from the Third Estate. Villers and Lauzun often discussed the fact that, for the first time, French noblemen could aspire to hold public office not on the sole basis of royal favour, but thanks to the suffrage of their peers.

Villers proposed another journey to Normandy, to which I agreed. Our rides by the sea, under the light snows of January, sealed our reconciliation.

"I have been thinking, Belle, of becoming a candidate for the representation of the nobility of Normandy," he said one day on the beach of Saint-Laurent. "But I will not decide on it without your approval."

"It is an excellent idea, my dear. I will be happy to return here with you at the time of the election. Or, if you prefer not to be seen with me then, you may also come back by yourself. You would not want to be accused of immorality for flaunting your mistress before your constituents."

"It is out of the question to leave you in Paris, Belle. I never want to be separated from you again. The nobility of Normandy will take me or leave me with whatever morality I can muster."

His new life with me, happy as it seemed to make him, must have felt a bit dull. Nothing of a serious nature had occupied him since he had left the army years earlier. Now everyone sensed that great changes were in store for France. These times were heady, for Villers and other noblemen as well as for commoners. Politics was open to all. It would provide a fresh outlet to his energy and intelligence.

Villers remained full of attentions during the rest of our stay in Dampierre. On our last night there, our embrace was more tender than ever. We found comfort in each other's arms. I fell asleep, content to feel him by my side.

I was awakened by a furious pull on my waist. My lips were forced open by other lips. I heard incoherent words, speaking of insatiable yearning, whispered in my ear by a hoarse voice. Heavy with sleep, I half opened my eyes. It was Villers's voice, his hands, his lips. In the hearth the fire had crumbled into a heap of whistling embers, glowing red. It must have been the early hours of the morning. I moaned, still drowsy.

Suddenly I was wide awake. He was already upon me, inside me. He had not given me time to take our usual precautions.

I pushed him away. "What are you doing? Do you want me to become pregnant?"

He kissed me wildly. "Oh, I do," he said, stopping to catch his breath. "Belle, my Belle, I want a child by you. I want it more than anything."

I stared at him. "I have no intention of being disgraced to satisfy a whim of yours."

"I will not disgrace you, my love. I will marry you. I will have the banns published tomorrow. Please." He pulled me close again. "I beg you, Belle. Let me take you like this."

"I cannot. The loss of my little boy left me dreadful memories. I do not wish for another child." I ran my hand on his face. "Please, my dear, be sensible."

He turned his back on me. I reached for his shoulder. He shrugged me off.

The next morning, Villers seemed happy and tender again. I wondered whether it had all been a dream. Although he was affectionate with Aimée and, in his own way, fond of his son, he had never before expressed any wish for offspring. He must have been driven by a desire to attach me in an irrevocable manner.

Upon our return to Paris, his behaviour changed. Before our separation, he had not seemed bothered by the attentions I received from others, and had even found them flattering. Now whenever other men spoke to me or even looked at me, I saw his jaw tighten and his fists clench. In particular he could barely bring himself to be polite to Lauzun.

Villers insisted on the benefits of a more retired life for my health and that of Aimée. He wished me to spend most of my time in his company at Vaucelles, with the Duchess as our sole guest. He attempted to dissuade me from attending entertainments I had no intention to renounce. He even objected to my meeting Emilie, who, he said, was a bad influence. I had concealed from him that it was to her that I owed the disclosure of his last known infidelity. I knew that he would never have forgiven her.

Villers had once promised never to hit me, but his temper seemed unpredictable whenever I was in company. My suspicions may have been unfair to him, but I could not help being influenced by my past experience of marital corrections. Moreover, my escape to the Duchess's, which had no adverse consequences for me, would have been a different matter had I been married. Villers, had he been my husband, could have me jailed as a runaway wife. I would have been separated forever from Aimée.

All those considerations led me to the conclusion that it would be more prudent to continue reaping the wages of sin rather than to become the new Countess de Villers. We are indeed strange creatures. What I had so dearly wished for a year earlier now seemed a step to be avoided.

Villers was well regarded by his peers in Normandy. He was elected a Representative of the Nobility to the Estates General in March of 1789. So were Orléans in Chartres, Lafayette in Auvergne and Lauzun in Quercy. All would be part of that famous assembly entrusted with the task of resolving the intractable budget crisis and restoring France to prosperity and happiness.

I taught Aimée, now three years old, to skate on the Seine, which had frozen solid during that terrible winter. My maids found unruly crowds, angered by the price of bread, massed in front of the bakeries. The populace cursed the Farmers General for increasing their enormous wealth by taxes on food at this time of famine. The wall built for their benefit now felt like a noose around the neck of the starving city. Wrapped in my furs, my stomach full, I could not help thinking of those who were cold and hungry. I asked Villers to forego my New Year's Day present and use the money to relieve the suffering of the poor, both in Normandy and in Paris.

The concerns of the day in Versailles were the ceremonies for the opening of the Estates General, the design of uniforms for each of the three orders and the protocol to be followed. The Estates General had not convened since 1614, and such details had been lost in the fog of time. Passionate debates were held under the Queen's direction. She insisted that proper attention be paid to distinctions of rank. Of particular import was the question whether the Representatives of the Third Estate should greet the arrival of the King on their knees. At the same time, the Duke d'Orléans spent 1,000 francs a day to feed the poor, which earned him the title of Protector of the People in Paris and caused him to be reviled as an opportunist and a rabble-rouser in Versailles.

I had intended to stay in Paris during the time of the meeting of the Estates General, which I did not anticipate to last more than a few months. Villers joined me one afternoon while I was reading *Paul and Virginia,* a new novel the Duchess had recommended. It recounted the adventures of a young noblewoman separated by her family from her

suitor, a commoner. I had never told the Duchess, or anyone except Hélène, of my first love. Now I found this melancholy romance too close to
my own story. I was not sorry to have my reading interrupted by Villers's
visit.

"Belle," he said, "we have things to discuss. I will rent a house for you
in Versailles for the duration of the Estates General."

I put away my book. "Why do we need a house in Versailles? You will
be less than an hour away from Paris on horseback. You could return
here every night, my dear."

"I expect the sessions of the Estates to continue late. I might feel too
tired to ride back to Paris in the middle of the night. At the same time,
dearest, I would not want to be deprived of your company."

"But you know that I am not fond of Versailles," I said, sighing.
"There is nothing there but the Court."

"I know that I am being selfish, Belle, by asking you to keep me company in that dismal place, but you are the one who encouraged me to
become a Representative."

I looked into his eyes. "Would you not trust me if I stayed in Paris?"

"I would, Belle, of course, but do you not know that I cannot bear to
be away from you?"

He bowed to the level of my waist to kiss my hand.

Villers rented in my name a fine house in Versailles, where I settled
with Aimée, Manon, Miss Howard and my maids on the 1st of May.
Only Junot, my footman, remained in Paris to mind my lodgings in my
absence. Villers did not secure separate accommodations for himself in
Versailles. He could be assumed to return to his Paris mansion at night.
Appearances did not matter so much to me anymore. I had been his mistress for a year and a half, and those who were offended by my morals
had already closed their doors to me.

On our first night in Versailles, Villers waited until we retired to present me with a pair of diamond bracelets in a trellis pattern. They were an
inch wide and seemed as valuable as the earrings he had given me.

"I wanted to thank you for coming here with me," he said, sitting on
the bed by my side. "I know, my love, that you did so only to please me.
Your sacrifice deserved a reward."

He reached for my wrists and, after kissing each of them in turn,
clasped the bracelets on them. I felt uneasy to wear this kind of jewellery
in bed.

"Thank you, they are beautiful," I whispered, staring at the bracelets.

"I had them made to your exact measurements, Belle. No other woman would have wrists delicate enough to wear them."

"You are very generous, as usual. I hope that you did not feel obligated to pacify me. I must have seemed ungracious in my reluctance to come to Versailles."

"You have never appeared ungracious, dearest. You made me very happy in accepting to accompany me. I wished to prove it."

He caressed me through my chemise, gently at first, then more urgently. He slipped it over my head. I reached for the bracelets to unclasp them. He stopped me. "No, my love. I want to see you wearing them, nothing but them."

The 4th of May had been set as the date of a grand procession of all the Representatives. The windows of my house offered an excellent view of the street on its path so I saw no occasion for Aimée and me to mingle with the crowd. I had invited the Duchess d'Arpajon to join us for that occasion. I am happy to have offered my dear friend this opportunity to behold the pageantry of the "Old Regime," as it would soon be called. This would be, unknown to both of us, the last occasion for its ceremonies ever to be held.

Villers, with all of the other Representatives, had waited since eight in the morning in front of the Church of Saint-Louis. The royal couple did not join them until eleven. The Third Estate walked first, dressed in plain black suits, hats and stockings. The Nobility followed, swords to their sides, in black coats, white breeches, lace neckties, gold cloth waistcoats and hats à la Henri IV, turned up in front and decorated with white feathers. Villers, with his tall, slender frame, having for once removed his earrings, looked very handsome. Lauzun, who gallantly bowed to us as he walked past my windows, was nothing short of dashing in spite of the fact that he was now past the age of forty. The Clergy walked behind, wearing the habits of their functions. The dignitaries of the Church, the red cardinals and purple bishops, were the only colourful notes in the procession.

The gold-embroidered canopy sheltering the Holy Sacrament was next, followed by the King's carriage and that of the Queen, wearing a dress of silver cloth and the *Regent* diamond, the largest of the Crown jewels. The King was saluted by endless acclamations, while not a single cry of *Long live the Queen* was heard. On the contrary, someone on the street shouted *Long live the Duke d'Orléans* as she passed. I saw her smart under the insult as one would under the lash, but almost immediately she recovered her disdainful composure.

The next day witnessed the opening session of the Estates General in the *Salle des Menus Plaisirs*, "Hall of the Small Pleasures," a vast ballroom within the Palace of Versailles. A dais had been prepared on which the King and Queen were to sit under a canopy. All morning the Representatives, one by one, had been assigned their seats in the cavernous room. The Clergy and the Nobility occupied the sides, while the Third Estate had been placed at the far end. It had as many members as the other two Orders together. The King, true to his character, had hesitated whether to accept or reject this measure. He supported and resisted in turn each position, before yielding to the majority view and agreeing to double the number of Representatives of the Third Estate. Altogether, over 1,000 Representatives were assembled, and as many spectators in the galleries behind the higher Orders.

I sat with the Duchess and the other ladies of the Court in one of the balconies that flanked the throne. My hair had been dressed, under Villers's supervision, in an array of loose ringlets and braids woven with the strings of pearls he had given me.

"It is not in fashion now," he said, "but you are beautiful enough to make it so after today."

I wore a new Court gown of white satin, made according to his specific directions. My bracelets circled my wrists and the *briolettes* of my diamond earrings brushed against my bare shoulders. Villers did not like me to wear necklaces, which, he said, interrupted the line of my throat and covered too much of its flesh.

"Look around us," the Duchess remarked. "All of the ladies of the Court are wearing their finest jewels, but they look tawdry compared to you in your white gown. You simply outshine everyone else."

Their Majesties arrived at noon. The King opened the session with a speech that lasted less than five minutes, counting the many interruptions by cheering Representatives. Again no voice was raised to cry *Long live the Queen*. I almost pitied her, but my feelings of compassion, as often when she was concerned, soon disappeared. The King, at the end of his speech, removed his hat as a sign of respect for the assembled Representatives. She turned to him with a frown and whispered to his ear, her opinion of his gesture unmistakable.

I marveled at her insolence in questioning the King's authority on so solemn an occasion. After some hesitation, he put his hat back on. The Nobility, accustomed to the Court's etiquette, followed the King's example. There was more confusion among the Third Estate, until some of its Representatives chose to remove their hats for the rest of the session, followed by the rest of their colleagues.

That awkward moment was followed by a speech by Monsieur Necker, the Comptroller General of the Finances. His tinny little voice soon gave way and a clerk endowed with better lungs droned on for three hours. My eyes were welling up with tears of boredom by the time it was over. The King rose, greeted by renewed acclamations. He took the Queen's hand in his to present her to the Estates and solicit their cheers. She made a deep curtsey, which at last drew scattered cries of *Long live the Queen*. It appeared to those of us close by that she left the room in tears. Unlike mine, hers were not caused by the tedium of Monsieur Necker's speech.

The Estates started work the next day. Villers had hired a private secretary, Monsieur Renouf, nearly sixty and owlish. Renouf, under his master's direction, prepared reports on each session of the Estates, which Villers in turn sent to his constituents in Normandy every few days. As their elected Representative, he felt much responsibility towards them and wished to repay their trust by keeping them informed of all developments.

Villers would join me for dinner immediately after the sessions closed for the day. He was more affectionate than ever towards Aimée. He sat her in his lap and took an interest in the progress of her studies. There was nothing she dreaded more than to disappoint him. Every night she would ask me to rehearse her lessons one more time in anticipation of his arrival. She insisted that many a page of handwriting be discarded as unworthy of his perusal and started afresh. She was almost four years old and, while Miss Howard continued her instruction in English, I taught her to read and write French. The hours of the day that were not dedicated to study were spent in long walks with Aimée in the woods of Versailles, now in all the splendour of their spring foliage, where we would gather bouquets of blue hyacinths.

"Look at me, my love," said Villers one night after dinner. "I have become a regular bourgeois now. I work all day and come home to your bed every night."

"You make it sound like a chore."

"On the contrary, Belle, I have never been so content, except maybe for the times we spent together in Normandy. The only thing that could add to my happiness would be to make you my wife."

I smiled. "Then, my dear, the picture of the Count de Villers, a reformed libertine, would indeed be complete. I would, I suppose, bear you a child once a year. You would also wear a flannel waistcoat and drink a cup of herb tea every night before bed."

He rose and came to sit by my side on the sofa. "Nothing wrong with any of it. Why wait to be married? I should begin to do all of these things already, Belle, so as to deprive you of any reason to persist in your refusal." He put his arm around my waist and pressed his lips upon mine. "Now, about that notion of fathering a child . . ."

The first sessions of the Estates had been dedicated to the verification of the Representatives' powers. The elections for Paris, delayed because of poor organization and the constant unrest in the capital, were still being held, almost two months after they had been completed in the provinces. Thus the Estates commenced without any Representatives from Paris.

Aimée and I, along with the entire Court, went into mourning at the beginning of June. The little Dauphin, Louis-Joseph, heir to the throne, had died of consumption. The disease had settled in his spine and bones. The poor child, tortured by an iron corset, had been so deformed that he had not been seen at Court for almost a year. He had been kept in the château de Meudon, a few miles away, where he had surrendered his soul to God. He was not the first of the royal children to die. Little Madame Sophie, his younger sister, had passed away a year earlier. She had been conceived around the same time as my poor little boy. The death of the infant princess, who was of no account to anyone, had met with the indifference of both the Court and her family. The Dauphin, heir to the throne, was another matter. His birth had been eagerly anticipated for over ten years after his parents' marriage and greeted by such joy that his death seemed a cruel mockery of happier times. It was a bad omen. I could not help but feel sorrow for the Queen's loss. I took Aimée to the Church of Saint-Louis in Versailles to light a candle and pray for the repose of both children's souls. The second son of the royal couple, Louis-Charles, a few months older than Aimée, became the new Dauphin.

The sad tidings from the Court had not prevented the Estates from continuing their sessions. The Representatives of the Clergy, in majority parish priests and commoners, had by the end of June joined the Third Estate. Together they now called themselves the National Assembly and had sworn not to dissolve before they had written a Constitution for the Kingdom. Villers was furious at those of his fellow noblemen who still insisted on holding separate sessions.

"The imbeciles represent less than one percent of the population, and they think they can refuse to join the Third Estate! What do they expect? That the King, prompted by the Queen, will support their position? He will abandon the nobility, as he has abandoned every cause he has ever defended. If we noblemen do not join the National Assembly, the Revolution will happen without us, and that will mean against us."

Everyone was now speaking of the "Revolution" as a matter of course. It was already a fact that admitted of no discussion. The King declared the deliberations of the National Assembly void in their entirety. He also threatened to dissolve the Estates General if they persisted in their position to meet as a single body. Nonetheless, a minority of the noblemen, forty-seven of them, led by the Duke d'Orléans and including Villers, Lauzun and Lafayette, seceded from the rest of their Order and joined the Third Estate.

Two days later, as Villers had predicted, the King reversed his position and invited the holdovers from the Nobility and the Clergy to join the National Assembly. He was thus placing himself at the head of the Revolution, or, depending on one's opinion, trailing it.

At the same time, the King ordered the regiments of the French army that were composed of foreigners, mostly Swiss and Germans mercenaries, altogether 20,000 men, to surround Paris. No one doubted that his real goal was to crush the capital if it showed any sign of siding with the new Assembly. Public opinion blamed that decision, which was to have such momentous consequences, on the Queen's influence. The bourgeois of Paris, meanwhile, started a militia, called the National Guard, to protect the city against the anticipated attack.

❧ 45 ❧

One night at the beginning of July, Villers came home from the National Assembly earlier than usual.

"Pack your things, Belle," he said. "I am taking you and Aimée to Vaucelles tonight."

"What is happening?"

"A German regiment has already set camp in the park of the Palace, and another has taken its quarters at the Orangerie there. The royal family is preparing to leave Versailles for a fortified city close to the Austrian border. You know what it means. The King will seek the help of Emperor Joseph, the Queen's brother, while the Swiss and German regiments are going to attack Paris and the Assembly here in Versailles. The Count d'Artois, the King's youngest brother, has publicly stated that all the Representatives of the Third Estate are going to be hanged. He is only saying aloud what the others are thinking." Villers took me in his arms. "I have been selfish to keep you here so long, my love. I would never forgive myself if any harm befell you."

Thus I spent those days of July 1789, which were to have such a bearing on the fate of France and Europe, in the safety of Vaucelles. Villers stayed with me the first night since there was no session of the Assembly on the morrow, which was a Sunday. He spent the following day teaching me how to load, aim and shoot a firearm, and insisted on leaving his best pair of pistols with me.

Villers left Vaucelles on the 13th to rejoin the Assembly. He had asked me, because he was leaving at dawn, not to rise to see him on his way. Yet I did. I kept him embraced a long time before letting him go. His eyes were red when he bid me good-bye. We did not speak much but parted with great regret and a sense of foreboding. So much had happened in the two months since the Estates General had convened and the future seemed very uncertain. All our grievances were forgotten in the sorrow of not knowing whether we would ever see each other again. He went on horseback to attract less attention than in a carriage. His plan was to reach Versailles through country roads without entering Paris, while trying to avoid the foreign troops massed to the south of the capital.

I spent that day in great anxiety and sent Lemoyne, one of the lackeys, to gather news in Paris. He had to turn around at the gates for no one was allowed to enter the city.

"I spoke to the guards at the Charenton Gate, Madam," he said. "Crowds have attacked the prisons and freed all the French Guards jailed for mutiny. They won't obey their Colonel anymore. The King's ready to have all the members of the Assembly arrested in Versailles. They also say that all the noblemen who have joined the Third Estate are going to be beheaded for treason. That means My Lord too, doesn't it?"

I thanked Lemoyne and gave him a silver *écu* of three francs for his pains. The following day, the 14th of July of the year 1789, was my twentieth birthday. I did not know whether Villers was arrested, sentenced to death or already executed. I was too anxious to read or sit down to any occupation. In an attempt to keep busy, I went for a walk with Aimée in the park. Around five in the afternoon, as we were headed for the river, we heard a booming noise.

"Listen, Mama," she said, "thunder. Why cannot we see the beautiful golden dragon?"

This was the name she gave lightning. I said nothing to disabuse her of this idea, although I knew that we were hearing the rumbling of a different kind of storm, one of far longer duration and greater import.

Again I sent Lemoyne, the lackey, to Paris. He returned before dark, flushed with excitement.

"The city gates are still closed, Madam," he said, "but the guards told me that the people stormed the Bastille."

"It is impossible, Lemoyne. How could the fortress, with its drawbridges and huge walls, be taken by force?"

"That's what they said, My Lady."

I went to bed uncertain of what to believe. When Manon helped me dress the next morning, I noticed that she was unusually silent. I saw her several times open her mouth and then close it without uttering a word.

"What is it, Manon?" I asked at last.

"I heard from Junot's niece, My Lady."

"Junot, my footman?"

"Yes, My Lady. He was injured in Paris yesterday."

"Nothing serious, I hope."

Manon blushed and looked down. "Please, My Lady, don't be angry."

I sighed, wondering what misdeed Junot, a man of mature years and placid temper, could have committed. "Tell me about it. Then I can decide whether to be angry."

"Well, Madam, yesterday morning, a huge crowd, over 20,000 strong, went to the *Invalides*, close to Your Ladyship's lodgings. There's an arsenal within the veterans' hospital."

I frowned. "I know. Are you telling me that Junot joined those people?"

"Yes, My Lady. But everything was peaceful. The French Guards took the lead and seized all the guns, pikes and sabres. We need some real soldiers, with real weapons, to defend Paris against those foreign mercenaries. Remember, three days ago, the Royal German Regiment shot at a peaceful crowd and killed a poor old man at the Tuileries. No wonder, their Colonel, the Prince de Lambesc is cousin to the Queen, and she—"

"So what happened to Junot yesterday? Was he hurt at the *Invalides*?"

"No, My Lady. The Governor there didn't resist. No one was hurt. The crowd took several pieces of cannon from the *Invalides*, but they were short of ammunition. So they went to the Bastille to find some. That's where everything changed. The garrison of the Bastille fired at the crowd and killed more than a hundred people. Everyone said that the fortress couldn't be stormed, but the brave French Guards directed the attack. It fell in half an hour."

"So it is true. What about Junot?"

"Oh, My Lady, people were running in a panic right after the garrison of the Bastille started shooting at the crowd. That's when he fell. He broke his leg. He was carried to his niece's lodgings. Now he's afraid you'll be angry because he took advantage of your absence to join the crowd. He begs you not to dismiss him."

I sighed. "At his age, a broken leg is no light matter. Yet he was fortunate. From what you say, he could have been shot dead. You may tell him that he is an old fool and should know better. Has he seen a surgeon?"

"Yes. He won't be able to resume his service for a month at least. So Your Ladyship won't turn him out then?"

"No, I will not."

"Well, to tell you the truth, he's mightily worried about My Lord. Of course, Madam, Junot is in your employ, but all the same . . . he would never lie to you, because you're so kind a mistress. But if you could tell My Lord that Junot fell in the stairs or something like that, he'd be grateful to you till his last day."

I could not help smiling. "Tell Junot not to worry."

What Manon did not say was that, after the fall of the Bastille, its garrison was massacred and its Governor beheaded by the crowd. I sometimes wonder what would have happened if the Queen had not used her influence to deny Lauzun his appointment as Colonel of the French Guards. He was always liked by his men for his bravery and cheerful temper. If he had been Colonel of the French Guards instead of the Duke du Châtelet, he might have prevented their mutiny at that crucial time. The course of events turned on small things indeed. A woman's spite was one of them.

The fall of the Bastille was the signal for the first wave of what would become known as the *émigration*. The Count d'Artois, the King's youngest brother and most fierce opponent of the Revolution, and other princes of the royal blood, left France. So did the Duchess of Polignac, the Queen's favourite, with her husband, lover, sister-in-law and pet priest in tow. She never saw her country again and died an exile four years later. I pity her for it, although she was no friend of mine, for it is a fate I now seem bound to share. I have tasted all of its bitterness.

On the 15th, Villers sent me a note informing me that he had returned to Paris with Lafayette and would join me in Vaucelles as soon as he could. At least he was alive. For how much longer I knew not.

Two days later at dusk, I heard the whinnying of a horse and the sound of hooves in the courtyard. I ran outside. Villers dismounted. I threw myself into his arms. He held my face in his hands and greedily kissed my cheeks, my lips, my eyes as if he could not feast enough on them. I had never seen him act in such a manner in front of the servants.

"Belle, my Belle," he said, "I thought I would never see you again."

"So did I. Oh, my love, I heard that you would be beheaded."

He put his arm around my shoulders as we went inside.

"The King has capitulated," said Villers. "He announced to the Assembly the withdrawal of all foreign regiments. Nothing will ever be the same, Belle. Bailly, the astronomer, now heads the city of Paris, with the title of Mayor, instead of that of Provost of the Merchants. The last Provost was shot dead by the insurgents after the fall of the Bastille.

Lafayette has been put in command of the new National Guard. So many things have changed since I last saw you, my love."

"So you are safe?"

"So it seems, at least for a while. The King went to Paris today. I saw him accept on the steps of the City Hall a tricolour cockade from the hands of Lafayette. The white, representing the Crown, is surrounded by the blue and red, the colours of Paris. Quite a powerful symbol: the monarchy besieged by the people of Paris."

"These also happen to be the colours of the American flag," I said.

"True, my Belle. It must be Lafayette's idea. I believe the events went to his head, which is not the strongest part of his person. He must now fancy himself the George Washington of France."

"Still, the fact that the King himself visited Paris is a hopeful sign. The city should be quieter now."

"Carriages are still not allowed on the streets, but I pinned a tricolour cockade to my hat and had no trouble returning here on horseback. Yet order is not restored. I met with a mob carrying at the end of a pike the head of Bertier de Sauvigny, the King's *intendant* in Paris, its mouth stuffed with hay. Of course, he had declared that the Parisians, if they were starving, could always eat grass. These words were not forgotten. The people of Paris are indeed hungry and angry."

The demolition of the Bastille was decreed. I joined the crowds that hurried to visit the fortress while it was still standing. I did not approve of the violence that had followed its fall, but, as almost everyone in Paris, I rejoiced to see it destroyed. It was the symbol of the arbitrary detentions of the Old Regime, of the dreaded *lettres de cachet*. Outside the dismantled fortress, little temporary cafés, sheltered under striped tents, sprang up in the summer heat. The site had become a fashionable excursion in spite of the dust and noise of the demolition. I bought Aimée a game of dominos made from the old stones of the Bastille, which had been turned into all sorts of mementos.

The situation had quieted by the end of July, to the point where I deemed it safe to leave Vaucelles and join Villers in Versailles. Yet the strangest rumours were spreading through the countryside. It was widely believed that the Queen was conspiring with the local nobility to massacre the peasants. As a result, they attacked many châteaux during the summer of '89, in what would be called *la Grande Peur*, "the Great Fear."

Since the opening of the Estates General, I had caught sight of the

Chevalier des Huttes from time to time in Versailles. We had barely spoken to each other since the duel between my brother and Villers. However, after crossing his path in the Palace, I began a conversation with him, awkward at first, but after a few minutes marked by some return of our former friendship. I knew that he did not wish to call on me in a house rented by Villers, and that Villers himself would not be any happier to know that I had received the Chevalier, so we agreed to meet in the salons of the Palace once a week.

The Chevalier remained staunchly loyal to his Queen. He expressed the point of view that the conduct of "my friends," as he called Villers, Lauzun and the noblemen who had joined the Third Estate in June, was tantamount to treason. I did not conceal my difference of opinion. We therefore agreed to never talk about politics, since it was a subject of conversation unlikely to give either of us any kind of pleasure.

Around the end of July, we met again. I was impatient to hear whether there was any truth to the rumours of the Great Fear.

"Have you received any news from my brother?" I asked the Chevalier.

"You need not worry, My Lady. He is unharmed, although the peasants did attack Fontfreyde. They intended to burn the old deeds proving the existence of your family's feudal rights. The Marquis, as could be expected, displayed great courage. Although he may not be popular with everyone, he has always known how to keep his vassals in their place. After he addressed them from the top of the outside staircase, they withdrew, their hats off, without causing any damage. Your sister, the Countess de Chavagnac, is also safe. The peasants also marched against the château of Saint-Hippolite, and her husband had a stroke during the attack. That scared the rabble away and saved the archives from destruction. I am sorry to report that he is not expected to live many weeks longer."

I wondered how much sorrow Madeleine would feel if she too became a widow.

"How sad," I said. "What about Cénac?"

"Things did not go well there, Madam. The current Baron is not so well liked as your late husband. He was made to watch, with the Baroness at his side, while the château was ransacked, the furniture thrown out of the windows and the archives burnt. The peasants even molested him."

It was with great relief that I learned of my brother's and sister's safety. Yet I pictured with some satisfaction the new Baron and Baroness de Peyre, pitchforks pointed at their stomachs, forced to watch the sacking of Cénac. My feelings, as usual, must have been easy to read.

"There is nothing amusing about it, Madam," said the Chevalier, frowning. "If the audacity of the rabble is not checked, both in Paris and in the provinces, the country is doomed. The King has shown towards those responsible for the troubles an amazing leniency, which those scoundrels have interpreted as weakness."

I opened my mouth to reply.

"I am sorry," he said. "I know that we agreed never to discuss that question. Please accept my apologies."

Madame de Gouville wrote me, for she found me a more reliable correspondent than her nephew, that most of Normandy had remained quiet and Dampierre had not been attacked.

"I have always been accommodating with my tenants, especially since the last harvest," said Villers when I read him her letter. "Moreover, I can hardly be accused of being part of an aristocratic conspiracy. And my aunt has knit enough stockings for little peasants to have gained some measure of goodwill."

The events of the following August are too well known to be related in detail here: during a late session on the night of the 4th and 5th, some of the Representatives of the nobility in the Assembly, led by the Viscount de Noailles, brother-in-law to Lafayette, proposed the abolition of the privileges of the old feudal society. The lords' private courts of justice were abolished. Access to the judicial system was to be free. Judges would no longer purchase their functions but would now be appointed on the basis of merit. Commoners would no longer be barred from any profession or place, whether in the army, the civil service or the church.

My friends, as the Chevalier called them, were all part of that movement. The Representatives of the Clergy likewise renounced its tithes. The members of the National Assembly had embraced in the middle of general rejoicing. When Villers came home after one in the morning and told me what had happened at the Assembly, I threw my arms around his neck and together we cried with joy. Everything seemed possible. A new era of happiness and liberty was opening before the Nation. Those who have not lived through such changes cannot imagine the headiness of those days.

The Assembly proceeded to draft a Declaration of the Rights of Man and of the Citizen, which was to inspire two years later the American Bill of Rights. It spelled out the right to resist oppression, the freedom from arbitrary arrest and detention, the presumption of innocence in criminal proceedings, the freedom of religion, the freedom of opinion and the equality of all before the law. I know that it is fashionable, now that France has been, for fifteen years, suffering under the yoke of Bonaparte's tyranny, to denigrate the legacy of the Revolution and the merits of its first Assembly, but the night of the 4th of August and the adoption of the Declaration of Rights remain unmatched achievements. They still make me, although I have not been allowed to set foot in my country in twenty years, proud to be French.

The Queen, however, made no mystery of her distaste for the new ideas. On the 25th of August was celebrated the holiday of Saint-Louis, the King's ancestor and patron saint. Upon that occasion, Their Majesties traditionally received the good wishes of the City of Paris, represented by its Provost. Of course, there was no more Provost since the fall of the Bastille six weeks earlier, but it had been decided that the Queen would greet delegations from both the National Guard and the new Municipality of Paris, led by its Mayor.

This ceremony was held in the Salon of the Nobles, the green room where I had been presented. The Queen, covered with diamonds from head to toe, had taken her place on a throne raised on a dais. I, in my best white Court dress, was standing behind the Duchess, who sat on a stool. An usher announced: "The City of Paris!" Bailly, the new Mayor, made his entrance. I was surprised to observe that, instead of kneeling before the throne, as was required by the etiquette, he made a deep bow. Curious to see the Queen's reaction, I watched her. Her face was frozen, but her entire body was shaking. After introducing the members of the Municipality, who also bowed, Bailly made a short speech in which he assured the Queen of the devotion of her subjects. She did not make any gesture or utter any word in response.

Then it was Lafayette's turn to introduce the officers of his staff. Again, all bowed to the ground. The Queen's face was now scarlet and livid welts were visible on her throat under her diamonds. This time she regained enough composure to stutter a few indistinct words and shake her head sideways to dismiss her visitors from her presence. All left promptly, astonishment and anger painted on their faces.

"Well," asked the Duchess once we left the room a few minutes later, "what did you think of this, Belle? Many of those members of the Municipality had never seen the Queen before. They asked to come to Versailles especially to be introduced to her. Now they have seen her indeed."

"She did look extremely upset. I was surprised myself by the fact that none of her visitors knelt. Yet, Madam, it was to be expected. Nowadays many consider those antiquated marks of respect humiliating and unworthy of a free country."

"Those poor fellows from the Municipality probably thought that they were showing enough deference by bowing." The Duchess shook her head sadly. "Now they will bring back to Paris a fine impression of the Queen. This does not bode too well."

∾ 46 ❧

Villers and I continued to live in Versailles until the autumn of 1789. Late in September, he expressed concerns that the Court had again resorted to its old tricks. The regiment of Flanders, known for its loyalty to the Crown, was called to Versailles.

"An attack on the Assembly must be imminent," he said. "The Queen has not abandoned the idea of seeing us hanged or beheaded, I suppose. The Bodyguards are to give a grand dinner to honour the officers of the Flanders regiment on the first of October. You should ask the Chevalier des Huttes for tickets. He cannot refuse since he is such a great friend of yours."

"I will ask him if you wish, though I will not much enjoy attending a dinner at which I am not to be a guest."

"Please, Belle. I am curious to hear what happens."

The event took place in the Opera of the Palace of Versailles. Tables had been set on the stage, with officers from the Bodyguards and Flanders regiment alternating. The National Guards of Versailles, for by then these militias had been instituted in all cities, large and small, had also been invited. I was sitting in one of the boxes. The orchestra played, while one heard cries of *Long live the King*. The spectators comprised both courtiers and members of the Assembly. Acerbic exchanges of opinions took place from one box to another.

I found the atmosphere unpleasant and was ready to withdraw when the royal family entered the stage. The acclamations, joined to the music, became deafening. The Queen took her son Louis-Charles by the hand and walked with him between the tables, smiling graciously as she knew how to do on occasion. Officers were throwing themselves at her feet and she gave them her hand to kiss. In the heat of the moment, some of the National Guards took off the tricolour cockades that decorated their hats and trampled them underfoot in the midst of cheering. I was shocked to see the King and Queen smiling and nodding in approval. I left in disgust.

I told Villers of the incident that night.

"This is a disaster," he said. "How could the King tolerate, much less encourage, such behaviour after he himself donned the tricolour cockade? News of this will spread to Paris in a matter of hours."

A few days later, I was teaching Aimée her letters when, some time after five in the afternoon, we were interrupted by shouts and songs coming from the street. I ran to the window. From the direction of Paris, thousands of women on foot, armed with pikes and scythes, their rags stuck to their meager frames by a chilly rain, were marching on the Palace. That display of poverty and anger froze me to the bone.

Around eleven that night, I heard more noise coming from the street and rose to see another cortege file by my house. A crowd, this time composed of men carrying lanterns, was headed in the direction of the Palace. A sullen Lafayette, riding at the head of the National Guards from Paris, closed the procession.

Villers did not return from the Assembly until late the next morning, his face drawn. He collapsed in a chair. Eyes closed, he reached for my hand and kissed it.

"What a night this has been, my dear Belle," he said. "You must have seen that mob arrive from Paris. The women were there first and set camp in the gardens of the Palace. The men joined them later. They were all clamouring for bread. Lafayette was granted an audience by the King and Queen. He assured them that there was nothing to fear. He himself retired around five in the morning."

Villers rubbed his face.

"One hour later," he continued, "a riot started after one of the men who had set camp in the gardens was shot dead by a Bodyguard. The whole mob stormed the Palace. The women in particular forced their way to the Queen's apartments, shouting that they would *make lace out of her bowels*. Two Bodyguards on duty that night at the door to her bedroom were killed."

I took a deep breath. "What about the Chevalier des Huttes? Is he safe?" I asked.

Villers shook his head. "I do not know, my dear. I would tell you if I did. What is certain is their sacrifice gave the Queen, barefoot and in her chemise, time to seek refuge in the King's apartments. Lafayette, awakened at last, arrived in time to save the rest of the Bodyguards from the mob's wrath."

"So apart from those two Bodyguards killed on the Queen's doorstep, all are safe?"

"I believe so. Later in the morning, Lafayette appeared with the Queen at the balcony of the Palace and kissed her hand. He may have saved her life then. He is in the unenviable position of attempting to reconcile the mob and Queen, who loathes him because she sees him as the symbol of the Revolution. The crowd, pacified by his gesture, began crying *To Paris!* The King ostensibly agreed to leave Versailles for Paris. Yet as usual, he tried to do the reverse of what he had promised. He argued that he refused to be separated from the Assembly. How convenient for him to forget that he would have been delighted to have us arrested or executed only hours earlier! We responded that we would follow him to the capital. He has no choice now but to leave for Paris."

I put my hand on Villers's shoulder. "Please take some rest, my dear. You look exhausted."

"I am, my love, but I must return to the Assembly now. The situation may change at any moment."

Early in the afternoon of that day, Aimée and I saw another parade under my windows, going in the opposite direction from the day before. Parisians on foot, Bodyguards and National Guards on horseback, all mixed together, were marching in the greatest disorder towards Paris. In accordance with the weather, which had turned dry and warm for the season, the mood of the crowd now seemed gleeful. I looked in vain for the handsome figure of the Chevalier des Huttes among the blue and red uniforms of Bodyguards. All I saw at first was the same crowd of bedraggled women as the previous day, this time cheering, straddling cannons or riding behind the soldiers. The carriages of the royal family and the Court followed at a slow pace, accompanied by men holding aloft on pikes two severed heads.

As soon as I recognized the nature of the trophies, I pushed Aimée away from the window, which was on the second floor. I was too horrified by the grisly sight to withdraw myself. I must have looked shocked, for the men holding the pikes paused in front of my house, pushed the heads into my face and, laughing and yelling, invited me to kiss them. I could not keep my eyes away from one of them. Its skin was grey, its hair matted with blood. The blade of the pike, like a steel tongue, was poking out of one of the cheeks. Disfigured as the poor remains were, I recognized the face of the Chevalier des Huttes. My knees buckled and I withdrew from the window, too stunned for tears. From the cries of the crowd I knew that the procession had resumed its march.

I had assumed, without any reason other than a desire to believe the best, that the Chevalier had been among the Bodyguards rescued by Lafayette. He had indeed been massacred by the crowd at the Queen's doorstep. It comforted me later to think that he had died bravely in the line of duty, as befits a soldier, and that his sacrifice had not been in vain. He had saved the life of Her Majesty, whom he loved so, by giving her time to escape.

As the street quieted, I looked out again, this time with tears for the Chevalier. All I remembered of him was his kindness to me, his fondness for Aimée and his help in bringing me to Paris. I was only beginning to understand that in the course of a revolution one should be prepared to lose one's friends.

The Assembly, true to its word, followed the King to Paris within days. So did Villers and I. Overnight the Palace of Versailles was deserted by the living and abandoned to the ghosts of kings long dead.

47

On our return to Paris, I found the same entertainments, balls, concerts, plays, as before. My enjoyment of them was dimmed by the impression the death of the Chevalier des Huttes had left on me. The events of the 5th and 6th of October spurred a second wave, more numerous than the first, of emigration. Many members of the nobility left France, some never to return. So did Madame Lebrun, who hoped to find new patrons for her paintings in Italy. The Marquise de Bastide, the Duchess's daughter, likewise left for Turin, the capital of the Kingdom of Savoie. Yet Paris society remained as elegant and cheerful as in the past, with the difference that politics was now the main topic of conversation.

The new liberty of speech, following centuries of royal censorship, had spawned hundreds of newspapers, pamphlets and satires. One no longer dreaded the *cabinet noir*, the "black cabinet," the division of the police that read and copied private letters under the Old Regime. I attended on occasion the sessions of the Assembly, now resettled in the former indoors riding arena of the Tuileries. The debates were rowdier than anything seen in England. The galleries reserved for the public were always full, as was fitting in a young democracy, and one had to arrive early to find room. The Representatives took their seats according to their political opinions: the party of the Court to the right, the Patriots to the left, and those who could not make up their minds in the center. The audience would cheer, jeer, whistle, clap, argue with the orators. Disputes, as is often the case among Frenchmen, could become quite heated. Once in a while a nobleman drew his sword and threatened to run it through a colleague of a different opinion. The "knitters," women of the lowest classes who would come each day to the Assembly, responded by shouting *String the aristocrats from the lampposts*.

From the galleries of the Assembly, I listened from time to time to the speeches of a carefully dressed young man, slightly built, with delicate features and not much of a voice. What he lacked in oratory skills was more than compensated by his conviction. His argument against the death penalty, which he called a barbaric form of punishment unworthy of a democracy, was particularly forceful. He was also passionate in his denunciation of slavery. He advocated the enfranchisement of all men, regardless of wealth, education or colour, although, to my disappointment, he did not mention female suffrage. His conviction moved me. I asked my neighbours in the galleries about him and was told that he was Robespierre, an attorney and the Representative for the northern town of Arras. Someone said: "Watch this young man, Madam. He will go far. He believes in what he says."

Villers, after our return to Paris in mid-October, continued to fulfill his duties as a Representative. Although they kept him occupied during the day, his old uneasiness returned. As I resumed my former life, he became incensed over the most insignificant details.

The Count de Maury had by then tired of poor Emilie. He often looked at me in a manner suggesting that he was considering me for the place she had occupied. One night, Villers, his face white, burst upon me while I was playing one of Mozart's sonatas on my pianoforte. I had forgotten that Maury had once mentioned that he liked the works of that composer. Villers slammed the instrument shut and insisted on receiving a full account of my feelings for Maury.

But this was nothing compared to the jealousy Lauzun inspired. He had once mentioned that blue was his favourite colour. I met him again at a dinner given by the Duchess, when I happened to wear a blue gauze dress. Also blue were the elegant heron feather in my hair and the ribbons that trimmed my long white gloves. Villers glowered at me across the table during the whole dinner. At the end of it, he seized me roughly by the arm and shoved me rather than handed me into his carriage. Once at my lodgings, he accused me of having some sort of secret understanding with Lauzun, of wearing blue that night to show him that I loved him, and of many other things.

In our intimate relations, Villers made increased demands, sometimes of a novel nature. Any reluctance, any hesitation in submitting to his summons were interpreted as a sign that I no longer cared for him or enjoyed his embraces. One night after a dinner he had given at his house, he told me in front of his guests: "I wish to show Your Ladyship a rather interesting book I just received from London. Please, Madam, be kind enough to follow me to my study."

I flushed with anger at the thought that he was flaunting our liaison and his power over me, when he had only half an hour to wait to be alone with me.

"You are very kind, Sir," I said, "but I feel a little tired. Some other time maybe."

Villers was ready to respond when Lauzun, who was among the guests, rose. "I must say that I am exhausted too," he said. "You will allow me to retire, Villers."

I expressed my gratitude by raising my eyes to Lauzun. He looked back at me in a rather sad manner. The other guests took their cues from him and left shortly. Another scene ensued, worse than usual because Villers had noticed the looks exchanged between Lauzun and me.

I tried to reason with Villers but came to realize the futility of my efforts. I would look away and wait in silence for the outbursts to subside. Before long he would acknowledge the irrationality of his suspicions and beg my forgiveness in the most contrite manner. I nevertheless learned to mind the most trivial details of my life and dread the results of an instant of carelessness.

Even my lady friends did not find grace in Villers's eyes. He believed them to induce me to betray him. The only one to escape his censure was the Duchess. I had missed her company in Versailles and called on her almost daily upon my return to Paris. After the emigration of her daughter, I was all the more sensible of the many obligations I had to my elderly friend.

It was during one of these visits that the Duchess told me, her eyes shining like those of a child: "I have a surprise for you, dear Belle. You are to be offered the place of lady-in-waiting to the Countess de Provence, with a stipend of 6,000 francs a year."

I remained silent for a minute. "I cannot express my gratitude warmly enough, Madam. I have no connections at Court that could explain such a favour. It is such an honour to belong to the household of the King's sister-in-law."

"Well, my dear, in truth these places are less in demand than they used to be. All I had to do was to suggest your name to some of my friends. When the Countess de Provence heard of it, she herself requested that you join her household as a replacement for my daughter."

"Why does Madame want me as a lady-in-waiting?"

"She has always been delighted with your beauty. Also of course, there is the fact that the Queen has never treated you well and hates Villers with a passion. That can only act as a recommendation in the eyes of Her Highness, who seems to have been infected by the revolutionary spirit. Finally, as you know, Madame de Gourbillon has been exiled to Lille since last February. The Countess de Provence misses her and thinks that she is owed some compensation for the loss of her dear friend's company."

I stiffened. "Does Her Highness expect me to provide the same services as Madame de Gourbillon?"

"Of course not, dear. It will be incumbent upon you to make things completely clear from the beginning. I am sure that Madame, who is far from an imbecile, has enough sense to respect your inclination."

"Are you sure?"

"I would not propose this otherwise," said the Duchess, smiling.

I trusted her judgment and gratefully accepted the place. True, I was taking a risk by becoming part of the Court at a time when the situation remained unsettled. Yet I still believed that the royal family's move to Paris, in spite of the violence that had attended it, would seal the reconciliation between the city and the monarchy. I saw more to admire in the Revolution than to fear.

Villers glowered at me when he heard my news.

"Have you taken leave of your senses, Belle?" he asked. "Why would you accept any position with such a woman as Madame?"

"It is worth 6,000 a year. That means a great deal to me."

"Do I not already give you an allowance in the same amount? Perhaps I should have increased it. Why did you not ask for more?"

"What you give me, my dear, is more than enough to satisfy my every need and whim, but I intend to save all of the money I will earn for Aimée's dowry. Her father, as you know, left her next to nothing. In ten years, when she is old enough to think of those things, she will have 60,000 francs, which may be enough to induce someone she likes to marry her. I want her to have better choices than I when I came to Paris."

He frowned. "You sound as if you had to bed Blue Beard. Was it really so disgusting for you to yield to me?"

"Of course not, but it was difficult to accept the idea of becoming your mistress."

"And pray whose fault is it that we are not married now? We need to seriously discuss these matters, Belle. You should know that I have amended my will to leave you Vaucelles and the Cantepie estate in Normandy, which brings 50,000 a year. I would make these gifts irrevocable by marriage contract. Moreover, I understand your concerns about Aimée, and I am ready to settle 60,000 on her as a dowry. So all you have to do is to marry me, thank Madame and tell her that you are, much to your regret, unable to accept her offer."

"You are very generous, as usual, but you have convinced me that matrimony would not suit you at all."

"That was years ago. I have changed, Belle."

"I am aware of it. Of late you have become jealous. Yet I have done everything in my power to please you, to the point of agreeing to be buried alive in Versailles for months."

"I know, Belle." He reached for my hand. "I have plagued you with my idiotic suspicions. Please forgive me. The truth is that I am afraid of losing you again. If you married me, I would feel assured of you."

"Can we not continue as we are? Are you not happy with me?"

"I am, but I want more. I need your promise that you will be mine and mine only, that you will love me, obey me and honour me."

"Do I not already do all of these things?"

"You do, but I want you to trust me enough to give me the power to enforce that promise. Is my proposal not generous enough?"

"It is, more so than I could ever expect or deserve. I thank you for it, but I do not wish to be so entirely dependent upon your kindness. I want to earn this money for Aimée. She is nothing to you. You should not be burdened with the expense of her dowry."

"She would be my stepdaughter if we married. That would be enough for me to want to see her decently settled. What I cannot fathom is why you will not accept this money from me, but are ready to throw yourself at the mercy of a woman who is a drunkard and a pervert to *earn* it, as you say. Have you any idea of what it entails?"

"Madame knows that I would never agree to anything of the kind."

"How would she? She has never met with much resistance from other ladies she has fancied. You are hopelessly naive, Belle, if you think that she does not expect you to be compliant, and much mistaken if you believe that I will tolerate such a ridiculous situation. I will not let you make a fool of me while you prostitute yourself."

"How can you speak to me in such a manner?" I could feel my anger rising. "Why cannot you trust my judgment?"

"Because you have none. Let me be clear, Belle. If you accept Madame's offer, your allowance will stop. You would not be a *sol* richer than if you had declined the place."

I looked straight into Villers's eyes. I remembered my feelings of desperate powerlessness when my brother had forced his will upon me, when I had been compelled to obey the Baron. That would never happen again.

"Fine," I said. "I will take the place. You may turn me out of here if you wish. I will find less expensive lodgings and pay for them out of my own pocket."

Villers rubbed his hands on his face. "So be it, Madam. I will put an end to Your Ladyship's allowance, which will be reinstated, with a substantial increase, should you reconsider your decision. There is no need for you to move. I will still pay for your rent and servants."

I held out my hand to him. "I am sorry to have angered you. Such was not my purpose."

"Maybe not, but you did not hesitate to do so. You are refusing, out of sheer stupidity and obstinacy, to grant a perfectly reasonable request I made of you. Do not ever suggest again that you honour and obey me like a husband. Good night to you."

Villers's jaw was tight as he left.

Yielding would have been giving up any pretense of independence. I hoped for a visit from him the next morning. He did not call. I have noted earlier in these memoirs, I believe, that I have no false pride. I wrote him a note stating that I begged his forgiveness for having offended him, that I was grieved to have done so, that I thanked him for his concern and that I hoped to have the pleasure of his company that night. He returned before dinner.

"Thank you for allowing me to save face," he said, smiling sadly. "I would have returned in any event. I cannot stay away from you for so long. You did not say in your note whether you had reconsidered your decision."

"I have not, my dear, but you need not worry. Rest assured that if anything inappropriate happens, I will resign my place with Madame immediately."

"I guess I will have to be content with this." He shook his head. "What a fool I have been not to marry you when you still wanted me."

The Court had moved to the Palace of the Tuileries, in the heart of

Paris. It had remained uninhabited for decades, except for an apartment set up for the Queen to spend the night when she attended the balls and plays of Paris. Even that part of the Palace had been unused for years because she had long quit attending public entertainments for fear of being insulted and heckled. She barely set foot out of the Palace. The King gave up hunting, which was, along with food and locksmithing, the great passion of his life. He became famous for his ability to keep his appetite, or "eat like a swine," as people would soon say, in the face of mortal danger. His stoutness turned to obesity.

Madame was under no such pall. She shared her time between the Palace of the Luxembourg in Paris, which had already been her residence before the Revolution, and her country house of Montreuil. Unlike her sister-in-law the Queen, she did not detest Paris. She and her husband dined almost every day at the Tuileries with the King and Queen, as they had done in Versailles. As part of my duties, I accompanied her during my week of service, which was, as before the Revolution, one out of three. After staying away as much as I could from the splendid Court of Versailles, I became part of its feeble shadow in the Tuileries.

Madame welcomed me warmly. She did the honours of her country house herself. Montreuil, although a pleasant retreat, was in my opinion less lovely than Vaucelles. Madame had successively added, following her whim rather than any design, a hermitage, a tower, a multitude of bridges over a tiny brook, a Chinese pagoda, an outdoors music pavilion and, needless to say, a mock farm, complete with dairy, barn, sheep, shepherds and henhouse. I expressed all of the expected admiration in spite of the artificial and haphazard air of the place, but was sincerely impressed by very fine vegetable gardens, which were the object of Madame's utmost care. She liked to cook with the produce of her little estate and made an excellent *pesto* soup herself, after a recipe from her native Italy.

I played the pianoforte and sang for Madame, which seemed to bring her comfort in spite of the fact that she had not much of an ear. She asked many questions about Aimée and requested that I bring her with me. At first, I had noticed that Madame often gave off whiffs of liquor, spoke rather too loudly, walked with an unsteady gait and in general acted in such a way as to indicate that she had *du vent dans les voiles*, "wind in her sails," as the saying goes. During those moments, the only company, beside mine, she seemed to tolerate with equanimity was that of Rosalie, a young Negress. She had been "given" as a little girl to

Madame, as if she had been a canary or a lapdog. Rosalie was about my age, graceful and delicate, with the darkest skin I had ever seen. She showed endless patience with Madame's bouts of temper. I did not want to expose my daughter, then only four years of age, to the sight of the poor princess in her cups, leaning on Rosalie for support. I have always found drunkenness unappealing, especially in a female.

Soon, however, Madame began to act in a more measured manner in my presence. Rosalie told me under the seal of confidence that Her Highness was indeed calmer and more manageable during my week of service than at any other time. After I became assured of her improvement, I humoured her by bringing Aimée with me on occasion.

After fulfilling my duties with Madame, I had to face Villers. He would wait for me at my lodgings, pacing the parlour, and demand a minute account of my day immediately upon my return. The same enquiries were renewed in bed.

"Why do you not trust me?" I asked, looking into his eyes.

"Trust you? You betray me with a woman, Belle, and you expect me to trust you?"

"I do not betray you with anyone. I never did. Never. Not once."

I held him against me to comfort him, to appease him. I wanted to reach for the part of him that was in pain. He drew back. "You have always lied to me, Belle. You are lying to me now. What exactly have you done with that woman?"

I sighed. "I already told you all about my day."

"Do you expect me to believe you?"

"Yes, I do. What have I ever done to deserve this? Please, my dear, trust me. You are making yourself, and me, unhappy over nothing."

He seized me and kissed every inch of my skin with a sort of frenzy. I knew that love or lust had nothing to do with it. He was searching for traces of Madame's odor.

"Please stop this," I said, shuddering. "You are tearing us apart."

48

One of the first acts of the Assembly after its arrival in Paris was to place the assets of the Clergy, worth hundreds, if not thousands of millions of francs, "at the disposal of the Nation," another way of saying that they were confiscated. For the first time, the government issued paper money, the famous *assignats*, backed on the credit of ecclesiastical property.

Around the same time, I started noticing in the salons an ever-increasing number of nuns whose convents had closed. Some were still wearing the habit. Others had given up any pretense of religious vocation and mingled freely in society. The only indication of their former status was that they sometimes forgot to curtsey and instead bowed, their hands crossed on their chests, in the manner of nuns. I wrote Hélène to enquire about her plans. I offered her, after securing Villers's permission, my hospitality in Paris. She responded promptly.

> *I thank you from my heart, dearest Gabrielle, for your offer. I am truly touched by your kindness and would like nothing better than to see again my little sister, too briefly met.*
>
> *Nonetheless I cannot abandon the remaining nuns of our little congregation in the middle of the current turmoil. Under the new regulations, we had to hold elections within the convent. I had the honour of being chosen as Mother Superior of our community for the next two years, a mark of affection and trust I cannot disregard.*
>
> *I must, with regret but without any hesitation, decline to leave Noirvaux. Since monastic vows are no longer enforceable by law, some of our nuns and lay sisters have already left. It will not dissuade me from keeping the convent open for those ladies who, like me, wish to remain within the fold of religious life.*
>
> *In truth, I am not without some apprehension of the future. I am sure that Monsieur de Villers has told you that the Assembly has begun working on what is called a "Civil Constitution of the Clergy." From what I understand, Bishops would now be elected by*

the laity, instead of being appointed by the King and ordained by the Holy Father. I cannot reconcile this with the absolute authority of Rome, which is an unshakable tenet of the Catholic faith. More importantly, I hear all members of the clergy, including nuns, would be required to pledge allegiance to the Constitution. I do not hesitate to tell you, dearest Gabrielle, that I would consider such a pledge a violation of my monastic vows.

Do not worry about us, Gabrielle. These new measures have not been adopted yet. We must all hope and trust in Christ's infinite mercy.

May God keep you, dearest sister, and Aimée under His holy protection.

† *Hélène, Abbess de Noirvaux*

This letter saddened me. Selfishly, I regretted not to be able to enjoy the pleasure of Hélène's company in Paris. I understood and respected the reasons that made her wish to stay in Noirvaux, but they filled me with foreboding.

The Assembly did adopt the Civil Constitution of the Clergy. Almost half of all clerics, including Hélène, refused to pledge allegiance: they would be called *réfractaires*, or "unsworn." They were allowed to practice the Catholic faith, provided that they do so without any financial help from the Nation.

In a desire to break from the Old Regime, the Assembly discarded the boundaries of the ancient French provinces, and instituted new territorial divisions called *Départements*. Likewise, the old Districts of Paris were replaced by forty-eight Sections.

All titles of nobility were also abolished. Commoners began to refer to us as *ci-devant*, meaning "former." I became the *ci-devant* Baroness de Peyre. The word would soon become a term of derision and insult. Servants' liveries were now forbidden, and coats of arms had to be erased from carriages, buildings and clothing. I had just finished embroidering a pair of white satin ribbons I used to tie my stockings. Out of habit, I had added a Baron's coronet on top of the blue monogrammed *G*. I should have discarded these garters but was reluctant to do so. They were very pretty with their pattern of forget-me-nots, and it seemed that what I wore under my skirts was no one's business but my own.

Preparations were made in Paris to celebrate the first anniversary of the storming of the Bastille. The Champ de Mars, until then a vast empty field reserved for military exercises, had been chosen as the location for the main event, during which the King himself was to pledge allegiance to the Constitution. An "Altar of the Homeland" crowned the summit of a huge step pyramid. Grandstands were built around it, creating an oblong outdoors stadium. A triumphal ark marked its entrance on the side of the river.

Parisians of all ages and all classes of society, crippled veterans from the *Invalides* Hospital, National Guards, butchers, their sleeves rolled up their muscular arms, charcoal deliverers with darkened faces, priests, students, children, society ladies participated in the construction. I shoveled dirt and pushed a wheelbarrow, with Aimée's help, for a few hours. A tavern keeper had brought a barrel of wine to quench the thirst of the volunteers. The atmosphere was one of rejoicing and hope, although I heard a *sans-culotte*, "without breeches," a man of the lower classes, so named because he was wearing trousers instead of knee breeches, sing a ditty I did not find to my taste:

> *Damn you all aristocrats,*
> *We'll fuck your women,*
> *And you'll kiss our asses . . .*

He seemed ready with more verses in the same vein, but was silenced in mid-song. Other men told him that he was offending the ladies and threatened to flatten his head with their shovels if he did not desist.

Every regiment in the army, every *Département* sent delegates, called "Federates," to witness the celebration. It was styled "Festival of the Federation," to signify the union of the whole country as one Nation. The King was now a constitutional monarch, subject, like all of his fellow citizens, to the terms of the Constitution. The people, through their elected Representatives at the Assembly, were now the sole sovereign.

On the 14th of July, 1790, the first anniversary of the storming of the Bastille, 400,000 spectators waited in the grandstands under the rain for the arrival of the Federates. I was seated in the Court's stands, in a white dress adorned with tricolour ribbons, to the side of the King's box, facing the triumphal arch under which filed entire regiments, followed by the delegates of Paris and all *Départements*. Finally, under deafening cheers, the members of the Assembly joined the official stands. I searched among the numbers and finally saw Villers and Lauzun.

Talleyrand, the Bishop of Autun, a tricolour sash tied around his priestly vestments, celebrated Mass, no doubt an unusual occurrence for him. The huge stadium was filled with the delegates and complete silence fell when Lafayette pledged allegiance to the Constitution in a voice loud enough for all to hear. I joined the crowd in the grandstands in rising and repeating "I do." Then it was the King's turn to raise his right hand and swear allegiance to the new Constitution. The Queen forced a smile and held the little Dauphin aloft to present him to the acclamations of the crowd. The rain had ceased. The sun's rays pierced the clouds to fall upon that unforgettable scene.

I joined Villers to a dinner of cold meats in the gardens of the château of La Muette, which thousands of Federates and other guests attended. A ball on the ruins of the Bastille concluded the festivities. Hundreds of trees, festooned with garlands lit by candles, had been planted for the occasion. Banners with the mottos "Liberty" and "Fraternity" floated in the warm summer breeze. Villers seemed to have forgotten our differences. We danced late into the night before returning to my lodgings. We then held our own intimate celebration in the privacy of my bedroom. It was my twenty-first birthday.

49

The royal family spent the whole summer of 1790 in the château de Saint-Cloud, two miles to the west of Paris. It had been purchased by the Treasury, a few years before the Revolution, as the personal property of the Queen. She had justified the enormous expense, made at a time of bankruptcy of the public finances, by the need for her to be "closer to the shows of the capital." In 1790, she no longer cared about those entertainments. I am sure that she would have liked to be very far away from them.

The Count and Countess de Provence went to Saint-Cloud every night for dinner, as they had done to the Tuileries, and I accompanied them during my week of service. With the other ladies of the Countess and the gentlemen of the Count, I sat at the royal table, a familiarity that would never have been allowed before the Revolution. I noticed that the King, who had resumed hunting, and the Queen, who took long walks in the park away from the hated Parisians, seemed happier than in Paris.

At the beginning of September, I let out a cry of indignation as I read the *Moniteur*. It related the execution of mutinous soldiers quartered in Nancy, in eastern France. A court-martial, under the direction of the Marquis de Bouillé, entrusted with the mission of restoring order, had tried the rebels. Their leader was broken and exposed on the wheel on a scaffold around which twenty-three of his comrades were hanged. Another twenty-nine soldiers were executed by firing squad. The remains of the regiment were also punished: every seventh man, picked at random, was sentenced to hard labour for life. I handed Villers the newspaper.

"What did you expect?" he said after glancing at it. "This kind of behaviour cannot be tolerated in any army."

"Those soldiers were only asking for their overdue pay."

"It would have been fine if they had acted with measure."

"That is what they did in the beginning, and all they received for their pains was a public flogging."

Villers put down the newspaper. "Rightly so, because they presented their request in a disrespectful and arrogant manner. Then they proceeded to take hostages and revolt against their officers. Those rebels received the punishment they deserved."

"But to have their leader broken on the wheel!" I shuddered. "One would believe we were still under the Old Regime. Such a hideous, protracted agony for the victim and such an infamy for those who ordered it. Bouillé is a butcher."

"Nonsense. Bouillé is a respectable man and a good General. My son serves under him and has nothing but praise for him. If your late husband had been in Bouillé's shoes, he would have had fifty men sentenced to the wheel, not just one."

"Is that supposed to reconcile me to this atrocity?"

"An example had to be made of the scoundrels who led the mutiny, or it could have spread to the entire army. You know nothing of military matters, Belle, and should limit your opinions to subjects you can grasp."

"This is not about military matters, but about common humanity. What a death for a soldier!"

"He should have remembered that he was one before rebelling. The Assembly, except for Robespierre and a few other rascals, is of one mind on this point. We are considering a special bill to congratulate Bouillé. I intend to vote for it."

I left the room in disgust.

The Nancy affair marked my first difference over politics with Villers. Tens of thousands of Parisians shared my opinion and demonstrated the next day to protest Bouillé's brutality.

⊸ 50 ⊱

The Court was much altered. Of the throngs of lords and ladies who had attended Versailles, only a few dozen remained in the Tuileries. The royal family was now mostly surrounded by ordinary servants and National Guards. The Queen's activities were ostensibly limited to knitting, tapestry, at which she was most proficient, and a game of billiards after luncheon. Madame Elisabeth, the King's younger sister, shared those pastimes, although in a more cheerful spirit. She could have emigrated then. Yet she chose not to leave her brother, to whom she was tenderly attached.

I remained on good terms with Emilie, although our fondness for each other cooled. She and I had shared a love of pleasure, of laughter, of life, and that similarity of temperament had brought us together. Now that times were becoming darker, differences came to the surface. Her lightness shocked me as foolhardy under the circumstances and she found me too earnest in my political ideas.

Among the remaining ladies of the Court was the Marquise de Tourzel, who had replaced the Duchess de Polignac as Governess to the Royal Children, much to their advantage. Madame de Tourzel was a widow, fifty years of age, a staunch proponent of the Old Regime, but also an affectionate mother who had presided over the education of her own children. Her youngest daughter, Pauline, a lovely girl of seventeen, still single, lived with her. I avoided discussing politics with Madame de Tourzel, but I often sought her advice on Aimée's courses of study. I compared my daughter's advancement to that of the little Dauphin, who

was only five months her senior. I was also on easy terms with other ladies of the Court, in particular Madame de Rochefort. She was about my
age, pretty and sweet-tempered.

I did not entertain any illusions as to my position. As a lady-in-
waiting to the Countess de Provence, I had to be tolerated. Yet because of
my association with Villers, Lauzun and other proponents of the new
ideas, I was not trusted. Many a conversation was abruptly interrupted
whenever I entered a room, a fact that I did not much regret because it
spared me comments I would not have cared to hear.

I once happened to overhear from the next drawing room a conversation between the Queen and Princess de Lamballe. The Princess, blonde,
blue-eyed and much given to what she called "nervous spasms," was a
member of the royal family and, according to widely accredited public
rumour, the Queen's lover. I did not believe that there was any truth to
this gossip although both ladies were indeed close friends.

"Yes, my heart," the Queen was telling the Princess, "when things
return to what they should be, we might forgive some of the commoners
who participated in the Revolution, provided of course that they repent
their errors and help us return to the old ways. Some of them have been
driven by ambition rather than by evil purposes."

"That is what I have always said, Madam," the Princess de Lamballe
chimed in. "They misbehaved more out of ambition than evil purposes."

"But others," continued the Queen, "will be shown no mercy. I am
thinking of those noblemen who betrayed the Crown, of which they
should have been the natural support. Men such as Lafayette, Lauzun,
Villers shall pay with their lives."

"True," said the Princess. "All of them shall pay with their lives."

The door to the drawing room where I stood was wide open, and the
Queen, who had spoken loudly and clearly, knew of my presence there.
She had intended me to hear these remarks. I excused myself to Madame
and went to the room where the Queen was sitting. I curtseyed and
stared directly at her. She pursed her lips like a petulant child and shook
her head at me in defiance. I almost pitied her for her illusions, for I did
not believe that things would ever "return to what they should be."
While generously handing out death sentences, she seemed unaware of
the fragility of her own situation.

51

I liked the sound of the church bells of Paris, their rhythm joyful for weddings and solemn for funerals. The *tocsin* was quite another thing: its urgent cadences served to warn the people of disasters, fires or other emergencies. It was also the name given to the largest bell in Paris, which was kept at City Hall and could be heard all over town. When it rang, all the bells of all the churches of Paris joined in. It was indeed a deafening, awe-inspiring sound.

I heard the dreaded peals on the morning of the 21st of June 1791, the longest day of the year. Villers and I were interrupted during breakfast by cries coming from the street. At the same time, we heard the sound of the cannon mingling with the *tocsin*. I ran to the window. Villers tried to stop me, but I opened it and looked out. A crowd was marching in the direction of the Tuileries. I called to a woman.

"The King was abducted!" she shouted. "The Austrian Woman has taken him away from us."

Villers blanched and departed in haste for the Assembly. Given the unprecedented circumstances, it remained in session for the following days without any recess. I would not see him during that time.

Junot, my footman, was still limping from the injury he had received two years earlier during the storming of the Bastille. His participation in that event had earned him a bronze medal, shaped like the towers of the old fortress, with the inscription *Victor of the Bastille* engraved on the back. He had shown it to me with immense pride and told me that he now felt personally responsible for the fate of the Nation. After liveries had been forbidden, he had asked my permission, which I had granted, to wear it on a tricolour ribbon on his coat.

I sent him to gather news. He returned before the morning was over, running as fast as his stiff leg allowed.

"Turns out the King wasn't abducted after all," he said. "He left a letter all in his own handwriting. It says that he never meant to pledge allegiance to the Constitution. He wants nothing to do with the Revolution. I still can't believe it, My Lady, but it looks like he quit Paris of his own free will." Junot paused to catch his breath. "The King's been deceiving us all along. And we loved him so! Everyone says he's reached the Austrian Netherlands by now. He'll place himself at the head of an army of foreigners and émigrés to attack Paris! See what I found lying on the ground by the gates to the Palace!"

It was a handwritten bill that read:

MISSING:

A LARGE SWINE THAT USED TO ROAM THESE PREMISES.
A REWARD OF TWELVE FRANCS IS OFFERED FOR ITS RETURN.

Indeed, the King was overnight revealed to be a liar, a perjurer, a traitor. The gutters of Paris were littered with his portraits, which had formerly decorated shops and private homes. They were now discarded in disgust for his treachery. I saw the *fleurs-de-lys*, emblems of the French Crown, taken down or covered with tar everywhere, while the word *royal* was erased from public buildings. Every name referring to the monarchy was changed, and even such an exotic character as the King of Siam, who could hardly be deemed a threat to the Nation, lost his street in Paris.

The Assembly, while preparing for war, had suspended the monarchy until further notice. Later during the day, Junot burst into my drawing room without knocking.

"My Lady, I just heard that the King's been arrested in Varennes," he announced.

"Varennes? I have never heard of it."

"It's a little town barely five leagues from the eastern border. The King came so close to crossing into Austrian territory! I hope you'll forgive me for disturbing you like this, My Lady, but I'm very upset."

"What else have you learned?"

"It looks like that scoundrel Fersen and the Queen hatched a plan to join the armies of Bouillé. You know, My Lady, that General they call the Butcher of Nancy."

The escape plan included the Count and Countess de Provence. They left separately in plain carriages, reached the border and crossed into the Austrian Netherlands without any difficulty. Madame, when I saw her again many years later, told me that she had been informed of the plan at the very last minute. Apparently, she was not trusted enough to be taken in her husband's confidence ahead of time.

The royal family, apart from the Count and Countess de Provence, now faced a most unpleasant return. Madame de Tourzel, who had taken part in the whole journey, told me about it later.

"Can you imagine, dear Madam," she said, "that we heard not one cry of *Long live the King*! I cannot recall a more painful journey. We had been boiling in the heat, choking from the dust for days since leaving Varennes. All the way, men kept their hats on. In Paris, a cook, who happened to be bareheaded, even covered himself for the occasion with a dirty towel he was carrying on his arm to show his contempt for Their Majesties."

In the meantime, at the Tuileries, the Assembly was debating whether to keep France a monarchy.

"How could the King be allowed to remain on the throne?" I asked Villers. "He tried to flee abroad to attack the Nation!"

Villers shook his head. "What is the alternative? A republic? Inconceivable. The abolition of the monarchy would lead to chaos, to civil war, to the reign of the lowest kind of rabble. Little as we trust the King, we have no choice but to tolerate him."

"Why does not the Duke d'Orléans avail himself of the moment? He is as popular as ever. Everyone would be happy to have him as Regent if the King were deposed now."

"A great many would even make him King outright, on the grounds that the Dauphin is a bastard, the offspring of the Queen's adultery with Fersen. This would indeed be the perfect time for him to make a move, but he is always paralyzed whenever action is required. Ask his warmest supporters, ask Lauzun. Orléans is an imbecile, my dear." Villers shrugged dismissively and finished his glass of wine. "Oh, he is ambitious enough. Yet, like the rest of the males in the Bourbon family nowadays, he does not carry much of anything between his legs. He must have consulted his astrologer and been told that the moment is not auspicious."

I frowned. "You cannot be in earnest, my dear."

"He is as superstitious as a scullery girl. I remember one night being dragged by Lauzun to the caves of Montmartre to attend some kind of secret ceremony for the benefit of Orléans, and of course at his expense."

I winced. "A black mass?"

"Nothing quite as gruesome, my love. Orléans is not cruel. It began with the christening of a toad by a man dressed as a priest, who then asked everyone to kneel and prepare to worship the Devil. I alone declined. Another fellow appeared, stark naked. He looked in every regard like a tall, well-built man, save for the fact that he lacked male genitals."

I stared at Villers, who seemed amused by my amazement.

"You did not know that the Devil was a eunuch, did you?" he continued. "*I* was certainly surprised. I had imagined the contrary. The Satan character, whatever it was, spoke in a booming voice and predicted great and terrible things for Orléans, who was shaking with fear and excitement. I had to pinch myself, or I would have laughed aloud. I was reminded of the scene between Macbeth and the three witches, though at least Macbeth was fooled free of charge."

Whether upon the advice of his astrologer, the Devil or anyone else, the Duke d'Orléans failed to seize the moment. The Assembly soon received a letter from Bouillé. In it, the General claimed the entire responsibility of the idea and organization of the King's flight. The Assembly, then controlled by moderates, hastened to use Bouillé's declaration to exonerate the King and Queen. Bouillé himself, along with those on his staff who had participated in the conspiracy, crossed the eastern border to escape charges of high treason. Villers's son, Charles-Marie, was among the officers who followed the General into exile.

I had met the younger Villers several times before, when he had visited his father in Paris during his leaves from his regiment. He had treated me with the icy politeness to be expected under the circumstances. I had not liked Charles-Marie much in return. Yet I felt for Villers. He was now separated forever from his son, not only by a border but also by an intractable difference of political opinions.

⚞ 52 ⚟

The flight of the royal family marked a complete change in the public perception of the King. A petition was to be signed on the Altar of the Homeland at the Champ de Mars, to propose the outright abolition of the monarchy. Villers had warned me to stay away, but I no longer listened to much of what he told me. I decided to see first-hand how much of a crowd the petition would draw. That day, the 17th of July, was a Sunday, and the Champ de Mars would be filled by the usual families out for their weekly walk. It would be interesting to see how many of those good bourgeois would be tempted by the extreme changes proposed by the petition.

I had an early dinner with Aimée and resisted her entreaties to take her with me to the Champ de Mars. When I arrived, I noticed nothing unusual. The day was hot; thunder rumbled in the distance. Small groups of people were milling around in a torpid manner. Some were resting, seated on the steps of the wooden pyramid that supported the Altar of the Homeland. Others had climbed to the top and waited for their turn to sign the petition.

Women pushing little carts were selling lemonade and biscuits. I stopped to speak with one of them.

"Is your lemonade made with spring water?" I asked.

"Certainly, Ma'am," replied the young woman. "That's why I sell it two *sols* more than the others, but it's worth it. Would you like a biscuit too?"

"No, thank you, I had dinner, but a glass of lemonade would be refreshing in this heat."

"Yes, Ma'am, it's been very hot. I wouldn't be surprised if we had a thunderstorm before long. It'll be night soon and I'll wheel my cart home."

"Things seem rather quiet around here."

"Mind you, the day started in a different manner."

"What happened?"

"Haven't you heard? I knew that it would be a good day for business, with the petition and everything, so I arrived early." The young woman handed me a tin cup full of lemonade. "One of my friends, over there, climbed the steps to the Altar. She wanted to be one of the first to sign. She felt something sharp under her shoe. She cried aloud. The crowd gathered around her and they saw a drill sticking out of the wood. They fetched the National Guard, who removed the planks. What do you think they found underneath? Two scoundrels were hidden there. They tried to explain that they wanted only to drill a hole to look under the skirts of the women who came to sign the petition. What do you think of that impudence?"

"It is indeed an outrage. What happened to those men?"

"They were hanged from a lamppost, that's what happened. Serve them right. The National Guards found a barrel with them under the planks. Some say it was full of gunpowder. The scoundrels wanted to blow up the Altar of the Homeland and the good people who came to sign the petition. One of the two brigands was a wigmaker. I don't need to tell you what those people are about. There are no worst royalists, since nowadays nobody decent wears a wig anymore."

"When did this happen?"

"Oh, it was all over before nine in the morning. First, the washer-women of the Gros-Caillou fetched their beaters to teach the two ban-dits a lesson. The National Guards tried to save them, but they were outnumbered. After the scoundrels were hanged, their heads were cut off and carried through town at the end of pikes. I won't shed any tears for them, let me tell you."

"And what has been going on since the incident of the morning?" I asked the lemonade girl.

"Not much, except that thousands have already signed the petition. Are you going to, Ma'am?"

"I will think about it."

"You should. It's time to rid ourselves of those Kings. Look, there's a man up there making a speech."

A man had indeed climbed midway up the Altar and was shouting at the top of his voice from the pyramid. I recognized Pierre-André. Indeed our paths had not crossed in years, since that day at the riverside *guin-guette*, when I had seen him in the company of the girl in the yellow dress. I felt a jolt of pain.

I promptly turned around and walked away. His speech was often interrupted by cries and jeering from the crowd, which only made him raise his voice more. He stopped at last. When I risked a glance, I saw him leaving. I stopped a man, who looked like a merchant and was walk-ing with his wife and daughter.

"Did you hear what that man said, Sir?"

"Oh, he was telling everyone to disperse right away, that he had just been at the Common House. You know that's what they call City Hall now. He said that a full regiment of the mounted Gendarmerie, with the Na-tional Guard, was ready to attack. According to him, martial law's been proclaimed and Lafayette's marching on the Champ de Mars with the red flag."

"Why were people jeering?"

"Nobody would believe him, of course. They shut him up at last. That was difficult, though, because of that big voice of his. He wouldn't quit." The man shook his head. "It doesn't make sense. The signing of the petition was reported yesterday at City Hall. Everyone's here lawfully. He must be some royalist agent, trying to scare people to prevent them from signing the petition. He left at last. Good riddance."

The red flag mentioned by Pierre-André was the signal that martial law had been decreed. The Gendarmerie was the new name given to the old Constabulary. My knowledge of Pierre-André did not lead me to suspect that he was a royalist agent. I was beginning to question the wisdom of my presence at the Champ de Mars. Yet I did not believe Lafayette capable of slaughtering unarmed Parisians out for an evening stroll.

My assumptions were put to the test. All of a sudden, shots were fired. The crowd started crying aloud and running in terror. Some fell and were trampled underfoot. Billows of gunpowder smoke burnt my eyes and prevented me from seeing more than a few feet ahead. People shouted that the Patriots were being massacred on the steps of the pyramid. Bloodied citizens, confirming this report by their appearance, ran towards the river to the west.

The smoke began to dissipate. All was chaos. Cavalrymen pursued the fugitives and hacked them down as they fled. The young woman who had sold me the lemonade fell before my eyes. The few *sols* she had earned that day cost her her life. A tiny white lady's dog was running around in all directions, yelping in a frenzy. People jumped into the Seine, and I heard more cries for help as they drowned.

Afraid of being trampled by the crowd, I sought refuge behind the cart of the lemonade girl. I watched the little dog bark in terror and run away. Two horsemen saw me and, sabres drawn, rode in my direction. I ran for the river, which the rays of the setting sun seemed to set ablaze. Several men were on my heels, also fleeing the gendarmes. I was wearing thin-soled silk shoes, unsuitable for this kind of exercise, but had never felt so light of foot.

All of a sudden, I felt something heavy hit me in the back. The wind was knocked out of me. I tripped. I believed at first that one of the gendarmes had struck me with his sabre. I said a silent prayer and prepared to die. I fell on my stomach as a mass collapsed on my back, followed by another one on my thighs. Only then did I understand that my companions had fallen under the blows of the cavalrymen. I closed my eyes and held my breath. The hooves of the horses raised puffs of dust inches away from my face. I heard cries a few yards away and the gendarmes rode off to turn their attention to other targets.

It was almost dark when silence, broken by the moaning of the wounded, finally settled on the Champ de Mars. I was unable to free myself from the weight of the men lying on me. No matter how fast or deeply I inhaled, no air seemed to enter my lungs. Panic engulfed me. After a few moments, I realized that I would die if I did not calm myself. Deliberately, I managed to bring my breathing under control. Time went by very slowly. Feeling was leaving my legs and my chest was sore. Although it was summer, I was cold and began to despair of ever leaving my position.

After a while, I heard the stamping of hooves again. I was able to lift my head to look in their direction. Soldiers had returned. They were plunging their bayonets into the chests of the fallen. The bodies next to the river were thrown into the water without ceremony. Covered by my companions, I escaped again the notice of the soldiers. New corpses were brought to the pile resting on top of me and left there. I barely felt the additional weight. At last I heard orders being yelled and the troops withdrew a second time. They were replaced by groups of dogs, content at first to silently sniff the bodies. Soon they began to growl at each other and fight. I tried not to imagine the object of their dispute. One quietly lapped blood from a puddle a few feet from my face.

Darkness enveloped me and, after what seemed like many hours, a half-moon rose, throwing a white light over my surroundings. The dogs barked, then ran away yelping. I heard men's voices. My heart skipped a beat. They could not be soldiers because there were only two of them. One was turning over the bodies and pawing them while the other was holding a lantern. They must be robbing the corpses. They would find me all too soon. I was not in the least concerned about what little money and jewellery I carried, but I pictured them stripping me of my clothes, taking turns to violate me and, once there was nothing more to be had from me, killing me. I dared not breathe.

"They are all dead," one of them said. "There is nothing for us to do here. Let us go."

"We can at least finish counting the bodies," the other one answered in a deep voice. "Many of them have already disappeared. Mark my words, the cutthroats will return before the morning to remove all traces of the massacre."

So the men were not thieves. Moreover, the deep voice was familiar. I took my chances and cried for help with all of my remaining strength.

"Listen," said one of them. "It sounds like a woman."

I continued crying out to guide them. I heard their footsteps. The corpses crushing me were lifted from my back.

"She is covered with blood," said the unknown voice.

"It must not be hers. Her dress is not even torn."

The man rolled me gently onto my back. It was Pierre-André, his face lit by his companion's lantern. My first reaction was to try to escape, but my entire body was so stiff that any movement was impossible.

"Fear not, Madam," said the unknown man. "We will not harm you. My name is Antoine Ferrat, and I am a surgeon. My friend Dr. Coffin-hal is a physician. We came here to treat the survivors, but it seems that no one, apart from you, is in need of our help."

"I believe you are right, Sir." I took deep breaths of the night air. "The troops came back already. I saw them finish off the wounded and throw bodies into the river."

Pierre-André was looking down at me. "What are you doing here?" he asked, frowning.

"Do you know her?" asked Ferrat.

"Oh yes. She is a *ci-devant* Baroness from my country."

"No matter who or what she is, we cannot leave her here. Even if she is unharmed, she must be stiff as a board."

"I am sure Her Ladyship can walk. These aristocrats may faint on demand in their salons, but they are sturdy enough when their lives are at stake."

I was still lying on my back. He bent over and caught me by the shoulders to raise me. The pain was so sharp that I let out a whimper. I was unable to hold myself and began to list to the side. Pierre-André stopped my fall with his arm. I was again on my back. He sighed.

"You may have suffered broken bones after all," he said in a softer tone. "I need to examine you. Do not worry. I will do so through your dress and keep it quick."

He knelt by my side and felt my thighs, legs and ankles. I do not think that I could have borne the embarrassment but for the darkness. He rose as soon as he was done.

"She may be bruised," he said, turning to Ferrat, "but she is fine. She can have another physician fetched once she is back home. You live on Rue Saint-Dominique, Madam, do you not?"

"How do you know?" I asked.

"You cut a prominent figure in the so-called Court, and your career is not difficult to follow. The day may come when you wish you had been wiser and less conspicuous in your choice of friends. Tonight, since we found you here, it seems that we have to offer you our help. Unless, of course, you prefer to wait for the soldiers to return."

"Of course not. I am most grateful for your assistance. I should be able to walk in a few minutes. Please, Sir, wait a little longer."

The two men stood looking down at me. "We should not tarry," said Ferrat. "I will carry her if you do not want to be bothered."

"No, I will do it. She must not even be half my weight."

Both men lifted me, this time more gently. When I was on my feet, Pierre-André put his arms across my back and under my knees. He carried me like a child. The numbness of my legs was subsiding and giving way to cramps. I was jolted with every step he took and felt the awkwardness of my position.

"If you would put your arms around my shoulders, it would make it easier for both of us," Pierre-André said. "You may rest against me if you are tired. I will not bite your head off."

I followed his invitation. My face was level with his neck. His hair was shorter now, cut above his shoulders. I could feel that mine was matted in places with blood. For the first time in many hours, I worried about my appearance. My straw hat with its pretty pink ribbons had been lost. The bodice of my white linen dress, wet and sticky on the back, was dusty in front. Unaccountably, a pink rose I had arranged between my breasts as a *babarel* was still there. It had been crushed in my fall and was beginning to fade but its fragrance was still sweet. Pierre-André glanced at it, then looked away. I had to speak before he could say anything.

"I apologize for this inconvenience, Sir," I said. "I must be soiling your coat with blood."

"These days one should worry about saving one's skin, not about the clothes that cover it. You have not answered my question. What were you doing at the Champ de Mars?"

"I went there out of curiosity. I knew of the petition, but I would never had imagined that it would lead to such a disaster."

"The petition did not lead to the massacre. What did is the desire of certain people, whom I believe to be your friends, to make an example of a few hundred Patriots. They wanted to teach the good people of Paris not to question the monarchy. We counted fifty-four dead before finding you, but you know that there must have been many more. The Nation will not forgive this atrocity."

"I can assure you, Sir, that I would not call anyone my friend who has been complicit in this."

"I almost believe you. The person you used to be would not have condoned the slaughter of innocents. If my memory serves me well, even the punishment of the guilty elicited your compassion." Pierre-André gave me a hard look. "But you are very naive with regard to your friends."

We had almost reached my lodgings.

"You may put me down if you want, Sir," I said. "I feel much better now."

"Are you afraid of being seen with us? Fine, run home by yourself then."

Pierre-André let go of me. I had overestimated my strength. My legs were still too weak to carry me. He had to catch me by the waist to prevent me from falling.

"It seems that you still need us for a few more minutes after all. Do not worry, we will leave you as soon as we can."

I bit my lip. "This is not what I meant."

Each of my companions took me by one arm. We arrived at my lodgings. Manon, still dressed, answered the bell. She put her hand to her mouth, silenced for once, and ran to open the door to the drawing room. Pierre-André and Monsieur Ferrat put me down on a sofa there.

"Please bring refreshments, Manon. These gentlemen saved my life."

"Certainly, Madam. My Lord was here half an hour ago. He didn't know you had gone to the Champ de Mars. He was beside himself when I told him. He went in search of you."

I wished Manon had not mentioned Villers in front of my visitors. Pierre-André, who had remained standing, was surveying the drawing room with a cold eye. He looked at the blue and white paneling, the silk drapes, the delicate porcelain-inlaid furniture. Colour rose into my cheeks.

"I had heard from my brothers that your late husband had not been generous in his will," he said. "They must have been misinformed. You live in the lap of luxury here. I should not be surprised, of course. These are the proper surroundings for a person of your rank."

"There are no ranks anymore. We are all equals now."

He shrugged. "How stupid of me to forget it! Equals or not, Madam, it seems that our intervention was useless after all. A few minutes later, you might have been rescued by your noble protector, instead of two strangers. When he returns, you might ask him why he did not tie you to a chair here instead of letting you walk into that butchery."

"I am sure that he did not know about it."

"And I am sure that he did." Pierre-André's jaw tightened. "This exploit had been planned for a few days by his friend Lafayette. He could not have been unaware of it."

"Who could plan such a thing?"

"That is a question you will have to ask your protector, or whatever other title you give your generous friend." Pierre-André turned to Ferrat. "We should go. Monsieur de Villers might be unhappy to find us here and have us arrested."

"On the contrary," I said, "he would thank you for rescuing me."

"It just happens that I do not want his thanks, or anything else from him. Keep your refreshments. I am sure that he has paid for everything here, including your person. Good night to you."

Monsieur Ferrat gave me a sheepish look and followed his friend out of the room.

I heard Villers's step and voice in the drawing room about half an hour later. He was speaking to Manon. I was in bed, wide awake, although I had blown out the candle on my nightstand. When he entered my bedroom, I pretended to be asleep. He sat on the bed and ran his hand on my cheek. I opened my eyes. He was bending over me.

"Thank God you are safe," he said. "I was sick with worry when Manon told me that you had gone to the Champ de Mars. Why did you not listen to me, Belle?"

"What exactly did you know? Had you been warned that peaceful, unarmed people would be slaughtered?"

"Do you mean the peaceful, unarmed people who killed those two men?"

"That happened in the morning. Everything was quiet by the time I arrived. Most people were there for a stroll and did not even care about the petition." I could feel myself colour as my temper rose. "You have not answered my question, Villers. Did you know of the massacre ahead of time?"

He frowned. "Of course not. Of what are you accusing me?"

"The men who brought me back here said that it had been planned. What did you know about it? Is that why you warned me to stay away from the Champ de Mars?"

"Any fool could have foreseen what was going to happen with the kind of rabble gathered there to sign the petition. Speaking of those two fellows, what were they doing there themselves in the middle of the night? Manon said one of them was addressing you in an insolent manner. She heard him raise his voice to you. Who is he?"

"He did not tell me his name. The other one said that he was a surgeon and that they had gone to the Champ de Mars to treat the survivors."

"I will have enquiries made about those men. Manon told me that the loud, rude one is six and a half feet tall, and built to match. That should make it easy. There cannot be too many surgeons in Paris answering to this description."

"What do you want from them? You should be grateful to them for saving my life. Do you not care about that at all?"

"I do, although I have no illusions about their motives. They probably brought you home with the sole idea of receiving a reward. Agreed, they deserve one and that is why I will have them traced. Good night, Belle."

Villers's tone was not one of gratitude. His answers had not dissipated my doubts concerning his advance knowledge of the massacre. I was certain that he wished to find Pierre-André and his friend to have them arrested.

It remained to decide how to express my thanks to Pierre-André. What surprised me was the strength of my feelings toward this man I had not seen in years. My first thought was to call on him at his chambers. Then I recalled his anger at my surroundings and the abrupt manner in which he had left. How would he receive me? What if he reproached me for the past? What if he upbraided me for my current position? I had never been proud of being a kept woman, but now I saw my own situation through his eyes. I resolved to write him.

> *Sir,*
>
> *Please excuse the awkwardness of this letter. The truth is that I do not know what to do or say to thank you for your help last night. I am mortified by the opinion you have of me. It does not diminish my appreciation for your assistance but makes any expressions of gratitude clumsy.*
>
> *Many times over the past years I have been tempted to call on you. Yet I have always been deterred by the fear of angering you or exposing myself to your contempt. The feelings of disgust you expressed last night, although they may be justified, proved me right.*
>
> *I know that I must have caused you great pain once. For this I beg your forgiveness. I would do anything, if you would let me, to atone for past or present offenses and regain some of your good opinion.*
>
> *If we never see each other again, I wish you the best and hope that in time you may come to think less ill of me.*
>
> *A thousand thanks to you, Sir, and to your friend Monsieur Ferrat.*
>
> *I would be honoured to remain, Sir, your humble servant.*
>
> *Gabrielle*

I could not bring myself to sign my married name. That letter, short as it was, required many drafts. All of my effort was in vain. For many days I hoped for a response, but none came. I concluded that Pierre-André either did not care enough for me to take the trouble to write back, or that he was still angry with me.

I was now a lady-in-waiting without any princess to wait upon. The flight of the Countess de Provence left me in an awkward position at Court. I felt compelled to approach Villers regarding financial matters, a subject we had not discussed since I had accepted the place with Madame.

"Do you remember saying that you would reinstate my allowance if I renounced my place as a lady-in-waiting?" I asked.

He was reading the *Moniteur* and did not look up from the newspaper. "I have been blessed with an excellent memory."

"So would you reinstate my allowance if I resigned?"

"Why would you resign? You would not listen to me when I requested that you decline the place. You knew what I thought of the Countess de Provence. You nevertheless chose to disregard my wishes. Now that she is gone, very likely forever, you may remain her lady-in-waiting as long as you wish. No one will object and I no longer care."

"But I do. It does not seem right to continue collecting 6,000 francs a year for nothing."

"Your delicacy of feeling does you honour, but I do not see why I should be the one to pay for it."

I bit my lip. "I am sorry I broached that subject, Villers. Please forgive me."

"Now, Belle, there is no reason to be cross because I do not immediately agree to your every whim. I cannot recall anything you did of late that would incline me to generosity." He looked straight into my eyes. "Yes, my dearest, you enjoy having your own way, regardless of what I think or say. That is fine, but, like any other pleasure, it must be paid for. Let me think about your request for a while." He resumed his reading.

I looked out the window. Why had my first impulse been to ask Villers for money? Had I become used to being a kept woman? I was reminded of Pierre-André's disgust at my lodgings and what they implied regarding my situation. Shame came to me belatedly, but with full force.

The next day, I spoke again to Villers. "I have given careful consideration to our conversation of yesterday. You were right. You have no reason to support me after I spurned your advice. You are doing more than enough by paying my rent and my servants' wages. I do not wish to impose further upon your generosity. Please forget the request I made of you."

"Does this mean that you have reconsidered your decision to resign your place?"

"I have not. I believe it would be unwise as well as dishonourable for me to remain a lady-in-waiting."

He smiled coldly. "May I ask how you intend to support yourself?"

"I have been able to set aside a few thousand francs over the years. It is not much, but I can certainly retrench on my expenses. That way the money will last several months."

"What will happen when you see the end of it?"

"I can sell some pieces of jewellery. Of course, I would keep the most valuable ones, such as the diamonds and the ring you were kind enough to give me, as well as the ruby earrings I received from my late husband. These, I believe, should go to Aimée as a memento from her father's family. However, I have many more, less valuable pieces with which I can part."

"Does that include some of my presents to you?"

"I would of course sell first the jewels I received from my late husband, but if I had to, yes, I might part with some of your gifts. What choice have I?"

"You could have waited for my decision before changing your mind so abruptly. Everything you have done lately seems designed to show me that you no longer care for me."

"You can hardly fault me for withdrawing a request that appeared to make you angry." I reached for his hand. "I do care for you and am grateful for your help."

"You have an odd way of showing it. Beware, my dearest, or you might see the well of my generosity run completely dry."

"I have always known that I might lose your affections any day. Love does not last forever."

"True, but even when it fades away, it is sometimes survived by friendship and respect. Often, like a bad wine, it leaves nothing behind but a sour aftertaste. It is up to you, Belle, to determine my future behaviour to you."

He shook off my hand, his eyes fixed on my face. I was surprised by his bitterness.

I also told the Duchess of my decision to resign.

"Well, dear Belle," she said, "you are right to keep away from the Court at this time. Things have been unsettled since the King's little escapade to Varennes and you cannot be too cautious." She shook her head. "I so regret having proposed you as a replacement for my daughter. It has caused nothing but trouble between Villers and you, and I hate to think of what might happen to you if you remained a lady-in-waiting."

I now limited my contacts with the Court to attending the monthly parties given at the Tuileries by the Princess de Lamballe, Superintendent of the Queen's Household. I went there out of a sense of obligation for my past stipend rather than for any pleasure I found in those gatherings. They were spent anticipating the gruesome punishments to be doled out to the "traitors" once the Revolution was defeated. Another topic of conversation was the situation in the colonies, where the Negroes were in full revolt. They had the audacity to demand the abolition of slavery without thinking of the damage it would cause their masters, and the sugar trade.

❧ 54 ❧

The Assembly completed the Constitution in September. This entailed the election of a new body, called the Legislative Assembly. No member of the old National Assembly would be allowed to seek another term.

This meant that Villers could no longer hold office. Many members of the nobility, including Lauzun, had long stopped participating in the deliberations of the Assembly, but Villers had remained assiduous in his attendance until the end. He had found great satisfaction in his functions as Representative, probably far more than he had expected. He was now left with as much time on his hands as before the Revolution, without any of the entertainments he had enjoyed then. He had to watch events unfold without being able to help shape the fate of the Nation. The consequence of this forced idleness was that he could now devote his full attention to me.

At the end of September of 1791, Emilie introduced me to Guillaume de Morsan, a young cousin of her husband.

"Do not talk to him if you do not want to, Belle," she whispered later. "Maybe it is not fair, but I cannot abide the sight of the man. One look at him is enough to spoil my appetite."

The marks left by smallpox on Morsan's face resembled burn scars and had spared only one of his cheeks. He was slightly built for a man and barely as tall as me. My first impulse had been to look away, but Emilie's remark had made me ashamed of myself. I made a point of sitting next to him at dinner.

"I am surprised," I said, "never to have met you before."

"I was a Lieutenant in the Bodyguards, My Lady. I have seen you on many occasions at the Palace when the Countess de Provence visited Their Majesties, but you may not have noticed me."

"One of my dearest friends, the Chevalier des Huttes, was also a Bodyguard."

"I knew and respected him, although I had been with the Corps only a year when he was killed. There is no finer death for a soldier, My Lady."

"I cannot bring myself to call any death fine, especially when I think of the Chevalier's end. I guess it is a female weakness. Are you going to be part of the King's new Constitutional Guard?"

"Unfortunately not. None of us Bodyguards are, I believe. We are suspected of harbouring hostile feelings towards the Revolution."

"So you find yourself out of a commission. It must be a great change for you."

"It is, My Lady, and not a happy one. If Madame de Brasson were not kind enough to invite me to her dinners, I would feel very lonely. Some of my friends from the Bodyguards have emigrated and invited me to follow them abroad. Yet I am reluctant to leave my country, although I see it daily take a turn for the worse."

"You are right. Not only have the *émigrés* left France, but they are ready to take arms against her. That I cannot comprehend or forgive."

"I understand your feelings, Madam. Yet someday, each of us gathered here tonight may have to choose between death and exile."

"What a terribly sad thought! I do hope that you are mistaken, Sir. The King has returned; he swore allegiance to the Constitution; the new Legislative Assembly has been elected. Hopefully things will follow a peaceful course now."

"Forgive me, My Lady, I did not mean to dampen your spirits. These days I let my personal woes colour my view of the political situation."

Our conversation turned to more cheerful topics. I found Morsan's company pleasant, to the point of forgetting his disfigurement. I noticed his fine grey eyes, always sad, but more particularly so whenever he looked at me. Villers claimed me promptly after dinner. I took my leave of Morsan, who bowed and kissed my hand.

"Thank you for the pleasure of your company, Madam," he said. "It is not very often that I have the honour of receiving such kindness from a lady."

"Who is that man?" asked Villers in the carriage.

"A cousin of Emilie's husband. He is a former Bodyguard."

He sneered. "I never saw anyone so repulsive."

"I found him quite pleasant."

"You must indeed have liked his company, for you have talked to him through the whole dinner."

"Yes, I like him."

"Has he asked for permission to call on you?"

"He has not, and you know that I would not have granted it. I am sure that he was interested in me only because I listened to him. Some people must shun him because of his looks."

"Your naivete would amuse me, Belle, if I were not beginning to wonder whether it is genuine. The man was watching you with hungry eyes. No wonder. When he looks at himself in the mirror every morning, he must thank God for the existence of whores. Without that convenience, he would never touch a woman."

"What a cruel thing to say, Villers!"

"Well, my love, truth is often cruel. But you are right. I should not have spoken it. The poor fellow's deformity does not prevent him from having the same needs as any other man."

It pained me to think of Morsan in the company of a prostitute. Villers seemed to have been either testing my reaction or trying to degrade my new acquaintance in my eyes. I saw Morsan again at Emilie's, and I always conversed with him, although I avoided sitting by him at dinner anymore.

When the weather was fine, I took Aimée for walks in the gardens of the Luxembourg Palace. The place brought to mind pleasant memories of my time as a lady-in-waiting to Madame. Aimée would bring her miniature boat, which she would push with a stick on the main basin. I had to watch her closely, for she was so entranced by this amusement that she had more than once come close to falling into the water. Once she had played to her heart's content, we would walk in the shade of the beautiful alley leading to the Fountain de Médicis, my favourite spot in the park. There we would sit on a bench and share almond biscuits we brought in Aimée's tiny basket.

During one of these impromptu meals, I saw Morsan walking in our direction. He bowed to us. "What a pleasant surprise, Sir," I said. "I did not know that you came here."

"My hours of leisure are many, My Lady, and Madame de Brasson says this is one of your favourite walks. I took the liberty of coming here in the hope of meeting you."

I felt myself blushing and saw that he too was colouring under his scars. To see a man do so added to my embarrassment.

"If my presence annoys you," he said after a pause, "I will leave immediately. It would be dreadful of me to repay your kindness by forcing my company upon you."

With a wave of the hand, I invited him to sit. "This is a public place. It would be rather presumptuous of me to forbid you to come here. And I do not mind meeting you. I would tell you if I did."

"I am very grateful for your forbearance. The pleasure of your company is my sole comfort now." He smiled sadly at Aimée. "I am delighted to meet your little girl. I hope she does not find my appearance disturbing. Most children are afraid of me."

Aimée was indeed staring at Morsan and holding fast to my hand. I pressed hers. She understood and curtseyed to him.

We saw Morsan again at the Luxembourg. Little by little, Aimée became less shy with him. He never failed to bring her pralines, her favourite sweets. His attentions won her good graces and she learned to smile at him. Our meetings were never arranged in advance, but we saw him whenever we went there. I assumed he was waiting for us every day. He was content to speak with me and then walk us back to the carriage.

I discussed my new acquaintance with the Duchess.

"Is this young man in love with you?" she asked.

"It is possible."

"I suppose it means yes. What about you, dear, do you love him?"

"No, Madam, I do not."

She put down her teacup and looked straight into my eyes. "Forgive me for asking an impertinent question, which only our friendship justifies. Why are you allowing his attentions?"

I blushed. "I cannot tell, Madam."

"You may be tormenting that poor man by letting him hope for what cannot be."

"Oh no, Madam, I do not believe that he entertains any illusions."

"How can you be certain of it? Have you discussed either his feelings or yours with him?"

"Never."

"Do you tolerate his presence because it flatters your vanity to have an admirer?"

"I do not believe so. You know me, Madam. I do not relish that kind of satisfaction. And I do not only tolerate him, I like meeting him. Here is a man who, while clearly admiring me, does not raise his voice to me, does not say unpleasant things, does not try to control my actions and thoughts. In his presence, I need not worry how my every word and move will be interpreted."

"What about Villers? How does he feel?"

"He seems very upset. I have noticed lately a stranger following me all over Paris. I suspect that he has been hired by Villers to watch me. A great deal of good it is going to do him, because I only meet Morsan in public places, and we do nothing but talk quietly."

"Still, Belle, regardless of what happens or does not happen between that man and you, Villers is bound to be jealous since you seem to enjoy Morsan's company so very much."

"But Morsan is disfigured."

"It makes it worse for Villers, dear, if you would prefer to him a man of such unprepossessing appearance. I am worried about you, Belle. Be careful. If you intend to leave Villers, so be it, but do not unwittingly make him angry over a man you do not even love."

I looked at the Duchess. "Do you believe, Madam, that Villers is thinking of leaving me?"

"I really cannot say, dearest. He no longer confides in me. I am only warning you to beware. In a way, he has lost his son, and there is no telling how he would react to losing you, or to imagining that he has lost you. What if he turns you out of your lodgings? Of course, you will always have a home here, but it may be a more temporary solution than you think."

"You are most kind, as usual, but I would not want you to worry about those things."

"How can I help it, dearest Belle, when I think of you and your daughter? Do you think that Morsan would marry you? Has he any fortune?"

"Emilie says he has next to nothing. He rents two rooms on Rue du Bac."

The Duchess sighed. "At least he has enough sense and decency not to propose. You have grown accustomed to luxury, Belle, whether you know it or not. Again, you are the sole judge of what you wish to do concerning Villers, but whatever you decide, keep your eyes open."

She patted my hand before reaching for her teacup.

❧ 55 ❧

The Duchess was right. I should have known myself better. The truth is that my mood matched the uncertainty of the times. I felt lost. I was on occasion tempted to leave Villers but had not the courage to do so. At other moments I reflected that our differences were trifling and that we were indeed quite happy together. Another event soon added to my confusion.

Emilie seemed to believe that the various political clubs that flourished at the time were kept open, like the theatres and the Opera, for the sole purpose of entertaining society ladies. She had once dragged me to the Cordeliers, who, she had assured me, were "very funny." That club had settled in the church of the former convent of the same name, which had been stripped of all religious artifacts. In the middle of the chancel was a rough wooden table serving as a platform from which the orators made their speeches. The pews remained. They were filled with men and women of the lower classes, who were not shy about expressing their opinions. Some men, armed with rifles, shot in the air when making their point. Before starting their speeches, the orators had to don a red bonnet, symbol of the freed slaves in ancient Rome, which was kept for that purpose on the table. I shuddered at the thought of the vermin that must infest that piece of fabric. I left without regret.

Emilie also suggested that we go to the Club des Jacobins.

"No, thank you," I said. "I did not much enjoy our excursion to the Cordeliers."

"Yes, but the Jacobins are different. They are bourgeois, you know, but with extreme views. I do not want to go there alone. Be a friend, Belle, and come with me."

"Curiosity will be your downfall, Emilie."

"Please, Belle. I do not know of anyone else who will go with me."

"Maybe everyone else is right. You can read an account of the speeches in the newspapers. Why go there?"

"Just this time, Belle dearest. I am sure you will like it. And you make me laugh with your newspapers. It is not the same as listening to the orators in person."

"All right, just this time then." She kissed me on both cheeks.

The Jacobins were indeed quite different from the Cordeliers. The Club was fitted to resemble the hall where the Legislative Assembly convened. The orator's lectern was situated below the president's pulpit. The regular members, all male, sat on benches in the hall itself, while a large audience, composed equally of men and women, gathered in the galleries. We found seats there.

At first, we listened to a speech by a thin man who, in a rather shaky voice, attacked Robespierre for having advocated the abolition of the monarchy. He was greeted by hoots from part of the audience. The president rang his bell, and ushers tried to restore order, to no avail. A tall man rushed to the pulpit. His voice dominated the uproar.

"President," he said, "let me respond to this scoundrel."

I did not hear the president's response in the middle of the racket. The tall man ran up the stairs to the lectern and pushed the first orator out of the way. He was now facing the public. I recognized Pierre-André Coffinhal.

"Friends and brothers," he said, "who among us, except Maillard here, still doubts that the so-called King is a traitor? Louis is the ally of the assassins of the Homeland; he is the worst enemy of the Nation. He is the accomplice of Lafayette and Bailly, the butchers of the people of Paris at the Champ de Mars. Have we forgotten how much innocent blood was shed that day? Some say that Louis is meek. They say that he has seen the error of his ways at last, that he will now abide by the Constitution. They are fools or rogues. Louis is a consummate liar; we all know it. He hides his duplicity under false airs of imbecility. Where do the *émigrés*, the unsworn priests, the conspirators of all stripes, within and abroad, find their warmest support? In Louis and his wife. We all know it. That Court of his is a viper's nest."

Cheers erupted. Pierre-André paused for a moment, surveying his audience.

"Yes," he continued, "the Court is a putrid sore on the face of Paris, an infection in our midst. It is the refuge of the hideous remnants of the nobility. We all know it, yet we are complacent. We are lulled into security while in Germany, in Austria, in the Palace itself, evil never sleeps. There, less than a mile away, plans are being drawn at this very minute to slaughter the Patriots. Let me ask you: how many more of us will have to die before we wake up? It is time, friends and brothers, time at last to overthrow the hated remains of the Old Regime. Let us begin with that most gothic of institutions, the monarchy itself."

Some men rose from their seats and cheered, while others cried in horror. Pierre-André's voice was echoing throughout the hall and drowning the shouts, friendly and unfriendly, the clapping of hands, the stamping of feet and the president's bell. He went on unfazed and in a thunder of applause demanded that a motion be put to the votes to exclude from the Club the prior orator, in whose direction he pointed an accusatory finger, and "all like-minded scoundrels." I was stunned by the violence of his tone.

"I have had enough," I told Emilie. "I want to go." I had to shout to make myself heard.

"Already? But we just arrived, Belle. I want to listen to this man. Are you not curious to find out who he is?"

She turned to the man seated to her other side. I rose without waiting for the end of their conversation. She caught me by the arm to stop me, but I shook her off. Our movements attracted Pierre-André's attention and for a moment my eyes met his. I looked away before I was able to determine whether his features reflected astonishment, anger or any other feeling. I was overcome by embarrassment. There was a short pause in his voice before he resumed his speech with undiminished energy. I ran away.

Back in the carriage, Emilie chatted on. "You are no fun, Belle. I take you to the Jacobins, and you spoil my pleasure! Why did we have to run like thieves when things were becoming amusing?"

"You found that speech *amusing*? Did you happen to notice that the orator was speaking of us when he was berating the nobility and the Court?"

"But have you ever seen anyone so ugly? His name is Corigal, or something like that. According to the man seated next to me, he was just elected Commissioner in the Second District. I would have learned more if you had not bolted. I have not heard anything so vicious; I am still tingling with excitement." She put her hand on my arm. "I have an idea, Belle. We will go watch one of his trials. I would love to see how he behaves on the bench. What do you say?"

"I say that we leave him alone."

"What is the matter with you? You are all pale."

"I am fine. I guess it was too noisy in there. That man frightened me, but, unlike you, I do not intend to follow him all over Paris."

That was the first I had heard of Pierre-André's election as Commissioner. He would, in addition to managing the police officers in his district, sit as a judge in Municipal Court. Of course, in the grand scheme of things, this could hardly be considered a function of the first magnitude. Yet Pierre-André was not yet thirty, and his career was taking a promising turn for someone so young. I had already read in the papers about his brothers. The eldest, Jean-Baptiste, my family's former attorney, had become the first *Procureur-Syndic* of the Départment of Cantal, which made him one of the highest officials in Auvergne. Another brother, Joseph, who had been a barrister in Paris before the Revolution, had become a justice of the new Supreme Court. Altogether, the Coffinhal brothers seemed to be doing very well under the constitutional regime.

↩ 56 ↪

The mood was changing. The bawdy celebrations of the Old Regime, such as the ones that had attended Mardi Gras, were now banned as indecent. Fashions too were different. Ladies' dresses became simpler and narrower. No one wore hoopskirts anymore, even at Court. The difference for men was still more striking. They wore their hair shorter, untied and without powder. They dressed in dark clothes of plain cloth, cut in the American style. Embroidered garments, for males and females, would now have looked very odd.

I was taken aback the first time I saw Villers go out with his hair loose on his shoulders and its natural reddish blonde colour, for there was no grey in it although he was past forty. Until then, I had seen him in this manner only in our intimacy. Oddly enough, Robespierre, the most extreme advocate of reform in some regards, remained faithful to the old fashions and wore his hair long, tied and powdered.

Many other changes of greater import occurred. The new Assembly was controlled by a group who would come to be known as the "Girondins," after the Department of Gironde, around Bordeaux, whence many came. They tended to be Republicans in their ideals, and were wary of the King's intentions. At the same time, they distrusted the people of Paris and wanted to reduce the influence of the capital to that of any other department.

The Girondins' grossest mistake was to declare war on Austria to "spread the ideals of the Revolution." The King signed a declaration of war against his brother-in-law, Emperor Leopold. I heard the Queen gloat about the superiority of the Austrian army. Both the King and Queen seemed to believe that the French would be speedily defeated, and welcome the foreign invaders as liberators, who would then restore the Old Regime. Everyone would then rally around the throne. Although I disapproved of the war, the Queen's words outraged me and gave me yet another reason to avoid the Court.

Villers and I were of one mind on this subject.

"This is one of the very few occasions," he said, "when you will hear me agree with Robespierre: spreading liberty by military force is a notion that could only have taken root in the head of a fool. No one abroad will welcome armed missionaries."

Indeed that war, which the Girondins expected so easily won, and the King and Queen hoped so speedily lost, raged on, interrupted only by brief truces, for twenty-two years. It ended last year, long after all of those who had wished it had perished.

The war had an unexpected consequence. Villers, now deprived of his seat at the Assembly, was supplying the army with horses, which often required his presence in Normandy. Aimée and I accompanied him there. I was happy to see Madame de Gouville again and never failed to be entertained by the sight of the aristocratic Villers turned horse trader. He greatly increased his already ample fortune during these months.

Such an interest in business affairs would have been deemed unbecoming, if not disgraceful, in a nobleman before the Revolution. Times were different now.

The Assembly decreed all assets of the émigrés forfeited. I sometimes thought of Villers's son, Charles-Marie, who had joined the army of the Prince de Condé in Germany. Although Villers never spoke about that topic, and I did not feel free to broach it with him, I knew that it caused him great pain to be estranged from his only legitimate offspring. I did not know what provisions he had made in his will, but he now had to disinherit his son, who, as an *émigré*, could no longer own property in France. I knew that he had large sums of money secretly transferred by his attorney to London, no doubt for the benefit of Charles-Marie. Villers still paid my rent and my servants' wages. I no longer expected to receive anything else from him.

57

In early June of 1792, I received another letter from Hélène.

> *I wish, dearest Gabrielle, I had better news to impart. Noir-vaux is closing. I am only allowed to stay here for the sole purpose of taking an inventory of our furniture and religious artifacts, which I must deliver to the Procureur-Syndic of our Départment in a few days.*
>
> *As to taking the "great pledge" of allegiance to the Constitution, as you suggest, it is out of the question, for me as well as for the twelve other remaining nuns of our community. We will never buy our safety by reneging on our vows. We all took the "little pledge" to liberty and equality, a step we hope will be sufficient to pacify the authorities.*
>
> *I thank you for proposing again to receive me in Paris. I would accept gratefully now, but I cannot abandon the twelve remaining nuns of our little flock. Fortunately the Countess de Lalande has offered us all her hospitality in her château once the Abbey is finally*

closed. There, with God's help, we will continue to serve Him as in Noirvaux.

Pray for us, Gabrielle, as I will pray for you and Aimée.

✝ *Hélène, Abbess de Noirvaux*

Hélène's assurances did little to cheer me. Who could tell whether she would find a lasting refuge in her new home?

The news from the front was no better. The Austrians and their Prussian allies were advancing into French territory. Reports of their atrocities spread to Paris. Along their path, villages were set ablaze, women were violated by entire battalions, civilians were slaughtered. All over France, Patriots volunteered to defend the Nation at this hour of desperate need. A law mandated the creation near Paris of a camp of 30,000 such soldiers. The King chose to veto this measure. I had opposed the war, but once it had been declared, I wanted my country to win and strongly supported the idea of the volunteer camp.

The populace was incensed by the King's veto. A mob, some said 100,000 men and women, invaded the Tuileries on the 20th of June, carrying signs of the most offensive nature. I was later told that among those was a miniature gallows from which hung a doll with a banner reading "String Marie-Antoinette from a lamppost." There was a display composed of a pig's ears, tail and genitals, referring to the King's lack of virility, and another with the horns of an ox, the symbol of cuckolds. The King drank from a wine bottle offered to him by an insurgent to toast the Nation, even donned the red hat of the *sans-culottes*, but refused to withdraw his veto. The crowd grudgingly retired at night.

Villers was outraged at the behaviour of the populace. He even requested an audience with the Queen to present his condolences for the insults she had suffered. To my surprise, she received him. He did not tell me what transpired, but I assumed that she was now desperate enough to accept the help of a man she had not long before wanted executed. Villers took Aimée and me to Vaucelles in June and spent most of his time there with us, only occasionally returning to Paris to attend to his horse supply business with the army. I would probably have remained the whole summer of 1792 in the country if word had not reached me that the Duchess's health was failing.

Over Villers's objections I left Vaucelles for Paris in early August to be close to the Duchess during what seemed to be her last days. I took Aimée to my friend's mansion. We arrived immediately after Dr. Jansaud had bled the Duchess. My daughter blanched at the sight of the red liquid in the porcelain bowl on the nightstand. The Duchess looked wan. Her blue eyes, which I remembered sparkling with kindness, were now dull, their light extinguished. Life had already deserted her. As we left, Aimée asked me tearfully why the Duchess had not recognized her. I pressed my daughter's hand without answering.

Thereafter I alone visited the Duchess every day, usually in the morning, because Dr. Jansaud's potions tended to make her drowsy later on. I returned to my lodgings and Aimée in the afternoon. I had not seen Morsan for over six weeks, although I had heard through Emilie that he was enquiring often about me. I had not many opportunities to think of him, absorbed as I was by the sorrow of losing a beloved friend of many years.

I was surprised when, on the 9th of August in the late afternoon, Junot announced that Monsieur de Morsan requested the honour of an interview with me. The footman should have turned him away, as he had been instructed to do with all male callers. The poor man was becoming forgetful and sometimes barely remembered the names of my visitors long enough to announce them. I would normally have refused to receive Morsan, but I reflected that he had too much delicacy to call on me without a compelling reason. I asked Junot to show him in.

"I beg your forgiveness," Morsan said. "I would have never, under normal circumstances, have taken the liberty of intruding upon you. The current situation justifies, I hope, my presumption in coming here." He hesitated. "A new attack against the Palace will take place within days. You must be aware of it."

"Monsieur de Villers mentioned it. I would not have left Vaucelles but for the Duchess's condition."

"I shudder, My Lady, when I think of you crossing the Seine every day to visit her."

I frowned. "Pardon me, Sir, but what gives you the right to be so solicitous of my safety?"

"Nothing, I am afraid. Yet I worry about you, Madam, with or without the right to do so. You do not seem to measure the gravity of the situation. Those of us who remain here are going to die."

"I will return to Vaucelles as soon as the Duchess no longer needs me."

"Going to Vaucelles is not going to do a thing. Do you think the

Jacobins' reach does not extend to the suburbs of Paris? Forgive me for being blunt, Madam, but you are blind to your own danger."

"The Jacobins do not control the Assembly."

"They control Paris, and it is all that matters. We will be swept away by the coming storm. By *we*, Madam, I do not mean only those who, like me, have remained faithful to their King. I refer to the whole nobility, including Monsieur de Villers and his friends. The great French Nation has tired of us, even of those of us who flatter the rabble. They will soon string us all from lampposts without making any distinctions between the ones who supported the Revolution and the others."

"Is it to share those dire predictions that you are disturbing me at this hour, Sir? They could have waited until our next meeting."

"I think not, Madam. In a matter of days it will be too late. Once the Palace is stormed, the royal family will be massacred, along with all of the nobility in town. I secured false passports this afternoon. I will be leaving by the stagecoach for Lille tomorrow and from there try to reach the Austrian Netherlands."

I stared at him. "You are going to emigrate?"

"If anything, I have delayed too long. Such a journey would have been safer a few months ago. You can probably guess at the reason why I was reluctant to leave Paris. I have secured, in addition to my own passport, another one for a Widow Durand, a lady traveling with a little girl. It is at your disposal and that of your daughter."

Morsan fell to his knees and seized my hand. "Please, Madam, hear me. I expect from you neither gratitude nor fondness. I know that you do not, you cannot love me. I am asking only that you to trust me enough to let me lead you to safety. I cannot bear the thought of you being hanged or torn to pieces by a mob. In my nightmares I see your head paraded through the streets by those cannibals. Horrible as it is to say, this is the fate that awaits you if you stay in France. Please, Madam, I beg you, save yourself, save—"

Villers, who must have been alerted to Morsan's visit by his spies within my house, burst into the room. I was wearing a light summer dress, made of several layers of lilac gauze. Startled, I rose from the sofa where I was seated. The flimsy fabric of my skirt was caught beneath one of Morsan's knees and tore with a loud noise. Villers ran to us, slapped the other man full in the face and seized my arm with such violence that I felt it pulled out of its socket.

Morsan rose. "You may hit me, Sir," he said, glaring at Villers, "but I forbid you to mistreat this lady."

"Forbid me? This lady, if you want to give her that name, is mine. I have kept her for years and will do what I please with her."

"Calm yourself, Sir," I told Villers. "There is no need for such language. Monsieur de Morsan was asking me to emigrate with him, and I was ready to decline."

"How clever of him! He knows he could never hope to approach you otherwise, but on the straw of a barn, while you are both hiding at night, he would only have to extend his hand, and then who knows . . . Maybe, with the excitement of fear, and under cover of darkness, you would not be too cruel. Or do you already feel for him a craving like that of a woman with child?"

Morsan drew his sword. "This I absolutely forbid," I said, looking into his eyes. "There will be no duels on my account. You can see that Monsieur de Villers is no longer his own master. You must leave, Monsieur de Morsan. I will not emigrate with you. You may be right in your assessment of our situation and I may be a fool not to avail myself of your offer. I thank you and wish you from my heart the best of luck, but I will not follow you. Please go, Sir."

Morsan was shaking with anger. After a moment, he sheathed his sword, bowed to me and before leaving, gave Villers a most unfriendly look.

"You should leave too," I told Villers. "I cannot reconcile myself to what I heard you say."

He was still holding me by the arm above the elbow and pulled me closer. "Not so fast, my pretty. I am not done with you. You have humiliated me by allowing the attentions of the most repulsive man in Paris, and now you dismiss me from your presence like a lackey? You will hear me first, Madam. Your ingratitude astonishes me. Have you forgotten what you were when I found you that night at the Opera? A little provincial goose, without any education, any experience of the world. A little nobody. The youngest daughter, unwanted and unheeded, of one of those families of aristocratic paupers still found in the most remote provinces of the Kingdom, with nothing to show for their arrogance but their titles. And what did your brother do for you? Give you, at the age of fifteen, to a brute like Peyre, and then abandon you after your husband left you penniless."

Villers's grip on my arm was so tight that it brought tears to my eyes.

I tried to use my free hand to disengage myself. He began to shake me. "For all your family cared, you could have starved to death or ended in a brothel, which might have been, come to think of it, the right place for a little trollop like you. You would have been hard-pressed to find a decent establishment to take you, though, because you had not even a maidenhead to peddle. A fine man, the Marquis de Castel, that brother of yours, who did not awaken until after I had bedded you, and then only because his honour was at stake."

I coloured from anger. "Do not speak in this manner. You know nothing of my brother's motives."

"The less I know of them, the better, I am sure. God knows what depravity lurks behind all that pride. But you are right, we were talking about you. You were pretty, you were eighteen and you were ready to sell yourself to me. That was all."

"It seemed good enough for you then."

"Like an imbecile, I had fallen in love with you. You were fortunate to look as fresh as you did after having passed through the hands of another man, and not any man, but Peyre! I should have made you confess what your husband made you do. I am sure such a tale would be entertaining enough. It might even have cured me of my infatuation. Yet it is not too late. Do not be shy, my sweet, tell me everything. Or, still better, you are going to show me."

My arm was hurting so much that I felt faint. "You are no better than him," I said, quivering with pain and anger, "if you can entertain the thought of tormenting me as he did. How dare you speak to me in this manner after I have shared your life for all these years?"

Villers stopped shaking me. His grip became still tighter. The pain took my breath away.

"The more I know you, Madam, the less I like you. Oh, you have given me my money's worth, I will grant you that. I was smitten in the beginning. Not enough, however, to be blinded to your limitations. As soon as I had decided to keep you, I had to give you some rudiments of education. Without me, you would still be more ignorant than the lowliest scullery girl in my kitchens. You could not open your mouth in society for fear of shaming yourself. Have you forgotten it? I made you what you are. You owe me everything." Villers was now shouting. "Do you hear me? Everything. And now this is how you are thanking me. Maybe you have not let that toad Morsan fuck you yet, although I would not swear to it, but you have been deceiving me since I started keeping you. I have for years shared your favours with Lauzun and half of the Court."

With this he let go of my arm. His rage turned to my dress. Seizing handfuls of the flimsy gauze around my waist, he tore away at it in a frenzy. Shreds of fabric fell to the floor. I ran from him to put the sofa between us.

"This is not true," I cried. "You know it. No man has ever approached me save my husband and you."

"You expect me to believe such a lie? To be a fool in addition to a cuckold? Come, little whore, how many lovers have you had?"

Villers was facing me across the sofa, out of breath, his eyes wild, his jaw tighter than I had ever seen it.

"I must ask you again to leave," I said. "You have now hurt me in every possible manner. I have no reason to tolerate your behaviour."

"You have far more reason for it than you suspect. You have pushed me to the limit and will regret it before long. Good night to you, Madam."

He slammed the door.

58

Shaking, I went to my bedroom. I did not wish to face Manon and removed the shreds of my dress myself. My arm was hurting from the elbow to the shoulder, the flesh red and swollen from Villers's grip. I lay on my bed in my corset and petticoat, reflecting that I had no choice now but to leave him. I felt dizzy and must have drifted off. Manon awakened me later that evening. She brought me a note from Mélanie, the Duchess's chambermaid, informing me that her mistress was not expected to survive the night. I rose and dressed in haste, relieved to have something other than the memory of Villers's madness to occupy my mind.

I asked Manon to put Aimée to bed without waiting for me since I did not expect to return until late. After kissing my daughter and telling her not to worry about her mama, I hailed a hackney and was off to the *Marais*. Even in the aristocratic Rue Saint-Dominique, groups of men were forming in the streets. I crossed the river and arrived at the Duchess's house, where Mélanie greeted me.

"I certainly didn't expect to see you tonight, My Lady, with everything that's happening. Picard, the footman, went out earlier. The volunteers from Marseilles have joined the rabble from the Faubourgs Saint-Antoine and Saint-Marceau. Together they will attack the Palace at daybreak. They will find it well defended, though. Picard says 8,000 National Guards have been called to the rescue."

I wondered how many of those would desert or even join the insurgents but kept my thoughts to myself. "How is the Duchess?" I asked.

"She received the last rites, My Lady. Father Martinet just left. He was impatient to go home, poor holy man, with being unsworn and all. Those scoundrels on the streets would make short work of him. He doesn't wear his cassock anymore, but they have a way of knowing." She shook her head. "It's a blessing for Her Grace to leave this world now."

The Duchess, when I reached her bedside, was too weak to speak. I took her hand and she pressed mine back. I asked her whether she wanted me to read to her. She moved her eyelids. I took her prayer book and read for a while. Mélanie brought me a light dinner on a tray and stayed with us. The Duchess was drifting off.

"You look so tired, My Lady," said Mélanie. "You should lie down on the sofa. I will rouse you if Her Grace awakens."

I did feel exhausted and went to sleep. I dreamed of my wedding day. Bells were ringing, but the church did not look at all like that of Lavigerie. I was not sure whether I would marry the Baron or Pierre-André. I was begging my mother to tell me. She seized me by the arm, shouting that I had disgraced my family. All the time church bells were ringing.

I woke to see Mélanie bending over me. She was shaking me. "Listen, My Lady, the *tocsin*." The bells of all of the churches of Paris were indeed ringing in urgent cadences. Drums were beating. The whole city must be awake.

"They're calling the Sections," Mélanie added. "They'll attack the Palace without waiting for the morning."

The Duchess was now moaning. I resumed my post at her bedside. Soon her breathing became more laboured. She did not regain consciousness. Mélanie and I knelt and together recited the Prayer for the Dying.

After an agony of twenty minutes, the Duchess passed away at two in the morning. To me, she had been closer to a mother than anyone I had met, except perhaps for Mamé Labro. I closed her eyes and tenderly kissed her hand, still warm and soft. Never again would it pat mine. She would no longer be there to smile at me, to listen to me, to comfort me. I sobbed when I tried to imagine life without her. I had lost her love and guidance at a time when I needed both more than ever. Yet I had to tear myself away from her bedside.

"I need to go home," I told Mélanie in the middle of my tears. "My daughter must have awakened. She will be terrified without me."

"Oh, you can't leave, My Lady. You won't find a hackney at this hour. What if a patrol arrests you for being out after dark? And what if those cutthroats find you? I can't bear to think of what could happen to you."

Mélanie was probably right. I remained with her to wake the Duchess until the first light of dawn. At half past five, I left and stopped a hackney.

"Are you out of your senses?" the driver asked when I told him my address. "You don't expect me to cross the river, do you?"

"We could reach the Left Bank through the Island of Saint-Louis. Everything must be quiet there."

"All right, I'll take you to the river. But if things aren't right, I'll turn back."

We were able to cross to the Left Bank, although we were stopped from time to time by bands of armed men who asked me why I was out at such an hour. They let us go when I explained that I had been attending a dying friend.

It was broad daylight when I arrived at my lodgings. Junot, hastening to tuck his shirt into his breeches, opened the door with his stockings down around his ankles. Manon was already dressed and looked at me with amazement.

"Why, My Lady," she said, "I didn't expect you so early. Mademoiselle Aimée is not with you?"

My heart stopped. "What do you mean, Manon? She is not here?"

"Well, no. My Lord came here last night before going to the Palace."

"Monsieur de Villers went to the Palace last night?"

"Yes, My Lady, around nine. I was ready to put Mademoiselle Aimée to bed, but he said you wanted her to join you at Her Grace's house. So I . . ."

"And he took Aimée with him?"

"Yes, he said he was going to take her to the Duchess's, and then go to the Palace by himself."

I had to lean against the wall for support. Villers had gone to the

Palace, knowing that it would be stormed in hours. Whether he had done so because he wanted to defend the monarchy, or as an act of despair, because he had lost me, I could not tell. What was sure was that, out of rage, of jealousy, of hate, he had stolen Aimée from me. He had taken an innocent child of seven, who loved him as a father, to a place where she would meet her death.

"Oh, my goodness," said Manon, covering her mouth with her hand, "what have I done? Where is she now? I should've taken her myself to the Duchess's house, but I was afraid of going out. Forgive me, My Lady."

I was so angry that I could have slapped her. I breathed deeply and made an effort to remain calm. "I must go to the Palace."

"Oh no, My Lady, you can't. Didn't you hear the *tocsin* ringing, the drums beating? That was the signal. The Palace is going to be stormed. Maybe it's already started. Then what will . . ."

"All the more reason to make haste. Perhaps it is not too late."

I left without paying heed to Manon's tears and entreaties. I was unable to find another hackney and ran in the direction of the Palace. I stopped a few times, my hand on my chest, to catch my breath, but images of Aimée dead, wounded, far from any help or comfort I could give her, spurred me on.

When I arrived at the Place du Carrousel, in front of the Tuileries, I gave a sigh of relief. Only regiments of the National Guard were stationed there. Everything was quiet and orderly. In spite of the early hour, the heat was already oppressive. I passed the gates and arrived at the Palace, where the Swiss Guards stopped me.

"No one may enter, Madam. We have orders."

"But I am Madame de Peyre, lady-in-waiting to the Countess de Provence. My little girl is inside. Please let me in."

"It is useless to insist, Madam."

I searched my pockets. By some miracle, my entrance card, bearing my name and rank, was there. I showed it to the Swiss Guard. He looked at it, but still refused to let me in.

"Fetch an officer," I said with tears in my eyes. "I am not leaving."

The guard went inside with my card while his comrade watched me. An officer arrived shortly, saluted and took me inside the post.

"I am sorry, My Lady," he said, "but no one may enter at this time, and no one should think of it. I would be doing you no favour by letting you in. We are going to be attacked momentarily." He lowered his voice. "In a few hours, I, with all of my men, may be dead. You have a chance to escape. Take it."

"I understand, Sir. Thank you for your concern. My little girl was brought to the Palace without my knowledge. Do you want me to let her die far from me, terrified among strangers? What mother would? Please, Sir, I beg you, let me in. What harm can there be in that, except to myself? You saw my entrance card. Do I look like an insurgent?"

"I did not need to see your card. I know you by sight." He paused. "I will let you in since you are determined to take that chance. God bless and protect you."

I barely took time to thank him and went in search of Aimée. Where would Villers have taken her? I ran to the Queen's Apartments, where I met with the Princess de Tarente, one of the ladies of the Court.

"Ah, here you are, Madam," she said, frowning, "and not a minute too soon. Your little girl will not stop crying and calling for you, to the point that Madame de Tourzel feared that she would awaken My Lord the Dauphin. Mercifully he slept through this horrible night. No one else, not even Their Majesties or Madame Elisabeth, went to bed. What possessed you to send your daughter here?"

"Thank Heaven. Where is she?"

"I left her with the chambermaids in the little entresol above Her Majesty's apartment."

A minute later, I was reunited with Aimée. Her face was swollen with tears. She had briefly gone to sleep on a sofa the night before, but had been awakened by the ringing of the *tocsin* during the night. She had not slept since. I took her in my arms to comfort her. Such is the resilience of childhood that she forgot her sorrows and dozed off in my arms in spite of the commotion.

I could hear orders being shouted and people running in all directions. One of the Queen's chambermaids told me that three hundred noblemen, most armed with only swords and pistols, had appeared the night before to defend their King. Villers was one of them. All of the men in the Tuileries, Swiss Guards, National Guards, servants and noblemen alike, had been assigned positions within the Palace and were ready to die in its defense. Entire battalions of the National Guard had already deserted, but the remaining ones, numbering a few hundred, seemed trustworthy. I did not see anything of Villers, but the chambermaid told me that he had been entrusted with the defense of one of the staircases.

I put Aimée, still asleep, down on a sofa and looked out the windows to see whether it was safe for us to leave. Everything seemed quiet. We were joined by Monsieur de Paget, Esquire to the King. He was carrying as his sole weapon a pocket pistol, and took his position with us in the entresol. I asked him whether he had any news.

"A delegation from the Municipality and the Department was received by the King," he said. "They convinced him to take refuge in the Riding Arena with the Assembly. The royal family, with the Princess de Lamballe and Madame de Tourzel, just left the Palace."

"Then there is nothing more for anyone to do. I am going to wake my daughter and leave the Palace. Will you come with us, Sir?"

"It would be folly, Madam. If you look out the window, you can already see the attackers massed on the other side of the Place du Carrousel. They are well armed with cannons and rifles. Weapon depots all over Paris have been pillaged during the night. The insurgents must be ready to attack by now. Anyone they see fleeing the Palace will be slaughtered."

"What do you think will happen to us if we stay here? And why did not the King, when he left, order the Swiss and National Guards to surrender? They are going to die here for nothing, to save the furniture."

"It is not my place, Madam, nor yours, to question the King's decisions. He ordered us to defend the Palace to our last drop of blood. We shall do so."

Cannon and musketry fire erupted outside. Aimée awakened shrieking. I heard thousands of voices singing in unison:

> *Arise, children of the Fatherland,*
> *The day of glory has come.*
> *Against us tyranny's blood-drenched banner is raised.*
> *Do you hear in our country*
> *The roar of those ruffians?*
> *They come into our midst*
> *To slit the throats of our sons, of our women.*
> *To arms, citizens!*
> *Form your battalions,*

March on, march on!
Let impure blood
Soak our furrows.

I was awed by its accents. Indeed I was listening for the first time to the "War Song for the Volunteers of the Rhine Army," or "*La Marseillaise*," as it would be called, because it had been first adopted by Federates from Marseilles.

Bullets shattered the windows and whistled past my ears. Without paying Monsieur de Paget any further heed, I seized Aimée's hand. Together we crawled across the room, careful not to cut our hands on the broken glass on the floor. We ran down a flight of stairs and found ourselves at the door to the Queen's Salon. I thought that other women might be gathered there, and that our best chance was to seek refuge with them.

I turned the door handle. It was locked. In a panic, I hammered at it with my closed fists, crying my name and begging for help at the top of my voice. The Princess de Tarente opened the door. Pushing Aimée in front of me, I rushed inside the room. The door was slammed and locked again behind us. The shutters were closed and all of the chandeliers and candelabra lit. Indeed a dozen Court ladies, including Madame de Rochefort, and the Palace chambermaids were inside. We huddled together in silence like a flock of sheep.

A long wait would have been unbearable, but soon we heard cries just outside the Salon. The insurgents had already taken the Palace. Blows resonated against the doors as the blades of axes shattered the white and gold panels. Shards of wood flew through the room. I took Aimée in my arms and covered her eyes. I felt her shiver against me. The doors gave way. Men burst into the room with yells of triumph. The sight of our group of women stopped them in their tracks. Madame de Rochefort, shrieking, fell to her knees. The attackers, past their first moment of surprise, seized one of the chambermaids and raised their swords. I held Aimée tighter, trying to steady myself. I expected us to be hacked to pieces one after the other when a man came running through the broken doors.

"What are you doing?" he cried. "You know the orders: spare the women!"

The insurgents let go of the chambermaid. All the ladies ran out of the Salon, I last of all, Aimée's hand in mine. In my hurry, I tripped over the bodies of two of the Queen's footmen outside the door. One of them, his forehead burnt and bloodied by a gunshot wound, was still holding a pistol. I stooped to take it from his hand. It must have been fired and be now useless, but it might serve to keep away attackers.

Gunfire and cries could still be heard on the Place du Carrousel. It seemed foolish to attempt to leave the Palace now. Still holding Aimée's hand, I ran back upstairs in search of a hiding place in a closet. We were following the main gallery when I heard a voice shouting behind me: "Another one there!"

I turned around and saw a bearded man. I aimed the pistol at his face. He was about twenty yards away, carrying a drawn bloodstained sabre but no firearm. He stopped and looked at me in amazement. Then a smile crept over his face.

"What would a little aristocrat like you know about pistols?" he sneered. "You'd only hurt yourself. Come, my pretty, hand it to me."

"I was taught to use a firearm," I said, still aiming. "This one is loaded. Stay away, or I will shoot you."

"Drop this thing, bitch, before I call the comrades."

He was approaching. I could probably have kept him at bay with the mere threat of the weapon, but lost my head and pulled the trigger. The pistol was indeed empty. I dropped it and fled down the gallery, dragging my daughter after me. The man was running after us. Aimée, whimpering, was slowing me down as I was pulling her by the hand. Without stopping or looking back, I took her in my arms and ran, my pursuer on my heels. Mangled bodies, as everywhere else in the Palace, were strewn across the hallway. I slipped on a puddle of blood, dropped Aimée and fell flat on my stomach.

My attacker reached me in an instant. I could feel him standing over me. He pulled me by my hair to raise me to my knees. I did not want to die without looking into his eyes. I wished him to remember my face and turned towards him. He raised his sabre and was ready to strike. I followed the movement of his arm. I imagined the moment, seconds away, when the steel of the blade would sever my head from my neck and my soul from my body. I was not frightened; I was already dead. When hope is lost, there is no more fear.

A voice shouted from the other end of the hallway: "Don't do that! Do you want to disgrace the Nation?"

My attacker stopped midway in his blow, which went astray onto my left shoulder. I did not feel any pain and believed that he had hit me with the flat of the blade.

"The little bitch shot at me," he said. "Those females deserve to die, just like the men."

"I told you already," replied my rescuer. "We don't kill the women."

Half a dozen men accompanied him. I was still on my knees, too stunned at the idea of being alive to think of moving.

"There, Citizen," one of them said, taking me by the arm to raise me to my feet, "you just need to cry *Long live the Nation*."

I did so with, I believe, a great deal of conviction. Aimée had witnessed the whole scene from a few feet away without a cry or a word. Her lips had turned white. I pressed her in my arms.

"We are safe now, dearest," I said. "These kind citizens will take us under their protection."

She did not seem to hear me. Her eyes wide open, she was looking straight ahead.

"We'll see you out of here," my saviour said. "Where do you want to go?"

The men took us to the Place du Carrousel. Through billows of white gunpowder smoke, I could glimpse the darker haze and orange glow coming from buildings on fire in the distance. The fighting continued before our eyes. Groups of women, armed with knives, followed the insurgents. They stripped the corpses of the Swiss Guards of their uniforms, decapitated them and cut off their genitals, which they pinned to the bodices of their dresses. Aimée and I, picking our way among naked, mutilated cadavers, had to walk in the gore spilled on the gravel walks of the gardens. The white marble of the statues was splattered with blood.

I shuddered. My shoulder was now throbbing. I put my hand there and felt something sticky. Looking down, I saw that the bodice of my dress, which had been light pink, was now soaked with blood. My skirts were likewise stained red from my fall in the gallery. My hair was loose and I had lost my bonnet and kerchief.

"I feel faint," I said to my companions. "Could we rest for a moment?"

"Certainly. With all the blood you've lost, you need some restorative. There's nothing like a glass of wine to put you back on your feet. We'll go with you to make sure you're all right."

One of them offered me his arm while another carried Aimée. We all repaired to the nearest tavern on the Terrace des Feuillants. I had never set foot in that kind of establishment, which would not have been deemed suitable for a lady. Tobacco smoke burnt my eyes and throat; men and women alike were yelling and cheering in celebration of their victory at the Palace. The owner glowered at me. "Who's this? She looks like one of those damned aristocrats trying to flee the Palace."

"Yes," his wife added while wiping a beaker, "Her Ladyship must be a friend of the Austrian Woman."

"Not at all," my companion said, "she's my sister and a good patriot."

I sat on a wooden bench and joined my companions in toasting the Nation a number of times. The wine burned my empty stomach and made me dizzier. I did not want to be accused of aristocratic aloofness, but there was nothing I wanted more than to lie down on my own bed. Aimée had fallen asleep, her head resting in my lap.

"Would you take me home now?" I asked, after imbibing what seemed a sufficient amount of drink.

"Maybe we should take you to a surgeon first."

"No, thank you. I will be fine. Please take me home."

"All right, we'll help you find a hackney then."

Two of the men volunteered to accompany us, while the others returned to the Palace to "finish the work." We arrived at my lodgings half an hour later, in the early afternoon. As the men helped me alight from the hackney, I saw a small crowd gathered on the street in front of Villers's mansion, a hundred yards away. People were cheering as furniture, paintings, drapes, books and papers came flying through the open windows.

59

"Oh, My Lady," Manon cried when she saw me, "what happened to you? My goodness, you're covered with blood from head to toe! Thank Heaven, you're alive, and Mademoiselle Aimée too. I was sick with worry, not knowing whether I would ever see either of you again. Let me send for Dr. Benoit right away. Junot said he just saw him come back from the Palace."

My bodice and chemise, soaked with blood, were already dry and painfully sticking to the wound on my shoulder. Every movement pulled on the inflamed flesh. Manon had to use scissors to undress me. I looked down at my left arm. The bruise, now dark purple, spread across several inches where Villers had grasped me the night before. The mark of his fingers was clearly visible. I shuddered at the memory.

Dr. Benoit was Villers's physician and, since our arrival in Rue Saint-Dominique, had attended Aimée through the usual ailments of childhood. He examined my shoulder and cleaned the wound with hot water.

"Do not worry, Madam," he said, "it will heal fast once I stitch it. You were fortunate not to be more seriously hurt. I do not know why you were in the Tuileries today, but it certainly is no place for a lady. I went there myself earlier to treat the wounded, but I found hardly anyone in need of my services. What a butchery!" Frowning, he pointed at the bruise on my arm. "What is this?"

I blushed and said nothing. Dr. Benoit took my arm and gently moved it. I winced at the pain in my elbow.

"The muscle has been crushed as in a vice," he added, "and the contusion has spread to the joint. This will remain painful for several weeks."

I looked away. "Have you heard any news from Monsieur de Villers?" I asked. "He went to the Palace last night."

"No, Madam, I have not seen or heard anything of Monsieur de Villers. You should rest and recover your strength before worrying about anyone else."

"Tell me. I will rest better knowing the truth."

He sighed. "I heard that all of the noblemen who fought at the Palace have been killed. Monsieur de Villers may have perished. I am very sorry."

I sent Manon to gather news. None of what she learned led me to believe that Villers could have survived. The King, from the Assembly, had waited until the afternoon to order the Swiss Guards to surrender. It was too late. Over 2,000 had died, including most of the defenders and 1,200 attackers. From the Assembly, one could hear cannon and musketry fire. From time to time, insurgents, covered with blood, brought to the Representatives news of the slaughter next door in the Palace, as well as objects, correspondence or documents they had seized. Some would, in later months, be used to prove the treason of the King and Queen.

There was a great deal of destruction, but no plunder, for all persons caught stealing in the Palace were killed on the spot by their fellow insurgents. The King and Queen were at first received with respect, but as the extent of the butchery became known, they were ordered to sit in the reporters' cubicle, a stifling space resembling a cage. All over Paris, the statues of the Kings, even those decorating the entrance to the Cathedral of Notre-Dame, even that of the beloved Henri the Fourth on the *Pont-Neuf*, the New Bridge, were pulled down and broken.

The next day, the Assembly suspended the monarchy. The royal family was imprisoned in the Temple, an enclosed compound in the middle of Paris, which, as its name indicated, had been the seat of the Templars.

The dynasty founded by Hughes Capet, Count de Paris, the most ancient reigning family in the world, had governed France without interruption for over eight centuries. It was overthrown in the course of these few days of August 1792. The former King was now a private citizen, and revolutionaries affected to call him simply Louis Capet, after the surname of his long departed ancestor. The Queen became "the Capet Woman."

The corpses of the noblemen found in the Tuileries were thrown out the windows. Then, along with the bodies of the Swiss Guards, they were taken overnight to the cemetery of La Madeleine, where they were buried in common graves. There rests to this day Charles Aurélien de Saint-Sauveur, Count de Villers.

I have at last found the strength to forgive him for the harm he intended when he took Aimée to the Palace. Did he want her killed? I hope not, for his sake. His final malice must have been directed at me, since he knew that I would follow her to the Palace in the middle of the storm. Did he want me killed? Did he want me to see him die? Did he want to die close to me? Did he repent before he died? He took the answers to his grave. So many, better or worse than he, have perished that none of it matters any longer. I can now mourn him as I mourn all the lives lost during the great Revolution.

60

Villers had often said that he would make sure Aimée and I lacked nothing after his death. Yet I received a note from his attorney, informing me that all provisions of Villers's will in my favor had been revoked on the 9th of August. Since none of his fortune could go to his son, who was an émigré, distant cousins would inherit everything.

The porter at my lodgings also told me that Villers had given my landlord notice for the 1st of October. He wanted to turn Aimée and me out of our lodgings without a *sol*. I kept busy, as much to discard the past as to prepare for the future. With Manon's help I sorted out which of my things could be sold to advantage and which should be kept for my new life. I had to find a buyer for my diamonds. They were now my only possessions of any value, and I intended to live on what I raised from their sale.

I visited Monsieur Boehmer, former jeweler to the Crown. His shop was as luxurious as ever, but it had an eerie, deserted aspect. He looked much thinner and older now. He smiled faintly when he saw the earrings.

"I remember these stones, of course, Madam," he said. "I have never seen the like of them. It seems so long since I sold them to Monsieur de Villers. When was it, in '87? Five years ago. And now . . ." He sighed as he put down the jewels. "I can offer you 10,000 francs for the *briolette* earrings, the bracelets and the ruby ring. All are amazing pieces."

I looked at him in shock. "But you told me, Monsieur Boehmer, that the earrings alone were worth at least ten times as much."

"That was certainly true before the Revolution, Madam." He shook his head sadly. "So many ladies are selling their diamonds these days, and there are no buyers."

I left, my eyes burning, and went to less reputable dealers. They all exclaimed at the beauty of the stones, but offered still less than Monsieur Boehmer. I decided to wait until the situation in Paris quieted in the hope of obtaining a better price. In the meantime I hid the jewels in fabric pockets I fashioned and sewed tightly into the lining of Aimée's skirts.

I followed the news in the *Moniteur* with great attention. I read that the old Municipality of Paris had been dissolved and replaced by a new one. A Council General, elected by the forty-eight Sections of Paris, now managed the capital. As I perused a list of its members, I paused for a moment. Among them was my former fiancé, Pierre-André Coffinhal. His election was reported as an acknowledgment of his role during the storming of the Palace. Pierre-André had rallied a group of Federates after a first assault had been repulsed by the Swiss Guards. His sword drawn, singing *"La Marseillaise"* at the top of his voice, he had led the insurgents to a second successful attack. We could have met in the Palace that day.

I also read that the Assembly, under the pressure of the new Municipality, had created a special tribunal to try the crimes committed on the 10th. There would be no appeals from its judgments. This court was called the Criminal Tribunal of the 17th of August and solemnly inaugurated that day in the main courthouse in the Island of the City. Again the name of Pierre-André Coffinhal stared at me in the middle of the list of the newly elected judges.

Those sentenced to die by the 17th of August Tribunal would be guillotined. That mode of execution had been invented as a humane substitute for the gruesome practices of the past. There would be no more hangings "high and short," where one slowly strangled to death, or interminable agonies on the wheel. Under the Old Regime, only members of the nobility were entitled to being decapitated. Even they remained at the mercy of the executioner's varying degree of skill. Now everyone would have a chance to have one's head cut off, cleanly and efficiently. Dr. Guillotin, the inventor of the machine, assured that the fall of the blade would give the victim a "pleasant feeling of coolness." How he knew I cannot say.

The new Tribunal wasted no time. Its first trial began two days later. The first three defendants were accused of forming clandestine royalist militias or corresponding with the *émigrés*. One after the other, they were tried, found guilty and guillotined.

"Can you imagine," said Emilie, "those trials begin at eight in the morning and then continue for forty-eight hours without even recessing at night!"

"True, Emilie, it must be awful to sit in that chair for two days and two nights at a stretch, listening to the witnesses and the attorneys.

And then to wait for the jury to return its verdict. But look, after the three initial death sentences, the Tribunal just acquitted the last two defendants."

"That is still three out of five sent to the guillotine. Mark my words, Belle: our turn will come. They will drag *us* before that Tribunal."

"Those tried so far, Emilie, have been influential characters, men who were linked either to the royalist brigades or to the *émigrés*. What can women like you or me have to do with such matters?"

"You, for one, were at the Palace on the 10th of August. *I* was not, but I am leaving all the same. I reserved a seat on the stagecoach for Lille in two days. I am going to Brussels. Morsan was able to reach it. He has already enlisted in the army of the Prince de Condé."

"I am glad to hear that he is safe, but I cannot reconcile myself to the idea that he joined the *émigrés*, those cowards who ran for their own lives, who abandoned their families, those traitors who fight against their own country. They have done more than anyone else to discredit the monarchy."

"You sound like a Jacobin, Belle. Those traitors, as you call them, have the support of the Prussians and the Austrians. They will hack the bedraggled French army to pieces."

"One would think, listening to you, that you want them to win."

"Absolutely, I do. That is the only hope to save the King now."

"Nonsense. The King made a huge mistake by failing to put enough distance between himself and the *émigrés*. He has convinced everyone that he, like the Queen, wishes the Austrians and Prussians to win the war."

"Of course he does."

I blushed with anger and fixed my eyes on Emilie's face. "Then he is guilty of treason. In any case, if the Prussians threaten Paris, the King, instead of being saved, will be treated as a hostage. His life will hang by a thread. Surely you must see it."

"Not at all. On the contrary, the rabble of Paris will be too terrified of the Prussians to harm the royal family. The King will be restored; the good times, when everyone was so happy, will return. There will be no more of that revolutionary nonsense. I will be back in less than three months, Gabrielle, with the victors. The Jacobins will be slaughtered. In the meantime, you should worry about saving your life and that of Aimée. Come with me to Brussels."

"I will not."

Emilie's words had shocked me. I could see how far we had moved apart in our ideas. I prepared my own move. It would be months before I saw a *sol* of what the Duchess had left me in her will, and her attorney had warned me not to expect more than a few hundred francs when her debts were paid. I had calculated that I would run out of ready money soon after the end of August. My lodgings were rented furnished. My only belongings, apart from my jewellery, were my clothes, a few trinkets, my books and a fine silver and crystal dressing-table set, a gift from Villers a few years earlier. Unfortunately, I was only able to raise two hundred francs from its sale.

I gave Manon, Junot, the footman, and both maids notice for the end of the month. Miss Howard left for England as soon as she was able to secure a passport. I presented Junot with one hundred francs because he was now too old, forgetful and crippled to find another place. His niece had agreed to take care of him, which at least guaranteed that he would not finish his life as a beggar. Usually elderly servants received a small pension from their masters, but Villers's death precluded that kind of arrangement. I would have liked to do better for poor Junot, but the state of my finances did not allow it.

Manon was crying. "It breaks my heart to leave your service, My Lady. After all these years. I'd gladly stay with you without wages, you know that. Now I won't see Mademoiselle Aimée grow up."

I took her in my arms. "I cannot accept, Manon. You should look for another place. Besides, I have barely enough money to support Aimée and myself. I expected to raise far more than I did. Please do not cry, my dearest Manon. We will see each other often."

It was therefore agreed that Manon would move in with her sister Louise, a lace maker whose services I had used in the past. Louise lived in Rue de l'Hirondelle, "Street of the Swallow," on the Left Bank, close to the river. As for Aimée and me, I still had until the end of September to locate something suitable, provided that I somehow pacify the landlord with regard to the rent for that month.

Those thoughts were on my mind when I went to bed on the evening of the 29th of August. Around two in the morning, I was awakened by a commotion. Someone was hammering at the front door. I heard feet shuffling down the hallway. Junot must have gone to see what was the matter. I rose in haste with barely time to throw a dressing gown on my shoulders. A dozen men wearing tricolour sashes burst into my bedroom. One of them, sporting a gold insignia, seemed to be an officer.

"What is this?" I demanded. "What do you want at this hour?"

"Are you the *ci-devant* Baroness de Peyre?"

"I am."

"We have a warrant for your arrest. Follow us."

"Why?"

"You are accused of being part of the Court conspiracies to kill the patriots on the 10th of August."

"That is not true. I have never been involved in politics."

"Save your arguments for the judges, Citizen. You will present your defense before the 17th of August Tribunal. I am giving you five minutes to dress, unless of course you prefer to follow us in your nightclothes."

"Can you please leave the room for a moment?"

"No. You might take advantage of our absence to destroy evidence." He smiled. "You need not pay attention to us."

Before the Revolution, ladies of fashion would disrobe as a matter of course in front of their menservants. It never entered my mind to follow that custom. I am naturally modest, and there is nothing I find more offensive than to pretend to forget that a lackey is also a man. Such were the petty everyday humiliations that made the lower classes hate us. The municipal guards seemed to assume that, being a noblewoman, I would have no objection to showing myself nude to strangers.

I asked Manon to bring me my warmest long-sleeved dress, which was "autumn leaves" in colour—the most prosaic things still had poetic names—and trimmed in pink and dark brown. It was too hot for the season, but I thought that I might be cold in whatever prison awaited me. The phrase *la paille humide des cachots*, "the damp straw of the dungeons," had come to my mind. While I was sitting on the bed, putting on my stockings and tying my garters, two of the men placed themselves a few feet in front of me. They were leering at my legs and bosom, giggling and elbowing each other. I could not imagine giving them the opportunity of watching me naked while I changed to my daytime undergarments. Since my summer chemise was sleeveless, I decided not to remove it and asked Manon to lace my corset on top of it, a sight that already seemed to entertain them a great deal.

I glared in the direction of the officer, hoping that he would order his men to turn around, but he was too busy going through my drawers to pay me or them the least attention. My lodgings were small. The search was soon concluded without producing anything of interest, except for Aimée's booklet of English exercises and multiplication tables, which were found in Miss Howard's deserted room and seized.

"A secret cipher to communicate with the enemy!" the officer said, waving the sheets of paper in my face. "This will be used at trial as proof of your activities, Citizen."

Manon had hastily prepared a traveling bag containing a spare set of clothes. The officer raised objections, but, yielding to Manon's entreaties, reluctantly agreed to let me take whatever fit in a small bundle. She was crying as she tied a kitchen towel around a pair of stockings, a chemise and a metal scraper to clean my teeth.

Aimée had been awakened during the search of her bedroom and had run to mine. She sobbed when she saw me escorted away by strangers. "Where are these men taking you, Mama? Can I go with you, please?"

"Your mother is going to prison, little one," said the officer. "That's where the enemies of the Nation belong."

"Do not worry, dearest," I said, kneeling to kiss her. "This is only a mistake which will be cleared in a few days. In the meantime, Manon will take care of you. You must be very good and obey her as you would Mama." I turned to Manon. "You know about the rent. The landlord, once he learns of my arrest, will not give you any delays to vacate these lodgings. You must leave by tomorrow."

A hackney was waiting for me. I settled in it, my bundle on my lap, a guard on each side of me. We crossed the river and took the direction of the Marais district. I was taken to the prison of La Force, a few hundred yards from the mansion of the late Duchess d'Arpajon. She had not been dead three weeks, but her passing seemed to belong to a different era. She did not witness the final collapse of her world or learn of my arrest. She was spared the knowledge of what awaited me.

61

I arrived at the prison of La Force around three in the morning on the 30th of August, 1792. I entered the echoing hall of the clerk's office. His wife, barefoot in shapeless slippers, was clad in a woolen robe thrown over her chemise. I recalled the high-heeled mules trimmed with swan down and the pink silk nightgown I had worn earlier during the night. Vanities indeed. I was entering a different world.

The clerk's wife opened a large register, in which she wrote my name, address and description. She asked the officer the reason for my arrest. Under his dictation, she added "*ci-devant* aristocrat, *ci-devant* lady-in-waiting to the so-called Countess de Provence, Court conspirator, present at the Palace on the 10th of August." The clerk untied my bundle and searched its contents. He nodded with an expressive smile as he unfolded my embroidered chemise and silk stockings. Watching him paw through my undergarments was no less humiliating than having to dress in front of strangers.

I was taken to a cell furnished with two iron cots. A female figure, prostrate on her stomach, lifted herself on her elbows. By the light of the turnkey's lantern, I recognized Madame de Rochefort. She rose and threw her arms around my neck.

"Oh, dearest Madame de Peyre," she cried, "I could not have remained apart from you a moment longer."

Madame de Rochefort was a pleasant woman with whom I had maintained a relationship of casual goodwill at Court, but I had never been aware of any particular fondness between us. I patted her in the back and invited her to lie down again. The wooden door closed behind us and we were left in the dark.

I reached for the other cot, covered with a foul-smelling mattress. Shivering with cold, I congratulated myself on the long sleeves of my dress. The din of the prison, even in the middle of the night, drowned my companion's whimpers. I listened, my eyes open, to a concert of shrieks, laughter and singing.

At last a grey dawn crept through the barred window. It was located just under the ceiling and lit the room enough for me to see the obscene pictures and inscriptions scribbled on the walls. The turnkey appeared, carrying on a tray two bowls of milk in which floated a few clots, along with two bottles of cloudy water. I looked at the liquid with disgust.

"Don't waste the water," he told me, "because that's all you'll have all day for washing and drinking. I am sorry, Citizen, but the allowance for the prisoners' food's just been reduced."

"Does the water come from the Seine?" I asked.

"Don't worry about it, Citizen. Some say it loosens your bowels, but I drink it every day, and I've never suffered anything like that. But then I let it stand for a while. That way, the filth settles at the bottom. If you do the same, you'll be fine."

Until then, I had drunk only spring water in Paris and refused to swallow a liquid into which 700,000 people emptied their chamber pots and garbage. I wondered how long I could survive on such a regimen.

I thought of Aimée. She would have to leave my lodgings, the only home she remembered, before the day was over. The poor child had experienced many shocks in the course of the past few weeks: the death of the Duchess, that of Villers, the scenes of horror during the storming of the Tuileries on the 10th, and now my arrest. Villers had told her that I was at the Palace on the night of the 9th and that he was taking her to me. I had explained to her that he had made an innocent mistake and did not know of my last visit to the Duchess. To Aimée, he had been almost a father. I wanted her to remember only his kindnesses.

Madame de Rochefort chatted on. She would speak of her husband, how much he must miss her, and how pitiable her own fate was. Not once did she ask me about my little girl or my circumstances. I rose to the level of the window by standing on tiptoe on my cot. Since my companion was too short to do so, I described to her the carts, carriages and pedestrians passing by in the street below.

Late in the afternoon, the turnkey returned and announced that we had permission to go down to the courtyard for an hour. There I met a dozen ladies of the Court for the first time since the 10th of August. The Princess de Lamballe, Madame de Tourzel, as well as the palace chambermaids were there. None of these women were in truth my friends, but we were all in the same predicament now.

The Princess de Lamballe and Madame de Tourzel had arrived from the Temple ten days earlier and gave me the most recent account of the King and Queen, whose captivity they had briefly shared. The King and his family were jailed in the grim medieval tower there, under the continuous surveillance of Municipal Guards.

My companions talked of the future. I kept my thoughts to myself. I reflected that the 17th of August Tribunal had tried only half a dozen persons so far, all prominent men. It would be months before I, an insignificant character, appeared before that court. Still, the idea of facing Pierre-André as my judge was not reassuring. Perhaps he would excuse himself on the grounds that he knew me. Or he might not say anything for fear of being compromised by association. He would sit on the bench, looking at me in an indifferent manner before signing my death warrant.

After an hour of looking at the sky, walking and talking, it was time for us to return to our cell. We watched the dim light of the day die out. I braced myself for another night of racket.

On the morning of the next day, a man brought us pieces of coarse white fabric.

"There, my pretties," he said, "now you will make yourselves useful. Quite a change for you, I bet. You'll sew shirts for the soldiers who risk their lives for us on the front. You are housed in luxury at the Nation's expense. You can repay this kindness by earning your keep."

I was delighted to have something to do beside listening to my companion. Madame de Rochefort went on complaining. The shirt she had started was soon soaked with tears and abandoned. I took it from her. By the time of our daily walk in the courtyard that night, I had finished my own shirt and hers. I gave them to the turnkey and asked for more the next day. I was becoming accustomed to prison life and resigned to the idea of spending some time there.

The third day, the 2nd of September, we were awakened by the urgent cadences of the *tocsin*. All the bells of all the churches of Paris, as during the night of the 10th of August, were ringing in unison. I shuddered at the memory. Soon afterwards, we heard a deafening noise coming from the street. I climbed on the bed and saw a crowd massed around the entrance. Many were waiving sabres, rifles and pikes, their words muffled amid the shouting. At one point, someone saw my head at the window and pointed in my direction. I retreated in haste.

Soon the same cries echoed inside the jail. The turnkey did not appear, nor did anyone bring us anything to eat or drink. All day long we heard doors slamming, things or people being dragged, and cries, both of fury and of terror. Madame de Rochefort had stopped crying. She was pale as a ghost and kept muttering, "Oh, my goodness, we are going to be massacred."

There was no arguing with her assessment, although I wished she had abstained from voicing it. We spent the day huddled together on her cot, expecting at any time our door to be kicked open. Darkness fell, but the shrieks continued into the early hours of the morning. Then they died too. For the first time since my arrival, complete silence closed upon the prison.

At dawn we were awakened by orders being shouted outside our cell. We jumped to our feet when a group of men, armed with sabres and rifles, burst into our cell.

"Your names," asked one of them.

"Marianne de Rochefort and Gabrielle de Peyre," I said.

"I see. Trollops from the *ci-devant* Court." He spat. "Don't worry, you won't have long to wait for your punishment."

The men left, slamming the door behind them. We looked at each other and knelt. We recited the *Confiteor* in unison. Together we remembered the agony of Christ on the cross, put our lives into His hands and beseeched Him to receive us. I recommended Aimée's fate to His mercy. I had often been lax in my religious practice, but now found comfort in prayer. I embraced my companion, who also seemed to have recovered her composure.

A few hours later, the men reappeared, accompanied by the turnkey. I asked him for something to drink and eat. My throat was parched and my insides rumbling. He returned with bread and red wine. Although I never had wine for breakfast before, the bread was too hard to be eaten dry. I dipped it into the beaker. The mixture burnt my empty stomach, but I forced myself to swallow it.

"Please take something, my dear," I said, offering the beaker to Madame de Rochefort. "We will need some nourishment to sustain our strength during the day. This may be our last chance to eat for some time."

I refrained from remarking that it might also be our last meal, though that thought was very much on my mind. My companion was unable to eat. As I handed back the empty beaker to the turnkey, I heard a voice outside the door shouting: "Send those women to the courtyard!"

We walked down in silence. Hundreds of male prisoners, as well as the other ladies from the Court, were already gathered in the courtyard. It now looked like the antechamber of death. Everyone was speaking, if at all, gravely and in low voices, as during a funeral. A number of armed men in civilian clothing, their shirtsleeves rolled up to their elbows, were watching us. They referred to their activities at La Force as "working" and to themselves as "workmen." Some seemed drunk although it was not yet midday.

"A *people's court* had been formed in the clerk's office," said one of them. "The crimes committed on the 10th of August won't go unpunished. All of you are going to stand trial for the murder of the Patriots."

They did not say what kind of penalty would be inflicted by the *people's court* or how swiftly, nor did I ask.

"The same's going on in all the prisons of Paris," another workman continued. "The unsworn priests have been dispatched already. Those traitors wouldn't even take the *little pledge* of allegiance to liberty and equality. They could've saved their lives, but they refused. Yesterday we also dealt with the worst scoundrels among you, the counterfeiters of *assignats* and the Swiss Guards. You're in luck, because they didn't receive any trial." The man glared at me.

The workmen decided who was going to appear next before the people's court. Two of them seized the *accused* and escorted him or her to the clerk's office. My fellow prisoners, one by one, left in this manner. Some went firmly. A few even affected a smile. Most begged for their lives and had to be dragged to face their judges.

A dozen Swiss Guards, still wearing their red, white and gold uniforms, had by some miracle survived not only the butchery of the 10th of August, but also the massacres of the day before. When their turn came, their courage failed them. These soldiers, who might have died bravely in the heat of battle, now sobbed and pleaded on their knees for mercy. I turned away.

"You weren't so meek on the 10th, when you were slaughtering the patriots," said one of the workmen. "Come. It's time to answer for your crimes."

"We were under attack," said a Swiss.

"Right. When we approached the Palace, you let us believe that you would fraternize with us, like the National Guards had done. That was just a trick to shoot us at close range. D'you know how many of the comrades fell before my eyes?"

"We were following the orders of our officers."

"You'll explain that to the judges. Let's go."

The Swiss remained huddled together, moaning in despair. At last more workmen, sabres drawn, came from the clerk's office.

"Hurry!" one shouted. "If these scoundrels won't budge, massacre them in the courtyard."

One of the Swiss rose, soon followed by his comrades. The men, ashen-faced, looked straight ahead as they were marched to the clerk's office. The pitiful human cattle in the courtyard made way for them.

I had kept my distances from Madame de Rochefort, who was almost paralyzed from fright. Her terror would have tested my own courage. I sat by myself on a bench. As the afternoon wore off, some of the workmen came to speak to me.

One of them was a cobbler from Marseilles named Elie Martial. He had come to Paris to join the Federate camp with the intention of going later to the eastern front. He had been outraged by the King's veto of the military preparations and had participated in the attack on the Palace on the 10th of August. Upon hearing that I was from Auvergne, he addressed me in the Roman language. He asked all kinds of questions about my life, my situation, how old my little girl was, and what she was like. His speech was only slightly different from that used around Vic, so we had no trouble understanding each other.

"Don't despair, little lady," he said. "The judges of the *people's court* will listen to you. Some of the prisoners are so scared when they appear before the court that they can't stand on their feet, let alone talk. *You* look to me like a brave person. You'll know how to explain your case."

"I hope so, but there is no telling how I will behave when my turn comes."

Another workman walked to me and demanded to inspect my nuptial ring. "Look at this!" he said, pointing at the writing inside. "It must be some secret password. That's the kind of tricks the conspirators use between each other."

"No," I said. "This is simply the date of my wedding."

"Where's your husband? Is he one of those buggering *émigrés* who are in cahoots with the Prussians?" He glared at me. "Those cowards always leave their women behind to do all the spying."

"No, Citizen, my husband died before the Revolution, in 1787. No one in my family emigrated. I am alone now with my little girl, who just turned seven. Look, here is her portrait."

I opened a gold locket I wore on a chain to show them a miniature portrait, painted on ivory, of Aimée. It also held a curl of her black hair. It was a present from Villers for the occasion of the New Year, only eight months earlier.

"There's no denying that she's pretty," said Martial in French. "She looks much like you. If she's already seven, you must have been full young at the time of your marriage."

"I was fifteen."

While Martial and the other workman were holding Aimée's portrait, I noticed that their fingernails were lined with red grime, and that their shirts were covered with splatters of the same colour. Martial caught my look.

"Me and my comrades have been working outside the prison door all morning," he said. He showed me his wrist. "See how swollen it is. That's why I've earned a rest; they've assigned me to watching the prisoners awaiting trial. It's easier here. Even those who cry and beg don't give half as much trouble as the ones who've already been sentenced and need dispatching." He frowned. "We need to act quickly. Messengers on horseback brought news from the front. The Prussians took Verdun two days ago. Some traitors there organized a welcome ceremony and handed them the keys to the city, along with candied almonds."

I looked at Martial in shock. "This is terrible news. Verdun was the last fortress defending the road to Paris. It is open to the Prussians now."

"That's right. Those ruffians could be here in three days. If they take the city, the first thing they'll do is free the prisoners, who will help them massacre all of us patriots. The Prussians don't even spare the women or children." Martial shook his head in disgust. "That 17th of August Tribunal is no good. It's not fast enough and it's far too lenient. Think of it: only three scoundrels sent to the guillotine so far! In the meantime thousands of conspirators remain in jail, snug and cozy, waiting for the Prussians. If we don't kill them, they'll kill us first."

"Do you think I would kill anyone?" I asked. "And I hate the Prussians as much as you do. What have you to fear from women like us?"

"You look harmless enough to me, but what do I know? It's up to the *people's court* to decide the fate of the prisoners."

"And who are the judges on the people's court?"

"They're appointed by the Municipality. Hébert's the President. You'll have to watch for him; he's a good-looking fellow with a pointy nose and long powdered hair."

I knew Hébert by reputation. He was a Deputy *Procureur-Syndic* for the Municipality and had been, according to Madame de Tourzel, put in charge of the royal family in the Temple. He was also a journalist, and his newspaper, *Le Père Duchesne*, "Father Duchesne," was full of daily encouragements, couched in the most violent language, to the good people of Paris to slaughter aristocrats. I had tried once, out of curiosity, to read that publication but had stopped midway, discouraged by both the substance and that various obscenities were found in every sentence. The fact that he was presiding over the *people's court* did not cheer me.

I hesitated before asking: "What happens after the prisoners are sentenced to death?"

"Depends. It's up to us workmen to decide the manner of execution. We don't use bullets because we can't waste them; they're needed for the war. Some prisoners are bludgeoned on the head first, so they don't feel a thing. Some are dispatched by the sword. Others have their throats slit."

My stomach lurched.

"Now, don't turn pale like this," continued Martial. "Since you're so pretty, the comrades would make it quick and easy. Just be sure not to run or fight. You'd make them cross without saving yourself. There's one thing you don't need to worry about: nobody's going to violate you. We're not brutes. Anyone who'd take advantage of a woman would be put to death on the spot. The other workmen would take care of that. All the same, I'll go with you if that'll make you feel better."

"Yes, if I am sentenced to death, please be kind enough to stay with me until the end. It will be less fearful since I already know you a little." I looked into his eyes. "I would take it as a great favour if you killed me yourself. I would prefer that to dying at the hands of strangers."

Martial shook his head. "I'd kill you if I had to, just like I killed the others, but I'd rather not. You see, I like you. I am clumsy when I don't feel good about something. I'd make a mess of it. You'd suffer more than needed, and I'd never forgive myself. You'll be better off in the hands of the others. If it comes to that, you can tell me which way you'd prefer to go. I'll talk to the comrades and stay with you to make sure it's done right, even though I won't like to see you die."

I tried to think of the mode of execution I would like best but could not settle on any which tempted me. I wanted to ask Martial's advice, based on his experience of the morning, but feared that I would begin crying if I said anything about it. All of my fortitude would be gone then. I put my hand on his. He patted it.

"I shouldn't have told you about all that," he said. "Anyway, you're worrying for nothing. Cheer up, little lady. I've a feeling you're going to be acquitted."

"What happens to the bodies of those who have been executed?"

"Why would you want to know?"

"I suppose you take their money and jewellery."

"I shouldn't be talking about that. I know it upsets you. Mind you, we're not thieves. Anyone caught stealing would be killed right away by the others. Everything is kept until the night and then sent to the Municipality."

"Then I want you to have this." I removed from my neck the gold locket with Aimée's portrait and handed it to him.

"You can't do that," he said, shaking his head. "We aren't allowed to take anything from the prisoners, dead or alive. Besides, it's far too valuable. It looks like gold and these must be diamonds around it."

"You would not take it from me. I am giving it to you. I want you to have it rather than it being thrown into a pile. You will have a memento of me when I am no more. Please."

"You don't understand. I won't accept anything from you, not when you're in this situation. It wouldn't be right. And don't worry, I'll remember you to my last day, no matter what."

I suddenly noticed Madame de Rochefort lying unconscious on the cobblestones of the courtyard. I ran to her, relieved to have something to distract me from the thought of my own death. A group of workmen gathered around her made way for me. I held my breath as I saw one of them, kneeling by her side, cut the bodice of her dress and the front laces of her corset with the point of his cutlass. I believed for a moment that he was going to violate her. Yet he only shook her by the shoulder. I realized that he had loosened her clothes to allow her to breathe more freely.

I knelt next to him. "Please, Citizen," I said, "you are very kind to help my friend, but she is extremely timid. Let me attend her instead."

I slapped her face. It took a long time to revive her, during which the man with the cutlass, now standing behind me and looking down at her, said to one of his comrades: "She's really pretty. A pity she's already married. She could've wed one of us to save herself."

The other workman replied, pointing his bayonet at my face:

"True, but her friend here, with the red hair, is even better. And *she's* a widow, although she can't be more than twenty. I wouldn't mind marrying her."

Still on my knees by the side of Madame de Rochefort, I raised my eyes to my admirer. He was no beauty and would not, under different circumstances, have tempted me in the least. Before I could say anything, a well-dressed man wearing a tricolour sash walked to us and said: "We are here to try these women, not to find them husbands. Leave this one alone, you two."

I never knew whether he was acting out of kindness, to protect me from unwanted attentions, or to prevent my escape. Regardless of his motives, his intervention put an end to any hope of the kind. The man with the bayonet gave me a resentful look and walked away.

Once Madame de Rochefort was able to stand on her feet, I did my best to rearrange her torn clothes. I brought her to my bench. With her head resting on my shoulder, I resumed my conversation with Martial and the other workmen, trying to delay my appearance before the *people's court*. Martial would leave from time to time to bring us back the latest news from the "courtroom."

I saw the Princess de Lamballe escorted to the clerk's office. After about an hour, it was the turn of the palace chambermaids, one after the other. Madame de Tourzel followed.

A few fortunate prisoners were freed after being claimed by delegates from their Sections and released to them without trial. I dared not ask Martial about the fate of the ladies from the Court. The fact that he did not volunteer any information about them did not seem a good omen. I regretted my suitor with the bayonet. Now I would have thrown myself into his arms without the least hesitation. I even wished Martial would propose, but he did not seem the sort of man to make an offer of marriage to a female under duress.

Madame de Rochefort, when her turn came, clung to me with amazing strength and tenacity. Her whimpers turned into shrill cries. They tore at my ears and put me in mind of the shrieks of a pig being bled to death. I watched with horror her fingers being pried from my skirts one by one. I begged the guards to let her go without trial, but they would not listen to my entreaties any more than to hers. At last she seemed to realize that resistance was futile, went limp and was carried, sobbing, to the tribunal in the arms of one of the workmen.

After her departure, I knelt against the bench, closed my eyes, traced the sign of the cross on my chest and recited the Prayer for the Dying:

> *O Jesus, I worship thy last breath;*
> *Please receive mine*
> *When I leave this world.*
> *I offer thee*
> *My agony and all the miseries of my death.*
> *As thou art my Father and Saviour,*
> *I release my soul into thy hands.*
> *May the last moment of my life*
> *Honour that of thy death,*
> *And my heart's last breath*
> *Be an act of thy pure love.*
> *Amen.*

I was the last one left in the courtyard from the group of ladies from the Court. At last, shortly after six o'clock, Martial walked back from the clerk's office.

"It's your turn, little lady," he said. "You'll be happy to hear that your friend, the one who cried so much, was acquitted. She couldn't even tell the judges her name. I'm taking you now because the tribunal just sentenced a thief to death. This gives you a better chance. They don't like to acquit two people in a row. Now, don't lose your head and say anything foolish before the judges. If you do, I'll squeeze your arm to stop you."

I hardly needed to be reminded of the possibility that I might soon lose my head in more ways than one. Martial and another workman took me by the elbows to lead me to the clerk's office. My knees were unsteady and I felt light-headed.

I faced my judges in the room from where I had first entered the prison. I tried my best not to appear frightened, which could have been construed as an admission of guilt, and clenched my fists to hide the trembling of my hands. It is said that courage is not the absence of fear, but the ability not to show it. By that standard, I was brave that afternoon.

I stood before nine men with tricolour sashes around their waists, seated at a long table. I recognized the one in the middle, from Martial's description, as Hébert. I had imagined, from reading the *Père Duchesne*, a coarse, unkempt *sans-culotte* instead of the well-groomed man I was facing. He was indeed handsome, an opinion I do not mind stating since I cannot be accused of partiality towards him. That did not make him any less fearsome in my eyes. Another man, standing, seemed to act as the prosecutor. I later learned that his name was Luilier and that he too was an officer of the Municipality of Paris. The registers of the prison were open in front of them. The room was full of onlookers, male and female. Workmen, sabres drawn, guarded the door.

"State your name, profession, age and address," ordered Hébert. He spoke in a polite tone, addressing me formally.

"Gabrielle de Peyre. I am widowed and have no occupation. I am twenty-three years old. I live Rue Saint-Dominique, number 132."

"Mind what you say, Madam, because the slightest lie will doom you."

"I have nothing to hide, Citizen President, and no intention of lying."

"That is what we are going to find out." He was looking down at the prison register. "Do you know the reason for your arrest?"

"I used to be a lady-in-waiting to the Countess de Provence."

The crowd jeered. Martial squeezed my arm.

"Did you receive a stipend?"

"Not this year. I resigned my place when the Countess de Provence emigrated."

"How much was your stipend?"

"Six thousand francs per annum, but as I told you, Citizen President, I have not received anything since last year."

"Did you keep going to the Palace after resigning your place?"

"No more than once a month."

"That is enough to participate in the conspiracies of the *ci-devant* Court. Where were you on the 10th of August?"

"I was at the Palace, but only because my little girl had been taken there without my consent."

"A likely story. Do not expect any mercy unless you reveal the plots to kill the patriots. Name your accomplices."

"I do not know of any such conspiracies, Citizen President. I have never been involved in politics."

"You, a member of the Court, a servant of the so-called Countess de Provence, claim be innocent?"

"True, Citizen President, I used to be an noblewoman, but I was arrested in my own lodgings. That proves that I was not trying to flee or hide after the 10th of August. I never had any correspondence with the enemy. I never left France, either before or since the Revolution. None of my family emigrated. Before my arrest, I was living quietly with my little girl without hurting anyone."

"Enough. You will have an opportunity to plead your cause later. Your turn, Citizen Prosecutor."

Luilier pointed his finger in my direction.

"Look at this woman, Citizens Judges, and look carefully because you will see the face of evil. By her own admission, she is an aristocrat and a member of the *ci-devant* Court. This, in itself, brands her a royalist conspirator, a traitor, a spy, an enemy of the Nation. But this is not all. You heard her; she tells us herself that she is a friend of the *ci-devant* Countess de Provence. You know what that means. She is a woman of perverted morals, of unnatural, revolting habits, which decency forbids me to describe, but of which you are well apprized."

Luilier paused. I heard cries of "tribade" and "whore" from the public.

"Raise your skirts, my pretty," shouted a woman, "we'll rub you the way you like."

"You'll see how good the blade of a knife feels down there," another chimed in. "That'll be a change from your other toys, I bet."

"Hand her over," said one of the workmen at the entrance. "We'll strip her and punish her where she lapsed, just like the Lamballe woman. That'll teach those bitches to despise men."

I was beginning to doubt Martial's assurances regarding the treatment of female prisoners. I felt faint. He pressed my arm and whispered: "Don't worry. I won't let them do that to you."

"Citizen President," I said, "what the Citizen Prosecutor says is not true."

"Silence," said Hébert, "let him finish. Quiet in the audience."

"And if that were not enough," resumed Luilier, "she also confessed to the heinous crime of receiving a stipend of 6,000 francs a year for no reason. She is a leech, a vampire, sucking the blood of the Nation while the patriots are starving. This alone merits a death sentence. Our brave workmen can be trusted to make the punishment fit the crime, or should I say, the crimes. Do not be fooled, Citizens, by her allurements, her youth, her false look of innocence. She is a menace, all the more danger-ous because she appears harmless. We will not be safe until the likes of her have been put to death. That is the only way to prevent her and her friends from destroying the Nation from within. Do your duty and show no pity. Justice demands it."

Hébert nodded to me.

"I am innocent of any crime and a good patriot," I pleaded. "I love my country, no less than you do. The last thing I want is the victory of the Prussians or the *émigrés*. I was widowed at seventeen, Citizens Judges, and left penniless by my late husband. My family tried to force me to enter a convent. They wanted to separate me from my little girl. When I refused, they would not take me back. They have denied me assistance of any kind. I accepted the place of lady-in-waiting only for the sake of my daughter. The Citizen Prosecutor is mistaken. I have never shared the tastes of the Countess de Provence. If I am sentenced to die, my little girl, who has no one else in the world, will be orphaned and destitute. I cannot leave her. She is too young. She is only seven. She is innocent. Please have mercy on her, if not on me."

There was a murmur of sympathy in the audience. Some of the women in the audience, perhaps the same who had hurled insults at me earlier, yelled: "Let her go."

"Do you swear to uphold liberty and equality?" Hébert asked.

"I do, Citizen President, with all my heart."

My fate was decided in minutes. The judges conferred between themselves and Hébert said:

"Let Madame be released."

I could not bring myself to believe that my life was going to be spared until my two guards, who had not left my side during the entire proceedings, warmly congratulated me. They took me outside the front door of the prison.

"I didn't tell you before," explained Martial, "but if Hébert had said instead *Let Madame be transferred to L'Abbaye*, that would have meant a death sentence. That makes it easier for the comrades outside. Most prisoners do believe that they're taken to another jail and don't understand until the last moment what awaits them. That way we don't have to chase them down the street. It's better for everybody."

A few yards from the entrance of the prison lay the headless, nude body of a woman, white against the dirt of the street. Her stomach had been sliced open and bright-coloured entrails were spilling out. Her legs were spread apart, her intimate parts had been cut off and the raw flesh between her thighs was buzzing with flies.

"It's the Princess de Lamballe," said Martial without any trace of emotion. "The comrades have taken her head to a hairdresser to make it all pretty again, and then we'll go to the Temple and show the whole thing to her lover, the Capet woman. Don't worry, I know you're not anything like her."

I felt a sharp pain in my stomach as if I too had been disemboweled. I wondered whether the Princess had still been alive when she had been mutilated. I could not avert my eyes from her body or reconcile myself to the idea that it had belonged to the silly, blonde, blue-eyed person I had seen in the courtyard only a few hours earlier.

I had not noticed at first anything but the poor remains, but my attention was drawn to cries nearby. Some ten yards away, corpses and body parts were piled high in the middle of the street. A man's head had rolled down from that heap into the gutter. It bore a large gash on the side. The force of the blow must have torn the eye from its socket, whence it hung by a shred of flesh. The street was slick with blood and reeked of death, for the corpses had begun to smell in the hot afternoon. Flies were everywhere.

All the cadavers were naked. Their clothes and possessions, pathetic as only inanimate objects can be, were neatly gathered against the wall of a neighbouring house. The body of a man was being stripped by two workmen at the foot of the pile.

"I know it's not a pretty sight, especially for a lady," said Martial, "with them being naked and all. We should be receiving straw anytime to cover the bodies. We can't leave them like this. They don't look decent. Now that you've been acquitted, you'll have to climb to the top of the pile and cry *Long live the Nation*. We'll help you if you're tired. After that, you'll be free to go."

A man I had seen in the courtyard was being dragged to undergo that formality. He had lost his shoes in the struggle and his white silk stockings, already soiled by the grime of the prison, were now stained by the blood of the corpses he was treading. He was offering a vigourous resistance but had to fight three of the workmen. They at last pulled him to the top of the heap of bodies, where they ordered him on several occasions to cry *Long live the Nation*. He refused with the utmost contempt. I tried to shout to him not to be so foolish but no sound came out of my mouth. One of the executioners, apparently tired of waiting, swore and plunged his sabre into the man's stomach. He collapsed. The executioner then drew a cutlass from his belt and began to cut off the victim's head. He had only fainted. The pain revived him and he began to shriek. Still held by my attendants, I turned my head away. The cries stopped. The executioner climbed down and took me by the chin to make me behold the trophy he was holding by its hair.

"Don't be shy, beauty," he said. "Look at what happens to the enemies of the Nation."

His two companions had already begun to strip the body.

My insides revolted at the sight of the head, blood still dripping from the neck. Spasms ran through my entire body. I retched. My breakfast of wine and bread, which had been churning in my stomach since the morning, splattered in a foul mess at my feet. I was shaking, my knees buckled, but I struggled to remain upright lest I should meet the same fate as the man in the silk stockings. I could already feel the steel of the cutlass against my own neck. I threw myself against Martial's chest.

"I will cry *Long live the Nation* as much as you want," I said, "but please do not make me climb there."

Martial caught me by the waist to prop me up. "She's been through enough for today," he told the others. "I'm going to take her home."

Carriages still drove up and down the street as usual, simply swerving to avoid the pile of bodies. Martial stopped a hackney, grabbed its occupant by his cravat, threw him out, pushed me inside and went in after me, while his comrade climbed next to the driver. I felt very cold in spite of the heat and was still shivering uncontrollably.

"Do you want to go to Rue Saint-Dominique?" asked Martial.

"No, please. Not there."

"Where then?"

My mind was blank. Martial must have seen that I could not take my eyes off the cadaver pile. He told the driver to move on, reached into his pocket for a handkerchief and wiped remains of vomit off my lips. He removed his jacket, which he wrapped around me in an attempt to make me warm. I rested my head on his shoulder without minding the bloodstains on his shirt or his smell of sweat.

"There, there," he said, "it's all over now. You just need to take some rest. Are you sure you don't know where you want to go? In Marseilles, I'd take you to my rooms and give up my bed for you, but I have no lodgings in this town. While I am working at La Force, I sleep on the straw in stables nearby with some of the comrades. I can't take you there. I wouldn't touch you, of course, and I'd keep the others away from you, but it's still no place for a person like you."

It was a while before I recovered my wits enough to recall the address of Manon's sister, on Rue de l'Hirondelle. When we arrived, I still felt dizzy. Martial took me in his arms and carried me to Louise's lodgings up three flights of stairs. Manon opened the door and let out a cry of horror. She told me later that she had believed at first that he was bringing them my corpse, for I looked like one. Everyone in Paris knew what was happening in the prisons and I had been given up for dead.

I will not attempt to describe the scene that followed. Aimée would not let go of my hand. The other workman left, but Martial carried me to Louise's bed, drew a chair and watched me for a while.

"Are you better?" he asked. "If you need anything, I'll get it for you."

I shook my head, unable to speak, and tried to smile at him.

"All right," he said at last, patting my hand. "I'll leave you with your friends. They look like they are going to take good care of you. I'd stay longer, but you'll want to undress. You don't need a man around."

≈ 63 ≈

My stomach was still upset. Manon made me sip some broth, undressed me and bathed me with a sponge. It felt very strange, after the squalor of the prison, to lie in Louise's clean bed, which she had insisted on giving up for me. I had trouble finding any rest. In the darkness, the memory of the agony of the prior day, the images of the pile of corpses, of the severed head of the man in the silk stockings, of the naked body of the Princess de Lamballe haunted me.

The next morning, to my surprise, Martial called.

"I was worried about you," he said. "I wanted to make sure you were recovering properly. You looked more dead than alive when I left last night. I'm still working at La Force, but I asked for a leave to call on you."

"I am feeling much better. There was nothing wrong with me, except for the effects of the fear I felt." I paused. "You were so kind to me yesterday. I can never thank you enough."

"Don't mention it," he said. "To me, the lives of those acquitted by the *people's court* are sacred. But, little lady, I also came to warn you. There are some who feel differently. They want to kill all aristocrats. *I* know that there are some decent folks among you, though not too many. It'd be a good idea for you and your little girl to leave Paris while you can."

"I believe you are right," I said. "I am grateful for your concern, and for your help yesterday." I hesitated. "I would like to give you something, if only to repay you for the hackney fare. I am sure that it came from your own pocket. I was too dazed last night to even think of it."

He raised his hand. "No, I won't take anything from you. There's no point in insisting. I did what I did because it was the right thing, and that's it."

"Then I am forever in your debt. May I ask another great favour from you, then?"

"What is it?"

"Can you be as kind to the other prisoners?"

"Not if they are enemies of the Nation. There can't be any quarter for those in wartime. I trust to the judgment of the *people's court*. Some of those priests and other rascals in the jails deserve no pity, yours or mine. *You*'re different. I'll soon be done working at La Force, because things are going briskly there. We'll run out of prisoners. Afterwards, I'll return to the Federate camp and ask to be sent to the army in Verdun. I'll defend my country to my last drop of blood."

"With men like you answering the call of duty," I said, "I feel no doubt of our victory. I do not know whether we will meet again." I took the jewel with Aimée's miniature from my pocket. "At least accept this. I am no longer a prisoner and you are free to take it now."

I wrote a note to prevent any accusations of theft and folded it inside the locket:

Gabrielle de Peyre to Elie Martial,
In token of her gratitude.
Paris, this 4th of September 1792.

I reached for his hand, opened it and put the jewel in it.

"Please accept it," I said. Tears came to my eyes. "For my sake."

He was looking at the locket, hesitating.

"All right then," he said at last, "since you wish it. I'll wear it under my shirt on the battlefield to bring me luck."

"I will be honoured if you do. May it protect you."

I held out my hand. He took it in an awkward manner, looked at it for a moment and kissed it. I embraced him and kissed him back on the cheek.

Martial and I had little in common, except for our native language and the feeling that neither of us might have very long to live. I do hope that he survived the war. He did kill prisoners at La Force. Yet during that terrible day, he was my sole comfort, the only voice of kindness I heard in the prison courtyard. If it had been my fate to die then, my end would have been less cruel thanks to him. He may have saved my life by taking me away from the pile of corpses and the murderer of the man in white stockings. Innocent or guilty, who cares now? Has there not been enough pain? Has not enough blood, on all sides, been shed to appease all thirst for revenge? Has not, after all these years, the time for forgiveness come?

I followed Martial's advice and sent Manon to purchase tickets for Aimée and me to depart on the first stagecoach for Auvergne. I knew that there was one leaving for Clermont at five every morning.

"May I go to Auvergne with you, My Lady?" Manon asked.

"There is nothing that I would like better, Manon. Yet I cannot take you away from Paris, where you have your sister, and a roof over your head. I am far from sure of my family's welcome."

After the events of the past weeks, I no longer feared anything my brother could do to me. I would have been happy and grateful to live with him if he had been willing to take me back. It remained to be seen whether he would help me after I had spurned his offers of assistance years earlier.

Manon begged me to reconsider, but I remained firm. She left for the coach office and returned an hour later in a state of great agitation.

"Oh, My Lady," she said, "what do you think? They just closed all the gates of Paris. Nobody can leave until further notice, even those who have a passport."

In all, the massacres in the prisons lasted five full days. All of the jails of Paris, which were overflowing after the recent wave of arrests, and some in the provinces, were emptied of their inmates, aristocrats, harlots, priests and common criminals alike. Some were released as I was, and over 1,000 "sentenced and executed per judgment of the people," as was written next to their names on the prison registers.

Outside the jails, life continued as usual in the capital. The shops remained open. The streets were still choked with carriages, pedestrians going about their business and vendors peddling their wares. In the cafés, Parisians gravely discussed the prison massacres as if they were happening in America. Ministers bleated a few speeches at the tribune of the Assembly, deploring "some excesses."

I often heard the 17th of August Tribunal mentioned during the days which followed my release. My thoughts then turned to my acquaintance on that court, but I was not desperate enough to risk applying for Pierre-André's help. I was hoping that those acquitted by the *people's courts* in the prisons would be immune from prosecution before the Tribunal.

The situation in Paris had now become dangerous enough for me to want to leave France. True, the French armies had won a decisive victory at the battle of Valmy and the Prussian advance had been stopped. Yet such success might not last. I wished to flee to England, which was not yet at war with my country. However, I could not imagine that a passport would be given to a person of my dubious credentials without the help of some influential character.

The only one of my friends who still had any position in the new regime was Lauzun, now called General Biron. Not only had he retained his rank of General under the Republic, he had been put in command of the Rhine Army. I had read that he had been called to Paris to report on the recent developments. I paid him a visit in his *little house* of Montrouge.

"My dearest," he said, embracing me, "what a relief! No one could tell me whether you had survived the massacres at La Force. You had disappeared and I hoped that you had managed to emigrate. What has happened to you?"

I told him of my adventures.

"I cannot imagine," he sighed, "you running for your life in the hallways of the Tuileries, thrown into jail, barely escaping the blades of the cutthroats. As for Villers, I always knew that he would repay your kindnesses by the most atrocious conduct. What has happened to our world, dearest friend?"

"I am afraid now, Lauzun. I should have fled after the 10th of August. I need a passport. Without one, I cannot leave Paris, let alone France."

"I have not the heart to deceive you, Belle. I cannot obtain one for you. All I can offer you is the key to this house. I must return to Strasbourg in two days, but you may stay here as long as you wish. The servants are trustworthy. No one will find you here."

"Thank you for your kindness, dear Lauzun, but all I would achieve by staying here is to compromise you. Right now I live with my maid's sister. I am safe there. I will not budge until I obtain a passport."

He shook his head sadly. "The young Republic needs generals and tolerates me, but everyone eyes me with suspicion because of what I used to be. I know of only one person who could help you: the Duke d'Orléans. Do you want me to speak to him on your behalf?"

I winced. "Only if you think that he would not expect anything in return."

"He is a better man than you believe, Belle. And he has retained much influence. He was elected to the new National Convention as a Representative for Paris. Have you heard that he asked the Municipality to officially change his name to *Philippe Egalité*?"

"I have." I could not help smiling. "And do you know what Hébert calls him?"

The *Père Duchesne* now referred to Orléans not as *Philippe Egalité*, "Philippe Equality," but as *Capet Bordel*, "Capet Brothel." Never before had I found Hébert's crudeness entertaining.

"Yes," said Lauzun, smiling, "Hébert does not seem to hold us libertines in high esteem. Yet the Duke d'Orléans, or *Egalité*, if you prefer, could obtain a passport for you."

"Please approach him on my behalf. But you know how I feel about him."

"You have always had exquisite taste, Belle. I will try my best." Lauzun reached for my hand and caressed it. "You declined the only help I can offer you, but would you please stop being so cruel? Would you at long last make an old man very happy?"

I laughed. There was something about Lauzun, a certain lightness, that always brought forth the happier side of life. I no longer cared whether he was married. He could have had as many wives as the heroes of the *Thousand and One Nights* without my thinking twice about it.

I shook my head. "Lauzun, dearest friend, I am as fond of you as ever, but I will not become your mistress at this time. You have a future in the Republic. I have none. If I were weak enough to link my fate to yours, I would drag you down without saving myself."

He did not take my refusal amiss and invited me to share his dinner, which I accepted. We reminisced about times past, their thoughtlessness, their sweetness, their frivolity, and spent a few very sad and very pleasant hours together. We both knew that these remembrances were our eulogy to a world that had just died before our eyes. He kept me in his arms a long time when I took my leave. I could feel silent sobs shaking him.

I never returned to my lodgings on Rue Saint-Dominique. Manon had left the place with Aimée on the day following my arrest and taken with her what remained of my belongings. Yet I could not stay much longer in Louise's lodgings without becoming a nuisance. They comprised a large all-purpose room and one bedroom and were not large enough to comfortably accommodate both sisters, Aimée and me. All Manon was able to locate on short notice and on my meager budget was a garret on the same street.

I sent her to sell my gowns, in particular the one I had worn in prison, to the used clothes dealers. With the money I purchased sturdy black cloth. I made a widow's dress, which I wore with a modest white muslin kerchief. That attire had the double advantage of making casual observers notice my clothing rather than my face and of allowing me to wear a widow's bonnet, a pleated white cap covered with a waist-long black crape veil. It would serve to hide my hair, which I had Manon cut six inches below shoulder length. It was thus less conspicuous and easier to dress now that I no longer had a maid. Aimée was sobbing as my locks fell to the floor of Louise's lodgings, but I was relieved to be rid of them. I stopped wearing any jewellery save my nuptial ring and tiny gold earrings.

I discarded all mementos of my life with Villers. Poor Aimée did not show such composure when I told her that we could not take all of her dolls with us, for she now had an entire collection of them. We kept only Margaret, the favourite. Many tears fell, but I remained firm. Even a single doll, especially one as large and expensive as Margaret, would be suspicious enough in our situation.

I called on Citizen Marcelin, the owner of the garret Manon had visited. The appellations of "Monsieur" and "Madame" were now officially discarded and replaced by "Citizen." Manon had found these lodgings deficient in many regards, but I was in a hurry and could not afford anything better. Aimée and I would have to share a bed in the only room. The rest of the furniture, coarse, scratched and grimy, consisted of a little table, two straw chairs, a portable alcohol stove, a nightstand and a chest of drawers with a washbasin on top. Its reddish paint was peeling, and in places even the plaster was missing. The room lacked a fireplace, and I could hear the wind whistling through the shaky window of the dormer. Yet it offered a view of the neighbouring roofs, the only pleasant thing about the room. I could imagine watching the swallows after which the street was named during the long evenings of the fair season, if I were still alive to see the next summer.

"Here it is, Citizen," said Marcelin. "A pretty room, as you can see."

He had used the familiar *thou*, which was becoming the preferred, "patriotic" form. It did not bother me much to be addressed in this manner by strangers. I did my best to return the favour, though I tended to revert to the formal, "aristocratic" *you* whenever I was not careful.

"How much is it?" I asked.

"Twelve francs a week. Mind you, if you can't pay rent, I'll throw you out without thinking twice about it, winter or no winter. Don't try to soften me by crying your eyes out. I've heard every story there is, and I just want my money." He scratched his neck. "Also, you should know that I'm a married man. I'm not interested in being paid in kind, if you catch my meaning."

The mere idea of paying Marcelin in kind made me wince.

"I hope at least," he continued, "that you're clean and won't damage my furniture."

"You will not find a more careful tenant than me, Citizen Marcelin."

"Your friend said you've a child. How old it is? Is it a boy or a girl?"

"A little girl, seven years old and very quiet."

"I hope so. I don't want any complaints from the other tenants about noise, or anything else for that matter." He wagged his finger at me. "If I find out that you're a harlot and receive men here, I'll report you to the Section. The Municipality just passed a new ordinance against whoring. I want none of that on my property. The last thing I need these days is trouble of any kind. Speaking of which, what did you say your name was?"

"Gabrielle Labro. I am a widow from Aurillac, in the Départment of Cantal."

"Don't worry, a pretty little woman like you can find a new husband in a trice. I'll need to see your passport. Like I told you already, I don't want any trouble with the authorities."

I took a deep breath. "Well, you see, Citizen Marcelin, my poor husband died last July. I found his affairs in a bad shape and discovered that his estate was owed over 1,000 francs by a caterer in Paris. The executor of his will is a rascal who declined to do anything to collect the debt. I decided to come here to take the matter into my own hands."

Villers had often said that I was a poor liar, but I had reached a time when telling untruths was a necessity. For inspiration, I recalled the fellow with large yellow teeth I had met on the stagecoach to Noirvaux five years earlier.

I looked straight at Marcelin as I continued: "On the stagecoach, I met with a stranger who proposed to help me find the caterer and assert my rights once we arrived. He seemed so very obliging. Unfortunately, he stole my portfolio, which contained my passport and most of my money."

"It's odd," said Marcelin, his eyebrow raised. "You don't look like someone who'd fall into that kind of stupid trap. But then you never know with women. Their brains seem to be located in their nether parts. Actually, it's true of many men too. So you want the room or not? I haven't all day."

"I will take it."

"It'll be twelve francs for the first week then, plus another hundred since you have no passport. And again, if you cause any trouble, I'll report you to the Section. Don't complain that you haven't been warned."

The same night, we moved our belongings, which were now reduced to my most treasured books, a few undergarments, shoes and jewellery, to our new lodgings. The doll Margaret of course accompanied us, hidden in a sack. Louise had handed me earlier that day a note from Lauzun.

> *I have spoken with the Duke d'Orléans. He is willing to help with your passport provided that you meet with him to discuss the matter. I had expected better from him.*
>
> *Please forgive me for failing you at such a time. I am sorry, Belle, more sorry than words can express.*
>
> *Good-bye, dearest, tender friend, for it would be too cruel to say farewell. Be safe.*

"It is ugly here, Mama," Aimée said when she looked around at the garret. "Can we not return to our old lodgings?"

"No, my treasure, we cannot. We should be grateful to have a roof over our heads. I cannot afford anything better than this."

"So we are poor now?"

"Yes, in a way, we are poor, but at least we are together. I am not in jail anymore. The prison was far uglier than this."

"You will not go back to jail, Mama, will you?"

"No. But we must be very careful. You have to tell everyone that your name is *Aimée Labro* and that your Mama is *Citizen Labro*."

"I liked my old name better."

"I find *Aimée Labro* very pretty too. Labro was the name of my nurse when I was little. I loved her and am proud to honour her memory in this manner. I am sure that you will become accustomed to it."

"And I do not like it when people are rude to you. Like Citizen Marcelin. Why does he not take off his hat when he talks to you? And he says *thou* to you. Why does he not call you *My Lady*?"

I could not repress a smile at the idea of Marcelin addressing me in such a manner.

"Because nobody says these things anymore, Aimée dear. Those who still do go to jail."

"But Manon calls you *My Lady*. Will she go to jail?"

"She does it out of habit, but it is a mistake. You are fortunate, because you are very young and it will be easier for you to accept these changes."

"But everything was so much better when we lived on Rue Saint-Dominique. I had you, and Miss Howard, and Manon, and all of my dolls."

"I know, dearest, but we have no choice. Also, please remember not to say *Rue Saint-Dominique*. It is called *Rue Dominique* now. We do not use saints' names for the streets anymore. Indeed it is better to forget that we ever lived there. And you must not mention Miss Howard to anyone."

"Why not?"

"Because she is English, and people think all Englishmen are spies. And the fact that you had a governess means that we were rich."

"Is it wrong to be rich now?"

"No, but when one has lost one's money, it makes people wonder."

"Did we lose our money because Monsieur de Villers died?"

"Yes, and it also has to do with many other things."

"Is he dead forever?"

I knelt in front of Aimée and looked into her eyes. "Yes, my dearest, the dead are dead forever. Their souls go to Heaven, and they do not come back. But we keep alive in our hearts the memory of those we loved. Then we join them for eternity when we die ourselves."

I saw tears in Aimée's dark eyes. "So the Duchess is dead forever too?"

"Yes, dearest. I know that it is very hard to lose the people we loved and the things we liked, but we must accept our fate and thank God for the blessings He still bestows on us."

I pressed Aimée in my arms, fighting my own tears.

On the 20th of September, the authorities created a new document, called a Civic Certificate, which was to be delivered by the Sections of Paris to good citizens upon their request. The next day, Marcelin popped out of his door as I entered his building. He lived in the porter's lodge, out of miserliness perhaps, and probably also to better keep an eye on his tenants.

"Citizen Labro," he said, "I've been thinking about something. Since you have no passport, it'd be good if you could procure one of those new Civic Certificates. You just need to go to the Section. They'll be happy to oblige a little widow like you."

"Certainly, I will go tomorrow."

"Fine, Citizen, but no later than that. You see, I like you because you seem a quiet sort of person, but I don't want to be accused of hiding aristocrats."

At eight in the morning the next day, I left Aimée with Manon and went to the Marseilles Section, which had jurisdiction over my new lodgings. I entered a vast hall, where a crowd was gathered. I walked to a guard seated at a desk and told him that I had come for a Civic Certificate.

"You're not alone, Citizen," he said. "All of these people are here for the same thing. You'll have to wait your turn."

He wrote my name, now Gabrielle Labro, on a sheet of paper. "Have a seat," he said, "if you can find one."

An old woman made room for me next to her on a bench. She was staring at me, and I was so afraid of being recognized that I almost left. Names were called, but things seemed to be proceeding very slowly. It was three in the afternoon before the guard called *Gabrielle Labro*. I followed him into an office where a man, smoking a long curved pipe, was seated. In a corner was a wicker basket filled with bottles of wine. He did not rise nor did he offer me a seat.

"So, Citizen," he said in the familiar mode, "where and when were you born?"

"In Aurillac, in the Départment of Cantal, on the 14th of July, 1769."

"Ah, the same day as the glorious storming of the Bastille. A good start. Let's have a look at your baptismal certificate."

"I did not take it with me when I left Auvergne. I did not think I would need it."

"You were very careless. All right then. Have you a residence certificate to prove that you have been honourably known in Paris since the beginning of the Revolution?"

"No, I only arrived last July." I told him the story of Widow Labro's woes.

"Are you telling me, Citizen Labro, that you arrived in Paris only two months ago, and that you have no passport?"

"It was stolen, along with most of my money."

"I don't care about your money, but without a passport, I can't give you a Civic Certificate. What proof have I that you are not an aristocrat or some other enemy of the Nation?"

"Citizen Secretary, you must believe me. My landlord threatens to turn me out if I cannot produce a Civic Certificate."

"Your landlord sounds like a good patriot. Listen, Citizen, I have nothing against you, but you are precisely the kind of suspicious character who should *not* receive a Civic Certificate. You say you arrived in Paris two months ago from Auvergne. How do I know that you are not an *émigrée*, illegally returned from the Netherlands or Germany? Can you at least produce a certificate of residence from Aurillac? Now, don't start crying."

Tears had come easily enough. I was hungry and my long wait had unnerved me. The man rose, offered me a chair in front of his desk and patted my back.

"I didn't mean to be harsh, Citizen," he said. "But even if I gave you your Civic Certificate, you'd also need the signature of the President of the Section. He wouldn't give it to you. So I'd be in trouble, and you still wouldn't receive what you want."

My tears redoubled.

"Do you know, Citizen," he continued, "that we must keep a list of the names, descriptions, and addresses of those who are denied a Civic Certificate? Believe me, if I were you, that's not the kind of list where I'd want to find myself. I'll tell you what I'll do, and that's already a great deal: I am not going to deny your Certificate, though in all fairness I should, so I won't have to put you on that list. I'll just prepare a Certificate, without giving it to you, and mention that you were adjourned until production of further proof. That way you won't be in trouble. Really it's all I can do for you."

I believed him. I dried my tears and, after fetching Aimée, returned to my lodgings.

Marcelin pounced on me before I could reach the stairwell. "So, Citizen Labro, do you have your Civic Certificate?"

"No, but it was not denied either. The Section needs to see my baptismal certificate. It will take only a little while to have it sent from Auvergne."

"So they wouldn't give it to you, would they? You look like you've been crying. I told you, it doesn't always work. All right, I'll give you a couple more days, but if you don't have it by the 1st of October, I'll report you."

September of 1792 witnessed the inception of the new National Convention that had replaced the old Legislative Assembly. The first act of the new Representatives was, by a unanimous vote, to confirm the overthrow of the monarchy and proclaim a Republic. The year 1792 became Year One of the French Republic, One and Indivisible.

Another event occurred, of lesser importance to the general public, but which would have a grave incidence upon my situation. During the night of the 15th of September, a gang of thieves broke into the *Garde-Meuble*, where the Crown jewels were kept. Diamonds, pearls, sapphires, emeralds and rubies were found on the streets of Paris. Good citizens returned them to the *Garde Meuble*. A beggar woman, having discovered "little stars" lying on the ground, brought them to the nearest police station and left without claiming any kind of reward.

The thieves were arrested a few days later. They were accused of being part of a royalist conspiracy to raise funds for the *émigrés*. The affair was thus deemed a political case and assigned to the 17th of August Tribunal, which sentenced them to death. A jeweler who had purchased some of the Crown diamonds at a bargain price was guillotined a few days later for receiving the Nation's stolen property. No one in Paris dared purchase precious stones. Overnight my diamonds, the sole source of my expected financial independence, became worthless.

Worse, I read in the *Moniteur* about the case of the novelist and royalist journalist Cazotte. During the September massacres, he had been jailed at L'Abbaye, where he had been acquitted. Following his release, he was arrested again and tried before the 17th of August Tribunal. Cazotte was found guilty and guillotined. The *Moniteur* listed Pierre-André as one of the three judges who had signed the death sentence. It was all too clear that the Tribunal did not intend to give any legal authority to the verdicts of the improvised *people's courts* formed in the prisons. My acquittal at La Force would not protect me.

Marcelin was ready to report me to the Section, which would lead promptly to a second arrest. The prospect of standing trial before the 17th of August Tribunal was dismal. My use of a false identity would make my case worse. After the theft of the Crown Jewels, Paris was abuzz with rumours of royalist conspiracies. Given my association with the Court, I would be assumed to be part of those plots.

Lauzun could do nothing. The Duke d'Orléans had put on his assistance a price I was unwilling to pay. Pierre-André remained my sole possible ally. If I wanted to appeal to him, I could delay no longer.

৺ 66 ৶

In the afternoon of the 27th of September, I prepared to go to the main Courthouse. My only hope was the memory Pierre-André had kept of me. I gazed at myself in the cracked mirror hanging above the chest of drawers in my garret. It reflected a pale, hollow-eyed face and a countenance matching my widow's dress. I shook my head in dismay. Would he recognize in me the blooming girl of fifteen he had met by the river, or even the young woman of the Champ de Mars, with a rose between her breasts?

I took Aimée to Manon and kissed my daughter good-bye, or farewell, depending on the outcome of my attempt. I repeated to myself for the hundredth time the reasons for my decision to seek Pierre-André's help. Aimée, poor child, saw my anguish and did her best to conceal her own. She held back her tears and threw her little arms around my neck. I left with Manon a note to my sister Madeleine, begging her to forgive my trespasses and to raise my daughter as her own. I asked Manon to find a way to send it if I did not return within twenty-four hours. Aimée squeezed my hand and I was off to the courthouse.

After entering the great gilded gates, I took a long look at the flights of stairs leading to the front doors. To my right was, through a small locked courtyard, the entrance to the prison of La Conciergerie, where were held those scheduled to appear before the 17th of August Tribunal. It might be the first step on their journey to the guillotine. I shuddered and looked away. I crossed the *Cour du Mai*, the main courtyard, and climbed the monumental stairs. Once inside the sprawling building, I asked an usher for directions to the premises occupied by the Tribunal. It was shortly after six in the evening.

A gendarme, who did not seem much older than me, was seated at a desk in a white and gold antechamber. I told him that my name was Labro and that I came to see Citizen Coffinhal to report a conspiracy related to the massacre of the Patriots on the 10th of August. The guard went down a hallway. He returned after a few minutes.

"Citizen Coffinhal has no time for you," he said. "You must report the facts to Citizen Fouquier, the head of the Grand Jury. You're in luck; he's still at work. I'll take you to him directly."

I sat in one of the chairs facing the gendarme's desk. "I am not leaving. I want to speak to Citizen Coffinhal and no one else."

The gendarme looked unhappy. "Well, when Citizen Coffinhal says no, I leave it at that. I don't see why I should make him cross. Citizen Fouquier, on the other hand, is good-humoured and soft-spoken, especially with the ladies, I mean female citizens. So it'd be wise of you to talk to him."

"No, that would not do at all," I said, looking straight at the gendarme. "Citizen Coffinhal and I are from the same country. I have documents of the utmost importance that are written in my native language, which is also his. If I cannot see him tonight, I will have to send him word that you would not let me speak to him. He will probably be very unhappy, because this is an urgent matter."

The gendarme hesitated. He sighed and disappeared once more. I heard a voice shouting upstairs. The gendarme returned, a little paler, and asked me to follow him.

We went down the hallway and up a corkscrew staircase. I was shown into a room on the second floor of one of the medieval towers. From the window, one could see the Seine glowing grey in the light of the late afternoon. Across the river, the ragged offerings of the used clothes peddlers, hanging from poles, floated gently in the wind like the flags of poverty.

The room was furnished with a marqueterie desk, in front of which were two chairs for visitors. A hat *à la* Henri IV, upturned in front, with black feathers, a matching cape and a gilded medal on a tricolour ribbon, all part of the new judges' uniform, lay on a small table. I could not help noticing that the hat was the same shape as the one worn by the Representatives of the Nobility at the opening of the Estates General, except for the dark colour of the feathers.

Pierre-André, dressed in black down to his stockings, was seated at the desk. He was reviewing papers and gave no sign of looking up when I entered. He said in the Roman language, without rising or inviting me to have a seat: "Come to the point, Citizen Labro. I hope for your sake that you are not disturbing me for nothing."

Pierre-André had used the patriotic *thou*. Yet, in his mouth, it brought to mind the past. I forgot all of the speeches I had rehearsed for the occasion.

"Citizen Judge," I said, also in the Roman language and in the familiar style, "you may remember me . . ."

He muttered an oath and rose from his chair, which screeched against the stone floor. For what seemed a long time, he stood glaring at me.

"As if one could forget the likes of you! How could I fail to recall the name of Labro? The very first lie you told me. And those amazing disclosures of yours are nothing but lies too, are they not?" He raised his voice. "Answer me, Citizen. You come here under an assumed name and false pretenses, and then you stand here stupidly staring at me. You are still the same, imagining that you can lie with impunity. But times have changed, if you have not. Answer me, or I will call the gendarme to have you arrested."

I mustered all of my resolve and fixed my eyes on his face. "Yes, Citizen Judge, I lied. It was the only way to see you."

"You wanted to see me! At last! After you have ignored me all these years! It must not have been worth your while to call on me after I rescued you at the Champ de Mars. That was after all only a minor service. I guess your situation feels a bit more unsettled these days, and this gives you a higher regard for my society. There is nothing I find so heartwarming as a disinterested visit from an old friend. So tell me what brings you here. Be brief. I have not all night to chat with you."

"I was arrested at the end of August and imprisoned at La Force."

"Ah, yes. Hébert and the *people's court* at La Force let you go. Not for long. We keep an eye on characters like you. You will find that real judges are not so easily mollified by your charms and your tears. Now let us come to the point. Why are you here? In one sentence."

"I need a Civic Certificate under the name of Labro, and my Section refuses to give it to me."

"What do you imagine?" he asked, sneering. "That the purpose of the Civic Certificates is to allow aristocrats to hide under a false identity? And what has it to do with me?"

"I thought that you might help me obtain mine."

"No less! How so?"

"By telling my Section that you can vouch for me. They will listen to you."

He stared at me. "You are asking me to lie to your Section? Have you taken leave of your senses?"

"You rescued me last year, Pierre-André. I thought that you might be so generous as to help me again."

I reached for his hand. He drew back. "I do not recall allowing you to use my given name."

"I am sorry, Citizen Judge."

"Spare me your apologies. Here is what I will do for you, and I hope that you will be grateful, for a change: I will let you go this time." He pointed towards the door. "Leave before I change my mind."

I looked straight at him. "No. Have me arrested if you want, but at least hear me before calling the gendarme. In any event, if I do not receive my Civic Certificate, it is only a matter of days before I go back to jail." I took a deep breath. "For years I have wished to tell you these things. I wanted to marry you. Oh, I wanted it so. I wanted to elope with you. I did not hesitate for a moment when I received your letter. I was on my way to join you at the crossroads of Escalmels that night when my brother caught me."

"I know. I knew the next morning. Your brother summoned Jean-Baptiste to Fontfreyde to tell him that you had tried to elope, that it aggravated my case because it established my *seduction* of you, a crime punishable by the gallows or the wheel." Pierre-André stared in the distance. "I waited all night for you at the crossroads. I kept hearing your step, your voice in the rustle of the wind. I thought I saw your figure in every wisp of fog, in every shadow. I waited for you until dawn. Only then did I abandon hope." He shook his head in anger. "What a fool I was! Two weeks later, I heard that you had married Peyre."

"But I was forced to do it. I remained locked in a cellar until the very day of my wedding. Even so, I would not have married the Baron, but my brother threatened to have you sentenced to death. I wanted to save you."

"At the time it drove me insane to think of you in that man's bed. But it does not matter now." A pulse was throbbing at his temple. "What matters is that, after your widowhood, when you were free, you became a whore."

I smarted under the insult. "I had but one lover," I said. "I became his mistress to support myself and my daughter."

"Let us not quarrel about my choice of words. Financial inducement is as good a reason as any for a woman to prostitute herself. I believe that it is even the most common."

"My husband had left me penniless. I had no other choice except entering a convent."

"No choice? You knew that I was in Paris, you knew of my profession. Nothing would have been easier than to find me. I lived less than a mile from you, but for all you cared, I might just as well have been in Persia."

"So you wanted to see me again?"

"Did I *want* it? I might even have been enough of an idiot to marry you."

Startled, I looked up at him. "You still loved me then?"

"Oh, I was cured of my illusions when I heard that you had become Villers's kept woman. That was better than marrying a lowly attorney, was it not?"

"I would never have guessed that you still cared for me." Tears came to my eyes. "If only I had known. . . . I too wanted to see you, but I was ashamed to seek you."

Pierre-André was gripping the back of his chair with both hands, his knuckles white. "But now you are not ashamed to seek me?"

"I am, but there is more than my life at stake. What would happen to my daughter if I died? I hesitated a long time before coming here. I knew that you would despise me all the more for it. Yet even if there were only one chance in a thousand that you would help me, I could not afford to let that chance pass."

"I see. Now, My Lady, you are desperate enough to humble yourself before the vile commoner you used to scorn. The stuff of tragedy. This brings us back to an earlier question of mine to which you have not responded. What made you believe that I would help you?" His eyes narrowed. "What do you imagine? That I have treasured your memory to this day? That I have hoped all these years for this moment? That I still love you?"

For a moment I caught myself wishing it were true. I shook my head sadly. "I only hoped that, even if you had stopped caring for me long ago, you might feel pity for my plight."

"Your plight! I feel exactly the same pity for your plight as for that of all other aristocrats, which is to say that it does not keep me awake at night." He walked from behind his desk and stood in front of me. "Now let us forget about pity, and love, and old times. Let us have a serious talk, Citizen. What have you to offer that could tempt me?"

"I have diamonds of great value."

"I take no bribes. I find it repulsive, as well as extremely dangerous, in my situation. Anything else?"

I hesitated.

"There has to be something else," he added, frowning. "What is it? It must be interesting, or you would not have so much trouble saying it. I am impatient to hear it. Come, Citizen."

I closed my eyes. "You may have me," I said under my breath.

"Louder, please. I am not hard of hearing, but when you mumble, I cannot understand you."

"You may have me," I repeated.

He raised his eyebrow. "*Have* you? I have not the advantage of understanding the jargon of the nobility. We live in a Republic now. Nobody owns anyone else. What do you mean?"

I bit my lip and kept silent.

"I might have some idea of what you propose," he continued, "but in matters of such delicacy, I would not want to be presumptuous and assume too much. Be more clear."

"You may . . ." I could go no further.

"All right, Citizen, I will help you of your little difficulty. Are you by any chance offering to have intimate relations with me?"

In spite of the humiliation, I was relieved. "Yes."

He paused. "Is your offer valid for one time only, or an entire night, or several occasions?"

"As you like."

"Excellent. And you would, I suppose, leave to my discretion the manner, or manners, in which I would have the pleasure to enjoy your person."

My cheeks were burning. "Yes."

"Really I am flattered by the improvement of my standing in your eyes. Last year, I did not deserve a simple visit, and now you find me worthy of . . ."

I drew a deep breath.

"My apologies," he continued. "I did not mean to shock you by the coarseness of my language. Let me rephrase in a genteel manner. You are offering me something of immense value, something more precious than your diamonds: the leftovers of the great lords of the Court. I should be grateful, I suppose, like a lackey who is presented with the scraps from his master's table. Truth be told, Citizen, I was beginning to worry whether such a proposal would be forthcoming in the course of our conversation."

He looked at me from head to toe. "I have not failed to observe the manner in which you are dressed. In itself, it did not seem likely to lead to anything. Then I thought again. A person of your experience would know that some men are aroused by modest attire in an attractive female. It does leave more to the imagination. There is still another possibility: you may have thought that your widow's costume would set forth your woeful situation and mollify me without any recourse to indecent offers. You know from past experience my delicacy of behaviour and may have hoped that I would help you without expecting a return. You were saving your interesting proposition for the very end, in case everything else failed. This must mean that you have played all of your cards."

"You have put more thought into this than I. This is the only gown I have."

"My mistake then. Forgive me. But how rude of me! Lost as I was in the meanders of your motives, I was forgetting to respond to your offers. Let me correct this omission. In addition to overestimating the effect of your charms, which are somewhat dulled right now, you seem to have forgotten that there is a great deal of competition in your field. What you propose, I can buy for five francs in any of the brothels of the *Palais-Royal*, excuse me, the *Palais-Egalité*. The ladies there are always happy to entertain me and they at least do not labour under the illusion that they are doing me the greatest favour in the world by spreading their thighs. I must decline. Anything else?"

His bitterness broke me at last. I burst into tears.

"No, nothing else then?" he continued. "Now that you have appealed in vain to my higher impulses, greed and lust, we have reached the unfortunate conclusion that I have no reason to help you. You were wrong not to accept my earlier offer to let you go. You are now guilty of an attempt to bribe a judge. It will add nicely to the other charges against you. You are going back to jail, Citizen Peyre."

I fell to my knees and rested my forehead on his thigh. "If you ever felt anything for me, Pierre-André, have mercy on me."

"Rise. Nothing disgusts me more than this abject servility inherited from the Old Regime. Look at me when you speak to me."

I was unable to move. He seized me by the arm to draw me to my feet.

"I am no brute after all," he continued, still holding me. "I will give you one last chance if you answer the following question to my satisfaction: would you ever have come to me if it were not to save your life? Think well. If you say yes, it might be one lie too many. If you say no, I might not find the truth palatable. Candor might not be a wise choice in your situation. A difficult decision, and you have so much at stake."

"Please help me. You cannot imagine what it was to be in jail during the massacres. I heard the cries of the other prisoners being slaughtered. I had to wait for days before my fate was decided. I do not want to go back there. Now you are telling me that you might help me if I give you the right answer. Is it true, or are you only tormenting me?"

"Why not humour me by giving me your response?"

"You will be angry whether I say yes or no."

"Perhaps. You will not find out until you answer. What is sure to make me angry, however, is the lack of a response."

"I cannot think right now. You are so harsh that I do not know what to say."

"Ah no, it would be too easy. You shed a few tears, you throw yourself at my feet, and you think you may dispense with any explanations. It will not do. I want an answer, not because I am harsh, but because I wish to know whether you take me for an imbecile, a fair query under the circumstances. Let me repeat one last time before I lose my temper: would you ever have come here if it were not to save your life? I want to hear it. What is it? Yes? Or no?"

"No."

He slowly raised his open hand. It came down so fast that I saw only a blur. My mother had often slapped me, and I remember to this day the stinging sensation on my cheek, but this was of a different order. The force of the blow stunned me and sent me tumbling across the room. I fell. Blinded for a moment, I heard Pierre-André walk briskly towards me. The correction would now begin in earnest. I raised my arm to protect my face.

He was content to raise me by the elbow and lead me to one of the chairs, where I collapsed. He took a handkerchief from his pocket, poured onto it water from a carafe on his desk and applied it to my face. I recoiled from his hand.

"I am not going to hit you again, Gabrielle," he said. "As a rule, I do not strike women. I made this one exception in your favour because I had wanted to do it for many years and you gave me ample provocation tonight. Keep this on your cheek for a while. The cold will prevent it from swelling. And stop weeping. You look awful."

I still could not see clearly. Tears were rolling down my cheeks in a steady stream, not from pain because I was too dazed to feel any, but from the shock of the blow.

"It was a mistake to come here," he continued. "I will not help you. Now before you go, I want to know your address."

I raised my eyes to him.

"Yes," he said, "out of the goodness of my heart, I will let you go. Do you still live on Rue Dominique?"

"No. I cannot afford it anymore and I am afraid of being arrested there."

"Where then?"

"Why? Are you going to have me arrested later?"

He dipped a quill in the inkwell on his desk. "Write it down. And do not ever lie to me again."

He handed me the pen and pushed a sheet of paper towards me. In a shaky hand, I wrote my new address. It did not enter my mind to give him a false one. He was sitting sideways on his desk, his arms folded, watching me while I struggled to regain my composure. I was reluctant to leave, to acknowledge my defeat. I cast one last look at him, the man I had loved many years before, the man I had bartered my innocence to protect.

He walked to the door, opened it and shouted the name of the gendarme, whom I heard running up the stairs as if all the hounds of hell were at his heels. I had no choice but to return Pierre-André's handkerchief. He picked up my widow's headdress, which had fallen to the floor. The gendarme appeared as I was trying to rearrange my hair.

"See Citizen Labro out," said Pierre-André. "She feels unwell."

The gendarme made a movement to offer me his arm, but after a glance at Pierre-André, thought better of it. He led me downstairs. Once we were out of earshot of the chambers, he began to talk to me.

"You look mightily shaken, but then Citizen Coffinhal has this effect on people. He's the judge they pick to examine witnesses in chambers. In the courtroom too, the accused are afraid of him, much more so than of Citizen Osselin, the President. It's that voice of his, and he's so tall and fierce. I tried to warn you, but you wouldn't listen when I told you to see Citizen Fouquier instead. From where I sit down here, I could hear Citizen Coffinhal shout at you. The way things were going, I thought he was calling me to have you arrested. You're lucky he let you go." He paused to look at me. "Citizen, you do look unwell. Let me call a hackney."

"You are very kind, but I live close by. Walking will do me good."

It was cool outside, and dark, which was a comfort. Once alone, I lost my way. The main courthouse is located on the Island of the City, and I lived on the Left Bank of the Seine. I had only to follow Rue de la Barillerie southwards, cross the Saint-Michel Bridge and turn right on the tiny Rue de l'Hirondelle to return to my garret. In spite of my familiarity with the streets of Paris, I no longer knew where my steps were taking me. The events of the evening kept recurring in my mind and erased any other thought. I walked for a while in the direction of the north. The stench of the *Châtelet* district brought me to my senses. I retraced my steps. My head was hurting and I was trying not to think of what the future held.

I reached my lodgings at last. I thought for a minute of going farther down the street to fetch Aimée, but I had not the courage to acknowledge my failure. Also, I did not wish to inflict upon my daughter, now that we slept in the same bed, the sight of a second arrest should it take place that night. I removed only my shoes, my cap and my kerchief and kept the rest of my clothes on. I lay on the bed, blew out the candle and remained in the dark, my eyes wide open, alert to any noises from the stairwell.

It was not long before I heard footsteps. There was a knock at my door. My hands were shaking so much that I had trouble lighting the candle. I did not ask who was there before turning the key into the lock. Pierre-André's figure filled the entire doorway. He was alone, wearing boots and civilian clothes. I stared at him in silence for a moment.

"Are you going to slam the door in my face?" he asked.

"I am sorry. Please enter."

He looked around. "Your circumstances, Citizen, seem less prosperous than in the past. Where is your daughter?"

"I left her with a friend. I thought that you would have me arrested."

"Not tonight. I am here because I have decided to save five francs after all."

I looked at him. "You are still angry."

"Have I not good cause to be?"

"Not anymore. I may be dead in a few weeks. At least, I will be in jail. I escaped twice, at the Palace on the 10th of August and then at La Force, but the end is near, I feel it. You will have your revenge without having to do anything. You can see me squirm before you in the accused's chair. You can watch my face as my sentence is read. So why be angry with me any longer? I know that you will not help me. It was stupid of me to expect otherwise. I was clinging to any hope, and you were the last one."

While I was speaking, he removed his coat, waistcoat and necktie, which he hung on the back of a chair.

"You are here tonight," I continued. "For this alone I am grateful, regardless of what you do afterwards. We have so little time left. Let us not throw it away."

"Let us not indeed. I, for one, intend to enjoy myself." He sat on the bed. "Why are you so demure? You proposition me, and then you say that you are grateful for my visit, but you have not kissed me, embraced me, undressed me. I have yet to feel your hands and lips caress me."

As much as I wanted to draw closer to him, I could not bring myself to cross the few feet that separated us. Everything I had said or done, or failed to do, had only driven him further away from me.

"I am tired of waiting," he said at last. "Since you do not want to do anything on your own, I will prompt you. First, I want a good look at you. Hurry now."

He watched me undress. He remained seated on the bed in silence, showing no emotion. It cost me great effort to remove each article of clothing under his eye. At last I was down to my chemise. I looked up at him.

He shook his head. "No," he said. "This is not good enough. I want to see you standing naked before me."

I took a deep breath and slipped the chemise over my head. I could not meet his eye.

"There is no need to be shy," he continued. "You are beautiful like this. Come here."

He reached for my wrist and made me sit in his lap. He slowly explored my breasts, my stomach, the inside of my thighs with his fingers. I kept my eyes on his hands, larger than any I had seen, dark against my skin. He encircled my waist with both of them.

"Stop shaking," he said. "I will not hurt you. I want only to *have* you, as you say, more thoroughly than any man ever had you. Nothing worse."

Pierre-André kissed me deeply, deliberately, as he had done the first time by the river, years earlier. The memory of that day rushed to me, so vivid that it was real. I could sense the heat of that June afternoon under the shade of the little wood. I was astonished to feel the same emotions anew. I kissed him back, hungry for him.

At fifteen I had not feared him. I had lain on the pebble bank by the Cère River, ready to let him take me. I had trusted him. I had loved him. He had loved me too, I was sure of it. I was also sure that he would have me arrested in the morning. I no longer cared. We were united again. The past and present were one. The future did not exist beyond the next few hours.

I wrapped my arms around his chest and rested my head against his neck. My lips caressed the smooth skin there, then moved up to rub against the roughness of his chin and cheek, and down again to feel the firmness of the muscles under the open collar of his shirt. He seized my head between his hands and kissed me more urgently.

"Now," he said.

"Oh yes, now."

He laid me down gently on the bed and, keeping his eyes fixed on me, rose to undress.

Naked, he looked still taller and stronger. The breadth of his torso tapered to a slender, muscular waist. His body was the same copper colour as his face and hands, with a narrow line of black hair running down the middle of his chest and stomach.

His arms closed around me. I was his. The promise made and breached years ago was fulfilled. His passion became mine. Through the night I clung to him as to life itself, to the last hours of my freedom, so few, so brief, so precious.

At last, Pierre-André drifted off. I watched him, fighting sleep as long as I could. Time was slipping through my fingers. I too must have dozed. He was shaking me by the shoulder. There was a faint hint of dawn in the sky. It was all over. Now that the time had come to be brave, fear had returned, like a fist in my stomach. I huddled against him, my eyes closed, to steal a few more moments of warmth and safety.

"Oh, please," I whispered, "not yet."

He shook me again, more forcefully. "Gabrielle, enough of this. I have to go. Awaken if you still want me to help you."

"What did you say?" I asked, startled.

"Did you not hear me?"

"I cannot believe it."

"You are wrong. I mean it."

"How will I ever repay you?"

He looked at me coldly. "You already did. I took you with great pleasure and will leave you without any regret. I do not need your gratitude, Gabrielle. After today, I want nothing more to do with you. Do you promise never, for any reason, to seek me again?"

"I do."

"It is half past five now. I arrive at the Courthouse at seven and do not want to change my habits today. I need to go to my lodgings first. I will meet you in an hour in front of your Section. Be on time, because I will not wait a moment longer."

He rose, poured water from the ewer into the basin and washed briefly. He ran his hands on his face, gathered his clothes and proceeded to dress. I did the same. I had put on my stockings and was tying my garters. They were the ones I had embroidered a few years earlier with forget-me-nots and a *G* crowned by a Baron's coronet. Pierre-André, tying his cravat, was looking at them.

"Show me your garters," he said.

I handed him one of them. He ran his forefinger on the monogram and coronet.

"Has it occurred to you that you could be searched if you were arrested? How would you explain this, Citizen Labro? Give me the other one."

He put them both in his waistcoat pocket. I tied on plain black garters.

"Should you have any other things emblazoned with this kind of aristocratic rubbish," he said, "now is the time to discard them. It makes no sense for me to take risks on your account if you do not pay attention to your own safety."

"You are right. I will be careful."

"I am starving," he said. "Let me have some bacon and eggs before I leave."

Meat and eggs were beyond my means. I now bought the cheapest bread, a brownish mixture of corn, oats, potatoes and, according to some, sawdust.

"I have only river water and bread to offer you," I said, "but if you wait a minute, I will run downstairs to buy something better at the inn."

Pierre-André glanced at the half-loaf on the table. "No, thank you. I have no time to waste. I will have breakfast at the Courthouse." He looked around. "Do you intend to stay in this hovel? There is no fireplace and it is right under the eaves. You will catch your death here this winter, especially if you do not eat properly."

"This is all I can afford until I can sell my diamonds. Even living like this, I will see the end of my savings before long."

I regretted these words as soon as I saw him search his pockets. He found an *assignat* of fifty francs, which he left on the nightstand. I took his hand in both of mine and pressed it to my cheek and lips. He withdrew it.

"I told you I do not want your gratitude," he said. "Use the money to buy decent food. Half past six in front of your Section."

✂ 68 ✂

I was waiting for Pierre-André well before the appointed time in front of the Marseilles Section. I breathed a sigh of relief when I saw him arrive precisely at half past six, wearing the black suit of his judge's uniform, but without the cape or medal and with a regular hat. He did not greet me, barely looked at me and pushed me by the shoulder in front of him as we entered the building. He paused to pull out of his pocket and tie around his waist a tricolour sash fringed in gold, the emblem of his functions at the Municipality. A crowd was already gathered in the waiting room where I had spent many hours a few days earlier. He spoke to the guard on duty, who disappeared into an office and, a minute later, invited us to enter. The Secretary rose.

"Greetings and fraternity, Citizen Judge," he said. "What brings you here?"

"Sit down, Citizen Secretary. This woman tells me you are giving her some trouble over her Civic Certificate. There is no reason for it. I know her; she is a good Patriot."

"Yes, that's right, I recognize her. She says she came from Cantal last

July, but she can't produce a passport or even a baptismal record or a residence certificate. Her papers were stolen, supposedly. She says she's the widow of a cheese merchant, but, if you want my opinion . . ."

"No, I do not want your opinion. As I believe I told you already, I know her. You would not doubt my word, I am sure."

"Nobody would, Citizen Judge. That's not what I meant. It's just that we need to see some evidence of what she says. Who's going to explain to the President of the Section that I gave her a Civic Certificate without any proof?"

Pierre-André rested both of his hands flat on the desk and threw his weight forward until his chest was only inches from the face of the officer. He lowered his voice. "You have all of the evidence you need right in front of you, Citizen Secretary. Are you telling me that you disregard my testimony?"

The Secretary drew back and muttered indistinct apologies.

"Fetch the President immediately," continued Pierre-André in a louder tone.

"I didn't mean any offense, Citizen Judge. Come to think of it, there can't be a better proof of Citizen Labro's story than your word."

The Secretary took out a portfolio with a shaky hand and retrieved my incomplete certificate. He crossed out "adjourned until production of further evidence," signed it and handed it to me.

"Now, Citizen Labro, all you need to do is go next door for the President's signature."

Pierre-André took the piece of paper from my hands and held it in front of the Secretary's face.

"So you want this woman to walk around with a certificate full of your scribblings?" he asked. "It would be worse than none at all. One would think that she carries a forged document. Give her a clean one. I will keep this one and destroy it myself."

The Secretary opened his mouth, but after a look at my companion, said nothing and hastened to prepare a new certificate. Pierre-André reviewed it and slapped the man in the back with such cordiality that he almost fell off his chair.

"Thank you for clearing up this matter so quickly, Citizen Secretary. When good patriots receive their Civic Certificates, it makes it easier to detect and punish the enemies of the Nation."

We went to the next office, where the President of the Section, sitting with several other men at a long table, also recognized Pierre-André, chatted with him for a minute, signed my certificate without looking at it and affixed to it the seal of the Section. I had received in less than fifteen minutes what I had waited and begged for in vain for hours.

Once on the street, I turned towards Pierre-André. He was no longer there. Towering above the crowd, he was already walking away. He had left without taking leave of me. I followed him at a distance in the direction of the river until I turned towards Rue de l'Hirondelle.

I could now fetch Aimée. With the precious Certificate in my pocket, my step felt quicker and lighter. I ran up the stairs to Louise's lodgings. When Manon opened the door, no words were needed. There was a smile on my face which nothing could repress. She cried with joy and we embraced. Aimée was waking. A new period of hope and happiness opened before me. Even my financial distress did not seem so dire anymore. Thanks to Pierre-André, I now had fifty francs in my pocket. Two months earlier, I would not have stooped to pick up that *assignat* if I had dropped it on the street, but as Pierre-André had observed the night before, times had changed. Now that I was in possession of the Civic Certificate, I could find work to support us. Manon herself was still without a place.

"Louise knows a laundress who needs a servant, Madam," she said, "but it's backbreaking work for very little pay. You wouldn't be able to do it for more than a couple of days without exhausting yourself. It'd break my heart to see your beautiful hands wrecked by those harsh soaps. Even I, after having been Your Ladyship's maid, have refused that offer."

"Manon, please stop addressing me as *Your Ladyship*. Those titles can only create trouble for both of us. Why not call me *Citizen Labro*? It is my official name now. And we cannot afford to be too fastidious about the work we can find."

"It will not feel right to call you *Citizen*. I will try, though. As for work, I would hope to find you something like sewing or embroidery."

"I have enough money to last a couple of months if I am careful, but I am more than ready to take any kind of work. Embroidery is less in demand these days, but sewing would suit me."

Aimée and I returned to our garret. I stopped by the porter's lodge to show Marcelin my Civic Certificate.

"Good," he said, returning it to me. "I knew you couldn't be an aristocrat. You're too decent a person for that."

I seized Aimée's hand and hastened towards the stairs.

"You had a visitor last night," he continued, "that great hulking fellow."

I turned around, looking straight at Marcelin. "He is a cousin of mine."

"Is he? He calls at odd hours for a cousin. Not that I mind, Citizen Labro. He must be on good terms with the authorities since you received your Civic Certificate." Marcelin grinned. "He may visit you every night if he likes. You did what you had to do, that's all. It's the result that counts, like they say."

I hurried upstairs. When I pushed open the door to the garret, tears came to my eyes. I was reminded of the night. How I wished Pierre-André had said that he still loved me, that he wanted to see me again. Now I realized that *I* loved him, that *I* wanted to see him again. In his arms, I had felt more than pleasure, more even than happiness. I had felt that we should never be parted. Then I chastised myself for indulging in such thoughts. Of course he did not want anything to do with me. He had put himself at risk to secure my Civic Certificate, a service I would never be able to repay. What right had I to hope for more? Once again destiny was tearing us asunder.

ঞ 69 ঞ

On the following Sunday, Aimée and I enjoyed a luncheon of boiled beef stewed with lentils and carrots, which I had purchased at the inn. It was a celebration, the first Sunday after I had obtained my Civic Certificate. We had nearly finished our meal when I heard a familiar step and a knock at the door. I ran to open it. It was indeed Pierre-André. In my confusion, I made a deep curtsey, my forehead almost touching the floor, as I had done before the Queen on the day of my presentation. Then I remembered what he had said about the marks of servility inherited from the Old Regime. My embarrassment increased. I rose in haste and gestured to him to enter. I still could not find any words to greet him.

"*Diou sia çains*," Pierre-André said. It is the traditional blessing in the Roman language, "God be here," that one speaks in Auvergne upon entering a house. I felt my eyes burning. I had not heard it in five years. It meant more to me than anything else he could have said. It was an expression of his respect, his goodwill, his remembrance of the old days and the old country.

He was looking intently at Aimée. "This must be your daughter."

"Yes. She is called Aimée."

I wanted to tell him that I had named her because of him, because that was the term of endearment he had used with me. Yet I could not. Aimée herself did not know it.

"She looks just like you," he said, "except for her colouring."

I was grateful that he did not mention her father. "Would you like to share our meal?" I asked. "I used some of your money to buy meat. No matter what you say, I will never be able to thank you enough for your kindness."

"I already ate, thank you. Can you take this child away? I need to speak to you."

I put Aimée's cloak on her shoulders and hastened to take her to Manon's.

"My goodness, My L— I mean, Citizen Labro, what's the matter?" she asked. "You look so pale. You're not going to be arrested again, are you?"

"I cannot tell yet, Manon. Something unexpected has happened."

My head spinning, I hurried back to the garret. Pierre-André was sitting on his haunches, looking out the dormer. He rose and looked at me. For a moment, we were both at a loss for words.

"What a surprise this is," I managed to say at last. "You did not want to see me again."

He smiled. "True. I did change my mind more than once in the course of our recent acquaintance. Can you not guess why I am here today?"

"No." Indeed the wild hope that he had returned because he wanted me had entered my mind. Yet I dared not believe it, let alone say it.

"When I came here the other night, Gabrielle, my intention, or so I believed, was only to humiliate you, to take my revenge for your abandonment of me."

"I know. I was convinced that you would have me arrested in the morning."

"Some idea you have of me! Why did not you tell me to go to hell?"

I had nothing to hide from him now. "I did not want to die without being yours, if only for a few hours."

He had walked to the other end of the room and turned slowly to me. "So you let me take you, believing that I was so depraved as to send you to jail after enjoying you all night." He shook his head. "I meant only to treat you like a whore and to leave as soon as I had enough of you. That was my first mistake. When I found you in this garret, in your plain black dress, stripped of your rank, of your luxury, of even the hated name of your husband, I saw the Gabrielle I had met by the river."

He sat on a chair and drew me to him. "I had yearned for you all these years and you gave yourself to me wholeheartedly. I could not abandon you to your fate. Yet after I had decided to help you, I resolved never to see you again. It seemed easy enough while I was still in your bed, feeling you, warm and soft, against me. I had not begun to miss you yet."

He tugged on my kerchief and touched the skin between my breasts. I shuddered. So it was true, he still loved me. I closed my eyes, dizzy with happiness, and stroked his hand.

"When I left you in front of your Section," he continued, "my resolution had begun to falter. It took all of my fortitude to part with you. That explains, if it does not excuse, the uncouth manner in which I went my own way. I reached the courthouse and went to work. I thought that I would erase you from my mind in the course of a day or two. I was wrong again. The more time passed, the more I thought of you." He sighed. "I had to remind myself that any association with you can destroy my position, even put my life in danger. I have managed to keep my mind otherwise occupied in the courtroom, but I cannot go to my chambers without remembering your visit there or lie in my bed without thinking of yours. I decided to break the spell. I went to the *Palais-Egalité* this morning, Gabrielle. I closed my eyes to imagine that I was holding you, and not some poor trollop, in my arms. All I achieved was to miss you more. Forgive me."

He was looking up at me, holding my waist with both hands. "So here I am, my beloved," he said, "three days after I asked you to seek me no more. I told you years ago that I wanted you forever. It is still true."

I reached for him and held him against my breast. "Pierre-André, never let me go again."

We spent the afternoon together. He was not yet thirty. I had turned twenty-three two months earlier. Life had separated us, tried us in different ways and taught us different lessons. He now held my fate in his hands. The world we knew had collapsed in successive waves of violence, to be replaced by a new one, governed by unpredictable rules that were unfolding before our eyes. Yet for a few blessed hours, we were once again the young man and the girl who had met by the river in Auvergne. I was his Gabrielle, his beloved, and he was everything to me.

⁓ 70 ⁓

Pierre-André needed to leave around seven that night to attend a meeting at the Common House. Before he left, I explained to him my dealings with Marcelin.

"I will find you decent lodgings," he said while dressing. "I cannot afford to keep you in luxury on a judge's salary, which I do not supplement as some of my colleagues do, but you and your daughter will lack nothing."

When Pierre-André returned two days later, he proposed to give my landlord notice on my behalf. I readily accepted since I was not fond of Marcelin's conversation.

"Here is your money," Pierre-André said when he came back fifteen minutes later, handing me one hundred and fifty francs in *assignats*. "I represented to Marcelin that the Municipality takes a dim view of those who prey on widows and orphans. He assured me that you had misunderstood him regarding the additional payment for lack of a passport. He was in fact on the verge of returning the hundred francs to you. He was very sorry to have given me the trouble to call on him, which I easily believe. He hoped that I would not report him to the Section for an innocent mistake. As a token of his good faith, he insisted on refunding every *sol* you ever paid him, even the rent for the time you spent here."

I hesitated. "I do not feel that it would be right to leave without paying him anything. And I am surprised. He seemed so fond of his money. Did you beat him?"

"I only caught him by the collar while I expressed my opinion of him.

It would have been unnecessary to push things any further. He was shaking in his trousers at the very sight of me. Do not feel sorry for him, Gabrielle. Those who take advantage of the helpless deserve no such concern."

Again I packed my things and Aimée's. They now fit in one trunk and one bag, which Pierre-André carried downstairs himself. After making sure that no one was following us, he hailed a hackney on the Place Saint-Michel. We crossed the *Pont-au-Change* and arrived in the Island of the City. We passed Notre-Dame and turned into the warren of narrow streets north of the cathedral. The lodgings he had found, on a second floor in Rue de la Colombe, "Dove Street," included a tiny kitchen, a water closet and a vestibule leading to two main rooms. One served as a dining parlour and had a couch on which Aimée could sleep, while the other was furnished as a bedroom. Over the last few weeks, I had almost forgotten the existence of such luxuries as drapes and carpets. I would not have felt happier if Pierre-André had offered me the Queen's apartment in Versailles.

"I am infinitely grateful to you," I said, sitting on the bed and patting the plump red coverlet. "And look, there are fireplaces in both rooms!"

"I am glad to be able to make you comfortable," said Pierre-André. "This is nothing out of the ordinary, but who needs more these days? It will be better for you to do without a maid. The last thing you need is someone to spy on you. This district is very quiet and conveniently located midway between the courthouse and my own lodgings on the Island of the Fraternity. You will find that, between my functions as a judge, my mandate as a member of the Municipality and my attendance at the Jacobins, I am a busy man. Do not imagine things, my beloved, if I cannot spend as much time with you as I would like." He stroked my cheek. "I would marry you tomorrow if I could. You know that it is impossible now: it would doom both of us. I will nonetheless regard you as my wife and expect you to keep faith with me."

He sat on the bed next to me. "If I discover otherwise, my love," he continued in a quiet tone, "I will take you to the river and drown you in the muck of the banks."

I shuddered at the idea of his hand holding my face down in the cold, foul slime. I wondered whether he had spoken in earnest and looked into his eyes.

"No, Gabrielle," he added, "I would never do it." He ran a finger on my cheek. "I was simply trying to tell you that I would be very unhappy if you strayed. My jealousy is in proportion to my affections. Until last year, I had a pretty little maid who also served me in another capacity. One afternoon when I came home early from court, I discovered the slut in *my* bed, if you please, with the butcher's apprentice. You should have seen their faces. They must have thought I was going to disembowel them on the spot and started begging for mercy." Pierre-André chuckled. "I was content to kick them both out of my lodgings without a shred of clothing on their backs. I threw their rags into the fire since I did not expect the turtledoves to come back. They must have had to hide until nightfall, and then hope not to meet a patrol. It was enough to assuage my lust for revenge. But that was Suzanne. I would take it differently from you."

"Did you hire another maid?"

"One fell into my arms, as it were."

I frowned.

"You need not worry about her," he continued, smiling. "She is not to my taste, although otherwise she gives me full satisfaction." He paused, looking grave again. "I might as well tell you that, since Suzanne's hasty departure, I have had a few mistresses. I may have acted a bit wild on occasion. I have also resorted to prostitutes. I am not proud of it and will put an end to it."

"Thank you for telling me, but you do not owe me any explanation. I am grateful and honoured that you want me now." I threw my arms around his neck. "And I will regard you as my husband."

He embraced me tightly.

I felt safe at last, as much as those times allowed. A new law required that a bill posted on the outside of each building indicate the identity of all of its occupants. Thanks to my Civic Certificate, Number 7 Rue de la Colombe reported as one of its tenants a Gabrielle Labro, age twenty-three, widow, living with her daughter, Aimée Labro, age seven.

Paris took a new look to me. The city itself had not changed, but the fashions, especially for men, were simpler, more somber than I had ever seen them. People walked more briskly. I had become wary of every stranger. A man staring at me on the street was no longer deemed an admirer, but could be a *mouchard*, a police informer, or a zealous patriot detecting in me an aristocrat in disguise. Until then, I had mostly traveled in carriages, isolated from any unpleasantness. I was no longer shielded from the hardships shared by all pedestrians. I had to be mindful of the offal overflowing from the rain gutters where chamber pots were emptied. I had to jump out of the way of horsemen and carts to avoid being run over, for Paris, unlike London, had no raised sidewalks. I often met with the former carriages of my friends, bearing half-erased coats of arms and now degraded to the rank of hackneys. Most trying of all, I had to endure, like any other female without a male escort, the insults and lewd gestures of men in their cups. Now that I was on foot, on a level with the street vendors, the beggars, the prostitutes, I came face-to-face with their deformities, their filth, their miseries, great and small. I could not look without queasiness at the offerings of the carts of the *regrattiers*, who purchased from lackeys the half-eaten leftovers from the kitchens of the rich and resold them to the poor. Without Pierre-André, Aimée and I would have survived on that disgusting fare.

My new familiarity with the streets also had some advantages. I came to realize how many of my countrymen lived in Paris. Almost all the water carriers were from Auvergne. Puech, who brought river water up to my lodgings, was from Murat, in the Département of Cantal, just twenty miles from Vic. He would stop to chat with me in the Roman language. He had never seen me before or heard of any person by the name of Gabrielle de Montserrat. Distances are not measured in terms of miles in the mountains. To him, I was simply Citizen Labro, a young woman from his country.

Many boatmen also came from Auvergne, bringing coal on barges down the Seine River. Once in Paris, the boats were taken apart and sold for wood. Some of the boatmen returned to our country on foot to repeat the process, while others settled in Paris. Indeed, all of the wine and coal merchants were from Auvergne, as well as a great many tavern keepers. Pierre-André seemed to know most of our countrymen in Paris. He liked to speak the Roman language with them, and me too. I had never felt so close to Auvergne since moving to Paris.

"Can you imagine, My Lady," said Manon one day, "the city is over-run by those foreigners from the provinces. They can barely speak French. They sound like those tigers at the King's Garden, the Garden of the Plants, they call it now."

"You forget that I am one of those *foreigners*. I was born and bred in Auvergne."

"That's not the same thing! You are a Baroness, for God's sake, and you speak so sweet, no one would ever know you come from that country."

I had kept Manon apprized of my move and new address, although not of the identity of my protector. Pierre-André had objected at first to my continuing this acquaintance.

"But she is entirely devoted to me," I said.

"Why? Because she had for years the honour of emptying your cham-ber pot every morning?"

I smiled. "Maybe. In any event, I am sure that she would never be-tray me."

"You and your stubbornness! You know that in your situation, you should trust no one."

"I trust you. And hopefully you trust me."

"Most of the time, yes, I am enough of an imbecile to do so. Indeed, my love, there is not one folly I have not committed for you."

"You are right to trust me, you know it. I owe you so much. Without you, I would be back in jail. I cannot bear to think of it after the Septem-ber massacres."

"Those were terrible times, Gabrielle. I came close to being killed myself." He was staring out the window.

"You? How could you, a judge of the 17th of August Tribunal, be in danger?"

"My function almost cost me my life. The mobs attacked the court-house on the first day of the atrocities, while we were in session during the trial of Bachmann, the Major General of the Swiss. He was the most hated man in Paris. Public opinion blamed him, with good reason, for the death of the twelve hundred patriots who perished at the Palace on the 10th of August. The trial had lasted three days and two nights."

"You must have been exhausted."

"I was beginning to feel some fatigue. The jury had retired to deliberate and the courtroom was silent. Yet I could hear cries coming from the jail of La Conciergerie below. I beckoned to one of the gendarmes and ordered him to go see what was happening down there. All of a sudden, a howling crowd, armed with pikes, rifles and sabres, burst into the courtroom. The public ran for the doors, screaming. The defense attorneys, the clerks and even the gendarmes also took to their feet. Bachmann, pale as a sheet, fled in our direction and hid behind the bench. Only the three of us judges and the prosecutor, all unarmed of course, remained at our places."

"Were you afraid?"

"Yes. For a moment I pictured myself hacked to pieces. I can stand my ground when attacked one on one, or even by several men, but I am no match for a mob armed to the teeth." He looked at me. "Yet, Gabrielle, I had to forget about my own safety. Yielding to that kind of violence would have made a mockery of the Nation's justice. My colleagues must have shared my feelings, for we all rose to protect Bachmann. A fellow walked to us from the crowd and demanded that we surrender the accused. We refused. He told us that we would be massacred if we insisted on protecting a scoundrel who had already been *tried and sentenced by the people*. We ignored that jackass and addressed the mob over his head. We demanded respect for the law, for the Tribunal's authority and for the verdict of the jury. The attackers listened to us. The crowd quieted and slowly withdrew. Bachmann thanked us profusely. There was no occasion for it, for the jurors reentered the courtroom and returned a guilty verdict. As you know, we sentenced him to death. He was guillotined later that day."

"Were you not tempted to spare his life after saving him from the mob?"

"No. We had protected him because it was our duty, not out of personal sympathy. After his trial was over, we decided to suspend the Tribunal's sessions until order was restored to the courthouse. I had been fully awakened and ran to the Common House to resume my functions at the Council General." He shook his head. "There, I learned that the events at La Conciergerie were not an isolated incident. Some scoundrels, all friends of Hébert's, on the Surveillance Committee of the Municipality had set up a provocation. They had dozens of unsworn priests transferred to L'Abbaye in regular carriages without sufficient armed protection. The convoy was surrounded by a mob. One of the priests hit a fellow in the crowd with his umbrella. They were massacred. The crowd then turned its attention to L'Abbaye itself and began to kill the other unsworn priests jailed there. From there, the slaughter spread to all the prisons of Paris, and all kinds of prisoners. By the time I arrived at the Common House, the situation was out of control. We dispatched envoys to stop the disaster, but they themselves narrowly escaped with their lives. The National Guards were on the brink of mutiny. If sent to the prisons, they would have joined the ranks of the killers. We remained in session all night, debating how to stop the atrocities and trying to organize the removal of the corpses, which could not be left to rot on the streets. Finally, we decided early in the morning to dispatch representatives to all the jails. The idea was to form *people's courts* to try the prisoners. Thus some of them, at least the poor devils jailed for debt, could be saved."

"I thought that the authorities had remained idle."

"The Girondin government certainly did nothing except make a few speeches at the Assembly, but we at the Council General tried to stop, or at least limit the massacres."

"So that is how Hébert came to preside over my trial at La Force. I would never have thought of his presence as good news."

"I cannot blame you. He, with his filthy rag of a newspaper, had inflamed public opinion, and his friends at the Municipality further stoked the Parisians' hatred of unsworn priests. Given the dismal news from the front, it was enough to trigger the slaughter. Yet he went to La Force with instructions from the Council General to spare as many prisoners as he could."

"Did you know that I was there?"

He stroked my cheek. "I did, my love, but had no way to save you individually. Only your Section could have claimed you. Yet before Hébert left for La Force, I drove him into a corner. I told him that, in his own interest, he had better not let any women be violated or killed. The scoundrel has always been mindful of me. He promised me in the most convincing terms that he would do all he could. When he returned that night, he reported to me that all the female prisoners had been released unharmed, except for the Lamballe woman. He assured me that he had acquitted her too. Apparently, like the imbecile she was, she had refused to pledge allegiance to the Nation and had been massacred by the workmen. I knew then that you had survived."

"Did it matter to you?"

"I was still angry with you, of course, but not to the point of wanting you killed, especially in such a manner."

"So you were trying to save me then. I never imagined it."

"How could you?"

He had given me his love, his help, his protection, and I had not even been aware of it. We held each other close that night.

~ 72 ~

Aimée and I avoided public entertainments. Monsieur Curtius's Wax Salon was more popular than ever, but I never set foot there for fear of being recognized by him or his niece. The royal family, along with the lords and ladies of the court, had been replaced by Generals and Representatives of the people. Even these had to be renewed from time to time as some were disgraced or guillotined. I hoped that my bust had been discarded too.

My main pastime, once I was done with Aimée's lessons, was reading the newspaper. I found that I no longer enjoyed novels, perhaps because the fate of my friends and the turns of my own destiny held all of my attention now. The news reported in the *Moniteur* every day was far more interesting than the plot of any fictional story. Aimée and I went out only to buy food in the nearby shops, to attend Mass or Vespers at Notre-Dame and to take walks in public gardens. Neither of us, after witnessing the carnage of the 10th of August, had fond memories of the Tuileries. We therefore went to the Luxembourg, which reminded me of my days as a lady-in-waiting to Madame.

After we returned home, I hoped for a visit from Pierre-André, who came to stay the night two or three times a week. On occasion he arrived early enough to share our dinner. He once told me that I was without exception the worst cook of his acquaintance, which reminded me of a similar assessment made by Joséphine years earlier. The playfulness of his tone did not fool me and, whenever he shared our meal, I bought food from a nearby inn owned by one of our countrymen.

Often I was already asleep when he unlocked the front door. That noise instantly roused me. I listened to his step, which I could recognize from any other. He undressed in silence, without lighting the candles. My heart beating fast, I waited for the moment when he would join me in bed and take me in his arms. I would awaken several times during the course of the night and listen to his breathing in the dark. His presence brought me strength, comfort, reassurance. I ran my fingers on his skin. I was not trying to wake him. I wanted only to touch him. I felt him, still asleep, stir against me. He moaned, his hands reached for me, his lips sought mine before he was even awake.

One night, he lit the candles after our embrace and raised himself on one elbow. He caressed the scar on my shoulder. I told him of the man who had hit me with his sabre on the 10th of August.

"Yes," he said, "at the Insurrectional Municipality, we had given instructions not to harm or violate any women found in the Palace. You know how it goes. Out of 100,000 people, you always have a few scoundrels who do not follow orders and go on a rampage. You were fortunate, my beloved, to escape with a flesh wound."

He then ran his forefinger over the scar under my left breast. I shuddered.

"This is something else," he said. "If it had been deeper, the apex of the heart would have been perforated. How did this happen?"

I could not bring myself to tell Pierre-André of the duel between my brother and Villers. I looked away as I said:

"Also on the 10th of August."

Before I realized what was happening, his hand had moved from my breast to my throat, which it held like a vice. I gasped and brought my hands to my neck in an attempt to defend myself, in vain. I abandoned the struggle and closed my eyes, ready to die. All of a sudden, Pierre-André's grip loosened.

"You are lying," he said coldly. "I told you to put an end to this habit of yours." I was still light-headed, trying to catch my breath. "And you take me for an imbecile. This is not a recent scar. I want the truth now."

I looked into Pierre-André's eyes. "My brother did it. Please do not be angry with him. It was an accident."

"Your brother? How interesting. Tell me about it."

Pierre-Andre listened carefully to the story.

"I beg your forgiveness for lying to you," I said. "I will never do it again. I was afraid you would create trouble for my brother."

"You should know me better than that. On the contrary, I commend him for trying to kill Villers. I thought that Castel had let you become that man's mistress without lifting a finger to stop that infamy. I would also have fought anyone who took liberties with the honour of a sister, with one difference: *I* would not have missed the scoundrel. Your brother, I will admit it, is no coward, though he lacks other qualities. I remember that fight we had in Lavigerie, after the banns for your marriage were published. He was not afraid of me in spite of my rage, and there are few men of whom I can say the same."

"So you think more highly of him now that you know about the duel?"

"I do, my beloved, which does not mean much. He is an arrogant, selfish, evil-spirited aristocrat, but he does once in a while, not often, display some feeling for you."

"Would you then, if I asked you, do a thing which would take a great weight off my mind?"

"If I understand you well, little minx," said Pierre-André, a thin smile on his lips, "you are asking for a favour to reward your lies. Granting it would not be a very moral outcome, would it?"

"I cannot hide from you the fact that, regardless of what he did, I love my brother. I was trying to protect him. I would lie to protect you too."

Pierre-André laughed. "Heaven help me if it ever came to that. You are inept at lying."

"So would you grant me that favour?"

"Ask, since you have no shame."

"Would you ask your brother Jean-Baptiste, who is now all powerful in Auvergne, to make sure that no harm comes to the Marquis?"

"That depends as much on the behaviour of the *Marquis*, since you insist on giving him that title, as on Jean-Baptiste's influence. He is not as powerful as you think. Moreover, your brother behaved to mine in an abominably insolent manner when Jean-Baptiste sought your hand in marriage on my behalf. Castel used still more offensive language after he discovered our proposed elopement. Jean-Baptiste is an even-tempered man, far more so than I, but those were words no one can easily forgive."

"Still, would you ask him?"

"Here is what I will do. Provided that *Citizen Castel* abstain from do-ing anything patently stupid, I do not mind asking Jean-Baptiste to cast an indulgent eye upon your brother's little aristocratic oddities. I am even willing to extend that favour to your sister, the *ci-devant* Countess de Chavagnac." Pierre-André looked grave again. "Now, my beloved, I want something to be clear."

"What is it?"

"I am prepared to extend some protection to your brother and sister, but this will stop here. In the future, some of your so-called friends may stand trial before the Tribunal for their crimes. I do not want to be pes-tered by any pleas for clemency. Not only would they fail to influence me, but they would greatly irritate me."

I made no response.

"Is it understood?" he continued, frowning. "Do you promise not to ask me to do anything I would deem contrary to justice?"

"I do."

My promise was not put to the test then. Pierre-André informed me that the 17th of August Tribunal was to be dissolved shortly.

"Are you unhappy about it?" I asked.

"No. I am to join the Court for the Second District as a judge, with the same salary, and I will of course remain a member of the Council General of the Municipality. To tell you the truth, most of the scoun-drels we should have tried were massacred by the mobs in September. To keep us busy, we were given jurisdiction over ordinary criminal cases, which was foreign to the purpose of the Tribunal."

Pierre-André shook his head. "And Osselin, the President, is not a bad man, but he could not manage a courtroom. He let the accused and defense attorneys rant for hours on irrelevant matters. Sometimes I would run out of patience and, although it was not my place, intervene to re-store a semblance of order. No, I will be perfectly happy to hear regular cases again. That is what I used to do as a Commissioner. Also, my be-loved, it will leave me more time to enjoy your company."

December 1792 saw the beginning of the King's trial before the Na-tional Convention. A month earlier, a cache of documents, known as the "Iron Armoire" had been discovered in the Tuileries following the dis-closures of the locksmith who had crafted it. It contained proof of the Court's schemes since the beginning of the Revolution, under the form of correspondence with the enemy, plotting the defeat of France and the arrival of the foreign armies as "liberators" of the country.

The deposed King was to be tried for his crimes, or mistakes, depending on one's opinion, before the elected Representatives of the Nation. He argued his case with composure and was defended by skilled lawyers. The result of that vote, which lasted many days, is well known: the National Convention, by an overwhelming majority, sentenced him to death. The issue of the stay of execution, however, was almost tied. Those in favor of immediate death were only one vote ahead. It was the Duke d'Orléans's vote that sent his cousin to the guillotine, an action that won him the enmity of the royalists and revolutionaries alike. With the King dead, his younger brothers in exile and the little Dauphin still a child, the Duke d'Orléans strengthened his position as pretender to the throne. His vote could hardly have been disinterested.

The King was guillotined on the 21st of January, 1793. The National Guard and all forty-eight Sections of Paris were on high alert, but no one made any gesture to save the former monarch or even to protest his execution. Whether one deemed it an act of justice or of cruelty, there was no turning back now.

I received the news with sadness, although there were loud celebrations from some quarters. In the Faubourg Saint-Antoine, an inn inaugurated a new manner to serve veal's head, in a *vinaigrette* sauce, in honour of the late King's execution. That dish became a staple on the 21st of January, which was proclaimed a national holiday. I have never been fond of that gruesome delicacy, for the sight of a severed head, even that of an animal, has always aroused my pity.

73

One would imagine that writing is an innocent enough activity. Yet it seems to irritate some. Aimée has been watching me with some curiosity, and now my granddaughter Gabriella is bemoaning the slow pace of my progress in making a new dress for her doll.

"Now poor Janie will not have anything new to wear this spring," she says, shaking her head sadly.

"Yes, she will, my treasure," I say, smiling. "My late mother, just like you, used to complain bitterly about my sloth. I will make amends for it and finish Janie's dress before Sunday. Now are you happy?"

"I have seen you write much lately, Mama," says Aimée. "What about?"

"It is a memoir of my life during the Revolution, dear."

"Why?"

"Why not? Writing pains me and soothes me at the same time."

Aimée rings for a maid to take Gabriella to her governess.

"It is time for your lessons, my dear," she says, without heeding her daughter's protests.

Once we are alone, Aimée looks straight at me. "Why, Mama, would you want to recall those times? Are they not better forgotten?"

"I have never forgotten them, Aimée. Have you?"

"I do not want to be reminded of them. And I do not want Gabriella to know anything about them."

"What do you remember?"

"Enough. I remember running with you through a gilded hall. You shot at a man and he tried to cut your head off with his sabre. You were covered with blood. I remember a garden strewn with naked cadavers."

"That was at the Tuileries, on the 10th of August 1792, my dearest, just before your seventh birthday."

"And I remember us moving to a hovel, and then moving again and again. We had to change names several times. We were always hiding, always fleeing. You were arrested before my eyes. I thought I would never see you again. Indeed, I was living with the constant dread of losing you."

I laid aside the doll's dress.

"It is not all," she continues. "I remember a dark-haired man, with a deep voice. To me, he looked like a giant. He was always dressed in black. He would call at night. When he had dinner with us, I was so terrified that I could not eat a thing or say a word." She shakes her head. "You would stop whatever you were doing when you recognized his step on the stairs. You would run to the door and throw yourself in his arms as if there were no other refuge in the world. I remember the way you looked at him. I have never seen you act in this manner with anyone else."

Tears fill my eyes.

"When he was there," says Aimée, "I no longer existed."

I rise to sit by her on the sofa. "How can say such a thing, Aimée? Since you were born, your comfort and safety have been my foremost concern. I have not made a single decision in my life without thinking first of how it would affect you. True, that man you remember was, with you, all I had. He saved my life on more than one occasion. You knew it, and should have been grateful to him."

Aimée rises and walks to the window. "What about my father? Why have you never told me anything about him?"

"I was doing you and his memory a kindness by sparing you the recital of my married life." I sigh. "Your father is indeed mentioned in my memoir. I had not intended for you to read it, but perhaps you should. You might understand why I kept silent."

Aimée, without leaving the window, turns towards me. "You must remain so. I do not want to know more about that other man."

"Would you, my own daughter, presume to tell me what to do?"

Aimée looks down. "No, Madam, but I do not wish to see the past revived."

"It is not for you to decide."

"You are writing about my life too."

"Maybe so, Aimée, but I will write what I want, whenever I want. It would pain me to see Gabriella and you leave, but I will not receive orders from my daughter in my own house."

Aimée is sobbing. I walk to her and take her in my arms. She apologizes. Maybe the feelings she expresses towards Pierre-André are normal. I have long suspected that she might have been jealous of him. Aimée's tears will not deter me from my purpose. On the contrary, there may now be another reason for me to write about the past.

On the night of the King's execution, Pierre-André handed me an *assignat* of 100 francs.

"Buy some fabric," he said. "I want you to rid yourself of your widow's costume. Anyone wearing mourning will be suspected of doing so on account of Capet's execution And you will make sure both of you pin tricolour cockades to your bonnets."

I bought fabric, one brown with a print of small pink roses and the other pale lavender with black dots, and sewed matching dresses for Aimée and myself. I hid my hair, whenever I went out, by wearing a *coqueluchon* of the same fabric. It was a waist-long mantle with a hood, which had just become fashionable. Pierre-André was right: mourning clothes were now deemed a display of royalist sentiment. I was, in any case, happy to return to more cheerful fashions.

I was pinning the hem of one of Aimée's new dresses when she asked: "Mama, do you think Citizen Pierre-André is a nice man?"

"Yes, I do. He is our best, our only friend now."

"Why did not we see him before, when we lived on Rue Dominique?"

"He and I did not meet often then, but I have known him for a very long time."

"How long?"

"I told you, Aimée, a long time."

"Did you know him before Monsieur de Villers?"

"Yes, dear, years before."

"Even before you married my Papa?"

I looked into Aimée's eyes. "Yes, I knew him even before my marriage. Listen, Aimée, you are too young to understand certain things. What you need to know is that I would have gone back to jail if Citizen Pierre-André had not helped me." I sighed. "He is also very generous to us. Without him, we would be on a bread and water diet, and only on the good days, because on the bad ones we would have nothing at all to eat. We would still be in our garret on Rue de l'Hirondelle. I remember that you did not like that place much."

She shook her head. "No, I did not."

"So we must not be ungrateful. We owe him everything."

"Are you going to marry him?"

"No, my dear, I do not think so."

"I used to think that you would marry Monsieur de Villers."

"Did you want me to?"

"I would have liked to have a papa. I know I had one, of course, but he is dead. I do not remember him at all. Monsieur de Villers was so kind to me. He gave me Margaret. He taught me to ride. I liked being at Vaucelles or going to Normandy to visit Madame de Gouville. Perhaps he would have been still nicer if you had married him. Citizen Pierre-André never does anything with me."

"Well, he has not much time. It does not mean that he does not like you. He does a great deal *for* you."

"I know. Oh, Mama, I am not ungrateful. You are the best Mama that ever lived. I am very happy because now you can be with me all the time, except of course when Citizen Pierre-André is around."

She threw her arms around my neck.

Pierre-André's career took another turn. Some Representatives, led by Danton, had insisted on the creation of a new tribunal, modeled on that formed on the 17th of August. Its mandate was to punish swiftly and without the possibility of any appeal "those guilty of counterrevolutionary schemes against liberty, equality, the unity of the Republic, the safety of the Nation and the sovereignty of the people." The National Convention agreed, and the Revolutionary Tribunal came into existence. Pierre-André joined the new court as a judge.

The circumstances were dire. After the victories of the autumn of 1792, the war against the Prussians and Austrians was taking a new turn for the worse. A new general-in-chief, Dumouriez, had betrayed the Nation, and, as Lafayette had done the previous summer, defected to the enemy. The whole west of France had risen against the draft of 300,000 men decreed by the National Convention to feed the armies. Civil war was now raging, with its center around Nantes. Thus a second battlefront appeared, this time on the west. It was marked by atrocities on both sides, too gruesome to be reported here. Royalist insurgents were ready to besiege Nantes, while an army of *émigrés*, supported by English ships, was rumoured to prepare to attack the city by sea. I heard again of a man I had long forgotten. Carrier, my late husband's attorney, had been elected as a Representative for the Département of Cantal to the National Convention. The violence and passion of his speeches at the Cordeliers Club had made him famous. He was sent as a Representative in Mission to Nantes to save the city from attack and quell the rebellion.

Lauzun, after various commands on the foreign fronts in the Netherlands and Italy, had also been sent to the west to fight the insurgents. There, he clashed with Jacobin officers, especially General Rossignol, a former goldsmith, who did not like to answer to a *ci-devant* Duke. More ominously, Lauzun won the enmity of Carrier, who revoked his command and had him arrested. I still had no news from Hélène, which, under the circumstances, I could hardly equate with good news.

74

Although Aimée and I never lacked any necessities, thanks to Pierre-André's generosity, I asked Manon to help me find a place. Her sister Louise had been a lace maker, but lace was no longer in fashion. Men no longer wore any. Even the ladies who could afford it did not want to make themselves conspicuous by flaunting such an aristocratic ornament. Louise had accepted a place as a dressmaker for the *Théâtre du Marais*.

"Imagine, My Lady," she told me while I was visiting Manon in her lodgings, "having to take such work! I never thought I would stoop so low. A theatre is no place for decent people. All actors are denied a Christian funeral."

"Not anymore. I am sure a sworn priest would give the last rites to any person, even an actor or actress, who would request them."

"That's what is wrong nowadays, Madam. Nobody respects anything. Thank Heaven, I'll be rid of the theatre in a week. I gave my notice as soon as I found another place with the widow of a surgeon."

"Does that mean that your place as a dressmaker is vacant?"

"I believe so. But you wouldn't do anything like that, My Lady, I hope."

"Oh, I would, Louise. I would be grateful for any respectable work that came my way."

I had to insist long and hard before Louise agreed to introduce me to Citizen Granger, the manager of the *Théâtre du Marais*. That establishment could hardly be counted among the finest of its kind in Paris. It had achieved a measure of fame the prior year by featuring *Robert the Republican*, a play in which Princess Theresa, young and beautiful, was held prisoner in a tower, while the eponymous Robert, a drunkard and an illiterate brute, was presiding over a "tribunal of blood," before which the supporters of the Princess were dragged. The people of Francovia, the country where those events took place, eventually freed Theresa, slaughtered Robert and restored her father, good King Ludovic, to his throne.

Needless to say, *Robert the Republican* did not meet with popular acclaim. It was booed during its premiere and failed to survive its second representation. A crowd of *sans-culottes* from the nearby Faubourg Saint-Antoine stormed the theatre, destroyed all the seats and threatened to string the Princess, along with King Ludovic, from a lamppost.

The theatre had closed for a few days. Under its new management, its repertoire was limited to romances between shepherds and shepherdesses, set in idyllic villages. The plays were now titled *Lisbeth's Cottage*, *The Lost Clog*, and *Virtue Rewarded*.

Granger, the manager, barely glanced at the samples of my handiwork I had brought with me. "I am sure," he said, "that a comely young citizen like you cannot fail to be a good seamstress. You are not a noblewoman, at least?"

"Of course not, Citizen Granger." I now lied with ease.

"Good. We do not need any more trouble with the authorities. You see, we already have a *ci-devant* Marquis as a prompter. He is a good patriot, and all that, but I don't want it said that the *Théâtre du Marais* is a den of aristocracy."

"I am no aristocrat, Citizen Granger. On the contrary, I received a Civic Certificate from my Section." I reached into my pocket and handed him the precious sheet of paper. He perused it and returned it to me.

"Everything seems in order, then. Can you start next week, when Citizen Picard is leaving us?"

"I would be grateful, Citizen. Would you mind if I brought my little girl along to help me? She is very quiet. I promise that she will not be in anyone's way."

He accepted, and I was introduced to the troupe. One of the lead actresses was Charlotte Tibaud, who had been Princess Theresa in the ill-fated *Robert the Republican*. I had no trouble recognizing in Charlotte the young woman I had seen in the company of Pierre-André in the riverside *guinguette* before the Revolution. Her hair was no longer a fiery red, but had turned blonde. This colour, I suppose, gave her the virginal allure required for her repertoire. It was no less difficult to imagine her as an ingénue than as royalty, but what she lacked in talent was more than outweighed by her personal advantages. I would soon discover that she was not shy about using the latter to forward her career. In particular it seemed to me that, in addition to allowing the attentions of a wealthy grocer and a member of the National Convention, she enjoyed a close relationship with Granger.

Her rival, in matters of the stage and of the heart, was Julie Morin, who had to be content with the parts Charlotte disdained. The other members of the cast seemed to stay for short periods of time, until they were able to secure employment in more distinguished establishments. I also met Citizen Lacoste, formerly the Marquis de Lacoste, now the prompter.

"Greetings and fraternity, beauteous young Citizen," he said.

"A good day to you, Citizen Lacoste."

"Congratulations. Granger did not waste any time in hiring you, I see."

"He needed someone to replace Louise in a hurry."

"No doubt. He must also have been impressed by your qualifications. Have you any experience as a seamstress?"

"I have sewn all of my life, but did not need to find work until I was widowed a year ago. The death of my husband left me in awkward circumstances."

"You express yourself in such a graceful, polished way, my dear. What was your husband?"

"He was a cheese merchant, but I was educated in a convent before my parents lost their fortune."

Lacoste arched his eyebrow. "It sounds like one of those stories one reads in novels. Very moving. Did you tell Granger about it? He could make a play of it."

"I do not want it published. Citizen Granger was satisfied when he saw my Civic Certificate." I looked straight at him. "What about you, Citizen Lacoste? I understand that you are a *ci-devant* Marquis."

"Indeed. A great deal of good it did me under the Old Regime. The onset of the Revolution found me in the dungeons of Vincennes, where I had spent the last ten years thanks to a *lettre de cachet* obtained by my mother-in-law, who is without any doubt the ugliest and most vindictive sow in all of France."

"Why did she request a *lettre de cachet* against you, Citizen Lacoste?"

He smiled. "With your permission, dear Citizen Labro, I will not tell you more until I know you better. The prejudices of old are not completely dead yet."

Pierre-André's reaction when I told him of my employment was what I had feared.

"What?" he asked, glaring at me. "You, a seamstress at the *Théâtre du*

Marais? I put everything I have at risk for you, I support you, and you cannot think of anything better than to find work in a theatre, of all places! Why do you not ask for a part in the next play and go on stage, while you are at it? And for what, please? A few francs a week? Are you ready to risk your life for so little?"

"But I will be very cautious, my love. The spectators will not even be aware of my existence."

"What about the actors, the manager, the stage hands? Are they ignorant of your existence?"

"They look like a decent lot and have no reason to suspect that I am an aristocrat. The manager was content with my Civic Certificate." I smiled. "I happened to meet an acquaintance of yours there, Mademoiselle Tibaud. She is in all the plays."

"Yes," he said, "I know she works there. Dear Charlotte, there is no better creature in Paris. It is not on her account that I am worried."

"Have you seen her lately?"

"A few months ago."

I frowned.

"Do not look at me like this," he said. "She came to see me after the disaster of *Robert the Republican*. Poor thing, she was afraid of being arrested. And the theatre was closed indefinitely. She was out of work."

"The stage does not seem to be her only source of income."

"Now, Gabrielle, is this a nice thing to say? You need not worry about her, my love. I helped her without any expectation of a reward."

"How long did she remain your mistress?"

"I had been keeping her for about two years when I happened upon you that day in 1788, at the *guinguette* by the river. It was quite a shock to see you, dressed like a fine lady, surrounded by your friends from the Court. I found a pretext to quarrel with Charlotte that very night. She certainly had done nothing to deserve it. She had been easily contented with what I could give her, while spurning the offers of far richer men. She had even agreed to dye her hair red to please me." Pierre-André smiled. "I could not look at a woman without trying to find something of you in her."

"Did you continue seeing Charlotte afterwards?"

"We remained friends, though there has not been any intimacy between us in years."

"What happened when she came to you after the theatre was closed?"

"I promised to do whatever was in my power to have the theatre reopened and to keep her out of trouble. Only then did she offer to resume our old relations. It was purely out of gratitude for my help, mind you, not as an inducement before the fact. I thanked her and declined. I had already renewed my acquaintance with you then." Pierre-André looked into my eyes. "And I do not wish to receive personal favours because of my function. I even refuse to see women I do not know in my chambers. It was only because of that concocted story of yours about documents in the Roman language that I accepted to receive you. As for Charlotte, she may not be a paragon of virtue, but she is harmless, if anything generous to a fault. I assisted her out of friendship. You should be the last person in the world to complain that I am so tender-hearted."

"I am not complaining. I am only afraid that you will tire of me someday and leave me for another woman."

He wrapped his arm around my shoulders. "I would never abandon you, especially in your current circumstances. Speaking of which, will you please renounce that idiotic notion of working in a theatre, or anywhere else for that matter? Sew to your heart's content, but do it from home without exposing yourself to unnecessary dangers."

"I know that you are thinking only of my safety, but I am going out of my mind indoors all day long. Please, my love, let me take this place. I promise I will be cautious and give it up at the first sign of danger."

He let go of me and shook his head in exasperation. "Go ahead, Gabrielle, act like a simpleton. But if you find yourself in trouble because of your stubbornness, do not expect any help from me."

Truth be told, I missed the pleasures of society. Manon had found a place as a shop girl with a linen draper and I seldom saw her. Apart from Pierre-André's visits at night, I barely had any contacts with other adults. So I became a seamstress at the *Théâtre du Marais*.

75

Under the Girondin government, the Nation was in shambles. The people lacked bread. The armies of the Republic were defeated. France was racked by civil war; the Prussians and Austrians on the eastern front threatened Paris. The Girondins hated the capital and the power of its Municipality. One of their leaders went so far as to publicly threaten the city with "annihilation."

On the 22nd of June 1793, the Sections of Paris, inflamed by such language, marched on the Convention with the support of the National Guard, led by General Hanriot. Under the threat of Hanriot's cannons, the Representatives voted to arrest their Girondin colleagues. The Jacobins, headed by Robespierre, took control of the National Convention. The former ministries were replaced by various Committees composed of Representatives. The most powerful was the Committee of Public Salvation, responsible for all matters concerning the survival of the Nation. It was led by Robespierre and his allies. The next in importance was the Committee of General Safety, in charge of the police.

The Jacobins inherited a disastrous situation. It was doubtful that France could survive as one Nation. Whenever I heard or read the phrase "The Republic, One and Indivisible," I was reminded of the dangers faced by my unfortunate country, which traitors wanted crushed and divided. It was a time of national emergency. The mood was somber.

It became mandatory for all theatres to play patriotic works at least three times a week for the edification of the people. These shows were paid for by the Municipality and free of charge to the public. At the *Théâtre du Marais*, they attracted a more vocal, more poorly dressed crowd than the other nights, mostly *sans-culottes* and their women.

At first, Granger had set his sights upon a play titled *The Pope in Hell*. Charlotte had been given the part of a nun who, after spurning the offers of the Holy Father, threw her habit by the wayside to marry a virtuous patriot. The play had been cleared for public representation by the

Municipality, but was soon withdrawn without any explanation in spite of its warm reception by the audience. I was not sorry to see the *Pope* fall into oblivion for I had hated sewing nun's garments for Charlotte. Apart from the disrespect to the habit, they reminded me of Hélène. The château of Lalande, where she had for a while taken refuge, had changed hands several times in the course of the hostilities before being set ablaze by the Republican troops. Even Pierre-André, whom I had beseeched to try and save my sister, had been unable to find any trace of her.

At the theatre, *The Pope in Hell* was replaced by *The Crimes of the Nobility*, a work of similar literary merit. Charlotte now played a shepherdess whose father had been hanged under the Old Regime, thanks to fraudulent charges filed by the Marquis de la Turpitude. The Marquis had unspeakable designs on Charlotte, eventually thwarted by her rustic suitor. The denouement consisted in the thrashing of the Marquis by his former vassals. The audience gave a standing ovation and proceeded to sing in unison *Ah ça ira*, "Ah it'll do":

> *Ah it'll do, it'll do, it'll do!*
> *Let's string the aristocrats from the lampposts.*
> *Ah it'll do, it'll do, it'll do!*
> *The aristocrats we shall hang.*
> *For three hundred years they've promised*
> *To give us bread;*
> *For three hundred years they've given parties*
> *And kept whores;*
> *For three hundred years they've crushed us;*
> *Enough lies, enough words;*
> *We don't want to starve anymore.*

The song hit close to home. I shuddered.

I complained to Lacoste of the new repertoire.

"Agreed," he said, "the plays are not very good."

"Not very good? They are dreadful."

"From a literary standpoint, yes, but that is not what matters. They educate the people, they expose the impostures of religion. You have no idea, dear Citizen Labro, how strong the prejudices bred by superstition and fanaticism still are."

"What do you mean?"

"Look no further than the relations between the sexes. It is clear that all women belong to all men."

"No, it is not clear to me at all. I have the good fortune to belong to no one."

"It is wrong, my dear, very wrong. You ought to belong to any man who wants you."

I raised my eyebrow.

"Yes," he continued. "You forget, dear Citizen, that we are all born free and equal in rights."

"What has it to do with me belonging to any man who wants me? Since I am free, I belong to no one but myself."

"Oh, but we are not talking about the liberty of women here. What matters is equality between men. If you allege your liking for one man to decline the proposals of another, you violate the principle of equality."

"Nonsense. I need not allege anything to decline anyone's attentions. Do you really believe then that a woman has not only the right, but the duty to give herself to any man who requests her favours?"

"Absolutely, my dear."

"What kind of liberty would I enjoy, if I could not use it to tell a man I dislike to go to hell?"

"Ah, but you would not do so for the sake of liberty. You would do it out of modesty. That despicable feeling is not found in nature. Look around: animals are not modest."

"Maybe not, but we are not animals. Your opinions, Citizen Lacoste, reflect the most absolute contempt for the rights of women."

"Women must not be selfish. They should subject themselves to the wishes of any man who fancies them. If I had my way, the law would establish houses of prostitution where any man could summon, by force if need be, any woman he likes to satisfy his wishes. I further contend that such rule should apply regardless of the age of the woman."

I stared at him. "Even if she were a child?"

"Even so. Even is she were the man's daughter or sister."

"So you are a proponent of incest?"

"Absolutely, if a man wishes to practice it. One of the greatest achievements of the Revolution is the abolition of all so-called religious crimes, such as incest, sodomy, blasphemy and adultery. Marriage, in my opinion, should be outlawed. It is nothing but a form of servitude."

"This is the only point on which we agree. One thing you should know. If such a system as the one you advocate were in effect to allow any woman to summon any man anywhere, I would never avail myself of it with regard to you."

He laughed. "So I feared, my dear. That is why it would be far better the other way around."

I doubted that Lacoste would have put his ideas into practice and found his opinions outrageous enough to be entertaining. I nevertheless made sure Aimée never strayed close to him. Maybe the sole reason why I tolerated, and even enjoyed the company of the *ci-devant* Marquis de Lacoste was that his manners faintly reminded me of the graceful world of the Old Regime, now departed beyond any hope of return.

Lacoste never made improper gestures towards me. I was less at ease with Granger, the manager, who never missed an opportunity to bend over my shoulder while I was sewing.

"What fine stitches you make, Citizen," he would say. "And you have the prettiest hands I have ever seen in a seamstress."

In the beginning, I would sew in an attic above the stage. I soon had to abandon that retreat because Granger posted himself under a small corkscrew staircase leading to it whenever I climbed there, no doubt to look under my skirts. I took to working in the wings, which afforded me both a view of the rehearsals and the protection of the actors against Granger's attentions. Aimée, with her beloved Margaret in tow, always accompanied me. She was a quiet child, absorbed by her lessons, and friendly to everyone. After a while, I taught her to sew and she began to help me with the easier parts of my task. She became quite a favourite with Charlotte, who had no children of her own, and indeed with the rest of the troupe.

76

Whenever I speak to my English friends of my homesickness, they seem to imagine that it is a general feeling of loss. They are novices in terms of bereavement. To me, homesickness is the recurrence, without warning or apparent reason, of a precise image of my country. It changes from time to time. These days, the figure of Notre-Dame with its flying buttresses, both massive and graceful, keeps appearing.

The ancient cathedral, which stood no more than a hundred yards from our lodgings, dominated our part of the Island of the City. In the beginning of our stay there, Aimée and I had without incident attended Mass at Notre-Dame. It had seemed safe enough since it was served by sworn clergy. However, a few months later, I heard in the middle of the service the braying of a jackass. The congregation froze. The liturgy stopped. A group of *sans-culottes* was leading the poor animal, a bishop's mitre on its head, priestly vestments on its back, down the aisle. My first impulse was to run, but I did not wish to attract attention by too hasty a retreat. The intruders reached the master altar, singing lewd songs at the top of their lungs. One of them, pushing the priest aside, drank the communion wine, unbuttoned his trousers and relieved himself in the chalice. I covered Aimée's eyes and resolved to no longer attend Mass. In any event, the cathedral was soon closed to the Catholic faith and dedicated solely to the meetings of patriotic societies.

Certain members of the Municipality seemed intent on restoring some kind of religious activity to the venerable building. One afternoon, while I was walking home from the theatre, I heard cheers coming from Notre-Dame. I headed cautiously in that direction, ready to flee at the first sign of danger. The crowd, although loud, seemed in a friendly mood. I saw a man wearing the distinctive trousers, short jacket and red hat of the *sans-culottes*. He was leading a buxom young woman, crowned with artificial flowers and clad in a Greek drapery girded by a tricolour sash, towards the doors of the cathedral. Hébert, who had presided over my trial at La Force, walked next to them. Behind came a procession of equally comely girls, all attired in the same manner, followed by a large group of men.

"What is the meaning of this?" I asked a woman next to me. "I did not know they still had weddings at Notre-Dame. The bride is pretty."

"You dullard," she answered, shrugging, "it's no wedding. The man there is Chaumette, the National Agent of the Municipality of Paris. And the citizen with him is no bride. She's the Goddess Reason. She's being installed in her Temple now that the blessed-asses have been expelled. And here's Hébert walking behind them."

I almost remarked that the Goddess looked like a regular mortal, maybe even like an actress or dancer, but did not wish to be accused of sacrilege towards the new divinity. Afraid that Hébert might recognize me, I left without witnessing the installation of the Goddess Reason in Notre-Dame.

I related the ceremony to Pierre-André the same night.

"I know," he said. "As a member of the Municipality, I was asked to attend that farce. I excused myself on the grounds that I could not be spared at the Tribunal. Robespierre is utterly disgusted. He thinks, and rightly so, that Hébert's Goddess Reason rubbish is nothing but thinly veiled atheism."

"But how is Hébert to be stopped? Every *sans-culotte* reads the *Père Duchesne*, or hears it read aloud. Also, along with Chaumette, Hébert controls the Municipality."

"Not for long. The scoundrel's days are numbered. I have been asked to denounce atheism as an aristocratic doctrine at the Jacobins Club. I would be surprised if Hébert's friends did not raise an uproar during that speech. Robespierre needs someone who can make himself heard in spite of the racket. He is a great man but, as you know, he has not much of a voice."

The appearance of churches was to be further altered. The National Convention passed a law mandating the destruction of all tombs and funeral monuments located within churches. I remembered the crypt under the chapel of Cénac where my son's coffin had been laid to rest. I could not chase from my mind the image of the tiny white box I had seen there during my husband's funeral. Now the idea of the profanation of his resting place tore at me. I paced the room, unable to find any peace. Aimée was watching me with uncomprehending eyes. After I put her to bed, I was overcome by sorrow.

When Pierre-André joined me that night, I was lying on my bed, fully dressed, sobbing so hard that, in spite of my efforts, I could not utter a word. He looked at me in silence, went to the kitchen and returned with a wet towel, which he applied to my face. He sat next to me and stroked my hair. My breathing slowed down. I took his hand in both of mine.

"Will you please tell me what this is about?" he asked.

"Do you know about the new law?"

"Which one?"

"The one that orders the destruction of all the tombs in churches."

"So this is what is upsetting you so. I thought that at least half of your family had been arrested. What is the matter?"

"The tombs of the Peyre family in Cénac will be desecrated. Your brother Jean-Baptiste, since he is *Procureur-Syndic* of the *Département*, could stop it if you asked him. Please."

"There is no need to ask him. Jean-Baptiste is a reasonable man. He knows that this measure targets the royal burials at Saint-Denis." Pierre-André frowned. "I did not imagine that the fate of your late husband's remains bothered you so."

I started crying again. "It is not about him," I said. "I cannot bear the idea of my son's bones, so little that they must already be reduced to dust, thrown away like rubbish."

"Your son? I never knew that you had a son."

I told Pierre-André of my second lying-in. His jaw tightened. "I should never have let you fall into the hands of that beast. I failed you. I should have prevented your marriage, if I had to crush Peyre's skull with my bare hands."

"But you would have died too. I know that, even now, you are still angry over my marriage. Yet all I wanted was to save you. You must believe me; you must forgive me at last."

Still seated on the bed, he raised me from the pillow and took me in his arms. "I believe you, Gabrielle, and I have long forgiven you. I am not even sure that there was anything to forgive. What could you have done differently, my poor love, at fifteen? What I cannot fathom is your brother's rage to separate us, when he knew that I adored you. And why? To condone the violation of his sister, of a girl barely out of childhood, by a drunken brute. All that misery because I had the misfortune to be a commoner."

I found the courage to utter the question I had wanted to ask many times before. "What about Villers? Have you also forgiven me for Villers? I should have sought you when I came to Paris, but I thought you hated me."

"I never hated you. Through my brothers, I had learned of your arrival in Paris and knew that you lived with the Duchess d'Arpajon. For months, I kept hoping for a visit, a letter, any sign that you still cared for me. Instead I heard that you had become a kept woman." He shook his head. "It grieved me as if I had learned of your death. I could not reconcile it with the memory I had kept of you. You were delightful when I met you by the river, Gabrielle. At fifteen, you were unspoiled, fearless, sparkling with intelligence, and also the prettiest girl I had ever seen. And a few years later, you let Villers turn you into a courtesan. How could you do such a thing?"

"I was no longer fearless when I met Villers. My marriage had robbed me of my innocence. I could not trust any man, not even you. I had not the courage to seek you."

"And what about the night when I found you at the Champ de Mars? I expected you to call on me afterwards, and all I received was that note!"

"I too was hoping that you would call on me. Oh, Pierre-André, I wanted to see you again. I wanted it so."

"Did you really expect me to visit you in the lodgings where that man kept you? Had you not noticed that the very sight of that place turned my stomach? And then what was I supposed to think of your little escapade to the Jacobins Club? Were you taunting me?"

"I never thought that I would see you that day. I did not mean to make you angry."

"Truth be told, I was more puzzled than angry. I had given up making any sense of your actions. But then you came to my chambers, begging for my help after shunning me all these years. I was wondering whether you would proposition me. And you did! You had stooped so low as to peddle your favours."

"You are right, Pierre-André," I said, hanging my head. "You have no reason to forgive me."

He raised my chin and looked into my eyes. "Listen, Gabrielle. I forgive you, and for good reason: I love you."

"So you do forgive me?"

"Yes. And I will write Jean-Baptiste to ensure that the burials of the Peyre family remain untouched. Now will you please calm yourself?" He gently pushed me down on the pillow and lay down next to me. "There," he continued, smiling. "I even forgive you for propositioning me. In fact, I am glad you did."

I huddled against him. His words had dissipated the misery of that day, of all those years spent apart.

The royal tombs in Saint-Denis were indeed opened and the bodies of the Kings since Dagobert in the 6th century thrown into a pit dug next to the Basilica. Many noble burials throughout the country met with the same fate. Yet my late husband and elder son still rest in the crypt of Cénac.

Some time later, attracted by unusual music, I noticed a gathering of hundreds of Negroes in front of Notre-Dame. By unanimous vote, the National Convention had just abolished slavery in all of the French colonies and territories. The Municipality had a stage built inside the cathedral to hold a celebration. I was watching from outside. Black women danced, to the sound of a kind of music I had never heard before, with both Black men and members of the Municipality. I saw the eyes of a Negress fixed on me. I looked back and, my heart beating, recognized the pretty face of Rosalie, whom I had not seen since the emigration of the Countess de Provence, almost two years earlier. Rosalie paused for a moment, considered Aimée and me, then resumed her dance. I shook my head in a brief sign of gratitude and turned around in haste. Doing or saying nothing was enough then to save another's life.

✺ 77 ✺

There was a sort of urgency to discard all reminders of the past, even the traditional method of reckoning time. The Gregorian calendar was abolished. The 22nd of September 1792, the day when the Republic had been proclaimed, marked the beginning of Year One. The months were now broken into three *décades*, composed of ten days each. The remaining five or six days of the year were called *sans-culottides*. Much fun has been made of that scheme, but I liked the new names of the months, which I found rather poetic: *Vendémiaire* evoked the wine harvest; *Brumaire*, the fog; *Frimaire*, the cold; *Nivôse*, the snow; *Pluviôse*, the rain; *Ventôse*, the winds; *Germinal*, the germination; *Floréal*, the flowers; *Prairial*, the meadows; *Messidor*, the harvest; *Thermidor*, the heats of summer; *Fructidor*, the fruits of the earth. The Saints' names associated with each day of the year had disappeared, along with the Sundays. From then on, one rested on *Décadi*, once in ten days instead of seven in the past.

The National Convention decreed that "terror would be the order of the day" against the enemies of the Nation. It voted a "law on suspects," encompassing the priests, the counterrevolutionaries, the aristocrats and anyone who kept company with them. Of course, as a *ci-devant* noblewoman, I was targeted. The new law gave the Revolutionary Tribunal exclusive jurisdiction to try and punish said suspects. It would become the main instrument of the Terror. Pierre-André's appointment to that court was confirmed on the same day.

Queen Marie-Antoinette, now called the Widow Capet, was transferred from the Temple to the prison of La Conciergerie within the main Courthouse. That step, for a regular prisoner, would have indicated that a trial was imminent. I could not help thinking of the sorrow she must have felt at being separated from her children, especially her son. She loved that little boy. If she had one quality, and she may not have had many more, she was a caring mother. In October, Pierre-André informed me that he would sit as one of the five judges at her trial. He had made it clear that he would not discuss any of his pending cases with me. I dared not ask any questions of him until the proceedings were over.

The former Queen's trial lasted from the 14th of October until the early hours of the 16th. She was guillotined around noon that day. I saw Pierre-André in the evening.

"She must have been exhausted," I said. "Fifteen hours on the first day of trial, and almost twenty-four on the second one."

"She seemed tired from the beginning. She was pale and bony, with greying hair, droopy eyelids and a puffy face. She looked twenty years older than her age. You know that she was not yet forty. A lifetime of depravity will do that to a woman."

"She must have been much altered since I last saw her at the Tuileries."

"That I cannot tell, because I never had the honour of meeting her there. The first time I set eyes on her was when I attended her official questioning a few days ago. She was clearly taking us all for idiots and acted with the same arrogance as if she had been surrounded by her courtiers. She retained the same insolence throughout the trial." He shrugged. "She called herself *Marie-Antoinette de Lorraine d'Autriche*. Herman, who was the presiding judge, let her use that name instead of *Widow Capet*. It was clever of him. What an imbecile she was to remind the jury that she was, had never ceased to be *the Austrian woman*. Herman addressed her formally and with courtesy during the entire trial. On many occasions, he let her respond evasively without pressing the point. She would have had a rougher time with Dumas or me presiding, but it is all for the better. Even the most hardened royalists will not be able to claim that she was not treated fairly."

"How did she argue her case?"

"Her main line of defense was that she was not responsible for any of her actions! She claimed she had obeyed her husband's orders when she prepared the flight to Varennes, or when she sent the French war plans to her brother, the tyrant of Austria. Her argument might have succeeded had she been any other woman. In her case, it was common knowledge that Capet had fallen entirely under her influence, that he was a hapless imbecile without any will of his own." Pierre-André shook his head in disgust. "Of course, that jackass Hébert had to disgrace himself by testifying that she had taught her son to pleasure himself. You may trust that scoundrel to bring up something lewd at every opportunity. Herman, who is no fool, let it pass without questioning Antoinette on it. The rest of us judges also ignored it, but one of the jurors insisted that she respond. That gave her an opportunity to feign outrage and appeal to the public."

"I am sure that this accusation was not true."

"Probably not. Boys of little Capet's age tend to do the same without needing much prompting. Robespierre was furious when he heard of Hébert's testimony and Antoinette's show of indignation. Of course, we decided not to include the accusation of incest in the questions put to the jury, which were limited to whether she had aided and conspired with the foreign and domestic enemies of France. Everyone knew the answers to that. Both of her attorneys limited themselves to repeating what she had been saying about obeying her husband and such rubbish. The jurors deliberated for over an hour. I was beginning to worry that they had been fooled by her lies."

"But they did not acquit her."

"No. The verdict was unanimous. As you know, the jurors always state their decision outside the presence of the accused. Herman warned the public to keep quiet before she was called back to the courtroom to hear the verdict. It was indeed read in complete silence."

"How did she react?"

"She looked stunned. I wonder what she was expecting. Then we deliberated on the penalty, which did not take long, and Herman pronounced her death sentence. She seemed to leave the courtroom in a trance. Around ten this morning, all five of us went with the clerk to her cell to read her the sentence again, as required by law. She did not want to hear it, but Herman made her listen all the same." He shook his head with contempt. "Who did she think she was? She must have imagined that she was still the Queen and could give us orders. To Herman, to me, to all reasonable men, she is a traitress, a vulgar felon like any other. Sanson, the executioner, arrived and tied her hands behind her back. Again she had to protest and make a fuss. Then she was off to the guillotine. I cannot think of anyone who had done more to deserve this fate."

"I know for a fact that she wished for the defeat of France's armies. She may have been guilty of high treason. Yet I was acquainted with her. Although she did not like me much, I cannot help feeling sorrow on her account. Imagine going from being the Queen of France to being treated like a common criminal."

"Everyone is equal before the law. I know that it is a principle she could never bring herself to accept, but it is the basis, along with liberty, of the Revolution."

"Do you ever feel any pity for the accused?"

"Of course, sometimes. What you forget, Gabrielle, is how the business of justice used to be conducted under the Old Regime. I was already a lawyer before the Revolution and I remember it well. The judges then, those judges who despise us for having been appointed by the National Convention, purchased or inherited their functions. There was no jury. Many defendants, especially the poor, had no attorney. Criminal proceedings were secret and even the accused or his lawyer had no right to know the charges against him. It would not have done much good in any case."

Pierre-André shrugged. "If the defendant had the insolence to claim his innocence, a little torture session brought him to his senses. Pounding iron wedges into the wooden *boots* tied to the poor devil's legs worked wonders. The bones were crushed without fail. Or, if the accused were deemed sturdy enough to survive the *water question*, he was tied, his limbs stretched out, a funnel was inserted into his mouth and he was forced to swallow over forty pints of liquid in a row. I need not tell you what damage this did to the internal organs. Once the investigation was deemed complete, the accused heard his sentence on his knees. If he were found guilty, he underwent a final, harsher torture session, again with the boots or the water question. This was allegedly necessary to obtain the names of any accomplices, or wrench a confession if one had not been secured earlier. Some defendants were by then too exhausted to speak. Others, after admitting to everything, were too weak to sign their confessions, or fainted outright. No matter: they were revived on a mattress by the fire and given a glass of wine before the torments resumed. I do not understand how anyone could condone such cruelty, but torture remained an official part of the procedure until '88."

Pierre-André shook his head in disgust. "When the time for the execution came, the accused, stripped to his shirt, a rope around his neck and a candle in his hand, climbed onto the executioner's cart. It stopped at Notre-Dame. There, on the front steps, the man was made to kneel, or was held in that position if his legs could no longer support him. He had to repeat his confession aloud in front of the crowd and ask God and the King to forgive his crime. Only then was he led to the place of execution to face a slow agony on the gallows. That is, if he were fortunate enough not to have been sentenced to the wheel. All that, mind you, to punish offenses sometimes no more grievous than stealing a few francs or hitting someone during a drunken brawl. And the procedure, torture included, was exactly the same for women, except that they could not be sentenced to the wheel."

I shuddered. "What you tell me is still worse than the hanging I witnessed as a child."

"You saw only the execution itself. Now look at what is happening today. No one who stands trial before us has been as much as slapped. The proceedings are public and everyone is entitled to an attorney of his choice. We appoint one for those who cannot afford one. The accused make their appearances unshackled and the only sign of respect asked of them is to rise when we enter the courtroom. No one is required to kneel, to beg for forgiveness or to die stripped of his clothes anymore. Those who claim that we are a *tribunal de sang*, a "tribunal of blood," and feign to regret the justice of the Old Regime are rogues. Most cases tried before us end in dismissals or acquittals." He sighed. "If anything, under the current circumstances I find the jurors far too lenient. All too often, following a verdict of not guilty, I have to release dishonest army suppliers. Those scoundrels become rich supplying the brave men who sacrifice their lives for the Nation with flimsy shoes or faulty guns. To tell you the truth, acquitting that vermin breaks my heart much more than the fate of the Capet Widow."

During the following months, the Revolutionary Tribunal tried many defendants, some famous and many obscure. Among the prominent characters sentenced to death were Madame Roland, the former queen of Parisian society under the reign of the Girondins, Philippe Egalité, the *ci-devant* Duke d'Orléans, accused of conspiring to restore the monarchy and make himself King, and Bailly, who had been Mayor of Paris during the massacre of the Champ de Mars. Pierre-André did not sit as a judge at his trial, for he was a witness for the prosecution.

All twenty-eight Farmers General, including Lavoisier, acknowledged the best scientist of the time, were also tried and sentenced to death. The Revolution had abolished their tax collection privileges; much of the hated wall that had choked the city for their greater profit had already been destroyed amidst general rejoicing. And there were the other enemies of the Republic, the merchants who refused to accept the Nation's paper money as payment for their goods, the bakers who let their bread become moldy rather than to sell it at the official price, the farmers who hoarded their corn while famine was still a daily concern for the poor.

I read that even Osselin, former President of the 17th of August Tribunal and now a member of the National Convention, had been arrested for harbouring the *ci-devant* Marquise de Charry, an aristocrat suspected of emigration.

"Well," said Pierre-André, "Osselin was an inept judge, especially in a presiding position, but he is not a bad man. He was caught. He had procured the Charry woman various hiding places under false identities throughout Paris and the suburbs. He finally hid her in his brother's rectory."

"Is it not what you have done for me?" I asked. "What if *you* were caught?"

"For one thing, you are not an émigrée like the *ci-devant* Marquise. In Osselin's case, the Charry woman was arrested several months ago. She had him called to the rescue. He vouched for her and talked the police officers into releasing her. Yet he was unable to have the case against her dismissed. He then tried to convince her to surrender of her own accord, but when she declined, he reported her himself."

"Was she his mistress?"

"What do you think?"

"Is she young? Pretty?"

"Both."

"Would you have reported me if you had been in Osselin's position?"

"Of course not."

I took his hand in mine. "You should think first of your own safety. If I were arrested, I would not even mention your name. I am grateful for all you did already and would never compromise you."

"I would try to save you till the end, Gabrielle, no matter what you say. I spoke to Robespierre on Osselin's behalf, but he was not inclined to let the case slip into oblivion. There are things you do not know about this business. Osselin's own brother, who is a sworn priest, also reported him. Finally, the Charry woman had a second, unrelated lover, whom she also entertained in Father Osselin's hospitable rectory." He shrugged. "Everyone betrayed everyone else in some way or other. The story, you see, is somewhat less romantic than it seems at first. Robespierre was not favourably impressed by any of the characters, and I cannot blame him for refusing to intervene. I still felt that I could not let Osselin go to the guillotine without trying to do something for him."

"What about Madame de Charry?"

"She went to Brussels for a while. She is guilty of emigration. She is doomed."

"Poor woman."

"The law is clear, Gabrielle. Any *émigré* caught within the territory of the Republic is subject to a death sentence. I need not tell you why. The only reason for them to come back to France is to spy for the foreign powers. So spare me the expression of your pity, and listen to me for a change."

Pierre-André grasped me by the shoulders and looked into my eyes. "If you are ever arrested again, I want to be informed of it immediately. Do you hear me? Immediately. I will face the consequences, whatever they may be. What I do not want is to find you without warning in my courtroom or to read your name after the fact among the list of those sent to the guillotine. The earlier I know of your arrest, the better chance I will have to help you."

With this he pulled me close.

The Marquise de Charry was indeed found guilty of emigration and sentenced to death. Osselin escaped with a deportation sentence, which was converted to life imprisonment. Madame de Charry's second lover, Osselin's brother and the arresting officers were acquitted.

It was not yet six in the afternoon, an early hour for Pierre-André's visits, when he interrupted our game of whist. To amuse Aimée, who has always been fond of cards, I had purchased a deck in the new style. The Kings had been replaced by the Genies of the Arts, War, Peace and Commerce, the Queens by the Liberties of the Press, the Professions, Marriage and Religion, all wearing tunics in the antique style. The Knaves had turned into the Equalities of Rights, Ranks, Duties and Colours, the latter represented by a Negro man holding a rifle and trampling his broken chains. There was not a crown in sight.

I rose to greet Pierre-André, who barely responded to my salutation. He was carrying a flat parcel, wrapped in the coarse canvas used for flour sacks, and did not look pleased. The size of the object, five feet in length by three in width, was familiar. My heart sank.

"Send your daughter to the other room," he said in the Roman language.

Aimée dropped her cards and ran without waiting for me to open my mouth.

"Are you not curious to see what I brought?" he asked. "Open it."

I reached for my scissors and with shaky hands cut the string tying the parcel. When the burlap fell to the floor, I saw myself, clad in a transparent drapery, my hair flowing down to my waist. The gilded frame bore the mention **The Baroness de Peyre** in bold black letters.

"So?" asked Pierre-André.

I hesitated. "I thought it had been destroyed." Indeed I had hoped so.

"Is this all you have to say?"

I was standing next to the table, toying with the Liberty of Marriage. The female figure wore a drapery similar to mine in the painting, although not so sheer. The words *Modesty* and *Divorce* were printed on the card.

"I am thoroughly ashamed of it, Pierre-André. I was only eighteen at the time. I would never let myself be painted in this manner now."

"Thank you for giving me this assurance. I already feel happier."

"Where did you find it?"

"I was walking on Rue Honoré, past a used furniture shop full of portraits of aristocrats and other discards from the Old Regime," he said. "Imagine my astonishment when I beheld, displayed in the middle of the window, a familiar face. Actually, more than a face, for the rest was familiar too. You had been given the place of honour. And rightly so, because I was reminded of what Romeo says of Juliet:

> So shows a snowy dove trooping with crows,
> As yonder lady o'er her fellows shows.

Of course I had to purchase this thing. I do not want a nude picture of you displayed in a shop window."

I looked at the floor.

"Also, your name on the frame might cause you to be recognized," he continued. "The merchant wanted two hundred francs for it. I told him that I would not pay more than fifty for the picture of a shameless little hussy. He argued, reasonably enough, that your state of undress was precisely what made this painting more valuable than the other portraits in his shop. We agreed on seventy francs. It was money well spent." Pierre-André pointed at the picture. "Observe how the painter rendered the roundness of your breasts, the elegance of your arms and legs, the thinness of your waist. The fellow did justice to your personal advantages."

"It was Madame Lebrun."

"At least you had enough modesty not sit naked for a man. But this masterpiece must have been commissioned by one. Was it Villers?"

"Yes."

"Did he decide how you would be painted?"

"Yes."

"So you let him do this to you?"

I made no response.

"My hand itches," he said, glowering, "when I think of the correction you deserve."

I dropped the Liberty of Marriage and drew back a few paces. "Villers is no more. Please do not be jealous of the dead."

"I am not jealous of Villers. I am speaking of *you*. And what about the living? By an unfortunate coincidence, I was reminded this morning of another of your suitors."

I stared at him. "Whom do you mean?"

"Guess."

"Lauzun? General Biron?" I asked after a pause.

"Exactly."

"I am very sad. I read about his arrest, but did not know that his case was coming to trial. He was, he is my friend."

"Your friend?"

"He never was my lover."

"You must have been the only woman at Court he did not bed."

"Perhaps. I did not keep a record of his adventures, nor did I care about them. I am telling you the truth."

I wanted to know whether Pierre-André would sit as a judge at Lauzun's trial but this did not seem an auspicious time to ask.

"You are dying to make some kind of request," said Pierre-André, his eyes narrowed.

I looked at him and took a deep breath. "You made me promise not to bother you with any pleas for leniency, and I would never ask for any favours of the kind. I know how angry you are, Pierre-André. But if you are to sit as a judge at Lauzun's trial, I beg you not to use your functions to harm him."

"Ah! Here we are!" Pierre-André's hands were clenched into fists. "If you must know, I was supposed to conduct his preliminary questioning, but I found an excuse not do so. I do not want anything to do with the trial of someone so closely associated with you. As to harming him, I would hardly need to do anything. It is all too clear that a General who repeatedly attempts to resign his command in wartime, as he did, is a traitor."

I now expected my portrait to be thrown into the fire as a sacrifice to the dark god of jealousy, but Pierre-André was content to leave it standing against a wall, staring at us. I had never liked it much, but now it seemed to be mocking me. I asked his permission to cover it again with the burlap before I called Aimée to dinner.

That night, I ordered from the tavern a dish of *tripoux*, an Auvergne specialty of which Pierre-André was particularly fond, and a bottle of his favourite Burgundy wine. I watched him from the corner of my eye during the meal. He barely said a word and did not look at me. He retired to the bedroom, a glass of wine in his hand, immediately after dinner.

I tidied the dining parlour and put Aimée to bed on the couch.

"Mama," she asked, fighting tears, "is Citizen Pierre-André angry with you?"

"No, dearest, he is only upset over that painting he brought here."

"Is he going to hurt you?"

"Of course not. He is a kind man."

I caressed her forehead and kissed her good night.

I was in no hurry to face Pierre-André's wrath, but had to confront the consequences of my past actions. Mustering my courage, I opened the door to the bedroom. He was seated cross-legged on the carpet in front of the hearth, staring into the fire. One of his large hands supported his chin while the other rested on his knee. I wondered how fiercely they were itching. Still worse than the fear of his anger was the thought that I had incurred his contempt or even lost his affections. I approached slowly and knelt before him.

"You may beat me, Pierre-André. I hope you will forgive me afterwards."

"Come here," he said, reaching for the back of my neck. I stiffened. To my astonishment, he drew me close. "Gabrielle, I told you already that I have forgiven you. True, at first I was a bit upset at finding a nude portrait of you publicly displayed." He smiled. "Now that the thing is no longer taunting me from a shop window, I might even take a liking to it."

I rested my head on his shoulder, tears of relief and gratitude spilling over.

"You are silly," he said. "Do you not know that I love you?"

He left early the next morning, the painting under his arm.

A week later, after a two-day trial, Lauzun was found guilty of having "left his armies in idleness" and sentenced to death. He was to be guillotined on the very last day of 1793. I could not let an old friend die without taking leave of him. Although I had never before attended any execution since the inception of the guillotine, I waited in the bitter cold at the corner of the Pont-Neuf, on the Right Bank of the river, and watched the cart, drawn by two large white horses, approach. Lauzun was alone on it, still handsome in spite of his now heavier features and greying hair. It had been shortened on the nape and the collar of his shirt cut off to facilitate the operation of the guillotine. He looked tired and bored. As the cart turned into the Rue Saint-Honoré, now Rue Honoré, he saw me and sat up. He smiled at me. A moment later, he closed his eyes, out of sadness or because he wanted to keep one image on his mind for the rest of his life.

I walked slowly home. I remembered the premiere of *Tarare* at the Opera, six years earlier. Villers had died at the Palace on the 10th of August. The Duke d'Orléans had been guillotined in November. And now, of the three men I had met that night, none remained alive.

ᘓ 79 ᘕ

One day in February of 1794, Pierre-André arrived at my lodgings and embraced me without saying a word. He sat down and took me in his lap. I immediately thought of the Osselin affair.

"What is it?" I asked, looking into his eyes. "You are in trouble because of me. Are you going to be arrested?"

He shook his head. "Thank you for thinking of me first, my beloved. No, it has nothing to do with me."

"Has something happened to my brother?"

"Confound your brother. He is fine, and will outlive both of us. No, this concerns your sister Hélène."

I closed my eyes. I had begged Pierre-André to find a trace of her, and now that he had done so, I did not want to hear his news.

"Oh, no," I moaned. "She is dead."

Pierre-André remained silent for a moment.

"Yes," he said at last, "it does seem that she is."

I sobbed while he rocked me like a sick child. At last I asked: "How did she die? She was killed, was she not?"

"You know Carrier, of course. He was sent to Nantes as a Representative in Mission."

"Yes, I read about it. I remember him from the time when he was the Baron's attorney."

"Apparently he remembers your family too. I did not tell you of this earlier, Gabrielle, because I did not want to worry you for nothing if it happened not to be true. Carrier is an excellent administrator. Thanks to his skills, neither Nantes nor the Republican army have lacked food, in the middle of a civil war, no less. His military decisions have been sound.

The rebels now seem likely to be defeated. Yet a few weeks ago, rumours began to reach Robespierre." Pierre-André shook his head. "They were too atrocious to be believed. Robespierre asked me what I thought of Carrier. The man is from our country, of course, but I do not know him well. He had a reputation in Aurillac for being a good attorney, but also a drunkard. That was the worst I had heard. Robespierre and I agreed that the rumours must be the kind of heinous lies the rebels spread to discredit the Republic. He nevertheless sent Jullien, in whom he has complete trust, as an envoy to Nantes to look into the veracity the stories."

Pierre-André stroked my hair. "They were true, Gabrielle. Carrier did not believe in the Revolutionary Tribunal or the guillotine, which he found too slow, too inefficient. He had hundreds, maybe thousands of prisoners, men, women and children, some no older than twelve, drowned without trial in the Loire River. He boasted that he had killed two birds with one stone by thinking of that mode of execution: he had resolved both the overcrowding of the jails and the disposal of the bodies. Jullien brought back a list of the persons presumed drowned. I saw your sister's name on it. Robespierre was appalled and recalled Carrier on the same day. Mark my words, the scoundrel will be put on trial; he will pay for his crimes before the year is over. Robespierre will not forgive this."

"What happened to Hélène?"

"She was drowned."

I looked into his eyes, trying to read the truth. "You are not telling me all."

"I am telling you all I know for certain."

"I have never forgotten the way in which Carrier used to look at me. What did he do to Hélène?"

"Only he can tell now."

"I think I can guess anyway. He wanted me. Hélène was very like me, only more beautiful. What did he do to her?"

Pierre-André sighed. "That is what upset Robespierre most among the horrors we heard. The prettiest women were taken from prison and brought to Carrier. They could win a reprieve or even their freedom if they pleased him. It seems that your sister fell into his hands. She must have resisted, for she was taken to the river the next morning."

Carrier had indeed turned into a lunatic in Nantes. He would draw his sword in front of the members of the local Revolutionary Committee and threaten to hack them to pieces with his own hand. In his calmer moments, he talked only of having them guillotined if they showed any reluctance in carrying out his orders. He plunged into drunkenness and debauchery. He had taken his concubine with him to Nantes, but that was not enough. He would, in addition to female prisoners, avail himself of the fine ladies of the aristocracy who threw themselves at his feet to beg for the lives of their husbands or fathers.

Pierre-André, although he must have known of it, did not tell me what happened to the women taken to the river. I learned later, at the time of Carrier's trial, that the criminals he had appointed executioners would strip them naked and violate them in turn before throwing them alive, hands and feet bound, into the Loire River. *Ci-devant* noblewomen suffered additional humiliations and cruelties, which I cannot bear to describe here. The thought of Hélène's final torments still keeps me awake at night.

Such would have been my fate had I stayed in Noirvaux with my sister. I loved her too well to abandon her in the middle of her dangers. I too would have gone from Carrier's bed to that, cold and slimy, of the river.

❧ 80 ❧

LONDON, THIS 15TH OF APRIL 1815

I just had a terrible dispute with Edmond Levassor, Viscount Morton. Although I should not speak of my own son in this manner, he is the most handsome man I have ever seen. He has my colouring, only his hair is a darker shade of red, between mine and that of Hélène. He has inherited his father's height and build, along with an aquiline nose and, I am afraid, a rather quick temper.

We received momentous news from the Continent: Napoléon Bonaparte has escaped his golden cage on the Island of Elba and landed in the south of France. Cities and entire regiments along his path have rallied to him. King Louis the Eighteenth has packed his trunks in haste and again fled abroad. Bonaparte has now reached Paris and settled in the Palace of the Tuileries. The war, that interminable war started in 1792, twenty-three years ago, has once more resumed. England is leading all of Europe in a coalition against France.

Edmond says that he wants to join the British armies. It is out of the question. No son of mine shall take arms against France, even when she is again in the grip of a dictator. Things did not go well. Edmond reminded me that he is, after all, half-English. He is twenty. Is he old enough, is he wise enough to understand the truth? Should I show him this memoir? Heaven help me, what is he going to think of me?

Time presses. I must resume my narrative.

After I finished my work at the theatre, Aimée would take her doll Margaret and me for walks in the Luxembourg gardens. Patriotic concerts there celebrated the victories of the soldiers of the Republic. We listened to the rousing accents of *La Marseillaise* and other patriotic airs, accompanied by fifes and drums. At that time, in 1794, the tide of war had turned in favour of France. The enemy was defeated on all fronts. Not only was the Nation freed from foreign invasion, but our armies occupied the former Austrian Netherlands and northern Italy.

During one of our walks, we found the aspect of the Luxembourg much altered. Throngs of workmen were digging out all of the lawns and flower beds. Astonished, I asked a guard what was happening.

"Orders of the Municipality," he said. "Citizen Chaumette's decided that there's no room for flowers in the gardens of the Nation when patriots lack bread. They're going to plant potatoes to feed the people."

Within weeks the Luxembourg and all other public gardens in Paris were covered with neat rows of potatoes. I am in no way adverse to that plant, but found the monotony of the landscape oppressive. Even the walkways had been narrowed to give way to Chaumette's agricultural zeal. I wondered what the Countess de Provence, who had been so proud of her vegetable garden, would have thought of these changes to her former residence. The Luxembourg Palace itself had become a prison.

Chaumette did not stop at half-measures. Our friend the guard, who always had candy in his pocket for Aimée, informed us that the beautiful old trees were to be pulled out.

"They make too much shade for the potatoes," he said.

I stared at him. "But this is appalling. The flowers and lawns can easily be seeded again, but it will take decades to replace the trees."

"Well, maybe, Citizen, but I'm not going to say anything about it. You should keep your opinion to yourself too."

That night I asked Pierre-André about it.

"Chaumette and Hébert, those rabble-rousers, are responsible for this," he said. "Those two hold crucial functions at the Municipality now. And Hébert uses his disgusting *Père Duchesne* rag to inflame the populace and aggrandize himself. As if a few acres of potatoes were going to alleviate the food shortages! Pure, outrageous demagoguery. And it is not their worst provocation. I am as fond of the trees of Paris as you are, but Chaumette has another idea: *cleansing* the capital of its harlots. He wants to send them to the Revolutionary Tribunal, because, he says, they harm the Nation by depraving the morals of the people." Pierre-André shook his head. "As if, with foreign and civil wars raging, and all of the real conspiracies afoot to destroy the Republic, we had time to try the 30,000 harlots found in the city. I, for one, fail to see why they should be sent to the guillotine. All of that animosity towards those poor women reeks of buggery. Add to that the Goddess Reason tomfoolery, and you will see that Hébert and Chaumette are intent on disgracing the Revolution. They use their functions to pander to the most ignorant segments of the people. Robespierre cannot tolerate this much longer. If we do not take control of the Municipality, we are going to see much worse."

Within days, Hébert was arrested and stood trial before the Revolutionary Tribunal for conspiracy against the Republic. Pierre-André was put in charge of the questioning of the accused and his nineteen co-defendants.

"By the time I was done with Hébert," he said, "the case was all but over. I know how to conduct the interrogation of scoundrels of that ilk. He looked stunned to find himself on the accused's seat, and still more so to face an old acquaintance like me as his judge. He could only stammer. Later, at trial, all he did was to stare blankly and respond by *yes* or *no* to the questions. He barely presented any defense."

Indeed all but one of the co-defendants were found guilty. Hébert, the idol of the *sans-culottes*, went to the guillotine. I expected the Parisians to rise in support of a man who had been so popular, but all remained quiet. Chaumette followed a few days later. The trees of Paris were saved *in extremis* by his demise.

After Hébert's execution, Robespierre was able to strike his more moderate enemies, those who, like Danton, demanded an end to the Terror. Danton, notorious for taking bribes, was an easy target for a criminal prosecution. He, along with his main allies, was also tried before the Revolutionary Tribunal for corruption, found guilty and guillotined.

The Municipality was now deprived of Chaumette, its National Agent, and Hébert, his chief ally. Robespierre had achieved a major victory in defeating his extremist enemies. He could now replace Hébert's friends at the Municipality with his own. Pierre-André recommended one of the jurors of the Tribunal, Claude-François de Payan, for the function of National Agent.

"Payan is a *ci-devant* nobleman," Pierre-André said. "Yet he is a true patriot, one of our most solid jurors. He is only twenty-seven, but he will be able to handle the function of National Agent. It was offered to me, but I can be more useful at the Tribunal. It is not always a pleasant function, but someone has to exercise it, and forcefully. In any event, I will not leave the Municipality. I will remain a member of the Council General and keep things in line there."

So Robespierre now controlled the Municipality of Paris through a group of men who were, and would remain till the end, entirely devoted to him.

More changes occurred at the Tribunal itself. Dumas, a staunch Jacobin, was promoted to the function of President and Pierre-André to that of Vice President, each in charge of one of the two Sections. His position in the new regime was becoming more prominent.

❦ 81 ❧

I had become Charlotte's friend at the theatre. She confided in me her liaisons with various characters and her many grievances against Granger. He was not, she complained, much of an athlete in bed nor did he know how to set off her talents as an actress at the theatre. She was not shy about disclosing the tastes and peculiarities of her past and current lovers.

"What about your late husband?" she once asked. "You never mention him."

"He was not as entertaining as your suitors."

"He mustn't have made much of an impression on you."

"Quite the contrary. He used to beat me without mercy."

"That's unfortunate. Still it's no reason not to remarry. Most husbands are better behaved. And then marital authority has been abolished now. They can't order you around anymore. And if you're plagued by a brute, it's easy to obtain a divorce these days. You don't even need a reason."

"You may be right, dear, but I am content with my current situation."

I often wondered whether Charlotte would reveal anything concerning Pierre-André, but she never mentioned him, maybe for fear of compromising him. I trusted his assurance that their liaison had ceased years earlier, but would have liked to know how he behaved with other women.

My conversations with Charlotte were always abruptly interrupted whenever Granger entered the room, for they often revolved around him. He seemed to guess it and looked none too happy about it.

"Citizen Labro," he said one day, "I need to talk to you in my office. Without your daughter, please."

I left Aimée with Charlotte and followed him with some reluctance.

"Have a seat, Citizen, have a seat," he said. "We are between friends here, are we not? There is no occasion for you to fret. Do you know that Julie is leaving us for the *Théâtre des Variétés*?"

"This is the first I hear of it. She did not confide in me. I hope that you will be able to find a replacement shortly for the part of Annette in *The Lovesick Shepherd*. We can use the costumes she wore in *Lisbeth's Cottage*, but I may have to alter them on short notice."

Granger smiled. "I would not worry about that. I believe I have already found her replacement."

He was clearly waiting for me to ask who it was. I remained mute.

"You should not limit your ambitions to sewing, my pretty," he continued, rising from his chair. He stood before me, the buttons of his breeches level with my face.

I looked away. "Indeed, Citizen Granger, I cannot think of anything else I could do here."

"What about acting, little goose?"

"I am flattered by your offer, but I am sure I have no talent at all for it."

"How do you know if you do not try?"

"I have always been told that I am a poor liar."

"What does it have to do with acting? And even if you were the worst actress in town, how would it matter? This is not the *Théâtre-Frauçais*. People come here to see a pretty face, and yours is lovely enough to make them forget their troubles."

He shrugged. "As if they cared about acting! In fact, it is a crime to hide as you do in the wings. Everyone should be allowed a good look at your charming person. Now that Julie has left, I cannot think of a better Annette than you. I saw you attend the rehearsals of *The Lovesick Shepherd*. You must know her lines by heart already."

"I cannot thank you enough for your kindness, Citizen Granger," I said, rising out of my chair, "but I have to decline. I cannot act, I am quite sure of it."

He was no longer smiling. "Am I hearing you correctly? You, a little nobody, are refusing a part for which any actress in Paris would kill? Are you out of your senses?"

I shook my head. "Please do not insist, Sir, I mean Citizen. I feel quite unequal to it."

A smile returned to his face. "All right, I understand. Poor little dear, I know you are shy. Do not worry, I will help you. I will be very good to you if you will let me."

He put his arm around my shoulders and tried to kiss me. I turned away and pushed him back. "What are you doing, Citizen Granger?"

"What am I doing?" He paused, glaring at me. "What about you? I saw you befriend Lacoste, that miserable old debris I keep solely out of pity. I have seen how he leers at you. Yet it does not disgust you, does it? Maybe it is because you are an aristocrat too."

He caught me by the arm. "Yes, my pretty, do you think I have not noticed those airs you give yourself?"

I shook him loose. "Leave me alone. I am not interested in acting. I am a seamstress."

"A seamstress! Tell a wooden horse that story and you will receive a kick. And now you refuse a part in one of my plays! You refuse me! I am not good enough for you, am I? And my theatre is not good enough for you either, perhaps? Your Ladyship was accustomed to something grander. Maybe you used to play in Versailles with the late Widow Capet." He was almost spitting. "Dirty little bitch! Harlot! Aristocrat!"

I fled, pursued by a stream of insults and profanity. In my retreat, I ran into Charlotte.

"What's the matter, Gabrielle?" she asked. "What have you done to Granger?"

"You should ask what he has done to me," I said, catching my breath. "He offered me a part in *The Lovesick Shepard* and propositioned me."

"To tell you the truth, I am surprised that he waited so long." She smiled. "What did you expect, Gabrielle, when he hired you? You should give it some consideration."

"Certainly not."

"But you will never become an actress if you act like a simpleton. How do you think I started in this business?"

"It was different, Charlotte. *You* wanted to become an actress. I do not. In fact, I believe that I will not return here at all tomorrow."

"You can't be serious." She frowned. "How are you going to live?"

"Do not worry for me, Charlotte."

"Let me at least lend you fifty francs. You will repay me when you can."

I took her hands in mine and kissed her. "You are very good, dear Charlotte, but I will be fine."

I usually left the theatre early in the afternoon, before the matinee audience arrived, but that day I decided not to tarry. I had put on my mantle and taken Aimée's hand in mine when I heard a commotion at the entrance to the theatre. I peeked from behind a door. Lacoste, one hand resting on his chest, his other arm raised to the heavens, was making a speech to a group of unknown men. I heard him declaiming at the top of his voice about "the immortal principles of liberty and equality." The men roughly pushed him aside. I seized Aimée's hand and ran to Charlotte's dressing room, where she was putting on her rouge.

"Oh, dear," I said, "I am going to be arrested."

She dropped her powder puff. "You, arrested? But why?"

"I saw Lacoste trying to stop a group of men. They must be the police. They are coming for me. Can you do me a great favour?"

"Of course."

"I cannot escape with Aimée. Would you take care of her until this matter is cleared?"

"Of course, but what's happening?"

"There is another thing, Charlotte, a very important thing. You know Citizen Coffinhal, the judge. Tell him of my arrest. Immediately. Please do not forget."

Aimée was listening to me, her mouth open, tears in her eyes. She was holding fast to her doll. I kissed her in haste and ran towards the public's entrance. Two men were posted there. I slipped behind the stage, where the sets were kept. I remained in hiding among the painted villages with their sunny skies, quaint cottages and grazing sheep. I wanted to wait until the start of the matinee, when I hoped to mingle with the public. I was crouching, my heart beating so hard that it felt like jumping out of my chest. I heard male voices.

"There she is," cried one of them. "Catch her."

The men were on my heels. I was fleet of foot with the laced shoes I now wore and I ran towards the artists' entrance. Two other men were waiting there. I turned around. They chased me and one of them caught me in his arms. He called the others to the rescue. Enraged, I let out a shriek. He put his hand on my mouth. I bit him with all the strength I could muster while kicking his comrade in the shins. I resisted until one of the fellows managed to seize my hands and tie them behind my back with his handkerchief. Apparently they had not deemed it necessary to bring shackles. Once I was bound, the man I had bitten slapped me. I was shoved into a waiting hackney.

The men took me to the Section of the City. Shackles were fetched to replace the handkerchief, but they were too large and would have slipped off my wrists. The man I had bitten held my hands behind my back while another bound them tightly with the end of a rope. I winced as it cut into my skin.

"There," he said, "this way you won't try to escape again. You must have much to hide to be so desperate to slip away. I'd be surprised if before long you did not dance a little jig on the Place de la Revolution."

That was the name of the former Place Louis the Fifteenth, where the guillotine now stood. Earlier, the grim machine had been taken apart after each execution. Now it was simply covered with a waxed cloth when it was not in use, both for convenience and to serve as a grim reminder of the fate that awaited the enemies of the Republic.

"I will be acquitted," I said. "There are no actionable charges against me."

"*No actionable charges*, eh? Listen to the way you talk. You were reported as an aristocrat and an illegally returned émigrée."

"That is not true. I have never left France in my entire life."

I was led by the rope, like an animal on a tether, into the next room. There several prisoners, all male, were waiting to be interrogated. One of them, seated on a bench close to the fireplace, rose and offered me his place. Four guards, smoking their pipes and drinking wine, were watching us. I sat down, enjoying the warmth of the hearth. Yet my wrists were hurting under the bite of the rope and my hands were becoming numb.

"We could untie her," said one of the guards, pointing at me. "She's the only one here who's bound."

"She resisted arrest," said another. "She even bit one of the officers. Mark my words, she's going to try and run away again. If the little bitch escapes on our watch, we'll be the ones with an assignation with Saint Guillotine."

"Please, Citizen," I said, "there are too many of you for me to escape now, and I am too tired and hungry to even think of it. And I would never repay any kindness of yours by causing trouble for you or your comrades."

The first guard, over the other's renewed objections, drew a knife from his pocket, walked to me and cut the rope. I massaged my wrists. He then brought me a plate of ham and eggs, with a beaker of water mixed with wine. I looked up and thanked him. It was several hours before I was called before the Revolutionary Committee of the Section, which held its sessions in the adjoining room.

My questioning did not elicit any new information. I denied everything. I was ordered to empty my pockets. Their contents, consisting of my Civic Certificate, a handkerchief, an *assignat* of ten francs, a lead pencil, a needle case, a thimble, some thread and a mother-of-pearl rosary, were inventoried before me by the president of the Committee.

"Look at this," he said, showing the beads to another man, "she's a fanatic." Then, turning to me: "All of this will be put in a sealed envelope. It'll be delivered to the clerk when you arrive in jail, and opened in your presence before the Revolutionary Tribunal."

✣ 82 ✣

It was past midnight when a group of police officers walked me to the prison of La Conciergerie. They did not take me up the monumental stairway I had climbed to visit Pierre-André in 1792. Like any other prisoner, I entered the jail through a small courtyard locked by a gate. A second gate, a few steps lower, opened into an office. There, the clerk, rubbing his eyes, wrote in a large register:

> *Gabrielle Labro, age twenty-four, born in Aurillac, domiciled*
> *Rue de la Colombe, Number 7. Height: five feet six inches. Hair*

and eyebrows: red. Forehead: average. Eyes: grey. Mouth: small.
Chin: round. Face: oval. Taken here by virtue of an order of the
Revolutionary Committee of the Section of the City, to be detained
until further notice by measure of general safety.

The police officers who had accompanied me signed the register and
left. The clerk's shaggy, filthy dog slowly walked up to me in the manner
of very old animals and licked my hand. I could hear the noise of a celebration coming from the bowels of the jail.

"Those," said the clerk, "are prisoners sentenced to death who are entertaining some of their comrades. They're going to the guillotine tomorrow. If you can afford it, you may do the same before you have your
pretty little head lopped off."

"There is no reason why this should happen. I am a good patriot."

"Everyone here claims to be a good patriot. Your case will be reviewed
by Citizen Fouquier, the Prosecutor. If he finds there's enough evidence
against you, he'll send you to be questioned by one of the judges before
you go to trial."

"Is it going to be Citizen Coffinhal?"

"Why would you want to go before Citizen Coffinhal?"

"I heard that he is very fair."

"He's the same way with everyone, for sure. He doesn't let the accused
rattle on, not that they feel much like it once they clap eyes on him. If it
was me, I'd rather go before Citizen Dumas. Now here's a man who likes
a joke. Even so, the accused don't always laugh with him either, mind
you. Anyway, you don't choose your judge. Whoever it is, he'll decide
whether to release you or to send you to stand trial. Then he'll let you hire
an attorney or he'll appoint one for you if you can't afford one. But that
won't be until tomorrow or the day after." The clerk reached for a key
hanging from a nail on the wall. "In the meantime, I'll find you an apartment. Speaking of which, I'm sorry to say, all of the paying cells with
cots in the women's section are taken. You'll share a *pailleux*, all expenses
paid by the Nation, with some other females. You're in luck: I have a cell
in the women's courtyard with three prisoners in it. You can make a four-
some and play cards together."

He laughed. The *pailleux* was the name given to cells without beds or
other furniture, where the floor, as in stables, was covered with straw—
paille in French—for the comfort of the inmates.

The clerk called two gendarmes, who invited me to follow them to an immense vaulted room in the Gothic style. My nostrils were assaulted by a smell of urine. I was reminded of the stench of the ménagerie at Versailles, which I had visited with Aimée in the old days. Iron bars, fitted between the columns that supported the high ceiling, formed a giant cage housing dozens of male prisoners. A layer of straw covered its floor. What was left of the room was a passage leading deeper into the prison.

My arrival, in spite of the late hour, was greeted by whistling and cheering. Some men, reaching through the bars, made obscene gestures and mockingly begged the gendarmes to lock me with them. I pulled my skirts away from them.

My guards, ignoring the racket, led me to the far end of the room and down several passages, all lined with cells. Most had no solid doors, but only bars. I could guess at human forms lying in the dark. Finally, we reached a paved courtyard, open to the sky. It was quiet there. The night was chilly and I gathered my mantle around my shoulders. The gendarmes opened one of the many doors opening into the courtyard and I found myself in a cell with three other women, whose shapes I distinguished briefly in the light of the lantern. The door was locked again behind me and I was left in the dark. A harsh voice yelled with an oath:

"Find a spot next to the door and quit making a damned nuisance of yourself."

I obeyed in silence, careful not to step on my companions, and hopeless of any news before the morning, fell asleep.

After daybreak, I had the opportunity to become acquainted with my new companions. I told my usual story. One of my fellow prisoners was an aristocrat, the Countess de Verneuil, who had been there for less than a week after spending three months at La Force, and another, Victorine Dubonnet, a woman of about fifty, a servant in a tavern. The third one, somewhat younger, was a lady's maid, arrested two days earlier with her mistress, who was imprisoned separately in the paying section. The presence of the Countess and the maid did not require much of an explanation, but I asked Victorine what had brought her there.

She sighed. "Well, Citizen Labro," she said, "I made uncivic statements in front of the patrons at the tavern. Someone must've reported me to the Section. I was drunk, mind you, else I wouldn't have said that the Republic's *assignats* were just good enough to be used as ass wipes. But that doesn't prevent me from being a patriot. I'd never have talked like that but for the liquor."

She was the one who had addressed me upon my arrival, but she soon took it upon herself to acquaint me with the customs of the place.

"I was transferred from L'Abbaye three days ago," she said. "Most people here don't stay more than a couple of days, because the space is reserved for the prisoners who go to trial before the Tribunal. It's odd, come to think of it, that they took you here directly after you were arrested. Maybe it's because you live on the island. I was questioned by a judge yesterday, so I expect to go up to trial today." She shrugged. "Not that I mind, because I've waited long enough. I'd rather know."

"I wish you luck from my heart, Citizen. I am sure that, when you explain that you were speaking under the influence of the liquor, the Tribunal will be lenient."

"That's kind of you to say that, but, you see, I have no family. If I did, perhaps I'd like to deceive myself. I was at fault when I opened my big mouth, no doubt about it. I'll accept the judgment of the Tribunal, whatever it is. If I'm sentenced before three in the afternoon, I'll go to the guillotine in the four o'clock cart. So maybe we'll never see each other again. If I'm sentenced after three, I'll have a reprieve until tomorrow."

The lady's maid seemed frozen, not as much from the cold as from terror, and was not saying much. The Countess was equally silent, staring at me in an unpleasant manner. I wondered whether we had met before the Revolution and I had unwittingly made an enemy of her, but neither her name nor her face were familiar. More simply, she may have thought that I was a *mouton*, a "sheep," a prison informant. I avoided her eye.

The guards brought us a bowl of soup in which floated pieces of spongy meat. It was, Victorine told me, the prisoners' least favourite food. I sniffed it with some curiosity. The lady's maid, watching me, declared in a dire voice: "It's human flesh from the cadavers of those sent to the guillotine. Those monsters are trying to send us to hell by making us eat other Christians."

I laughed—no one in jail should waste any opportunities to do so, which are rare enough—but checked myself when I saw her looking at me grimly.

"I've never heard anything half so silly, you dullard," said Victorine to the lady's maid. "You believe any lie your friends the blessed-asses tell you, don't you? It's true, though, that nobody knows what's in the soup, except the guards, and they won't tell."

"I cannot be sure," I mused, sifting through it with my spoon, "but it does look like *mou*."

Mou, "soft," is the name given to beef lungs, a delicacy Joséphine used to serve—uncooked, of course—to the cats in Fontfreyde. They would run to her, tails up, meowing with delight, when she put their plate down on the floor of the kitchen. For an instant I was transported to my girl-hood, a happy time when no one spoke of beheading me. I forgot the bare walls of the cell, the straw on the floor and the stench of the bucket in the corner. I was back in Joséphine's kitchen, sitting in the warmth of the *cantou* and playing with the cats. The *mou* had brought tears to my eyes.

Victorine broke the spell.

"That may be," she said. "Regardless, eat it in moderation, Citizen. I had the same thing yesterday and the day before. It turns your bowels to water. That's mighty inconvenient if you have to stand trial. I won't take any, in case I go up today."

Not knowing what to expect myself, I followed her example. The maid was still considering her bowl with revulsion, as if touching it would have sealed her eternal damnation. Only the Countess, without a word, finished her soup. Either her innards had been toughened by months of prison fare, or she was showing aristocratic fortitude in the face of adversity.

After breakfast our door was opened and we were allowed to go to the courtyard. In the light of day, I saw a large fountain that occupied a cor-ner of it and was surrounded by a small crowd. That was one of the luxu-ries of the women's quarter. We were allowed to wash in it, and the fortunate ones who owned a change of clothes could clean those. The pris-oners with most seniority behind bars used it first. Since I was the latest arrival, I had to wait until all of my companions were done before using the fountain. The clean water refreshed me. Looking at my reflection, I did my best to pick off my clothes and hair the pieces of straw that had gathered there during the night. I wanted to look neat, regardless of what would happen later.

We were allowed to walk all day in the courtyard. There was no hope of escape, for the walls were high and fitted all around with iron spikes turned downwards. The women were only taken back to their cells and locked in at dark. That arrangement was much more pleasant than anything I had known at La Force. Some of the male prisoners were likewise allowed a walk in a nearby passage closed by an iron gate that opened into our courtyard. Thus they could communicate with the women for some time every day. Some were kissing ladies passionately and holding their hands through the bars.

"Do you think these people knew each other before arriving here?" I asked Victorine.

"Most of them, no. People fall in love quickly here. Chances are at least one of the turtle doves is going to be guillotined in a matter of days. That makes romances brisk." She chuckled. "The only one who remained for months here was the Widow Capet, and she didn't even find a lover. The first time in her life she had any rest from that quarter, I bet. But then they must've kept a close eye on her."

I was surprised to notice that, in spite of everything, the atmosphere of the prison was not mournful. The nearness of death made the sweetness of living all the more precious.

I wondered whether Charlotte had informed Pierre-André of my arrest. If she had, his silence implied that he did not wish to save me at a terrible cost to himself. I remembered that he had told me not to expect his help if I ran into trouble at the theatre. He had been right, of course. I could not blame him for declining to intervene after he had warned me of the danger and I had spurned his advice. I might now pay the ultimate price for my imprudence.

With the Osselin affair fresh on my mind, I did not want to compromise Pierre-André. I loved him too well to cause him any harm. Not a word would pass my lips to indicate that I knew him. I needed to prepare for the worst, which included the guillotine and the final thought of leaving Aimée adrift before her ninth birthday. I trusted that, even if he did not want to help me, he would make arrangements to send her to my sister Madeleine. I did not think that Pierre-André wished to see me on his docket. What man, in his position, would have the courage to look me in the eye as he read my sentence? So we might never see each other again.

"You look worried, Citizen Labro," said Victorine as we were walking in the courtyard. "Cheer up. Your situation is not hopeless. I am too old, nobody would believe me, but at your age, you can always claim to be pregnant. You say it right after the President reads the verdict if things don't turn out too well for you."

"But I am not with child. I would be examined by prison physicians. They would report their findings to the Tribunal."

"In the beginning, physicians or no physicians, they can't see a thing, so the Tribunal would give you three months' reprieve. That's plenty of time to bribe a turnkey or a gendarme to impregnate you. With a pretty young thing like you, I'm even sure that more than one would do it free of charge, for the pleasure of taking you, of course, and also out of pity."

"I cannot imagine giving myself to a stranger and bearing a child under such conditions. Further, I could not be sure to become pregnant. The lie would be discovered three months later."

"Here's what you'd do, Citizen. When the physicians come back to visit you, you say you miscarried and had yourself impregnated again. A woman in my cell at L'Abbaye told that story. A turnkey sold her a fetus in a jar, pickled in spirits. It cost her fifty francs, but it was worth it."

I stared at her.

"She showed it to the doctors," continued Victorine, "as proof of her miscarriage. They must've known she was lying, because it was almost full term. Yet that earned her another three months' respite. After six months, of course, if your pregnancy is still not confirmed, the Tribunal would become suspicious."

I put my hand on Victorine's arm. "Maybe it is misplaced pride, Citizen; maybe I should not be so fastidious, especially since I have a little girl. Yet I could not bring myself to say or do the things you suggest. I thank you, nonetheless, for your advice and concern."

"It's a pity, but I don't blame you. I'm not sure I'd do it myself, even if I were younger." She laughed. "Also, with my looks, the turnkeys would charge too much. I couldn't afford it."

Victorine's name was called soon afterwards. I rose to embrace her, but she gently pushed me away.

"You're a kind person, Citizen Labro," she said, "but if you kiss me, I'll become soft-hearted and lose my courage in front of the judges. That's the last thing I have left. I wish you luck. Don't forget what I told you about being with child. You've time to reconsider."

She was taken away by the gendarmes.

I missed Victorine and, to avoid reflecting upon my own situation, kept thinking of her trial. Around noon, the gendarmes put an end to my anxiety by calling my name. I followed them upstairs through a labyrinth of passages and corkscrew stairwells. Some doorways were so low that they had to remind me not to hit my head. My heart was beating fast as I wondered whether I was being taken to Pierre-André's chambers. I went instead to the ground floor of the other round tower.

I waited, standing between the two gendarmes, next to an open door. I heard a man's voice, not Pierre-André's, swearing inside the room and understood that I had some time left to myself. I fell to my knees, facing the wall. My eyes closed, I whispered the Prayer for the Dying. Its simple words comforted me as they had done in La Force. One of the gendarmes grabbed me by the shoulder to raise me, but the other stopped him.

"Leave her alone," he said. "She's not hurting anybody."

At last a clerk, white in the face, left the office, carrying a pile of papers. The voice shouted, "Bring her in." I blessed myself, rose and followed the gendarmes inside. A man was seated behind a desk covered with papers.

"Wait outside, you two," he told the gendarmes, "and leave the door open."

He did not rise but looked at me with some interest.

"I am Fouquier, Public Prosecutor of the Revolutionary Tribunal."

He was by then one of the best-known men in Paris and the simple mention of his name was sufficient to inspire terror in the bravest hearts, for he could bring anyone to trial before the Tribunal. I was, of course, apprehensive, but could not help feeling a great curiosity towards him. Pierre-André had told me that they had been friends since before the Revolution. Fouquier was rather tall, well built, and not young anymore, as revealed by deep vertical wrinkles on each side of his mouth. His hair was still black, his eyes dark and intelligent, and his nose, a prosecutor's nose, long and pointy.

"What were you doing out there on your knees?" he asked in the familiar mode.

"I was saying the Prayer for the Dying, Citizen Prosecutor."

"Do you expect to die?"

"It will be for you, Citizen Prosecutor, and for the judges and jurors of this court, to decide."

"I saw that a rosary was found among your things. Have you any connections to unsworn priests?"

"I never had any. I used to attend Mass served by sworn clergy. Now I address my prayers directly to God and His Saints without recourse to priests of any sort."

"All right. Make yourself comfortable and tell me why you find yourself here today."

I sat down. "You will be the one to explain why I am here, Citizen Prosecutor," I said, "because I do not know. I am a widow and lead a very retired life. I am a seamstress at the *Théâtre du Marais* and only stir from home to go to work or buy food. I have no relations with the enemies of the Nation. I am as good a patriot as you will find anywhere. That explains why I had no trouble receiving a Civic Certificate from my Section."

"Your Section must have been deceived, because there are strong suspicions of aristocracy, maybe even of emigration, against you."

"It cannot be, Citizen Prosecutor. I have been a seamstress at the *Théâtre du Marais* for over a year. Before that, I used to live in Auvergne."

I told again the story of Citizen Labro, her early widowhood, her woes, her ill-fated journey to Paris. While I was continuing my narrative, to which Fouquier listened carefully and without interruption, I saw on his face the look of someone who has heard many stories, and not believed them all.

"I will be more candid than you," he said when I was done, "and tell you why you are here. Citizen Granger, your employer, has reported you as an aristocrat in disguise, which of course raises suspicions of emigration. That good patriot says that you give yourself *the airs of a Marquise*. Those are his words, and I cannot say that I disagree with his assessment."

I took a deep breath. "I am not surprised to hear that Citizen Granger is at the root of my troubles. The truth is that he is unhappy with me for reasons that have nothing to do with my supposed aristocratic airs. I spurned his advances yesterday, Citizen Prosecutor. He must have reported me out of spite."

A thin smile appeared on Fouquier's face. "I have no trouble believing that a man could be tempted by a juicy little morsel like you. If true, it makes Granger a swine, but in no way does it preclude your being an aristocrat. A search of your lodgings produced sheets of a child's lessons. You have obviously received an excellent education yourself. You express yourself very well and without any country accent. Now would you like to explain to me where the wife of a cheese merchant would have learned to speak like this?"

"I was sent to a convent for a few years as a child. There I learned to speak French. My parents used to have a bit of money, but I was orphaned early and had to marry Citizen Labro when I was fifteen. I am in turn striving to give my daughter a decent education."

"Where is your child now?"

"I do not know, Citizen Prosecutor. We were separated when I was arrested at the theatre."

"Why did you resist arrest if you were innocent?"

"I was terrified of going to jail."

He arched his eyebrow. "You do not look terrified at all. Indeed it has been some time since I have seen anyone answer my questions with such composure."

"It is only in your presence that I am not terrified, Citizen Prosecutor, because you are speaking to me with great kindness."

"Have you been imprisoned before?"

"Never."

"I will make some enquiries to verify your story. Until then, you will remain here as a guest of the Nation in our *pailleux*. If you are telling the truth, you have nothing to fear and will be released. If not . . . Now it would seem that we have a visitor."

I turned around in my seat. Pierre-André bent slightly to go through the door frame. It was the first time I saw him in his full official dress. Whoever had designed the judges' uniform had not had a man like him in mind. The plumed hat added another foot to his height, and the cape hanging from his shoulders made him look like a tower draped in black cloth. He slammed the door closed. Everything in the room shook. He walked directly to Fouquier's desk.

"You and your mania to keep your door open!" he said. "This woman is a good patriot. Let her go."

Fouquier smiled again, this time broadly. "So you know this pretty little fish I caught in my nets, do you not? It was kind of you to recess your trial to inform me of it in person. She is, if one is to believe her, a Citizen Labro, a seamstress, the widow of a cheese merchant from your country. Do you want her sent to your courtroom for trial? Or, I can, if you prefer, ship her to Dumas. I guess it would not make much of a difference."

"She is telling the truth," said Pierre-André, looking straight at Fouquier. "There is no need to try her before anyone."

"Now, friend Coffinhal," said Fouquier, "I would be the last man to accuse you of lying to protect the enemies of the Nation, but she looks like the widow of a cheese merchant as much as I resemble the Pope. I was thinking of sending for some of the National Guards who were on duty at the Palace before the 10th of August. I believe, I do not know why, that they might recognize her. Many, especially those partial to red hair, would consider her rather attractive. The National Guards will remember her better than her plain friends."

Fouquier rose from his chair to sit on his desk before me. "If I am not mistaken, not only is she an aristocrat, but she might be one of the ladies of the Court. Look at her hands, so soft and white, with long, tapered fingers. I have never seen such delicate wrists in a grown woman."

He had taken both of my hands into his, turning them over and considering them with great attention. Pierre-André wrenched them away from Fouquier and took them in his.

"Never touch her again," he said.

Fouquier grinned. "There is no need to be cross with an old friend. I was only testing you. I knew she was yours from the moment you stormed my office."

Pierre-André let go of my hands and looked at the Citizen Prosecutor as if he were ready to seize him by his necktie.

"Congratulations," continued Fouquier, "quite a prize you have here! But if you want to save her, why not wed her as well as bed her? You know that I married a noblewoman myself. Those who are cured of their aristocratic prejudices make excellent wives. Provided that this one has no connection with the conspirators of the *ci-devant* monarchy, you have nothing to fear by taking that step."

"I am old enough," said Pierre-André, "to manage these matters without the benefit of your advice."

"So I was right, was I not? You, of all men, with a lady of the Court! I know that you stopped, some time ago, patronizing the houses of convenience of the *Palais-Egalité*. Let me assure you, by the way, that you are sorely missed there. Your custom was very regular and you left nothing but good memories. And your more elegant lady friends, one in particular whom I will not name, also lament the loss of your society. What was I supposed to think? That you had suddenly converted to continence? In all the years I have known you, it has never struck me as one of your many virtues."

"How kind of you to take such a keen interest in my affairs!"

"It is one of my duties to be well informed. I have long suspected that you were discreetly keeping a woman somewhere, not at your own lodgings of course, but probably not too far either, because you are a busy man. And why such secrecy, except to hide a liaison with an aristocrat? But I must confess that I would not have imagined anything like this one. You make a fine couple together." Fouquier chuckled. "Beauty and the Beast, if you do not mind my saying so."

"Instead of making stupid jokes," said Pierre-André, "you should be thinking of a way to resolve this. One thing I know. She is not going back downstairs to that squalid hole you call a prison. I want her out of here before the day is over."

Fouquier, in excellent spirits, and Pierre-André appeared to have become the best of friends again. They agreed that Pierre-André would keep me for the rest of the day in his chambers and assume all responsibility to take me out of there after dark. Fouquier would have the clerk record my transfer from La Conciergerie to the jail of *Les Oiseaux*, "The Birds." Pierre-André asked who had reported me.

His eyes narrowed. "Granger, is it? The promoter of *The Pope in Hell*. Probably a friend of the late Hébert, intent, like him, on discrediting the Revolution. And now he wastes the time of the Nation's magistrates by filing idle reports to harass patriots. A provocation too many. Have him arrested. Today."

Fouquier concurred. He rose to bow to me. "It was an honour and a pleasure meeting you, Madam. I hope to be, someday, the best man at your wedding."

Pierre-André marched me out of Fouquier's office. He ordered the two gendarmes who were still waiting for me outside to escort me to his chambers. There he dismissed them and locked the door.

Without a word, he took me in his arms and held me tight for several minutes. My cheek pressed against the black silk of his waistcoat, I could barely breathe, both from the strength of his embrace and the sudden relief of my escape. Then he made me sit in one of the chairs. He opened the door and called a gendarme.

"Fetch something to eat," he said. "I have no time to go down to the *buvette* today."

The man came back with a basket containing a bottle of red wine, a cold chicken and a loaf of fresh bread, as well as plates, a glass and silverware. I could not imagine a finer or more joyful meal, which we shared on his desk.

"I only learned of your arrest today," he said. "Charlotte sent a note here last night, but I had left early for the Jacobins. I found it when I arrived in the morning. I had enquiries made at your Section and learned that you had been taken to La Conciergerie. From there, it was easy to track you to Fouquier's office." He ran his finger on my cheek. "All of this is my fault. I should have kept a closer eye on you, and of course absolutely forbidden that nonsense about working at the theatre."

I stared at my feet.

"From now on, my love," he continued, "you will obey me. And I will come by every night, regardless of the hour, to make sure that you are safe. For this afternoon, I will keep you locked here while I am in court. After dark we can go to my lodgings. You will stay there until I find something else for you."

"Why can I not return to my lodgings?"

"Fouquier knows about that place, Gabrielle."

"Are you not friends? He arranged everything to let me go."

"Indeed. He must be delighted to have learned about you. Not that he would necessarily use it, but he likes to be well informed about his friends and enemies alike. He is the creature of the Committee of General Safety. That gives him a hand in all police matters. He had me followed once. There he found some difficulty. I may be easy to spot, but I can tell a *mouchard* when I see one. One night, I caught one by the scruff of the neck after retreating into a carriage door. I cured him of the desire to ever follow me again. I let the scoundrel escape in one piece to make sure he told his colleagues of his unpleasant encounter with me. No one has bothered me since. Police informers have been content to ask about me where they know I can be found." Pierre-André shrugged. "You heard what Fouquier said about my former habits. It amused him to shame me in front of you. I am glad I already told you about them; otherwise I would not have liked you to learn of them in this manner. Every bit of knowledge makes Fouquier more powerful. I do not want him to be able to find you."

"What about Aimée? I left her at the theatre with Charlotte."

"I know. I will fetch her tonight."

I hesitated. "Pierre-André, how will I ever thank you?"

I took his hand in mine, caressed it and looked up at him.

"What now?" he asked, frowning.

"I am ashamed, after all you did for me already, to request still another favour from you. Please do not be angry. In any case, you can always refuse."

"May I ask the purpose of these preliminaries?"

"This morning I met a poor woman who was kind to me. She made unpatriotic statements under the influence of liquor. Yet I am sure that she never meant any harm. She went up this morning and may be called to your courtroom. Perhaps she has already been sentenced and it is too late."

He withdrew his hand. "What is her name?"

"Victorine Dubonnet."

He shook his head. "Ah yes, the woman who voiced her opinion of the Republic's paper money. She was questioned yesterday and admitted everything. She is indeed on my docket this afternoon. You are right, Gabrielle. I already did much for you today. And you may recall that I expressly forbade this kind of plea."

"I did promise not to ask you for anything you would deem contrary to justice. By bringing Victorine's case to your attention, I do not feel that I am breaching my pledge. She was speaking as a true patriot and expressing remorse for what she had said about the *assignats*."

"The jurors usually take a dim view of those cases," he said. "They think, with good reason, that those servants are all royalists."

"But she is no lady's maid. She is a servant in a tavern."

He sighed. "So what exactly do you expect me to do?"

"You told me that sometimes, to save the accused's life, you add a question for the jury as to whether the defendant acted with malice and counterrevolutionary intent. Also, you might show leniency in the sentencing. Again, I am sorry to bother you. Now that, thanks to you, I will escape, I cannot let her go to the guillotine without trying to do anything for her."

He rose. "Rest easy then. You tried. I am not angry with you, but I am not promising anything. I will form my own opinion of your friend when I hear her. If she deserves to die, she will. I have to go. Do not make any noise or light the candles."

Pierre-André returned after five o'clock.

"The Dubonnet woman was acquitted," he said. "I did add the intentional question. She cried when I read the verdict."

ᨌ 84 ᨏ

We had to wait until after dark to leave through a little door opening on the *Quai de l'Horloge*. He went first and I followed ten feet behind. We crossed the *Pont-au-Change* in the direction of the Right Bank and then walked back south towards the neighbouring Island of Saint-Louis, or Island of Equality, as it was then known. In less than ten minutes, we reached the *Rue de la Femme Sans Tête*, or "Street of the Headless Woman," where Pierre-André lived. I found that name a bit unnerving given his judicial functions. He was greeted by a maid, around fifty, her face slit by a harelip.

"This is Pélagie," said Pierre-André. "Pélagie, this citizen is a friend of mine who is going to stay here for some time. Be good to her."

Pélagie nodded at me and responded with garbled words I did not understand. The lodgings were clean, comfortable and pleasantly located in the quaint island, just a stone's throw from the banks of the Seine. On the walls of the dining parlour hung an assortment of swords and pistols. In the drawing room, a fine picture of a woman in a black dress and a white bonnet had been given the place of honour. Pierre-André informed me that she was his late mother.

Pierre-André left again and came back an hour later, holding Aimée's hand. She held her doll tightly against her breast. It had been more than twenty-four hours since we had seen each other. When she saw me, she dropped Margaret, shook Pierre-André loose and ran to my arms.

"Mama!" she cried. "Charlotte would not tell me why they took you away again. She said only that you would be back. But she would not say when."

I kept her embraced a long time. "So you see, my treasure, she was right. We are together again."

"I could not sleep last night, Mama. I thought I had lost you forever."

"I was not lost. Citizen Pierre-André found me. He saved my life, Aimée. Again."

Aimée raised her eyes to Pierre-André. "Thank you, Sir," she said in a small voice.

He patted her head. Pélagie had prepared dinner, which Aimée ate sitting on my lap. She clung to me after I put her to bed on a couch in the parlour. Pierre-André was watching us from the door.

"You must be exhausted too, Gabrielle," he said. "I am expected at the Common House and will come home late. Do not stay up for me. Go to bed."

I started when I recognized my own portrait by Madame Lebrun in his bedroom. The gilded frame, which had borne my name, was missing. I blew out the candles but could not find any sleep. I heard him come home much later, although he was trying not to make any noise. He undressed in the dark. The bed shook under his weight. I huddled in silence against him. Without a word, he took me in his arms, caressed my face and kissed my lips. The French say: *Il n'y a pas d'amour, il n'y a que des preuves d'amour.* "There is no such thing as love, there are only proofs of love." I needed no other proof.

I remained a week, the happiest in my life, in Pierre-André's lodgings. Aimée and I, of course, could not stir, but we kept busy with her lessons. All of our things had been left behind in Rue de la Colombe, except for the clothes we wore and the precious Margaret. I sent Pélagie, whose speech I was beginning to understand, to buy remnants of fabric and all three of us went to work sewing a new set of clothes for the doll.

"So she is the servant you mentioned," I told Pierre-André the following night. "She seems very kind."

"She has been with me for over two years now. Shortly after Suzanne's departure, I was walking home when I saw a band of street urchins throwing stones and rubbish at Pélagie. They ran as soon as they saw me. The little scoundrels always do. I brought her here and stitched a nasty gash on her forehead. To thank me, she cleaned my lodgings while I was in court. It was becoming necessary since I had not had time to hire a new maid. Like most men, I am not neat when left to my own devices. I had intended to keep her until she healed and send her on her way with a few francs in her pocket, but she made me understand that she had nowhere to go. She had been a servant in an inn before being thrown out when her old master died. No one wanted to hire her, and she had been begging for her bread in the streets. So I have kept her."

"Can you understand her?"

"I have become used to her speech. I gave her wages and Suzanne's room. She has replaced that little minx to my advantage, though I have not invited her to share my bed. She is clean and the perfect maid for a man in my situation. People think she is a half-wit, so Fouquier's *mouchards* do not think of using her to spy on me. Speaking of Fouquier, he wasted no time. Your friend Granger is in jail already."

"What will happen to him?"

"His case can hardly be a priority these days. He will stew in his prison for a while, until Fouquier either releases him or indicts him as a counterrevolutionary conspirator. But if you want your revenge, I can ask Fouquier to schedule him for trial immediately."

"No, I do not wish Granger any harm. What about Charlotte? Will she be in trouble?"

"I spoke to Payan. His brother supervises of all the theatres for the Municipality. The *Marais* will be closed until they find a replacement for Granger, but it will reopen in a few days. Charlotte will be fine. Payan knows that I do not want her harassed. The rest of the personnel was investigated, though, and a *ci-devant* Marquis de Lacoste, allegedly the prompter, was arrested."

"But he is a patriot and an ardent Republican. Before the Revolution, he spent years in jail under a *lettre de cachet* requested by his mother-in-law."

"Do you know why?"

"He did not tell me."

"No wonder. He disgraced his wife's sister, who was fifteen, and eloped with her to Italy. That may explain his mother-in-law's animosity. The morals of the aristocracy never fail to appall me."

"I am still sorry that he was arrested because of me."

"I, for one, will not shed any tears over the fate of that lecherous old goat. And you must understand that your whims, like that notion of working at the *Théâtre du Marais*, have serious consequences. Not only for yourself, but also for others, including me."

"Are you in trouble because of me?"

"I will try to stay clear of it."

Two days later, Pierre-André returned home with news.

"First," he said, "you must be impatient to go out. I found you new lodgings on Rue du Bourg-Tibourg, to the north of the Common House. The location is convenient, and you will have an additional bedroom for Aimée."

"Thank you. Still, I will be sorry to leave this place. I am very happy here."

"And I was happy to come home to you every night. Yet it is too dangerous for both of us, you know it. As for tonight, we have to go out together."

"Are you not afraid of being seen with me?"

"Not by the man we are going to visit. I already told him of your existence."

I paused. "Who is it?"

"Robespierre."

"Why did you tell him?"

"I had no choice, Gabrielle."

"Yes, you had a choice. Fouquier had not said anything."

"I had no intention of spending the rest of my life wondering whether he would change his mind. That would have given him more power over me than I am willing to grant him."

"Remember Osselin. Remember how he paid for the same kind of indiscretion."

"Osselin hid everything from Robespierre. I will not make the same mistake, especially now that Fouquier knows about you. In fact, I should have told Robespierre from the start."

"Why does he want to see me?"

"He wishes to make sure that I am not taking advantage of your circumstances." Pierre-André shrugged. "Other men seem to think, because I am no classic beauty, that any female found in my bed has been forcibly dragged there."

"Do you mean that Robespierre has time to worry whether a former aristocrat is coerced into a situation she does not like?"

"He is a man of the utmost delicacy of feelings. And seeing what kind of woman you are will help him determine what kind of man I am. You have nothing to fear. He assured me that he wishes only to speak to you outside my presence."

I looked at Pierre-André in horror. "You will leave me alone with him?"

"What do you imagine he will do to you? He will meet with you in the Duplays' dining parlour to avoid giving you any uneasiness. He usually receives his visitors in his bedroom, but he does not deem it proper with a woman."

"What if I am at a loss for what to say?"

Pierre-André grinned. "That would be the first time, my love. You will do fine. In any event, I have no choice now. Neither do you."

"What did you tell him about us?"

"Everything." He handed me my mantle and pushed me firmly by the shoulder. "Come, Gabrielle, we are going to be late."

During the hackney ride, I thought of what the impending meeting with Robespierre would entail. Pierre-André had risked everything to save me. Now his career, his freedom, even his life depended on a few sentences I would exchange with a stranger. I had no idea of what might doom him in Robespierre's eyes. Never before had my words carried such weight. I rested my head against Pierre-André's chest. He patted my back in silence.

We stopped in front of the Duplay house, where Robespierre rented a room. Darkness had fallen. We passed through a doorway between two shops and crossed a small courtyard. Pierre-André rang the bell. The door opened so fast that we must have been expected. The figure of a woman was outlined against the yellow light of the hallway. Once inside, I saw that she was about my age and brown-haired. She looked at me with rather unfriendly curiosity.

"You know where to go, Citizen Coffinhal," she said before disappearing.

I felt panic rise in me. I had bravely faced Hébert at La Force and

Fouquier at the Courthouse, but only my own life had been at stake then. Now I was frozen with terror. Pierre-André seized my wrist and pulled me up a flight of stairs before opening a door on the second floor. We found ourselves in a comfortable dining parlour. My eyes closed, I gripped his hand. I heard the door open.

"What is the matter?" asked a quiet voice.

I opened my eyes and recognized the slight man with delicate features whose speeches I had followed at the National Assembly a few years earlier. A mongrel looked up at me from behind him.

"She is afraid of you," said Pierre-André. He was addressing Robespierre in the familiar mode.

"Of me?"

"I would not say it otherwise. I explained to her that you wish to meet her, but as you can see, the feeling is not mutual. Come, Gabrielle, this is not like you." Pierre-André disengaged himself from my grasp. "I will be waiting for you. Be brave, my love."

My eyes followed him until he closed the door.

"Would you like to have a seat, Madam?" asked Robespierre.

He pulled a chair for me. It had been some time since anyone had addressed me formally, and still longer since I had been called Madam except by Fouquier, who had done so only to mock me. Robespierre, on the contrary, was watching me seriously. Reassured by the presence of the dog, I held out my hand to him. Wagging his tail, the animal briefly sniffed my fingers. My composure returned.

"I did not expect to cause you such uneasiness," said Robespierre, who also took a seat.

"I am not afraid on my own account, Sir. Do you mean Pierre-André any harm because of me?"

"There are very few men I call my friends, Madam, and those I want to be able to trust beyond any doubt. I had always believed Coffinhal to be one of them. Yet when he told me that he had been hiding an aristocrat for over a year, I realized that I did not know him as well as I thought."

"No one can entirely know another," I said. "Yet you may be assured that he is entirely loyal to you."

"Now that he made what he tells me is a full confession, I want to know whether he has told me the truth."

"I am sure that he has. He respects you too much to fail to tell you anything of significance."

"So what is of significance in this affair?"

"I can only speak from my standpoint, which may be different from yours or his. I am a former noblewoman, Sir. Yet I am no conspirator, nor do I entertain any relations with the émigrés. Pierre-André would not have anything to do with me otherwise. I cannot say why he has taken such risks for me. We met in Auvergne when I was fifteen. We fell in love then and wanted to marry. My family would not hear of it and forced me to wed another man. I was widowed before the Revolution. In spite of everything, when I sought Pierre-André's assistance after the September massacres, he helped me. He did not need me. He did not even want to see me at first. He did not force me to do anything." I looked into Robespierre's eyes. "I could not bear the thought of any harm coming to him by my fault. Even the loss of your trust and friendship would be a terrible blow to him. I beg you not to withdraw either. If any-one is to be punished, let it be me and me alone."

Robespierre was petting the mongrel's head. "So you take upon your-self the entire blame for this business." The animal closed his eyes.

"I do. I took advantage of the feelings Pierre-André had retained for me. The only fault which can be laid at his door is weakness."

"He too blamed himself for what happened."

"I am not surprised, but I am sure that you will not be fooled by it. None of this would have happened if I had not sought him."

"He says that you have a little girl."

"Yes, by my late husband."

"He begged me to spare you for her sake."

"Again I am not surprised. Yet I have not done anything to deserve his kindness."

Robespierre rose. "Well, Madam, I have heard enough. I will let you go back to him."

He opened the door to the dining parlour. "You may take Madam home," he told Pierre-André.

Before I knew it, I was back in a hackney.

"Does this mean he has forgiven you?" I asked Pierre-André.

"It seems so, although I will know more tomorrow. He must have liked you." He laughed and bent to kiss my cheek. "Who could resist you?"

Before taking me to my new lodgings, Pierre-André provided me with a residence certificate in the name of Jeanne-Françoise Dunoyer, which had been his mother's maiden name. He also gave me a duplicate key to his own lodgings and showed me a cache in the floor of his bed-room, where he kept rolls of gold coins and a portfolio full of *assignats*.

"You never know what may happen," he said. "Do not hesitate to come here in case of an emergency."

~ 85 ~

LANGTON COURT, THIS 12TH OF JUNE 1815

I hold in the palm of my hand a man's gold watch, engraved with the initials *P. A. C.* and the motto *Vivre libre ou mourir,* "Liberty or death." It stopped at twenty past eleven on a rainy summer day over twenty years ago. I have never rewound it. I am also looking at the fine black and white antique cameo you have always seen on my right hand. This ring I will keep till my last breath, but the watch should go to you. I will find a way to give it to you in the course of this day. Oh, Edmond, I have now reached the part of my narrative I do not want to write. Those who say that time dulls the pain of bereavement know nothing of sorrow. I had the maids light a great fire in spite of the season, but no matter how close I stay to it, I am shivering. Tears blind me. Yet for your sake I must find the courage to continue. God, as always, will lend me strength.

I settled in my new lodgings on Rue du Bourg-Tibourg, which were more spacious and better appointed than the previous ones. Pierre-André, as promised, now visited me every night. After the disaster at the *Théâtre du Marais,* it was out of the question for me to seek another place. Aimée and I resumed our daily walks to the Luxembourg. The following weeks saw the eradication of potatoes and the reappearance of flowers and lawns.

"It's the same thing in all public gardens now that Chaumette and Hébert are gone," said our friend the guard. "And there's no more talk of cutting the trees. Citizen Payan's in charge now. You should see what they're doing at the Tuileries. It's beautiful. That's where they'll celebrate the Festival of the Supreme Being."

On a beautiful spring day, Robespierre led a procession of all the members of the National Convention to solemnly set fire to a colossal cardboard allegory of Atheism. The same morning, a declaration stating that "the French people recognize the Supreme Being and the immortality of the soul" had been posted all over town. The entire choir of the Opera, eight hundred strong, sang hymns to the glory of the Supreme Being. Tens of thousands of Parisians watched Atheism go up in flames. I decided not to join the crowd and was content to hear the account of the festivities given by Pierre-André, who attended as part of his official functions.

Two days later, Couthon, Robespierre's most trusted ally within the Committee of Public Salvation, introduced before the National Convention what would become known as the Law of the 22nd of Prairial. That bill completely reformed the procedure followed before the Revolutionary Tribunal. Indeed it became much harsher. Dumas and Pierre-André were again appointed by the National Convention to preside over the two sections of the Tribunal. That time would be known as the *Grande Terreur*, the "Great Terreur." For the first time the Tribunal would sentence more defendants to death than it acquitted.

Madame Elisabeth followed her brother and sister-in-law, the King and Queen, to the guillotine. She was tried before Dumas for sending her diamonds to her brothers in exile to support the armies of the émigrés. Pierre-André told me that Robespierre had attempted to save her, but that influential members of the Committee of General Safety, in charge of the police, had insisted on the execution of all adult members of the Bourbon family.

A few weeks later, Pierre-André handed me a sheet of paper.

"What is it?" I asked.

"A passport for a Jeanne-Françoise Dunoyer, widow, and her daughter. It is authentic. Those are the actual signatures of two members of the Committee of General Safety. You have nothing to fear by using it."

I stared at the document. "What do you want me to do with it?"

"It might save your life if you had to leave Paris."

I shook my head. "Thank you, but I will not leave. Not without you."

"You know that my functions require my presence here."

"What are you hiding from me? Do you want us to be separated?"

He put his arm around my shoulders. "Of course not, my love," he said, "but one thing matters more to me than your company. It is your safety."

"Have you reason to think that I am not safe in Paris?"

"Strange things have been happening."

"What strange things? The Royalists have been defeated in Vendée. The armies of the Republic are victorious in the Netherlands. The Austrians have been routed."

"Thanks to the Tribunal. There is nothing like the fear of the guillotine to refresh the zeal of those generals and remind them of the expediency of winning battles. The same is true of army contractors. We keep them honest." He paused, staring in front of him. "But Paris is restless. I know this town, Gabrielle, I can feel its pulse. For one thing, the situation is out of control at the Tribunal. Since the Law of the 22nd of Prairial, defense attorneys are no longer required. Defendants can now be convicted upon the basis of written evidence without witnesses being heard. Moreover, the questioning of the accused by a judge before trial, which led to many dismissals, has been eliminated. This means that all cases come to trial. And we lost our discretion in sentencing: we must send to the guillotine any defendant found guilty by the jury. We would need ten times as many judges, clerks and jurors to handle the caseload these days."

"But why is this happening at this time, when the situation is improving?"

"Robespierre has decided to empty the prisons before the year is over. It is laudable, of course, when you consider the number of conspirators, spies, *émigrés*, royalists and like scoundrels housed there. Yet, with less judges than before, we cannot keep pace with the number of defendants. Herman, who is now in charge of the prisons, wanted to send me one hundred and fifty per day. Fouquier even proposed to have scaffolding—*scaffolding*—installed in my courtroom to accommodate these numbers."

He was now pacing the room. "I made it clear," he continued, "that it was out of the question, regardless of what Dumas might have agreed to. I told Fouquier that I will not let him turn my courtroom into a circus, with the accused perched in midair like monkeys. Finally, he agreed to *limit* the number of defendants to no more than thirty per day, which is already impossible to manage."

"Why does not Robespierre show more leniency after the victories?"

"We are close to reaching the goals of the Revolution, Gabrielle. Now that we are winning the war against the foreign tyrants, our last obstacle is the existence of the scoundrels who conspire from within against the safety of the Nation. That is why Robespierre wants all of the prisoners tried by the end of the year. The innocents will be acquitted and the rest guillotined. What I do not know is how the Tribunal is going to achieve this goal. The other day, I had the surprise to see a boy of fourteen, a *ci-devant* nobleman, with barely a moustache, among the accused. I added a question for the jurors, reminding them of his age and asking whether he had become an enemy of the people *with discernment*. What do you think? They answered in the affirmative! I could not believe my ears when I heard the guilty verdict. I had to break the law. I sentenced the boy to twenty years in prison. I should have sent him to the guillotine, since now it is the only penalty we may impose. I looked Fouquier's deputy in the eye while I read the sentence. He kept quiet."

Pierre-André shook his head in a worried manner. "And Robespierre has been acting in a rather odd manner lately. He barely shows his face at the National Convention anymore. That is where he is vulnerable. He can now count on the loyalty of the Municipality and the Revolutionary Tribunal. I am part of both and do not worry about either. My colleague Dumas behaves in an improper manner on the bench and his jokes are in the worst taste, but at least he is completely trustworthy. The other judges are insignificant. Fouquier, although he receives his orders from the Committee of General Safety, where Robespierre has many enemies, is too busy to take the helm of any movement. It is not in his nature anyway. Yet many scoundrels infest the ranks of the Convention. Some are as corrupt as the late Danton; some are cowards who keep quiet and bide their time. I told Robespierre to begin by sending Carrier, along with all the other Representatives in Mission who are guilty of atrocities, to stand trial before the Tribunal, but he would not listen to me. He wants to wait for the right moment to strike them."

Pierre-André sighed. "Also, Robespierre has been sick. And he is in love with Eléonore, one of the Duplay girls. You saw her that night when we called on him. Nothing wrong with that, of course, but he needs to bed her. I told him, as a friend and physician, that nothing is more detrimental to a man's health than continence. *Semen retentum venenum est.* He should marry her if he does not want to make her his concubine. I am sure she would be delighted to have him. I even offered to speak to the girl on his behalf if he were too shy to do it himself. He was horrified by the idea." Pierre-André shrugged. "Other men always underestimate my powers of persuasion with the fair sex."

No one except Eléonore Duplay, who is still alive and has never married, knows what happened between herself and Robespierre, but what is sure is that he decided to come out of his isolation. At the end of July 1794, on the 8th of Thermidor, he gave a speech before the National Convention in which he denounced unspecified "scoundrels." Many Representatives felt targeted. It was almost midnight when Pierre-André, looking concerned, arrived at my lodgings. I was very surprised when he announced that he would not go to the Tribunal the next day but had to see Robespierre instead. He did not volunteer more information nor did I feel free to pry.

A suffocating heat hung over Paris the next day. Around three in the afternoon, I heard in addition to the rumbling of thunder, drums beating and the *tocsin* ringing. The sense of foreboding that enveloped me since the day before became unbearable. I took Aimée by the hand and almost ran with her to the Island of the Fraternity. I opened the door to Pierre-André's lodgings. Pélagie looked at us with surprise. Barely taking the time to greet her, I opened a chest and took out a change of clothes and linen for Pierre-André. There, between two shirts, I found one of the embroidered garters he had taken from me. I had not time to wonder about what had happened to its twin, but tears came to my eyes as I looked at the blue embroidery and the monogram. I then lifted the carpet in the bedroom and emptied the cache of gold and *assignats* Pierre-André had shown me. I threw the money into a traveling bag, along with his clothes, my garter, razors, some toiletries and a pair of pistols. Pélagie was watching me with uncomprehending eyes.

"Follow me," I said. "You are in danger."

She shook her head. I held my hand to her. "Come with me. Citizen Coffinhal would want it."

I was ready to leave when the face of Pierre-André's mother caught my eye. I seized a pair of scissors and cut the painting out of its frame. I did the same with my own portrait by Madame Lebrun. I rolled both canvasses, which joined the rest of my loot in the bag. I was done in less than five minutes. I left in haste, dragging Aimée and Pélagie behind me. It was not yet four o'clock in the afternoon of the 9th of Thermidor when I returned to my lodgings.

There I waited for hours, racked by anguish. At last, at three in the morning, I heard a key turn in the lock. I was wide awake and jumped out of bed in an instant. I threw myself into Pierre-André's arms. He smelled of sweat and of gunpowder. His coat was already wet on the shoulders. It had just begun to rain. He kept me embraced for a long time without speaking.

"I wanted to see you one last time, my poor love," he said at last, "but I must leave. I have already compromised you enough by coming here. I will go before dawn. Everything is lost."

"Not if you are alive. You must stay here. You will be safe. I went to your lodgings and took everything you will need."

He collapsed on the couch. His shoulders were shaken by sobs. Without a word, he wrapped his arms around my waist and cried in my lap. It was the only time I saw him weep. I held his head against my breast. Finally, exhausted, his eyes closed, he let go of me and rested against the back of the couch. I fetched him a glass of wine and sat by his side.

"What happened?" I asked. "Why did you say that all is lost?"

"Robespierre was prevented from speaking yesterday at the National Convention. Tallien, who was presiding, must have been part of a conspiracy with some other former Representatives in Mission, the Carriers, the Fouchés, the Collots. They all began shouting at the same time while Tallien was ringing his bell like a maniac. Couthon, who is usually energetic, just remained seated in his wheelchair and watched the disaster unfold without taking any action. Before you knew it, the Convention had decreed the arrest of Robespierre and his main followers. I would be surprised if I were not included in that measure. I had warned him that the Convention was the viper's nest where the scoundrels had regrouped. Men like Carrier knew that their days were numbered."

"Did you not meet with Robespierre yesterday morning?"

"I did. He was concerned about the Tribunal. I agreed to keep an eye all day on Fouquier, whom he particularly distrusts. I asked a common friend, a countryman of ours, to invite Fouquier and me to luncheon. I think I mentioned that man, Vernhes, who lives in the Island of the Fraternity. Around three, in the middle of the meal, we heard drums beating."

"I heard them too from here."

"I sent for my sword and tricolour sash and ran to the Common House. There I heard the news of Robespierre's arrest. Worse, that imbecile Hanriot, who had gone to free him, had managed only to be caught himself. Payan and I, with seven other patriots, formed a provisional Executive Committee to take charge of the affairs of the Nation. Men from all the Sections of Paris had responded to the call of the drums and were gathered in front of the Common House. I harangued them and asked for volunteers to save the Nation in its hour of peril. Over 2,000 men, altogether seventeen companies, armed with twelve cannons, followed me, cheering. I also convinced a detachment of the mounted Gendarmerie to join us. I was riding at the head of a little army, Gabrielle, more than enough to carry the day."

Pierre-André rubbed his hands on his face. "The first order of business was to free Hanriot. He was, after all, the Commander in Chief of the National Guard. I stormed the offices of the Committee of General Safety, where I found him tied like an idiot to a chair. I spoke to the gendarmes who were guarding the Convention. I shamed them for arresting patriots instead of the conspirators who wanted to lead the Nation to its doom. They too cheered and abandoned their posts to follow me. The scoundrels of the Convention were completely defenseless. I had the cannons pointed, loaded, ready to fire in their direction. What followed, Gabrielle, I will never forgive myself."

He stared straight ahead. "We needed Robespierre. There are not two men like him. And I am only a judge, Hanriot was the General. I took only a dozen men with me, including Sanson, the executioner, and his brother, to go free Robespierre who was still held at the Courthouse. The rest of my troops, the cannons, the gendarmes, I handed over to Hanriot. I gave him instructions to open fire on the Convention if the scoundrels who had attacked Robespierre were not immediately delivered to us. He had done it last year with the Girondins, I thought he could do it again. I left. I found Robespierre at the Courthouse, freed him without encountering any serious resistance and brought him back to the Common House."

He was now shaking. "There, what did you think I saw, but the troops I had left into the hands of Hanriot, the cannons, everything! I could not believe my eyes. The soldiers were idle, some were beginning to drink, others were leaving. Hanriot had been content to bring them back to the Common House without attacking the Convention. Now, even with Robespierre there, the occasion was missed; the battle was lost."

"How could Hanriot fail to act?"

"He drank himself silly, no doubt out of fear. He could barely ride his horse. The Convention was able to muster a force to attack the Common House after two in the morning. We heard gunfire outside the door of the hall where we were gathered. It was clear that we were all going to be killed or arrested. Robespierre blew his brains out. His younger brother opened a window and jumped. The others, I believe, were arrested without offering any resistance. I, for one, was not going to give the scoundrels that satisfaction. As I was running down a hallway, whom do you think I saw? Hanriot! That coward, that drunkard, that imbecile who had destroyed all of our hopes! That piece of rubbish was not even worthy of the guillotine. He fled from me, but I was faster and caught him in a moment. When I was done with him, I sent him flying through a second-floor window."

"Did you kill him?"

"I did not take the time to ascertain his condition. I can find my way around the Common House blindfolded and had no trouble escaping through a back door. Now you know everything. Robespierre is dead; the Nation is in the hands of scoundrels."

I undressed Pierre-André like a child and joined him in bed. He went to sleep immediately, his head on my shoulder.

The next morning Hanriot was found in a gutter, one of his eyes torn from its socket, but alive. Robespierre, against all odds, had also survived. He had only shot himself in the jaw. He was taken, along with his younger brother, Dumas, Hanriot, Payan, Couthon and sixteen others, to the Revolutionary Tribunal. Sellier was acting as President now that both senior judges were unavailable: Dumas was among the accused and Pierre-André missing. Upon Fouquier's request, all of the defendants were sentenced to death without trial. They were executed during the afternoon of the same day, the 10th of Thermidor. That night, I learned that Madame Duplay, whose sole crime had been to be Robespierre's landlady and Eléonore's mother, had been thrown into jail. A mob of women stormed the prison and hanged her from the bars of her cell window.

A vast conspiracy had been forming for several days to overthrow Robespierre. It comprised members of the Committees of Public Salvation and General Safety, former Representatives in mission like Carrier, steeped in blood and afraid of answering for their crimes, friends of the late Danton, and rich people who were tired of the price controls imposed under Robespierre's leadership. All of that disparate group would be called the Thermidorians. They were the victors.

I did not feel the least doubt that Pierre-André, if he were discovered, would meet the same fate as his friends. He was the last of the Jacobin leaders still at large. I offered to call on his brother Joseph, since he had prudently kept to his judicial functions on the 9th and 10th of Thermidor. Pierre-André reluctantly accepted.

I visited Joseph Coffinhal at his home in the *Marais* district, Rue Beautreillis. Pierre-André had told me that his brother had married well. The fine house into which I was shown had been part of his wife's dowry. I had never met Joseph before but would have recognized him without difficulty. He was well over six feet tall, a slightly shorter model of Pierre-André, as broad in the shoulders, though not as lean around the stomach.

"Jeanne-Françoise Dunoyer?" he asked coldly, his eyebrow raised. "How is it that you bear my mother's maiden name?"

"Pierre-André chose it when he procured my residence certificate."

"Who are you really?"

"Gabrielle de Montserrat."

His eyes narrowed. "Now this is familiar. You are the youngest sister of the *ci-devant* Marquis de Castel. I remember that scandal. Almost ten years ago, was it not? Pierre-André almost went to the gallows because of you. I have never met anyone more adept than my younger brother at creating trouble for himself and his family. So he has laid his hands on you at last. How long have you been his mistress?"

"I have been living under his protection for almost two years."

"Well, it seems that *he* is the one in need of protection now."

"That was the purpose of my visit."

Joseph shrugged. "What does he expect me to do? To help a fugitive, a man who is already under a death sentence?"

I shook my head. "He is your brother. He saved my life. These claims are higher than any set by the laws of men."

"I find it imprudent to disregard the laws of men. I may be more attached to my life than you are to yours."

"Can you not arrange for him to go abroad?"

He sniggered. "Pray name a country that would give him asylum. He has made himself rather conspicuous these past few years. Everyone knew him to be an acolyte of Robespierre long before the events of the 9th. He might have saved himself by keeping quiet that day. But no, instead he was riding all over Paris, rallying the enemies of the Convention, his sword drawn, his tricolour sash waving in the wind."

"What about Auvergne? Your brother Jean-Baptiste would hide him."

"And how would you send a man like my younger brother, who is so easily recognizable and whose description is posted throughout France, safely to Auvergne? Even *I* do not dare stir from this house for fear of being mistaken for him. No, the only thing I can suggest is that you continue hiding him until further notice."

"Can you at least write Jean-Baptiste?"

"Let us assume that I do that. How would I let you know of his response? Where do you live?"

"I cannot tell you."

"What do you fear? That I will warn the authorities of Pierre-André's whereabouts? I will not betray him. Come back here in a week."

That week was the strangest, the most intense, the most dreadful of my existence. It changed me forever. For the first time, Pierre-André and I could spend as much time as we liked together. I kept bringing him news. On the 11th of Thermidor, seventy members of the Council General of the Municipality were sentenced to death, also without trial, the largest batch ever to go to the guillotine. Another twelve followed the next day. All were Pierre-André's "friends and brothers," as the Jacobins called one another, his comrades in arms. Sometimes he was lost deep in his own sorrow and sometimes he clung to me as if I alone could shield him from death, his own and that of all the others. We were each other's sole comfort. There was something approaching happiness in our despair.

I took Pélagie with me when I called again on Joseph Coffinhal. He glanced at my companion.

"Who is that? Why did you bring this woman here?"

"She is Pierre-André's maid. I thought that you might hire her as a servant. She has nowhere to go now. You have nothing to fear on her account. She is entirely devoted to your brother. In any event, no one can understand her speech."

"Thank you very much, but we have all the maids we need. Why on earth would I want such a freak in my house? You seem to forget that I have two young daughters."

"She is very kind and hard working. I am sure that your children would grow fond of her in no time. My own little girl already likes her."

He shrugged. "Keep her then."

"I may flee Paris if Pierre-André leaves. I do not want to attract attention by traveling with someone so conspicuous."

"And why should I want someone so conspicuous, as you put it, around my house? She might be recognized as Pierre-André's maid. My connection to my younger brother cannot be forgotten too soon." He looked straight at me. "But you came here, I believe, to discuss his fate, not this woman. I was able to make arrangements. A countryman of ours by the name of Lescure owns an inn on Rue Croix des Petits Champs. Pierre-André is to knock at the back door at one o'clock tonight. The man has a false passport for him and will take him, hidden in his cart, to Clamart. There Pierre-André can catch the five o'clock stagecoach to Clermont. Jean-Baptiste will have a manservant meet him there. Pierre-André will have to hide in the mountains until things settle."

"Can that man Lescure be trusted?"

"I have known him for years, and so has my brother. Pierre-André lent him money on more than one occasion, and even helped clear charges against him when Lescure was in trouble with his Section for hoarding flour."

"So you are certain that the man will not betray Pierre-André?"

"I would trust him with my life."

Pierre-André was pacing the parlour when I returned to my lodgings. I told him of Joseph's plan.

"Something does not sound right," I said. "I cannot bring myself to trust your brother. Please, I beg you, stay here with me."

He sighed. "It is useless to insist. I have made up my mind to go. Lescure owes me more than money, after all, and in any event I have no choice. Please do not make it more difficult for me. Take care of yourself, Gabrielle, for your daughter's sake and for my own. I put a great deal of effort into saving you, my beloved. Do not let it go to waste." He reached into his waistcoat pocket. "There, keep these in memory of me."

He handed me his watch and removed the antique ring from his little finger. "My body will go to the scoundrels who will kill me, but I want you to have these."

I shook my head, refusing to take the objects. He put them in my hand and closed it around them.

"So you know that this so-called escape scheme is a trap," I said. "Please, my love, listen to me. Do not go."

"What else can I do? Stay here? Make you run the risk of being arrested for hiding a fugitive? You know that you would be sentenced to death too. Do you think I want you to be guillotined with me? Worse, to be massacred by a mob in jail like Citizen Duplay?"

"I am willing to take that risk."

"I know. But what for? What kind of life is left for me? I still have you, my Gabrielle, my poor, my tender love, but my friends are dead, all of them. Can you imagine how it feels to be the last one standing? The Revolution is over; the Nation can fall prey to a dictator. Now that the fear of the Tribunal is gone, any victorious general may use his popularity to seize power. Liberty and equality are defeated, perhaps for decades. For me it is too late. I will not see them reborn. You may, but only if you live."

He raised my face, forcing me to look at him. "You must live, Gabrielle. I beg you. You have done so much for me this past week, these past years. Now I am asking you to do still another thing. Please let me go, my beloved." He pressed his lips on mine. "We will be reunited someday, I am sure of it, though maybe not in this world."

I ran my hands on his face, kissed it, smelled it, filled my eyes with its image. I thought of the children we would not have, of the years we would not spend together, of all the things that take a lifetime to share. Words I had never spoken came to my mind, words he would never hear if I did not say them now. I needed to tell him all.

"You will never know . . ." I was shaken by sobs. "I will never see you again, and you will never know . . ."

He pressed me in his arms. His embrace was stronger than the crushing feeling in my chest. "I do know, my love. I have long known. Stop this. You are killing yourself, and me too." He held my face in his hands. "Look at me. Promise me to live. I need to hear it."

I could only moan. He held me by the shoulders and shook me.

"Do you promise? Say it."

I caught my breath. "I promise."

He left just after midnight. From the doorstep, I watched his large frame receding into the shadows of the stairwell. I listened to the sound of his footsteps, fainter and fainter. At last there was nothing left. He was gone. All was empty.

Finding any rest, any occupation was impossible. At dawn I dressed and woke Pélagie. I gave her a note, with instructions to take it to Manon if I did not return by nightfall.

I am sorry to have left you, dear Manon, without news for many months. I know that you must have worried about me, but please understand that I had no choice. You may trust the woman

who will bring you this. She will lead you to Aimée. I may not live
to see the end of this day. If I do not, I count on you to tell my sister,
the Countess de Chavagnac, of my daughter's whereabouts.
God bless you, dearest Manon, and Louise.

I left for the Tuileries while Aimée was still asleep. I went to her bedroom and took a long look at her before setting off. I passed the Common House, followed the banks of the river until I reached the hall of the Convention in the Tuileries. I remembered the 10th of August, the bodies of Swiss Guards, the man who had wanted to behead me with his sabre, even Villers.

Wrapped in my mantle, I sat with the public in the galleries of the Convention, waiting for the session to begin. I knew that there I would be able to follow the evolution of the general situation, and, as much as I dreaded it, obtain the first news of Pierre-André's arrest if his fate was indeed to fall prey to his enemies.

The session opened at nine in the morning. The Representatives were still congratulating themselves upon the fall of the "tyrant" Robespierre eight days earlier. I was too numbed by sorrow and boredom to pay much attention to the speeches. Suddenly, a man, out of breath, ran into the hall and shouted, "Coffinhal was arrested. He has been taken to La Conciergerie."

That announcement drew cheers from the Representatives. For a moment, the hall seemed to swirl around me. I saw the panting man climb the stairs to the President's chair and whisper in his ear. I heard the latter ring his bell to demand silence.

"It seems that we have a difficulty," he said. "Since the Revolutionary Tribunal is temporarily closed pending its regeneration, Coffinhal was taken to the ordinary Criminal Court."

"To death!" yelled several Representatives. "No trial for the traitor!"

The President again rang his bell to call for order. "It is not so easy as it sounds. Oudard, the President of the Criminal Court, has declined any jurisdiction over political crimes. He refuses to sentence Coffinhal to death."

Oudard must have been a brave man. For a few minutes, I entertained the hope that Pierre-André could be saved.

One of the Representatives stood from his seat and shouted: "The traitor must perish *today*. We cannot wait for the Revolutionary Tribunal to reopen. Let us put to the votes a special bill ordering the Criminal Court to sentence Coffinhal to death."

Cries of "Death to the traitor!" echoed through the hall.

I have since read that bill. In it Pierre-André's name was misspelled *Coffinal*, another indication of the urgency the Convention felt to put an end to his life. Pierre-André Coffinhal, who had presided over so many trials, was denied one. For him there would be no evidence, no witnesses, no arguments. He was sentenced to death upon the declarations of two clerks who merely attested to his identity.

✌ 86 ✌

After hearing that the bill sending Pierre-André to the guillotine had passed, I ran in a heavy summer rain to La Conciergerie. I knew that he would be executed immediately and prayed that I was not too late. When I reached the courthouse, a group of women had gathered around the prison entrance in the *Cour du Mai*. I had heard of that hideous crowd. They were called the *lécheuses de guillotine*, "guillotine lickers" and waited there every day to escort the prisoners on their last journey on earth. The cart, with its large white horses, was ready.

I held my breath as Pierre-André appeared, his hands tied behind his back, surrounded by a dozen guards. A slash cut across one of his eyebrows. He was greeted by the cries of the women. He climbed alone the steps to the cart and sat on one of the planks, sullen, facing backwards. The cart, escorted by rows of mounted gendarmes, slowly crossed the *Pont-Neuf* and turned into Rue Honoré in the direction of the Place de la Révolution. The rain drenched Pierre-André, gluing his black hair to his face and his shirt to his chest. The weather had not discouraged a howling crowd from gathering. The sight of human suffering is too alluring not to attract spectators. Cowards who would not have dared come within ten yards of Pierre-André if he had been free sidled between the horses of the gendarmes and climbed onto the cart, shouting insults. A well-dressed man was trying to poke him through the bars with a closed umbrella. I remembered witnessing similar behaviour towards a caged lion at the ménagerie of the Garden of the Plants. People were yelling:

"Coffinhal, you are out of order!" and repeating to him some of the jokes Dumas had made on the bench. Pierre-André looked around with contempt and shrugged in silence at the jeers.

I followed the cart, my knees unsteady, leaning on strangers in the crowd to keep from stumbling. Midway to the place of execution Pierre-André saw me. His look pierced me. I started, but his face relaxed and from then on he kept his eyes fixed upon me. My strength returned. I had to be brave for his sake. He would leave this world assured that I would not give in to sorrow.

When the cortege reached the guillotine, placed next to the bronzed statue of Liberty that had replaced that of the late King Louis the Fifteenth, Pierre-André looked up with what seemed like relief. His lips moved as he took one last look at me. I will never know whether he was saying a prayer. Perhaps he was bidding me farewell or telling me to remember my last promise to him. Then he shook his head sideways as if to tell me to leave. I did not. In spite of the throbbing pain in my chest, I had to stay till the end. I could not even look away.

Disdaining the ladder pulled by the executioner's aide, Pierre-André jumped off the cart. He climbed the stairs to the scaffold with a surprising lightness for a man of his bulk, as if impatient to be done with the business of dying. He stood, face forward, against the plank. It swung down, the neck was adjusted inside the *lunette*, where it barely fitted, and the triangular blade dropped a moment later with a dull noise.

The crowd roared. I still watched as Sanson, the executioner, retrieved the head from the leather bag where it had fallen. He walked around the scaffold, holding it aloft by the hair, blood dripping from the neck, for all to behold. The body was rolled sideways into a wicker coffin by the side of the dreadful machine, and from there pushed into a second waiting cart. Sanson and one of his aides climbed next to the driver.

I had not given a thought to what I would do after Pierre-André's death, but now I could not bring myself to abandon his remains. Free at last from the cries of the crowd, I followed the cart carrying the head and body under the relentless rain. I had no umbrella and was by now soaked to the bone. Yet I felt neither cold nor weariness. At last we arrived in sight of the graveyard of Les Errancis. The entrance portal bore the inscription *Champ du Repos*, "Resting Field." Once inside the gates, I saw two separate trenches, each about thirty feet deep and square, both surrounded by barrels of quicklime.

Sanson looked at me with curiosity. "Did you know him?" he asked.

"He was my best friend. I believe you knew him too."

"True. I've never met a more resolute character. I might still be in trouble because I helped him on the 9th."

"Do you mind if I stay a moment?"

"Suit yourself, but it won't be a pretty sight."

"I have not seen any pretty sights today. I want to say farewell to him."

"All right then. That pit over there's reserved for those who die a natural death. This one was dug the other day for Robespierre and his friends."

"So they are all buried right here?"

"That's right. All of them."

The back of the cart stopped at the edge of the pit. Sanson and his aide cut the leather strap tying Pierre-André's wrists and proceeded to strip his body. Because of the weather or the unpleasantness of the task, they made haste. I could not keep my eyes off the naked flesh, glistening in the rain, whiter than I had ever seen it in life. The downpour washed away rivulets of blood flowing down the chest. Even decapitated, the corpse, broad in the shoulders, slender in the waist and hips, looked strong and tall. I was struck by its beauty despite the horror of the red gash at the neck.

"You're not going to faint, are you?" asked Sanson. "You look as pale as he. Do you want any of his clothes? The Nation lets me have them, but I donate them to hospitals because they are ruined by the blood. You can have your pick, except for these fine leather boots, which might fit me."

I was tempted to ask for the shirt, a wet heap of white material, stained red. It could not be of any value with its mangled collar, but I thought of the watch and ring Pierre-André had given me before his appointment with fate. I preferred to remember him alive.

"Thank you," I said. "Keep everything. If you want to do me a great favour, you can let me hold his head for a moment."

"Are you sure?"

"Please."

He delicately seized the head and gave it to me. I held it between my hands, surprised at its weight. The expression was serene now, the dark eyes half-open and not yet cloudy. I kissed the cold white lips and touched the forehead with mine as I had done when Pierre-André was alive. With infinite regret I put the head down on the floor of the cart. I closed the eyes and for the last time caressed the cheeks.

I turned away when it was thrown, along with the body, into the pit. At the time I shuddered at the thought of the immediate destruction of his flesh. Yet the lime that burnt his body spared it the slow indignities of putrefaction.

My solace is that he joined his friends Robespierre, Payan and the members of the Council General of the Municipality of Paris. He rests in the company of the men who shared his ideals and his death. All are buried in that pit, separated from him only by thin layers of dirt and lime.

How I left the graveyard and returned to my lodgings I know not. I remember awaking in my bed, feeling nothing but exhaustion and an overwhelming desire to die. I was drenched in sweat, shaking with sorrow, cold and fever. A cough would not leave me a moment of rest. Breathing seemed to bring water instead of air into my lungs. I was suffocating. I could not distinguish between the light of the candles and that of the sun. My surroundings were bathed night and day in a yellow glow, the colour of urine. I had taken leave of my body, so unbearable was the pain of living.

I must have remained three weeks in this condition. Manon reappeared. She was, as usual, most attentive and talked without respite "to entertain me," as she would say. The only way to bear her chatter was to listen to none of it and turn my head away in spite of the effort and pain that movement entailed. Pélagie, when Manon left, would take a seat by my bed and knit in silence. She stopped only once in a while to pat my hand without trying to meet my eye. Every day she would take Aimée to me and put a finger to her lips. Their silent presence soothed me.

One day at the very end of August, Pélagie gently rolled the bedsheets and rubbed my stomach through my chemise. She had never done anything of the kind before. She was nodding at me, smiling. It had not escaped me, even in my condition, that I had missed my monthly curses. Yet I had not thought anything of it, attributing their absence to the effects of my sorrow and sickness. Pélagie's caress made everything clear. For the first time since the death of Pierre-André, tears rolled down my cheeks. They would not stop. They saved me. I knew then that I would live, for you, because of you. Pélagie took me in her arms. She too was sobbing.

I recovered. During my first outing after my illness, as I was walking past a wall covered with bills, the name *Coffinhal* caught my eye. Posted there were various court orders. I forced myself to read. One of them reported that *Pierre-André Coffinhal, former physician, former attorney, Vice President of the Revolutionary Tribunal, member of the Council General of the Municipality of Paris, outlawed on the 9th of Thermidor* had been sentenced to death on the 18th of the same month by judgment of the Criminal Court of Paris. It was his obituary. He was thirty-one. Life was atrociously short then.

You understand all by now, Edmond, my poor love. He was your father. The portrait of the lady in the black dress you have seen all your life in my bedroom is indeed that of your grandmother. But she is not the Marquise de Castel, my mother, as I told you. She is Jeanne-Françoise Dunoyer, Pierre-André's mother. Forgive me for lying to you. Forgive me for not telling you of these things earlier. Forgive me for telling you the truth now. You have to know.

ᔰ 87 ᔱ

Pierre-André was executed on the 18th of Thermidor of the Year Two of the Republic, One and Indivisible, the 5th of August 1794, old style. I have learned since that, upon his arrival at La Conciergerie, he kept shouting at the top of his voice that he had been hiding on the Island of the Swans for a week, that all of his former friends had either shut their doors in his face or betrayed him, that he was starving and that he considered the prospect of the guillotine a kindness compared to the hardships he had just endured. A meal was brought in haste to silence him. He ate, but his clamours lost none of their violence. They only turned to the subject of Hanriot's cowardice. For hours they echoed through the jail, so frightening to the other prisoners, the turnkeys and the gendarmes assigned to guard him that no one thought of questioning him about his whereabouts during the week of his disappearance. It was the last proof of love I received from him.

Life goes on. It was growing within my womb. I had to make plans for you, for Aimée, for poor Pélagie, whom I could not abandon, for my own safety. I was sitting in my bed, thinking of what the future held for all of us, when Manon, looking very pleased with herself, entered and handed me a letter. I did not expect any and opened it with great curiosity when I recognized my brother's handwriting.

Madam,

I received from your maid news that you are unwell and a request that I allow you to return to Fontfreyde when you are again able to travel. I do not know whether her letter was simply a ploy to appeal to my love for you, or whether you are indeed too sick to write. If the latter is true, I am sorry to hear it and wish you from my heart a full and prompt recovery. Whatever the case, I want to make my feelings clear.

Do not believe me ignorant of your conduct during these past two years. I know to what, and to whom, you owe the preservation of your life. At a time when the King and Queen, our sister Hélène, and so many of our friends confronted the gravest dangers and met their deaths with heroic courage, you found your safety in the bed of a man whom I had detested long before the true extent of his depravity became public knowledge. You enjoyed, thanks to his protection, your own little island of comfort in an ocean of innocent blood. This I know for certain, but I suspect worse.

I suspect that you eagerly threw yourself in the power of that man whose name I cannot bear to write, that scoundrel, that cutthroat, that murderer of thousands. I suspect that you enjoyed your degradation and that your present illness results from its sudden ending, although his death is considered a blessing by all decent persons. How you could have sunk so low is beyond my comprehension. Have you no conscience?

If you are in need of money, I will send you all I can spare. It will not be much, because the peasants have become insolent beyond belief nowadays and seem to think that the abolition of our ancestral rights absolves them from paying rent. As to giving you the protection of my roof and my name, it is out of the question, now or at any time in the future. Your company would be unbearable to me. The truth is, Gabrielle, that I never want to see you again. My anger may fade in time, but the disgust I feel for you is so deep that I cannot imagine it subsiding.

During these two years, how many times have you thought of me? You have been constantly on my mind. I spent sleepless nights worrying that the brute, your love, would tire of you. I feared that he would on a whim sentence you, still fresh from his embraces, to share the fate of his other victims. I pictured you, your hands tied behind your back, climbing the stairs to the scaffold. I tried in vain to prepare myself to hear the ghastly news. Yes, little sister, sometimes I prayed for the continuation of your disgrace, if only it could preserve your life, and sometimes I cried for you as one cries for the dead. You made me wish for what I hated most.

I believe in the forgiveness of all offenses. Yet I cannot forgive you. I have no more ardent desire than to see my beloved Gabrielle again, to feel her presence next to me, but pray tell me, what is left of her now? I am happy to know that you are safe, but I would not be able to look at you without thinking of what you did; I would always picture that man touching you. His shadow will forever separate us.

I beg you not to renew your request. It hurts me to deny it, but my answer is firm. Have your maid write back: I will do everything in my power to help you, except what you are asking. You have always enjoyed an excellent constitution, which leaves me no doubt of your recovery.

May God keep you, Madam, and my niece under His holy protection.

The Marquis de Castel

P.S. I enclose the note he had the cruelty to send me, along with its contents. Why I have not burnt both I cannot say. Please imagine what I felt upon receiving them.

Within my brother's letter was a note, dated of the 28th of September 1792, and addressed to the "so-called Marquis de Castel."

Citizen Castel,
You will be happy to learn that I am extremely satisfied with your sister.
Greetings and fraternity,

Pierre-André Coffinhal

Folded within was the white and blue garter he had taken from me, and whose twin I had found in his lodgings. Pierre-André's note was written, as an added mark of disrespect to my brother, in the familiar style.

I put both letters down on the bed covers. I was angry with my brother; I pitied him. The sight of Pierre-André's bold handwriting made me cry. I understood now why he had asked for my garter. In one sentence, he had taken his revenge for the humiliation received years earlier, for the destruction of our hopes of happiness, for the long misery that followed.

Suddenly I was freed of the ties that had bound me to my brother. All that mattered was to keep the last promise made to Pierre-André. I had to live and to leave France.

ꙮ 88 ꙮ

LANGTON COURT, THIS 14TH OF JULY 1815

The rest you know. As a child, my love, you made me tell many times the story of my escape from France thanks to a passport in the name of Jeanne-Françoise Dunoyer and Pierre-André's pistols. You know how Aimée, Pélagie and I reached the Netherlands, sometimes on the stage-coach, sometimes on foot; how I was arrested again as an Austrian spy close to the frontline; how I arranged for us to cross the Channel from Ostend on a smuggler's boat. What you did not know, Edmond, is that you were part of that adventure. I was carrying you, my most treasured possession, the memento of my dead love, the token of my pledge to live.

At last we arrived in London, where I found many of my old friends, including Emilie, now widowed, and Morsan, among the French *émigrés*. There I met the Earl of St. Ives. I told him of you. I told him everything. He cared enough for me to offer me and my unborn child the protection of his name. He proposed. He has raised you as his son and heir; he has loved you no less than if you had been his own. If these memoirs serve only one purpose, it should be to make you aware of his goodness and the debt we owe him.

You may have heard of what happened to the remaining characters of this story. Carrier, the murderer of my sister Hélène, the man who conspired to assassinate Robespierre and your father, quarreled with the other Thermidorians. Soon after their victory, they had him tried for the atrocities he had committed in Nantes. Pierre-André was right: Carrier did not live to see 1795. He was guillotined in December of 1794.

Fouquier too was arrested once his services were no longer needed by the Thermidorians. He languished in jail for almost a year. He was tried in May of 1795, along with Herman, Sellier and the remaining judges of the Revolutionary Tribunal. Like them, he was doomed. He and Sellier must have hoped to save their lives by sending Robespierre to his death, but the guillotine was their sole reward. I thank God for sparing Pierre-André the slow agony of those months in prison.

During the year that followed the fall of Robespierre, many of the Jacobins who had not been guillotined were summarily executed or massacred in jail by mobs, all with the active participation or tacit approbation of the Thermidorians. Thousands died in what was called the *White Terror*.

Dear Manon chose to remain in France. She inherited a tidy sum of money from an aunt and married a fellow twenty years her junior. They have an umbrella shop in Paris. She writes that they are very happy.

Many others survived. Mesdames de Rochefort and de Tourzel, my companions at La Force, were jailed in 1794, during and after the Great Terror, but both are alive. Pauline de Tourzel married the Count de Béarn and, like some members of the old aristocracy, joined the new Court of Napoléon Bonaparte after he proclaimed himself Emperor of the French in 1804. I always thought with some amusement of that disparate assemblage of the ancient nobility and a crowd of upstarts. Former washerwomen, whose husbands had become Dukes, rubbed elbows with *ci-devant* ladies-in-waiting to Queen Marie-Antoinette. Repentant Jacobins fawned at the feet of His so-called Majesty Emperor Napoléon.

My brother, the Marquis de Castel, still lives in his château of Fontfreyde. He never married. His heir is the Count de Chavagnac, Madeleine's elder son, who is almost my age. I have never corresponded with the Marquis since leaving France, but my sister Madeleine keeps me abreast of all the news from Auvergne. She had the sorrow to lose her younger son, who had become a Colonel in the armies of Napoléon and was killed at the Battle of Austerlitz in 1805, almost ten years ago.

In 1808, I saw again Marie-Joséphine de Savoie, the former Countess de Provence, now Queen of France in exile. She had just arrived in England, worn down by sorrow and bitterness. I would visit her on occasion at Hartwell House, where she had at last joined her husband. They had lived apart during those years when she had been driven away from one country after another by the victorious armies of the French Republic, and then those of the Empire.

"Goodness gracious, Baroness, I mean Lady St. Ives, is this you?" she exclaimed when I first called on her. "I am so happy to see you; you were always so good to me. How is it that the years, those terrible years, have spared you? You are as beautiful as ever, my dear angel, maybe even more so, in a different way."

"Your Majesty is very kind."

"Yes, they call me the Queen now. Look at me, a shrunken old woman! What a cruel mockery that is, a Queen of France with only a few acres of English land to call her own."

"With all the respect I owe Your Majesty, I must admit that, when one speaks of the Queen of France, I always think of the late Marie-Antoinette."

"So do I, dearest friend. I never understood my sister-in-law, but what a fate! Did you know that the poor woman had already passed away when she went to the guillotine? Yes, she had bled to death during her monthly curses. Can you imagine such an atrocity? They decapitated her corpse."

I did not argue with poor Queen Marie-Joséphine, grateful that she had at least recognized me. Dear Marguerite remained with her till the end, which followed two years later, in 1810. Queen Marie-Joséphine did not live to see her husband restored to the throne. Along with all of the French *émigrés*, and all of Napoléon's spies in England, I attended her funeral at Westminster Abbey. I do not know which was more mournful, the occasion or the gathering of the debris of the Old Regime. I could not behold my fellow *émigrés* without a mix of pity and contempt. Even those who had lived here for twenty years had not learned a word of English, for they had been too busy commiserating with each other and recalling the days of the "sweetness of living." These are lost, gone forever.

Last month at Waterloo, the defeat of the French armies, outnumbered almost two to one, heralded the final fall of Bonaparte. Forty-five thousand men perished on the day of that butchery. The war, started twenty-three years ago by Queen Marie-Antoinette and the Girondins, has ended at last. The powers of the victorious English-led coalition, like the witches in *Macbeth*, are to meet

> *When the hurlyburly's done,*
> *When the battle's lost and won.*

The Bourbons are restored for the second time, once again brought back to France in the luggage of foreigners. The fact that they owe their throne to the enemies of their own country never seems to disturb them.

Your paternal uncles have done very well under both Napoléon Bonaparte and the restored Bourbons. Jean-Baptiste Coffinhal was a member of the Legislative Assembly under the Empire and is now the Chief Prosecutor of the Court of Appeals of Riom. Joseph is not even called Coffinhal anymore. He became a State Counselor under Napoléon, who later made him a Baron. Both brothers, as you can guess, promptly switched allegiances when the Empire fell. Joseph recently received from King Louis the Eighteenth permission to drop the name Coffinhal altogether "due to the disgrace attached to it by his younger brother during the Revolution." He is now My Lord the Baron du Noyer, plain and simple. Many of the opportunists, the cowards, the traitors, the men who abandoned their ideals, their friends, their brothers, survived and prospered. So did I. Today is my forty-sixth birthday.

I often wonder what would have happened if I had been allowed to marry Pierre-André at fifteen. He would likely have remained a physician in the high country. Both of us would have spent the years of Revolution safely in Auvergne. Would he have been content with domestic happiness in a small town while events in Paris shaped the fate of the Nation? You would have been born, Edmond, but in very different circumstances, one of a country doctor's many children, to follow your father's profession, or perhaps to become an attorney.

And what if I had sought Pierre-André when I arrived in Paris at seventeen? He would have wed me. Would he, married to a noblewoman, have become such an implacable enemy of the Old Regime, a friend of Robespierre, an insurgent, a judge of the Revolutionary Tribunal? Instead of perishing on the guillotine, would he have lived to enjoy as successful a career as his elder brothers? Or would his passionate belief in the new ideals have led him down the same path, to the same death, regardless of the vagaries of personal destiny? No one can answer, I least of all.

I am an aristocrat again, now an English Countess, but I still cannot return to France. My country is in the grip of a second *White Terror*. Atrocities are committed there against the remaining Jacobins and those who supported the Revolution. The fortunate ones are executed by firing squads, others slaughtered with refinements of cruelty, some bled to death like swines. If it were discovered that I aided and sheltered your father, one of the judges of Marie-Antoinette, my life would be forfeited. So, Edmond, I will die an exile here.

Emilie called last week. She once boasted, on that day of August 1792, that she would be back in Paris with the victors in three months. Little did she know that she would have to wait over twenty years. I envy her: like the other *émigrés*, and unlike me, she may now return to France. Yet the country she will find across the Channel has little in common with the land she left. The tricolours are outlawed, replaced by the white flags of the old monarchy. The Revolution has been defeated, those who fought for it have been put to death, but its mark is imprinted on all minds, even those of its enemies. One does not kill ideas.

My soul remains in the country I will never see again; my heart is wedded to that of a dead man. Yet I have the memory of love, and I have hope. As he once said, we will be reunited someday, though not in this world.

HISTORICAL NOTE

Mistress of the Revolution is based upon the true events of the French Revolution. Many characters in the book, Marie-Antoinette and Louis the Sixteenth, of course, and also the Coffinhal brothers, Robespierre, Carrier, Fouquier, Hébert, Lafayette, the Duke d'Orléans, Madame Lebrun, the Duke de Lauzun, the Chevalier des Huttes, Madame de Tourzel, the Princess de Lamballe, among others, are inspired by historical figures. The little town of Vic really exists in the mountains of Auvergne, and the fine houses of the Chevalier des Huttes and the Coffinhal family can still be seen there. Gabrielle, however, is entirely fictional, though I like to think of her as an imaginary ancestor of mine.

Pierre-André Coffinhal was indeed the vice president of the Revolutionary Tribunal and a close friend of Robespierre, whom he freed from jail on the ninth of Thermidor. He was the only Jacobin leader to escape that night. He remained in hiding for a week afterward before being betrayed. As in the novel, he spent his last hours roaring in his cell, was sentenced to death without trial, and promptly executed. He shrugged at the jeering crowd on his way to the guillotine.

This is a novel, not a scholarly work. Nevertheless I tried, whenever possible, to follow firsthand accounts, such as the numerous memoirs written by eyewitnesses. To my regret, I had to leave out many events and many fascinating historical characters, such as the journalist Marat. Including them all would have made an already long book too cumbersome.

I strove to write this novel in the British English Gabrielle would have used in 1815, an endeavor that deepened my knowledge and appreciation of this rich and evocative language.

ACKNOWLEDGMENTS

A novel is a labor of love. Not only the love of the writer for her characters, but also the love she draws from her family, her friends.

I wish to thank my first American readers, who, after reviewing a few chapters, encouraged me to persevere in this endeavor. I am thinking of Dr. Andrea K. Scott, and others who will not be named here.

Some of the more pleasurable, stimulating moments in the conception of this book were the conversations during wonderful French dinners at the home of Christiane David and Philippe Lemaître. Thanks to Philippe for his many trips to the Research Library at UCLA.

Later, my life plunged into darkness, and I abandoned the novel for months. Then my son told me that he missed seeing me writing, and the happiness it had brought me. It was the incentive I needed to return to the story.

My mother helped in so many ways while I completed the novel. My thoughts go to my father, a native speaker of the Roman language, who shared with me his passion for history. Sadly, he did not live to see this book published.

Pam Sheppard taught me much about the craft of writing. I cannot thank enough Stephanie Cabot, my agent; Julie Doughty, my editor; and all of the people at Dutton who helped turn my manuscript into this book. I am grateful to all for their support, enthusiasm, and great work.